Preface

The Network began life as a simple sequel to my fir
Ten Wickets. All of the characters in that novel reap,
years on. However, the five major new characters, who act as its narrators,
took over **The Network** and turned it into a sprawling narrative of
Dickensian length and sentimentality. I published this, Dickens-style, in
episodes, on www.epublishingonline.co.uk but many of my friends expressed
the wish to see it in a printed book. This edition is for them. I attempted to
shorten it, without much success. I liked my characters too much and the
narrative and dialogue which they supplied to me. A few of their more
saccharine passages did end up on the cutting room floor but the book is still
unashamedly sentimental, and I doubt if anyone has written a more
optimistic book about the power of cricket (or any sport) to change lives.

The customary author's disclaimer applies with more force than usual: this is
a work of fiction. A few real people appear but all the others have no intended
resemblance to any actual person, alive or dead. Because I have played cricket
for many years for Parliament's team, the Lords and Commons, many readers
have guessed at the "real" identity of the loathsome politician. There is none:
he is simply a logical continuation of a character in A Tale Of Ten Wickets.
One character, Howard Foy, is a successful writer: his triumphs are all
unpublished or unperformed works of mine.

The Network is narrated entirely by five different characters, with their own
font. All direct speech appears in upright Palatino Linotype: "Howzat?" My
principal character, Steve, uses *italic Palatino Linotype* to speak to the reader:
Don't know why I bothered to appeal.

Cal, a 12-year-old boy, narrates in Comic Sans MS. (I chose this before
discovering that this font is frowned on by serious typographers. It seemed to
work for him).

Cal's mother Alice, a lawyer, speaks to the reader in legally sound Times New
Roman.

Zoe, a teenage girl given to colourful speech, delivers her narrative in
Bradley Hand ITC.

Howard, a screenwriter, speaks to the reader in Courier New.

Richard Heller September 2010   richardkheller@hotmail.com

The Network was first published online in episodes by
www.epublishingonline.co.uk

This edition is published by

Bearmondsey Publishing
204 The School House
Pages Walk
London SE1 4HG
England

ISBN 978-0-9556740-1-3

Printed in Great Britain by the MPG Books Group, Bodmin and King's Lynn

For Eddy

Enjoy, I hope, when rain stops play

Richard Heller

THE NETWORK

The delayed sequel to <u>*A Tale Of Ten Wickets*</u>

Best wishes

Richard

Cover illustration by Will Tubby

Bearmondsey Publishing 2010

Chapter 1   Opening bowler

Dear Uncle Frank,

I have just bowled the greatest delivery in my career. Correction. I have just bowled the greatest delivery in the history of the universe. Wordpower - you told me never to undersell myself! Anyway, it totally castled Brendon (I think I told you, he's a Grade 2 opening batsman in New Zealand) and if the middle stump had not been attached to the base it would have gone right through the back of the net into the High Street.

"Too good, mate. I think it reversed."

"The only thing that reversed was you, bro, backing away."

"Where I fell over the big heap of shit <u>you</u> left outside leg stump. You were poop-scared of the piethrower."

"Well, he ain't a piethrower any more. Did you spike his lemonade?"

Brendon and Daniel argued for a bit but I just stood there after my follow-through, acknowledging the crowd. Except of course there was no crowd, because we were the only people using the nets. This little kid rode by on a bike and I wanted to stop him and say "Did you see that?" but that felt a bit weird so I let him go. Brendon and Daniel stopped arguing and Brendon gave me back the ball.

"Don't bowl another ball, end it there. Just remember what you did."

But I can't remember anything. Something just took over and everything felt perfect. Like Frank Tyson, in his book you gave me: "glad animal action." If I could just be a glad animal...

"You're really only 16?"

"Yeah."

"And you're not playing for a team? You just come to these nets?"

"Yeah. My school didn't have a team, and I did play for two clubs but it didn't work out and I haven't got transport and Dad thinks there's no future in cricket and I'm supposed to get work experience this holidays..."

"Take it easy, mate, you don't have to spill out any personal stuff. Look, Brendon and I are going to find a team to play for this month while we're in

London and we'd like you to play with us and if you bowl like that we'll hire a stretch limo to take you to the matches."

And I really believed him. And all of a sudden I lost it. I started crying and I couldn't stop. How was I going to explain it to Brendon and Daniel, two strangers I met in the nets a few days ago that they have just changed my whole life? I mean, there's thousands of kids with real problems and I'm strung up just because I can't find a cricket team to play for? They'll think I'm some total saddo.

"Hey, mate, don't cry, you're not allowed to water the pitch."

It made me laugh and Brendon gave me a T-shirt to wipe my face. Then Daniel said again "You don't have to spill any personal stuff, but if you do it stays here."

And I almost told them right there and then. Everything for the last three years which stops me playing for a team. Why I ran away from you-know-who, why I walk for miles to use these nets instead of the ones nearer home, why I changed schools, what happened when I started playing for the Ahmads, what's happening at home… I felt I could trust them, but why should I park any of that stuff on Brendon and Daniel, they've come all this way from NZ to have a holiday?

"Sorry. It's just that every time I get into a team a lot of bad stuff seems to happen."

"Steve… Give us your mobile number. When we find a team, we'll call you and we'll see you right, and make sure you play every game. Listen, Daniel's a law student when he's not partying or playing sport. If someone tries to stop you playing cricket he'll sue them for… for… "

"Restraint of trade. Open-and-shut case." *It made me laugh again.*

"'Close of play, and the New Zealand batting shattered by that fierce spell from England's teen bowling sensation Steve Helson. None of them will be looking forward to facing the mean machine tomorrow with a new ball in his hand on his favourite pitch with the famous pothole just on a length on off-stump.'"

Daniel passed me an address book and a pen. "Phone and email, please?" *I wrote them down in the section for H - where was an entry for Hadlee, Sir Richard!!*

We packed our kit away and took the stumps back to the office. "Same time tomorrow?"

"Forecast isn't good, but we'll book anyway." *He rang the bell and the curmudgeonly curator [Wordpower!!] shuffled to the counter.* "You know the name now. McConnel."

"Can't I pay this time?"

""You keep your hand in your pocket. We'll be back when you're 18."

"Now Steve, how are you getting home?"

"Walk."

"Where's home?"

"Kenborne Vale".

"That's a fair step with your kit bag. Are these your nearest nets?"

"No… but they're … better."

They didn't really buy that, but they didn't ask any more. We walked out of the park and the McConnel twins turned away. Suddenly my phone rang.

"It's Daniel. Do me a favour, put that number in your list, and phone it when you get home."

"Don't worry. I've done it loads of times. I'll be right."

"'I'll be right'. He's learning our language."

I'll be right. I _will_ be right. I am a great fast bowler. I've got two real mates, watching out for me. I am free, I have total power. I am a glad animal.

I dragged my bag back. Hell, it is a long way home but I didn't notice. I just bowled Brendon in my head over and over again. I finally got to our street and dumped my bag at the corner. I glared at the lamppost. I ran in ten paces, took off and delivered. A gun in each hand. Look over the left shoulder. Left arm high. Shoot him with your left hand. Right arm high. Shoot him with your right hand. Just like you told me. The lamppost had no chance.

"Where have you been, your dinner's cold?" *Sorry, Mum, the dinner you shopped for with such care and spent hours preparing so lovingly? No, not that dinner. The one that you could have stuck in the microwave whenever you liked, the dinner that could have waited for me. But she cannot take this moment from me. I am still a glad animal.*

"Sorry. But I just bowled the best delivery in the history of the universe."

Dad had a spreadsheet at the kitchen table and Mum of course had the manuscript of her Novel. "Look how hard we have to work. Can't even take time off for meals." I get the message, Uncle Frank. Just like when they told me there would be no summer holiday this year. Apparently we have to redecorate the house, although I haven't seen any signs of anticipated ameliorations [Wordpower!] I mean, no catalogues, no samples of carpets or fabrics or paint colours, no one measuring things or drawing things. But definitely no summer holiday. I don't mind really, our summer holiday is just here in a different place.

"Did you hear what I said, Steve?"

"Sorry, Dad." *He folded the spreadsheet and looked at me directly.*

"I said, have you just been playing cricket all day or have you done anything about finding a holiday job?"

I don't know where all this has come from, me getting a holiday job. I've already agreed to go to business college and forget asking for a trial at a cricket club. So why do I need a holiday job? It's not about the money. We've got money. Hell, I've got the money you gave me. Dad doesn't even have to pay me an allowance. I thought hard and I remembered a notice in the park.

"They want sports coaches and play leaders in the park for the kids' summer scheme."

"Do you think that is a realistic hope when they look at your school record?"

That was a low blow. It even made Mum look up from the Novel and Dad made a judicious [Wordpower] retreat. "I'm sorry, son. We said that was past. But it is a practical consideration. It will come up when you look for jobs, especially with children or young people." *Again Mum rattled the pages of the Novel and Dad hurried on.* "I don't mean to go on about getting a job. It's more about being ready to take on some responsibility."

"They need extra lifeguards in the pool. That's pretty responsible, isn't it, making sure people don't drown?"

"Don't be snippy with me. You're sixteen. You're about to make your way in a tough world. You need to prepare. You need to make choices that will help you get on in life, not just hang around that park all day."

Finally Mum put down the Novel. "For goodness sake, he only broke up a week ago. Can't he have a little bit of holiday?" *I wish I could believe that Mum was actually interested in me. Our family's a battlefield and I'm just a small hill which each side tries to occupy to fire on the other. [Wordpower? Or showing off? Maybe. But it really feels like that, Uncle Frank. Was it always like that?]*

"When I was his age I had already worked for three years." *Ah. That's familiar. Dad, the self-made man, having to carry the selfish wife and the idle, unthinking son. Do you want to trade me? What about one of the other school leavers in my year? Would you prefer Mick the shoplifter, or Denny the pimp, or Carl the drug dealer? No. Don't get sucked in to the battle on Dad's terms. Or Mum's. Open another front.*

I pushed my plate away and put on my Good Smile. "Thanks, Mum. That was brilliant, even though I let it get cold. Sorry." *I can't even remember what it was supposed to be. Mum ruffled my hair.* "In war the situation changes from moment to moment. Every advantage must be seized, however temporary." *I think that was in your Clausewitz book. Mum is now an ally. I have become the Sensitive Son, appreciating her as a creative artist who still finds time to be a caregiver.*

"Dad. I know you think cricket's a waste of time, but it did bring you a big client once." *Dad flushed. I didn't need to say who that client was, and what happened with him two years ago. I tensed up and I wanted Mum's hand, like when I was little, but she was back with the Novel. So I swallowed and pushed on.*

"Dad, can we make a deal? I really want to play cricket in the park with Daniel and Brendon. And then play for their team when they find one. They are quality, Dad, I mean just below first-class in New Zealand, and they really have brought me on in just a few days." *I was losing my audience.* "Besides, Daniel and Brendon are really rich, I mean they're going round the world and their dad owns this giant farm and a winery. I'll bring them round and you can meet them" *and their money.* "And there will probably be other rich people in their team and you can meet them as well."

"So what is the deal?"

"I introduce you to a new prospective client and you let me play cricket for the rest of the summer whenever I want. And if I find a job I want to do, you let me do it, no questions, so long as it's legal."

Dad looked away and said nothing. Good interrogation technique, you taught me. Silence is very powerful. Mum was scrawling something in the Novel. I had to say something to break the silence.

"I will pay all my cricket expenses. Kit. Match fees. And travel. I know how much time it takes for you and Mum to take me to matches." *This time they both flushed. Weren't you glad, two years ago, when someone offered to drive me everywhere? More silence. Dad is a good negotiator. I suppose you have to be when you build a one-man business. I blurted something else.* "You can cancel the deal if I get bad GCSEs. Anything below C." *That's a fair offer – I'm doing ten of them. I had to fight that school for the right to take them. It was afraid I would fail and drag it down the League table.* "D or below in any subject and I do what you want in terms of holiday job and going to business college afterwards or any other plans you have for me."

Another silence. "Agreed. But I have to meet this Daniel and Brendon first." *And inspect their money.*

"Thanks, Dad. You won't regret it. And Mum, it's good for you too. It means I'll be out of the house when the decorators come in." *She flushed. Couldn't resist that. Wrong, I know. Your Clausewitz again: "a commander should not waste effort on ephemeral successes." I withdrew from the battlefield lest I dissipate [Wordpower] the real victory.* "I'll clear and run the dishwasher."

In the kitchen, alone. It never takes me long to clear it up and leave everything spotless. You taught me to be neat and put everything away, just so. When I finish all the chores, I suddenly notice I'm sweating furiously, way more than bowling flat out at Brendon and Daniel.

Why do I have to work so hard to get a game of cricket? What's with my dad? I mean, loads of dads dote on their kids playing cricket. In the nets I've seen this fat little kid called Robert and he's got all the best kit, and his dad bowls to him for hours and Robert whines at anything faster than a lollipop and his dad slows it right down so he can hit it back past him. Was I like that with you, Uncle Frank? If so, I'm real sorry.

Stop it. Now. You told me ages ago: "Play with the cards you got dealt. Make what you can from them and wait for a better hand". And haven't I just been dealt a great hand? In a team with Brendon and Daniel… It will take me into a new orbit, like the Voyager spacecraft slinging itself round the planet Jupiter [Wordpower!!!]

Still the Good Son, I remember to offer them coffee. No takers. Dad is back on the spreadsheet, sipping mineral water and Mum has opened a bottle of white wine to accompany the Novel. Both fighting again on familiar ground. Dad: look how hard I

have to work. Mum: you're driving me to drink. But they seem genuinely pleased at
my offer. Dad puts down the spreadsheet and clasps me round the shoulder.

"Steve. That was a very mature discussion. I'm proud of you." *The clasp gets a
little firmer. Enough to make me believe it might be a hug. Mum's turn.*

"Come over here, handsome." *She holds my face in her hands and checks it against
Dad's. I think she's confirming that her family genes won out. I do look just like you
at my age, don't I? Another ruffle of my hair, and a kiss. More than a duty one.*

*Years back, we might have played Monopoly at this stage, but now nobody's sorry
that I'm tired and I want to go to bed early. I treat myself to the massage unit on the
shower and a very hot full bath with Mum's special oil which she doesn't know I've
discovered. Bad Son! Muscles uncoil. Hot, muggy night. I walk naked to my bedroom
window and simply drip dry.*

*There's just room enough for my delivery stride. Watch myself in my little mirror,
bowling the magic ball once again at Brendon. Glad animal action. Turn to salute the
crowd and crash onto the bed.*

Glad animal inaction.

Chapter 2   Match Abandoned

I woke up in the early dawn. The air in my room was thick and clammy. A miasma [Wordpower!] formed of my sweat and stolen body oil and spilt linseed oil. I stuck my head out of the window. The air outside was no better. It had that metallic smell that you get before a storm. Please not today, I'm meeting Daniel and Brendon.

I reached in your trunk for your next book. I told you I finished <u>All Quiet On The Western Front.</u> I really liked the bit where they take revenge on that stupid schoolmaster. I'm sorry it's taken me so long to read all your books, Uncle Frank. I've only finished letter R. But be fair, some of them were well big! "Scribble, scribble, scribble, Mr Gibbon. Here's another damn, thick, square book!" Thanks for giving me the abridged edition! Are there really people who've read the whole lot? Anyway, I'm now past authors R and into authors S. Salinger J D. <u>The Catcher In The Rye.</u> Nice and short. It's about a lonely, misunderstood teenager. I will give it my expert opinion!

But I didn't feel like reading right then. My whole body was still alive with glad animal action. I threw on some running stuff, and tiptoed down the house. Past her bedroom. Past his bedroom. Trainers on. Remember my key on the string. Remember to switch off the burglar alarm. Now's your chance, lads! You can steal Dad's spreadsheet or Mum's Novel. Take anything except my cricket bag and my uncle's trunk.

Into the street. Check at the corner. Make sure you-know-who's car isn't parked nearby. No worries. There's no one around except the Mad Person and the winos waiting for the corner shop to open. I don't need a warm-up. I just go straight into my action. The commentators on Test Match Special are in rhapsodies again. "Astonishing, the pace this great bowler can generate from just a ten-yard run up. Helson to Brendon McConnel, New Zealand's finest batsman. Beats him, all ends up, full length on off stump, past the outside edge, keeper has to leap to take it…"

On my way back to the house, I take the fifth New Zealand wicket. One of the winos applauds. Was he a cricketer once? It makes me sad. I stop bowling and jog the rest. Five for 21, the New Zealand top order blown away by the England opener, already a legend at 16.

Let myself in. Remember to reset the burglar alarm. Nothing missing. Shame. Trainers off. AAGH! Not just cheesy, they're positively mephitic [Wordpower!!] Into the bathroom, pinch Dad's special cologne which he doesn't know I've discovered. Bad Son. A splash in each trainer. A splash over me.

Back into the bedroom, strip off. A final look at my glad animal action in the mirror.

Flop onto bed. The great bowler sleeps. In faraway New Zealand cricket fans view his opening spell on the TV highlights and despair at his carnage of their champions.

I wake up and they've gone. He to his office to make more money for rich people. She to her office to market cosmetics. Sorry, Uncle Frank, I know you hate "she". My mother, your sister. But I know that I am "he" to her. I've heard her on the phone to her girl friends. Dad is one kind of "he" and I am another kind of "he." Never Donald or Steve. She doesn't like her job, although I thought it was fun when I had a day in her office. She seems to be really good at marketing cosmetics, but she still hates it. It's as if she were saying "Look what I have to do for you" to Dad. And to me.

She's left me a note telling me where to find breakfast. Thanks, Mum, just in case the Bad Breakfast Fairy decided to move it. Pint of milk straight from the carton, banana, muesli, freshly squeezed OJ, wholewheat toast. This great bowler's body is a temple.

It's raining hard. Shit! Please lay off in time for me and Daniel and Brendon. A good time to start <u>The Catcher In The Rye.</u> *I crack up at the fart in the sermon but I can't sit still. I decide to hit the pool. Walk. I don't mind the rain, I'm going to get wet anyway.*

A pervo checks me out in the changing room. It creeps me for a minute, then I realize it's not me specially, it's everybody. And besides, who wouldn't check out the physique of this magnificent fast bowling machine? An Italian (I think) boy comes in and gives him a show. Bloody hell, I couldn't wear Speedos like that. The Italian boy asks for 20 pee for the locker and the pervo takes his chance.

Oh shit. That bitch Angie's at the fun pool, with some of the other girls from my school. Not swimming, just posing. Before long, they're going to be fat. Head down and walk to the length pool. They won't follow me there.

Phil's on duty today. "Hey Psycho!" There were only two kids at school whom I liked to use my nickname. Phil was one and Nick was the other. Me and Nick were Psycho and Weirdo. Phil was called the Sheriff. Two years above us. He hated bullies. Nick and I generally got left alone, because bullies are afraid of kids called Psycho and Weirdo but if we did get bullied we never went to the teacher, we went to the Sheriff and he sorted it. And he was actually interested in the stuff that mattered to us, like if I wanted to talk about one of your books or if Nick wanted to talk about one of his planets or galaxies we would go to Phil again, not to a teacher.

So there's Phil. He's a leader with a mind and our school gave him no more aspiration than being a pool attendant. And he is still a pool attendant at the same pool, two years on. All right, he's a bloody good pool attendant, but was that all our school could offer for his whole life after?

"Howdy, Sheriff."

"You coming to work here? We're still short."

"My dad's not keen. Besides, I'm playing cricket. Met these New Zealand guys at the nets and they are complete gods and they want me to play for them."

"Great. You deserve it." *I dove in the fast lane and didn't bother again with a warm-up, just churned up and down the pool. The pervo (Speedophile?) and the Italian boy wouldn't let me overtake, but Phil whistled them into the medium lane out of my way. The Test Match Special commentators started up again in my head, praising the great fast bowler's high arm action. Finally I hauled myself out beside Phil.*

"Hey Steve, what was the hurry? Anything wrong?"

"No way, Phil. I feel great. I've taken all ten New Zealand wickets in my first Test innings."

"I get my break soon. Tell me about it."

I met Phil and he bought me lunch at the staff rate and I told him all about the McConnel twins and the best ball in the history of the universe.

"Steve, I would love to hear more but my break is over and if someone drowns they take it out of my pay."

"Make it Angie and I'll pay you."

"Let her go, Steve. She was a slag and pretty soon she's gonna be a fat slag. Do you hear from Nick?"

"Not much. He thinks he's discovered an asteroid. He's going to name it for me."

"Asteroid Psycho?"

"Asteroid Toecrusher."

The rain had stopped but the sky still looked very portentous [Wordpower!] I got home and had another go at <u>Catcher In The Rye</u> but I dozed off. I was woken by my mobile going off. This does not happen often. I was a bit disoriented.

"Daniel? Shit! Are you waiting for me?"

"Not in this, mate." *I looked out of the window and it was chucking down.*

"Shit!"

"Listen, Steve. We want to tell you something. Can you meet us in the Kenborne Arms? Big pub in Rendell Avenue. Can't be too far from you."

"I don't know… I don't go to pubs."

"You're sixteen, you're allowed. Steve, this is serious and we ain't got too much time." *So of course I rushed out and ran to Rendell Avenue and found the pub and Brendon pulled me into a corner booth and Daniel asked what I wanted to drink and I said lemonade because I can never think of anything else and he brought it over.*

"Is this about the team?"

They both looked really miserable and they both tried to speak at once and finally Daniel said slowly "Steve, we've had some bad news from home. Our dad's had a heart attack. He's not in danger, but he needs us back home to work the farm."

"So, we're really sorry," *said Brendon,* "But that means no more cricket and we know you must be gutted and we're gutted too, because we really liked playing with you."

Don't cry. That would be so selfish. I mean, their dad might be dying and I'm upset about not playing cricket? Anyway, Uncle Frank. I held it together and said "That's awful. About your dad, I mean."

Daniel said quickly "Look, we didn't have much time but we got you a few things," *and he reached into a big plastic bag and pulled out this one-day cricket kit in this weird colour.*

"Who plays in this? White coffee."

"Beige. You're now an official member of the Beige Brigade. That was NZ's one-day cricket kit in the 80s. Isn't that the worst strip ever?" *Then Brendon pulled out a sheaf of comic books.*

"Footrot Flats. A national institution in NZ. That's what life is like on our farm, except that Dad's a lot brighter than Wal Footrot and our mutt's a lot stupider than The Dog. And here's an aerial shot of our farm."

"Bloody hell! How big is that?" *Daniel thought and said* "Let's say you could play five cricket matches at once and still have plenty of room for the stock. Now something else. You've seen what me and Brendon wear round our necks."

"The pendants?"

"That's a maniah. It's a spirit, half man, half bird, and it looks out for you. Now you can never buy one for yourself, someone has to give it to you. So we got you this one." *They handed me one like theirs, only a bit different, and slipped it round my neck.* "Now, all these spirits know each other and they can talk to each other from far away. And they know when it's time to meet again and so they come together."

"But just as a precaution, these are our emails and this is the address and phone number of our place in NZ and when you want to drop by, you get in touch and we'll say 'G'day Steve, what day are you coming?'"

Then I did lose it and I started to cry. "You mean… you want me to visit you? But … you hardly know me. We've just played a bit of cricket. I mean … do you know I'm called Psycho? You know why I haven't got a team?"

"Don't water that lemonade, the barman did enough of that already," *and I started to giggle.*

Daniel said, "Look Steve, we're Kiwis. We say what we mean. Of course you can come to our farm. Mind, it's not going to be a free ride because there's a shit load of work to do on a farm. When you have to carry a wounded sheep up the hill-face, it's not like pushing the supermarket trolley."

Brendon said "But it's not all work. I hope you can swim, because we got the best beach in the world near our place. And you can join our cricket club, and I told you we got the grade system, so you're playing in the same club as first-class and Test players, and you practise with them in the nets regularly and when you're good enough in one grade you go up and eventually you play with them for real. You'll be playing Tests for NZ in no time, you're better than the piethrowers we got now."

I started to giggle again but then Daniel said very seriously, "Listen mate, if you go to NZ no one cares about Psycho or any stuff like that over here. No, if you come to NZ all we care about is talent and hard work and character. We'll have you, mate, any day of the week." *Then they gave me a giant double hug. I was surprised but I didn't care who saw us. Then they broke away.*

"We've got a flight to catch and we have to pack." *I stumbled out of the pub, with the stuff they gave me. Then you'll be glad to know I remembered and rushed back and hugged them both again and said* "Thank you. You're the best. I hope your dad's okay."

But when I walked back home in the rain I felt miserable all over again. And I felt like a shit for being so selfish, and then I felt even more miserable. But I just couldn't take another false dawn. As if I could ever get to New Zealand. As if I could call up Daniel and Brendon and say "Remember me? The kid you met in the nets in the park and we played a few times? I've come over to join the rest of your life."

When I got home the Western Front was active again and it actually cheered me up to be back in the war zone. Mum opened fire first.

"You're all wet. Don't drip all over the place."

"Sorry. But I thought we were redecorating so does it matter where I drip?" *"Fire was successfully returned, and our forces were able to reach their objective [my bedroom] without further opposition."*

Dinner was pretty much a repeat of yesterday. Dad with his spreadsheet, Mum with her Novel. Dad asked me "Did you see those New Zealand people?"

I almost blurted out what happened and then realized that would end the deal with Dad and I would have to look for a job again. "An army faced by overwhelming superiority may practice deception to avoid encirclement and annihilation." *Your Clausewitz again – or maybe it's me.*

"Oh yeah. But they've had to go away to… inspect their property in Ireland. They're an Irish family. The McConnels. They've got a pile of real estate in … in County Meath." *The first Irish county I could remember.* "But they would really like to meet you when they get back." *That might give me a bit longer.*

"Irish property is heading for a fall. They should have a spread of securities."

"I'm sure you could help them, Dad." *Now I'm Dad's Good Son, so naturally Mum is annoyed.*

"What's that round your neck?"

"They gave it to me. It's called a maniah. That's a protective spirit."

"It makes you look like a chav."

"It's actually quite valuable, Mum. It's carved from stereated obsidian." *[Wordpower!!! I completely made that up].*

"Do you want to give it to me to put in the safe?"

"No thanks, Dad. That would be really unlucky. In fact, the McConnels would never speak to be again because I would be under a curse." *[Genius!!! Maybe you were right, Uncle Frank, I am going to be a novelist.]*

"Well, take good care of it, at least till they get back."

Mum decided to abandon this sector of the front (ie me). "I've had a bloody day. I am going to bed."

"Do you want me to bring you a hot drink, Mum?" *Good Son!*

"No, thank you, sweetheart." *She held out her arms. I went over for the ritual kiss. She fingered the maniah.*

"You know, I take it back. It's really quite distinguished." *She framed my face again and repeated her genetic inspection.* "You could make something of your appearance" *glaring at Dad, as if to contrast his sartorial nullity [Wordpower!]* "Would you like to shop this weekend and have a giant makeover?"

"Mum, that would be awesome." *Good Son! Having partially retaken the lost ground on my sector of the front, Mum withdrew with the Novel. Dad had no better counter than to pick up the spreadsheet and announce that he had a pile of client work to get through in the study. He gave me one of his near-hugs.*

"I'll clear up," *I announced, as if there were massive competition for the task.*

I left the kitchen immaculate as usual and went up to my bedroom. I stripped naked again and went into my delivery stride again, to bowl the magic ball that castled Brendon.

My little mirror showed me no glad animal action. Just a scrawny kid waving his arms. Waving goodbye to life?

"You pathetic snivelling little drama queen", I said to the image and then burst into tears. I said it again when I sobbed into the pillow, and I only stopped when I looked at your photo.

Then I said "Dear God, I am not a very nice person and I don't believe in you but I would like you to give Daniel and Brendon a safe flight home and make sure their dad's okay."

Chapter 3   Unexpected Bounce

I felt great next morning. For a start, it was a beautiful day and I owned it. Thanks to my splendiferous subterfuge [Wordpower!] with the McConnels Dad would not nag me about getting a job. I could probably spin out the subterfuge for at least a week.

They had both gone to work. I owned the house. I walked naked around all the rooms, even the ones I don't like. I finished in Mum's and admired myself in her full-length mirror. That slag Angie was right. I was the fittest boy in our school. Running, swimming, fast bowling. No booze, no chemicals, no junk food, no wonder I'm a god.

I bowled in slo-mo at my mate in the mirror. Yes, it's back. Glad animal action. But still stuck on five-feet-ten, curse it! Who's going to give the five-ten bowler the new ball ahead of the six-five hulk?

I bet Brendon would, or Daniel. I fingered the maniah around my neck. Brendon and Daniel gave that to me and all the other stuff just because I bowled at them in those nets. And they offered me a new life, and they meant it. Just for those nets.

I'm going there again to bowl at someone else. I just hope it isn't that fat whiny kid Robert and his dad who does not know how to manage him. I feel great, but not quite great enough for that pair. Anything over 50 and the Whinometer starts up. The sad thing is he is quite a decent bat for anything slower.

Still naked, I fortified my fabulous physique with my usual sportsman's repast and admired it again in a series of reflecting surfaces. Then I dressed for the nets. The Beige shirt in honour of Brendon and Daniel. The material was as horrible as the colour so I put on my white undershirt in high-tech spacecraft fabric. My trainers. Wow, they still smelt of Dad's special cologne which I had splashed into them like the Bad Son I am. Should I send an unsolicited testimonial: Dear Mr or Ms Chanel, Have you thought of promoting your male fragrance as a teenage trainer tamer?

I hauled my cricket bag out of the house and into the street. Hot already. Even with the wheels it was a long trudge to the nets but I won't use the other ones. I lengthened my stride as I finally approached the nets and listened for the sound of the crimson traveller connecting with the wooden lance or crashing through the wooden castle [Wordpower]. Silence, and I felt a bit deflated. My eyes confirmed that there was no one at the nets. A fabulous sunny day in the school holidays and no one at the cricket nets. No wonder we cannot produce a Test team.

I didn't bother collecting the stumps from the office and helped myself to the wicket-sized traffic cone instead. I put it in Net One, the best of an indifferent selection. The nets in the other park are actually better as well as nearer but I don't like them any more. At least these nets have creases marked at both ends, and give you a decent run-up. I picked six cricket balls out of my bag and marked out the ten paces from which I generate such astonishing speed. The Test Match Special team started up again in my head. My third over had the crowd humming like angry hornets. [Check whether hornets hum]. Three late outswingers and then a searing break-back crashed into the hapless traffic cone. "Wow!" said the crowd.

The crowd was this skinny kid on a bike, with a backpack. He looked about ten. Big wide eyes and mouth open, like a cartoon character. He had this really trendy bike helmet on, and for some reason I felt glad that someone had given it to him and made him wear it. He took it off and he had this long blond hair but cut so that it fell away from his face.

"Australia lose their first wicket," *I said,* "Simply destroyed by England's new fast bowling sensation," *and got rewarded by a giggle.* "I like your shirt." *It had a mushroom cloud on it and a slogan: One Nuclear Bomb Can Ruin Your Whole Day.*

"Thanks. I nicked it from my mum." *Another Bad Son!* "I don't like yours."

"Respect from you, it's the Beige Brigade."

He stepped off the bike and left it by the side of the net and dumped his backpack beside it. Then he bounced around from one foot to the other for a while and looked away from me at the ground. Then, still looking away from me, he said in a rush "Can I bowl at you? I can actually bowl and there's no one else here and I'll go away again when those Aussies arrive…"

I was puzzled for a second and then I remembered glimpsing this little kid on a bike when I bowled my wonderball at Brendon. "Aussies? Those guys are Kiwis, New Zealanders. Don't call them Aussies, they'll go mental and you'll be killed to death!" *Another giggle. Bright kid. He understood my purposeful pleonasm [Wordpower!] The one you taught me.*

"I saw you before. I nearly asked to play then but I didn't think you would want a little kid and besides I was poop-scared of those Aus… Kiwis." *Poop-scared – a Brendon/Daniel expression. He must have been listening really hard.*

"You were poop-scared of them but not of me?"

"No. You're awesome but not scary." *I wasn't sure whether to be miffed or pleased with this remark, so I said* "Can you stay here and mind all our stuff while I get the stumps? Then bowl and see if you can scare me." *He looked as if I had given him the Universe as a Christmas present.*

I fetched the stumps and set them up in place of the devastated traffic cone. I collected the cricket balls and offered him a selection. "I'm sorry, I've not got a junior ball."

Mistake. "I never use a junior ball. Look at my hands." *They were gargantuan [Wordpower!!] He put my best slightly-used ball in his left hand.* "Small kid, big hands, so I had to be a spin bowler." *I nearly added "Big mouth" but he was such a happy little guy I blocked it.* "Slow left arm."

"Monty Panesar? Daniel Vettori?"

"There's more."

"Ooh, I am scared. Try a few practice balls." *I watched him. Not so much a run-up, more a series of bounces. Nice delivery action but trying too hard (like me when I was little) and scrunching himself up. I remembered us, in the years back.* "Take it easy and keep yourself tall. Use all of your four foot."

"Four-foot-nine and a bit more!" *Your wind-up worked again. Indignant, but he got the point. Some better balls followed but both arms still a bit low. Time for your two-guns routine. It seemed to work. Full length deliveries, off stump, no special spin. Suddenly I remembered something else.*

"I'm Steve."

"I know. I'm Cal. Cal Devane. As in Cal Devane the rock star. He was my mum's uncle." *It meant nothing but I managed a suitably impressed* "Cal Devane!" *and started to pad up.*

"What are those?"

"They're called Padman shorts. Under your whites or ordinary shorts today and they hold everything in place, two thigh pads, box. Gives you just a tad more confidence."

"I want some."

"Be extra good to Mum and Dad and see what happens."

"There's only Mum." *Shit.* "It's fine. Mum's brilliant. You should meet her."

"I want to." *And I did. Who got this chirpy kid here on her own? It wasn't the time to tell him that two parents aren't always better than one. Or even none.*

"You're wearing a helmet against me?"

"Definitely. Always respect a new opponent. Besides, you have to wear one in matches until you're eighteen, unless your parents write a note and say it's fine for our kid to have his face smashed into a pile of putrescent pulp." *[Wordpower!] Giggle.* "Have you got one?"

"No. Bat, pads, gloves, box. But no helmet. The club gave them to us, but I don't have a club any more." *His face suddenly darkened.*

"Me neither." *Mine did too.* "We'll get you a helmet… I mean, I'll go with you and your Mum to a shop and make sure you'll get the right one." *His face lit up again. I picked up gloves and bat and walked into the net.*

"Is this leg stump?" *You-know-who told me to try leg stump against slow bowlers. It worked. Whatever else, he was a bloody good batting coach.*

"Left arm, round the wicket." *His first ball. Nice and full but wide of off stump. I could have reached it and driven it hard but why deflate him on his first ball? Exaggerated leave-alone. Second ball, decent line and length. A bit of flight. Right forward, ostentatious footwork, soft hands, smother any spin (not much of that). Third ball, half-volley. I'm afraid he's got to learn. Crashing straight drive. Oh please don't try to stop it. Phew, deflected past his hand.*

"Sorry. Couldn't help it. Glad you didn't stop it, that would have hurt. Don't be upset, it wasn't that bad a ball."

"I'm not upset." *He walked back slowly after the ball, which had crashed back off the tall tree. I felt good. You swine, feeling good after battering a little kid? But I couldn't help it after such a great shot. I was still living with the shot as he started his run-up again. Fourth ball. Thrown high, around off stump. Left foot forward again for another drive. Suddenly the ball was not there. It jagged back in off the pitch, bounced over my bat and hit me in the left inner thigh. A huge squeal from the bowler.*

"Too high for lbw and probably spinning past leg stump as well, but fantastic delivery!" *I meant it.* "Chinaman. You hardly ever see them."

"You didn't!" *Giggle.*

"Who taught you to bowl the Chinaman?"

"No one really. I was really bored at home on my own and was just fooling around with a tennis ball and discovered I could flick it out of my wrist as well as my fingers. Then I did it with a cricket ball. A full-size ball." *Glare.*

"When you can do all the orthodox left-arm the Chinaman's a great surprise ball. Lots of batsmen wouldn't have a clue."

"You didn't have a clue and you're an awesome batsman."

"I'm not an awesome batsman…" *But then it seemed wrong to take any of his triumph away from him. And I did average 20 going in number 8 for Mr Ahmad's team.* "But I am probably one of the best batsmen you've ever bowled at." *Time again for Test Match Special.* "Steve Helson. Scorer of the world's fastest century, totally at sea against England's new mystery spinner." *Giggle. Grin.*

The day got hotter and the park got fuller but we still had the nets to ourselves (do I have cricket halitosis?) He bowled a really long spell to me alone – much more than he'd be allowed in a match. (Even I have to go and lie down after 6 overs!) I was in control but he made me work and he kept throwing in that bloody Chinaman to keep me honest. I tried taking guard outside the crease and the little bugger threw in a really fast one outside offstump and squealed for a stumping. Not out on referral (by me to me). Eventually his arm got lower and I started smacking him about.

"Okay. One over. Eight to win, one wicket to fall any result possible." *He took a deep breath and went right through his repertoire. I second-guessed when he would bowl the Chinaman but he deceived me with his arm ball. Last ball, two to win. Yorker! Brave decision. I jammed it away and ran one. He picked up the ball and broke the stumps as I turned for the second.*

"And it's a tie! Only the third in Test Match history! Really well bowled. Terrific spell. Hardly a bad ball. Loads of good ones. Why aren't you in a team, you'd be a star?" *His face clouded. Stupid question.*

"Why aren't <u>you</u> in a team, you are a star already?" *Deserved it.*

"Have some water." *I passed him my bottle and he took a big glug. I was sweating so I slipped off the Beige shirt.*

"What's that?"

"Under shirt. Made of some kind of spacecraft fibre. Supposed to regulate your body temperature." *I pulled it off and threw it to him.*

"I want one."

"Be even nicer to your Mum."

"Impossible." *And I bet he was right. He peeled off his funny Nuclear Bomb T-shirt, and flopped face down on the grass.*

"Sunblock?" *He sat up and sighed.*

"Mum always makes me…" *He fished in his backpack and brought out some Factor 30. He smeared his face and front.* "Will you do my back?" *I froze for a minute. I wondered about how to warn him about asking strangers to put suncream on his back.* "Come on, I can't reach." *Well, who else could do it?*

"Don't do a silly face on my back." *Giggle.* "Here, I'll do yours." *He took the tube and did something much more elaborate on my back. Without looking round I could make out the design.*

"That's me batting! An original from Britain's leading suncream artist. That will be worth millions." *Giggle and smirk. He moved across to rub it in and I froze up. You know why. He looked surprised.*

"Gosh, I won't hurt!"

I recovered quickly. "I want to keep it! I won't burn because of my saturnine complexion *[for some reason I was just on maximum Wordpower that day!]* but you need protection." *I rubbed my silly face into his back, very gently with the back of my hand, and he almost purred like a little cat.*

"How about riding your bike home and getting your batting stuff?" *The sudden dark face again.*

"What about your friends? The Kiwis. Won't they want to bat when they come?"

"They're not coming. Their dad's ill, they've gone back to NZ. May never see them again." *That snivelling self-pity again. I felt ashamed. And with this great new cricketer I've just met.* "I want to bowl at you. Just you see if I'm not scary! Get your stuff. Do you live far away?" *More of those nervous bounces and darting looks at the ground rather than me.*

"You come with me, and we can raid the fridge. Mum makes brilliant leftovers."

"I'm sure she does, but if I come with you I've got to schlep my bag there and back and I came a long way already and I honestly don't feel like another schlep." *That and the thing about not taking a stranger to your house. Even a stranger who's only a few years older than you.*

"Oh. Yeah." *More bounces and darting looks.* "Look, you're going to think me a total baby but there's a big dog in our street and I'm scared of him." *Not very convincing. Something else was going on.*

"Just keep eye contact with that dog and don't make sudden movements." *Your advice.*

"I don't think I can. It's… too much for me." *The start of tears. What was going on? What had defeated this brave little soldier?*

I almost hugged him but then said quickly "Tell you what, use my stuff. I think it will work for you. First, try my bat. It's very light." *On your recommendation and you-know-who's. He did know his stuff.* "You will be able to use it with a low grip. Now those Padman shorts have a drawstring and if you're not embarrassed you can put them on over your shorts." *No embarrassment at all. He strutted around in them.* "Now my pads will be a problem around those Twiglet legs." *Pout. We just managed to get them tight enough.* "Gloves. Shit! Wrong way round. No protection for the thumb that needs it. I really wish you would get your own stuff."

"I'll be right." *Another Brendon/Daniel expression. Did he listen to everything we said? It could have been creepy but I just felt sad that he had been too shy to ask to join us. They'd have loved him.*

"Now, helmet."

"It's so hot."

"If I turn your face into a pile of putrescent pulp you will lose your ten-million-dollar movie star contract." *Your answer when I used to protest. Giggle. I jammed the lid on him and fiddled with everything until it sat on him properly and he could see over the visor.* "A few throw-downs to see if you can move at all and use the bat." *He barely lifted the bat out of the blockhole but he could move his feet, and he did, properly, right forward or right back. No scampering to leg.* "Okay, now the real thing. About your kind of pace. With that heavy bat, try to hit straight and not too hard. Definitely no hooking." *I didn't try much spin, just flighted filth. He dealt with it very easily. I eased up into second gear.*

"Come on, this is pie-throwing."

"I'll show you pie-throwing." *I moved up into third gear. The medium I bowl on wet wickets. Pretty quick to him. More hurry from him and some play-and-miss but no whining and no running away. Half-volley. Smashed straight past me. What every fast bowler hates, especially when followed by a victory squeal.*

The next ball my body took over. Same run-up, still well below the pace, but a little extra body action and a flick of the wrist. Definitely quicker, back of a length, rearing up and hitting him just above the elbow. Another squeal, but pain not victory.

You total, unmitigated shit. I rushed down the net. He had dropped my bat and was rubbing furiously. The start of tears. "God, I'm so sorry. Where does it hurt? Did it hit your elbow? Take your time. Breathe slowly. Count to ten backwards. Come out of the net. I'll get ice from the café. There's arnica in my bag."

"Don't wet yourself. It's only a bruise. I want to go on. It was fun until then."

I went right back to first gear.

"Oh come on, those aren't even pies, they're lollipops." *Back up to second gear.* "Cream pies." *Very cautiously, back up to third gear.* "That's better. Bread rolls." *He nicked the one I swung away from him, but so do lots of bigger people. He missed my yorker, but so do lots of bigger people. He did not run away, as do lots of bigger people. He played a few tired cross-bat shots and I said* "Okay, last over. You cannot hit hard with my stuff, so just three to win, one wicket to fall." *I set my umbrella field. Seven close catchers. The little guy showed really good judgement and picked off two singles. Last ball. My Slower Ball. Same action from the palm of my hand. He attempted the same push past me to win. Too early. In the air. I flung myself wide and low and caught it inches off the ground. Squeal.*

"Incredible. The second Test Match ends in a tie like the first! What odds could you get against that? The bookmakers have been ruined and police are anxious to interview players from both teams... Get some water."

I helped him out of all my kit and passed him water. "Finish it, I brought tons. You mustn't dehydrate. That was a very, very good innings. With your own kit, you would have scored buckets of runs. I wish you had played with me and Brendon and Daniel. You could have faced them, and they are way better than me." *Once again, Uncle Frank, I have never seen anyone as happy. I felt a bit dizzy. Low blood sugar? What about him, he had way less stored energy than me?*

"Luncheon interval. Have you got stuff to eat?" *He pulled a big plastic box from his backpack and extracted two big obviously home-made roast beef sandwiches. I must have drooled because he offered me one on the spot.*

"Go on. Mum made it."

"Your Mum made it for you, to build rippling Superman muscles of steel like mine." *Giggle and shy peek at my admittedly magnificent upper body. I scarfed down some cereal bars and threw him one of my bananas.*

"Why do fast bowlers eat bananas?"

"They get sponsored by the Banana Marketing Board." *Actually I hadn't a clue. Biology is not one of my GSCEs. I think it's something to do with potassium.* "I'm getting some more water."

"We don't need it."

"We do now," *and I emptied the rest of my bottle over him. Massive squeal. I escaped. He ran after me but I waved him back to watch over our stuff. I came back from the café with masses of water, and more cereal bars and bananas. He was stretched out in the hot sun with no top on. I made him take more water. Me too.* "Into the shade. No arguing." *I checked the sun, tried to remember your lessons, and finally worked out which direction it would take. (Westward.) We dragged all our stuff into a shady spot where I calculated the shade would last.* "A little nap would refresh us before the next session. You will be surprised what a good pillow you can make from a cricket bag." *I repacked mine as you taught me and stretched out with my back and shoulders against it. He made as if to lie beside me. It signalled total trust, maybe more. Either way I wasn't ready and I had not met his mother.* "No, we both need a little nap and I am a terrible thrasher when I sleep and I don't want to pulverize your face by mistake. Only when I bowl. Make yourself comfortable on the other side of the bag." *He did so, a bit reluctantly, and we both dozed off. I had a short vivid dream of dealing myself a poker hand and finding it was a straight flush.*

Chapter 4   New Partnership

I was wakened by a shower of water on my face and a squeal.

"Revenge!" *He finished emptying the water bottle.* "You've been asleep for hours. You're not fit like me. One spell and you're stuffed."

"If I've really been asleep for hours, why didn't you do something useful like going back home and getting your own kit?" *Another shuffling silence.*

"I ... only want to bowl. And you don't want to bowl at a little kid so that you have to bowl lollipops and pies."

"I really enjoyed bowling at you, just as much as at bigger people, no - more. And I need to practise bowling bread rolls as well as my ... heat-seeking missiles." *Giggle.* "So go on, back home on your bike, come back with your own kit, so you can bat properly."

"Come with me, you didn't get any real lunch and there's loads in the fridge."

Deadlock. I really thought I would have to warn him about taking strangers to his home, then came salvation. I never thought I would be glad to hear the whiny voice of fat Robert.

"Not fast, this time."

"Don't worry, darling."

"I know those two. Come and meet them." *I knew cricket net etiquette would take over. Cal would bowl at Robert and then Robert and his dad would offer Cal an innings, and Cal would borrow all of Robert's kit (approximate value £200), especially his beautiful correctly-sized bat.*

"Is he any good?"

"Nothing like you as a bowler. Decent enough batsman, but terrified of anything faster than a cream pie. So he'll be fine against you." *Glare.*

Robert had added much extra padding to a body which carried a lot already. I felt sorry for him for the first time. Fat kids have a hard time, even when Daddy spends £200 on their kit.

"Hello again. This is Cal. Do you mind if he bowls at you for a bit? He's a spinner." *Robert sized up the smaller, thinner boy.*

"Go on, darling, and then you get more bowling and I bet his spin is better than mine." *I picked up the secret message: father would stay there with the speed gun.*

"Okay. Spin?"

"Slow left-arm. Round the wicket." *Cal cleverly stressed the word "slow."*

"And can I just turn my arm over?" *Instant resistance. I added hastily* "No run-up at all. Just flighted filth for you to hit."

"That would be brilliant, because then I could practise keeping." *The father looked animated for the first time, rather than anxious. He held out his hand.* "We didn't really do names when you bowled to us last time. Steve, isn't it? I'm Joe Barnes and this is my son, Robert. And Cal is your…?"

He cut in instantly. "Friend. Cal Devane."

"Any relation to the rock star?"

His face lit up again. "He's my mum's uncle!"

"Well, let's rock and roll. Now darling, I'm going to keep wicket instead of bowling. The Frenetics have pulled me out of a deserved retirement and I haven't kept for years." *He extracted gloves, box and keeping pads from their bag, put them on, moved the stumps forward and crouched.* "Remember, I'm an old codger and it would be cruel to make me dive down the leg side."

He libelled himself. He clearly knew his trade as a keeper. I was pleased for Cal to have an ally. I bowled lollipops at Robert. The Test Match Special team spoke again in my head: painful to see this great fast bowler reduced to a one-pace run-up. Robert swatted them all away. But he and Cal had a proper contest. Cal bowled in his orthodox style, occasionally being driven off overpitched balls but winning one caught-and-bowled and a smart stumping. He threw in a few Chinamen, which spat past Robert (who skipped backwards) and his father (who admired). After each Chinaman I put in an extra-pathetic lollipop for Robert to smash. His father gave me a little nod of recognition.

The ball slipped out of Cal's hand and stopped dead in front of Robert. He swiped it back hard straight at Cal. Within the rules but, I thought, bad manners. What would you have done, Uncle Frank? I decided to step up a gear, from lollipops to pies. Robert turned his back on the first pie and I hit him. Shit. Force Eight on the Whineometer.

"It's too much for me!" *His father flapped around and then shot me an angry look. Shit in spades! I had made a powerful enemy. Maybe he would get me banned from the nets. Maybe Cal too, guilty by association. I flapped as well.*

"I'm so sorry. I didn't mean to hurt you, but it's really important never to turn your back on the ball. Breathe slowly, count to ten backwards, you'll feel better. Then have another go, you were batting really well."

"It's not fair! Just because I'm fat!" *This was a new agenda.*

"You're not fat, you've just got muscle-in-waiting." *Wordpower, I thought, but it did not work.*

"It's too much for me!" *Cal then took charge. He pulled Robert aside and had a long whisper. It made him giggle, and he resumed his place at the crease.*

"Does this mean you want to carry on?" *Nod.* "Do you want revenge?" *Nod and fierce stare.* "Cal, can you take a break? Mr... Joe, do you mind coming out of the net for a while?" *They both obeyed.* "Robert, this is your chance for revenge. You're going to hit the ball back at me and hurt me. You are going to hit the ball hard before it hits you. Therefore you are going to walk out and meet it and hit it just after it bounces. First, a few throw-downs." *Nod.*

After a few miscues he hit one of my throw-downs at me. I fielded it casually. "Nice shot, but that didn't hurt at all. I thought you wanted to hurt me. Even that little weed can hurt me and you are much stronger." *Exaggerated pout from Cal.* "So I want you to try again." *More throw-downs as Cal rummaged in his backpack. Joe watched silently. Robert made some decent straight drives and again I fielded them quite easily.* "These are good shots too but they don't give me any pain. Would you like to try some real balls instead of throw-downs? No run up but proper action." *Nod.* "Okay. Same idea. Hitting the ball before it hits you and making it hurt me instead of you." *He struck a few lollipops at me and off his best shot I pretended to misfield.* "Better shot, but still not painful. Why not?"

"Because you're tough."

"Because there was no pace on the ball for you to hit. To prove it, do you want to try hitting some quicker balls in the same way?" *Dubious look.* "They will be just the same as all the others, right up there in the slot for you to drive, you'll just have to do it a little sooner." *Reluctant nod. I moved up to pie* mode. *He missed a few but at least he still tried to meet them. The first one he hit decently I stopped, then winced ostentatiously and flapped my hand.* "Ouch. Annoying but not painful. Maybe still not enough pace on the ball to start with. Do you want to try the same with something a little quicker?" *Positive nod.* "I'm now going up to third gear. That is as fast as anything you will ever face from anyone your age. That is what I bowled earlier to him." *I moved from pies to bread rolls. He missed the first few but stood his ground. Eventually he hit a clean straight drive. I put my hand on it and howled with pain (almost for real). I dropped the scalding projectile [Wordpower] and jammed my inflamed digits into my armpits. I saw a little gloat, and a big smile from his father.*

"Is that enough revenge?" *Nod, with added gloat.* "Do you see? The faster the ball the harder you can hit it. Pace is your friend." *Nod.* "It won't always be that simple, and we did not try anything off the back foot, but the principle is always the same. Hit the ball before it hits you." *Nod.*

"Thanks. Thanks a lot. Would Cal like to bat?" *Cal jammed something into his backpack and joined us.*

"I haven't got my stuff."

"Use mine. It's the same as Tim Morrow uses." *England's new batting genius. I remembered reading a story about him and his dad and his toy tiger.* [1]

"Gosh. Are you sure?" *Nod.* "Can I have the Padman shorts?" *We fitted him out and Robert handed him his expensive bat.* "Wow, is that real?" *Inscription to Robert from Tim Morrow. Wow indeed! These people are well-connected.*

As I hoped, my little guy batted really well with the right-size kit. I bowled my bread rolls, Joe Barnes was a decent off-spinner (leg-spin to Cal). Robert was all over the place until I tried out your "two-guns" idea on him. He improved but was still low in confidence. Cal used his feet and dealt comfortably with Joe and me but was surprisingly clean bowled by Robert's first straight ball.

"Reverse swing!" *This time Robert looked as though he'd been given the Universe for Christmas.*

The sun began to sink (in the direction I had predicted) and I stepped up my pace. Not heat-seeking missiles, but certainly heated bread rolls. I made sure that they were up in the slot and Cal met them on the front foot. The first full half-volley he crashed back at me. I stopped it and howled in pain (pretty genuine). "That must have hurt! The

---

[1] See "The Tiger Will Bite Your Legs" from <u>A Tale Of Ten Wickets</u>

same hand that was damaged earlier today. And he signals – he cannot carry on. The world's fastest bowler destroyed by England's new partnership of Barnes and Devane." *Double set of giggles.*

"We have to go, darling." *Protest, and then suddenly the sun went behind a cloud and Robert noticed something on my bare back, while Cal unpadded.*

"Look, Dad, it's a design in sunblock, like that ad you did. It's a batsman. Who did that?"

"Cal. He is Britain's leading artist in the medium. My back is insured for twenty million pounds."

"Can he do one for me?"

"Too late, the sun's going down."

"Will you be here tomorrow?"

"Yes," *shouted Cal before I could say anything.* "And the day after that, and the day after that, and the day after that…"

"Can we come?"

"We're going to see Chemical Brothers."

"I'd rather come here." *Joe Barnes pulled out a £20 note.*

"Take Cal to the ice cream stand, and trade phone numbers and whatever else, and we can fix another time to see Cal and Steve."

"What about my diet?"

"We won't tell the Diet Fairy." *The two kids trotted off, and Joe turned to me.* "That was the best afternoon he's ever had here. He's got a new mate, which he really needed, and you're a brilliant coach. Did you think all that up yourself – hurting the bowler and the two guns?"

"My uncle Frank taught me that way, but I have made some additional adjustments and adornments." *He smiled.*

"Did your uncle also teach you alliteration?"

"My uncle Frank was mad about words and if he ever found any he really liked he would give them to me and then say 'Wordpower!'"

"Words are my business. I'm a writer. Well, a copywriter. Have you heard of Barnes Dorman Sharp?"

"Sorry."

"My advertising agency. It is … not inconsequential."

"Wordpower!" *we both said, and he added* "Litotes." *Then he sighed deeply.* "Wordpower isn't everything. Sometimes words stop you saying what you want to say. I used a bunch of words once to avoid saying 'I love you and can't live without you.' I carried them around me for a long time. They were in an airletter.[2] Then, thank God, I got another chance." *He brightened up.* "You and Cal aren't related? How long have you known each other?"

"Since this morning. Well, he saw me before with those New Zealand guys you and Robert once saw me with, but he didn't speak to me. But this morning he asked if he could bowl at me, and well, we just carried on."

"I thought you must have known each other for years."

"He's … really likeable. And he's really good at cricket. As you saw. And… well, he was on his own and I wanted to make sure he was… safe. I'm going to meet his mum before we play again."

"That's very responsible." *He pulled out a card.* "That's my private number and email. Please use them and leave your details. I would be delighted if you coached Robert again, although we're going on holiday soon. If you're interested, you can come to the agency and do a trial as a copywriter. And if his mother agrees, Cal can come and work in the art room the next time we do a sunblock ad. Robert's done shifts for me – he's a snapper. So has Zoe, his sister, a writer. Sadly, not together. They don't get on…" *His face clouded but then brightened again.* "Also, I would like to introduce you to a real writer. Howard Foy used to work with me and he owns shares in the agency. But he became a real writer. Do you know the Rob Patty stories?"

"Yeah. The hopeless screenwriter. We used to watch them on TV every Sunday. They were brilliant." *They must have been. Even Mum and Dad stopped arguing when they were on.*

---

[2] See "Air Letter" in <u>A Tale Of Ten Wickets</u>

"Howard wrote them. They're based on a character we used to play cricket with. He stole my screenplay, so Howard stole him back. [3] Howard's the real deal as a writer, although he hasn't written much since his wife died." *He sighed again.* "Howard is also the real deal as a cricketer and a big shot at the MCC. If he respects you, and I'm sure he will, he could get you on a programme as a player and as a coach." *I felt dizzy and then some tears started up again. What a wuss I'm turning into!* "Something wrong?"

"Sorry. It's just that … cricket's everything to me, but every time I get something going for myself, something happens. A door slams in my face."

"Howard will hold the door open for you. What happens after is up to you. Put those numbers in a safe place. Email your contact details as soon as you can. I will pay back what you did for my boy." *The two kids bounded back.*

"Cal helped my diet by eating my ice cream as well! Can Cal come to our house? And Steve? Can they stay over?"

"We'll sort something with Cal's mother. Ifֽ Cal wants to come." *Big smile.*

"Thank you for the ice creams. And thanks for letting me use your kit. Your bat is awesome."

"Do you want to borrow it?"

"No, thanks a lot, but Tim Morrow signed it for you and besides we're going shopping for kit." *I worked out the cost of a new Tim Morrow special and hoped that Cal's mum had a good amount of plastic in her purse. Which reminded me that I didn't have any plastic of my own. Why not? Why does Dad dole out my money? I went off into une petite reverie [Motpouvoir!] and scarcely noticed the remaining goodbyes. Cal woke me up.*

"Are we going home now?"

"Will your mum be back?"

"Should be. Unless she's on a case."

"Case?"

---

[3] See "Pat Hobby Runs Out Of Luck" in <u>A Tale Of Ten Wickets</u>

"She is one of the top children's lawyers in the country." *Loyal of him, but maybe true. I remembered what Brendon had said. Perhaps she could sue Dad for restraint of my trade as a cricketer. We gathered our stuff. I put the Beige shirt on very carefully over his design on my back. He picked up his backpack, bike and trendy helmet, and I started to shlep my cricket bag.*

"Robert turned out to be a nice kid, after all. I always thought he was a pest, but you got to him in five minutes. Have you got some kind of Nicedar? And what did you say to him which stopped him whining when he was batting."

"I told him when I batted against you I peed my pants."

"Not true at all."

"I thought it would make him feel better."

"And you let him bowl you."

"It reversed."

"Not true at all."

"I thought it would make him feel better." *I pondered this for a while and then said something which had been on my mind all day.*

"I'm really looking forward to meeting your mum, and it's … important she should meet me, and if… she doesn't like me we won't play cricket again."

"I <u>know.</u> Of course she'll like you. What's not to like?"

"You have not seen my dark side. When the moon is full, I… I… I don't recycle newspapers." *Giggle. We reached the big tree where two kids, a bit smaller than him, were staring forlornly at a football stuck in the uppermost branches.*

"It's my brother's. He didn't know I took it. He'll kill me." *I waved everybody away and pulled my worst cricket ball out of my bag.*

"This might work." *I wound up and threw as if from the boundary, only up rather than in. On my third attempt I hit the football, but jammed it further into the branches. Cal elbowed me aside.*

"This is a job for… The Cat! Give me your shoulders." *He climbed on them and just reached the lowest branch. He hauled himself up and worked up the tree. A rotten* branch cracked under him. *I turned white, but he grabbed another one. He climbed upwards and was practically a speck [hyperbolic Wordpower] when he reached the captive football and released it to its grateful tenant.*

It was harder coming down. When Cal reached the broken branch he could not go any further. "Steve? Ready? Catch!" *and he jumped off into my arms. I just managed to catch him and fell on my back.*

"Are you okay?"

"Of course. It was an easy catch but you made a meal of it. Are <u>you</u> okay? You're hyperventilating!" *He got up and waved aside the thanks of the kids with the football.* "All in a day's work for … The Cat!"

We walked on slowly, him pushing the bike, me pulling the bag. I stopped and looked at him for a while.

"Who are you looking at?" *The yob's challenge to a fight, from the least menacing yob in the Northern Hemisphere.*

"You. Where do you get room for that outsize heart?"

"I haven't got an outsize heart."

"Have too. Risk your neck for some other kid's football."

"I wanted to show off to you."

"Not true."

"Why did you lie about yourself to Robert and let him bowl you?"

"Wanted you to think I was a nice kid and like me."

"Not true."

"You don't think I'm a nice kid and you don't like me?" *Mock alarm.*

"Not true as to motive." *Long pause.*

"My mum told me when I was little that if I ever felt small and sad I should try to do something good for someone and it would make me feel strong and happy. Even if it's just … letting a bug out of a matchbox. And she was right."

33

"Did you feel small and sad this morning?"

"Yes, before I met you."

"Why?"

"Oh. Just because I do sometimes. And what about you?" *Diversionary attack.* "Don't talk to me about big hearts." *He put his bike down.* "You play cricket with a little weed like me all day. You teach me good stuff. You look after me. You go to pieces when you think I've got hurt. You're really nice to Robert, even though you think he's a pest. You're a total softie! You couldn't even squash a tomato!"

He threw himself at me and for the second time I had to cope with his massive 80 pounds. (Estimate). He tried to wrestle me to the ground. I made him work for a bit then let him win. Just like you with me, when I was little.

Was this what you aimed to do, Uncle Frank? Make someone feel totally excited and totally safe, at the same time?

And is this what it felt like for you?

Chapter 5   Crowd Disturbance

I beat the big softie easily and pinned him to the ground. I lay on top of him for a bit. I <u>so</u> wanted to kiss him and then thought, what would he think of me, and we're right in the middle of the park! So I jumped up quickly and picked up my bike.

"Look, I want to show you a stunt." Actually I didn't know any stunts..

"Helmet on."

"You're worse than Mum!"

"Every trip, never mind for stunts. I always wear mine." *Lies on my part, Uncle Frank! But I will now.*

So I stuck it on and whirled round the park and tried to think of a stunt and of course just fell off my bike in front of him.

"Gosh, I could never do a stunt like that." But not sarky.

"I want to try again." Actually, I wanted to delay going home. Maybe <u>they'd</u> have gone...

"I want to meet your mum." So he pulled his cricket bag and I put my backpack on and started pushing my bike. I told him where I lived and how to get there. When we crossed the busy road he slipped his spare hand onto my bike to help me and I felt... looked after.

As we got nearer our street I slowed down and listened. Maybe for once they'd have gone... But then I heard those bloody skateboards. Fuck. Fuck, fucking fuck! They're going to call me names and I'm going to cry and he's going to know about me and see that I <u>am</u> a baby and I can't stand up for myself. He stopped and put his hand on my shoulder.

"Are you worried about the dog?"

"What dog?" Fuck again. Stupid! Forgot what I told him. He looked at me for a bit.

"Are you being bullied?" I nodded and really tried for once not to cry.

"How many?"

"Two."

"Bigger than you but not as big as me? On skateboards?" **I nodded again.**

"Now, can you be extra brave for a few seconds? Walk past them with your bike, just go where you're going and don't look at them or pay any attention to what they say. I'll be right behind you and I want to surprise them."

"All right." **So I walked on, and of course there they were, fat Ed and spotty Peter, and they started up.**

"Watch out, it's Fairy Boy... mind your backs it's Fairy Boy... how's your arse, Fairy Boy, is that why you can't ride your bike?"

"He's still wearing his helmet. Does Mummy make you wear it, Fairy Boy?" **I nearly flared up when they mentioned Mum, but then Steve stepped up. He dropped his cricket bag and crouched a little, like fighters on TV. Our road's a dead end, that's why they come here to make me go past them, but it meant they had no escape from Steve.**

"Why are you talking to Fairy Boy? I don't see any Fairy Boy here. His name's Cal, he's my cousin, and I'm Steve. And your names would be... Boobs, and... Pusface? Or Tits and Zits?" **They looked a bit sick, and Steve went on** "Not much fun being called names, is it?" **They nodded.** "So I think we'll stick to real names all round. So again, Cal, Steve, and...?"

"Ed."

"Peter."

"Well, Ed and Peter, I need your help. I went to prison for a year and I don't want to go back there. You don't want to know the ways people fight in prison and to get through it you have to fight dirtier than everyone else. Anyway, I went to prison for smashing another kid's jaw (and he's still having surgery). I hit him because he dissed my family and when that happens I go a bit psycho. So what would really, really help me is for people not to diss my family. Don't have to like my family, just not diss them. Do you think you could tell your mates about Psycho Steve?" **They nodded.**

"Does that mean yes?"

"Yes."

"Yes."

"Good. Everything will be fine now. No dissing my family, no Psycho. Oh, and there's lot's of other kids in my family, so you would not want to pick on one of them by mistake, would you? Now, you know Rainborough Street, near the main road? It's got a slope and if you're any good at skateboarding you could go well fast and do stunts. Why don't you guys try it? Of course, that would need guts unlike being two-to-one against my cousin who's smaller than you." **He gestured with his thumb and they skated off fast.**

"Was that... true?"

"My uncle Frank said that when you are being interrogated you should use as much of the truth as you can. Do you mind being my cousin?"

"I wish."

"Bullies don't like trouble. You won't see them. Now you're king of your street again." **That's when I lost it and started to cry. He hugged me.**

"How long has it been going on?"

"All summer."

"It's over. They'll tell everyone about Psycho Steve."

I hugged him back. "What if they find out you're really a big softie?" **For a second I thought he was going to cry. Why?** "Let's go and meet my mum."

I find it hard to write about my son Cal's bad summer. I am a lawyer and I am supposed to use neutral language. But to my dying day I will be furious at all those responsible, including myself. I will try to be factual and not to direct the jury.

For some years, Cal had a best friend of his age called Ben. They went to primary school together, played cricket together and created comics together – Ben supplying the words, Cal the drawings. They also had frequent sleepovers in each other's houses. Cal was a popular kid and had plenty of other friends, but Ben was the special one. At his pleading, I worked my socks off to get him into the same secondary school as Ben, which also offered an excellent art department.

Ben's parents did not approve of me or Cal as a single-parent family with a liberal-minded attitude to most things. It would be fair to describe them as members of the Moral Majority, and as ostentatiously religious. But Ben's friendship for Cal was so strong, and so creative, that they allowed it.

Like virtually all boys, Cal and Ben did some exploration and experiment together on their bodies, and at twelve, in their first year of secondary school, they had reached the stage of mutual masturbation. Ben was bigger and more advanced physically than Cal, but Cal was far more mature and aware emotionally. At eleven, he told me that he believed he was gay. He believed he was in love with Ben, and looking for more than physical satisfaction. I didn't listen to him as I should have done. As I would have done for a client. But in my mind Cal was still my little boy, years away from big grown-up emotions. If I had listened better, I might have warned him against declaring his love to Ben, as he did on a sleepover, one weekend near the start of the summer term. He asked Ben if he could kiss him and if they could be boyfriends.

Ben roared for his parents, and claimed that Cal (smaller and lighter) had attempted a sexual assault. They actually yanked my little boy out of bed in his nightwear, threw him into their car and virtually dumped him on my doorstep without even checking if I was at home. I was too busy comforting my traumatized, sobbing son to take in their version of events. I heard Cal's truthful account, in dribs and drabs over the next two days. He did not go to school on Monday, but that evening he had rallied to my pep talk. He had done nothing wrong, Ben and his parents were totally stupid and we would not have anything more to do with them. He could do so much better than Ben as a boyfriend and he even started making a list of possible candidates at school.

Neither of us were prepared for that little shit Ben to have outed him to the school on the Monday. Cal was greeted on his return to school on Tuesday with a volley of homophobic abuse. He collapsed in tears, not so much because of the abuse but because of the betrayal. I have never bothered to work out Ben's motives. Essentially, he was a weak character and I've learnt over the years that weak people are the ones who betray you. The vicious ones will hurt you, maybe even kill you, but it's the weak people who betray you. Anyway, I yanked Cal home again.

Of course I took the issue up with the school and they promised to take action. I should have known that the action would be worse than useless. Cal's school was an academy. That meant that it had outside sponsors, who were given effective control of it in exchange for a one-off payment of £2 million. (Some sponsors never coughed up, but they got control of their schools anyway.) Cal's school sponsors were a group of evangelical Christian businessmen, the Companions, who did not like homosexuals. They appointed a head teacher of their kind, a creeping Jesus with more experience of business than teaching, and similarly-minded staff. I should have known these people would let down my gay son. At an interview I did ask how they handled gay issues and the head prattled about their policy of tolerance. Tolerance – as if being gay was some kind of weakness. Why didn't I scream there and then: "he's left-handed, too, do you tolerate left-handers?"

Cal had to recover at home for the rest of the week, during which time the whole of years Seven to Nine were made to listen to a long presentation about tolerance. No attempt to screen out the ringleaders or make Ben face up to the consequences of his actions. Needless to say, years Seven to Nine took it as a collective punishment, and that made Cal really popular on his return.

Every day for the next few weeks, he endured name-calling, physical assaults, and damage to his property, whenever a teacher wasn't looking and often enough in full view of a teacher. He had to give up his local cricket club, where he had been a star, because some of his chief tormentors were in the team. Because we live in a cul-de-sac, some kids took to hanging around all day at the corner of our road, so he could get the treatment at weekends and holidays as well. By courtesy of modern technology, they were also able to bully by text and online. Worst of all, they defaced his drawings – his greatest talent.

I think what really got to Cal was the treachery, and not just Ben's. None of his friends stood by him. Nobody wanted to get the treatment, especially the friends he knew to be gay.

After a few weeks of this my bouncy little boy was destroyed. He became tearful and clingy, and could not bear to go outside. His appetite was ruined and he had regular episodes of vomiting and bedwetting. The school offered him counselling: I suggested they might prefer to counsel the bullies and the homophobes rather than the victim. We had had enough and I pulled him out of school. As a children's lawyer with contacts in the media I was not the sort of parent schools liked to challenge. They agreed to treat him as absent ill (which was true enough). A home teacher made some visits – a nice grandmother who happened to be an amateur artist. She spent most of their sessions admiring his drawings, which restored some of his self-esteem.

I hoped that the bullies might forget him when I pulled him out of school, but this was not so. Cal had been one of the most popular kids in his year. Bullying him was a revenge for the losers who had been in his shadow. For other boys, nervous about their sexual identity, bullying Cal was a statement that they were "normal". And almost certainly the worst bullies were being bullied by somebody else. Bullying Cal was their payback and their only source of self-esteem. For whatever reasons, there were always enough bullies in my son's world and sometimes in his physical space to make him miserable, humiliated, afraid and alone. I offered to get the police and the law in motion against the worst of them. He thought it would just make things worse and he was almost certainly right. If I had got an injunction or an ASBO against them they would have treated it as a badge of honour.

He would not leave the house except with me. At weekends I drove him a long way from our neighbourhood so that he could feel safe in the open air. We went for long walks and he would draw and draw. On one walk we saw a cricket match in progress with kids of his own age and I saw his eyes fill with tears.

"Sweetheart, the fielding side looks as though they really need you. Why don't you ask if you can play for them?"

He thought about it for a while and then said sadly "Mum. They'd ask why I wanted to play for them, all the way out here, when we live in London and they'd find out all about me and then it would all start up again."

So there was no cricket for him that summer, except spinning a ball endlessly against our back wall. It was a really irritating sound and I wanted it to go away but I bit my tongue and simply asked what he was doing and he said, with a tiny flash of pride "That's my mystery ball. The Chinaman."

The school term ended with him still officially on their books, but I would not send him back there even if I had to go to jail. I would rather have him in care than in The Companions Academy. Private school was out of the question. I had an offer of a place in a poor school a long way away from us. I investigated home schooling – a sad choice for a gregarious twelve-year-old.

The summer holidays were the worst period. Last summer I had hardly seen my boy: he was outdoors somewhere all day. Now he shut himself away, doing nothing but draw or practise that infernal ball against the back wall. I was frazzled myself by this stage and we started to get on each other's nerves. I got too tired to drive him to places and in any case, I wanted him to reclaim our neighbourhood.

About that time I found a big pile of drawings he had never wanted to show me. They were technically very accomplished, but they showed his ex-friends, especially Ben, being terrified or even tortured. I called him over.

"Cal, darling, these drawings tell me they're winning. They want you to be one of them, unhappy and hated. If you want to gain power over them, do you want a suggestion?"

"Yes."

"Try to make someone else happy. It will make you feel big and powerful, even when you're small and sad. Trust me on this. Anyone can be cruel but only a great king can show mercy."

"That's what you said when I was little and put the bug in the matchbox."

"And do you remember what you felt like when you let him out?"

"I remember what it felt like when you gave me an ice cream." His first joke for a long time. He gave my idea a try. He did some gardening for our nice neighbour and got her garden looking really good and then sketched it for her, even colouring it in and that meant a lot because he doesn't really favour colour, only line.

"Was she happy?"

"You bet!"

"And how do you feel?"

"Brilliant. Two ice creams!" He thought for a while and then said "Mum. What could I do to make you happy?"

I hoped this might be coming, so I took a deep breath and said "Go to the park by yourself. You can ride your bike – with your helmet on – and if those little shits are on the corner, just ride past them and ignore them. I know it will be hard but I know you can do it. And when you get to the park I suggest you head for the cricket nets, and who knows, there might be somebody who might want to play with you."

"Suppose… they're in the park?"

"That's a risk but the park should be crowded and bullies don't like crowds. And you told me they never favoured the cricket nets. Will you be brave for me and give it a try?"

"It's still sunny. Can I go now?"

On return: "Mum! There was this kid bowling who's a total god!" and he went on breathlessly about this boy a bit older than him who was an awesome fast bowler, with two Australian brothers, young guys, who were even more awesome.

"Did you ask if you could bowl at them?"

"No. They wouldn't want a little kid."

"Cal, did these people look like they would be mean to a little kid?"

"No. They all seemed really nice. They made lots of jokes and they all wound up each other but they didn't mean it."

"I bet they would appreciate a fielder to get the ball back for them. And at best you would bowl at them and try out your mystery ball. Now, do you think they'll be back?"

"Yeah, I think they go loads of times."

The next day was wet, but the one after was sunny. I made him a big picnic lunch with enough to share for the others, packed him off on the bike, nagged about the helmet, and went to work hoping for the best.

I got a text at work saying "AT NETS PLAYING WITH GOD."

Chapter 6   Fast Bowler In New Contract Talks

"We're home! He's with me! What's for dinner?"

My son has a big voice when he's excited. That meant the end of my session at the piano. Just as well. Bach is a land of lost content. I headed out to the hall. Cal was bouncing around, showing off his prize exhibit, who was hovering, shyly, in the doorway. The god was a little shorter than I expected, although of course I had to look up to him (I am usually described as petite). He was a good-looking, very athletic boy, with a short, nondescript haircut, wearing a surprisingly horrible beige shirt.

"Trainers off!" I called automatically, and the god looked embarrassed.

"Are you certain? These trainers could be not just malodorous but mephitic."

I smiled at the god's vocabulary. "In that case, Cal will remove them for you and take them to the back door."

His little disciple removed the god's trainers and actually inhaled deeply. "Gosh, mum, they smell like your perfume," and the god blushed, guiltily. Then my son remembered to say "This is Steve. This is my mum," before rushing off.

"Very pleased to meet you, Mrs.. Ms Devane…"

"Alice, please. I am very pleased to meet you, Steve. Thank you for playing cricket with my son – and all day. Was he a pest?"

"Hell, no! He's… brilliant. It was great playing with him. And then we met some other people I sort of know. Anyway, I thought… you'd want to meet me… I mean, with me being with him all day…"

"Steve. I wanted to meet you to say thank you. Cal's had a rotten summer. It's been all I can do to get him outdoors at all. Eventually I forced him out to the park and he saw you with two Australians…"

"New Zealanders!"

"Sorry. And he was really excited for the first time and I actually urged him to find you again. The park's a public place and if you had been the wrong kind of stranger he would know what to do. Actually, I was much more worried about something else," at which point Cal bounded back.

"Mum, Steve got rid of the bullies! He made them pee in their pants," and he told me the story of Psycho Steve.

"I'm sure you defamed yourself, Steve, but in a good cause and I think it should work. Now, did you do or say anything to cause those two boys, bearing in mind their physical and intellectual maturity, to apprehend an immediate act of battery?"

"Wordpower," Steve blurted, and then added "What does that mean?"

"It's lawyerspeak for, did they think you were about to hit them?"

"No. Just if they dissed Cal or you."

"That's fine. For the future, it's potentially a crime to make somebody think you're about to hit them, as much as actually hitting them."

"Oh. Doesn't that mean that you might just as well hit somebody?"

"Threats, assault without battery, have a lesser penalty than hitting someone as well, especially if you cause wounding or actual bodily harm."

"What penalty would there be for actual bodily harm?" There was clearly a point to that question but this was not the right moment to answer it.

"If you want legal advice you'll have to pay me to be your lawyer."

"Go on, Steve, she's the tops. Oh and Mum, we met this really nice kid called Robert and his dad and he was really nice and they want us to have a sleepover at their place and they're going to call you."

"That's wonderful, sweetheart." The first sleepover since the fatal one with Ben, I hoped that Robert really was a nice kid. Anyway, he was someone new and not part of a circle where he could betray Cal, even if he was a shit. "Now then, Cal, show Steve your room and Steve, park your cricket bag there. Then Cal will show you the shower."

Cal eagerly pulled him away. A handsome, accomplished young man, but why was he so nervous? I went to the kitchen and wondered what I could offer him for dinner.

I was so embarrassed when I took Steve to my room. Bungle was on my bed! Maybe I could distract him and get him into the shower before he noticed. He parked his cricket bag somewhere (my clothes were all over the floor!) and I pulled my sketch book out of my backpack.

"Look, I did this. Would you like it? You don't have to, I mean, it's not very good and I can do a better one..." **But his face lit up.**

"This is fantastic. You've got... my glad animal action."

"Glad animal action?"

"That's from a book by a great fast bowler. My uncle Frank gave it to me."

"So you actually want it?"

"Of course I want it! When did you do it?"

"When I was watching you with those two New Zealand guys."

"I want it framed."

"OK. And do you think Robert will like this?"

"That's great too. He'll love it. That's when I got him to straight-drive me and hurt me, right? You've flattered him, you've slimmed him down a lot."

"No. That's what I can see. Muscle in waiting." **He seemed pleased that I remembered. Now, could I get him into the shower?**

"What's your teddy bear's name?" **AAAGH!**

"Bungle."

"That's a funny name."

"Mum sort of gave it to him. When I was little ..."

"You mean last week?" **and I gave him my most savage punch.**

"When I was little years ago and I did something wrong, like spilling a drink or breaking something, I always said it wasn't me it was him, and Mum would always say 'That bear is such a bungler!' So he became Bungle."

"Don't ever lose Bungle. I can still remember the terrible day I lost Sergeant Bear," **and he looked really sad.**

"Mum! Mum! This is really important!"

"I'm on the telephone."

"Sergeant Bear's gone. Have you seen Sergeant Bear? He was on my bed this morning. Oh bloody hell! Did he get in the bag with that stuff for Emma's charity shop? Who put him there? I didn't. I packed the bag with my stuff for that charity shop. Somebody took Sergeant Bear. Did Emma go into my room? I hate her. I hate you!" *and I ran out, leaving my mum still on the phone. Then I rushed back in again.*

"Mum! Quick, which is her charity shop? Just tell me which one…" *and she told me and I grabbed my bike and zoomed into the High Street and pushed into the shop. My mum's friend Emma, who's a cow, complained about my bike but I just said* "Never mind that, where's Sergeant Bear, the teddy bear you took from my room?" *and just then I saw a little girl pick him up in the shop and hug him and look at her mum. So I went over to her and knelt down and said* "Do you like him?" *and she nodded and I said* "That's Sergeant Bear. He used to live with me. My uncle Frank gave him to me. He's been in the Special Bear Squadron and he's trained to do this special kind of combat called tedkwando. So if a monster gets into your room at night, he can fight it." *The little girl started to smile.*

"What's your name?"

"Francesca."

"Gosh, that's like Frank. Frank to Steve to Francesca. Do you like Sergeant Bear?" *She nodded.* "And Sergeant Bear, do you like Francesca?" *I made him nod, madly. Francesca's mum started to say something, but I said* "It's time to say goodbye Sergeant Bear. Please look after Francesca the way you looked after me," *and I took my bike and went home.*

***

"But I still miss Sergeant Bear sometimes," and he looked really sad again and I really wanted to hug him but then he said "Are these all your clothes?"

"Yes. Mum says I'm not Cal Devane, I'm Cal the Vain."

"And a lifejacket." **AAAAGH! Mum made me try it on to see if it still fitted. Serves me right for not cleaning up my room.** "Do you do any water sports?"

I thought about lying but it wouldn't have worked. "No. It's because I'm poop-scared of water." **Oh God. He knows now I'm a baby and a wimp.**

"I'm glad you've got that. A lifejacket is brilliant. I mean, you can swim as far as you like but if you get tired or if it gets rough it will hold you up."

Then Steve looked at me for a bit and said "I'd like to be your lifejacket." *That just came to me.* "I love swimming. When it's wet, we might go to the pool together."

"Good, I'll watch you."

"What are all those hooks and things on the walls and the ceiling?"

"Mum put them up for me when I was little. Years ago. Look, I can go right round the room without touching the floor." **And I did.**

"You won't catch me doing that. I'm poop-scared of heights."

"You? No way. You're just saying that to make me feel better."

"It's true." *And it is true, isn't it, Uncle Frank? Remember that awful day at the base when I froze on the climbing tower and you and Sergeant Kwame had to get me down? I cried and cried because I had let you down and you said no, you had let* me *down.*

"What's that picture?" *Amazing. A giant picture of some people hunting. Most kids would have rock stars or footballers. Not that I ever did.*

"That's Paolo Uccello. A Hunt In The Forest. It's totally … brilliant. Mum took me to see it in Oxford when … I wasn't going out much. Uccello went mental about perspective. Look, see how everything looks as though it's disappearing towards the centre?"

"Yeah. Like it was getting sucked into a black hole."

"Gosh. Maybe. Anyway, that's the vanishing point. And look, it could be miles away. That's perspective. Imagine discovering perspective. You've got a flat surface and just by drawing a few lines in the right way you can make it look really deep. And look, see, there's a river in the picture with a different perspective and it looks weird, doesn't it?"

"Like a dream."

"Maybe. Anyway, I tried to do something like it." I went over to what Mum calls my studio, where I keep all my drawing stuff and sketchbooks. It's the only part of my room which is tidy, and I easily found what I wanted.

"This is me and Bungle in this imaginary forest, with one perspective for me and another one for Bungle so it's like... two worlds in the same place."

"That's totally brilliant." I'm pretty sure he meant it. He was right of course! And I pulled out some other drawings and he seemed awestruck.

"Gosh, sorry. You wanted a shower," and I showed him ours, which isn't bad actually and how everything worked and gave him a towel. And I so wanted to get in with him to help save the planet but I didn't and let him have a really long shower. He sang, but really badly. "There's a towel and a T-shirt Mum says you might like to wear." I left them and went back to my room, and he came in wearing his shorts and the T-shirt.

"My Folks Went All The Way To The Tao And All They Got Me Was This Lao-tzi T-shirt."

"Mum told me it's a joke. The old guy is Lao-tzi who was the founder of Taoist Buddhism. So it's a Lao-tzi lousy T-shirt. And there's another joke because Tao means the Way."

"Wordpower!"

"What's for dinner? Have we got something decent for Steve?" When Cal bounced into the kitchen with that request I knew that Steve had passed the teddy bear test. I set it up myself by putting Bungle back onto the bed. If there had been any hint of disdain, Steve would have been out of the door.

"Don't worry, Alice, I've got to be home. I've got things... to settle with my parents. And I've got to write to my Uncle Frank."

"But we are playing tomorrow? And the day after? And the day after? And the day after?" Steve looked pensive.

"It all depend on how things go. With my dad. He wants me to get a holiday job."

"I'll offer you a job right now. Cricket coach and bodyguard to my son at national rates per hour."

"I don't want any money to be with him! I had a brilliant day. He's a great cricketer. A great person who is a cricketer. But I don't know how many more I can do. You see, I did make this kind of deal with my dad. I promised to introduce him to some new clients – actually those New Zealand guys – but now I can't so I'll have to get a job instead."

"Do you want to get a job?"

"Only playing cricket. And not with Cal, because that's not a job that's what I want to do. And Dad doesn't think cricket's any kind of job, anyway."

"Hmm. I don't want to pry but did your father offer you anything as his side of the deal – like money or anything else that you could value in terms of money?"

"Well, not really. Just the right to play cricket."

"And were you forced into it?"

"Kind of."

"Hmm. In a court of law, you might challenge that contract with your father. It might be void for lack of consideration – your father did not give you anything of value in exchange for doing what he wanted. Alternatively, it might be void for duress – he forced you into it. You could even have a shot at saying it is void for public policy, in that our country believes that all teenagers should be encouraged to play sport."

"Daniel, my NZ mate, said something about restraint of trade."

"That's a good angle. But you're not yet in trade as a cricketer. You have not earned any money from it. Wait! Take this." I handed him a pound coin. "Your first fee as a cricket coach. You are now a professional cricketer."

"Mum, you're such a cheapskate, professional cricketers earn squillions of pounds," and we all laughed.

Then I said seriously "Steve. It's not for me to pry into your home life. It's up to you to work things out. But we would both like to see more of you. How old are you?"

"Sixteen."

"Then it is reasonable for you to have some independent choices in your life, especially if they are good choices like playing cricket and spending time with Cal and me. I think we are pretty good people for you to meet." Suddenly his eyes welled up with tears. What sorrow had we unlocked? This was not the time to find out and I changed the subject. "Are you sure you won't have something to eat? What did you have for lunch?"

"What I always have for cricket – cereal bars, bananas and buckets of water."

"Not enough protein. Cal, get out the smoothie machine and make a Humungous. One for you too, if you want, and bring them into the living room." I motioned for Steve to follow me and he took the cue.

"One thing I have to ask you alone. You've probably realized that Cal is gay. Do you have any kind of problem with that?"

"Hell no! He's … just… amazing."

"Good. But I'm also pretty sure he has a massive crush on you already. Is that a problem?" He looked really anxious. "Steve, don't worry about what you say, so long as it's the truth. Nothing will make me think worse of you."

"It's just that … do you want him to have a crush on me? Are you sure you even want him to see me? There's things you should know about me."

"Do you have a criminal record? I can find out."

"No. But I did something bad once. And there's other stuff…"

"Honest answer: is there anything about you that might harm Cal?"

"No! The minute he talked to me I just wanted to … look after him. Like my uncle Frank used to look after me. I'd go mental if something happened to him. I did, I mean in the park, when I thought I'd hurt him and when he jumped out of this bloody great tree."

"Did he do Cal The Cat? Poor Steve. Do you have any brothers or sisters?"

"No."

"I thought not. And have you ever had a pet?"

"No."

"Then this might be the first time you've ever looked after a … small creature who needed looking after. It's a very exciting experience for anyone with a heart, especially a big one like yours."

"He's the one with the giant heart. We had a fight about it." Suddenly I hugged him. He was surprised at first and then let himself melt into it. "Thank you for looking after my little one. And doing such a great job." Cal came in with the smoothie and parked it instantly and got a piece of the hug. We did not let Steve go until all his anxiety had melted away and he was as floppy as Bungle the bear.

"I really must be going."

"Get his smoothie down you." He took a big gulp.

"Wow! What's in this?"

"Three kinds of yoghurt, vanilla ice cream, milk, grapes, oranges, bananas, apples, pears, and a chocolate squirt."

"Where's yours?"

"There was only enough for one. And you're the fast bowler, you need more than me." Steve finished it off.

"Thanks a lot. That was… quintessential." I smiled again at his vocabulary.

"Now, Steve, do you want a lift home? He's okay on his own."

"No. Thank you. I'll walk. I want to think about … stuff. I've never had a day like this." My heart went out to him.

"All right. But Steve, please put our numbers on your mobile." We gave them to him. "And please call me when you get home." *Why is everyone suddenly looking after me? First Daniel and now her?* "If you're picking up Cal for cricket tomorrow, leave your bag in his room. Please keep that T-shirt. It suits you. And you will stay to supper tomorrow or else I'll sue you. Goodbye Steve. I'm glad we met you."

"Goodbye Steve. Come early tomorrow." *And they both gave me another giant hug. For time and strength I think they've already overtaken Mum and Dad this month. Sorry to say that, but I think it's true, Uncle Frank.*

I replayed the whole day on the walk home. Four brilliant new people on the same day and they all seemed to like me. Why? Anyway, you were right. I have dealt myself a new hand. I turned into my street and remembered to phone Alice.

Fire was being exchanged along the whole length of the front when I arrived home. Then it stopped and for a second, I thought that both armies would train their fire on me. "The weaker army must seize on any momentary hesitation by its opponents."

"Mum. Dad. I'm sorry I'm late, but it's not like it spoils my dinner because you could microwave it any time I come in. I met some new friends playing cricket in the park, actually four of them, and they wanted me to spend time with them afterwards, at least two of them, and I did, because it is good manners and that is a reasonable way for a 16-year-old to behave. I won't need any dinner tomorrow, because they have invited me to eat with them. I may not be here very much because they have asked me to play more cricket with them over the next few days. But I will be back to mow the lawn." *On which we never sit or play.*

"Dad, I am sorry to tell you that the McConnels, the rich New Zealanders, have had to go home, so I won't be able to introduce them to you. One of the new people I met is called Joe Barnes and he is head of a big advertising agency, Barnes Dorman Sharp. He is probably very rich. If the opportunity arises, I will give him one of your business cards, but not if it feels wrong.

"And Dad, I am cancelling our deal because I don't think it is reasonable for me to have to find you a new client every time I want to play cricket. And I am advised that our deal may not be a contract because you have not given me anything of value in exchange and because I was under duress and because it's against national policy to stop teenagers playing cricket or sport generally. And it might also constitute restraint of my trade as a cricketer."

"What on earth are you talking about?" *And suddenly Dad stopped being cool and sarky, as he usually is, and looked enraged and I felt scared. I tried to focus on the four new people I had met* "You have decided to break an agreement. And how do you think that will prepare you for your future – if you have one? Whatever you do in life, you have to keep your word. You take a job, it says you have to clock in at 7 am, you clock in at 7 am, or you get fired. And then you try to get another job – a sixteen-year-old who cannot keep his word – do you think you'll get any offers?" *I prepared myself for more heavy shelling from the self-made man against the feckless son, but suddenly Mum opened up from behind the inevitable pages of her Novel.*

"Oh for God's sake! Can't you two ever stop arguing? I do a crap job all day and when I come back to my home I want to do something creative. That may not mean much to either of you, but it means a lot to me. And how can anyone create anything in this house, with you two arguing the whole time? For God's sake, let him go and play cricket. And see these other people if they want to see him. At least it will stop all this arguing. Oh, and give him some money so I don't have to listen to more arguments.How much do you need?"

"I don't really know but I don't want my friends to pay for everything."

"Give him one of your spare cards and put a thousand on it. That should keep him quiet." *A thou? Ya-hay! I would never have asked for that. Dad scowled but put through some calls to his 24-hour bank and then threw me my first bit of plastic. He scribbled on a piece of paper.*

"That's your Pin number. Change it if you want to something memorable, but not your birthday. This is good for a thou. You want more, you earn it."

"Wow! Thanks Mum! Thanks Dad. I really appreciate that." *Good Son, but this time I didn't wait this time for his semi-hug or her social kiss.* "Here, I'll clear." *I made jobs last in the kitchen and listened out for one of their arguments. But evidently this was their night for silent mutual martyrdom. [Wordpower? Just don't seem to care right now]. While I worked on an imaginary grease spot on the oven top I heard them both leave the table. I made my escape to my bedroom. Escape? In my own home? I nearly lost it and got weepy again [what a total mush I've become lately] but then replayed my day once more. Cal. Robert and Joe. Alice. Four people who saw me today and want to see me again.*

When I gave my little one his goodnight kiss I was not too surprised to see what he was wearing but I pretended to be, to tease him.

"Cal The Vain you have more clothes per square inch of you than anyone else in Britain but now for the first time in your life you are wearing beige. This can only be love."

"Oh, Mum. I love him so much my teeth ache."

"Good heavens, did you kiss that hard on your first date?"

"I wish!" and he burst into tears. I had been wrong to tease. This was deep emotion. I held him for a long time and ruffled his hair, which Yasmin shaped so devotedly.

"Oh sweetheart. It really is too early for you to fall in love that deeply. I don't want you to get hurt. Steve has a life of his own. We don't know what other people are in that life – people of his own age. One of them may be special to him already, and even if there is no one, what you want just isn't fair to him. He may not be ready for that kind of responsibility. I have a feeling that Steve's life has had much loneliness and sorrow. People like that cannot be rushed into relationships. You, little one, have to make Steve feel safe just as much as he made you feel safe – as if nothing bad can ever happen. That's what it was like for you, wasn't it?"

"Yes."

"So why not stay there for a while? Enjoy it, day by day, having the great summer which you thought you'd lost."

"Okay."

"And now please take off that shirt. It must mean something to Steve and he won't want your bodily essences all over it. And it's also a horrid fabric and I don't want it in the way when you give me the biggest, longest hug of your life."

Chapter 7 Sudden Collapse

We had another brilliant day at the nets, except that he was really late.

"What time do you call this, you slacker? I've been up for <u>hours.</u> You are so dead, I've been practising my new mystery ball."

No bullies at the street corner, of course, and when we saw one of the others in the High Street they saw Psycho Steve and ran away. We did see a crazy drunk and Steve took my hand and I kept it there even though I wasn't scared.

We had the nets to ourselves for a bit and he was <u>so </u>lbw to my new mystery ball.

"It was a good ball, all right a great ball, but there's no mystery, it was a topspinner."

"A lot you know. That was the zooter."

I batted, and he went right up in pace to heated bread rolls and I hit them all before they hit me, although three would have been caught behind. We had a break and I climbed the big tree again just to show off and to make him catch me, and he almost wet himself again.

Then we started again and this Asian man came along with his two sons. One was about Steve's age and the other a bit older than me and I think the older one was a bit ... slow, and his younger brother was sort of looking after him, and Steve was really patient with him even when he made him miss his run-up. They were all really good, well, except the father who was a bit fat, and they all liked Steve (of course) and the father kept saying sorry to him about something.

When they left, I asked Steve what that was about but he just said "That's Mr Ahmad. He had a team I used to play for but… things didn't work out. Thank you for being so nice to Fazal. He's a bit … different mentally. But he's brilliant at gardening. They've got a little gardening business and the younger boy, Ijaz, is his manager. Don't even think of bargaining with Ijaz!"

We played on a bit and then had lunch. "Mum says the second sandwich is for you, and don't argue!" but he didn't argue, he just drooled.

We had a little nap again, only not together, but it was still nice and then this American family came along and we taught them all how to play cricket, only they still thought bowling was weird, although they thought Steve could make it as a pitcher, as if he'd ever want to be a chucker. Then right at the end Robert came by with his mum, Belinda, only without his stuff, so he used mine and then he asked us to a sleepover at his house before they all went away and that would be my first since ~~Shithead~~ Ben.

Robert's a photographer, He had this fantastic camera and he took a great picture of Steve (of course) and me, which he will email, so I must give him my drawing. Then we walked home. This time I took his hand and I didn't care who saw.

"Steve?"

"Cal?"

"Wouldn't you rather play on a team than just play with me?"

"I would like to play for a team again, but I would rather play with you than anyone else. I would rather play with you than with... Tim Morrow."

"You would?"

"Well, I've got more chance of getting you out."

"You didn't get me out once today."

"I so did."

"So did not." And we went on like kids until we got home.

Mum was playing the piano again. I think she misses it sometimes.

"Easy Favourites By George Gerswhin". That's more my style, these days, and sometimes I have to fake it. "We're home! What's for dinner?"

"Your spag bol." Brilliant choice, Mum. Now he'll know that I can cook. He remembered to take off his trainers and we went to my room and he said hello to Bungle. We had a shower (not together, I wish) and Steve put on a clean T-shirt (boring plain black). When we got to the kitchen Mum had unfrozen a big pot of <u>my</u> bolognese sauce and it was starting to simmer and she boiled water for the spag. She made Steve grate the cheese and I washed the salad stuff and then whirled it around in the metal thingy to dry it only I tried to show off and all the salad flew all over the kitchen. Pillock! But he just laughed and I picked it all up and I washed it all again.

He wolfed everything down.

"Did you really make this? It's brilliant."

"Yes. And the salad dressing."

"He's going to make someone such a wonderful wife!"

"MUM!"

I told her about our day and Steve looked a bit sad about the Ahmads. She told us about her day. She has this little kid as a client who wants a divorce from his parents, and he looked a bit sad again, so I gave him a second helping (and one for me) and Mum told him to eat more protein. There was still some left and he and Mum didn't want it so I had thirds.

"You're going to get fat!"

"No chance. Look," and I threw off my top, "Rippling Superman muscles of steel!"

"I've seen more muscles on a teddy bear!" So I started fighting him again but Mum stopped us. "I'll prove it. Into your room," and we followed him.

"This is for the world tedkwando championship. In the red corner, at a fighting weight of eighty pounds, the challenger, Cal 'The Cat' Devane. In the blue corner, at a fighting weight of one pound, the reigning champion, Bungle The Bear. This is a sudden death contest, the first submission wins it."

I picked up Bungle and as I expected Cal made a mad rush. It was easy for me to make Bungle hold him off and then lift him up and fling him onto his bed. I followed up and the bear won a submission with a lot of squealing and giggling from the loser.

"The winner – once again – Bungle The Bear! I told you he had more muscle."

"Loser cleans up the kitchen and sets up the Monopoly board. You do play Monopoly, don't you, Steve?" Cal scooted off.

"Yeah." He looked really wistful. I ruffled his hair. He should grow it longer.

"I used to have a bouncy, noisy kid who loved being outdoors. Then I lost him for a while. Thank you for bringing him back." He looked round Cal's room as if he was trying to memorize it. "I'm glad that Bungle won. Cal mustn't win every time." I scooped up the bear and we both looked at him. "He looks like a Bungle, doesn't he?"

"Not totally gormless but not exactly full of gorm."

"That's funny, Steve."

"It's one of Uncle Frank's."

"Did you write your letter to him last night?"

"Yeah." He looked wistful again but Cal shouted "Ready!" before I could say more.

"It will be nice to play with four again."

"Four?"

"Yes. We always play with Bungle."

Cal had tidied the kitchen in record time and set up the Monopoly board. I sat Bungle on the table.

"I'm the hat, the Cat in the Hat. Mum's the iron. Bungle's the dog, chasing me the Cat. You're going to be the car because you're a fast bowler." He gabbled through our special rules for Bungle. "I didn't know which ice cream you liked so I gave you all three."

"And you still don't know which ice cream you like so you have to try all three?" *Complacent smile.*

"He never puts on any weight."

"Ectomorphic."

"Thank you." *He thinks any new word is a compliment.*

Their Monopoly was way noisier than we used to play at home. "Bungle's won a beauty contest!.... Steve's in jail, Mum, keep him there, don't sell him the get-out card… Income Tax – I'm not paying… Cal, you can't borrow from Bungle, you'll have to get a mortgage… Just £10 for my birthday present?" *It ended up head-to-head between me and Bungle. I was wiped out when I landed on his Mayfair.*

"Fancy losing to Bungle. You've got less brain than a teddy bear!"

"Yeah, well I lasted longer than you."

"That's only because I missed my rent when I went off to get more ice cream."

"I never thought teddy bears could play. I wish I'd played with Sergeant Bear. We used to play a lot at home. Dad always won because he was so good at money and I always lost and Dad said I shouldn't buy so much property because it made me short of liquidity." Another wistful look. Imagine getting finance lessons in family Monopoly.

"I want to play again."

"I want never gets, and Bungle's getting tired. We're going to the sitting room, and I'm having coffee, and Steve?"

"I'm not really into coffee much."

"Bring Steve a peppermint tea. You might take one, as well, to settle those five helpings."

I took Steve to the sitting room couch and he sat bolt upright on the edge. "Steve, this isn't a job interview, it's a family couch and it's meant for people to sprawl in and be comfortable," and I forced him to lie back and sat next to him. "Now pretend you're Bungle." I had taken him with me, and made him flop on a cushion. Steve slowly uncoiled. "Comfortable? Floppy?"

"Positively ursine." I smiled again at his language.

"Steve, you are amazingly fluent. I talk to a lot of people your age and it's hard to get a consonant out of them, never mind a vocabulary. I bet your uncle Frank enjoys your letters."

"I don't know. He's been dead for three years." And he burst into tears, which turned into racking sobs, gasping for air. Oh hell.

Chapter 8   Bad Light

Cal came in with a tray of cups.

"Oh my god! What's wrong with Steve?"

"Nothing, sweetheart, just letting go for the first time." I made Steve lie on the couch and took his head in my lap. His sobs ended and he said something strange.

"The head must lie upon the block that was wont to lie in Queen Catherine's lap." I said nothing: I knew he would explain. Cal put the tray and cups within reach and sat on the floor, holding Steve's hand.

"It's from a story Uncle Frank told me. Queen Catherine was the wife of Henry V, only he died young and she was sent away to a castle in Wales, without even seeing her baby son, the new king. And she fell in love with the castle musician, Owen Tudor, and they had children. Then she died and the new king's council found out that she had taken a lover who was only a musician, after being married to the big hero, Henry V. They were so angry with Owen Tudor that they had him beheaded. That's what he said when they took him to the block. And Uncle Frank said he asked to face upwards ' that I may see my lady's face again before I die.'"

"That's very sad and very beautiful." Then I was silent again. There would be more. I signalled to Cal to stay silent too, but I didn't need to.

Eventually Steve said "My uncle Frank was everything to me. When he died, it was like the sun going in, for good." More silence. Cal passed the cups. Steve sat up and drained his tea, now pretty cold, at one gulp. "Everything good about me, everything I can do came from Uncle Frank. He taught me to play cricket. He could do everything. He could bowl fast or slow, he could bat, he could field anywhere, even keeping wicket. He got a match for the Army against the RAF. Youngest player. I didn't say he was in the Army, did I? He joined when he was 16, my age. He wasn't happy at home, he wanted to get away. He was Mum's brother, but much younger. They weren't really brother and sister."

I listened. Children in deep emotion don't organize facts – only when they're guilty of something do they have a story prepared. I knew Steve would empty things as and when he remembered them. It would be up to me to marshal them. Cal sat on the floor again and took Steve's hand.

"Frank did his basic training and he got lots of cricket. But he found ordinary soldiering a bit boring even with the cricket, and he was always a loner – like me - so he got accepted by the SAS. And he did loads of secret missions all over the world, and I don't know about them because they're still secret, only

I know he got the MC because I've got it in his trunk. It's not the VC but it means a lot." Cal and I ignored our cold drinks and waited again.

"Uncle Frank never married and I don't think he had anybody in his life, although he had a few really close mates in the Army, like Sergeant Kwame and Corporal Austin. He could have been an officer several times, but he didn't want to be and also he got a bad disciplinary record when he punched out an American in Iraq about torturing people." He closed his eyes.

"I was the only person he really loved. He told me. And he spent every leave he had in London with us. With me. Ever since I was born. I think my first words were 'when's Uncle Frank coming back?' That's all I ever said. I must have driven my parents mental. And they could never answer because Uncle Frank was always on some mission. He would just arrive suddenly, like the sun coming out.

"Uncle Frank gave me all the toys I really loved, like Sergeant Bear." Cal squeezed his hand and gave me a little glance to tell me he already knew about Sergeant Bear. "And my first cricket bat. And tons of books. Anything he thought I'd like to read. Cricket books especially but not always. Uncle Frank loved reading. And words. As soon as I could write we wrote long letters to each other and then emails and if we used a word we really liked we would write Wordpower, straight after." He started to sob again, first softly and then rackingly. Then he broke off and almost shouted "I still write to him because no one else gives a toss about my life. No one! Maybe he knows what's going on for me. Probably not. I don't believe in God or heaven or hell or whatever. But I still tell him. And no one else."

Cal and I stayed silent and waited again. He calmed down and lay his head again in my lap. "I'm reading all the books he didn't give me. They're in his trunk. In alphabetical order. It's taken me years and I'm still only on S for Sartre." I couldn't help smiling. No wonder he had a vocabulary.

"Uncle Frank took me out loads of times, to bases where he knew people. An army base can be pretty much like a holiday camp for a kid, with sports facilities and all kinds of other stuff you can play with. We went swimming a lot. He didn't have to teach me to swim, I can't remember not swimming, but he taught me every other sport I can do, I'm not bad at football, I was the school left back, and tennis and squash and snooker, does that count as sport? And chess and all kinds of card games when it rained and he taught me how not to lose shed loads of money. And how to drive a car and a motorbike. And some SAS stuff, only it got me in trouble." He stopped dead and I made a mental note. Then he brightened. "Whatever we did, it was always really exciting but I always knew nothing bad would happen." Cal gave his hand another big squeeze. "Except on the climbing tower. God, I so lost it on the tower and I cried and cried afterwards.

"But what we always really wanted to do, summer and winter, was play cricket together. Just the two of us. I asked him, didn't he miss playing for the Army and maybe he could have gone pro, but he said no, all he ever wanted to do was play with me. And Cal knows how he taught me, and Robert, because I passed it on to them." This time he squeezed Cal's hand.

"Just the two of us. That's what we both wanted. I could have asked my mates at school, but I always wanted Uncle Frank to myself so I never asked anyone. And so I never got any mates. Serves me right for being greedy." A question formed in my mind. I left it unspoken and he answered it.

"I never asked kids to my home. There was nothing to stop me and my parents would feed them and talk to them and add them to the Monopoly. But they did all that stuff as if they felt they had to, as if they were thinking 'God, as if one kid in the house wasn't enough.' So I kind of stopped asking and I lost my mates, even in the sports teams. I was in them all at prep school." I picked that up – he was privately educated. "I broke the school bowling record two years running."

"Only two years?" Cal could not resist breaking in.

"They kept taking me off in my last year to let others bowl." After this retort he sighed deeply. "Uncle Frank eventually left the SAS, and rejoined his old regiment, the Halbardiers. Actually, they've got some other name now but he always preferred the historic one. They were having a hard time, first in Iraq and then in Afghanistan, and Uncle Frank thought it was wrong to go on doing what he called 'glamour stuff' in the SAS. So he rejoined his old mates in Iraq and Afghanistan, and they were glad to have him.

"Some really bad things happened to him and he nearly got killed by a roadside bomb and he saw a lot of his mates wounded and dying. And just the daily life out there was pretty terrible the way he told me, the heat, and not enough of anything, and sleeplessness and feeling surrounded by people who hated him, and thinking anyone – I mean any Afghan or any Iraqi – who came near him might want to kill him, even little kids.

"When he came back to us – to me – on leave he was really stressed out. He'd have bad visions and nightmares any time of day or night, and I used to hold him and say it was all right. Me protecting Uncle Frank who always looked after me. We did nothing but play cricket, that leave, because that calmed him down. It got me to a new level, but I didn't care because I was so sad for Uncle Frank. I begged him to quit, but he said he couldn't walk out on his mates, and besides, he wanted to finish his 22 years, to get his full leaving gratuity and pension, and I said 'Never mind the money, Uncle Frank, Dad's got buckets of money and I'll ask him to pay you, and I could live with you and he wouldn't have to spend on me.'

"I urged him to train as a teacher or as a cricket coach. But he said, no, it wouldn't be safe for him to be near kids – not even me.

"Not even me, he said again, and then he started to cry, right there in the cricket nets in the park where we used to play. And we went home and Uncle Frank suddenly said 'Goodbye, Steve. I love you. Don't join the army. It's not what it was. They don't know what they're asking us to do. They've ground us to pieces, Blair and Brown. The messiah and the miser. And then they lie about us. They say they give us everything we need and we have to borrow bandages from the sodding Afghans. Listen, Steve, if there's another war and they come for you, hide in the cupboard with Sergeant Bear.' And that's the last time I saw him." He struggled for a long time, coming to terms with what he had to say next.

"Uncle Frank just disappeared. He didn't answer letters and his Army e-mail didn't work. And then, around a year later, Mum and Dad called me in and told me he was dead." He began to breathe rapidly.

"He wasn't even in the Army any more. He got through Iraq and Afghanistan, and all those secret missions, and he was killed in a road accident. In London. In London. I didn't even know he was here. He didn't come to me. Why didn't he come to me, I could have taken care of him?" He was almost hyperventilating. He counted backwards from ten and his breathing slowed to normal. "Uncle Frank taught me that. He didn't even have a military funeral. Just me and Mum and Dad in a crematorium and a few of his Army mates and his new employer. He'd gone into private security. Minding celebrities and Russian billionaires and that kind of thing. Sergeant Kwame told me about it. He said Uncle Frank got through his 22 years and then didn't know what else he could do except security and the money was great, especially the tips from the Russians. But he hated it. He lived alone in a little bedsit, with nothing but his books in a trunk. Sergeant Kwame didn't want to tell me, but Uncle Frank had been drinking and the driver had no chance.

"After the funeral there was a bit of a party at some pub and Mum made small talk and I hated her so much although I suppose she had to. Sergeant

Kwame asked me if I wanted Uncle Frank's trunk and I said of course and he drove it to our place that evening. And no one else has ever had Uncle Frank's keys. It's almost nothing but books. And his medals. And some pictures. Nearly all of me. I didn't remember them being taken. Sergeant Kwame told me that he had witnessed Uncle Frank's will. He had given £20,000 to a forces charity called Combat Stress[4] but everything else was coming to me. I didn't think there would be much left and I didn't care anyway."

I could not help cutting in. "Were you not at the reading of the will?"

"No."

"That is quite wrong."

"I had a kind of breakdown. I was like a zombie, apparently, I didn't eat and kept on saying I could have taken care of him. Mum took me away to the seaside. I can't even remember where and it wasn't summer so it was bloody cold but she bought me a wetsuit so I could go swimming anyway and I just swam for ever and ever. There were times when I didn't want to come back, but I wanted to play cricket for Uncle Frank so I did. Mum did a lot of writing. She's writing a novel. She's been at it for ages. She's like Flaubert – a sentence a day." That nearly made my heart break – this sad boy with his sudden flash of literary history.

"I wanted to talk about Uncle Frank and his childhood, but she actually did not know much about him. And I don't really think she liked him. So I started reading Uncle Frank's first book, A for Aldington: Death Of A Hero. Good title to start with, right after Uncle Frank died." A brief, twisted smile. "I wanted to talk about it, but she hadn't read it. I suppose it is not very well known now. But then I found she'd hardly read any of his books, even though she did English at college. Uncle Frank was an auto-didact. Wordpower!" Suddenly it became a real smile.

"When we got home, Dad told me that Uncle Frank had left me a bit of money and that he was looking after it. That's what he does, looking after people's money. But I would get an allowance from it until I was 18."

I couldn't help cutting in. "So you get your allowance from your own money?"

"Dad gives me more, for jobs like mowing the lawn. And he pays for big ticket items like my bike. But I don't spend my allowance on anything except

---

[4] A real charity which does excellent work: see www.combatstress.org

cricket stuff. I mean, I don't care about clothes." Cal The Vain blushed guiltily. "Or music." I blushed guiltily, thinking of the piles of piano music I buy and don't play. "And I don't need anything to read because I have all of Uncle Frank's books. I simply wolfed them down in the months after his death – B for Bunyan and Byron, Robert; C for Camus and Chandler and Chekhov's short stories and Conrad; D for Defoe and even D for Dickens. I became a speed reader and a speed bowler. That's all that was left to me from Uncle Frank.

"I haven't had a happy day since Uncle Frank died." He spoke coolly and scientifically. Without self-pity. "Correction. I've not had a happy week. I've had days that were happy and it looked as though life might be looking up again, but then everything got snatched away. I've had days and weeks that are OK, like... holidays. Mum and Dad always take me on good holidays. Always somewhere hot near the sea and I swim for ever and Dad fishes and sometimes we even go spear-fishing together. Except that I hate killing fish." Cal nodded. "And Mum reads magazines and writes her one sentence a day. And everything's ... all right. But it's not happy, like Uncle Frank happy. And if I get any Uncle Frank happy, it never lasts a week. I suppose it's just like cricket. You're batting, and you score century after century. But then it all averages out. You get a run of low scores and ducks. You get down to your real average. I had all my hundreds with Uncle Frank. I can't expect more."

He sighed and sank back again into my lap. I have listened to many children tell me about bad experiences. By now, Steve should have been feeling relief and escape but he was still tense.

"There's more to unpack, isn't there, Steve?"

"Oh yes. Shitloads. Sorry. There's loads of really bad stuff." He glimpsed at Cal.

"Do you want this to be for the two of us and no one else?" He nodded.

"Do you still have the pound I gave you yesterday as your cricket coaching fee?" He fished in a pocket and gave it to me. I darted over to the wordprocessor and typed him a receipt on our firm's stationery. I gave it to him. "Steve, you have just engaged me as your lawyer, indefinitely, for a fee of one pound. Our conversation now has absolute privilege, which means I tell nobody about it, whatever you say. If you tell me you've murdered someone, it stays with me." He looked startled.

"Tell Mum everything, Steve. She's the tops. And you're always going to be the tops for me." Cal squeezed his hand one more time, stood up and reached for Bungle. Then he went to his room, leaving his precious bear for someone in greater need.

Chapter 9   Bad Light Continues (Replays)

After Cal left, I went to pick up a new legal pad and pen.

"I'm your solicitor. I need a record of our conference. I could tape it, but I think that notes will be enough." Bullshit, of course, but with a purpose. I thought that the formality would make him more confident about opening up. "Of course these notes are confidential and privileged. Do you need a bathroom break?"

He did. He returned purposefully and sat in an upright chair.

"My life fell apart after Uncle Frank died. Cricket was the only thing that kept me going. It was winter but I went to the nets anyway in our local park with some balls and just bowled and bowled at ..." At whom, Steve? "At nobody. Just into the empty net. At weekends, I mean. I was a weekly boarder at X." I whistled. I hope he did not notice. X is a very expensive independent school. I am not naming it because what follows is still potentially defamatory.

"I got a bursary there for cricket. It was really sporty. I did okay there, nothing special at anything except English and cricket. Not many mates, even for cricket. I offered to bowl at people in the nets but nobody wanted."

"That could have been a compliment."

He thought for a second and smiled. "Yeah, maybe... After Uncle Frank died, my bowling went up a yard in pace. Because I was bowling for him. And my batting. I had some lessons, that is, well, I really worked on it." All the while I took notes, sometimes making my special mark to come back to something. "When the new cricket season came round I was way above my age group. I took 20 wickets in two weeks in all matches. And got a fifty against another school in six overs. They promoted me to the Development Squad – the players they were grooming for the first team. All the others were two years older than me, and they all hated me. Especially the captain. I had pushed out one of his mates. And he let me know he hated me. Like in the nets, I had to bowl so that he could practice his shots, and the same way at his mates, bad balls like half-volleys outside offstump so that they could play wonderful cover drives. Mind you, be fair, he was a bloody good batsman. He could have gone on..." Suddenly he looked very troubled. I waited, using the weapon of silence. "And they stuck me at Number 11 although I was a better batsman than some of his mates.

"In matches, the captain never gave me the new ball. Or the end I was best at, or the field I wanted. If the oppo were rubbish I never got put on but if they were belting us I got a long spell. And I was always given a long walk in the field. And I knew I was the best bowler – well, the best pace man, we had a fabulous legspinner. The captain was injured in one match and so was one of the other pace men so the vice-captain had to bowl me and I got their top four for 18 and we won by ten wickets. But the next match it was back to normal."

"Surely there was a master in charge? Didn't he see what was happening?"

"He was weak. Totally. He was good technically as a coach, but he couldn't stand up to the captain. The captain's parents were bloody rich and his dad was chairman of some county – and kids like that got what they wanted at that school." He shut his eyes for some time. Something bad was coming and yet again I waited in silence.

"We had a home match and the captain made a century for the first time. And it was a bloody good innings. Then we just rolled them over and I didn't even get to bowl." He shut his eyes again for a moment, but forced himself on. "Well, of course everyone was all over him and he spent a lot of time with his fan club, still in his whites. And by the time he got back to the dressing room to change, there was just me in the shower. I was the junior in the team so I always got the last shower and I like to spend a lot of time in the shower. Well, you know that, don't you?" A proper smile. I was moved. He had had two showers in my home and still hoped I might have noticed his routine. The smile disappeared quickly and he looked away from me into space.

"There was another kid hanging around the dressing room. Not a cricketer. This kid around my age. Blond. Long floppy hair. Floyd. He called himself Pretty-Boy Floyd The Outlaw. That's a folk song. About an American gangster." Another attempt to delay the inevitable and I did not respond to it.

"Floyd was the school tart. He used to sell himself to other boys. So much for a show, so much more for a feel, so much more for a hand job, top rate for a blow job. Nothing else. I didn't tell you X was still all boys. He had a good… business. He especially liked hanging round sports teams.

"The captain comes in, still in his whites, and he says 'Floyd, how delightful! I've just scored my first century and now I can score my first butt.' And Floyd says 'You know the rates and I don't do it up the butt' and the captain says 'Come on, Floyd, you love it and you should pay me," and he went on and it really creeped me out and I came out of the shower and started changing, just thinking he'd stop if I was there, but he went on as if I wasn't there at all, and he looked really weird, and maybe he was on some kind of drug, there were loads of drugs flying around that school with all the rich kids, and he kept saying 'Come on Floyd, you love it,' and Floyd looked really scared, so I had to do something and I stepped in and pushed the captain away and said 'He doesn't want it, so leave him alone.' And the captain noticed me for the first time and he said 'Fuck off, Helson, it's nothing to do with you. And as if anyone would fuck you.' And I said, 'Well, nobody fucks <u>with</u> me either.' Wordpower!" A flickered smile, proud of his literary skills even in crisis.

"Well, we started fighting and Floyd ran away. And the captain was two years older than me and bigger and he was soon beating the crap out of me. And, remember I told you Uncle Frank taught me some SAS stuff, self-defence? Well, there was one move he said I should never use unless I was desperate. I pulled it out then, and smashed his face. And he collapsed and he writhed and he screamed, God that scream, and I ran out screaming myself and I saw someone and yelled for them to ring 999. I could have done that myself on my mobile but I couldn't think about anything except that scream."

I dropped my pad and pen and went over to hold him. Very unprofessional, but I now had a boy in a nightmare, not a client. He stood up and clung on for a long time, before letting go and sitting back. I picked up pad and pen again and waited.

"It turned out that I had broken his jaw. Not just cracked it but practically broken it in two. A bit lower in the carotid artery, a bit higher in the temple and I might have killed him.

"An ambulance came for him and they took me away into the San. Like I was infectious, had to be isolated. And a master came and asked me some questions and then he came back with a statement for me to sign."

I could not let that go. "No call to your parents? No other adult with you? No sort of caution, warning that the statement might be used against you? No suggestion that you should have a lawyer? No tape recording?"

"No. They told me next day that my story hadn't stood up. There was bad blood between me and the captain and that's why I had fought him. I suppose Floyd didn't say anything. He'd have been afraid that the school would find out about his ... business. And my dad came and took me home."

"And you got no chance to make any further defence for yourself? In a court of law, Floyd and the captain would have been cross-examined. So the school said you had suddenly decided to attack a boy who was bigger and stronger than you in a spurt of uncontrollable rage. So probable."

"Without Floyd it was just my word against the captain."

"In hospital, not capable of being interviewed."

"Well, I mean it was him or me, and which kid would you want at your school, the rich kid with the powerful parents, or me?" A flash of anger and then he shut his eyes again. "Besides, they were right. I actually didn't care a toss about Floyd. He was a tart. I hated the captain."

"That's not why you fought him. I know you well enough by now. You were protecting a scared boy."

"I don't know! There was all kinds of stuff going on in my head... The captain needed reconstructive surgery. I think it's still happening. He never played cricket again. They wouldn't let me see him. I wrote to him to say sorry but I never got a reply. I destroyed another cricketer."

"He destroyed himself, Steve. He was on a destructive path and you were unlucky enough to be in the way. That school should have stopped him, and his parents. Not you. Please think about that. Anyway, what happened next?"

"Dad told me I was leaving that school for good and I should be grateful that they were not going to bring charges. Oh. Alice? Could this stop me working with kids? Dad thought it would."

"No. You're not a criminal. It's not going to show up on a CRB check. And tell me, were you formally expelled? Did you ever see a piece of paper or hear a formal statement from that school that you were expelled?"

"No. Dad just took me away."

"They never did anything formal. Formality would have given you rights. If they had brought in the police and the law you would have got a proper defence and in a court of law everything would have come out and the whole world would have known that that expensive school was a shower of shit. Instead, they transferred all the guilt onto a vulnerable boy, still in grief and shock. How convenient! And no one at that school spoke up for you? None of the masters, none of the boys?"

"No. And no one got in touch after I left. I went home. Some old biddy – sorry, that's unfair – a retired teacher came to tutor me at home, but mostly she just left me alone to read Uncle Frank's books. I was at D for Dickens. Bleak House. Right enough. Home was pretty bleak and I was grounded for cricket. That was the worst. So I just read on and on for Uncle Frank. Bleak

House. I wondered if he related to the character of Captain Hawdon, you know, the ex-soldier living in poverty under another name…" This time a literary diversion, to postpone something bad. I cut him short.

"That was a terrible thing, but it's not all. Something else happened, didn't it, Steve?" I looked at the pad and my special marks. "Something about bowling at someone in winter in the park nets. Something about improving your batting."

"Uncle Jimmy." The bare words seemed to release him. He told me the next thing in a calm, detached way, and sat Bungle upright on the couch. As another listener or as a proxy for Uncle Jimmy? Either way, it seemed a good sign.

"Like I said, after Uncle Frank died I often went to the nets in the park and bowled cricket balls on my own. One afternoon there was a man there in a track suit. A bit older than Uncle Frank. I think he had been running. He asked me if I wanted someone to bowl at. And I said, sure, but I didn't have any stuff, but he did and he went away and came back with it. And he batted against me and I was fast and in bad light but he still hit me all over the place. No helmet. He was fantastic, I'd never seen anything like it, I mean Uncle Frank was brilliant but I think he held back against me. He would not let me bat because I didn't have a helmet. He said I was a really, really good bowler and he could only hit me because I bowled so straight. And would I like to play again, only indoors was warmer and maybe I would like to go to the Indoor School at Lords, but he would have to meet my parents first." I twisted uncomfortably. I could guess what followed but I had to let him tell it.

"He said he was Jimmy and I said I was Steve. And he gave me a card with his name and address, which was close by and he said get your parents to call me. We left the park and he put his stuff back into his car. It was amazing – a vintage sports car, an Alfa Spider 2000 – and he said it was his 'fun' car and maybe I would like to drive it one day.

"Well, you bet I wanted to play cricket with him again, and at Lords, so I begged my parents to get in touch and he came round for dinner and they really liked him. He talked to Mum about fiction and asked to read her novel and he talked to Dad about money and gave Dad some money of his to manage." I twisted involuntarily and put a big scrawl on the bad. He bought Steve.

"Sorry, Steve. Writer's cramp. Fine now."

"My parents were happy to let me play cricket with Jimmy. We weren't really speaking much because I was still angry with them for not mourning Uncle Frank the way I did. I went to Lords regularly on weekends with Jimmy. He took me in the 'fun' car and he even let me park it in the car park. He was kind of replacing Uncle Frank but I always knew when he was coming. And he helped my cricket a lot, got me to shorten my length a fraction because I was overpitching and really brought on my batting. I knew the basics from Uncle Frank but I didn't work on it much, because I was a bowler, but Jimmy said I was good enough to aim for 25 each innings, and he got me to use a lighter bat and move my feet more decisively."

"Was anyone with you?"

"Not at first. Just the two of us. Like Uncle Frank. And it wasn't just cricket, he belonged to this fabulous gym with a pool, or going to places – he knew everything about London – and even letting me drive the Alfa. But the best thing was he let me talk and talk about Uncle Frank and he'd read a lot of Uncle Frank's books, so we could talk about them too."

"You were a weekly boarder, so in school term this was all at weekends. You can't have been seeing much of your parents?"

"I guess not… but they didn't seem to mind not seeing me. And they really liked him. He always stayed on when he dropped me off and he listened to Dad talking about the economy, or Mum about writing. He told her how much he enjoyed her novel. 'Very deeply felt, and so much detail about the heroine's life.' IE Mum, wittering on about herself."

"So there is this man out of the blue making a huge effort to be the new Uncle Frank. Were they curious about him at all? Did they check him out?"

"Dad checked out his money. Does that sound cynical?"

"Not if it is true."

"He had inherited a fortune from his father. Oil, I think. And he made more himself, investing in the theatre and films. He called himself an angel. Mum checked out this part, and said he had really good judgement."

"But nothing about his personal life?"

"Not really. Mum said he'd been married and divorced. No children." I made another note and waited some more.

"As it got nearer the cricket season some other people came to Lords with us. He had this team called the Gin and Limelight Eleven. Theatre people. There was this huge fast bowler called Xan McVeigh, way faster than me, only it was really funny when he wasn't bowling fast he was a total screamer, sorry, can you say that about someone, only he put on this high voice and treated everyone as a girl? Jimmy was Jemima and when Xan met me he said 'Who brought Miss Butch Teen Dream?' and called me Stephanie. He made me laugh. But Y was there too." A famous actor, who could sue. "He made a pass at me in the dressing room and Jimmy got really angry, and I was a bit creeped out but Jimmy made me feel okay again. I think that's when he let me drive the Alfa for the first time. Alice, have you ever driven an Alfa?"

Another attempted diversion, which I ignored, He rearranged Bungle on the couch and resumed the story.

"The cricket season began at school and Jimmy came to those early matches when I took tons of wickets. My parents couldn't … didn't come… and when people thought he was my real Uncle Jimmy it was just sort of easier and he was all right about it, actually he was pleased. And he got on really well with everyone and it was the only time I was ever popular at school.

"And I played in the first Sunday match for the Gin and Limelights, just outside London, and Xan blew them away, five wickets. He'd have got more only the umpire didn't like him saying 'Howzat, girly?'" Another delaying tactic. "And I got two cheap wickets at the end and a catch in the deep and Jimmy got a quick fifty and he was really pleased with me. He took me home, because he had fixed it with the school for me to come back on Monday, and asked my parents if I could play in the next match, which was all day at some castle and there would be some ex-England cricketers on the castle side, and he would fix another Sunday exeat with the school, and I pleaded and pleaded and eventually they said yes. Dad had to be away with a client next weekend, so it didn't matter to him, and Mum was glad to have more time alone with her novel." He gripped Bungle very hard, and then remembered that was my boy's friend and actually apologized. He sighed and forced himself to finish.

"Jimmy said that it was a long way off and they would need a very early start and it might be convenient if I stayed overnight with him. And they agreed.

"During the week Jimmy emailed me the match programme for Sunday, and there were pen portraits of all the players and I was in them with the England stars. I was described as 'teen pace sensation with a Tom O'Ryan action.' Tom O'Ryan's England's fastest bowler only they keep dropping him for going to night clubs." One more sidetrack.

"Mum picked me up on Saturday and I was really keyed up and I got on her nerves, so when Jimmy rang and suggested we have a net and then dinner she was glad. We played in the park and he said I had an extra yard of pace, and this blond kid about my age asked if he could play and he wasn't much good but Jimmy gave him some tips and told me to save my express stuff for tomorrow, so he could just about keep me out.

"Then we went to his place. It was the first time I'd seen it and it was huge. A big house, all to himself. The basement was a gym, with a hot tub and a sauna and a massage table. He showed me his 'boring' car, a Lexus, which we would use tomorrow. He showed me right round and there were pictures in every room and there was one I really liked and he said it was a Leger. He took me to the spare room and said he was sorry it was so pokey only it was as big as our living room at home, with a big bathroom of its own and he told me to take a shower and I could just wear shorts afterwards because we were eating at home. I had one and came into the sitting room and we watched a bit of the Test on this giant TV. When I sat on the couch he said I didn't have to be so polite, and asked me to sprawl out and be comfortable." Just as I had. Did I bring back a bad memory? But he did trust us enough to sprawl on our couch.

"He said it was very important for fast bowlers not to stiffen up, and said we would do some relaxation exercises before going to bed. And he moved the cushions around on the couch and made me move around until I was comfortable. Then he looked at me for a bit, and said if I got bored with the Test, try surfing the other 400 channels, and he went into the kitchen. He called me in after a bit and said we were having a fast bowler meal, and there was this giant steak and a baked potato and salad. But the dressing wasn't as good as Cal's." I was touched.

"Then he said he knew I didn't drink but champagne didn't count and he opened this wee bottle and gave us both a glass and actually I had had some before at a wedding only this was way better. Dom something."

"Perignon." I sighed.

"He said he would bring some bottles for when I took my fifth wicket in the match, so I would not be accused of jug avoidance. You know that bowlers have to buy a jug of beer for everyone if they take five wickets?" Still another attempt to delay the inevitable.

"He told some really funny stories about the rest of the team, especially Xan, and I was literally rolling on the floor. Then he took me in the living room again and we watched a video of Bradman and the Bodyline series and he told me I was already as tall as Harold Larwood and I felt great. " A deep breath, and his eyes shut for a time.

"Then he said he would teach me to relax and he took me down to the basement. He made me do a bit of light work on all the machines. Then he said I should try out the sauna, and people took their clothes off for the sauna and would I mind? So I did and he gave me a towel. I went into the sauna and it was really hot and I think there was some kind of herb burning because there was a really thick smell and I felt a bit woozy. Then he told me to come out, and he looked at me and said my muscles were still very tight and he asked me to stretch out face down on the massage table and put the towel over my bum.

"'Steve,' he said, 'I'm qualified as a therapist and I want you to trust me and trust your body. Don't do anything, I'm going to unclench all those fast bowler muscles.' And he put his fingers and thumbs on my neck and shoulders and pressed and pushed and it was brilliant, I felt really good. Then he worked his way down my back and sides and it didn't feel quite right and he said again 'Trust your body, Steve, and let things happen.'

"Then he got nearer my bum and my balls and I asked him to stop but he said again 'Trust your body, Steve, it's enjoying this,' but I jumped up and screamed 'Leave me alone!' And I gave him a smack across the face, like Uncle Frank had taught me, and it wasn't hard but he burst into tears, and he kept saying sorry, and I said 'Don't come near me,' and I picked up my clothes and dashed into the spare room and picked up my cricket stuff, and he was still crying and saying sorry and I said I was going home and he said he would drive me and I said 'I'll fucking walk!' and I slammed out.

"I was a bit frightened that someone might have heard but there was no one in the street, except some kid at the corner and he walked away.

"I walked back home and Mum actually looked annoyed." Bloody hell. "Well, only a second, but I could tell. She had two of her friends with her. She said Uncle Jimmy had phoned and he was worried about me, and I said I didn't want to talk to him or see him again ever. And she said she was sorry after all he'd done for me. Or was it for her? Anyway I went to my room and she brought me a cup of tea and asked if I wanted to tell her anything and I looked at her and suddenly thought 'No. You're only asking because you have to. You'd rather be with your friends.' So I didn't and she went back to her friends. And I still felt a bit shaky, but I fell asleep.

"The next day she asked me again but I still didn't feel like talking to her, so I just said I didn't want to see him or talk to him ever. And I wanted a new mobile number and a new email. She took me back to school early. I went to the Library and read one of Uncle Frank's books. D for Defoe: Journal of the Plague Year, and I thought I've got the plague, I mustn't see anyone."

"Steve. You didn't have the plague. You were a victim of a predator and a traitor, who pretended to be your Uncle Frank. He set you up. And your parents. But you got free. Because you were brave and stood up for yourself."

"But I still felt dirty. He was right, I did enjoy it and I was getting … hard."

"Steve, your body is programmed to respond to certain touches and getting an erection was a normal response from a healthy teenager. It didn't mean that you wanted sex with him. It doesn't mean that you're like him."

"I knew that in my head but I still felt… diseased. I almost gave up cricket but then I thought that was wrong to Uncle Frank. But when I wanted to bowl a really fast ball I used to put Jimmy in place of the batsman."

"When you had the fight with the captain, were you really fighting Jimmy?"

"I think so."

"Two people trying to use power. Is this the first time you've talked to somebody about Jimmy?"

"Yeah. Except to Uncle Frank when I'm alone. My parents knew that I hated him and was scared of him, and they probably guessed why, but they never heard it from me. Dad told me next weekend that Jimmy wouldn't be part of my life again. But he was. I could see his sports car sometimes in the street. And he was in the nets. With the blond kid that I talked about and I wanted to go to the blond kid and say something but I couldn't because I felt sick."

"Steve. The blond kid was not your responsibility. You had it all to do to protect yourself. Other people should have confronted Jimmy. What about your parents? Did they never challenge him?"

"Mum still liked him. And Dad went on managing his money." I scrawled my pad again. "I found out later when I did a bit of work in his office." I fought really hard to say nothing. "I suppose they thought I was … OK, so they didn't need to do anything more. And I just got on with things. Uncle Frank had this saying 'if you get a bad hand, play it as well as you can, and deal another.'

The worst thing was not being able to use our local cricket nets to bowl in, because I was afraid of seeing him again. That why I walked for miles to get to yours."

"And that's why you met Cal."

"Yeah! And you." His face lit up. I went over and hugged him.

"Steve. You're safe now. I'm going to keep you safe. Just give me that man's full name and his address. I'm going to make sure that he doesn't harm you or any other kid. I can do that. You don't have to. Now, are you ready for bed? There's a spare room we can make up."

"No. There's more … stuff."

"Well, I don't sleep until my client does."

Chapter 10   Bad Light: Final Session

My client took another bathroom break and I made us some more tea and coffee. As well I had a light schedule the next day. He returned and gave a rueful smile.

"I'm sorry there's so much of this. Like Dickens."

"Maybe if Dickens had had some one to talk to when he was a teenager we wouldn't have had all those novels." I picked up my pad again. "What happened after you left the X school?"

"My dad told me I would be going to Cibber Comprehensive." I whistled. A poor reputation – many of our firm's criminal clients go there – and a long way away. "He said nowhere else would take me." I wondered if that was true.

"It was, well… different from X. It was pretty much a school for no-hopers – kids and teachers. It was the sort of school you went to because you had to go somewhere and teachers were always coming and going. We had a lot of supply teachers. All the teachers just tried to get through the day. They were always knackered. I heard one say if it wasn't the kids it was the paperwork.

"There were a lot of rough kids there but in a way I was lucky. Somehow they got to know why I left X. I wouldn't be surprised if it was Mr A" (name withheld again, for legal reasons). "He used to leak gossip and personal stuff to be popular with his class. Anyway, as soon as I arrived I became known as Psycho. People thought I was dangerous so they left me alone. I had precisely two mates – mind you, that was two up on X. One was called Weirdo. Psycho and Weirdo. Nick, really. He used to sing or say long strings of words, just whenever he felt like it and we became mates by trading words. Everyone else thought he was weird but he was cool about it, because he got left alone like me. He was American and both his parents were visiting professors. He was nuts about astronomy. One clear night he got me onto the roof of their apartment block. I had to climb this tiny iron ladder and I was poop-scared but he was so excited he got me up there and pointed out all the constellations and the planets and he went mental over light pollution. 'They've poisoned the sky, Steve!' He went home and they live in the desert and he thinks he's discovered an asteroid and he wants to name it after me.

"That's wonderful, Steve. Be sure to tell that to Cal." He told me about his other mate, an older kid who's now working at a swimming pool and I made a little note to see if he could help Cal.

"I just kind of got by at Cibber. Nick the Weirdo and Phil the Sheriff. I didn't need anybody else. I got into the football team, which helped, because they didn't have a better left back, but I was never one of the football set. Nick should have been goalie, he was an amazing shot-stopper, but he did loopy stuff and he let in a soft goal once because he was looking at a satellite.

"There was only one really bad thing about Cibber. They had no cricket team. I offered to set one up but you needed a teacher and none of them were interested or had the energy." His face darkened again. "I think that's why Dad wanted me to go there. Why does Dad hate cricket so much? Mum doesn't mind it, she just thinks it's boring, but Dad actually hates it. Why?" I could see tears starting and I had no answer.

"I can't tell you. I doubt if he can tell you. Maybe he was jealous of Uncle Frank. Maybe he was jealous of you – achieving something which he couldn't do or even understand. People are very odd. They latch onto things that mean nothing to anyone else. I had a client once who wanted to divorce her husband because he sang off-key in the shower."

"God, she'd divorce me!" Big smile, which is why I had invented that client.

"Anyway, no cricket team at school. And I couldn't practice at our local nets because of Jimmy so I walked over to yours. And I couldn't sign for a local club because they used our nets, and also I thought, who's going to drive me to away matches and suppose it's another Jimmy? Was that being stupid?"

"What you feel deeply is never stupid. Misguided possibly but never stupid."

"Anyway, I just ran and practised my action and whenever I could I went to your nets and bowled at anyone or no one. Nick came sometimes but only because he was my friend and I could tell he didn't really like it and I couldn't bowl fast at him because he was my friend. Then in the spring I met the Ahmads. Cal's met them."

"He told me about them. Father and two boys, right?"

"I really liked them. Mr Ahmad, Imtiaz, and the younger boy, Ijaz, kind of … looked after the older boy, Fazal, who was a bit… different. And they seemed to like me."

"Don't be surprised. I'm not."

"Anyway, Mr Ahmad had his own team and he asked me to play for them. And I told him I didn't have transport and he said he would drive me and I felt safe because he was really ... paternal. And it was OK with Dad because Mr Ahmad was rich and might become a client." Another flash of bitterness.

"I really liked playing for them because they were short of fast bowling and I got lots of work and the end I wanted. And some were a bit fat, like Mr Ahmad and didn't catch much, but his brother was a brilliant keeper. He stood up to me! He's the only keeper who's taken a stumping off me!" I tried to look impressed. I still don't understand the game very well.

"And they needed my batting as well. For a while, after Jimmy, I didn't give a toss about my batting but Mr Ahmad's team needed it so I kept my head down instead of just having a whack and tried to give them 20 minimum.

"Mr Ahmad's team played in this sort of Asian business league and most times I was the only ... white person at the match, but I didn't mind. Unlike that fucking slag Angie!" A new departure. As usual, I waited for him. He resumed in a faraway voice.

"Like I said, most people ignored me at school and I ignored them. When I got into the football team there were these groupies, who followed us. Mostly girls but also a couple of boys. Be fair to that school, it didn't matter much about being gay. But none of the groupies were interested in me.

"The biggest groupie was this girl called Angie. Big, busty blonde with this kind of baby-doll face. She thought she looked like Marilyn Monroe. Nick said she looked like a drag queen doing Marilyn Monroe. Anyway, she was going out with our midfield schemer, although everyone said she was working her way right through the team. I think it was a bit like getting your colours, getting a shag with Angie.

"Anyway, we had this match at home and we got thumped and the groupies turned on us and everyone tried to get away early but I was last in the shower and taking my time as always and when I came out, Angie was still there." He looked far away and I think he was talking to Uncle Frank again.

***

"Ooh, Psy... Steve! You scared me." *But she didn't look scared, and she gave me a good look. For some reason I only had a really small towel that day, so there was plenty to look at. I trained a lot harder than the rest of the team, what with running and swimming and bowling, and no junk food or whatever, and when I saw her looking me over I started to feel really good.*

"You scared <u>me</u>, Angie. Who are you waiting for? Johnny's gone." *Her boy friend. He'd had a really crap game and probably couldn't face anyone.*

"I was waiting for you, Steve. I want to ask a favour."

"Well, if you could just let me change, Angie, and ask me then." *I was embarrassed. I was getting stiff and that towel was taking the strain.*

"I'll turn my back but you've got nothing to be ashamed of." *She did this prancing pirouette [Wordpower!] and I hurried into my clothes.*

"Okay, Angie, what's the favour?" *She pirouetted again.*

"Steve. I think there's this guy stalking me. I see him outside the school and I'm sure he's following me home and I would really like you to take me home because I would feel really safe."

"So you're afraid of a psycho and you ask another psycho to protect you?" *She started to cry and I felt sorry for her.* "No offence, Angie. I know my nickname. Of course I'll walk you home. Where do you live?" *And she told me, and it would take me way longer to get home, with soccer kit and school books.*

We walked out of the school.

"Can you see him?"

"See who?"

"The guy you think's a stalker."

"Oh. It's hard to pick him. He changes his clothes. But he always looks really creepy. That's him!"

"But he's almost a midget. You could knock him over with one fingernail." *Actually, she could have taken out Osama Bin-Laden with one of her fingernails.*

"But he really creeps me out." *I knew the feeling.*

"Don't worry, Angie. You're safe," *and I put an arm around her. She slipped her arm round my waist.*

"You're the only one on that team with a real six-pack, Steve."

"Go on, Angie, I bet you say that to all the six-packs." *She giggled.*

"You're funny, Steve. You're so quiet but you're really funny." *We walked on and she played a little tune with her fingers on my side.*

"Do you play the piano, Angie?"

"No."

"Me neither. Gives us something in common." *She giggled again.*

"Funny." *We got to her street. It looked really run down. There were loads of rubbish bags in front of her house. She rang one of the bells and then fished out a key.*

"Well, you're safe now, Angie. I've got to get home."

"Come in and have a cup of tea."

"I've got shed loads of homework."

"We can do some together."

"We don't have the same homework." *I'll say. I think she was on colouring books. Sorry, that sounds cheap. But she was way below, academically.*

"You can help me. You're a boff. It takes me ages and the teachers are crap. I bet I could learn stuff if you taught me." *And I felt sorry for her again.*

"Okay, Angie, and I could use a cup of tea." *Her flat was a tip. It smelt bad. There were dirty dishes on the floor, I hate that. And bowls of dog food.*

"Mum's usually out now with the dogs. She looks after them for people. It's hot in here." *It was.* "Do you mind?" *She took off her top layers, leaving just a thin blouse over a black bra.* "Don't be shy, Steve. Make yourself comfortable." *I took off my top layers, coming down to white school shirt over white muscle top.* "Shirt too, Steve. Watch me." *She slipped off the blouse. I knew she was giving me a show but I still liked it. I let her take off my shirt.* "God, you're fit, Steve."

"I work out a lot, Angie, and I don't eat junk."

"No, not fit as in fitness but fit as in hunk, fit as in big sex god." *I bet she had said that before but I still felt good.*

"Come and sit here, Steve." *She sat on this tatty couch. There were dog hairs on it. Suddenly, she looked really beautiful to me.*

"Angie, can I ask you something?"

"Go ahead, hunky."

"Could I lie my head in your lap?" *She looked puzzled.*

"Whatever." *And I did, and I couldn't smell the dogs any more just a big cocktail of smells from her – perfume, shampoo, make-up and … her. And I told her the story of Queen Catherine and Owen Tudor.*

"Sad." *But I think she meant it as in "sad bastard" not as in "makes you cry."*

"Steve. Stay right there." *And she slipped from under my head and took my shoes off and then my school trousers and then everything else. And sometimes she touched parts of my body, and I felt really tingly and I started to get stiff long before she reached my boxers. Then she took the rest of her clothes off. She went through the pockets of my clothes and my wallet.*

"No condom, Steve? Don't worry." *She fished in a drawer and brought some out.* "Ooh, Steve, I think we need Mr Extra Strength, don't you? Let's do this together." *We slipped one on. I'd seen it in sex-ed.* "Now, Steve, this is your first time, isn't it? But I know you're not gay – I checked – and I'm sure you're Mr Natural. I'm going on top of you and I'll .. guide everything. Just relax and trust your body."

Well, she couldn't know what those words meant to me. Jimmy. I nearly pushed her off but then I thought no, I'm a man and I fought Jimmy and this is what I want, so instead I pulled her down and gave her a fierce kiss on the mouth. It lasted a long time, with a lot of tongues.

"Ooh, Steve. Such passion!" *But then she took over and worked my body, especially nipples, and showed me what she wanted me to do in reply and then she guided me in and eased herself up and down and we were both moaning and gasping and I'd read somewhere that you had to make it last, but I just couldn't, I just exploded and she screamed and I started to stammer I was sorry and she shut me up and said I was brilliant and she always knew.*

"Hurry up, we can have a shower before Mum gets back with the dogs."

So we did and I'd read somewhere that people find this a real turn-on and do it all over again, but somehow it didn't work for me. I kept noticing that the shower wasn't any good, not nearly as good as ours at home, and the toilet smelt worse than school. And she didn't look as good in the shower, more droopy and kind of fuzzy. I was still really excited and kept telling her how wonderful she was, but I was sad too. Like when I was little, and I got the birthday present I'd been begging for only it wasn't as wonderful as I thought.

"Yeah, thanks Steve, and thanks for the shag, it was quality, but my mum will be back any minute and she doesn't like … She always wants the bathroom." *She hurried me away and we were dressed again when her mother arrived, with a couple of dogs.*

"Hi, Mum, this is Steve. He's helping me with my homework." *Her mother was really tired-looking and struggling to control the dogs.*

"How do you do, Mrs…" *I was really embarrassed. I mean, I had just shagged her daughter and I didn't even know her surname. But I didn't do any classes with Angie, so why should I? Fortunately I was saved when the big Labrador jumped up on me and licked my face. He had really bad breath.*

"He likes you. He doesn't like many people." *I pushed down the Labrador myself, since she made no effort.* "Is Steve eating? I don't know what there is." *But I didn't fancy eating there. At least my mum's microwave specials were clean.*

"Oh, no thank you very much, but I've got heaps to do at home. See you, Angie."

"See you, Steve. And thanks for helping me with the… Biology."

It wasn't original, but she had made the effort, so I said "Funny." *I left and started to walk down the street and then heard her running after me. I turned round and we had a long snog, more tongues, and I didn't care who saw.*

I went home in a daze. I was a man. Was that all there was to it? I thought about Julien Sorel in Scarlet and Black. *(Why did you file it under B for Beyle instead of S for Stendhal?) Anyway, it took him for ever to do what I had just done, and worrying all the time about what sort of man he was. And for me, it was all over in four pages. I felt brilliant, but when I got home, I felt sad. What would I do for the rest of the story?*
***

My client returned to me. "You know the rest of the story, don't you?" I did, but he had to tell it.

"The next day at school was kind of brilliant. Everyone seemed to know that I'd done it, and even though people kept saying 'Angie's latest', which took some shine off it, I got a lot of respect. Except from Nick and Phil, the only people I really liked. Phil thought I'd made a big mistake and Nick hated her. He said he'd got himself dropped from the football team to avoid having to do it with Angie.

"I took her home again, not every day but a lot and she never talked about the stalker again. We did it again, different positions, and it was great while it lasted, but then nothing else to talk about. And always that terrible flat and her mum coming back with dogs, didn't matter what breed they were they all came with bad breath and were all trained to jump on me. I finally found out their surname – Carstairs. Her mum had nothing much to talk about, apart from the dogs. And sometimes I'd stay on to eat, except all the food there was really nasty, processed and full of fat and sugar and chemicals. And I felt really sorry for them both. Her dad had run off and gave them no money and I really wished I had some money to give them so they could get somewhere better to live and eat better food. Am I a snob?"

"Possibly. But it's not snobbish to dislike dirt and dogs and dire dinners."

"Wordpower, Alice! I took Angie home once. What a disaster! Dad made a point of discovering that she had no dad and no money, and Mum kept asking her which novelists she liked to read, knowing that there weren't any. And I took her up to my room, but she didn't want to take her clothes off because she said she was cold. She didn't want me to open Uncle Frank's trunk, and she didn't want to talk about him. She just wanted to go home because mine was so cold. Actually, she was right. Her home had some life in it. Mine had none.

"I stayed with Angie because my parents disliked her and I thought they were snobs and had no right to judge her. So I defied them, and really tried to convince myself that I loved Angie. And she said my … performance was getting better and better. But it meant getting maybe, ten minutes which would be fantastic and electric and then hours which were really boring and got on my nerves. Mind you, be fair, I must have been really boring for her." I really warmed to this boy, taking his share of responsibility for a failed relationship.

"I could never talk to her about stuff that mattered to her, like soaps, or music, or celebrities. Or school gossip. I couldn't even give her the football team gossip because I wasn't interested and I could not remember who was going out with whom." I smiled: how many other British teenagers today would give you a 'whom'?

"I was useless at shopping because I had no eye for clothes and didn't know which labels were in and out. And I never wanted to see the same films that she did. I was useless at parties and clubs, although I was good at looking after her and getting her home.

"But the worst thing was cricket. She just didn't want to know about it. The one thing I'm really good at. She could handle football, because it didn't last too long and she knew enough about what was happening. But cricket? 'Boring.' And when the spring came along and I started putting in more time at the nets, she really resented it. That's why Nick came with me, even though he didn't like cricket, because he knew she wouldn't be there.

"When I met the Ahmads I was well made up and I told her that I was going to play for them and that it meant everything to me to have a team and I'd really like it if she came to the first match and she said 'You mean you're playing with Pakis?' and that finished it. I actually wanted to slap her, but I held it in and said 'The Ahmads are my friends and no one calls them Pakis. I don't want you to come to my match. It's over between us. I don't know why you ever started it. Was it a dare or a bet? What did you get from your friends for scoring with Psycho? Or were you trying to work your way through the football team?' That was cheap, wasn't it? Giving myself a good exit line. But I did exit and I could hear her screaming 'Fuck you, you're so up yourself!'

"She told the school that I was gay all along and that Nick and I were lovers. I didn't give a toss but Nick was upset. So I decided to play it for laughs, and I made a big show of coming out and I pretended to be Xan, the screamer fast bowler, and Nick became Nicola the Star Queen and all the other boys got girls' names, and everyone did laugh and went on our side."

"That was a very mature thing to do, Steve. And Xan came to you from Jimmy. So you were selecting something from your memories of Jimmy. That was very powerful and very healthy for you." He thought about this.

"I suppose so. And my batting improved. Jimmy corrected some things. Anyway, my life seemed to be looking up a bit. I'd got shot of Angie. Nick and I were officially a couple and we could do what we wanted, which was really just talking for ever, but once – all part of having a laugh – I snogged him in the school playground and we both... enjoyed it.

"And best of all, I was playing for Mr Ahmad's team. I had to do a lot of work on his team because some of the uncles were a bit fat and useless. Sometimes when they dropped an easy catch off me it was really difficult to say 'Good try, Mr Khan!', but I loved all the work and they all seemed to like me. And Mr Ahmad took care of me. He bought me a chest protector before one match because the other side had a really fast bowler. And he got on with my dad, talking about business, so I got no strife at home about playing for him. And then it all fell apart.

"One match Mr Ahmad had his nephew from Pakistan playing for us. He was a young guy, a religious student, and he didn't like me and he said something in their language to Mr Ahmad, and I could tell it was about me, and Mr Ahmad said something sharp in reply. We batted first and the young guy was a bloody good batsman and he scored a century. I joined him at number 8 and he ran me out with a bad call, but Mr Ahmad saw him to his hundred.

"We were all out and we had tea. Except it wasn't just tea it was more like a restaurant, with loads of samozas and bhajis and different kinds of curry. I wish Cal had been there. All I could manage was a bit of rice because I would be opening the bowling.

"And then suddenly Mr Ahmad's nephew starting talking about Afghanistan. Some British soldiers had been killed and he was really happy about it because they were enemies of Islam. And of course I thought of Uncle Frank and I really lost it and started shouting at him. 'You fucking bastard!' and that was really bad, because there were lots of women and children around and Pakistani people hate swearing in front of them but I had totally lost it. 'My uncle Frank was a soldier in Afghanistan and it's a toilet of a country and do you think he wanted to go there? Do you think that's why he joined the army, to go to Afghanistan and kill Muslims? Because if you think that you're not only a shit, you're stupid too!' And I burst into tears and went off and grabbed my clothes and threw them into my cricket bag and ran away from the ground. Mr Ahmad followed me, but I just kept running and he was a bit fat so I soon got away. I really make a habit of running away from cricket matches, don't I?

"I wandered about for a bit, looking a bit stupid in my whites, and eventually found a Tube station and worked out how to get home. I felt really guilty because Mr Ahmad's team wouldn't have their fast bowler, and then I felt sad because I could have had some of that beautiful food.

"I got home and Dad wasn't best pleased that I had walked out on Mr Ahmad. And then Mr Ahmad came by and asked if I was OK, and he told me his team had won, because of course the nephew was an ace bowler as well and had taken six wickets. And Mr Ahmad said he was really sorry about what had happened and he really liked me but he had to stand by his nephew, because his nephew was family… And I said I was really sorry to swear in front of everybody, because it wasn't respectful. And we just sort of agreed that I couldn't play for his team any more, but he hoped we would meet again at the nets and he was sure I would find another team.

"But I didn't get another team because Dad was angry that I had lost him a good contact and in any case, I should be concentrating on GCSEs.

"So all I could do was go back to those nets and just keep bowling at people. Or even at nobody. And then I met the McConnel twins – the New Zealanders that Cal saw me with and they were going to form a team with me in it – and then they had to go home suddenly because their dad was sick, and this is pathetic but I thought I was under some sort of cricket curse. Every time I thought I had a good thing going, it would be snatched away."

"But you fought the curse. You came back to the nets and you gave my little boy his life back again. That's what knights do in legends. They fight curses and save people." I went over and hugged him again.   "Are we done?"

"I think so."

"Steve, you've taken a battering in the last few years. You are still in grief for your Uncle Frank and you have had to cope with one problem or crisis after another. I have to ask you something. You don't seem to have had much support from your parents." He broke away from my hug and stood up.

"No. It's because they hate me." Matter of fact.

"It's easy to believe that. They may not be demonstrative or empathetic, some people aren't, but it doesn't mean they hate you."

"It's easy to believe because it's true. I didn't want to believe it for a long time. I thought it was, like you said, they're not demonstrative. I've seen parents who really love their kids, Nick's parents and now you and Cal. They hug and kiss their kids, like it's for nobody else and they might never see them again. My mum kisses me like one of her friends. And Dad gives me these almost-hugs. And I thought, well, maybe they're not demonstrative.

"And like everything they do as parents, like birthdays, holidays, Christmas, playing Monopoly, it was like, well, we're parents, this is what we have to do.

"And when they argue, which is virtually all the time, and I get really knotted up, I used to think, they don't know what's going on for me and if they did, they would just stop. Then I began to think they knew I was unhappy but they went on arguing anyway, but I thought it's because they were unhappy themselves and they couldn't help passing it on to me, like measles.

"Then I thought it had something to do with Uncle Frank, because I had loved him instead of them, and if I was a good son they would love me. And then all the bad stuff kept happening, and I thought if the bad stuff would stop happening they might see I was a good son.

"After Uncle Frank died, I read Mum's novel, as much as she'd finished. Guess what? It's about a creative woman, dragged down by a boring husband and a stupid, selfish son. I was Fred who cared about nothing except football. But she got all the football bits wrong. And then I realized Dad had a kind of novel going too, although he never wrote any of it: hard-working self-made man supporting pretentious wife and a stupid, selfish son who cared about nothing except cricket. And I thought – well, they've got a make-believe idea of me and if I could just get rid of that idea, they might love me.

"But then I realized that they hated me and that was all there was to it. They didn't hate me because of Uncle Frank or because I was a bad son or because they had an idea of me. They just hated me." He was holding desperately to the matter-of-fact analytic tone.

"I heard them arguing with each other one night. About my… conception. Each was saying it was the other's fault. They were sorry I'd even been born," and there he could not hold out any longer. The racking, gasping sobs returned. I held him tightly and silently for a long time. Eventually his breathing slowed down and I pulled him beside me onto the couch. I cradled his head on my lap, as he seemed to like and spoke to him softly.

"People say crazy, twisted things when they argue. I've seen them in evidence. Things they don't really mean and then try to remove."

He started to protest and I hurried on. "But even if they meant it, they were the losers not you. They lost the joy of knowing their wonderful son and seeing him grow up into a wonderful young man. Their wonderful son, who's clever and inventive and funny, who's brave in adversity, who's so kind and loving when he could be enraged at the world. Their wonderful son, with the Scarecrow's brain and the Lion's nerve and the Tin Man's giant heart."

A flicker of a smile. "But I haven't seen the Wizard. Every time I get near the Emerald City the door slams in my face."

"You didn't watch the film closely enough. The Wizard doesn't give them anything. They had the brain and the nerve and the heart right from the beginning. Don't ever let on that you know this, but when Cal and I watched the film on video, Bungle got scared of the Witch and Cal had to hold his paw behind the couch."

A real smile. "Now, Steve sweetheart, the conference is over. You've had your pound's worth. It's way too late for you to go home. There's a sofa bed in my study which I will make up and you crash on it. And you are now on holiday here, until further notice. Sleep in, I'll tell Cal not to wake you. Your cricket stuff's already here so go home tomorrow and get anything else you need for a week's holiday. If there's any problem – call your lawyer."

He gave me a real smile, stood up and hugged me.

"Thanks for listening to all that."

"I'm sorry you had to wait so long. But I hope you will feel better now. And remember, you are now on holiday, which means not just being away from home, but away from your past."

He broke off the hug and picked up Bungle. "I kept him up too. He'd better go back to base."

Chapter 11   Resumption Of Play

Mum said Steve was in the spare room (!) and don't wake him up, so I
mooched around and I even tidied up all my clothes and he still wasn't
awake so I left him a note: "Gone to Mrs Kundera's, neighbour No 23," and
then wondered for ages and then I finally wrote "XXXOOO Cal" because
it's true and I don't care! I did some gardening and Mrs K gave me two
ice creams because I was looking thin. Then Steve rang the bell.

"You must be Steve, the god. Cal's been talking about you for an hour,"
AAGH! Thanks, Mrs K! But it's true.

"I hope you're a cricket fan, Mrs Kundera, because there's nothing else about
me that would be worth an hour."

"Martina, please. I didn't understand a single word he said but I know a lot
about you." Then he saw my pictures. She had framed them really well.

"Martina, those are beautiful. Are they valuable?" Silly question!

"They will be. Cal did them for me." He looked at them more closely.

"Sorry. I don't know much about pictures. Well, anything. Those are the first
I've seen of yours in colour."

"It's only a wash. I don't normally do colour, it just seems to get in the way.
But you cannot really do a garden without colour."

"Cal not only did the pictures he did the garden itself. This is the best it's ever
looked."

"Cal does your gardening? Gosh, I hope you don't need any muscle," so I
punched him and he staggered back and crumpled.

"Just for that, you can move the rubble." And he picked up all the big sacks
full of concrete stuff as if they were Bungle and put them in the skip.

"Steve, would you like some coffee, proper coffee, not English?" And she
brought us all coffee and pastries from Havel's and I had two.

"Martina, that was wonderful. I never liked coffee before," and she took him
into her kitchen and showed him how to make real coffee.

"Steve, Cal is the grandson I wanted and I spoil him. You make him very happy, so you must come here too and be spoilt too. Don't wait to be asked and you can come on your own."

We went home and he seemed really puzzled about something. "She was really nice. Why are people so nice to me, all of a sudden?"

"God, you're stupid, sometimes! You're a nice person."

"Your mum's been fantastic to me. She stayed up almost all night, listening to me. Piles of … stuff. And all for a pound. She didn't know me! And she asked me to stay for a week. If that's OK with you?"

"As if," **and I couldn't stop it and gave him my biggest hug, the one that makes Mum say "What have you broken?" I finally let go and said** "Sorry. Was that embarrassing? I promise I won't do it if there's people."

"Of course, it's not embarrassing. It's totally brilliant, but it's become strange, that's all. Since my uncle Frank died."

"Well, we do loads of hugs Mum and me, so you'd better get used to it." **And suddenly he gave me one right back.** "Come on! I'm quite strong, really, and you're not going to break me," **and he made it tighter.** "Much better. Almost as good as Bungle," **and we had a fight, and he broke a mug.**

"Cripes! Oh God, I'm so sorry, I've got money now, I'll replace it."

"Don't wet yourself! We get them from the supermarket, Value White Mug, one pound. As if Mum would have valuable china with me in the house. What are we going to do now? It's raining."

"Pool? Shallow end until you're ready for more?"

"NO!" **He's not going to see me clinging to the steps. Instead he taught me a card game called gin rummy and won three million quid.**

"I'll settle for a signed drawing."

"That's worth way more than three million." **I made us bolognese sandwiches (!) for lunch.**

"I need to go home for a bit and pick up some stuff."

"Can I come with?"

"Do you mind if I say no?" **He looked really uptight.**

"Of course I do but I know you've got to be alone sometimes. Hurry up back, it's stopped raining." **And he gave me a hug.** "Improving."

I ran home even though it was getting hot. I didn't even stop to rehearse my bowling action. It would just be a quick in-and-out. As if I were a burglar in my own home.

No one in of course. Two notes waiting for me. Those bloody notes. "S. Gone to writers' retreat for weekend." *So what happened to our shopping trip and my makeover?* " Food for you on top shelf of fridge." *Ooh, suppose I helped myself from the second shelf! Bad Son!* "Mum." *Just that, not "Love Mum" or any Xs and Os. Am I getting hyper, Uncle Frank? It never got to me before. Read Dad's.* "S. Lawn needs you! Dad." *At least a gleam of humour. It stopped me saying "Fuck the lawn!" I so wanted to get back, but they're never going to say I let them down. Sorry about the "they." I did a cracking job on the lawn. Two cuts.*

I wrote a note back. "Mum/Dad. Lawn got me! Gone to cricket retreat for a week." *Payback! Was it a bit cheap?* "Staying with friends. On mobile if GSCEs come in and you want to congratulate me! Or ring friend's number (she is top children's lawyer – see card.)" *A little warning. Hope it wasn't necessary.* "Don't worry about me – not doing anything stupid. For emergency garden care – see other card. They are quality." *I left them one of the Ahmad brothers' cards. I wished I could see Dad trying to bargain with Ijaz.* "Love, Steve."

I went up to my room. Yours when you visited. Hell, it is small. What would I need for a week's stay? Not the smart suit. One smartish pair of black jeans, one smartish shirt. A few T-shirts, boxers, socks. Hell, almost my entire casual wardrobe fitted easily into my backpack. Toilet bag, toothbrush (well-used), razor (hardly used!) Deodorant (seems to work, never any complaints). Your current book: S for Sartre, The Age Of Reason. *Hard work! I looked around the room. Was there anything else? My cricket trophies? They'd think I was vain. Your photograph? Yes. I want them to see it. I wrapped it really carefully in my clothes and wedged it into the backpack. Brilliant. Now I could bike back and regain the lawnmowing time.*

"Why weren't you wearing your helmet? Fine of three million quid!" *Shit! Caught out. If I say something to him, like always wearing my helmet, I must come through.* "Suppose you fell off and turned into a zombie and could never bowl fast again? But cool bike! How many gears?"

"Eighteen. My dad gave it to me." *Well, gave me the money and let me pick it.*

"Put it with mine and Mum's at the back. Lock it, just in case. Hurry up, we're wasting valuable cricket time."

We rushed to the park and I smacked him about and bowled him three times with my orthodox stuff. "God, you're crap today. And you mixed up all the Test Match Special commentators. One ball you were Henry Blofeld, then the next you were Victor Marks."

"Sorry. Thinking about stuff."

Steve spent the evening brooding and even Cal lost his bounce. I gave them both some good news.

"I talked to Robert's parents. They've invited you both to their house tomorrow evening, to stay over. They really wanted to see you before they go off on holiday on Monday."

"Brilliant!"

"Steve?"

"Oh sorry, that's nice of them." Something else was going on for him. I hoped I wouldn't need another all-night conference to draw it out.

"Handy for me, as it happens, I have to go out tomorrow evening. With a client. Steve, I don't really know the Barneses. Are they easygoing or do you and Cal have to be on best behaviour?"

"They seem easygoing. They're both nuts about Robert. There's an older sister as well."

"They're not members of any evangelical religion?" He looked understandably puzzled.

"I don't think so. They're both in advertising."

"Guess what they asked me?" I told him and got a flicker of a smile.

Steve's mind went AWOL again during Monopoly and he twice forgot to claim rent from Bungle.

"You really are crap today."

"Steve, what's on your mind? In five minutes or less."

He wrestled around in his head and suddenly blurted "Notes! I went home today for my clothes and my bike and they'd left me two notes. Completely impersonal. Not like Cal's which he left for me here this morning. Hell, I'm their son, in my home, not the hired help." He was getting shaky again. "Why do you want me here? My parents don't want me, I haven't got a home. I haven't got a future, just being packed off to business school. The only thing I'm good at is cricket and I haven't even got a team… I'm just a casualty."

"Don't be a pathetic little drama queen!" He was shocked, as I meant him to be. "Steve, sweetheart, we like having you here, but only if you're happy. If you cannot trust yourself to be happy here, I'm afraid you'd better leave. You've had a lot of unhappiness and it's probably become familiar. People stick to what's familiar even when it's bad for them, because they feel safer. But when people are determined to be unhappy … well, they just suck the air away from those around them. So I want you right now to think of something that would make you happy."

He closed his eyes and then said "I'd like to try Cal's method. Make someone else happy. So could I take Cal to the Oval cricket shop tomorrow and buy him new cricket kit?"   We both hugged him. I agreed to his proposal, but only if I paid. He fought back at the Monopoly board and took Bungle to the cleaners.

Before we all went to bed he showed us a photograph of his uncle Frank.

"That's him with his medal. The MC. He got it for a mission in Bosnia but he wasn't officially there so I don't know exactly what he did."

"You take after him. But … I could never see you in the army."

"No way, he's a total softie!"

We looked at Uncle Frank again and I took a chance. "Steve. This may be hard for you but I think you should stop writing to your uncle Frank, either for real or in your head. It's helped you come to terms with everything that's happened to you. It's certainly improved your vocabulary. But now I think it's time to let go. You won't lose your uncle Frank. Love really does last for ever and the love he gave you is always with you. Your uncle Frank lives every time you play cricket, every time you use an interesting word, every time you do anything happy or creative. Most important, he lives on in everything you pass on to Cal, and Robert. And they will pass him on too, even though they did not know him."

We were all a bit choked by now so I brought it to my conclusion. "Steve, it's time for the living to take over. Think of all the people who care about you now and want to know what's going on in your life. Me and Cal, of course. The Barneses. Mrs K next door. She stopped me in the street tonight and asked about 'that handsome devil.' Watch her, Steve, she's a real party girl. Your friend Nick in the States. And what about those New Zealanders?"

"Daniel and Brendon? God, I never emailed them. They must think I'm a total shit."

"I doubt it. But feel free to hit the computer. Don't take all night, we have to shop tomorrow." Another collective hug and then he hurtled off to my desk.

Cal wanted us to go to the Oval shop long before it was open. "Hurry up! Don't pretend you need to shave!"

"Cal, don't make personal remarks. Take your time, Steve, I hate men with stubble." Cal was right but Steve still needed all the ego he could get.

When we got to the shop there was this guy around Steve's age and Steve knew him.

"Bloody hell! It's George. Sorry, we never got beyond George and Steve. Steve Helson."

"George Dabby. I'm doing work experience here. Do you still go to the nets?"

"Yeah. This is Cal. Cal Devane. Left-handed all-rounder. Orthodox and wrist spin. He goes to the nets too. Alice, Cal, this is George. He's going to open the attack with me for England in five years time."

George found everything like Steve's in my size, including the space shirt and the Padman shorts. And there was a Tim Morrow bat and it was perfect and they made me hold it out in my right hand for a minute and Steve said it was an amazing price and Mum said I should have it.

"Alice, can I pay for the helmet? And I'd like to add an arm guard and a chest protector? Just in case he faces a fast bowler on a bad wicket. Even if he uses them just once it would be worth it."

"Steve, Cal's right, you are Mr Softy. I can't believe you're a fast bowler."

George said we'd spent so much that we ought to get a free test of everything in the nets and David, his boss, said yes.

"You can't use the new bat. Two coats of oil and six hours knocking in, minimum, with an old ball. Alice, it's the most maddening sound in the world, you might go mental." So I used my old bat which I'd brought to compare and George gave me a new grip for free. "If you wear all of the padding, George and I will bowl full pace. Heat-seeking missiles."

Bloody hell, they were fast but they pitched everything up and I managed to hit most of them before they hit me – and all the padding worked when I didn't! David bowled a few (slower, big breaks off the pitch) and he said I had great footwork (true) but my head was falling away (it was) and I should look up and over my right shoulder (and I got better). Then Steve and George batted for a bit so I could bowl and David said I had a lovely high action (true) and I told him about Steve and the two guns and he was impressed. George smashed me a bit but he swept too much and I bowled him with my arm ball. David told me not to overbowl my zooter. Steve and George bowled short at each other and called each other pie-throwers but I'd have been poop-scared. It was the first time I'd ever seen Steve bowl short and he looked different. Maybe he is a Psycho after all.

I watched them from the gallery. I so nearly rushed down to protect my little baby when he got hit, but he was fine, so I spared him the shame. He was much better than I remembered. Steve must be a brilliant teacher. It was the first time I had ever seen him bowl. He turns into some kind of animal. All the gear took a big bite out of my plastic but I'd have paid it ten times over for getting Cal's summer back again. The boys had a long argument in the car on the way home.

"George was faster than you."

"So not."

"You didn't let go when I was batting and he did." That was true. Even I could see that. When Steve bowled at George he was different. He must not make things too easy for Cal.

Quick lunch at home (but enough protein for Steve) and the boys crammed all of their cricket gear into Steve's bag. Steve did his overnight stuff and I dealt with Cal's, remembering his drawing of Robert and adding a secret. Then I drove them to the nets.

I really liked all the Barneses. Joe used to know Portia. He was an energetic, nervous man, Belinda serene. They adored Robert and I wondered at first if he might be spoilt, but he had nice manners. There was an elder sister at home. She sounded like a problem.

Robert was fatter than Cal's drawing, but he would be solid when he lost it. Is my boy a seer as well as an artist? Robert has such a crush on Cal – and he didn't even notice. I hoped things wouldn't get complicated. Of course he has a crush on Steve too. Steve is indeed a brilliant teacher. He thinks he is just passing on what his uncle Frank told him. There's much more. Belinda broke in on my reverie.

"Meeting Cal and Steve has been such a boost for Robert. He really needed it. He and his sister have been at each other's throats all summer. It's been really quite poisonous at home," and I learnt that they had been bullied at school (doesn't any school get a grip on this?) and that Zoe (the girl) had taken it out on Robert. They had been pulled out, and would be going to a new, private, "progressive" school called Marian's, founded by their friend Howard Foy in memory of his wife. The name left a vague memory – writer, perennial panellist on "serious" radio and TV programmes. Widower. Devastated by grief. The school made me envious. It sounded perfect for Cal – and totally out of reach.

"Mum! Look at Robert's bat! That's Tim Morrow's signature. They <u>know</u> him!" Just to wind him up, I pretended to know nothing of England's latest batting hero. Robert gave me all of his statistics.

The net session finished. Joe fussed the younger boys into drinking a lot of water. So did Steve. Relax, young man, there's plenty of parenting around here. Everyone collected their stuff. The Barnes lived right on the edge of the park. I did a quick estimate of family house prices and felt another flash of envy.

Chapter 12   Rest Period

Dear Zoe Future (Mrs Stephen Helson?),

If you don't get this letter, it means that I have just ruined my entire life!! And serve me right for being a cow and a moron!!!

I was in my room this afternoon, half reading and half sulking (as usual), and 100 per cent angry with my little brother Robert because I knew he had been in my room, where he's banned. And I heard Mum come in and head for the kitchen and then Dad and Robert came into the hall with some other people. And they stopped and looked at Robert's red squirrel photograph (boring). One of the visitors had a nice, husky voice and I thought it might be a voiceover actor for one of Dad's commercials.

"Robert, that is astonishing. Did you have a long lens?"

"Not specially. I just hid in the tree and waited for him." Actually, it is pretty amazing. Then this woman started talking about the cricket team picture and she really seemed to know her stuff.

"Steve, that's really good. Look, very few lines but they're all doing something. They tell you everything about everybody. Look, there's Joe, he's really beating himself up about something. And that guy in the shades is really powerful and completely ignoring the guy next to him. And the scorer with his arms out – he owns everybody."

"Good spot, Cal. That was our cricket team, the Frenetics, around fifteen years ago.[5] The artist was called Anthony Hodge and he played for us too. Big loopy legbreaks. Sadly, he died. But do you recognize the boy?"

"No."

---

[5] See the cover of <u>A Tale Of Ten WIckets</u>

"That's Tim Morrow."

"No!"

"You played in the same team as Tim Morrow."

"Sure. We know him very well. His stepdad is the third partner in our agency. We always knew Tim was way too good for the Frenetics, but he played to be with his dad. He's now our President."

"Oh my god, oh my god, he's played with Tim Morrow, we are not worthy."

Strange. Who was this mad cricket groupie? I came out and went downstairs to have a look. And it wasn't a woman at all, but this cute little blond boy about Robert's age. And the other voice belonged to the most divine boy in the universe!!! Amazing body, everything perfect, and his face,,, Not just handsome but BEAUTIFUL, and noble, like a mediaeval paladin doing battle for good against evil (although not a very good haircut). They had moved on to the portrait.

"Look Steve," *Steve. My favourite name.* "That's really well drawn too. If there were no colour and tones you would still know everybody. And the grouping's really important."

"He put me behind the chair to hide my fat tum!"

"No, he put you behind the chair because you make a triangle with your mum and your dad. And look, Steve, everyone's got something with them to say what they do. Robert's got a camera, Belinda's got designer paper, Joe's got a laptop, Robert's sister's got a pen and notebook. So she's a writer, and Joe's a writer but he does other stuff too, which you can do on a laptop. Oh and look, that's really clever, they're right by the finished portrait, and in that finished portrait there's another finished portrait and if you scunch up really close, that's got a tiny finished portrait too. That's called an infinite regress. Diccon Swan. God, he's really good.[6]"

---

[6] A real and excellent artist: see www.jenniecohen.co.uk/dicconswan

Now wasn't that a perfect time to slip into the conversation about the family portrait and be part of the nice warm circle? But no! I was still in a red rage with Robert, so instead I blurted out "Wow! Who's this? Mr Cutie and Mr Hunky? What are you doing with Mr Lardo?"

"Fuck off, Miss Bitch! It's actually muscle-in-waiting but you haven't got anything in waiting, you'll always be Miss Bitch!" This took me by surprise. Robert never had a good comeback and he usually ended up crying.

So I couldn't let that go and said "You've been in my room again! I could smell!"

Dad was furious, of course, but before he could say anything the little blond boy cut in "My name's Cal and this is Steve. I think you know your brother Robert. And Robert, this must be your sister…?"

"Zoe."

"Robert and Zoe, go straight to your rooms and come out when you've learnt how to receive guests to our house. Steve, Cal, I'm really sorry." So I went back to my room, of course, and looked at Steve on the way and he looked totally sick, as if he absolutely despised me and why not and I threw myself onto the bed and burst into tears. It meant goodbye Future Zoe… Goodbye for ever. A knock at my door. "Go away!"

"It's Cal. Can I talk to you?" I let him in. He looked a bit amazed at the books. Then he looked at the only poster.

"Who's she?"

"Emily Dickinson. A poet. She lived in her room most of her life. Like I'm going to do."

"Have you been bullied?"

"God, does it show?"

"I'm an artist. I'm an expert at faces. I can read yours. And I'm an expert on being bullied. The worst thing is when your friends join in, isn't it? My best friend – my ex best friend – started it for me. And it never stops, does it? Pushing you, hitting you, wrecking your stuff. And names. All the names. If they don't get you at school they get you with texts, emails, whatever. And they get you on the street or in the park."

"You know."

"Robert too."

"Yeah. He was already getting a hard time in his first year so he asked me for help and that is such a mistake and they had already started in on me in my year so Robert just made it worse and I hated him." Cal started bouncing from foot to foot and he looked at Emily Dickinson so I knew he must be struggling with something important.

"Robert's my friend and I know that you don't really hate him only he's just there all the time for you to lash out at but it's not fair and it's not right and it means they're winning. The bullies, I mean. They always want to turn you into one. Like vampires."

"That's really interesting. Where did you get that from?"

"My mum and I talked it over."

I thought about this for a while. To gain time I said "We're going to a new school. Marian's College. It's independent. Our friend Howard Foy set it up in memory of his wife. She was a teacher. He wanted it to be her dream school where she would have loved to teach. The number one rule is that you have to be happy. If you're not happy, you get savagely punished to within an inch of your life!" The head said that to Robert and me when we first met him with our parents. It made Cal giggle. I looked at him. Robert and I have had professional counselling over our feud, our whole family's had therapy, Had this little cutie-pie got the answer in five minutes?

The next thing he said completely made up my mind. "Steve hates bullies. He goes completely psycho. He saved me from the bullies," but I didn't let him tell the story. I simply grabbed his hand and towed him towards Robert's room.

I could hear him snivelling at somebody – presumably Steve!

"I hate her so much! I can't do anything right and I'm always fat or stupid. I know she's had a bad time but it's not my fault and I've had a bad time." I knocked. "Fuck off!"

Deep breath. "Robert, I'm really, really sorry. Sorry to die for. I want to tell you face to face but I'll go on shouting through the key hole."

A beat. "Come in." Steve had his arms around him! A stab of jealousy. Why couldn't it have been me first? Because I didn't deserve it. Steve turned him round, gently, and I took over hugging Robert. My brother.

"Robert. I'm really, really sorry I have been a crap sister. I'm proud of you. I'm glad you're in my family. You don't have to be my friend, but can we stop the war?" I meant it, but I couldn't help checking whether Steve had heard it too!

"Yeah. I'd like that. And you don't have to be my friend. Shall we tell Mum and Dad?" Steve and Cal caught each other's eye and stayed behind when Robert and I went to the living room. Steve looked at me as if I wasn't a total cow. Perhaps there's hope.

"Mum! Dad! We've come to tell you the war's over."

"Yeah, and we're sorry we're such crap kids."

"You're not crap kids, you just do crap things sometimes," and we had a big soppy family hug.

Robert had this humungous room.

"He's got five teddies!"

"And you were worried about Bungle."

"I feel a bit mean leaving him behind."

"You didn't! Check your bag." **He was there!** "Your mum packed him. She checked with Joe and Belinda and they checked with her."

"As if I'd make fun of a teddy bear!"

"They didn't know you then. Robert's had a hard time."

"I know."

Robert came back, looking well made up. "What have you guys done to my sister? She's all right again! Is that your bear? What's his name?"

"Bungle," and I told him why.

His bear had a mac and a gun! "This is Ted Luger, Bearvate Eye. He was huge in the 90s, a big cartoon series, only you don't see him now because they took his gun away. Dad plays cricket with the guy who thought of him.[7] This is Caspar the Camel, this is Victor the Giraffe, this is Manfred the Dog, and this is Arthur the Stegosaurus."

"You've had a very important ted in here, haven't you?" **Steve pointed to a big photo on the wall. It said "Robert. Thank you for looking after Tiger so well. Love from Tim." Morrow!**

"Wow! Almost no one's allowed to even touch that tiger."

"Tim's my there-is-no-godfather. We'll play cricket with him when he's free. And maybe Tom O'Ryan."

"Did you take all the photos, Robert? They're wonderful. Like the ones you took of me and Cal."

"I'm glad you like those but I don't really rate them, because they were digital, and it feels… too easy on digital. This is the camera I really like, the

---

[7] See "Lift Off" in <u>A Tale Of Ten Wickets.</u>

one I used for all the ones on the wall. It's a classic Leica. Over fifty years old. Stephen Duveen gave it to me."

"Stephen Duveen? As in The Road Of Silk?"

"As in."

"He's a really famous author, Cal. That was one of my uncle Frank's books. The only travel book."

"I'm going to do that journey myself, one day. It's changed."

"You know everybody. How do you know Stephen Duveen?"

"He watched one of Dad's cricket matches and got to know everyone and stayed in touch.[8]"

Then I remembered my drawing of him. Gosh, did Mum pack it? Phew! Why do I always hate giving people my drawings? I mean, they are brilliant and worth millions. But I made a complete prat of myself again. "Look, do you want this? You don't have to, it's really rough, I can do it better…"

But he was gobsmacked, just as Steve had been. "You've made me… slim."

"Muscle in waiting. I can see it when you hit the ball." And then he hugged me!

I slipped away and wandered by mistake into their sitting room.

"Sorry…"

"Sorry, nothing Steve, the whole house is yours. Whenever you like. You just gave us our family back."

"It was Cal, really. He does that to people."

"It was you as well. And in five minutes. They should send you two to the Middle East. Listen, you've already done us a huge favour but I would like to ask another. Can you babysit, tonight? Well, not babysit, but can we leave you

_____

[8] See <u>A Tale Of Ten Wickets</u> passim.

here tonight? Belinda and I would really like to look in at Matthew Neal's party. He's the hottest PR in town and everybody will be there and if you're not at his party people think you're dead. We couldn't ask you when Zoe and Robert were at war, but now you should have no problem."

"We'll feed you all before we go. There's tons more if you get hungry again. Robert knows what he should eat. I'm afraid there's no junk."

"I hate junk! But are you sure... I mean, you hardly know me?"

"Steve, we would feel very happy to leave you looking after our house and our kids."

Later

Mum and Dad went to their party after all.

"Steve's in charge! You will experience his iron discipline." Cal snickered. "No teenage party movie will be shot on this set."

They gave us supper – my fish pie. He liked it!!! But it was Cal who really put it away. Poor Robert was so envious. We had some dessert and cleared away. Steve's a real housewife! Then we went to the sitting room and the giant TV. We argued a bit over channels and then I said "Let's show them Howard's movie."

"Which one?"

"The Speculator."

"That one's ancient. Ricky Rubato."

"But it's so romantic."

"Zzz." We argued for a bit but I let Robert win because I had been such a bad sister (only I let Steve see).

I put the DVD in of <u>Your Very Own Ricky Rubato</u>.[9] "I'm surprised you never saw this, Steve. It did great box office. You'll meet Howard. He's my there-is-no-godfather. He'll really like you."

"How do you know?"

"I know Howard and I know you. Don't argue." Steve moved for the armchair but Robert and I grabbed him. "Sorry, Steve, but this couch needs four people" We threw him on the couch and arranged him and then the three of us arranged ourselves on top of him!

"Do I get any say in this?"

"No! You're just furniture!" and we all squealed with laughter. Eventually we settled for a share of him (I copped a shoulder and part of his big chest!) and we watched the DVD. He stretched his arms out as if he was trying to encircle us all, and with that and the movie (a Howard Foy "feelgood" special) it felt as though nothing bad could ever happen again. We got to the payoff and the multiple happy ending. We stayed on the couch, each in the moment.

Finally Cal said "My mum would like that. She plays the piano."

"She should meet Howard. But don't let him anywhere near a piano. He's worse than Ricky Rubato."

Steve said "That was great. Brilliant dialogue. Just a weeny bit sentimental?"

"You cried when Beppo The Wonder Dog started singing again. Admit it!"

"Of course he cried, the big softie. He's so soft you could put him on toilet paper instead of that puppy." Cal and Robert went into hysterics.

---

[9] Howard Foy's smash hit <u>Your Very Own Ricky Rubato</u> is available from www.richardheller.co.uk

"You are both so dead when I bowl at you tomorrow." **No chance, and they knew it. That's when I fell completely in love with him.**

To my huge joy, Robert took Cal off to his bedroom. I got a nice hug and kiss from them both but they insisted that Steve come and say goodnight. "You have to, you're the babysitter!"

Alone together for the first time! He looked really thoughtful.

"Anything wrong, Steve?"

"I just feel a bit … dizzy. I only met Cal a few days ago, and Alice, and now you and your family, and it's like being in another world. You all act differently, as if you were happy all the time and you wanted everyone to be happy around you."

"Sweet of you to say that, but I was a bitch to Robert for months. And to Mum and Dad. This house was really poisonous. You and Cal got us back."

"But you say 'got us back'. This is how you always were, right? Something went wrong and it got fixed and things are back to normal. It's been normal for you to be happy… well, it's not been normal for me."

"Well, get used to it, Steve. You make people happy and they want you to be happy. What did it feel like when we were all on the couch?"

"It felt great."

"Good. We felt great too. We all wanted a piece of you."

"I know and I wished I could grow and give you more. I seem to be stuck on five foot ten." **He doesn't realize it's quite enough when you're PERFECT!!!** "I wanted my arms to get longer especially so that I could get them right round you all."

And wouldn't this have been a great moment to say "They're quite long enough for one" **as I would have done in a Howard Foy movie and we would have melted into a clinch? But this was**

real life and I didn't think of it. Steve went on "I just finished one of my uncle Frank's books. S for Salinger, Catcher In The Rye."

"Oh, I read it too, I loved it." *Fool! Now I had got us into Lit Crit instead of Life.*

"Lots of it was really funny, but I thought he was a bit of a … prat, Holden, I mean, just talking about himself all the time and almost as if he wanted to be confused and not do anything about himself. But there was one bit which really got to me, the bit which explained the title, when he wanted to be the catcher who stops the kids getting hurt. That's what I feel like, a lot. Which reminds me – I'm the babysitter and I'd better check on the babies."

When I got to Robert's bedroom, he and Cal were lying side by side on the floor on these little mattresses. All the available teddies were around them.

"Futons. They're brilliant. I want some for my room. Steve?"

"Cal?"

"I always get really scared on my first night in a new house."

"And when someone near me gets scared I get scared too, and I go to the fridge and eat and that's why I'm so fat."

"So do you think you could sleep in Robert's bed and we would feel much safer?"

"Pitifully bad. You are two of the bravest kids in the world, you're in the room Robert sleeps in every night, and you have a huge bodyguard of teds."

Long hug for Robert. "Goodnight, Robert. I'm really glad you're Cal's friend."

"Cal's my best friend, ever."

Long hug for Cal. "Goodnight, Cal. Thank you for bringing me here."

"Improving. But you still need more practice."

Will close for now, Zoe Future. Saved from disaster. Waiting for Steve on the couch with all to play for!!!

Chapter 13   Close Catching

To Zoe Future (Dear Mrs H?)Steve came back with a book and I so nearly asked him about it and we would have been in Lit Crit again instead of Passion!

Instead I said "Now Steve, it's my turn to be furniture and it's your turn to be comfortable," and beckoned him to the couch.

"Zoe? Can I... lay my head in your lap?"

"Sure." And he did and I stroked his hair, which he has got to grow longer. And then he told me this story about Owen Tudor and Queen Catherine.   "Oh, Steve, that is terribly sad but terribly beautiful," and I think I passed some kind of test because he looked really happy.

"Do you think that it's possible to love somebody that much?"

"Oh yes."

"I often wonder why Uncle Frank told me that. I don't think he loved anybody. Well, except me."

"Perhaps he loved you that much." And I barely stopped myself from adding "I do." Instead I said "Your uncle Frank meant a lot to you, didn't he?"

"Oh hell, yes..." and he choked up for a second and then he started to tell me about his uncle and being together and playing cricket and reading books and using interesting words and I went on stroking his hair and I wanted to make him feel really safe and comfortable when he told me, and know that he could trust me with his life and his secrets. And I knew Uncle Frank was going to die, so I tried to listen really hard without thinking about my own feelings, because I have never lost anyone I really loved. I didn't even cry with him, because it was his grief and I had no claim. I just stayed as part of the furniture.

"Bloody hell!" He sat up suddenly. "Thank you for listening for so long. Is my head really heavy? Here, why don't we both get comfortable?"

And he stretched out and pulled me to him and we both made little adjustments until we were both totally relaxed and I fetched up with my head on his shoulder and his arm around me. And could we have had the Kiss of the Century? Yes. But of course I had to blurt out "What's the book, Steve?"

"S for Sartre. The Age Of Reason."

"I've not read it."

"It isn't about all that much, there's this bloke called Matthieu and he lives in Paris just before the war and he teaches philosophy only he never seems to do much work, just hangs around cafes and spends money and he's got friends and lovers but he tries to avoid being involved with them because he's obsessed with his freedom, and he keeps his freedom but he spends most of his time feeling guilty about it." He thought about this for a while. "There's two more but I don't think I'm going to read them because there's a big S for Solzhenitsyn coming up."

"Are you really reading all of your uncle's books in alphabetical order?"

"Yeah. Uncle Frank left me to me that way. Everything in alphabetical order in the trunk, and he even put S for Stendhal under his real name of B for Beyle. He read millions of books, but I know that these are the ones he wanted to keep and wanted me to read. So I'm going to do them all and think what they meant to him."

"Steve, don't bite my head off, but it sounds a bit like work."

"Zoe, I'd never bite your head off. I love talking to you. Especially here." He gave me a teensie extra squeeze with that muscly arm.

"You were ready to bite my head off when I was horrid to Robert. Did you totally hate and despise me?" *I had to know!*

"I was really upset for Robert and I wanted to take care of him," *Of course!* "But if you really want to know, I didn't really think about you. I was more confused and sad about… stuff in general."

"What stuff, Steve?"

He struggled for a while and then things came again in a rush. "When Uncle Frank died I realized that our family is fucked up. Mum hates Dad, Dad hates Mum, they both hate me." *I tensed up. I wanted to scream at them. But Steve seemed quite matter-of-fact about it.* "I was pretty much a loner, so I thought our family was normal. Then I met Cal and Alice and Robert and your mum and dad and I thought, families are great after all, and ours is abnormal. But then I saw you and Robert and I thought, no, they're fucked up after all, and fucked-up is normal and I felt completely … paralysed. Cal had to take charge."

"The little genius." *Cal saved my life! Must pay him back.*

Steve's life was way deeper than mine. I didn't know about losing someone precious, or not being loved by my parents. Except through books. Books! Suddenly that seemed to be a more comfortable place to be. "Have you found out what Uncle Frank wanted to tell you, Steve? Through the books, I mean."

"Not always. He didn't leave GSCE Pass Notes with them," *Sudden gorgeous smile!* "A lot of them are books about war and military life. Especially novels about the First World War. I know that when he was in Iraq and Afghanistan he thought a lot about the soldiers being ground down in the trenches and the incompetent leaders and the people at home who didn't know what was going on. And some are about young men trying to work out who they are. And some he just thought were fantastic bits of writing. No poetry and no plays. He thought poets and playwrights had it easy."

"Had it easy? They've got the toughest job of the lot. One mistake in a poem or a play and it's wrecked but in a novel you've got a chance to recover."

"You make it sound like batting and bowling! Anyway, we were both bowlers, Uncle Frank and me."

"So what do you make of Sartre, Steve? You – not Uncle Frank."

"I'm beginning to think Matthieu's got it all wrong. I think... you become free when you actually commit yourself to someone."

"Oh so, totally."

"Cal made me see that. The first day I met him I was feeling really sorry for myself but then we started playing cricket I forgot about everything except helping him to play better, and giving him a great day and well, taking care of him. And then Robert came, with your dad, and I had never actually liked Robert before, but then I wanted him to have a great day too because I would then feel great and now I want to make life better for everyone I meet."

"You've made my life better, Steve. But you should think of yourself too."

"Yeah, but what makes life great for me is making it great for someone else."

"You're not being very logical, Steve, because if you get off on doing stuff for other people maybe they would get off on doing stuff for you."

"I suppose so... Do you like reading, Zoe?"

"Is it cold at the North Pole? Do dogs have bad breath?" He winced for a minute. Not a dog person! Me neither! "I gobble books, like ... a shark. It didn't make me popular." Suddenly I had to let things out. "At my old school you had to pretend to be stupid the whole time. You couldn't be interested in any subject. And I loved English, even though they taught the books from worksheets. Pot Noodle literature. David Copperfield in a sachet. And I knew more than the teacher. She was wrong about Lady Macbeth. Sheila Fereday's a friend of ours.[10] She played Lady Macbeth and talked to me about her..."

"Sheila Fereday? As in Mrs Rob Patty? You know her?"

---

[10] See "An Excellent Moment" and "Final Score" from <u>A Tale Of Ten Wickets.</u>

"Sure. She's married to Alex Bramley, who's in Dad's cricket team." **He looked awed.** "Anyway, I thought everyone would be really interested to know what Sheila Fereday said about Lady Macbeth. God, I was so wrong. She turned the whole class against me. Every lesson she would say 'does Miss Barnes agree?' or 'does Miss Barnes know someone who's more expert?'"

"Some teachers stitch you up."

"My parents complained but it was too late. I was now the target. You know, Steve, girls bully in a different way to boys. It's less about physical intimidation, although some girls have a nice line in pinching and scratching, and it's more about isolation. You don't have any friends at all, even best friends walk away from you and people talk about you as if you weren't there. I was rich, I was stuck-up, I dressed badly, I was a lesbian, I smelt. I looked like a monkey. I stopped being Zoe and just became the Monkey. 'Monkey's here, watch out for fleas… What's that smell? Oh, it's Monkey.'" **I shuddered and he tightened his arm around me.**

"I like monkeys." **True or was he being kind? Did it matter? Be still, my beating heart!** "And it's better than my nickname."

"Which is?"

"Psycho."

I hooted with laughter. "You? Psycho? You great big… teddy bear!"

His face darkened for a second. "I'm not always like this, Zoe." **He thought about something and then headed back to a safe place.** "What's your favourite book?"

"Madame Bovary."

"Oh my God, that was one of Uncle Frank's top picks. He told me if I only read one from his trunk, that had to be it."

"And what did you think of it, Steve?"

"I couldn't stop reading it, even though I didn't like her. In fact, I even hated her. I don't think I liked anybody in the whole book and I don't think Flaubert liked any of them either. But he makes you understand everybody."

"You actually hated her? Didn't you think she was a prisoner?"

"She made herself a prisoner, of all those novels she read and all those fantasies. I hate people like that, who think they're better than the people around them and think they deserve to be somewhere else." **He obviously knew someone like that.**

"But she at least tries to make life a little more interesting, not just for herself but for her husband, and he doesn't even notice and he's so boring and he's not even any good as a doctor."

"But she marries him and has his child and she should just make the best of it. Especially for the child."

"What, like Madame Homais?"

"Well, maybe."

"But she's so boring. Good but boring. Do you think Flaubert could have written a novel about her?"

"No. I suppose not."

"That sort of France is still around, Steve. We drove through it last year and our car broke down in this little town and I could swear that Emma was there, dying of boredom."

"I think Emma would have died of boredom wherever she was. Even if she had got to Paris. Alice and I talked about this a bit. People write scripts for themselves and they stick with them even when they poison their lives. Oh God, it's so symbolic, isn't it? Emma takes poison, but her whole life has been poisoned already. With all those fantasies."

"But are they total fantasies, Steve? I don't mean the silly stuff like being an aristocrat but the idea that there are finer things in life, the idea that you can experience beauty or passion?"

"I don't think those are fantasies but the idea that you are some kind of superior being because you understand beauty or passion…"

"Steve, we're still arguing about her. So do millions of other people. Why do you think that is?"

"Well, he was just so fucking brilliant, wasn't he? Sorry. Flaubert. At writing. You can tell that in translation, imagine reading it in French."

"I tried to but my French isn't good enough and I really wanted to know what happened next."

"I didn't even try. I just piled in and I'm sure I missed a lot and yet… I don't think Flaubert ever wants you to stop and say 'wasn't that a great piece of writing?'"

"That's what great style is about, don't you think? Not noticing the author at all. And yet some great authors make themselves noticed, like Tolstoy or Dickens."

"I always got fed up when Dickens starts talking. I sometimes thought he must have been having trouble making up that episode and chucked in a thousand words from himself."

"Don't be too hard on him, Steve. He had a public to satisfy. Suppose he'd written like Flaubert, one sentence a day."

"That really got to me, that one sentence a day. And often going back on it and correcting it. Caring that much about characters you don't even like. God, if I had written Madame Bovary it would be over in about five minutes. Stuck-up cow reads too many fantasy novels, marries this dim doctor, lives out in the sticks, and then she moves but it's still in the sticks and then… and then…" *And all at once my beloved was asleep with his arm around me. Good old Flaubert!!*

Chapter 14   Change Of Kit

Cal's sleepover was convenient for me. I was meeting my French fancy man. Claude is a married businessman who visits England regularly. We met at a piano recital by someone I knew as a student. For two years we have had a discreet, civilized relationship, based on music, food, sex and a total absence of commitment. He has never been to my home or met Cal. I have never asked him to leave his wife, who set him up in business. As it happens, he is also my client – my only commercial one. I saved him a great deal of money when I stopped him from doing business with a flake. I can spot a flake at 500 metres at twilight. It makes me a little easier for his wife to accept: my husband's in conference with his lawyer does sound a lot better than my husband's in congress with his mistress.

"Alice, you are not enjoying yourself. Have I done or said something wrong?"

"No, Claude. You are charming, attentive and very sexy as always. You found the right concert for both of us as always, the food and the room were perfect as always, you made a daring but totally right choice of wine, as always. We will do something new and something familiar when we make love, as always. It's me. I am not as always."

"Can you tell me why?"

"Only by breaking the pact. We say nothing about our lives at home."

"I am your friend, Alice, I hope. We made that pact when we first made love because we were afraid of making claims on each other. I don't think we should be afraid any more. I think we should trust each other."

"You're right. As you might expect, it's about Cal. He has found himself the perfect elder brother. He is a talented, caring, very lovable boy … young man. He is not loved at home and for three years he has had nothing but trouble, injustice and sorrow. He had supper with us and he opened up to me. Oh, and I'm his lawyer, too. I shouldn't be talking about one client to another."

"Very well, you're fired! I do not see what is the problem."

"I feel responsible for him. But I cannot do anything for him that would make a difference – give him a home, sort out his education, support him in his future. He is staying with us for a few days – on holiday. I could ask him to join us when we go away to Devon. I think he would love it, I know Cal would be thrilled and it would give me a better holiday too. He is very protective towards Cal and I would get free child care and could flop around drinking gin like a bad mother. No, I'm being unfair. I don't like Steve just because of Cal, I like him in his own right."

"I think you wanted to say, love him in his own right. Don't what I think. How could I mind whom you love, in your own life when I'm not there?"

"You're right again. What made you so wise?"

"You never asked me for wisdom before."

"So what do I do, my oracle?"

"Take him on holiday. Will his parents object?"

"I doubt it. But what happens when the holiday is over?"

"Invite him to supper, as your friend and Cal's. That may be enough to make a difference to him. That makes a difference to me." For the first time in our relationship he looked wistful. "Do what you can, Alice. No one can ask for more. Give this boy a corner of his life that works well: the rest he has to manage for himself."

"There is something else on my mind. Cal's already in love with him. Do I want that to get deeper?"

"You cannot control that. Do you think that this boy, Steve, would … do anything with Cal?"

"God no! Cal has much the stronger will."

"Alice, I've not been a parent, but I know that you cannot control your children's emotions, only their behaviour. You lay down some basic rules about what they can do, and then step back. They will have to work through their feelings for themselves. Now do you want dessert?"

"No, I want room service."

Thanks to Gustave Flaubert, my beloved was asleep with his arm around me. He looked amazingly peaceful. It would have been cruel to wake him by a thoughtless movement. So I simply melted into him and fell asleep myself.

"You bounder! You rotter! You villain! Unhand my daughter at once!" We both woke up with a start. My parents were back and doing their awful Victorian melodrama schtick.

"My child! My innocent che-ild! What has he done to you?" Steve, for whom this was new, blushed scarlet.

It was nothing new to me, but I did the same. "Mum! Dad! That's awful. I can't believe you got Sheila to act with you. You're embarassing Steve."

"No we're not, dear, we're embarrassing you." Mum sounded a bit squiffed but Dad had no such excuse.

"How long have you been here?"

"Five minutes. You looked so peaceful, like the little munchkins downstairs."

"Joe, I'm so sorry, I don't know what happened. I remember we were talking about Flaubert..."

"Steve, please. You are not the first visitor to fall asleep on that couch. If you want to say good night to Zoe, Belinda and I will disappear."

But Steve didn't wait. He just picked me up and held me to him in the air, as if I weighed nothing (not true, alas, I am Miss Slacker Queen), and said "Good night, Zoe, I really enjoyed talking to you until I fell asleep." Then he whispered "Pscyho must lie upon the bed Who would rather lie on a monkey's lap" and I giggled and he gave me a soft little kiss which still registered 13 on my Richter scale!!

Mum followed me to my bedroom. Oh God, please don't talk to me about sex.

"I'm not going to talk to you about sex. You should know by now how to avoid a baby and how to avoid a disease. So should he. We are going to talk about love. You are in love with him?"

"Oh God yes," **and I burst into tears.**

"What is that all about? You should be happy. I'm certainly very happy that he is your first love. If he is your first and last love, that is fine by me. And your father. But I must advise you - give this one plenty of time."

"Mum, you should talk! You and Dad met and married in six weeks!"

"Your father was in a hurry – you know why. He was terrified of losing me. As if! And he had Howard nagging him. Steve's different."

"Why?"

"Steve has had many troubles in his life."

"I know."

"You don't know them all. Neither do I. Alice gave me a hint when we watched the boys play cricket. Anyway, Steve's had trouble and sorrow. Then suddenly he gets released – like a prisoner on parole. Prisoners often have trouble adjusting to life outside. Steve's had just a few days of … happiness. I'm sure he feels disoriented. Give him time to sort himself out. He took a huge step tonight."

"How?"

"He fell asleep with you. It's a huge sign of trust for any creature to sleep with another. Much more than having sex. Do give this one time, sweetheart. You won't regret it." **Mum decided that was a good exit line. Of course I'll give him time but will he know that I'm giving him time or will he think I'm not interested in him? Shouldn't I first throw myself at his feet, and then give him time to pick me up?**

I still felt totally embarrassed. First night in their house, they've trusted me, and they see me on the couch with Zoe. As if she were Angie. Will they think we were making out? Joe seemed really cool – or was he just toying with me?

"Steve, Belinda was the designated drinker tonight and I was the designated driver, so I'm awarding myself a whisky. A 12-year-old Macallan. Can I put something in a glass for you?"

"Not whisky. I mean, thanks. I just… don't drink. Water, please. Thanks." *God, now he thinks I'm an idiot as well as a sex maniac.*

"Good idea. Not drinking. Drink is bad for cricketers and bad for writers. It's pretty bad for everybody. My firm doesn't do drink advertising. But I still enjoy a drink, or even two or three." *He passed me a water. He poured himself a whisky, very reverently, like a priest serving Mass [Wordpower, not that I've ever been to Mass.]* "Two rules, if you're ever going to drink. Rule One, never drink when you're thirsty. Alcohol, I mean. Say, after you've bowled 20 overs in the day. Have a pint then and it just drinks itself and you're on the way to being boozed without any pleasure. Make the first two pints water or juice. Rule Two: never drink anything cheap. Drink quality stuff. You'll enjoy it more and you won't be able to afford much – especially if you buy a round of it - so you're less likely to get shit-faced." *Come on, put me out of my misery.*

"Steve, we shouldn't have surprised you. It was unfair. But you looked sweet together. Our girl's been unhappy for a long time."

"You didn't mind?"

"Not what we saw. Trust. Security. Intimacy. That is so important. That's really what holds people together. Not passion, intimacy." *Belinda came in. On cue? I wouldn't be surprised. But when she sat beside him and held his hand it looked right.* "Not what you do when you go to bed together but how you feel when you wake up together. The way you move together, the rhythms as you talk together, putting your attention in the same place. Never having to make conversation or small talk together or put on a performance, like we did for strangers at the party. Never having to be polite to each other. Being able to say 'God, I hate that dress,' or 'you're talking complete crap.'"

"Don't be too sure of that! Try and end every argument with 'you're right, dear. As usual.' Try that one out now."

"You're right, dear. As usual."

"Promising. Shall we have him as a son-in-law?"

"Could he support us all when the agency tanks? Seriously, Steve, you've started things the right way round. Intimacy first, passion later." *They both started to move out of the room together, then he said over his shoulder* "By the way, Steve, if you ever make a move on Zoe she doesn't like, watch out for her right knee. Unless you want to be a professional falsetto, like that other boy... You're welcome to sleep on the couch, but you know where the spare room is. Get up as late as you like."

I must have had a few good hours sleep in their spare room but it seemed I'd only dozed off when Cal crashed in. Robert followed him with a tray.

"I told you, he's a slacker. We've been up for hours. Here's your breakfast, if you don't want those croissants, I'll have them."

"He ate mine already. Cal's brilliant for my diet."

Robert poured me some tea. Cal added milk and three sugars (I have my vices). I scarfed the croissants before the shark got them. "Thank you very much. Now I want a very small snooze."

"We'll have one too, just to make sure it is very small," *at which Cal jumped into the bed. Before I could protest Robert was in there too.*

"God, this bed's crap. No wonder we never have any guests." *They bounced around for a while.*

"Don't make a noise. Everyone's asleep." *They started saying "Sssh!" to each other, louder and louder, until they got hysterics.*

The guest room is right underneath my attic space and I could hear a commotion. I hurtled down in my PJs to rescue Steve. As I expected, the boys were all over him.

"What are you doing to my beloved?"

"He's our beloved today, and you can't have him!"

"Don't be silly, there's plenty of him left over," so I dived in as well. Shameless hussy! We got ourselves arranged again, and he folded us all in.

"If you've all finished, can I have my very small snooze?" And we all lay still. I think that our heartbeats actually synchronized. We dozed off for a tiny bit. "Cal, stop twitching! If you're that hyper, I'm taking you on a run."

"Us too."

"All right. Outside the front door in five minutes. No noise."

"I'll do the burglar alarm and bring a key."

"Good thinking, Zoe." Now he knows I can be practical!

Cal doesn't really run, he bounces and glides. Like Legolas! Which of course means that Steve is Aragorn, the warrior and the king in waiting. Which of course makes me Arwen. And Robert, puffing desperately? (Me too – must get fitter!) Poor Robert must be Gimli, the dwarf! Unfair. Maybe he can be loyal Sam Gamgee. Cal sometimes bounces and glides backwards, so Robert doesn't get left behind. Sweet! Steve checks on us all regularly. When he sees this weirdo on the other side of the street he runs to our left, to screen us.

There was only one thing wrong with my beloved and I had this dramatic idea and I was really pleased that Mum was awake when we got back.

"Now you're talking, sweetheart. Leave it to me. Your father will agree." One simple reason why Mum and Dad get on so well.

We had showers and changed and ate a bit of breakfast (Steve's a health nut and Cal's a guts!) and mooched and watched some crap cartoons and Cal said "Can we play cricket?"

"Later, sweetheart. First, we're all going shopping. Without my husband. He would have one of his fainting fits. Front door in five minutes!"

Mum piled us into the BMW. Steve got the front seat so I only got the little boys. Curses! Steve and Cal went a bit white. They've never driven with Mum before. We screeched into the car park at Megamall just as it opened. "You don't know this, Steve and Cal, but I'm in Britain's shopping squad for the Olympic Games. This training session is for you both. This is to say thank you from all of us. We want you to shop for clothes as you have never shopped before!"

"Mum, can we go straight to Ursinho's?"

"You know best."

"It's the new, hot Brazilian label. They've got a complete store in here. It means 'little bear'".

"Sweet!" Cal was pleased, Steve looked a bit bewildered.

"Can I help you? Are you looking for anything in particular?"

"We're looking for everything in particular! T-shirts, tops, shirts, pants, shorts, swim trunks, trousers, shoes. Some in his size – midget – and some in his size – god." The assistant's eyes had already lit up but when he saw Steve he almost started to shake! Fair enough, but don't hit on him!

We wouldn't let Steve choose anything. "Sorry, Steve, but your clothes are drab! You're getting a new look!" The assistant, whose name badge said 'Emerson', fluttered around us and we soon stuffed our cart with god-sized clothes. Robert (the photographer) advised on colour, Cal (the artist) on line, I (the worshipper) on fit. Mum and Emerson sometimes put in a veto or insisted on a choice of their own. I wouldn't allow anything shapeless – only form-fitting stuff (including pants!) Cal and Emerson supported me.

Our only problem was picking stuff for Cal. He did his bouncing from foot to foot routine and looking away and

Mum took him aside. They had a whispered conversation and she said "Sure, darling, if that's what you want."

The cart was full in no time. "Okay, Steve sweetheart, before I burn my husband's plastic, is there anything else you'd like?"

"Oh no, I couldn't, but… It's stupid but I've always wanted to have… a leather jacket."

"Don't move! I'm going to the stock room!" Emerson hurtled away and fluttered back with a black leather jacket. "This is it. A classic. And it's discounted. Take off that beach shirt, superb though it is on you, and wear this free white T-shirt. Now try this." Steve slipped it on. "Now look angry. No, that's still happy. Angry."

"I've dropped an easy catch off your bowling." Glare!

"Yes! Young Marlon Brando. I knew I was right." Emerson took us to the pay point and totted up. I went a bit pale at the total but Mum didn't turn a hair.

"I can't let you pay for all this…"

"Steve. It would be our pleasure. Please don't deny it to us. And besides, Cal has something to tell you. "

Mum really dropped him in it. He blushed deep and did his usual bounce-and-look-away act. "Half was going to be for me but I'm Cal The Vain already and I've got heaps and Mum said no more till I grow out of everything so I wanted you to have my share too."

Steve scooped him up and hugged him. "Now who's the softie?" He put him down, thoughtfully. "All right. Thank you. I can't believe it. Gosh, I was due a makeover and then… it fell through, but now I've got it after all. But, listen, I'm going to put all this stuff back," Emerson turned pale! "unless you let me buy something for each of you. On my plastic."

"I don't need anything."

"Wait up, Robert!" Cal jumped up. "The purple shirt that we wouldn't let him have. I think that colour would look great on you." Emerson rummaged in our big discard pile and then found a smaller version for Robert to try on.

"Hey, hot stuff!" My brother, of all people.

"Great. Now Cal."

"I honestly don't want anything except one of the T-shirts with their bear logo because he looks like Bungle."

"Those are free, sir."

"Try again, Cal."

"No, honestly. Just the T-shirt."

"I know. Pick out some swimming trunks."

"What for?"

"Doh... Swimming."

"I love swimming. I'm a mental swimmer. I'm going to swim to Albania this year. Let's go swimming after this."

"Er... Cal can't swim.... In pools! He reacts to the chemicals. Only in the sea."

Phew, thanks, Steve. Saved from bad shame. And I do need some new trunks just to lie on the beach.

"Can you all help him choose? I saw something for Zoe, well maybe, in another shop and I want to see if it's still there." We forced Cal to get a snazzy pair with an Amazon forest print. What had Steve picked for me? He returned. It must have been very small.
"Now, Belinda."

"Oh Steve, not here. This is a young person's store."

"And the problem is?" **Mum was eventually nagged into a man's "unstructured" jacket.**

Steve then went into Cal's nervous routine. "They had it. The thing for Zoe and look, you might absolutely hate it but it can go straight back…"

I opened the little package and gasped. He looked terrified! I put him out of his misery. "He's beautiful! I love him!" **I showed the others the brooch – in the form of a monkey! We had the huge movie clinch we missed last night. Off my Richter scale!!!**

"I hoped… you could own the name they called you."

"I do, Steve. Thank you. But one problem."

"What?"

"Where am I going to find a Psycho brooch to give you back?" **We both laughed (he has great teeth too!)**

I went to the nets with them, and joy! Steve took his shirt off.

"You've still got Cal's picture on your back!" **A cricketer in suncream. The little cutie-pie is a genius, too. He did one on Robert's back (a camera) and one on mine (a monkey!) We'll keep them for Corfu.**

"You've got all those fabulous tops and you're wearing that horrible beige number?"

"This one's lucky. I met Cal in it and he led me to you."

"Aaah!" **I watched. Robert's way better than before, even I could see, and he doesn't whine. I'd forgotten that Dad's really good, especially for an ancient (sorry Dad!) Cal's so sweet when he** does something good. Steve's a fabulous teacher. He makes them feel brilliant even when they do something crap.

When Dad batted, Steve gradually went up to full pace. His face became an angry mask. He seemed to hurl himself at my dad, not just the ball. Robert told me "That's around 80 miles an hour." Bloody hell! Steve was bowling as fast as Mum on a motorway. I was glad he made our dad wear a helmet.

Cal's mum, Alice, came to watch. Steve's staying with her. I was glad: I really liked her. They live on the other side of the park. We went to the car and picked up the boys' overnight stuff and Steve's wonderful new clothes.

"Great makeover, guys."

"It's not finished, make him grow his hair."

"Yeah, he can go with me to Yasmin."

We had a little more chit-chat, but finally we had to say goodbye. Both boys said really nice thank-yous (not like some). Steve hugged everyone and I tried to make mine last longest and then Cal hugged everyone and then Cal hugged Steve "by mistake".

"You're not saying goodbye to him, silly, he's staying with you!"

"Doh! Cheers, Robert."

And finally we had to go home. We're going to Corfu tomorrow for two weeks, fabulous villa, own pool, own beach, own boat, but totally Steveless so I burst into tears as I packed. Next year, he's coming. I don't care if it's two weeks in Bovary Town.

Chapter 15 Risky Single

"Daniel and Brendon

Thanks for the email and brill pictures. I am really glad that your father is on the mend. Your farm sounds insane. Why did the bishop let the goat into the living room in the first place?! I have been having a pretty crazy time myself…"

"Nick

It's brilliant that they have given you the run of the observatory. I got really choked up when you told me that the IAU had recognized your new asteroid and you still want to call it Asteroid Steve. If you come back to the school playground I may snog you for real! Listen, can you also find an asteroid named Zoe and one for Cal, Alice, Robert, Belinda and Joe? …"

"Young Steve, get off that computer right away!"

"Sorry. Have to go. More news to follow. Yours in orbit Steve."

"Come into the garden and model all your new clothes."

So I wore them all.

"Well, look who's turned into Mr Yummy! Is that everything?"

"Apart from some pants."

"I think we can take the pants as read."

"Well, actually they're mostly black."

"Ha-ha. You're a lucky guy, Steve, you have wonderful stylists in your team. But you must grow your hair. There's not enough to ruffle. Yasmin will fix it. Now, have you considered modelling? Or a career in porno?"

"Mum!"

"Kidding, Steve, but do you feel good in those new clothes? Different?"

"Yeah."

"Clothes. That's all it takes to feel good. Why is this little guy so cheerful, Cal The Vain? If you ever need to pick yourself up, just try on some new clothes. But stay out of mine! Now can you guys feed yourselves? I really need to play the piano for a little while…"

Cal and I went into the kitchen. I listened to her playing something. I didn't know it. I probably wouldn't unless it was a TV commercial! It was very fast and seemed to have a lot of notes in it.

"Your mum's in a good mood today."

"I think she's been seeing her French fancy man, whom I don't know about only she always talks about him to Portia."

"Portia?"

"Head of her law firm and my sort-of aunt."

"Do you mind? About the Frenchman?"

"Hell no!"

"Sorry. Not my business."

"Is too. If you're my friend you can ask me anything."

"Sorry."

"Don't say 'Sorry' the whole time!"

"I won't. Sorry." **So we had a fight again and I almost let him win.**

"Are you hungry?"

"Not really. I ate most of Robert's food all day!"

"You're so good to him! I'm not hungry, either. Why don't you make us each a smoothie? Just something simple, not a Humungous."

He made something simple, we drank it, I washed up and suddenly he crashed.

"Did you sleep at all last night or did you chatter all night with Robert?"

"Chattered all night with Robert because you're such a crap baby sitter."

"Bed."

"Carry me." *So I did.*

"You are strong."

"Not specially. You're an ectomorphic weed. Now teeth."

"Do them for me?" *He got hysterics. Finally he agreed to do his teeth if I carried him to the basin and carried him back. I wondered if any man had done that job before me. He held on for a long time before I could release him to Bungle.*

Alice was still playing the piano. I watched and listened. It was beautiful. Eventually she looked up and noticed me.

"Oh Steve, you're such a treasure for a Bad Mother. Did you put him to bed?"

"He's crashed."

"I'll do my goodnight kiss even if he doesn't notice." *She went out. I looked at the music on the piano. Visions Fugitives by someone called Prokofiev. There were heaps of other sheet music on the floor.*

She came back. "He looks about 8. Did you like that? Prokofiev is one of my favourites but he's too good for me now."

"I hardly know any music. Just the Test Match Special Theme. Who was Prokofiev?"

"A great Russian composer. He died on the same day as Stalin, which ruined his obituary coverage. Steve, you don't really want to talk about Prokofiev."

Deep breath. "Does Cal know his dad?"

"No. They have never seen each other. Cal's father was … is American. I'm pretty sure. His name is John Smith. At least that's what he told me. He made a joke of it. He was really good at making jokes. In the four months I knew him I never saw any ID – not even a utility bill." *I already thought, what a tosser.* "Do you really want to hear all this?"

"If you want to tell me. It's only fair – you listened to me all night."

"You love Cal, don't you?"

"Yes."

"Good answer. And no hesitation. So you had better hear his story." *She sat at the piano again.*

"I met John, Cal's father, at a party where I was playing the piano. A lot better than I do now. There's a rogue musical gene in our family. My mad uncle Cal had it. He was a rock musician. He could play virtually anything and sing, and write songs. He was known as the poor man's Steve Winwood. He knocked around with all kinds of rock legends from the Sixties, Winwood and Clapton, Ray Davies, the Animals, Steve Marriott and the Small Faces. He so nearly became a legend himself. He had a band called Calamity and they got into the top 50 with one of his songs: Anywhere But Here.[11] Listen, I'm doing what you do, Steve. Finding something else to talk about when I've got something painful to say."

"Is he still alive?"

"No. I wish I'd known him better. He died when I was fifteen. At least he heard me play the piano. He wouldn't teach me. He insisted on proper lessons and said I had to become a 'real' pianist and not a fake like himself, who never made anything of his talent."

"That's sad. He sounds really good. He shouldn't have beaten himself up."

"If you're interested in my uncle Cal, there's a trunk full of his stuff in the cellar… Yes, Steve, you and I have something in common. A fabulous uncle who left a trunk of memories. But mine was not as disciplined as yours. He didn't organize things into alphabetical order. He just left a mass of diaries, letters, pictures, tapes. And there's piles more stuff in storage."

"Has Cal seen it?"

"Of course. He had a good laugh at the clothes. He's not all that interested in music. His dad's genes won over mine. Now Steve, don't let me get off the point again." *She sat up. This meant business.*

---

[11] Lyrics at Appendix

"I was saying… I met John, Cal's father, at a party. I had just started as a piano student at the Royal College of Music. I was never going to make the top flight but I think I would have made a decent accompanist, or rehearsal pianist, or teacher. And possibly composer or arranger: I did a lot of theory and composition. But I was a real little provincial mouse and I had hardly even been to London, let alone lived there, and I knew almost no one at the party except another student who had dragged me there, so I went to the piano more as a hiding place than for any other reason.

"I didn't think anyone was listening but I looked up and there was … Brad Pitt, looking spellbound!

"Well, not quite Brad Pitt. But drop-dead, movie-star beauty. And charm. Charm without even speaking. That man … dripped charm like sweat. Wordpower!" *We had a laugh. I had her doing it too.*

***

"Can I turn your pages?"

"I haven't got any pages."

"Could I get you some pages and then I could turn them and if this were a hundred years ago people would say 'she's letting him turn her pages' and we'd be virtually engaged?"

"That's kind of you but I'll just carry on from memory."

"You're leaving me with a great memory. What was that you were playing?"

"I'm worried that you have to ask. It's very well known. Mack The Knife by Kurt Weill."

"Tell me about him."

"German. Started out as a serious composer but wrote jazz operas with Berthold Brecht and then stage musicals in the USA. Listen, this is a much better song of his. Surabaya Johnny…"

***

"Steve, why didn't I listen to that song? It's all about betrayal. Listen…" *She played this slow, sad song and sang some words in German.* "But once again, he looked spellbound and I could not believe that I had done that to him."

***

"That was so beautiful. Look, don't laugh but my name's John Smith."

"Alice. Alice Devane. Why should I laugh at John Smith?"

"Because if I took you away to a hotel, which I would like to do right now, and signed the register as John Smith the clerk would assume it's made up and that I'm a married man who's cheating on his wife. But I'm not married and if I were married to you I would never go to any hotel without the real Mrs John Smith."

***

"Was that tacky, young Steve? Because to me, right then, little Miss Scared Mouse at the piano, it wasn't tacky it was… Wordpower!" *No laugh this time, from either of us.*

***

"Can I get you a drink? There's some good stuff left. When they open the bottle I brought, it's time to leave."

"No, thank you."

"Alice? Are you enjoying this party?"

"Not specially."

"I didn't enjoy it at all until you started playing, but it's hard to hear you through all these people and that piano's on its last legs. On its last legs…"

"I got it."

"So would you like to go to a better piano? In a less crowded room?"

***

"I'm trapped in this heaving room, full of ugly people I don't know, and this sensationally beautiful man asks me to go away with him? No contest. So we slipped away, and he asked if I'd mind walking because he loved London at night, and it was cold but he pulled his coat around me, which meant his arm around me, and it felt very warm and safe. And as we walked along he told me about all the painters who had lived in a place or painted it, which led to him telling me that he was an art student, and having private lessons with Juan Medina." *I must have looked blank.* "A Great Artist, capital G, capital A.

132

Came to Britain as a child after the Spanish Civil War." *That comes into the Sartre book. Matthieu keeps wondering if he ought to be there.* "And he was absolutely fascinating. Not charming at all. Just pouring out everything he knew and believed about painting.

"Finally, we came to this terrific house – not flat, house – in Mayfair, and I was just gobsmacked and I asked if it was really his, and he said he was housesitting for a cousin who had become some kind of ambassador but he had it to himself for a year, when he would either make it as an artist or go back home to the family business."

"What was that?" *It just came out. Maybe I'm like my dad after all.*

"I never found out a damn thing about it – how it made money or even where in the States it was. It could have been the Mafia. All I knew was that his mom was the brains of the business and the family. Anyway, I didn't really take in what he was saying, because I was still in awe of the house. It had some terrific pictures, even the little provincial mouse could tell. I remember a Klee and a gorgeous Signac. And of course loads of Medinas – John's teacher.

"And then he took me into the piano room and there was a concert Steinway. Better than anything at the College. I went weak at the knees."

***

"Do you play?"

"No."

"Your cousin?"

"I don't think so. He has parties… It's looked after and I had the piano tuner just a week ago. But it's really just sitting there, as furniture. It seems cruel to do that to a piano. I was going to put in a lonelyhearts ad for it: 'Concert Steinway, fit 60-year-old, WLTM beautiful pianist, F, for fun nights in.' But now I can save my money. I hope. Please play him."

***

"I loved calling the piano 'him'. And it was almost… human. Gorgeous and mellow and responsive and as I went through my little repertoire from memory he made me believe I was a concert pianist after all. So suddenly I'm in a dream house, playing a dream piano for a dream man. And John said I was wonderful and begged me to play for him regularly, and guess what? He was an amateur ventriloquist and he made the piano beg me as well, like

Sparky's Magic Piano, and it made me laugh, and I was still laughing when we had a bath together, and still laughing when we went to bed together…"

"That's right, young Steve, I went to bed with him on our first date. Not even a date. He picked me up, I went to bed with him. I'm a slut. No excuses, but I will just tell you that laughter is a powerful aphrodisiac. If you laugh together. Laughing for one is a real turn-off.

"So I went to bed with him and to go with everything else he was a considerate and inventive lover. And a joy to wake up with. That's as important – probably more so."

"Joe told me that."

"Well, they have a great marriage … Anyway, we started dating, and he took me all over London, giving me more of his painters' history, and I took him to concerts and he said none of the pianists were as good as me, which was silly but sweet, and I honestly think he did prefer to listen to me, alone, on his cousin's wonderful piano. He did a great drawing of me playing it. He made me look beautiful."

"You mean it was realistic?"

"Sweet. I mean, seriously, that he caught the glow that was in me, being with him and playing the piano. And I'm still glad that I know that Cal's father was a fine artist, whatever else he was."

"Do you still have it?"

"No, but let me get to that. We saw more and more of each other and eventually it seemed natural for me to move in with him and play that beautiful piano. I pretended it was for my music, but actually that got worse."

"Why?"

"I never wanted to do scales and technical exercises on it. I just wanted to please my lover, so I did lots of 'Easy Listening' Classics, the kind of stuff they put out for Christmas and I'd start to fake all the difficult passages…"

"Like Ricky Rubato!" *And I had to tell her about the movie at the Barneses.*

"That sounds like fun. And their friend Howard must know something about the piano. My teachers were furious, but John and the house and piano suddenly counted for more than my career. We had a great time together."

***

"John, you've got to stop spending so much money on me."

"Why? You're a poor student and you probably have to sell matches at night to survive, and I'm a rich dilettante."

***

"And I always saw his point. So I stayed on in his house, spending his money. Listen to this." *She played this spiky sort of tune and sang another bit of German.* "That's more Kurt Weill. The Ballad Of The Easy Life. That was us. A perfect routine, on his money. A bit of sightseeing, a bit of shopping, a nice dinner, make love to the piano, make love to him. And he was mine! He never even looked at anyone else. Total attention on me, wherever we were. God, that is such a turn on as well." *She played some clashing notes and I jumped.*

"There was only one thing wrong with John. I actually didn't know anything about him. I shared his money, his house and his bed but nothing else in his personal life. He went away to study with Medina – he never took me with him. He never showed me any other drawings or paintings. He never introduced me to any friend of his. He met some of my College friends and they fancied him rotten (both sexes!) But he never wanted to meet my parents. They spoke on the telephone and he was very charming but he clearly did not want to go to Sheffield, where I came from, and he even more clearly did not want to ask them to the Mayfair house.

"He told me nothing about his origins. He never got any mail at the house – everything was addressed to his cousin, the ambassador. I didn't care then. I just romanticized him as a man of mystery. I knew just one thing. His Mom was the biggest force in his life. If she ever called him he would always take it in another room away from me. They had long conversations I could never hear. He never told me anything about them, or her, he'd just say 'Mom's not herself.' And right after any of those conversations, he always wanted to take me shopping and insist on buying really classy, expensive stuff. Especially shoes and accessories – his mother said that women judge accessories.

"All the time we were having a great sex life. Sometimes we just could not keep off each other and one day we made love on the kitchen table and I think that is when Cal was conceived. Maybe that accounts for his giant appetite." *Wry smile.*

"I was overjoyed when I discovered I was pregnant. I wrote this little script that I would give up the College (I was only hanging in there by a thread) and we would find somewhere else to live when his cousin came back and I would make a home for him and do all the boring child care while he did the interesting Dad stuff and he would have time and space to become a Great Artist. This was the Nineties, remember, and I'm trying to be Doris Day.

"But he wasn't reading that script at all." *She played a few more big chords on the piano. I remembered her waiting for me to tell my story and waited in silence.*

"John said nothing for a while. Then he offered to pay for an abortion. He didn't notice my feelings or ask about them. Just offered an abortion as casually as... calling for a plumber to fix the sink. And I got hysterical and ran into our bedroom and cried and he came and held me and cried too. And eventually I stopped crying and just felt all the familiar sensations of being in my beautiful bed with my beautiful man, and he stopped crying, and we made love, really tenderly, the most affectionately we had ever been."

***

"Darling, I did something unforgiveable but will you forgive me? You gave me a shock, a wonderful shock, but still a shock. I never thought I'd be a father this early, never thought I'd get so many perfect things this quickly... first you and then our child and this great life together. Maybe at some level I was saying 'wait, I haven't earned all this yet.'"

***

"And you know, Steve, I believed that flim-flam, just as I believed him when I asked point-blank if he wanted this baby and he said yes."

***

"Then he gave me more flim-flam about being worried about me having to give up my career, and I told him about my script and he promised me that he wouldn't be the kind of Dad who only does the fun-type parenting and I guess that came out true because he didn't do any type of parenting.

"Then I decided to force the issue about our families. Could we break the news together to his and mine? He finally agreed to go to Sheffield. We spoke to my parents together and they pretended to be delighted at the news and then I said we should phone his mother, and he said no, we would fly over together and she would meet the mother of her grandchild."

***

"Darling, let's celebrate. I want you to shop as you have never shopped before."

"You bought me clothes last week."

"But those were only to wear to go shopping today!"

***

"So he propelled me down Bond Street and he developed this funny idea that people should buy their clothes in stages, and change outfits at each stage up, so that they would start in Poundstretcher and then throw that stuff away in Matalan and then throw Matalan stuff away in M&S until finally they would throw away a Ralph Lauren in the Chanel shop... But actually he seemed very set on what I should buy and he wouldn't let me choose anything..." *I started to say something but she was ahead of me.* "Steve! You had a great time having stuff chosen for you today, didn't you?"

"Yeah."

"Why do you think that was?"

"Everyone had way better ideas than I did." *She sighed.*

"And you were sure that they would use those good ideas and not make you look like a pillock, because?...."

"They all... loved me." *It still gives me a surprise.*

"Ding! Well, I got the wrong feeling with John. I didn't like the clothes he chose for me. They were expensive but very fussy and well, too old for me. I was hardly older than you but he wanted me to look ... at least 25. His age. And then he wanted me to have a big expensive hair-do. And for the first time I didn't feel loved, I felt controlled...

"Well, he booked the hair-do at this salon full of women with three-decker names and we fixed to go to lunch after at this fashionable restaurant, so I wore one of the new outfits and I saw his first reaction to the new look and it was shock. Hardly an instant, but I saw it, and then he was full of compliments and said I would totally knock out his mom...

"But the next day he was back early from Medina's studio. Message from his brother, their mother was sick. Nothing serious but he would fly back right away, and send me a first-class ticket when she was better, and would I mind if he took the drawing of me, because it would make her better right away..."

"So he flew off and I waited and waited in that beautiful house, and of course he never sent a ticket, never wrote, never phoned, never left a message."

"Could you get back to him?"

"I had no contact details for him. To John Smith, somewhere in the United States, art student, quite a challenge for the mailman."

"What about the famous artist he was studying with?"

"Sir Juan Medina would not see me and his secretary told me that he would never interfere in the personal life of another artist."

"Bloody hell! Not even to pass on a letter?"

"Yes. Some people think that Great Artists, capital G, capital A, have the right to behave like prize shits. I'd simply hate it if Cal turned out that way."

"No risk."

"Sweet to say that, but he is good at getting what he wants. Anyway, I had plenty of time to work out that John was back in his mother's control. I realized what he was trying to do in the final shopping spree – make me look like someone his mom would want him to marry, some American society princess. And it hadn't worked and he had panicked.

"A few weeks later I got a very stiff letter from an American law firm, with a cheque for $50,000, in final settlement of any claims against John and that I would signal my acceptance if I cashed it. Now I knew enough about law even then to realize that was bollocks, and my friend's fiancé, who was a solicitor, drafted me a letter to send back to John and them, and I cashed the cheque without prejudice to future claims. They were cheap enough to suggest that I had got myself pregnant to trap John into a commitment." *Another crashing chord and then she replayed the song called Surabaya Johnny.*

"So that is Cal's father. A shag on the kitchen table. He gave his son a great bone structure and artistic talent. And dangerous charm. God, I would so hate Cal to use charm the way he did, to make people do what he wants. Once again, Steve, say no sometimes. Don't always let him win."

I thought about this for a bit. "You've never heard from him?"

"No."

"You never tried to find him?"

"I left messages when Cal was born. Just in case he was interested. And I always left new contact details when we moved, which was pretty often in the early days. But he disappeared without trace. Didn't even leave me the drawing.

"I have a bad feeling that it had all happened before. He was so careful not to leave any means of finding him. I don't think you can manage that so well, unless you've had practice. Imagine, Cal might have an older half-brother or half-sister."

"I hope… they're happy."

"Me too."

Chapter 16   Sharp Single

Suddenly she seized my hand and pulled me to Cal's bedroom. We watched him asleep with Bungle. She was right: he did look about 8. We tiptoed away and we went back to the living room. This time she took the couch and I took a chair.

"Every time I get angry with him I remember that I've had my wonderful son to myself and he's missed him. And if he suddenly turns up and thinks he might enjoy his son the artist, he can fuck off. He didn't do his son the puker and the crapper and the wake-you-up-all-nighter."

"And Cal's never had a stepfather? I mean… you must have had thousands of offers."

"Thank you, sweetie. No. We had a near-miss. In the end a lucky miss. But we're out of sequence. We have not had him born yet."

"I quit the College and went back to my parents in Sheffield. We never got on well and I always favoured Uncle Calum, who was funny and sweet when he was in rehab, over my dad who was never especially funny or especially sweet. Uncle Calum was Dad's brother. Dad was a lecturer in economics who never made prof and Mum worked in a bank, but what they really wanted to do was to retire to their flat in Majorca and I knew that they wanted me off their hands and now they were stuck with me and a baby. I've got an elder brother, but he never liked me much and in any case, he's in Capetown. So Cal ended up being born in Sheffield."

"That means he's qualified to play cricket for Yorkshire."

"I knew everything was meant to be. I gave him all of my uncle's names. Calum Nolan Devane – exotic, aren't they? – to annoy my parents. We spent his first year in Sheffield. I did some odd jobs and some piano teaching, and he was a sweet little baby and very easy. Then my parents decided they did want to go to Majorca after all and they wanted to sell the house in Sheffield and I thought it might be good to try living in another country so I followed them out there. Have you ever been to Majorca, Steve? On holiday?"

"Yeah."

"Was it a good holiday?"

"Yeah. But I spent most of it under water."

"That's the best way to see Majorca. I hated it. We traded a decently built house in Sheffield, which is a real city, for a badly built flat in a new development with no plan except taking money from suckers. We were living on top of each other and there was no insulation, and every time Cal cried or got toothache you could hear him all over the flat. And I didn't like any of the neighbours, who were boring and whiny. I learnt Spanish to try and get away from them, but it took ages to find any Spanish-speaking people apart from the cleaners and shop staff. Sorry, nothing wrong with cleaners and shop staff – I've done both – but that was just to show you what kind of place it was. Nobody even wanted piano lessons. I played a bit in the pub. Yes, the British pub, not the Spanish café.

"And worst of all, my parents. They took care of Cal, and did a perfectly good job, after all they had raised two of their own, but out of duty. I could tell. And I can't stand that. People who accept him out of duty. And I knew when he was two years old, when kids scrawl with crayons, that Cal was a genius.

"I stuck it out as long as I could and then hauled him back to London. I rented quite a good flat with John's money, sorry, Cal's money. We needed a decent space to live in. I did some more piano teaching and I got a job accompanying a funny guy called Ray Corvino. He loved Cal and spoilt him. Never had a problem about Cal coming with me. When we needed to, we parked him somewhere with drawing materials.

"Ray had had a shot at being a rock-and-roll star, and he had known Uncle Calum, but now he was wearing a bad toupee which itched and doing imitation Sinatra. He had no illusions about himself. He used to say 'There are good Sinatra imitators and when you can't get them you book Ray Corvino. If Sinatra was the Chairman of the Board, Ray's the office boy.'" But the sad thing was – I wasn't good enough for Ray. He was too kind to say so, but he deserved a better accompanist, and I left him. I also gave up on the idea of being any kind of professional pianist.

"I moved us to a smaller flat and started doing odd jobs – baby sitting, cleaning, waitressing, receptioning. I walked away if the boss gave me the creeps. I got lucky with child care – a retired lady upstairs who fell in love with Cal. Just like Mrs K. Sometimes she could not manage and I had to take him to work. If that was a problem, I left. He was a total cutie-pie and very low maintenance – if he could draw. I landed one job receptioning at an art gallery and the owner told me what I already suspected, that he was a genius. He offered to sponsor him and educate him, but I wasn't ready to sell my little boy so I walked away.

"Cal and I got by. No, I think, better than got by. Bungle was a big help. Cal saw him in a toy shop and he was the one toy he ever really pleaded for. And if Cal ever did something stupid and annoying, it was blamed on Bungle so that Cal could understand what he had done wrong without feeling guilty about it. Bungle will never leave us. If Cal ever gets too old for him, Bungle will stay with me." *I remembered my Sergeant Bear, casually abandoned to the charity shop, and had a flash of bitterness.*

"And since you're wondering, I dated some men and brought some of them home. And none of them seemed to care for Cal. At best, they tolerated him. I could see it in their eyes 'oh, there's a child in the deal.' So they got chucked. One was pretty rich and we could have lived well, but just as with my parents, no one's allowed to tolerate my boy."

"Cal went off to primary school. No worries at all for a chirpy little kid. I met other parents and we formed a little self-help network, taking in each other's kids. With that and the neighbour I was able to do a secretarial course and start temping. And one job took me to Portia Harper. She's a solicitor and she married one of her clients – Alan Harper. And I just discovered he used to play for Joe's cricket team."

"Everybody's played for Joe's cricket team!"

"He was known on the team as Death Wish because he used to field so close to the bat. And he used to do lots of crazy sports apart from cricket, which involved jumping off cliffs or out of aeroplanes. But when he married Portia he gave all that up.[12] They had a terrific marriage – for less than a year. He went into hospital for minor surgery, in overnight and out the next day. But he picked up a hospital infection and it killed him." *I jolted upright in my chair.* "Yes, it is shocking, isn't it, Steve? The black irony, dying in hospital after years risking death.

"Portia sued the NHS and it was slow torture getting them to disclose records and own up to anything. But she won in the end. She set up a practice which specialized in helping victims of bad health care. She actually called it 'Britain's leading ambulance chasers' and Cal later drew their logo of her running after an ambulance with a writ in her hand." *Brief smile.* "Portia has won millions of pounds for clients. She strikes terror. The other side usually settles as soon as they see her name on the case. Actually, Portia says that her clients want first to be heard and to have someone take responsibility when things go wrong. That matters more to them than the money.

---

[12] See "Death Wish" in A Tale Of Ten Wickets.

"Portia and I hit it off right away and I took Cal into her office one day and she adored him. I think she offered me a permanent job just so she could spoil him. I took it and I started to get interested in the law. Especially the law relating to parental responsibility. Portia helped me write another letter to John's American lawyers. By then I had already decided that I did not want him to move into Cal's life, but Portia told me to go for his money first and fight about access later.

"Portia nagged me into getting the qualifications to become a para-legal. That means doing a lot of the work that solicitors do but without the status (or fees) of an admitted solicitor. She more or less tutored me – and Cal did little drawings to help me remember leading cases, like a snail in a ginger beer bottle for Donoghue v Stevenson 1932 on product liability. I somehow scraped through the exams." *I bet she sailed through!*

"By now her firm was not just chasing ambulances but also bad employers, bad parents, and bad companies who mistreated poor people. She chose partners who had been victims themselves, who would be obsessive about getting justice for victims like themselves. I got through a lot of work. They used me to interview children, which I seemed to be good at." *We both smiled.*

"Portia never remarried. She enjoys what she calls 'liaisons paresseuses.'" *I made a mental note to look that up and understand the joke.* "But she urged me to find somebody permanent. There were good men around, who would be there for me and for Cal. And of course she found one for me. He was a client – a young guy who had been misdiagnosed in hospital and needed emergency surgery – and she asked me to take over his case. It was open-and-shut and the NHS surrendered without a fight but the guy thought I was a genius and took me out to dinner.

"He was John too but totally unlike the first one. John the Second was quiet and serious and when he tried to tell a joke, it had as much chance as a hedgehog on a motorway. But he wasn't in love with himself and he asked questions about me and Cal that suggested he was really interested in us. He was a banker before that became a term of abuse and he seemed to be really good at his job. All his family were high achievers and had been for generations. Some of them are in the National Portrait Gallery… If you were a Westaway you always had a top education, you always hit the top of your profession, and you always married someone who would produce another Westaway. They had lived in the same house in Kent since Queen Anne gave it to the first General Westaway for helping the Duke of Marlborough out of a jam at Malplaquet. Bear with me, Steve, this is important.

"I didn't know any of this on our first date. John's mother told me later. She was more Westaway than the Westaways. Of course, she was a high achiever – she was a codebreaker in intelligence. She was the first person in Britain to know that there was going to be a Berlin Wall.

"I really liked John and I was glad to go out on other dates and Portia always baby-sat and pumped me afterwards. Finally I put him to the Cal test, and he passed brilliantly. He played with him and talked to him and Bungle and admired his drawings and listened to him describe them and asked intelligent questions. And I was sure that was all genuine and not just an act for me and that he actually enjoyed being with Cal. As you do, Steve.

"Best of all, he introduced Cal to cricket. He played with him for hours, and bought him his first bat. John's bank had a sports ground and nets and lots of teams and Cal played for the kids and did really well and John was captain of the second eleven and I watched both of them and my legal studies slowed down a lot, but Portia cut me a lot of slack.

"Before very long, John asked me to move in with him. He had a big place in a better part of London, near a better primary school, with a piano for me and a garden big enough to play cricket with a soft ball. And it seemed perfect but Cal was unhappy. I thought at first it was homesickness, and missing familiar places and people and our nice neighbour and his old friends. But it went on for a long time. He was always nervous in John's place and was very clingy and got into our bed a lot. John could not have been more patient with him, but it gave me the first feeling that things were not right."

"You mean John was tolerating him again?"

"Yes. Cal's an artist. He sees things I don't. Perhaps I should have asked him what he saw, or asked him to draw it. One thing made me uncomfortable, literally – the furniture. It was all wrong for John's place and all of it was discards from the Queen Anne house and from all the older Westaways. He was the youngest of that generation. All the others had married suitable vehicles for the Westaway genes.

"God, those Westaways. They just dropped in whenever they felt like it and chatted away to John and each other as if Cal and I were not there at all. They had loads of family slang so we could not understand what they were saying and join in, even if they invited us to.

"One thing about them – John always made love to me more energetically after any of them came round. As an act of defiance."

"Like me and Angie?"

"Yes. And it didn't work for either of you, did it? You should make love to somebody because you adore them, not to defy somebody else.

"Finally, we got the summons to the Queen Anne house to be presented to his mother. Muvvy. That's what he called her. A private name, not for sharing with me. Virginia was the chicest woman I've ever known. She was wearing cashmere as if she had just thrown it on and I was wearing jeans for the car journey and she let herself be kissed and she looked me up and down and said 'my dear, I'm sure you would like to slip into something more comfortable,' as if jeans were my formal outfit.

"She had a genius for making people feel that they were badly dressed or in the wrong place or simply not Westaways. And she turned it on Cal, who was just nine. She pretended to be surprised that he was there, although we had told her ages ago to expect him, and she went into a little tizzy: 'what a nice surprise, but where are we going to put this young man?' as if there were not stacks of rooms in the house.

"That was one of her weapons, pretending to be absent-minded. So she always called him Carl instead of Cal and she kept thinking that I had gone to Cambridge, like a previous girl friend who had nearly made it into the dynasty. And she pretended not to understand what a para-legal was ('my dear, do explain it because in my day solicitors just had clerks and secretaries... so you do take notes, like a secretary?')

"And then she awarded herself the right to be an outrageous snob ('my dear, it's the way I am'). The English are brilliant at that. 'My dear, I'm afraid I'm a mass murderer. It's just the way I am'. So when it came out that I came from Sheffield she pretended that it was somewhere in the Arctic and asked how I coped with the tundra.

"Then the dogs came in to inspect us. I don't know what breed they were. One was small and yappy, the other was big and clumsy, both had bad breath." *I grimaced.* "Yes, you've been through that as well. There's no excuse for it, you know. It's the fault of the owner. And she could tell that Cal hated the dogs instantly but she ignored this and pretended that it would be a big treat for him to walk the dogs, and poor Cal looked absolutely desperate until

John stepped in and said he would like to show us the grounds so we would all walk the dogs.

"It was a pretty poisonous weekend, but in her way Muvvy was a genius. She never missed a chance to make us feel like interlopers. Worst of all, she turned on Cal, because of the Romney.

"He and I found ourselves alone in front of this big portrait of a young woman: Miss Westaway. Late eighteenth century. In the garden of that house, with a puppy. And Cal suddenly blurted 'Mum, that's awful,' and he told me why. Well, you know he has got rather a penetrating voice and he went on about her nose being like a clown and her feet size 13s and the puppy looking stuffed and either the house was the wrong size or the girl was eight feet tall. And suddenly Muvvy was there.

***

"Young man, that is a Romney."

"Gosh, was he famous?"

"Very. That cost the family a thousand guineas, which was a huge sum. What a shame you were not around to paint Miss Westaway instead. But would you like to try your hand now?"

***

"And Cal did a sketch of Miss Westaway and I am not saying this out of loyalty, it really was better than the Romney. And instead of being awestruck at the nine-year-old she just said 'how charming' – and commissioned him to sketch the dogs. Knowing that he hated them. To make it all worse we visited her neighbours, the Dagincourts, and they had an ancestor painted by Gainsborough and Cal loved it and said so in the same penetrating voice.

"That doomed Cal with the whole family. He was never a genius to any of them, he was simply the rude brat who trashed the Romney.

"And so it went on. Muvvy having endless family conversations with John, and getting Cal's name wrong, and talking to me about the Cambridge I had never been to, and when I dressed for dinner, giving me the name of 'such a clever little woman who runs up copies of all the great couture houses.' And she talked about an acquaintance who had wrecked his career with a bad marriage ('a positive leech, my dear, she brought him nothing and selected the most hideous wedding presents. I palmed them off with one of Ethel Dagincourt's watercolours to blend with their napkins.')

"And she and John went to church the next morning but she made it clear that Cal and I were excused ('my dear, I'm actually an atheist too, but it used to be the family living and I want to be sure that the new vicar is not a happy-clappy'). She obviously did not want the village to see us. So I walked the foul dogs and Cal did his sketch and he made them both look rabid.

"At lunch they discussed a new Westaway baby and worked out how many famous people he was related to and she asked if I knew any of them at Cambridge and apologized again for being so absent-minded.

"At last we were able to go home. Poor Cal was actually sick a few times. Hatred does that to him. It happened regularly when he was bullied. Finally I settled him down with Bungle.

***

"John. I love you very much and Cal does too, but please don't ask us to visit your mother again."

"She wasn't really herself this weekend."

"Yes, she was, John. That is herself. She's your mother who's so funny and charming and totally loves her youngest boy and totally hates me and Cal. You know that's true. We're leeches. Marry me and she'll give us an Ethel Dagincourt. I'm sorry Cal was rude about the Romney but I don't think it made any difference. We're not Westaway material, are we? Single mother who's not much better than a secretary, boy whose father's disappeared, so we don't even know whose blood will come into the family. I'm not angry about it, John, and I still love you but that is her script and I'm afraid your whole family feels the same way."

"Fuck the family. Fuck them all."

***

"And as if to confirm that, he immediately fucked me. Afterwards he held me for a long time and said over and over again that I and Cal were worth a million of them and meeting us was the only good thing that had happened in his whole life. I told John that I didn't want him to lose his mother and his family but I didn't want to see any of them, still less expose Cal to them, unless they accepted us as part of the family on equal terms."

"Not tolerated."

147

"Not tolerated. God, that's such an English virtue, toleration. 'You're not really in the top drawer, but we tolerate you.'

"So the Westaways stopped dropping by his place, and I got rid of some of their cast-off furniture and bought some better stuff. And the three of us had a very good summer, lots of cricket, lots of shopping trips, lots of sex. We went out with Portia and her latest liaison, I reconnected with some of my fellow students making their way in the music world. One was thrilled at getting a hot new agent – Ray Corvino. We met my old friend again, no longer faking Sinatra, but promoting real talent. He had given up the toupee and was completely bald. He said 'you don't have to itch when you're rich.'

"At the end of that great summer, John took us away on this fabulous holiday in Grenada. Luxury hotel with its own cricket teams for him and Cal, a grand piano for me, private beach for all of us. And we had a very, very good time as a family, and I think John was on the point of proposing.

"But then we had a row because Cal nearly drowned. John used to take him swimming a lot and he was OK but not brilliant, and one day he got too far out off the beach and we weren't paying enough attention and he started swallowing water and panicking and thank God, some other guests got to him and hauled him back to shore.

"Cal's been terrified of water ever since. He'll go in about waist high, wearing his lifejacket, if I'm in grabbing range. The terror is genuine but I also think there is some payback going on – against me. For letting him down when he really needed me. And for setting him up with fathers who let him down. Anyway, Steve, I'll be very happy if you even get him to try to swim again, because he won't for me.

"The row really shook John. He had no practice with boiling rows, with shouting and swearing. Westaways have controlled, simmering rows with delicate sarcasm. When I started swearing at him, it made him realize, I think, that I would never be a Westaway and that my first loyalty would always be to Cal, who would never be a Westaway either. And he didn't shout back, he tried to reason with me and that made me angrier, and then I felt guilty for being angry and then I felt angrier again for being made to feel guilty, and I needed him either to shout back or to listen but not to reason with me… Steve, when you have a serious relationship, find a way of handling rows."

"Joe always ends every argument saying 'you're so right, dear. As usual.'"

"Well, that's a very good way. Anyway, I eventually cooled down but John was still shocked and he never proposed. Now all this time he had been seeing his family. He went to birthdays and weddings and such – without me and Cal. His mother would run up to London for lunch with him – without me and Cal. And it's hard to move at all in the top tier of English society without meeting a Westaway."

"Gosh, I remember now there was one at my first school."

"There would be. Anyway, all through the time we were living together, John was still in the orbit of his family. All following his mother's script: me and Cal were not right for him, were dragging him down. They didn't need words, they could deliver the script subconsciously, just by a fleeting look of worry or contempt when me and Cal were mentioned.

"One of the clan was a director of John's bank and he arranged for him to go to America on a six-month project. I am sure Muvvy put him up to it. And when he told me I got a terrible echo of John the First and I started to shake and cry, and John couldn't understand why I was being so unreasonable, it was just for six months and there was no point in hauling Cal out of school and we would both go there for Christmas and do some giant shopping trips and Cal could learn to ski and make snow sculptures.

"'Oh yes, that will be nice, John', but I knew that once again I would be waiting in a beautiful house for an air ticket which never came.

"John the Second behaved a little better than John the First because he actually telephoned and he was so terribly sorry but he had found somebody else.

"I had prepared myself for this phone call for a long time, so I didn't even listen to his carefully prepared clichés … knowing we could never really be happy… wanting the best for all of us… never forget me… I could ask him for anything…"

***

"John, you can save your nickel. You're leaving us. Thank you for the good bits – the treats, the holiday, our sex life, Cal's cricket. I don't trust myself to say anything more. I am not a Westaway and it may not be polite. I don't want to live here, in your space, so if you want a housesitter perhaps you could find one of your family to take over. That's it. Goodbye."
***

"I told Cal and all he said was 'does this mean we can go home?' and that's when I broke down because I had given up our old flat where he was happy, and traded that for a flake who had run out on him. God, what is it, Steve, this fatal attraction for men named John with dominant mothers who run away from me to the United States?"

Something told me to get up and hug her, and it was right. "Thanks, Steve. Portia took over. She moved us in with her for a bit and she took us to the Alps for Christmas and Cal actually did learn to ski after all, and do snow sculptures. She gave me a big pay rise which I didn't deserve. I know she felt guilty about having thrown me and John together.

"John sent me a cheque at the firm and I wanted to tear it up, but Portia said 'make him double it, he fucked over two people not just one, and if he is buying himself forgiveness it will make him feel twice as forgiven.' So I followed her advice and then, of all people, my dead uncle Cal came through for us. One of his old songs called 'Short Story' was used in that teen movie 'First Love Forever.'"

"God, that movie was so crap! Angie made me see it. But is that the song about the really short kid and the tall girl? That was… decent. Your uncle wrote it? That's so cool."

"Decent enough to be a global hit,[13] and I was Uncle Calum's sole heir. It paid the deposit for this place and it still earns money from places I cannot even find in Cal's atlas.

"That's virtually Cal's whole life story, and mine. Portia worked me hard and made me qualify as a solicitor. I specialized in family and child law and when she decided that I was obsessive about getting justice for wronged children she made me a partner.

"John the Second married an American society princess with two historic names. Exactly the sort of woman which John the First wanted me to imitate for his mother. Quite a lot of Kennedys went to their wedding. I've not brought any man into Cal's life since. I tried out Portia's liaisons paresseuses. I have a French fancyman called Claude, who comes over here on business and gives me a good time. Cal knows nothing about him." *I couldn't help blushing!* "For goodness sake, Steve, don't tell me you're embarrassed! Young people are so puritanical today. I suppose we've left them nowhere else to go.

---

[13] Lyrics at Appendix

"John left Cal a legacy. Not just the fear of water but confusion and guilt. It's very common for children to blame themselves when a parent's relationship fails."

"I know, I did."

"He also gave Cal a picture of what it was like to have a dad. Especially in cricket. You had better take note of that, Steve. He's asking a lot of you already. You're four years older, not even that, and you're being asked to fill in some of the squares as a dad. Step away if it's too much."

"I wish... I could be everything he wants. I want to try, until you get someone better."

"I thought you would say that. Don't forget to have fun."

Chapter 17   In The Deep

Steve sleeps the whole time. He was asleep when I woke up, asleep when I had my breakfast, asleep when I said goodbye to Mum and still asleep when I ate his breakfast. I went for a bike ride because there were no bullies any more and he was still asleep, so I jumped on him in bed and he hugged me to shut me up. (Yes!)

"You're so boring! You talk to Mum all night and then you sleep all day and you'll get fat and you'll bowl even slower than you do now!"

So he took me for a run and we went flat out with no bowling and I got a stitch and serve me right. Then it rained so no cricket and I took him to the National Portrait Gallery which he had never been to. Bad shame!

"You don't have to look after me quite so much. I come here loads of times on my own." He seemed a bit sad so I took his arm all over again! I only let him go when I went to the face I wanted, and took out my sketch book and pencils. "Now I'm going to give you a drawing lesson. Who's this?"

"Richard III."

"I'm going to draw him now like the artist." I did. "Okay, how does he look? I mean, what sort of expression."

"Hmm… worried about something."

"Now I'm going to change a few tiny lines." A quick rub-out and some new lines. "Now how does he look?"

"Sad. As in sorrowful."

"Good. And now once again, a few new lines…"

"Evil."

"And again…"

"Mad."

"See. Just a few lines can change his whole personality. Now, do you think he's a hunchback, like they said?"

"No. He's got one shoulder higher than the other."

"Now look… Hunchback!"

"Hell, it's so easy to destroy somebody."

"A few lines, that's all. And now look…"

"Drunk, but that's…"

"Silly. Yes it is. I've given him plus signs instead of eyes. Can't happen in real life but it works when you draw it. Plus-sign eyes mean drunk. An American cartoonist called Peter Arno invented that and we've all copied it since." *I loved the 'we' – him and all the other great artists!* "You see, you can always invent some new way of saying something when you draw."

I took him round and made him look at faces and say what they meant and when he got stuck I helped him with a drawing. But then I saw it, General Westaway, and I felt a bit sick again. "We knew some Westaways, but they didn't think Mum and me were good enough to be in their family."

He was going to lose it so I hugged him tight right there in the gallery, and I replayed something his mum said to me. "Well, they were the losers. They never got to know your mum, who's so totally brilliant and loving, or you, who's the same and a cricket player and I got you to know you both instead."

He held on for quite a time. Fuck those Westaway snobs. It must have really hurt. "I've had enough faces. Let's go to the National Gallery."

We bought a big drawing pad at the art shop and then I hauled him in front of Seurat's Bathers. "Everyone raves about the colour and the light in this, and they're fantastic, but I want to show you how well drawn it is. Now go away and look at something else."

I sat on the floor and drew. I had to throw away two because Seurat's so good. Then I got him back. "I thought you'd be here. Everybody likes Rousseau's tiger but he's crap. He looks like a paper cut-out. Now come back to the bathers… Now look at the picture again. Do you think they're having a good time?"

"I suppose so. They're having a day out."

"Now look at my drawing. Don't tell me it's good, even though it is, just tell me something you can see about the people."

"They're ... not looking at each other."

"Got it. When you look through the colour and the light you can see it in the drawing. Seurat was wonderful at drawing. He made hundreds, maybe thousands of drawings, before he did his pictures. So - they're not really having a very good time. Imagine being on holiday and not talking to the people you're with."

"I've been on holidays like that."

"The boy's not shouting to his dad, if it's his dad, he's just shouting. All the others are looking into space. Even the dog. And what can you tell me about the clouds?"

"They seem to be part of the smoke from the train."

"Got it again. So they haven't got very far, have they? They're not in some big open space where there's nothing but clouds. They're in the city and there's a train belching smoke over them."

"Wow!"

"You can see it in the drawing." There was quite a crowd around us by now. Mum says I'm a bit loud sometimes. And this lady came forward, Small, a bit like Mrs K, only with reddish hair and lots of scarves. And she turned out to be American.

"That was a wonderful lecture, young man," Not sarky at all! "I lecture about art too and I'd like to steal it. And I would like to buy your sketch. Is this your agent? Would $100 seem reasonable?" I would have given it to her, but Steve cut in.

"Thank you. We can take dollars or a traveller's cheque but not credit cards."

Cheek! But she just smiled and pulled out some dollar bills. "Now, would you please sign it and date it?" I was so gobsmacked I forgot to do the fancy signature. "Cal Devane? Thank you. You're right about Seurat. He was a great draftsman. We had a wonderful show of his drawings in the Museum of Modern Art."

"I'll never draw that well. Let alone paint."

"In a hundred years or less when you're hanging in here or the Tate, people will say 'I'll never draw as well as Devane.' Now could you both be very kind and walk me back to the Cavendish Hotel? It's not far." **We did and she gave us tea and cakes! She gave us a card.** "Ask your mother to get in touch and I'll have them send you the catalogue of the Seurat show. And tell me when you're having a show of your own…"

Dear Zoe the Monkey

You were right and I didn't want to get an email from you so of course I deleted it and I never read about the pool or the boat or the tortoise or the Durrell house or your dad falling off the banana or your mum overtaking on the hairpin bend or your new hair style and I didn't bother to download the photo or drool over it so I never saw that you swept it back from your face. And yes, it was really boring reading about all that stuff, especially for the 97th time.

And you won't bother to read this email and know that Cal took me to the National Portrait Gallery and the National Gallery and we met this amazing woman called Professor Linda Nochlin but if you've got this far Google her because she's totally famous as an art historian and a feminist critic[14]…

… maximum good luck to Robert on the swim to Albania but half way is fine. Cal's going on a long swim soon, but he doesn't know it. He and Alice are going on holiday in Devon somewhere. I suppose I will go home then, but it does not matter if I can see you again and if I can't see you again nothing matters anyway. TRUE!! Tell Robert I'm amazed at his fitness regime and I couldn't do it and it's sweet of you to do it with him, but you don't have to for me because holding your body again whatever its shape will be quite enough to make me

Your very own Psycho [all of your Xs and Os squared]

"Wake up, Cal! You're such a slacker!" *Revenge on my part!* "Get ready for a bike ride. Meet me outside in five minutes – with your helmet on. Do your teeth. Do not wake your mum."

He was ready in under four minutes. "What's in the back pack?"

---

[14] True.

"Materials. Follow me." *Traffic was light and we soon got back to my part of the world. Kenborne Vale. I watched out for the early morning winos and even more carefully for Jimmy's Alfa. No worries on either front. Down Rendell Avenue, Burden Road, and finally I stopped at the Wexford Street pools.*

"You're not getting me in there!"

"Do you trust me?"

"Yes..."

"Nothing bad will happen and you don't have to do anything which is too much for you. You won't be embarrassed because we've got the length pool to ourselves. I sorted it with my friend Phil, who works here. The Early Bird club has cancelled and he's given us their booking."

"Did you bring my lifejacket?"

"I told you before. I'm your lifejacket. If you need it, I'll hold you up."

"You better." *Phil let us in. I introduced him and explained why he was called the Sheriff at my school. We got changed, and we traded compliments on our new Ursinho swimwear. Vanity overcame fear, until he got to the steps of the pool.*

"I can't do this."

"You're not allowed to say 'I can't'. Either 'I'm scared' or 'I don't know how.'"

"I'm scared."

"Of drowning?"

"No – of being hit by a giant meteor."

"Well, you have more chance of being hit by a giant meteor. First, the water here is three foot deep and you are four feet tall."

"Four feet ten and a bit more!"

"Second, Phil is right there in the water and he's a trained lifeguard and he would lose his job if he let you drown. Third, if I let you drown your mum would sue me for all your worth and I can't afford fifty pounds."

"Hah! Three million at least." *But he got down the steps and stood beside me in the water.* "Well, if I have to die at least I'll die in your arms."

"Don't be a pathetic little drama queen!" *He actually looked shocked. I reached over to the backpack.* "We're not swimming anyway, to begin with, we're playing cricket." *I pulled out the plastic bat and tossed him the plastic ball. I swam towards Phil at the deep end and trod water.* "I'm batting. Show Phil your beautiful action." *Again vanity took over, and he let go of the edge and bowled to me.* "Nice flight, isn't it, Phil?" *I knocked the ball in front of him, so he had to go a little deeper to retrieve it.*

By the end of the first over, he had loosened up in the water, although he still hadn't taken his feet off the bottom. "Good over. Maiden. Now, I have to try to score in this over, so I may hit some catches. Go for them. Remember to call 'Cal's!' or Phil might go for them too, and crash into you."

"Cal's!... Cal's!..." *He started going for the catches and his feet left the bottom. For the fourth one he made good distance and actually caught it.*

"Not out. That hit the water first."

"It so didn't!"

"If you're not certain, you shouldn't claim a catch. Not out."

"I am certain!"

"Not out. No more arguing and catch this instead." *As I hoped, indignation took over. He thrashed through the water and caught my next one cleanly and some distance away.* "That is out. And notice where you caught it. You have just swum five metres. Was that so hard?" *His eyes lit up.* "Okay, next over you can catch it or you can do a run out. Phil is the wicketkeeper. You have ten seconds to field the ball after I hit it and either throw it into Phil or pass it to him."

We did another over. I made him go a little further each time to catch the ball or throw it. He got one catch and I credited him with two run-outs. "Nice throw. And you swam eight metres."

"Ten!" *It was, but I wanted another argument.*

"Eight."

"Ten! At least. It was twice as far as five!"

"Phil, could you settle this please? You're the expert. Could you measure out ten metres at the edge of the pool and go there?" *He did.* "No way did you manage the distance from us to Phil."

"Did too!"

"Prove it." *He did, although Phil had to catch him at the end.* "That was the slowest ten metres since Olympic records began, but I suppose it was ten metres. Now – another version of the game. This time you're the ball. Phil's going to throw you to me, I'm going to throw you back to him. Ten seconds to complete the run out." *After two successful run outs we increased the distance between us. He managed twelve metres but fifteen brought panic. I grabbed him.*

"You cheated!" *Another splutter and a desperate clutch. I had forgotten how strong people are when they are afraid of drowning.*

"Don't talk with your mouth open." *Giggle.* "I've got you." *He stopped strangling me but kept his arms around me. I carried him back to Phil at the deeper part of the pool.* "Phil, do you think he's tired after all that swimming?"

"Definitely. He's done well over a hundred metres today." *Eyes lit up again.*

"Do you think he should have a nap?"

"Distance swimmers always take naps."

"You're going to fall asleep in the water. First, make yourself all floppy like Bungle." *Blush. I had let out a terrible secret, not that Phil would mind him having a teddy bear.* "Lie on your back, look at the ceiling. I've still got you. Go floppy and when you fall asleep I'll let go." *The second attempt worked and he floated on his back.* "Now kick your feet up and down very slowly and push your arms in and out very slowly…. Keep going…. Stop! Fifteen metres. Was that hard?"

"No way."

"Steve's taught you the same stroke I always use for beginners. You can do that for ever and you don't have to worry about breathing. Now try floating on your front." *He went through all the front floats. Cal enjoyed the Dead Man's.* "Notice how much easier it is to float in deep water than shallow?" *Nod.* "Good, because you're going to swim a whole width at the deep end… no,

158

not near the side, between Steve and me." *Thrash, thrash, gasp, squeal of triumph.*

"Now straight back again!" *Initial protest, thrash, gasp, thrash, gasp, thrash, thrash, squeal.*

"Twenty metres." *Triumph.* "But totally crap swimming! Zero points from all the judges for artistic impression." *Pout.* "Serious. Your leg kick is crap, your arms are crap, your breathing is crap! Phil will sort all that out while I do a few lengths for fitness." *He watched me do a show-off crawl and then turned to Phil. I churned up and down the pool, ignoring them, until I got a signal from Phil.* "Do you think you're any good?"

"Phil told me how to avoid your bad technique!"

"Then show me. Swim down to me. On your own." *I swam about half way and faced him. He came towards me, pull, breathe, kick, glide. He was in his own zone, so I slipped backwards, still watching him. Neither of us stopped until he had finished the length.*

"Congratulations. One whole length, 33 metres and a third. Now was that hard?" *Like the first day we met, he looked as if I had just given him the Universe as a Christmas present. I rummaged in the backpack again and pulled out the floating shark.* "Now this is Jaws, and you've got to escape." *Actually Jaws looked more like one of the Pathetic Sharks in Viz, but Cal didn't seem to mind. I held it with both hands.* "Jaws and I can only kick, you can kick and use your arms too. If you reach the other end before Jaws you've escaped, if Jaws touches you you're eaten. You get a start of three seconds, no more." *He hurtled away towards the deep end and I let him escape by inches.* "Oh my god, there's Jaws's evil brother right here, so you'd better escape again. No, not behind Phil. Throw him away!" *Phil chucked him a little way back towards the shallow end and I let him escape again, just. Phil followed us.* "Two lengths. Sixty-six metres."

"And two thirds!"

"We're docking that, because Phil chucked you. But 66 is enough for a badge, isn't it, Phil? He's a swimmer." *I copped a giant hug and kiss. I didn't care that Phil saw, especially when he copped one right after! We did stunts and mucked around until it was time for Phil to let in the regulars. Cal chattered away non-stop and wanted to come to the pool again and again, just as when we first played cricket.*

We changed and I bought a few cereal bars and the healthiest drinks I could find at the pool's vending machine. "Do you want to thank Phil in your usual way? I brought your sketch pad and pencils." *He pulled off a sketch of Phil from memory, and he did his usual bouncing-around-and-looking away routine when he gave it to him, and Phil was delighted and Cal said it was crap and he would do another when we came back. I phoned Alice and told her Cal could swim.* "Are you OK, Alice?"

"Just stunned. We'll celebrate this evening."

We went for a long aimless bike ride and then went back and flopped around. I think we knew that nothing else that day would match up to that swim. We eventually found some cricket on TV and crashed onto the couch to watch it. Which is where Alice found us, fast asleep! What is it about me and other people's couches? I've never dozed off at home.

"Don't be embarrassed, Steve. You've earned a little nap. So have you, sweetheart. I'm proud of you. Did he really do fifty metres?"

"Sixty-six!" *I nodded agreement.*

"In that case, I keep my promise. You can have anything you want."

"Three million pounds!"

"Don't have it on me."

"Asking Steve to come with us on holiday."

"I was going to do that anyway, so you can ask again."

"Don't want anything else. You want to come, don't you, it's a brilliant house and there's beaches and I can swim now so you don't have to watch me the whole time and a haunted house and tons of places you can go on a bike and there's a cricket team and they're crap and they really need you, they even need me?... " *Gasp.*

"Okay. Remember to breathe, like when you're swimming."

"I think you'd like it, Steve. We've been there two years running and we don't want to go anywhere else. It is an unusual house and off the beaten track. The owner rents it out in summer and we share a month with Portia, my boss. If you have no other plans, we'd like you to join us. There's plenty of space and you can go off on your own when you want to." *I gaped for a bit and she must have thought me an idiot.* "I'm going to take looking like a goldfish as a Yes."

Chapter 18 Substitute

Steve's house felt chilly the moment we went in. I thought at first they must have air conditioning. Everything was immaculate and in excellent, expensive taste. There was no evidence that a family lived there – no photographs, no childhood trophies, no mess. It was a good house in a mixed area: Kenborne Vale had never quite arrived. Steve ruefully pointed out the winos and crazies in the streets.

Parking Cal with Mrs K, I had fixed a meeting with Steve's parents to agree and arrange the holiday. I was surprised that neither had been in contact with me. Their son disappears for days with a stranger and they are not even curious? During the trip in the car, Steve had given me a little of their back story.

"This is only what I picked up from Uncle Frank. Mum never wanted to marry Dad. She was in love with this guy called Fred at uni. Dad never went to uni: he started work at 13, he always says. He met Mum at a party and he fancied her and he just hung in and she went out with him when she could not get Fred. And this went on for years, after Mum left uni, Fred first, Dad as substitute, until Fred suddenly told her that he had found someone else, and she was really broken at first but Dad was still around and already making money. I think she married him to show Fred she didn't need him.

"But all the time she really wanted Fred and a few years later Fred's marriage hit the rocks and he might have been available again – except that she got pregnant with me and Fred didn't want to be stuck with someone else's child. I suppose I'm lucky she didn't get rid of me..."

Luckily I saw a car park. I pulled in, stopped, and squeezed his hand. "Steve, don't be a prisoner of what you don't know. Real life is hard enough, don't think the worst until you have to. If this meeting is going to be too painful I can fix things without you. Go home if you want." Shit! What a mistake.

"I *am* going home. I can bloody well take people to my bloody home."

"Too bloody right."

Steve introduced me to his parents with a lot of formality and an edge of defiance. His mother – did her parents really name her Desiree? – was an attractive woman who clearly spent a lot of time on her looks. (I'm a bitch as well as a lawyer). Steve had inherited his good features from her. His father, Donald, was a nondescript man but I could sense a powerful will. Steve seemed to have nothing from him, until I remembered seeing him bowl fast in the nets, when he had his father's expression – focused and implacable.

I felt myself being appraised and was glad that I had elected to stay in a business suit. She offered me wine from her already open bottle. He countered with an offer of mineral water from his bottle. I could sense Steve tensing up, and I asked for tea to get him out of the room.

I decided to take charge. "Desiree, Donald, it's good to meet you. To come straight to the point, my son Cal and I have enjoyed Steve's company so much over the last few days that we would like to keep him a little longer. I understand that you have no holiday plans, so I hope that he could join us in Devon for two weeks."

"That's very kind of you, Alice. Our holiday this year is a victim of the downturn." She shot a venomous look at her husband as if he was author of the downturn. "We were going to redecorate instead, but that too fell victim of the downturn."

"I am surprised that you felt you needed to redecorate. I think your house is beautiful. I'm sorry about the downturn but you must have had an upturn to go down from." Neither of them reacted to the compliments. I rattled on quickly. "My practice doesn't really notice upturns and downturns. Sadly, there's always a supply of families and children in trouble. What does hurt us is cutting the legal aid budget. Then we really have to bear down on costs." Donald looked interested in me for the first time, but I didn't want to drift into a financial discussion. "Anyway, we really hope you can spare Steve a bit longer. He's made a huge difference to my son, Cal. And I like him very much too."

"Steve?" His mother seemed genuinely surprised that anyone would want to spend time with him. He came in with two teas: I hoped that he had missed that.

"There will be no extra cost involved. We would be driving down in my car and we are staying in a house with plenty of space, not a hotel. If there is any extra cost for his food, or excursions or whatever, Steve will more than pay it back as a childminder, although you had better not use that expression to my son. Maybe I should say 'teacher.' Steve is a brilliant teacher. Have you considered that as a career for him?"

"Steve's career has been a worry to us." His father spoke for the first time. Despite the 'us', he never glimpsed at his wife. "It's been hard to get him to think about anything other than cricket. It may seem harsh on my part, but over my life I have seen many young people throw their lives away on some impossible dream. It might be sport, it might be … drama or art or … inventing perpetual motion. And some of them have had talent. But they don't know how much the odds are against them. And eventually they're on the scrap heap – and all their friends who just plodded along at something boring, they're the ones who have got ahead." Well. I recognized the story of his life. But must Steve replicate it? "My wife talked about the downturn but I see it at first hand. I have to protect my clients from the downturn. And believe me, it's worse than anyone admits. It will last for years and years. I don't think Steve understands the world in which he's going to have to make his way. There will be no market at all for the kids who chased their dreams. Only the kids who dug into something."

"Steve has told me that you're very keen for him to get some kind of holiday job before he goes to business college in the autumn. But I think he has been too modest to tell you that he landed one." Steve looked bewildered. "And he's still too modest! It's a cracking job as well – he's going to be an intern at Barnes Dorman Sharp." Donald looked blank and Desiree looked amazed. "Desiree, I sense that name means more to you than to Donald."

"My husband is not very up in the creative world. Barnes Dorman Sharp is a highly successful advertising agency."

"They turn clients away, don't they? And they have several hundred kids each week, begging to work there for nothing." Only a slight exaggeration. "Joe Barnes will pay Steve for his time. He will join one of his creative teams and write copy."

"Steve? A writer?" She was amazed. Clearly, that was her space. "He's certainly no end of a reader. My brother's library… But I've never seen anything he's written. I mean, apart from the odd school essay."

"Joe Barnes has been a professional writer for years," I could not resist the implied comparison. "He thinks Steve is worth a chance, and I hope you would agree it would be terrible for him to pass it up."

"That is unthinkable." She shot a glance at her husband, as if certain that he was thinking it.

"Now if that does not work, and Steve is not a copywriter after all, I would like him in our office. We always need extra hands just for filing and administration, and we need proof readers for documents. Even one misprint or comma out of place on a document and we could lose a case. If Steve does a shift at our office he will develop an eye for detail and a sense of discipline. Otherwise we will cut him loose." This seemed to play well with Donald. "We deal frequently with family finances so he will learn some accounting skills. I might ask him to 'devil' for me – look up cases and legal reports – and he will learn some law. And, because he is brilliant at talking to children, he might help me in some of my interviews, which means that he will also pick up secretarial skills. Oh, and we'll pay him. Steve, have I missed anything out?"

He still looked absolutely bewildered, and with good reason, since I had invented everything, but like a good trouper he came right in on cue. "No, I don't think so. Mum? Dad? I don't think I could get any better jobs this holiday, and I'll work at them flat tack, and they're going to look good on my CV."

"What about clothes?" Desiree's question threw me for a minute, and then I realized I had won.

"He will not need anything much for Devon, and actually he's done rather well in the clothes department. The Barnes family decided he needed a makeover."

She blushed. "Oh goodness. We were going to do that, sweetheart, but then I had to go to my writers' retreat." No, you didn't. You chose to. "That's a new shirt, isn't it? And trousers. I'm impressed. Where from?"

"Ursinho. It's a new designer label. From Brazil."

"Did that come out of the money I gave you?"

"No. Belinda paid. She wanted to. But I bought something for everybody."

They both fell silent. Yes, it's worth thinking about. Other people love your son. They want to buy him clothes and give him a holiday. "If it's all right with you for Steve to go on holiday with us, I do need you to sign this form, in case he needs emergency medical treatment." Donald read it very carefully and signed. I could see Steve unclench. "I think that will be unlikely, he's a strong, healthy young man. Does he have any allergies? Phobias? Anything at all I should be aware of?"

They thought hard and shook their heads. It was Steve who shouted "Heights!"

Steve was fretful in the car. "Alice? Me working for Joe Barnes and for you. Wasn't that... well, lying?"

"Don't think of them as present lies but as future truths. Both of those things will happen if you want them to. Joe thinks the world of you. So do I. You will have to meet my boss, Portia, but she will do the same. I thought those things would seal the deal for your parents without a confrontation."

Cal was at home waiting for us. Mrs K could not keep him and he was bouncing off the walls.

"Well, is Steve coming?"

"Yes." He burst into tears.

"Well, if I knew it was going to upset you so much, I'll stay here."

"God, you're so stupid sometimes," and he ran out of the room.

"Don't go after him, he's just been overwrought all day. He'll be fine."

A minute later he was back, very cool and poised. "I'm afraid I was a baby. But I am delighted that you will be coming and I trust that the arrangements will be to your satisfaction."

"Wordpower, Cal!"

We tried some Monopoly but Cal was still over-excited and Steve was still pensive.

"Alice? Do you really think I would be good at teaching?"

"You'd be brilliant at teaching. You even taught me to swim. That's like teaching Bungle ... nuclear physics."

"Not every kid's as brilliant as you are."

"But you'd make them think they were."

I was struck by Cal's perception, although typically he accepted at once that he was brilliant. "Steve, I know that you would be brilliant at the actual teaching. But I would be worried how you would fit into the English school system as it is now – the paperwork, the bureaucracy, the endless testing, the endless targets, the endless people telling you what to teach and how to teach. And don't go near an academy. Oh, don't start me on that... Steve, your father has an idea of what you should do, and there is some force in what he says. I've got an idea of what you should do. But what do you want to do?"

"I want to be a professional cricketer. I thought about asking for a trial at Lords, but I haven't played any match cricket for ages."

"Just walk in there and bowl and they will see you're a god."

"Cal. Honestly, there are stacks of bowlers my age who are better than me. And even if I were a god, I'd still need someone to recommend me."

"I'll recommend you."

"Thanks, but I think it needs to be a member of the MCC."

"Tim Morrow! Robert knows him. Write to him now. I'll write too and I'll tell Robert to write."

"Sweetheart, I think we need to run that past Robert and Joe first. That's good manners when you want to use someone's name to influence somebody else. But don't worry, Steve, we will get you a trial at Lords. Now is there anything else you want to do?"

"Well, I thought I could take a coaching course."

"Excellent. But is there anything you want to do outside cricket?"

"Yes. But only if I find I can't do anything inside cricket."

Daniel and Brendon

Thanks for your great email which cracked me up again. Does your father not like that bishop? I was amazed that he came back at all after being chased by the goat, so why did your father ask him to help out at the beehive? Was he wearing his robes and mitre when he jumped into the pond? I've done a lot of jumping into water myself because Cal's now got a mania for swimming since Phil and I taught him and Alice came with us last night .."

"Bloody hell, Alice, you're good!"

"Mum was under-14 Freestyle Girls champion of Sheffield."

"I always thought she was a freestyle girl."

Zoe

Please ask Robert not to snatch such sultry snapshots [Wordpower] of you on the beach because when I downloaded them Alice's computer overheated (like me).

I'm really glad you're having such a great holiday and even gladder that you have survived your mum's driving. And to Robert, major herogram! Getting to mid-

channel means that he reached Albanian territorial waters, which is epic. A hundred metres is still an epic for Cal. He managed it, just, for me and Alice…

"Brilliant, sweetheart! I'm so proud. Now do it again." *Protest.* "Again." *Reluctant crawl.* "It is brilliant, but he needs more stamina. Don't be too soft on him, Steve. Make him do lots of lengths, not just stunts and tricks."

I still can't believe I'm going on holiday with them but I haven't believed anything that's happened for the last ten days, and maybe I'm only having an immensely long dream. Perhaps I'm in a coma somewhere, but that's a small price for dreaming about you…

"Steve, are you awake?"

"No, I'm asleep."

"I'm not."

"But your mum is. If you want to talk, come over here and whisper." *He dived onto my bed. He had something big to say, but there was no room for his usual bounce-and-look-away routine.*

"Steve?"

"Cal?"

"Do you really want to come with us on holiday?"

"Yes."

"You won't feel … stupid, having to hang out with a kid?"

"No. Totally not."

"What if people look at us or say stuff?"

"I'll tell them to get stuffed." *Giggle.*

"Steve?"

"Cal?"

"Do you mind that I love you so much?" *I gave him an outsize hug.*

"No. Only if it blocked you from seeing and knowing all the other people who love you and are going to love you."

"Steve?"

"Cal?"

"Would you like to live here always?"

"Cal. It doesn't matter where you live but how you live. If you and your mum want to see me I will always want to see you. We're going to play cricket, go swimming, visit art galleries, play Monopoly, hang out. I will always want to see you, for the rest of my life, and when you don't want to see me any more I will always want to know what's going on for you. Cal?"

"Steve?"

"I never knew when I was going to see my Uncle Frank but we still loved each other. Maybe more than if we'd lived together. And I will love him for ever." *I could feel him dozing off in my arms.* "Cal, don't fall asleep here. There isn't room and Bungle will miss you."

"Carry me."

"You are a baby sometimes."

"Carry me while you still can. I'll be carrying you before you know it."

The day before going to Devon Alice asked me to come to her office to meet someone. I didn't have to, but she thought it would be important. Should I get my suit? Not necessary, just clean trousers and clean shirt.

I found her law firm easily. It had a big sign, drawn by Cal. I met Portia Harper, her boss. She wasn't old but her hair was white. There was a big photo of a man in a cricket shirt on her desk. I remembered her losing her husband and I felt she would not want to talk about cricket, but she started on it and asked a lot about Joe Barnes. She was really friendly, but I knew I wouldn't want her on the other side in a legal case.

"Ten minutes, Steve, well done. Fools and bores last less than two in Portia's office, unless they are paying clients. Now, your next meeting could be painful, but I set it up because I think it will be good for you. I will be there. It will be informal. Nothing on the record, and nothing will go further."

She took me into an interview room and there was a blond kid around my age. Then I recognized him and got a shock.

"Hello Steve. I'm Alan. We played cricket in the nets. With Jimmy." *I felt guilty again. Seeing him with Jimmy all those times at the old nets and never speaking to him. Never warning him.* "I live with Jimmy." *Bloody hell!* "Steve, I know what you feel. We've seen you turn away as soon as you see us."

"Not you…"

"You don't have to talk to me. But I really want to tell you how things are. Maybe you will still hate Jimmy but I don't think you'll be afraid of him. And whatever happens you never have to see him again or hear from him."

"You live with him?"

"Yes. Ever since the day you ran off."

"But that was three years ago…"

"And you think I was under age? How old do you think I am?"

"Same as me – sixteen."

"I'm nineteen, Steve. So I was sixteen then. Legal. I've always looked younger than I am. Jimmy likes young-looking boys. Let me tell things as they happened, and then make up your mind about us."

"Okay."

"When I first met Jimmy – and you – I had left school with no qualifications. And my parents had thrown me out of home."

"Bloody hell, for being gay?"

"No. For being impossible. For drinking and drugs and stealing from them. Stealing from my kid brother. For making life hell for my family. I lived on friends' sofas for as long as they could stand me, and sometimes on the street. I wasn't exactly on the game but I did make some money out of men. Nothing more than a blow job." *He took a big gulp of water.*
"I saw Jimmy a lot in the neighbourhood. He's not difficult to miss. And I had him lined up as a … client. But then I saw him with you, both having a great

time, and I knew that's what I really wanted – him giving me a great time and taking care of me. Now I didn't want to push you out, I thought, maybe I could become your mate and get a part of everything. So I stalked him and you, as much as I could. And I saw that you both really loved cricket, and I spent every bit of money I had on some cricket stuff and hung around those nets. And one afternoon I played with you, Bloody hell, you were scary!" *I couldn't help being pleased.* "When we finished I was really hoping that he might ask me to tag along but he only wanted you." *I felt really sorry for him.*

"I watched you drive off in that wonderful car and then I walked to his street. I knew where he lived and I knew a place where I could hide and watch. I actually thought that at some time one of you would come out into the street, and then I would casually walk out and meet you accidentally and get invited in to whatever you were doing. But neither of you came out until I saw you storming out into the night."

"I knew you had had some kind of fight, and I'm afraid I thought that was my only chance."

"It was you I saw in the street."

"Yes. You didn't recognize me, you were in a red rage. You'd actually left the front door open, so I pushed in. Jimmy was hysterical and sobbing and cursing himself and I just held him for a long time until he calmed down. Then he started beating himself up again because he was afraid something would happen to you, on the streets at night. And I told him that I lived on the streets and that nobody ever messed with people like you, in a red rage, and if they did you would sort them out." *Again, I couldn't help being pleased.*

"He calmed down again and then I took a big chance and said that I really liked him and I really wanted him to teach me cricket and I would do anything for him, and if he didn't like me I would go but could I just spend one night on his floor first? And then he asked me for my story and I told him and we went to bed and held each other and fell asleep." *I took all this in. I wanted to ask a question but it seemed so silly.*

"I know what you want to ask. What happened in the match the next day?"

"Yeah."

"I played instead of you. Jimmy had some whites that fitted me. And when we arrived Xan was there. You remember Xan?"

"Of course."

"He looked me up and down and said 'Well, who's Miss Teen Prom Queen? And what happened to Miss Butch Teen Dream?' and I said you were sick, but we had played together and I was a substitute. And Xan called me Eileen and we just carried on." *We both laughed.*

"It was the poshest place I had ever been to and full of famous cricketers and other people and I knew Jimmy – Jemima – was on hot bricks in case I showed him up on or off the field. But I worked really hard, and nobody thought I was trade. I wasn't nearly as good a cricketer as you and we were a bowler short but Xan tore in and took six wickets. He had to bowl them all, because Darrel Hair, the celebrity umpire, didn't like Xan calling him Doreen. I chased everything in the field and took quite a good catch and made ten not out and scored the winning run with Jimmy at the other end. " *Suddenly I felt really happy for him.*

"Jimmy and I have been together ever since. And I've never shown him up. On or off the field. But I'm still only the substitute." *He looked wistful.* "He adored you, Steve. He still does. There's a drawer in his desk that is kind of a shrine to you. It's full of photographs, scores from your school matches, the programme for that big match, with your name on it, not mine. He really, really loved being your sort of uncle and being your coach and giving you treats. He never forgave himself for … letting go. He hates himself for poisoning your life. It's torture for him to know that you're afraid of him. He wants that lifted. So do I."

I thought for a long time. "Does he think… I might come back to him?"

"No. I have asked him. He expects nothing from you. Nothing at all, not even knocking up in the nets. He just hopes that you will not run away every time you see him or the car."

I thought again. "No offence, but… do you mind being a substitute?"

"No offence. Yes, sometimes I do. But he has been good to me and I've had a great three years – hell, way better than living on the streets or being on the game. Luxury home. Loads of treats. Fabulous holidays. Meeting famous people. And discovering I could do something after all. He let me drive the Alfa and I was not only a really good driver but I actually understood that car and I learnt how to care for it and service it. Jimmy's putting me through a proper course and I am going to become a specialist car mechanic. And he'll always let me drive the Alfa."

"I don't see that. Why shouldn't you drive the Alfa?"

"I'm leaving him, Steve." *I must have looked gobsmacked.* "I know he's tired of me. He likes young, fit boys. Look at this." *He pulled out his shirt.* "It's called a paunch. I'm losing my looks and my figure. He feeds me too well. I work out like crazy but I'm not an athlete like you, Steve. I know he wants somebody else. So I will find him someone. Not like you. Like me. Another substitute."

"Bloody hell! He's chucking you out after three years …"

"No Steve. I'm walking out when I know I have found the right person for him. And then I will live with Xan. I don't live in a good world, Steve, but there is honour in it."

"I'm sorry, Alan. I didn't mean to judge you. Thank you for telling me all this. I really hope everything goes right for you. Say hello to Xan from Stephanie."

"I will. Have you any message for Jimmy?"

"Tell him… I'm OK." *I looked at Alice.* "Better than OK. I went to some other nets and it was the best thing that could have happened to me. Tell him… I'm OK about seeing him but I don't want to talk to him. Tell him I still take guard on leg stump to spinners."

Chapter 19   New Pitch

Brendon/Daniel

Thanks for another great email. Great news about your dad. Is he a militant atheist (like me?) First that bishop and now the Jehovah's Witness! But how did he accidentally get locked in with the pig? Do pigs have flats in NZ? Explain please! In haste because I am packing for Devon. Can't believe they wanted me to go with them. But then everything lately's been brilliant for me – I think it's the maniah you gave me. But you must know that already…

"Cal, I'm going to teach you how to pack like my uncle Frank. If you really need all those clothes you can easily get them into that case. Listen to that shirt and it will tell you what shape it wants to be."

"Don't really want it, anyway. Steve, will you show me how you pack your cricket bag?"

"We've packed the cricket bags already."

"Yeah, but even so, how do you pack yours?"

"I have a ritual, I do everything feet upwards. Boots first, socks, trousers, Padman stuff, shirt and so on. Finally towel, shampoo, make-up." *Giggle.* "Helps me remember."

He immediately unpacked his cricket bag and solemnly repacked everything in my order. "Do you think I would look good in make-up?"

"No. And don't you dare practise with mine!" *Repeat giggle and girly pose.*

We went back to his suitcase. Alice came in to check progress. "Neat job, Steve. And good grief, neat job, Cal."

"Steve taught me."

"Did you pack your lifejacket?"

"Don't need it. I can swim now."

Sudden tension. I cut in quickly "You actually need it more because you'll be much braver in the water. More good swimmers drown each year than non-swimmers, because they get confident and do dangerous things." *He did not* buy this, and fair enough, *I had completely made it up.* "If we both got into trouble that jacket could save my life as well as yours, because if you started going under you could drag me down. Remember in the pool when you got a scare? Drowning people have awesome strength."

"Okay."

"What about Bungle?"

"Steve, how could you? Bungle never gets packed. Hand luggage if we're ever in a plane, extra passenger in the car."

"Just like me with Sergeant Bear."

"In ten minutes, everything you guys are taking to Devon has to be in the hall. Then sleep because the alarm is set for 4 am, in the futile hope that I can get on the road before all the other punters."

I'd never have believed it would be so easy to wake up at 4am! Perhaps I was excited... It was a real struggle loading the car.

"Steve, you're taking that leather jacket? We're having a heatwave."

"It makes me feel good," *and I blushed.*

"Have I got two fashion queens with me? Just stay out of my make-up." *Cal and I got hysterics.*

"Sorry about all the cricket stuff, Alice."

"I'm not. Next year I'll get a bigger car." *You mean, there'll be a next year?*

She parked me in the front seat next to her. Cal and Bungle scunched into the crowded back seat. Even at 4-30 the approach to the M4 was slow-moving. We drew up alongside Jimmy's Alfa, with him and Alan. He tooted and they both waved! Two days ago I would have cringed. Now I waved back.

"Where are you off to?"

"Devon." *I had spoken to him – and nothing happened.* "You?"

"Morocco."

"Enjoy," *and I meant it.*

"Who were they?"

"Just some guys I once played cricket with."

"Cool motor." *And that's all they were. Two cricketers with a cool motor. From my past. The traffic moved again and they were gone. Alice flashed me a smile.*

At last we hit the motorway. I let her make a few miles and then I couldn't resist it. "Are we nearly there yet?"

"Cal grew out of that years ago. Try it again and I'll find an Easy Listening radio station."

"Sorry. Do you want the radio?"

"Try Jazz FM."

I found it and this amazing pianist came up. I recognized the tune. "Day In, Day Out. Ricky Rubato! The Barneses know Howard Foy, who wrote it. He's Zoe's there-is-no-godfather."

"I've heard him on radio. He does a quiz called You're Booked! and blows a whistle as the referee."

"Would you like to meet him?" *As if I could introduce her to a famous person!*

"Yes. He sounds fun. I'd love you to fix that for me." *She meant it. As if I did know famous people. I thought about this for several exits. She tapped me and made me look backwards. Cal had fallen asleep with Bungle. As before, the years melted off him and they looked uber-cute. [Wordpower].*

"Steve. I'm really glad to have you with us, but will you make a promise? Please treat this as your holiday, not ours. Don't just fall in with what he or I want to do. If you want to go to a teen rave, I'll drive you there and pick you up again. If you want to lie in bed all day, go ahead. If you just want to be alone, just walk or take the bike, there's one your size. If you meet someone you want to be with – go away and be with."

"Alice, you said there's a beach and a cricket club. Believe me, that's all I need. And being with you and him, that's a holiday. All the time." *She got a bit teary and I hurried on.* "Do you know what the pitch is like? Do they have a good team? Is there a sea mist, it's supposed to be good for swing?"

"Steve, I haven't a clue. You hurried away, didn't you, because I got emotional? Try not to do that. I know why you do, but you're safe now. There are no bad emotions. You paid me a beautiful compliment. I reacted emotionally. Be there with me, in the moment, and don't run away."

"Okay."

"Now add the words 'and quit bugging me you stupid bitch.'"

"I can't."

"Of course you can."

"Can't because I don't feel that way."

"Good answer! And what do you feel?"

"You're totally wonderful and brilliant all the time and I never met anyone like you!" *and I burst into tears. I keep doing that! Why, when my life is so great? Simultaneously she squeezed my hand, cussed out a Lexus, and pointed me towards the Kleenex. It must be true that women are multi-taskers.*

We had a Welcome Break [not so!] and I let Cal and Bungle take over the front seat.

"I need him to navigate."

"Why have Sat-nav when you can have Cat-nav?"

"If he's been anywhere once he can remember how to get there. Ever since he was little. Stunning visual memory."

He proved it when we came off exit 24 of the M5 and started drifting through Somerset. "Left at the post office … ignore the road sign and go straight on at this roundabout …. right at the house with the giant gnome…" *The road got twistier and turnier. I caught glimpses of the sea through woodland. Finally we saw a sign for Glendon Courtenay.*

"The Courtenays were a big Devon family, they ran everything in the Middle Ages. I don't know who Glendon was."

"Mum! There's a Chinese restaurant instead of the post office! The pub's got karaoke! Don't let Steve in! Stop at the cricket pitch... Wow! They've redone the nets. Can we try them, they won't mind?" *She stopped the car and we had a little knock-up, no pads. It was a way better surface than the park nets.*

I looked at the pitch. "This looks as good as the first eleven pitch at my old school. Somebody takes real care of this." *I felt an instant loyalty to a club I had never played for. Might never get a game for.*

"Come on, guys, you'll be back. We need to set up the house."

We drove a little way out of the town, and she stopped.

"What do you think of the house, Steve?"

"What house?" *They thought I was joking but I really didn't see it at first.* "That is so amazing! It almost disappears."

"Brilliant landscaping. Lots of levels and they all seem to burrow into the earth. I think the architect was a Hobbit. Now if you're nervous, start walking because Cal's going to drive to the door." *He could barely see over the wheel but he didn't hit anything and even changed to second.*

It didn't look like a big house but there were tons of rooms. Cal bounced on all the beds and gave me the room with the best one. It was a double. It made me feel ... tall. Cal's drawings were hanging everywhere. "Helena, that's the owner, has the largest collection of Devanes in private hands."

I heard Alice playing a piano somewhere and went to investigate. "This is a much better piano than mine and she's had it tuned."

"What was the piece?"

"Petrushka's dance, from a ballet by Stravinsky. I persuaded Cal to go because there's a dancing bear but he was furious that it wasn't a real bear and he's never been to a ballet since."

The hallway had a giant map by him, with important local landmarks. On the cricket pitch he had added a small left-arm spinner clean bowling a batsman. "I wonder who that is? And the cat up the twisted tree? Beach... ice cream shop... cliff path (no thanks!) ... Haunted house? Serious?"

"It's just derelict."

"There's definitely a ghost, but Mum doesn't want to go there."

"Hmmm…. Who had to sleep in my bed last year when this house started creaking?"

"Bungle." *Blush.* "Steve – beach first or cricket?"

"Cricket, don't you think? Then we can cool off in the sea."

"Mum? Please can we go now?"

"Wait up, sweetheart. Make some tea and bring it into the living room." *When the tea was ready she made us all sit on the couch and sip it slowly.* "We're having this tea to say that this is our home for two weeks. It's not a hotel where we just charge in and out. We respect it and we enjoy it. We do things slowly. Welcome to our home, Steve." *I got all teary <u>again!</u> I really am turning into a silly little drama queen. We finished the tea, slowly.* "Now, I am going to make a shopping list, and you and Steve will test all the bikes. I will then leave you at the cricket and do a giant shop."

"Don't you want me to come?"

"Sweetheart, when you shop with me the bill is double."

"Well, remember that Steve's here. Don't be stingy on helpings."

All the bikes were fine but something was missing. "No gears! These must be antiques. But they'll make us fitter. You might even get leg muscles." *I let him beat me up again.*

It was only mid-morning when Alice took us to the nets, but it was already hot.

"Are you sure they don't mind?"

"I'm a member." *Grandly.* "You can be my guest. I'll bat first."

There were some proper stumps set up and all the netting was in good order. Again I knew that somebody took pride in the place. I felt totally brilliant. My glad animal action took over. The ball flew from just back of a length past the batsman's throat. Cal's throat.

"Steve!" *He was pale under the helmet.* "That was the first time you've scared me. Not just the speed but the way you looked. It was…"

"Psycho?"

"Psycho." *I was scared too. Was that what it meant to bowl fast? Being possessed and not even caring that your best mate is the batsman?* "Bowl some more like that."

"Come out of the net."

"No. At me. I'm a batsman not a baby. I've got to take anything that comes."

I was so proud of him. I made him check his helmet and all the protective gear. There was not much of him I could hit! "Okay. I'm bowling flat out. Now you're a good batsman with good footwork. Do everything you normally do but just do it quicker. The good thing about the extra pace is you won't have to hit the ball hard. Just get behind everything and make a good contact with the bat."

I bowled a full length ball. His stumps clattered. "Perfectly good shot. Just not in time. Make your decision earlier and move your feet."

I stayed flat out but on a full length. I could not bring myself to give him another throat ball. I bowled him one more time and claimed a few edged catches but he met more and more of them successfully on the front foot. "Come on, bowl it short. You would in a match."

"All right. On your own head be it." *[Wordpower. Suddenly I've been making puns.]*

Just back of a length, and it flew. He kept his eye on it and jerked his head away at the last moment. Still at full speed, I mixed them up. He was happier on the front foot but he got behind the short stuff and none of it got him out. He squealed a claim for a top-edge six.

"Can I bowl too?" *I looked round and it was a girl! Bad shame on me for being surprised, but I could not remember playing with a girl. She looked a bit younger than me. Pretty. Athletic. Fair hair. Tight T-shirt with a gap above her shorts. She bowled a slow-medium good length ball. He took a giant swipe and lost his off stump.*

"Cal, that was crap! After you did all the hard work."

"Cal! Is that really Cal? Ohmigod! And who are you, trying to kill my toyboy?"

"Marjorie! My fag hag!"

"I couldn't believe it was you. When did you learn to bat like that?"

"This is Steve. He's the best teacher in the world. And get this, he taught me to swim! Wait till we hit the beach."

"Respect! How did you do that? He used to be terrified."

"I didn't really teach him, we just played cricket, sort of, in the water."

They had met last year. Marjorie lived in the village. Her dad was the local pharmacist. She filled him in on local gossip, mostly about the cricket team. They were having a bad season. It had lost a young mechanic and gained a retired businessman. Some people called Davison were malcontents. Sam Carter, the captain, had sold more land. He might be forced to sell the cricket pitch, which belonged to him and which he cared so lovingly. His son Edwin was still a drip. "How long are you here for? Would you play for us? You're awesome and Cal's way better than Edwin, who's scared of the ball."

"You bat, Marjorie. Don't worry about him, he is the world's biggest softie!" *He took off all his armour and fetched some water and his sketchbook.*

I offered her all of my stuff. We had a job getting my chest protector over her tits. I felt wrong about bowling full pace at a girl but she had no worries with my fast-medium. "Not even heated bread rolls!" *I felt great that he remembered.*

"Okay, Marjorie, if you're ready I'll crank it up."

Full pace, full length, past her defensive shot, crash into her pads. I appealed. Cal looked up from his sketchbook. "Not out. Going down leg."

"Crap umpiring!" *I bowled some more, full pace, full length. Two clean bowled and three more appeals.* "Marjorie, you can't count on a biased umpire like Cal and most of these are out. You're trying to whip everything to leg, which makes you play round your pad. It works great on my slower stuff but at this pace you haven't got time. Try and play everything full face towards me." *She did and I got almost nothing past her.* "Brilliant. You're winning the contest and the bowler has to shorten his length. Now the only way I can get you out with a short ball is a catch. Bowled, lbw are out of the picture. So you don't have to hit anything you don't want to."

"I know." *And she did. She watched all my short stuff over her left shoulder. I slipped in a yorker to keep her honest and she dug it out.*

"You're hopeless." *Cal threw down the sketch book and picked up a ball. I knew what was coming but she didn't. Huge squeal for lbw.*

"Not out, going down leg."

"Don't be silly, that was the zooter."

"Did you teach him that?"

"No. I practised it on my own. I was having a crap summer until I met Steve." *He hugged me.*

"Aren't you my toy-boy any more?" *He hugged her and she lifted him off the ground. She had to be strong, even though he was an ectomorph. She kissed him and put him down and we bowled at her again.*

"You're a really good bats…person."

"Thank you. It's way easier since you made me play straight. And what have you done to my toy-boy's bowling?"

"Not much. Just made him taller. Use all of his four feet!"

"Four feet ten-plus! Mum measured last night." *He did the bounce and look-away routine I had learnt to recognize and gave her his sketch of her batting.*

"Cal, this is brilliant! Way better than last year!"

"I know. I'm not doing anything different. I think it's just because… I'm happy." *We both hugged him and held it for quite a long time.*

"Oh hell, there's that drip Edwin." *A skinny boy about her age was shuffling nervously towards us.* "He's all right, really, but his dad's a bit hard on him. He does loads of work on the ground and he plays with me whenever I want. Shame he's so useless."

"Er… sorry… do you want me to bowl at you, Marjorie?"

"That's sweet of you, Edwin. This is Steve who is a god and this is Cal, you remember from last year, who's turning into a god."

"Gosh. I'm Edwin." *I felt sorry for him. He had less self-esteem than a dead gerbil. Was he always like that or was it just with Marjorie?*

"Marjorie told us you do a lot of work on the pitch, Edwin. It's fantastic. I used to go to a posh school and this ground's as good as our first eleven."

His face lit up. "Thanks. It belongs to our family. Dad really wants to keep cricket going but it's hard. We're selling land. I understand money, Dad doesn't…" *Me in reverse!*

We all bowled a bit more at Marjorie. She was respectful to me and Cal but smashed Edwin's very ordinary medium. I took him aside. "Edwin, you're not bowling badly but she has lined you up and you look beaten. You can't let her dominate. You must hate her and crush her."

"No chance."

Only too obvious. The poor goop worshipped her. "Well, at least make her work harder. Tell me, is Marjorie tall? Has she got a big stride?"

"Not really."

"So what if you made her reach for the ball outside off stump? And how about taking pace off the ball, so she has to hit it harder?"

He tried and on the fourth ball it worked. She sliced an obvious catch and they were both awed by my tactical genius [hyperbolic Wordpower].

"That's the first time I've got her out since primary school."

"It won't be the last. Now you bat."

I made him wear all of my protective gear. "Dad thinks I'm a wimp."

"I wear all of that. Am I a wimp?" *Snort from Cal.* "Do you feel safer?"

"A bit."

But I was hardly out of second gear when he started backing away. Marjorie looked scornful. I whispered to Cal "Could you tell him what you told Robert?" *He whispered to Edwin, who laughed. I replayed the rest of my pace-is-your-friend routine with Robert until Edwin hit a straight drive off a quickish ball and hurt me. I dropped the commentary: it seemed a bit babyish for an older boy but he smirked just like Robert. Suddenly I wanted to try something else.*

"Okay, Edwin, you've driven a well-pitched up ball, but what if I drop short and make it fly? Are you going to back away again?"

"You bet."

"I can make the ball follow you. Try it." *I tried three short fast ones. He backed away and each time the ball flew past his helmet. I tried one more and he flattened himself.* "Running away simply does not work. I will always bowl faster than you can go backwards. Now, try taking guard on off stump and force yourself to stand still. You might get hit. If it's too much for you, don't do this."

He looked at Marjorie. "Okay."

"Keep your eye on the ball. Hit it if you want to but otherwise watch it go past your left shoulder." *I really hoped this would work. I still couldn't guarantee where my fast ones would go. Phew! Three safely watched over his left shoulder. A fourth knocked down safely in front of his face.* "Brilliant! Now is it easier to see the ball in that position?"

"Yeah."

"In a match you wouldn't take guard on off stump. That was just to show the principle of trying to watch the ball past your left shoulder. Now take centre. Some more short fast balls. Try to stand still, but if you must make a move head for off stump." *Three more short ones whizzed safely past his head. He watched them all. I pitched one up and to my joy he drove it past me. Cal's right, I am a hopeless softie. Even Marjorie applauded and his face lit up.* "Brilliant batting. You made me waste three balls at full pace. You made me change and hit me for four. Am I the fastest bowler you've ever faced?"

"You bet."

"You crushed me. If you can crush me you can crush anybody." *Smirk.* "Now prove it. Crush us all. Express pace from me, honest seam from her, mystery spin from him. You are not going to give an inch to any of us. You are not going to be out. You are going to smash every bad ball." *He pumped out his chest. I pumped out mine for another reason. Instead of using a lesson from Uncle Frank I had just used one from Jimmy. I had power over his memory.*

Edwin batted out of his skin. He milked Cal and crashed into Marjorie. She looked bewildered. There was a new balance in their relationship. "Have you tried holding it across the seam?" *Coach Helson was on fire that day – her first attempt skidded under his drive and bowled him, but he just laughed and stayed in the zone. So did I. Glad animal action unleashed. The other two slipped away and we fought it out. I think I reached 80 again but he stood his ground. He straight-drove an overpitched ball and it was fielded by a tall man.*

"Dad!" *He looked proud of his son, as he should have done, and I felt all gooey again. We stopped and I got introduced to his father, Sam Carter, club captain and ground owner-keeper.*

"Steve, did you just teach my son to bat?"

"Not exactly… I think I just showed him he can bat."

"Steve's the best coach in the world!"

"How long are you here for? You could be the answer to years of prayer."

Chapter 20   Perfect Pitch

In the two hours I had been shopping Steve had acquired two more worshippers. He did not realize. The poor boy still seems surprised that people even like him. Cal and I have more work to do.

At the cricket pitch I recognized Marjorie, the pharmacist's daughter, and Edwin, the son of the club captain. I always thought that each father got the child the other wanted, Marjorie sporty and outgoing, Edwin studious and a whiz at figures. But now I saw a new Edwin – bouncy and assertive. Steve had taught him to bat, in front of his father. Just like Robert. He should get a career as a cricket therapist.

We went off to the pub and talked about the cricket club's forthcoming match against a visiting team, Undecim. Pretentious name – Latin for the Eleven. Did they think they were the only eleven in the world?

"Public school twerps – mind you, I'm one myself." Just when I was ready to dislike Sam Carter he had a knack for making fun of himself. "I went to the same school as their captain, Paul Russell. Same house, actually. I worshipped him. He was funny and clever and a rebel. Then he turned into a bigot and a pillock.[15] The Right Honourable Paul Russell, former Conservative minister, turned banker. And the only good word in that collection is 'former.' Steve, will you play for us and hit him? In fact, could you kill him? Then I needn't pay back the money I owe him."

"Be careful, Sam and Steve, that could be incitement and conspiracy."

"Who plays for our team?" Sam was quite choked when he heard Steve say 'our.'

"You're looking at most of it. Me and Edwin. Marjorie and her dad. Johnny behind the bar. Mr Sawyer the painter and Mr Painter the carpenter. True – it's a local joke."

"Only Mr Painter the carpenter is a much better painter than Mr Sawyer the painter!"

"Cal!"

"But it's true!"

"Maybe, but not so loud."

---

[15] See "The Undisputed Champion Of The World" from <u>A Tale Of Ten Wickets.</u>

"Our President, Ernie Walt, still plays when we're short. He has to be at least 70. Luke Marriott has just joined. I don't know much about him. He's a retired businessman. Then there's the bloody Davisons. They object to everything I do. Unfortunately we need them. If you come to our practice session on Friday evening you should see everybody. Look, Steve, could you do some coaching?"

"Me?"

"You did more for Edwin in half an hour than I've ever done."

"Coach grown-ups?"

"Just analyse and advise and motivate."

"You know I'm not qualified?"

"You're a natural. If it makes you feel better, I'll tell them you're on the MCC ground staff."

"I wish... Sam. Is Cal going to play?" Sam twisted and turned and so did Cal. "Sorry, I've no right to ask. Cal is good enough to play for any side I've ever played for, as a spin bowler who can bat." I knew he meant it.

"The selection committee meets after the Friday practice. Could you join us?"

We broke up. I made plans for Marjorie and Edwin to meet us on the beach and invited them both to dinner at the house. Marjorie accepted on the spot. Poor Edwin was gagging to accept but his father needed him at home. Things were not well in that family. Money worries or something more?

"First one into the sea gets an ice cream!" Cal hurled himself in, no lifejacket, no clinging hand. My heart leapt. The rest of us caught him up and we did a lot of infantile stunts. "First one to the buoy gets another ice cream!" He churned towards a red buoy, about two hundred yards out. We followed. He almost made it, but started to splutter. I froze but Steve caught him quickly and eased him to the buoy. He made long efforts to sit on it, trying to catch his breath and his nerve.

"Get on my back instead." Did Steve really intend to carry him that far? I knew he would try.

"I'm OK now." He let go of the buoy and swam slowly back. We all grouped around him in close escort.

"Cal, don't hold your breath so much. Try like this." Surprisingly it was Edwin. He had a very graceful style. I realized for the first time that as a fellow ectomorph he might be a better swimming model for Cal than Steve.

We flopped on the beach and baked. I ordered everyone into sunblock. Cal did pictures of cricketers on Edwin's back and Marjorie's, but this time in reverse, as blanks in the sunblock. It must have been harder. We dozed for a while..

I woke up first. I looked at Marjorie. She looked stunning. Just like Zoe in her beach photo. Like Zoe – Guilt! Shame! Two-timing bastard! I hadn't thought about her for hours.

We hit the sea again. This time staying within Cal's depth. Edwin gave another demonstration and he started to swim more rhythmically. He finished a long stretch and clung onto Marjorie for a bit to recuperate.

"It's getting wavy."

"I know. Do you like my hair that way?"

"Yes, but I meant the sea."

"I know. Do us all a favour and test your lifejacket now. No one here thinks you're a wuss and everyone here wants you to stay alive." He dashed back to the beach, strapped it on and jumped into the waves. It was not a great surfing beach, like some of its neighbours, but they were respectable. He bobbed around without moving a muscle.

"It still works."

Steve organized a contest. Each of us to launch him on a wave and see how far we could get him. "No cheating by swimming. Arms out in front of you and ride the wave as far as you can." We each had two tries. We got better and gave him some long rides. I heard a lot of squeals, but the happy ones, not the scared ones. I won the contest (but I think he cheated). Finally we all body-surfed ourselves and with the help of the jacket he made it right onto the beach.

"That was the best day I've ever had here!" and we all got a hug and kiss. Edwin looked a bit startled but he took it well.

Back at the house, we each showered and changed quickly. Cal took charge of dinner and ordered me out of the kitchen with a gin and tonic. He made Steve peel potatoes and sent several back. Marjorie did better peeling carrots. He roasted a large chicken with lemon and garlic, alongside potatoes and we adjourned to play Monopoly. Bungle wiped him out again and he retired in a huff to do the carrots and finish off the rest. I opened some special-offer claret and issued it in varying amounts, alongside water. I drew out Marjorie over dinner. She told us of her own dreams of becoming a cricketer and how distant they were: Steve hung on every word.

We devoured all the food and Marjorie asked Cal to marry her.

Cal brought out all the ice cream I had bought. As usual, I had underestimated.

The children ordered me out of the room with the remainder of the wine, They cleared the table and loaded the dishwasher. I drifted out towards the piano. It occurred to me to open up the piano stool.

"Oh my God!" Someone had slipped in a giant Sinatra songbook. The children rushed in. "Ray Corvino, where are you in my hour of need?"

"Mum used to play with a professional singer. He was a legend." Marjorie looked awed: Ray would have been so proud. I broke into <u>All Or Nothing At All.</u> Shyly, Marjorie sidled up to the piano. "Can you sight-read, Marjorie? This one isn't hard and I'll help you as much as I can."

"All or nothing at all, half a love never appealed to me…" She sang a little hesitantly but in tune.

"This was in Ricky Rubato as well…"

"Shut up, Steve! Sorry, but Marjorie's good."

"You are. You have perfect pitch. You need much less help than Ray. Attack the song, make it yours."

We did <u>I've Got You Under My Skin,</u> <u>Just In Time</u> and <u>You Make Me Feel So Young</u> with growing confidence. Steve looked mesmerized. We finished with a tricky selection (which often defeated Ray): <u>In The Still Of The Night.</u>

"I hate to say it, sweetie, but it is the still of the night and I'm not sure I should drive you home."

"I can easily walk."

"I'll walk with you." Only I caught the flash of jealousy from Cal as Steve leapt to his feet and slipped out of the room.

"You're very talented, Marjorie. Not many people could tackle those songs cold. My friend Ray is now a top music agent. I would be glad to introduce you or give him a tape."

She looked stunned and stammered out thanks. Was she a kindred spirit to Steve – unable to believe that anyone would want to do things for her?

Steve returned in his leather jacket. The night was stifling hot. I could not help smiling. It did look great on him, but Marjorie would have admired him in a bin liner.

We walked along for a bit. It was really hot in the leather jacket. She must think I'm a total prat.

"I love your jacket, Steve."

"Thanks. I had this big makeover. Zoe..." *Aaagh!*

"Who's Zoe?"

"A friend." *Lying, worthless shit...*

"A friend who bought you a great leather jacket? Steve... I've met other boys here from London. They've all had girl friends, except for the one who had a boy friend. You're a god compared to them. It would be unbelievable if you didn't have anyone in London. Is your girlfriend called Zoe?"

"I don't know ... " *Suddenly I just had to hug her. Then I let go and looked at her.* "Less than two weeks ago my life was going down the toilet. I was a complete loner, my parents hate me, I had just left a crap school with no future. Cricket's the only thing I'm good at but I haven't got a team and my dad doesn't want me to play. Oh look, there's much more but I'm leaving it out. Then I meet Cal at the cricket nets in a park, and my whole life turns brilliant. Everyone I meet is wonderful ... and now you... and it's making me dizzy. It's like a dream – that's so corny but it's true. I'm scared it's got to end."

She slipped her arm around my waist. "Real enough for you, Steve?" *I pulled her closer and slipped some of my jacket over her. We walked along for a bit. Suddenly she stopped.* "You mean you don't play for a team?"

"School didn't have one, and other teams... just didn't work out and now my dad doesn't want me to play."

"You don't have to listen to him. Sign up for a team and tell him to fuck off. That's what I'd do. You know something, I wish it were like that with me and my dad."

"But doesn't he play in the team?"

"Dad doesn't really like cricket. He took it up for my sake, to give us something to share. He works terribly hard at it, so I don't get embarrassed, but I know he doesn't really like it."

She stopped suddenly. "My brother walked out five years ago. No argument, no warning – he suddenly had enough of living here. Look, Steve …" *Her arm swept over the view.* "Our little town and the beach under the moonlight and the stars… Gorgeous, isn't it? Paint a picture, but don't put in any people. Our little town's dying on its feet. There's no jobs going, no new business. Nobody's making a living. My dad has to do two jobs, my mum works, I work most days in the shop. The farmers are all stuffed. We don't get many tourists. It sounds wonderful being undiscovered unless you're the undiscovered." *She made us walk on.*

"Paul didn't like cricket. He surfed, every moment he could. You can't surf on our beach, so Dad would drive him to catch a wave, sometimes for miles. No one else in our family liked surfing (I was a bigger scaredycat than Cal). At first we all used to watch him, but then Mum and Dad got busier and busier so they started just dropping him and as soon as he could drive he drove himself. So he was … away from us. Then one day he left. Nice thank you note on the table as if he'd spent the night. We get postcards and phonecalls from him, but he's never come back.

"Mum and Dad were really cut up and Dad thought maybe if he had surfed Paul would have stayed. I know that's wrong but when I got mad on cricket, Dad was determined to share it. So he made himself play for the team, and he drives me miles to practise indoors each week in the winter." *She stopped again.* "Do you see why I would rather have your dad than mine? You don't feel guilty about playing cricket. I do. I feel it's eating into Dad's life. And Mum's. And where's it going to take me? I'm a girl. There's no money in it for me unless I get right to the top, into the women's test team. Some chance. You're a boy. You've got eighteen first-class counties to try for, plus loads of clubs. There's villages near here that have a professional in the summer for League matches." *She walked on.* "I could play for one of them. The bloody Davisons are always threatening to do that. If I played for a bigger club with a women's team I would get better cricket and better practice and coaching and maybe get discovered. But if I left our club Dad would stop playing and I think Edwin might too and I think we would just fold up. It wouldn't be fair. Sam works so hard."

"Marjorie, I once went to a posh school and I was in the development squad for the first eleven. You're better than lots of their players. Especially as a bats…person." *We both giggled.* "They must have trials for women in Devon. You could just walk into one. Honest, I'm not just saying that. Just as you could sing for that guy… Ray Corvino."

"Do you think Alice meant that?"

"Of course. She always means what she says. Your singing … made my hair stand on end."

"That's not saying much." *She ran her fingers through it. Tingle, but more guilt!* "You should grow it."

"Everyone says that."

"Does Zoe say that?"

"Well… yeah."

"Sorry. It was bitchy of me to ask."

Now we were both feeling guilty. Something said hug her again. "Where did you learn to sing?"

"My gran taught me a bit. She used to sing in pubs. I mean people paid her, not because she was drunk. She left me her record collection. I was in the church choir for a while, but Dad didn't like it, he's a militant atheist."

"Just like Monsieur Homais."

"Who's he?"

"The chemist in Madame Bovary."

"What's Madame Bovary?"

"It's one of the greatest novels ever written." *Disappointed. What right have I got? Why should she be a reader as well as a cricketer?*

"What's it about?"

"A bored, frustrated woman living in a little country place who has fantasies about a better life and keeps looking for a man to escape with."

"I used to think like that. The boys I met from London each summer, one of them would be my white knight and take me away. And now you Steve, the biggest white knight of them all…" *Yikes!* "Don't panic, Steve. It's fantasy. If I get away it will be under my own power. Besides, you're here with Cal. He has to come first. He loves you to pieces. And you love him."

"Yes. I do."

"I'd have hit you if you'd said no."

"Is it that obvious?"

"Yes. It's not sick or weird. You two fit together."

"I've never met anyone like him. When he's happy he lights up the world."

"And as soon as you met him you wanted to make him happy and take care of him?"

"Yeah."

"I felt the same way last year."

"I'm glad. I think when you love someone you want the whole world to love them."

"Yeah, but not all at the same time." *We laughed.* "I'm home. We live above the shop. Are you going to the nets tomorrow?"

"Yeah."

"Can you make it noon? Dad will give me an early lunch hour."

"Sure."

"Well, see you then."

"See you." *Don't be stupid. Give your friend a goodnight kiss. So I did. Quite long but no tongues.*

I walked right past our house. What an idiot! Of course the brilliant landscaping made it hard to see in the dark but it was really because I was thinking too much. I saw the car and retraced my steps.

"I was beginning to worry. I know he's still awake even though he's zonked. Can you bear to say good night?"

"Of course." *I hung up the leather jacket and had a quick wash. I was sweating, and serve me right for vanity. I padded into his room.*

"Bungle was getting worried." *I hugged them both.* "Steve?"

"Cal?"

"Are you glad you came? Was today all right?"

"Best day I've ever had on holiday. Except when you were struggling in the water and it became the worst."

"I panicked for a second but then I knew you would get me. Steve?"

"Cal?"

"Do you think I'll play in the match?"

"I would be amazed if they've got a better spinning all-rounder. But some teams play people because they've been around a long time or have given something to the team. Or because they know somebody. All you can do is turn up to the team practice and do your best." *Only I'm not playing for them if he doesn't.*

"Steve?"

"Cal?"

"Do you love Marjorie?"

"I love everyone who loves you. I love Bungle." *I hugged the bear passionately.* "Bungle, my darling, my one and only."

"Stupid."

I put Bungle back on his pillow. "Cal?"

"Steve?"

"Thank you for having me." *Giggle. He recognized my ironic use of a conventional formula [Wordpower]. I ruffled his hair and switched his light out.*

I really needed to talk to Alice, but first I needed a giant glass of water.

"Was she worth sweltering for under that macho jacket?" I regretted the tease. Poor Steve clearly wanted a Serious Conversation.

"Alice. I really like Marjorie and I want to be with her again and she told me loads and I'd really like to do something for her. But I feel really guilty about Zoe."

"Steve, did you make some pledge to Zoe never to speak to another girl? Never to make another friend in your whole life, without her approval?"

"No."

"And she would never ask you for such a pledge. You ever meet someone like that, run away."

"I shouldn't have worn Zoe's jacket."

"Your jacket, Steve, not hers. If you're crazy enough to wear it on a hot night, that's your call not hers."

"But to impress another girl…"

"Steve. People like you with giant hearts can be very destructive without knowing it. They love everybody and they can't bear to disappoint anybody. That's you, isn't it?"

"I guess so. I've been really happy lately and I want to make everyone I meet happy."

"Can't be done, Steve, and if you try you'll get exhausted and resentful. You have to think of yourself. Meet your own emotional needs, don't always put others first. It's not even fair on all the other people, never to give them the chance of putting you first. Go back to that leather jacket. Didn't Zoe and Belinda get pleasure from meeting your wish?"

"Yes."

"When you have kids. That's when you decide to sacrifice anything for their sake, even your life. But not before. Above all, don't get into a relationship with anyone because you feel sorry for them or grateful. I meet couples like that regularly in the divorce court."

"Joe said the key to all relationships was intimacy."

"Good thinking. So – Zoe or Marjorie? Who makes you feel – intimate? At ease."

"Well, they both do. They're like two halves of me, Zoe's the book half, and Marjorie's the cricket half."

"So meet both of your needs. See them both. Don't be afraid to disappoint one of them, or both of them if you meet someone else. Don't be afraid to disappoint me, or Cal. That's the toughest one, isn't it?"

"Yes."

"Because he's so happy when he gets what he wants. Don't protest – I know him better. He can sometimes turn that on, making people want to make him happy. His father had that terrible gift. I couldn't bear it for him to turn out that way. Say no sometimes – and when you want to, say goodbye."

I know a good exit line, and I kissed him and strode out of the room. Over my shoulder I said "Sleep as long as you want tomorrow. As long as you want."

Chapter 21   Close Of Play Scores

I let him sleep in. I know I can't have Steve whenever I want him (all the time). I must let him do what he wants, even if it's going out with Marjorie. Or Zoe. I mean, I like M and Z so why shouldn't he? (Mature!)

I ate my breakfast and I left his alone. I didn't bounce on his bed but went on a bike ride with Mum. I see what Steve means about no gears.

He was awake when we got back and looking at my map.

"Where would you like to go, Steve?"

"Haunted house?" Mum won't take me but she might let him...

He looked at her. "I promised Marjorie we'd be at the nets at noon."

"Let's go now!" Then I could get an hour without Marjorie! (Immature!)

"One more cup of tea."

He's a ridiculously long tea drinker, but we still got there by 11-30.

"Edwin! Weeding the pitch by hand."

"Dad's really proud of it. Well, so am I. And it beats working on the farm. I don't know why Dad keeps it going. It loses money and none of us enjoy farming. I suppose it's been in the family."

"Come and bat. You can use my stuff and Marjorie's coming at noon." He looked well made up. Could I get Marjorie and Edwin together? But who would have Edwin when they could have Steve? (Sorry Edwin!)

"This will be good for you because you'll have to adjust each ball from express pace to flight and spin. So concentrate."

He did. It was really hard to bowl at him even when I did all my mystery balls. Steve made the ball fly around, but he didn't run away and blocked everything or let it go by.

"Stop. Edwin, you've done half the job. You've frustrated both of us and we're getting desperate to get you out. But you've hardly scored a run. Two long-hops from Cal," (True) "string of half volleys from me," (Exaggeration!) "Nothing punished. Think about some run-scoring shots. Next one from me I overpitch, I want to see a drive or at least a push and follow-through."

Straight drive. Almost as good as mine!

"Cal, another long hop please. Cut, slash or drive off the back foot. Your choice."

Clean bowled! "Cal! I asked for a long hop, you produce the perfect arm ball."

"Sorry! It was an accident."

"Okay, at least it showed Edwin you can't make up your mind what shot to play in advance. Wait for the ball and make a decision."

Marjorie came and watched and he didn't even notice. Concentration! I gave up and took a little break with my sketchbook. At last he nicked one off Steve. "Great batting, Edwin. At least 30 against a quality attack, and the mystery spinner took himself off!"

I batted and Steve said it had to be a long innings so I really tried not to show off and he was pleased. "Great work, Cal. Taking the easy single." He put on full pace over the wicket, pushing it across me, but he wouldn't give me a throat ball.

"Come on. You did yesterday! Don't be a softie piethrower!"

Finally he let one go and I made room and smashed it!

"You forgot I'm left handed! Bowl one round the wicket at me!"

Wow! Scary again, but I watched it and pulled my head back.

"I can't do another."

"Stuffed again. Not fit like me." The others laughed but he and I knew what he meant. Steve hates hurting people. He shouldn't be a fast bowler.

We made him bat. "See if you can play a long innings."

We bowled and bowled and he hardly said anything. "Edwin, I can reach out there and drive you, so think of another plan... Marjorie, how about across the seam or an off cutter?... Cal, don't overdo that zooter!"

"Just because you can't pick it!" But he could. He was picking everything and hitting us where he wanted. He looked grim, like when he wants to bowl really fast.

"You say you can't bat!"

"You made me bat well, and Edwin and Cal. You hardly bowled a bad ball, you kept going. Did you notice my feet? I did. They wanted to move today and carry my body into the right shot. Trust your feet when they talk to you." He says silly stuff at times, but you remember. "Marjorie, Edwin? Can you do me one more favour? Bowl at me from 18 yards and make them fly."

They flew at him and he hooked them all. Marjorie tried a yorker and he crashed it off the back foot. "Good idea, Marjorie! I saw it late." Trying to make her feel good. I would have gloated. Why is he so nice?

Mum arrived with a giant picnic and for once I didn't eat the last sandwich.

"I need to get back to Dad's shop."

"Not fair, you haven't batted!"

"I'll fill in for you, Marjorie, for an hour, if your dad will have me."

"Alice, you can't!"

"Who says? I've been a shop assistant in my time. And I can have a talk with your father."

After initial shock, David Court the pharmacist accepted my temporary services for an hour. There were not many general customers and the medicines and prescriptions he had to do anyway. An over-conscientious man, working desperately to stay afloat.

"You've been very kind to Marjorie," a little surprised.

"We like Marjorie very much. Me and Cal and Steve."

"We've heard no end about Steve this morning. We didn't meet him last year. Is he your other boy?"

I really should have been ready for that question but it made me stumble. "No, a friend. Anyway, we would all love to see more of Marjorie. Can you spare her occasionally over the next two weeks?"

A wry smile. "I might just as well let her go altogether. Since she met Steve, she can hardly think about me or the customers. And she sings non-stop."

"That might be my fault. We did a few numbers last night. I've been a professional accompanist and I think she has great talent. She's ... fifteen and she was rattling off Sinatra standards. With your permission, I would like to introduce her, live or on tape, to a top agent."

"Marjorie? Are you sure? She used to sing with my mother, and in the church choir, until ... I asked her not to. Would it mean her going to London?"

A strange question. "For a day, perhaps. I could look after her."

"Thank you, but it's not that. She would have better chances at cricket too."

"I suppose so."

"Why would she come back here?" His hands swept over the old-fashioned shop. "Her brother never comes back."

"I'm sorry if I caused you pain."

"No, no." He wrote something slowly and precisely in a register. "Alice. I can just about share my daughter's cricket. But when her world takes in London and a singing career and agents and you and Cal and the miraculous Steve, I haven't a place any more."

"You are totally wrong." He looked amazed. "Pardon me for being blunt. David, I am a family lawyer. I have interviewed dozens of girls Marjorie's age who cannot wait to get shot of their parents. She is not like them. You and your wife will always be a big part of any world she creates."

When I got back Marjorie was smashing Steve's bowling all over the place.

"Alice! Get us out of here, I'm being battered." I didn't know much about cricket, but I felt that Steve was bowling at exactly the place where he wanted to be battered.

Edwin was wide-eyed and Cal was zonked. I made everyone re-hydrate. Cal revived and began his usual embarrassed ritual of giving someone a drawing.

"Is that really me?" Poor Edwin! No self-image.

"Totally." Oh good, that was from Marjorie. Cal had made him look fierce and determined. And a bit taller.

"That's what you look like when you decide to dominate the bowler. Look at it before you next go out to bat. Now Cal's having a nap." No protest. "We might have a dip at 5. Then Chinese takeaway. Then whatever... You two are welcome to join us if you have permission."

"Can we do some more songs?"

I had a major nap and Mum took us to the beach. The others were there. No waves so I went in without my lifejacket. I think Mum and Steve organized a patrol because there was always someone right by me. Edwin gave me another breathing lesson.

Marjorie helped me make a sand cat.

"I think Edwin swims better than Steve. Steve's got more power but Edwin has better technique. And he's a brilliant teacher." Marjorie looked impressed. My cunning plan was working. I signed the cat and Edwin took pictures on his awesome mobile phone. I made him do one of everybody and then mail them to us.

Mum took us home for showers and ordered takeaway. We ate it in the garden as it was still hot and I offered everyone the last spring roll before I ate it. (Manners). Mum took us into the piano room and looked in the stool.

"Marjorie, those Sinatra songs last night were mostly meant for a man. These might suit you better." She held up a music score by someone called Peggy Lee. "This was her standard. Fever. I'll play it once, excuse my voice. Then choose your time, I'll fill in."

Marjorie sort of whispered at the beginning and then got louder. She looked really far away and I drew her without making a noise. "You give me fever..." But I couldn't tell which one she meant, because she was still looking far away!

"I love this one, Marjorie. It's stolen from my favourite, Kurt Weill. You have to talk it as well as sing. Is that all there is…" Steve and Edwin were both staring at her but she still looked far away. "This one's from a cartoon. Lady And The Tramp. I took Cal to this years ago at the NFT."

It was a cute tune but I could see Mum getting a bit teary. "He's a tramp… But they love him… Breaks a new heart every day… And I only hope he'll stay that way". I knew she was thinking of my dad whom I've never seen. I put an arm around her and Steve joined me.

"Sorry, Marjorie, lost the tempo. Try not to shack up with a rover. They're not always as nice as the Tramp. Find a stayer." She pulled out more music from the piano stool. "Oh my god!" She held up the music score from Your Very Own Ricky Rubato. "This one would be good for you, sweetheart."

"I've got a crush on you, sweetie pie…"

"Not as good as Beppo the Wonder Dog!"

"Cal! Rude!"

"She didn't make Steve cry but he cried when Beppo the Wonder Dog sang this in the movie." Marjorie gave him a huge smile. Aagh! Bad move by me.

"This one looks good. Howard Foy wrote this one himself. With Daniel Hill. There was a Daniel Hill who taught at the College. Great guy. Hope it's him and that he made lots of money out of this. This one's tough, Marjorie, moves between two keys. If you can pick up this one you have to turn professional."

She stopped and asked Mum to start over. It sounded OK to me but she was not satisfied. "I'm on the Blue Train, From Nothing to Nowhere…"[16]

"Wow! Honey, you've just delivered a torch song. You'll have to sing it to Howard Foy. Steve's going to fix a meeting." Aagh! Mum! Now she'll hang on to Steve more than ever. She looked harder inside the piano stool. "There's some really old stuff here. Oh hell, tricky piano part. Give me a rehearsal and then try."

"Easy come, easy go, you are here, so darling let's be clear and as we came, let it go…" But I still couldn't tell which one Marjorie was looking at!

---

[16] See Appendix. Daniel Hill is for real.

"And here's a pretty waltz. And a good closer."

"Who's taking you home tonight, after the dance is through…" **She finished and I pinched Edwin!**

"Ow! I mean, sorry. But can it be me? I mean, taking you home? After the dance. Not that we danced. Just as well, I mean for you since I can't."

"I could drive you both, I'm not drunk." **Mum! Give Edwin his chance!**

"Mum, you said the car's making a funny noise. You don't want to break down in the middle of the night."

She gave me a funny look and then one at Steve. "Well, if you don't mind, Edwin."

"Oh no, we'll be fine. If anything happens, I'm sure Marjorie can take care of me." Edwin. I'm so proud. It took real confidence to make that joke against yourself.

She gave Steve a long kiss goodnight but Edwin had his chance! Mum sent me off to do my teeth. "Steve, in case you had not noticed Cal is jealous of you and Marjorie and he has practically pushed her into Edwin's arms. Don't let him control your life. If he wins with Marjorie, he'll try it again with Zoe. Some time I would really like you to take Marjorie on a date. Alone."

"Okay."

"No. Steve, not okay just for my sake. How about your feelings? I've seen the way you bowl at Marjorie, asking her to hit you."

"I do that to lots of bats… people when I'm coaching."

"All right then, what did you feel when she sang?"

"Excited. Like… reading a book I really like and wanting to go on."

"So wouldn't you like another chapter of Marjorie? To yourself?"

"Yes."

Chapter 22 Selection Problems

I vetoed beach and cricket and haunted house and took the boys to Castle Drogo. Small protest from Cal, ready acceptance from Steve. I wish things were the other way round sometimes. As I expected, Cal furiously sketched the fantasy castle and the dead but gorgeous rooms and Steve was absorbed in the story of the people who created it, the effervescent Lutyens with his endless puns and the rich, obsessive owner Julius Drewe.

"I would have hated this house by the time it was finished. Twenty years? He must have thought he was trapped for ever in his life before the war. When his son was alive." Steve glared at the castle. "Hell, I wouldn't want to be stuck in my life twenty days ago." He took a few paces as if starting his run-up and then remembered where he was and blushed. "You know, Alice, I'm always going to be a bowler, not a batsman. You always get a chance to start all over when you're bowling. You get hit for six, the next ball might take a wicket. In batting, you're out once and your life is over."

Cal was almost sick with nerves when we got back. "Sweetheart, I've no idea whether you will play in the match tomorrow but you will play really badly in the team practice tonight if you keep jumping around. Either you have a nap or you have floppy time."

"What's floppy time?"

"I think you young people call it chilling. Doing no kind of purposeful activit. Cal and I have quite a lot of floppy time, especially in winter. Don't you?"

"Not really. I think I'm always doing something – school work, cricket, swimming, fitness, reading, jobs at home."

"What did you do when you weren't doing any of those things?"

"Writing or talking to Uncle Frank."

"We'll have to teach you to flop. Lesson one, it's better to be horizontal. Cal, set up recliners in the shady part of the garden. Lesson two, keep a supply of liquid on hand. I'm going to make real lemonade. Lesson three, light reading only. What are you reading now?"

"Lord Slim: Defeat Into Victory."

"One of Uncle Frank's?"

"Yeah, he commanded the Forgotten Army in Burma in the war. He has a really clear style – I bet he gave good orders. Did you know that Stendhal modelled his style on Napoleon's orders?"

"Steve, stop. I'm giving you some trashy magazines."

I lay out in the recliner in the shade. It was really peaceful, just a hum of something in the background. I wanted to tune into it, but Cal kept twitching and bouncing.

"You're crap at flopping and you're supposed to be teaching me. Still thinking about the match?"

"Yes."

"Your mum is right. You really are wasting energy. Come over here. You're my favourite cricketer in the whole world. You always will be. Doesn't matter what team you play for or don't play for. I don't know what's going to happen tomorrow. Selectors do funny things sometimes. But if you don't play in the match, I know that in ten or fifteen years when you are England's spinning all-rounder they will be mourning in Glendon Courtenay the day that they dropped Cal Devane." *I eased him onto his recliner. It didn't take long for him to fall asleep. Alice came back.*

"Well done, Steve. Now try and do the same yourself, but if you fail dip into these." *She gave me some magazines called* Romantic Interlude. *I started to read a story called "Only A Factory Girl" by Rosie M Banks. The background hum turned into a piano: I recognized some of Marjorie's songs last night. Rosie's story lost its grip.*

I woke to the tinkling of fresh lemonade. Cal and I gulped it down. He was fine, but suddenly I was a bag of nerves.

"What's with you, Steve?"

"I'm coaching grown-up people. Why should they listen to some strange kid?"

"Because you're a god. Why do you think I listen to you? I never listen to anyone else."

"That's true enough." *Alice whispered something to me. I slipped away and changed into my space-fabric top and my Beige Brigade shirt. The outfit when I first coached Cal and my life turned around. She was right. I felt great.*

Alice drove us to the nets. I had no idea how long their practices lasted. I asked her to come back at dusk. Marjorie and Edwin were already there with their dads. She introduced me to hers and I felt myself being examined. Sam introduced me to Johnny, the barman, who was the team's wicketkeeper. I did some catching and throwing drills. Marjorie threw like a man and Edwin threw like a girlie. I realized I had never done any fielding practice with Cal. Bad coach! Alice was right, I've been too soft on him. He had a surprisingly hard throw but wild. Johnny was a fine wicketkeeper, which gave me some hope.

"Stop! Johnny has saved at least twenty in overthrows. We are really making life hard for him. We love our wicketkeeper. Everybody say 'I love Johnny.'"

They obeyed, although the locals sounded embarrassed.

"Let's now prove that we love Johnny by putting all the next throws right into his gloves. That means we look at his gloves at the moment of release. It means we throw on-balance, trying to drive through the front foot. From distance it will help to do a little bunny-hop, like this one," *Giggle.* "It will probably help all of you, especially the young slackers, to throw with a high elbow. From distance, it's no disgrace to throw first bounce rather than direct. But it is always a disgrace not to back up the wicketkeeper or the bowler. Let's see what happens when I try."

Long throw. Please let it go right. It's not the best part of my game. Zoosh! Thank you. Right into the gloves. "Now everybody. I'm hitting the ball anywhere, you don't know when it's coming to you so watch. Marjorie … brilliant as usual. David, good choice, first bounce… Cal, way better… Edwin, perfect. I knew you loved Johnny… Everybody, I love you all for backing up each time."

They seemed to be having fun. Two men arrived, Mr Painter (Zeke) and Mr Sawyer (Adam) who were the wrong way round. Mr Painter was black. Sam whispered to me that he had had a match for Barbados. I wondered when. An elderly man arrived in cricket whites. He moved as if there was all the time in the world. Everyone else stopped and stared.

"Mr President. What a pleasant surprise!"

"Wanted to meet the new coach."

"Ernie, this is Steve Helson. MCC trialist. Our revered President, Ernie Walt."

"And who's the other young chap?"

"Cal Devane. Mystery spinner and left-hand bat. He was here last year."

"Surprised he can see through that hair. Would you like a trim? Still got me clippers." *Poor Cal looked terrified.*

"That's an honour, Cal. Ernie has cut hair on many famous cricketers."

"Really? Who?"

"Me for a start." *Groans and boos from his team.* "I had some to cut then. When I was a boy at Upvern School. And somebody even more famous."

"Who?"

"Tim Morrow." *Cal was gobsmacked.*

"When I had the shop in south London. He was only a boy, younger than you. That was before his mum re-married and he went away."[17]

I rescued Cal's hair. "We're doing some fielding drills, Mr... Ernie. Will you join us?"

"First slip. That's my position." *Not to me, I hope! Mustn't be ageist, but couldn't help it. I remembered the fumbling uncles in Mr Ahmad's team.*

"A few high catches. We're going to call our own names as we catch them. We're going to be balanced, preferably standing still, because we've watched and judged the ball. We're catching them at eye level, and I prefer to do them baseball style, palms out. But above all, we're catching them because we love the ball. We love it to bits. In fact, it's not a ball it's our favourite teddy bear and as soon as we catch him we give him a big hug." *Blush from Cal.* "Nicely, Adam, now hug the bear... Good one, Sam... Edwin, remember the hug! ... Cal, you don't need a victory roll... Ernie, good decision to leave it to Johnny. If it's in range of the keeper, he has the best chance."

A big Merc drew up and this tall guy came out. He was in whites – just washed. No, more than just washed. Immaculate. Even angelic. [Wordpower]. He hugged and kissed a dark-haired woman and a boy about eight, wearing a swimsuit and a

---

[17] See "The Undisputed Champion Of The World" and "The Tiger Will Bite Your Legs" from <u>A Tale Of Ten Wickets.</u>

lifejacket. On the way to the beach, but why did he need to wear it in the car? I heard the woman say "Into battle, my hero."

He ran up to us with an old bat in his hands. Fit. "Sorry to be late. Our boy was not having a good day. Luke Marriott." *Sam greeted him and introduced him to the people he did not know. Cal and me. There were some weird letters on his cricket shirt. I could just make them out.*

"F-R-E... Frenetics! Did you know Joe Barnes?"

"Of course. He did our advertising. 'When perfection isn't good enough, ask for Luklora...' That took us to the top of the laundry market. That's what we do. Did. We were in the laundering business. Clothes, not money. And do you know who designed this typeface?"

"Belinda?"

"Correct. It's actually called Frenetic script. But there is not much demand for a typeface which is designed to look all over the place."

"Did you play with Tim Morrow?" *From Cal.*

"Loads of times. When he was about your age."

I could sense the others getting restless, so I organized a rota of bats...persons and bowlers in the two nets. There were not many bowlers. Zeke Painter was half of the opening attack – the other half, the younger Davison, was AWOL. Marjorie was first change. Sam bowled off-breaks. Edwin could hold an end. Adam Sawyer bowled very slow loopy spin. Ernie Walt had bowled for Devon in the 1950s but now performed only a ritual over in his President's match. These people needed Cal very badly. The batting was more promising – they could afford to hide Marjorie at number 8.

"Before we start, I would like everyone to watch Edwin against me." *He looked shy but Marjorie and Cal urged him to pad up.* "Edwin never did much for you as a batsman. Did not like pace bowling of any kind, right?" *Nods.* "I am now going to bowl full pace against him. Some of the balls will fly about." *He still looked nervous. I whispered to him* "I know you're not scared. It's the audience, right?" *Nod.* "They're not bowling at you. I'm bowling at you and you hate me and want to destroy me. Think of Cal's drawing of you." *Intense glare.*

I held nothing back. "Four off the opening over, no chance, no retreat, met everything or watched it go past. It was a good over but Edwin won it. He was good technically but much more important, he had character and heart. What you want in your opening batsman. Hint!" *Sam and Edwin looked startled.* "Sorry, that was not my place to say. Now, in this session I will make suggestions about technique when I notice something, but nothing about character and heart because I know you've all got them." *Where did that come from? Anyway, they seemed to respond. I could see chests puffed out.*

"Steve, do you mind if I bat first and then practice keeping?"

"What, in the net?"

"Sure. Not to you, but I stand up to all the others. And I want to keep to the new mystery spinner." *One chest puffed out further.*

"Respect! I haven't seen Zeke but plenty of keepers would stand back to Marjorie. Will you wear a helmet?"

"Steve, I'm over eighteen and you're not my dad!"

"Just in case. You don't know what's coming with these bowlers. Get hit in the face and you might lose your ten-million dollar movie contract." *Laugh. Stuff seems to work just as well on grown-ups as on Cal.*

I tried to give just one point to everyone. "David, you're working so hard to get behind the ball that your head is falling away to the right. Stay tall and keep looking over the left shoulder… Zeke, I bet you scared them shitless in Barbados but on a slower surface, maybe a fuller length? … Sam, you're a mean off-spinner but how about the one that drifts away? … Adam, you can't always be an artist! Don't try to flick or glide everything. I want to see boring shots only from now on…" *They seemed to enjoy it. I got a real education, having to bowl exactly the balls I wanted them to hit. I tried to persuade Ernie Walt to join in, but he wanted everyone else to have their turn first.*

Sam was a good batsman but needed to relax more.

Luke was real quality but rusty. "The crowd are jeering. Can't get the bloody thing off the square."

"You're trying to hit too hard, Luke. You have so much time for your shots. Just wait and stroke the ball around for a bit."

There were many squeals from Cal's net. Johnny was a superb keeper: it really lifted him. "Johnny and I have secret signals! Bet you can't read them."

Marjorie danced down the track and hit him over his head. "Shame Marjorie can read them."

Suddenly the mood changed. A truck drew up and two men stepped out, one middle-aged and one young. I knew it was the infamous Davisons.

"Sorry, I'm late, skipper." *He wasn't.* "Jobs on the farm. And I'm not a gentleman farmer." *Sam looked furious.*

"Not a gentleman, anyway," *Luke whispered, and I giggled.*

"You're the city gent who's bought Illsleigh House. These two your kids?"

"I'm Luke Marriott and you have met my son."

"This is our new coach, Steve Helson of the MCC." *Blush. Not yet!* "Cal Devane you met last year."

"We are not worthy."

"I assume you are the Davisons. We are nearly finished. You can join the rest of the session or we can give you one net and you can practise on your own. If you join in you do it on my terms."

"I'm sure we can learn from the MCC. What would you like me to do, coach?"

"I would like you to call me Steve, for a start. And him Cal, and everyone else by their right name. What do you both do?"

"I bat." *Snort from Marjorie.*

"I open the bowling."

"Good. He can bowl at you."

"No point. I've had plenty of him."

"All right, me and Cal. The bowlers you don't know."

"I didn't come here to face kids!"

"Lesson one, respect the bowler until you see the ball. Assume he can bowl, whatever his size. First, one over from me."

I did it at medium pace. I thought I knew what would happen and I was right.

"Are those your only shots? Pull or slash?"

"Worked, didn't they?"

"You hit one six and one four. Two complete misses and two easy catches. That was against medium. Do you think you can play me at full pace?"

"I've seen plenty of fast bowlers, sonny."

"From the other end," *Marjorie whispered and I laughed and let go the "sonny."*

"Try me." *As I expected he tried his two shots. When they did not work and the ball flew at him he backed away. It was pathetically easy to york him.* "No hits, two clean bowleds to me."

"Light's going."

"Who arrived late? Okay, umpire accepts your objection to the light. Captain has to bring on his slowest bowler. Cal?" *I whispered to him* "You've had a look. Now make a plan." *The plan needed only three balls, two short, one arm ball. The victory squeal was cut short when the batsman flashed a look of hatred and stormed out of the net. I heard him muttering about toffs and City boys. I may also have heard "little queer" but I decided to store it.*

"I take it you've retired. You have a good eye. My guess is that you make two fifties each year, very quickly. Against bad bowlers on a slow pitch. Against any decent bowler I bet you average less than 20. You're a specialist batsman, you owe this team more."

"I've scored a thousand runs for this bloody team."

"In how many years?" *Laughter.* "If you bothered to learn some defence and some straight-bat shots you could get your average into the 30s. Do they have good bowlers tomorrow? They'll buy your wicket for ten or less." *He muttered about toffs again.* "Okay, I've seen the specialist batsman, how about the opening bowler? Marjorie, are you okay to carry on? The light is poor."

"Yeah, I've faced him." *The younger Davison charged in.*

"Stop! I make that 20 off the opening over. Twelve to Marjorie, eight wides. Is that the way you normally bowl for your team?"

"Can't get my rhythm in these nets."

"These nets are as good as the MCC's." *As if I knew! But Sam and Edwin got a big lift.* "If you want rhythm, cut your run up in half. Get both arms up high. Feel your body pivoting on your left leg and through your left side. And you might like to look at the target. Top of off stump works well for some people. You have pace, but it is useless without control."

He looked interested for a second. Maybe I could work with him, but then his dad cut in. "Listen, sonny, have you ever done a job of work?"

"No, but I know how to bat and bowl."

"I mean, work on a farm. A real farm, not a gentleman farm. You might learn something, instead of poncing down from London with your little friend and telling people what to do."

"I've had enough!" *It was Ernie Walt.* "This young man's given us three hours of bloody good coaching for nothing. You've never done a hand's turn for this club. I've listened to you for years, bellyaching and calling Sam a toff. Well, I'm not a toff, I cut hair all me life. And I say, fuck off! Sorry, there's a lady present. But fuck off to Illsleigh, if they'll have you."

"I bloody will. This club's dying on its feet." *He flashed another look of hate at Ernie Walt.* "Come on, son."

The son hesitated. He looked tormented. Go on, you must be 20 at least. Say no to your dad, for the first time. He looked up at me, but I couldn't do it for him. He looked away, and shuffled off in his father's wake. Shame. You had a chance to leap to freedom. The farm truck screeched away.

"Drip," *said Marjorie.*

"I guess that's it. Well played, everybody."

"Excuse me, but I haven't batted."

"Mr Walt, Ernie. I'm so sorry."

"I'm not a complete pillock with the bat."

"I'm sure you're not, and thank you for what you said. Now, the light isn't good and in real life, I wouldn't be allowed to bowl against you. How about Sam, Adam, Cal, Edwin?" *Johnny slipped back behind the stumps. They bowled for ages. Ernie stayed on the crease and played each ball at the last possible moment. At last something bounced on him and he was caught behind.* "Bloody hell, Ernie. You're almost unbowlable. With just a little footwork you would score runs as well and you would get on top of the ones that bounce."

Sam whispered something to me. "Now Ernie, I've just learnt you're a ballroom dance champion. What's your favourite song?"

"Who's Taking You Home Tonight?"

"Gosh, Alice plays that!"

"It was always the last one of the night and I always felt happy because it was always with Dorothy and I was the one taking her home. Still do." *I got teary again. Wuss, drama queen or what? But imagine still being in love with the same person at his age?*

"That's wonderful, Ernie. Do you think you could dance with the bat for a minute, as if it were Dorothy? Move your feet and lead the bat. Forward or back and across. Marjorie, could you help us for a minute?" *She looked startled and then got the point and started to sing.*

"Who's taking you home tonight, After the dance is through…" *Ernie started to glide and when I thought the moment was right I tossed one up and he danced towards it and hit it straight past me. Mass applause. Sam silenced it.*

"I don't think we need the selection meeting. Can everyone be here tomorrow at 1-30 for 2?"

Chapter 23　Throat Balls

Dear Zoe Future (Mrs S Helson?)

Heard from Steve at last! Terrified that he had been snared by some local Devon hussy. And he sent insanely bad pic of himself on beach, he says in retaliation for ones I sent of me! Drool! Also one of cutie Cal which Robert drools over, poor fish.

They are playing a cricket match tomorrow. He won't admit it but he is nervous. Told him he's a god but not the same as being there and screaming from the boundary. (Or would that embarrass him?)

The match seems to have more backstage drama and secret history than a Dickens novel...

"Lemonade thanks, Sam." *I could never think of anything else in pubs.* "Look, I'm sorry that I seem to have lost you two players."

"It was going to happen anyway, and I would rather have a dead gerbil in the team than a live Davison." *He stomped off to the bar.*

"You drifted into a long feud, Steve. Will Davison hates my dad."

"Why?"

"Because my dad went to Upvern school. Because his middle name is Courtenay. Mine too. The Courtenays of Devon. Only a cadet, collateral branch, but the county family. Will is a self-made man. His father was a labourer on our farm. Now he owns more land than my father and is much richer. But he still thinks my father... and me ... are keeping him down."

"He might keep him down in the batting order, because he belongs there."

"I wish it were that simple. I can understand Will sometimes. Dad gets all the respect here, but he has achieved far less. Dad made a pretty good mess of everything he tried – the City, the travel business, selling cars, selling wine.

Dad inherited our land from a distant cousin. He had to come out and live on it because he could not make a go of anything else. And he's making a pretty good mess of our land, too. Steve, I love my dad but I see things as they are."

"Okay, but what's that got to do with the cricket team? What's so hard about accepting that your dad runs the cricket team? Because he's a way better player, because he works his guts out on the ground. Like you."

"I wish my dad were a groundsman. That would make him really happy and he would be brilliant. On his own or running a team of people..." *He looked wistful.* "Steve, Will Davison is out to finish my dad. He would like to buy all of his land. He bought a piece last year – I forced Dad to make him pay over the odds. Will wants the cricket field. That will be the last thing to go. My dad would sell our house first and live in a caravan before he sells the cricket pitch. If Will gets the pitch, it will be the end of the Carters. The Courtenay Carters. I'm not sure what he'll do with the rest of his life. Probably fuck up his son. He hasn't finished that yet. Mark can be quite human when his dad's not around."

Sam came back with a big tray of drinks. I took a gulp of lemonade. It tasted crap after Alice's homemade. I'll have to think of something else.

"What are you drinking?"

"Double cranberry juice and soda. Adam put me onto it. Adam gave up drinking to concentrate on his painting." *I could tell what he thought of Adam's painting.* "Try it."

"Umm." *Whatever his merits as an artist, Adam was a whiz in the beverage department!*

"Finish it! I'll take the lemonade. Thanks for teaching me to bat. It means a lot. And to my dad."

"Where's he gone now?"

"To finish buying a round for everybody. Because he's the captain. No, because it's a compulsion. Getting your round in first, and for all the people who never buy you one. Look, tomorrow's match. Against Undecim. You had better know that they cheat."

"How?"

"They bring their own umpire. He used to do first-class so he does both ends. But he's paid by their captain. Paul Russell." *He stopped. He looked fierce again, like Cal's drawing.* "I don't know why they bother. They are way better than us. Including Russell. I so, so wish Russell were a crap cricketer but he isn't. He's a top batsman. But they cheat. We never get a decision, they always do. You have to bowl them or get an undisputable catch. Or get them retired hurt. You could do that!"

"Why do you play them?"

"Russell's given money to our club. And an interest-free loan to Dad personally. They were at school together. The same house. Dad used to idolize him. I think he still does, or rather, what he remembers... Anyway, he comes here with his team and they're allowed to play by their rules. Listen, we've all learnt to live with this. You and Cal don't have to. You're both a bit special. You'll be playing for loads of great clubs. England eventually. You don't have to play for a team of ... beggars."

"I really want to play for you. Cal too. And I like the idea of retired hurt."

Steve says he met a great bloke called Luke Marriott who knew Mum and Dad.

We went out into the garden. Cal was literally sitting at Luke's feet.

"Did you really play with Tim Morrow?"

"Loads of times. He was really too good for us even at eleven. He played for us to be with his dad. His two dads. I'm sure he knew he was always going to play somewhere better. But we weren't rubbish."

"What was he like?"

"Lovely kid. Like you." *Smirk.* "Bouncy but not cocky or lippy. He did fall in love with my wife. But then so did I. When I met her she was working in a laundrette and I collected laundry from somewhere every day just to see her."[18] *Giggle from Cal, respect from me. That's love.* "We got married. We went into the laundry business together. We had a chain of laundrettes, but then we sold them and went into the high end of the market. Specialist laundry for top-class hotels and restaurants. We just kept the one laundrette where we

---

[18] See "Love In A Spin" from <u>A Tale Of Ten Wickets.</u>

first met. We have our anniversary there each year." *Smile. No giggle this time, respect all round. Marjorie looked a bit awed.*

"We took our business into Europe and the US. We did brilliantly. I did miss playing for the Frenetics but I played overseas. I had a season for the Hollywood cricket club when we went for laundry contracts in the movie business. When you see a Hollywood movie, watch the credits for 'Laundry services by Luklora'. I played with Russell Crowe once. Before Gladiator."

"What was he like?"

"Quality but a bit up himself. He was furious with our fast bowler for calling him Rosalie." *Xan, I bet! But somehow I didn't want everyone to know that he called me Stephanie. Coward! Traitor!*

"I had a great life, terrific business, great lifestyle, wonderful marriage. We wanted children and we had a few setbacks but eventually we had a boy. We were warned against having another, but we now had a boy like Tim for Laura to spoil and tease and me to play cricket with." *His face clouded.* "Things average out. You can't always score a century." *I'd used that image myself.* "Our boy is not Tim. Billy is … not normal. They say that he is 'on the autistic spectrum.' They didn't say whether he's on the red end or the violet…" *Flash of rage. I had a picture of evasive doctors and consultants.* "Billy hardly speaks, and it's not usually coherent. He is physically un-coordinated. He has deep anxieties and compulsions. There are good days and bad days. We have money. We can buy a lot of help and care. But it is still exhausting."
Cal squeezed Marjorie's hand.

"We sold our business. Got a fabulous price but I don't like the way they run it now. I dabble in venture capital. I'd like to invest in … well, human beings, talented people I believe in. But Billy is pretty much a full-time job. We're here because of Billy. We were driving to Bude to see Laura's mum. Our car broke down and Billy got hysterical. Some nice people took him and Laura into their house while I was waiting for the AA and he calmed down, miraculously. It turned out they wanted to sell their house and we bought it on the spot. Surroundings make a big difference to children like Billy. And air, I'm sure. We sold our London house. He seems much better already, and he loves the beaches." *I tried to imagine dropping your whole life, and living somewhere totally different for the sake of your child. He must have read my mind.* "I don't want anything different. Billy's our boy."

Right on cue his wife waved across the pub garden. Closer to, I could see she was a real looker. Dark hair, sharp features, big, wide mouth. Like Zoe! Guilt! But no wonder Tim Morrow fell in love with her. She led Billy by the hand. He was still wearing the swimsuit and the lifejacket. He made a strange sound and dived into his father's chest.

"Sorry, we're late. He didn't want to leave the rock pool. And he didn't want to change clothes. I'm afraid I let him keep them."

"Hello, Billy. I've got a lifejacket too. Only I can swim now. Would you like to swim? Steve can teach you. And Edwin and Marjorie and me." *Billy looked at Cal for a second and then grabbed at his T-shirt. It was the Ursinho one, with their little bear mascot.* "Do you like that, Billy? That's a bear. Have you got a bear? I've got a bear called Bungle." *He didn't care who was listening!* "Do you want this T-shirt, Billy, I can get another?"

"No!" *Laura cut in firmly.* "He mustn't just take things."

"Sorry. Okay, Billy, I can't give you this bear, but would you like to have his brother?" *He gently pushed Billy's hand away and pulled out his sketchbook from his back pack. He stripped off the T-shirt and quickly copied the logo.* "Here, Billy, do you like this bear? You can have him." *Billy took the picture with a big smile and gave another sound.*

"We think that means thank you. I'm amazed, Cal, he's never taken to a stranger that quickly."

"Maybe it helps that I'm not much bigger than him because I'm such a weed."

"No, Cal. He's not normally at ease with children his size. There's more."

Billy was reaching for Cal's pencil and pad. "Do you want to draw something, Billy? Another bear? Let's go somewhere quieter. How about that table near the barbecue?" *He took the smaller boy's hand and led him gently away.*

I felt Marjorie suddenly clench my shoulder. "God, I hope Cal becomes a dad." *We watched them both, in their own world, drawing.*

"Steve, a quick word?" *Sam Carter took me aside.* "We did not have our normal selection meeting, because we didn't need to. But the committee did meet and we decided unanimously to offer you the post of club professional."

"Me? I'm sixteen, I'm only here for two weeks and I'm not qualified, certainly not MCC…"

"Don't get excited, Steve, it's not much of a job and we could only pay you £20 for each match and coaching session."

"I don't want to be paid. It's an honour to be in your team."

"Then can we just put you on the fixture list and notify the county? Club professional: Mr S Helson?"

"On one condition. You offer the job to Marjorie when I resign." *Club professional… I rehearsed my TMS interview. 'Well, Jonathan, I got my first professional engagement at sixteen at Glendon Courtenay…"*

"Don't hesitate to give advice when the amateur captain makes a mistake. For a start, do you really think Edwin should open?"

"Definitely. He's got the technique and the attitude and it would deepen your whole batting order."

He told Edwin in front of Marjorie. They were both well made up. Then he took Edwin home. "We've still got a farm to run. Unlike you gentlemen of leisure." Jeers. I suddenly realized that I hadn't bought Sam a drink. Nor had anyone else.

The Marriotts had been having a long chat with Alice. I noticed that neither of them touched alcohol. That had to be because of Billy. But for the first time they both seemed really relaxed. They hardly even glimpsed towards the far table, where Billy was drawing with Cal's pencil and paper. Finally he stopped and Cal led him back to his parents.

"Which bear is Billy's and which is mine?"

"Oh my God!" *The two drawings were almost the same.* "He likes playing with crayons but he has never done anything… like this."

"You can never tell when an artist will emerge. I was early but he might just have been … waiting for something. He likes bears. Get him lots of different bears and see if he'll draw them. By the way, he's left-handed, like me."

Steve told me all about Cal and Billy and we all cried (including Mum and Dad).

He almost crashed out in the car and did not even want to drive the last bit to the house.

"Can I go to bed now?"

"Of course, sweetheart. Was it really tiring looking after Billy?"

"No. Yes."

"I'm so proud of you."

"It wasn't hard. They worry about him too much, Luke and Laura. I suppose I would too but Billy's okay and they should just let him do things his way unless they're dangerous. Anyway, everyone looks after me, you and Steve, and Marjorie and Edwin and Mrs K at home, and maybe it was time for me to … pay it on. Look after someone else."

"That's called maturity. Does it mean you're too old to be carried to bed and tucked up with Bungle?"

"No." *I moved to do the carrying part but she scooped him up like a cushion. Respect! He's not a total weed! Did my mum do that to me? I wish I could remember… She detoured to let him hug me. I'm still amazed at the way they live.*

I said good night myself and had a glass of milk. I had another go at Lord Slim and at Rosie M Banks. Neither lasted long.

Four-thirty. Awake and nervy. Pathetic for the club professional! Go for glass of water. "Can't you sleep, either?" *Jump out of my skin!* "Scaredycat!"

"Am not! Just startled."

"Wet yourself!" *Start of hysterics.*

"Don't wake your mum. I'm running. Come with, if you want." *Nod.* "We had better leave a note." *4-45 RUNNING Back 5-30. S C. He added tons of Xs and Os.*

It was set to be another scorcher. We jogged uphill and looked down at the village. On the level we rehearsed bowling actions. "Devane… bowls to Pratface. Big swing, Helson's under it. Caught. The sixth wicket for Devane, Undecim all out 70 on this perfect pitch. What's that funny twisting path?"

"It leads to the haunted house. Shall we take a look?"

"No."

"Scaredycat!"

"Can't get spooked on the day of the big match."

Back to the house, quick sluice. Agree to attempt short snooze.

"Good afternoon, people. I let you sleep in for your big match but there is now no time for a cooked breakfast." *We shared my healthy sportsman's repast, and packed cereal bars and bananas for later. Alice hoisted a giant pack of water and insisted on sunblocking us both. I felt little and looked-after again.*

There was an odd booming noise in the pub. I thought the sound system had gone wrong. "Now I could have been with the IZ at Highclere today. But I said 'No, I'm booked for my favourite ground and my favourite tea – and my favourite bowlers!" *Horrible cackling laugh. I saw Sam looking glum with a man about his own age in whites. He had an MCC sweater, and an MCC tie holding up his trousers.* "Three centuries in a row. That's what I call good manners!" *Alice bought me my new cranberry mixture. Cal wanted one too. Sam gestured us over.*

"Alice, please meet Paul Russell, the visiting captain. Alice's son, Cal. And our new club professional – Steve Helson." *He looked me up and down. I felt creeped out suddenly. Not one of those? I remembered someone saying he was homophobic.*

"That's an MCC sweater, isn't it? Steve wants a trial there. Steve's a god. He's our fast bowler. I'm the mystery spinner."

He looked down at Cal. "Well, a mystery spinner! But can you do it with a full-size ball on a full-size pitch?" *Microsecond of rage followed by angelic smile. Very mature, Cal!* "Trial at Lord's, eh? Let's do a deal, you two give me another century and I'll arrange a trial at Lord's!" *Another cacophonous cackle [Wordpower]. But he meant it. I just didn't want to be there any more.*

"Let's warm up". *Cal was eager but I felt ashamed for slinking off. So much for the club professional. He had spooked me.*

We changed quickly. Edwin and Marjorie were already warming up in the nets. (Surprise). Cal and I loosened up. "Ah, the mystery spinner and the would-be trialist! Care to bowl me some half-volleys on off stump? I'd like to re-tune my cover drive."

"I think I should bowl at my own side." *No return of his smile.* "But as you're the opposition, we'll give you the nets and perhaps one of your bowlers might do the half-volleys."

The rest of our team were on the ground, apart from Luke. Our best batsman. Their players had arrived too. They had a lot of different coloured caps. Sam pointed out three who had played first-class, and their paid umpire, a ferrety man with insignia and impedimenta [Wordpower]. We repeated last night's catching and throwing drills. "We love Johnny… remember to hug the bear…"

Cal dropped a sitter. I was about to remonstrate but I saw what he was looking at. Luke had arrived with Laura and Billy. And twelve teddy bears. Billy solemnly lined them all up behind the boundary. Laura took off a scarf. "Make this your talisman, my hero." *She tied it round his neck and they kissed passionately. Yes, that would be a good warm-up routine. He bounded onto the field, full of apologies, pausing only to catch a huge skyer casually with one hand.*

Sam lost the toss and they batted. "Now Sam, as always, Ron will do both ends as the professional umpire. We'll fill in at square leg."

"Opening bowler, S Helson," *Sam called to both scorers. It occurred to me that I hadn't met ours. He passed me a new ball. Ohmigod, I'm opening the bowling in a real match. I've waited for this for ever. What do I do? Which end do I take? What field do I have? Panic. Oh very professional.*

"How about the pavilion end, Steve? Give you what wind there is. Zeke, fine leg. Ernie, first slip." *Groan, but maybe Johnny will go for everything.* "Me second, David gully. Luke cover point." *Sam now needed my guidance. Don't be stupid, you know how you want to bowl.*

"Could I have Edwin as short mid off? Short as you feel comfortable. Adam, square leg, on the single. Marjorie, patrolling just about all of leg side. And can I have Cal as a sort of deep gully, left of David?" *He looked disappointed but I directed him. Luke said something to him and he brightened up.*

Jonathan Agnew on Test Match Special gives my field to listeners.

Their number one is one of the first-class players. He could take me to the cleaners. Better throttle down and bowl line and length… No. This is the best day of my new life. I'm a glad animal fast bowler.

Great. First ball on target. And it hurries him. The first-class player. Stabs it in front of him. Next ball. Another stab. Rolls out on leg side, between Marjorie and Adam. Easy single. "No!" from his partner. They don't fancy me!

"Top fielding, Cal!" *Glow. Good stop, saved my maiden. My first professional over. Approval from Victor Marks on TMS.*

"Bowling, Steve!" *Sam sends me to the fine leg boundary. Much squarer than Zeke had been. Zeke a bit stiff. Number two helps himself to a boundary and a two. But on the last ball he doesn't want a single.*

Second over. I know I'm getting faster. Am I bowling downhill? Feels like it. Beat him for pace alone. Johnny makes a big show of taking it above his head. In again. Shit! Over-pitched. Straight past me for four. Hardly tapped it. Well, he played first class.

"Good comeback, Steve!" *It was. Jagged in. Where did it hit him? Inner thigh, I hope. Hurts there. He leaves the next one. Pretty close to off stump. I might have played it, but he was first class. Try yorker. Dug out. Easy single. I've given Marjorie too much to do.*

Better over from Zeke. Mostly defended. One quick single. Then a push wide of Marjorie. Easy single. Striker wants another! Not there and not his call! He really doesn't want my end! Marjorie fields. Remember you love Johnny! Oh yes. Into his gloves, bails whipped off. Big appeal. "Not out". Their square-leg umpire. Bloody hell, Edwin was right. They cheat.

"That was out!"

"Can't see from there, sonny. Have to be certain. Over."

My next over. I sense Cal still seething. The rest of our team seem to take it as normal. Something tells me to take a few extra paces. Move back my marker. Make sure the batsman sees it. Feeling great. "Truly fast bowling carries with it a sensation of pleasure: it is to be borne along in a sense of elation." Frank Tyson. Start the run-up, gather momentum. Umpire stops me, batsman not ready. Oh yes, you were. Just trying to break my rhythm. Not angry. Still in elation.

"Sorry, Steve." *Johnny's let through four byes. Not ready for the extra pace. He retreats a little. Next ball, full length, off stump. Drive. But it's too quick for him. Edge. Over Cal's head. Desperate leap. Finger tip. Four lucky runs.*

"Great effort!" *But he's heartbroken. My fault. Why didn't I trust him at second slip and put Sam there instead? Good decision by the professional! Breathe. Back slowly. Remember what you told Alice: in bowling you always get another chance.*

Same ball a little wider. Nicked! Regulation catch for Johnny. Concerted appeal. "Not out."

Remember your manners. "Thought I heard a nick."

"Have to be certain." *Force myself to smile. But elation has gone. All right, I'm only allowed to bowl you. So - fast and straight on middle stump. But of course that makes me drift down leg. Effortless four for the first-class man. Twelve off the over! Well done, the professional.*

"Great over, Steve. No luck." *Nice of you to say so, Sam.*

Zeke bowls wide of off stump. We need dot balls after the professional's last over. Batsman goes after one. Edge. All along the ground. Past Ernie Walt at slip. Poor old boy doesn't move. I run a long way from fine leg to retrieve. Two runs. Sam pushes back the field. There's an easy single. Thanks, Sam. Bring number two to my end. Zeke bowls. A little closer to off stump. But he isn't interested in the single. Tries a big shot – drags it on. Bowled! No appeal necessary. "Over."

Big huddle. I congratulate him. He says "Thanks for my wicket, Steve."

Next man in is their captain. The Right Honourable Russell. Wearing an MCC sunhat. Both openers had helmets. Sunhat. Tempting target. Or does he want me to be tempted? Not bowling at him anyway.

First-class opener pushes me to Marjorie. Easy single. "Can she come in now, please Sam?" *I'll give him everything front of the wicket on leg side if he plays a shot.*

"Beautiful wicket, Sam. As always. Thank you so much. One leg, please?"

I hate batsmen who ask for one leg instead of leg stump. And does he think I'm a spinner? "That is leg stump. Right arm over, five to come." *Elaborate marking of his guard, using a bail. Who do you think you are, Shivnarine Chanderpaul? Don't get angry. Stay elated. Walk back slowly to my new mark. Something catches my eye. He has shifted his guard to middle. Crafty sod. Trying to mess up my direction and maybe con the umpire that he is still on leg stump.*

Want to fine tune your off drive? Try this one! Full length, fast. "Offering to shape" *as they now say. Meaning what? Text book forward defence. Shit, he can bat. Same again, next ball. Same stroke but now some follow-through. Good shot. No hesitation in taking two.*

I'm not planning the next ball. Just run in and see what my body wants to bowl. Full length, fast again but moves back on him. Hit on the pads. In front. Another concerted appeal. He looks up at his umpire. "Not out. Going down leg." *Shall I point out that he changed his guard to middle? No. Will make no difference. But why bother to con the umpire when you own him?*

I bowl the next one wide of off stump. Give myself a dot ball to calm down. Exaggerated leave-alone. Last ball. Yorker. Perfect! Hit his toe. He's hopping about. Another concerted appeal. It was right on the crease. Can't refuse this one. "Not out. He hit it. Over."

Sweet smile. "Sorry, ump. Didn't hear the nick."

"Those were both out!"

"Keep your voice down. I was warned about this. We're playing with a stacked deck. We'll get him my next over. Don't tell anyone but move as I walk back to my mark. Go deeper and squarer. Backward point. Quite deep. That's actually unfair play, but against this lot…"

Decent over from Zeke but they milk it for six between them. They are quality. Right Honourable Sunhat ends up back at my end. "Sam, can I have four slips just for one over? David to three, Luke to four? Cal, staying just where he is." *I say this a little louder. Did anyone notice?*

"If you're sure, Steve." *Edwin is still short mid-off. I've left big gaps on off side.*

Now for my cunning plan I actually want a half-volley on off stump. Get Sunhat to tune his cover drive. Damn! He doesn't buy it. Forward defence. "Edwin, much straighter. Regular mid off." *Now he's got a free hit to most of the off side. Same ball, please. He can't resist. Four to vacant cover boundary.*

Please make my next ball work. I'll sacrifice the rest of my career. I'll work for sick children, I'll wash the feet of beggars. Push the ball into the palm of my hand, but change nothing else. Same run-up, same action, same follow-through, same intensity.

Thank you, whoever you are. Perfect slower ball. He attempts the same shot. Way too early. Miscue. Looping over my new fourth slip. Cal's moved to his secret position.

He hasn't picked it up. Now he has. Got ground to make. Ball dying. Throws himself full length. Fingers under it. Mega squeal!

Sunhat has not moved. "Fine effort, young man, but you mustn't appeal unless you're certain you caught it."

"I am certain!"

"You can't be certain in that situation."

"Are you saying he's cheating?"

"Not at all. But it's part of the spirit of the game that you don't appeal for that kind of catch unless you're certain. Important for a young chap if he wants to play for the right sort of team. Anyway, if he's not going to withdraw the appeal the umpires must decide."

"You know that neither of them could see, Paul. And we haven't got the funds for cameras and a third umpire." *Sam is white with fury.*

"Not out," *say both umpires. I think Cal might cry. Luke puts his arm around him.*

Breathe slowly. Time for another cunning plan. Walk down the pitch. Look at a place half way down. Glare at the batsman. "Okay, Sam, could I now have Zeke at deep backward square, Luke at short square, David at short mid wicket, Marjorie deep mid by the boundary marker? Cal, everyone else, as before." *Jonathan Agnew predicts a bouncer.*

But I bowl the same slower ball. Sunhat has moved back and across in anticipation. He changes his shot hastily to aim again for the vacant offside. A horrible smear. Looping up again towards Cal. He charges in. Oh hell. Too excited. Overruns it. Has to backpedal. Offbalance. Grab. Drop.

"Throw it in, Cal!" *Zoosh! Well gathered, Johnny. At least they did not get a run. Looks away. I think he is crying now.*

"Very bad luck, young man, but I don't think your big friend's very happy."

Is that your idea of cricket? Messing the mind of a twelve-year-old? No more elation. "David, back to gully. Zeke, short fine leg. Luke, Marjorie, come in short where you feel comfortable. Edwin, back to short mid off. Cal, point. Yes, same level as David." *I don't want him moping. I want him involved. Ready to attack the ball. And with a good view of what's coming.*

Same offer. Sacrifice the rest of my career, the children, the beggars, and I'll rescue endangered species. Only this time I want a throat ball. One.

Same run up and delivery stride but this time something tells me to flick my wrist forward. Ball on a length. He starts forward.

Yes! The ball explodes on him. Startled squawk. The ball would have crashed into his face, if he hadn't jumped back – and fallen on his arse. "Steve!"

"Great take, Johnny!" Overhead again. Saved four byes.

The batsman takes his time getting up. Next ball, still full length but from wide of the crease. Same flick of the wrist. Explodes again. He's retreating but it follows him. On his arse again! Yes! Johnny can't take it this time but Zeke fields and Sunhat isn't going anywhere. "Over!"

Thank you. Whoever. Two throat balls. Who says I'm not Psycho?

Chapter 24 Tea Time Score

First Class picks up six from Zeke's next over. That leaves me the Right Honourable. He delays me. "Not like you, Sam, to leave a spot in the middle of the pitch." *He prods an area a long way from where I landed the throat balls.* "For once, makes it worth having a helmet."

Good decision. It makes a satisfying clang when I hit it. Second ball – on his arse again! "Are you letting him have another? Persistent short-pitched bowling."

"These are well up, Paul. He's getting life. If you're a bit shaky, retire. We'll let you back."

Nice one, Sam. Third ball, fended away off the glove. Caught by Johnny. Hardly worth appealing, but we try again. "Not out. Forearm." *To be fair, he had guts. Some batsmen would have walked to get away from me.*

"If that hit his forearm it would be broken," *says Luke to no one in particular. Ball five. Not trying a throat ball this time. Inside edge, just past the stumps. And Johnny. Jammy four. He has the grace to look sheepish. Ball six – cut him in two! I wonder what make of box he wears? Shit, twinge of pain in right shoulder. Must bowl through it.*

A cheap over from Zeke. And I've still got the Right Honourable. "Hold it a moment. How many overs has he bowled?"

"Five."

"Then this is his last. His little friend's mother told me he is only 16." *Oh Alice! You thought you were just making conversation and you've forced me out of the attack!*

"He's right, Steve. ECB rule. They think you're a delicate little flower." *Giggle from Cal and Marjorie. Hell, I haven't taken them a wicket. Back to the mark. Throat ball – just past helmet. Throat ball – clangs helmet. Yorker – uproots middle stump. Even his paid umpire cannot give him a reprieve. Venomous look at me, being hugged and feted. Number four takes guard, honestly on middle stump. Three balls to get them another wicket. Suddenly I'm totally spent. Two total pies. I think he was too surprised to hit them. Come on, something to remember last ball. Oh yes, a full toss. Four. Well worth remembering.*

A glimpse at the scoreboard. 44 for 2 off the first eleven overs. Not bad, but now I'm off for twelve overs and Zeke can't go on much longer. One first-class bat well set. Loads more batting to come. Can't see where our next wicket's coming from.

"Sorry, Sam. You needed more wickets from me."

"Steve. The sight of Paul Russell on his arse is the summit of my cricket career. You'll be back. The rest of us will try and hold things for you."

"We need wickets too. Think about Marjorie. She uses the seam and the ball's still got one. And this lot are arrogant. I bet they think she's no good because she's a girl. And Cal might give them a shock."

"Maybe…" *Obviously unconvinced.*

Alice has water for me on the fine leg boundary. Huge gulp and pour on the rest.

"Steve! That was terrifying! What happened?"

"He's a cheat. And he played mind games with Cal. But that wasn't professional, having my private feud with him. I didn't do enough for the team. Scuse me!" *Pick up and hurl it in. Ow! Hurt right shoulder. And why? They had settled for one.*

"It's a game, Steve. Don't beat yourself up. There are other things in life. Look at that!" *Billy was paying no attention to the match. Instead, in deep concentration, he was marching all his teddy bears one by one right round the field.*

Sam puts himself on as first change. Decent enough off-spin but no threat and field spread. A short inspection and then they milked him for eight an over. Zeke getting tired and dropping short. Eight an over the other end. Hundred up. Both batsmen well set. First-class opener close to 50. And my shoulder really hurts. They get two runs because I have to bowl the ball in from the boundary. I haven't got a second spell.

Drinks break. "You got a problem, young Steve? Shirt off, and hit the floor."

"Yes, sir, Mr President!" *Ernie worked his fingers into my shoulder.* "Owww!" *But relief!*

"We had massage in one of my shops. I learnt a few things."

Marjorie on for Zeke, I think a few overs too late. Johnny comes up to the stumps. Cordon on the offside. Oh-oh! Right Honourable Sunhat replaces the square leg umpire.

As I hope, their number four is a sexist. Without waiting to see whether the girly can bowl he decides to charge her and smash her over her head. She sees him, pushes the ball wide, swinging further away. Brilliant take by Johnny, bails off! "Not out." *We are all sick, but Luke, at cover point, looks thunderous.* "You might get a better view from here, Mr Umpire, where the sun isn't in your eyes." *Sputter.* "Enjoy the rest of your innings," *he murmurs to the batsman. Flush. The next ball he runs a single to hide at the non-striker's end. Partner watches the remaining balls carefully, contenting himself with 2.*

Number four still feeling guilty. I can tell by the way he starts slogging. Clearly in torment he takes 16 off Sam's first three balls. Another crazy swing. Miscue. Colossal skyer. Whose? Please not mine! (They've picked a wimp as their professional). "Edwin's!" *You beauty! He does everything right. Hugs the teddy bear and then disappears as everyone hugs him. Marjorie and his dad the last to let go.*

Luke turns to the Right Honourable. "Are you sure that wasn't a bump ball?"

Over number 24 came up on the scoreboard and I knew Steve could come back to kill more people. But Sam wants me! All I've done is drop an easy catch. What if I get spanked?

"Sam wants to save me for the death. You're on because you're the mystery spinner, so spin it. Give it lots of air. Don't overdo the zooter. Bowler's name – Devane!"

Steve and Sam help me set a field. I wanted Ernie closer at slip but I didn't think I could ask.

"Don't be mean to my little cutie-pie!"

"Marjorie! They'll think I'm a baby!"

Secret whisper back. "That's what we want them to think."

Remember to stay tall. Both hands high. Yes! Surprised, weren't you? It was a good ball. Had to defend. Same again, a little spin! Edge. Ernie too far back. Bounces in front of him and spins away. He turns to chase it –

and crashes to the ground, holding his knee. Oh poor Ernie! But the shits take a run.

We help Ernie off. Marjorie's dad, David the pharmacist, gives him a big pill. They take ages to give us a sub – and then Right Honourable says we cannot put him at slip!

I wanted Sam there anyway. Next ball at their number-one batsman. Four!

"Don't worry, it was a good ball."

"I know." He was not really watching me because I'm a little kid. I knew what to do next.

Chinaman! Just like he did to me in the nets. It seems years ago. He misses. Stranded out of his crease. Easy stumping and even he can't refuse it! Shit! Johnny hasn't read it either. Fumble. Escape.

"Hell! Really sorry, Cal."

"No, it's my fault. I forgot the secret signal." *Sam has to stop them arguing.*

Right. Time for the zooter.

Oh, Cal. Don't try the zooter. To a bloke this good it's a long hop. Six!

"Good idea, Cal." *No it wasn't, Sam. Yorker. Good comeback, but still 11 off the over.*

"Sorry, Sam".

"Why? One bad ball. You're getting another."

Marjorie fights really hard to bowl dot balls. Three dot balls, then a two. Should have been one, but the sub didn't try. She's angry. Bloody hell, she's bowled a throat ball! Surprised. Fended away. Lobs straight up. Caught by Johnny. She gets a group hug. This time me and Cal get the longest.

Cal's next over. At the good opener. Strictly orthodox, changes of pace. Off drive, too high off the splice. All right, it was a tough chance but the sub might have gone for it. Two runs, no apology. Next ball, looped up, really inviting. Straight drive. Not quite at the pitch. Skyer. Luke running frantically along the boundary. Caught above his head! Magic! What are they protesting about this time? "Sorry, Cal. Stepped on the boundary rope." *Six again!*

"Have a blow, Cal. Well bowled. You'll be back." As if. Two overs, nought for 19.

Ernie returns. "I'm faster on one knee than their bloke."

"Thank you, sub," *from Sam.* "For your contribution," *adds Luke.*

The new batsman's another sexist, I can tell. And Marjorie's bowled him! "Across the seam. Your idea, Steve." *And of course Right Honourable notices that this is her last over. Stupid ECB. But I want her end, anyway.*

"Adam, next over?" *Oh no. Whisper from Sam:* "Five pounds says he'll get a wicket."

Wide-wide-four-four. Long hop. Miscue. Zeke's under it. Another teddy bear is hugged. At least our team can catch in the deep. Six wickets down for 180. Me and Zeke back for second spells. We could just get them all out for less than 200. "Give me some magic, Ernie."

He inflicts more pain ("Baby!"*) but my shoulder loosens up.* "No treatment on the field, please!" *I'll assume Right Honourable meant that as a joke. Re-set field, just a slip and a gully. Almost everyone else on one. Make them hit to get a run. Henry Blofeld gives field to listeners.*

To the first-class opening bat, approaching his century. I seem to be completely weightless as I run in. Yes! Another throat ball and you didn't like it! But mustn't waste my second spell working him over. Keep the throat ball for surprise. Enforcement. Give him everything. Outswinger, inswinger, slower ball, cutters. Hit him on the pads. Appeal (just for the record). Umpire's hand twitches! He's going to give us a decision. "Not out." *Can't bear to look at me or give an explanation. Yorker, dug out. Plain straight ball. Forward defence. Last ball. He looks round the field for a single.*

"This one's mine. Watch for the single!" *Wide of off stump. Chase that if you want your single. Maiden over.*

"Bowled, Zeke!" *A little faster. Refreshed by his break. Or was it me? Anyway, just one lucky four off the over.*

"Sam, can I have two slips and bring up Zeke to leg slip?" *Let me get the opener and they're finished. Number eight is rubbish. Zeke will get him. Give him everything this over. He tries a leg glance. In the air, just wide of Zeke. Damn! Four runs, could have been one. But Sam's giving me leg gully as well! Offer him the same shot. He takes it on the hip instead. Wide of off stump again for the last ball.*

Zeke bowls well again. Our whole team's on fire. "Great throw, Adam… Stopped, Ernie!" *And I meant it.*

Hell, he is good, the first-class opener. I'm giving him everything I know. He meets it. Just the odd single. Protecting his partner.

Zeke yorks the number eight. Seven wickets down. Score 210. Good performance. And number nine looks hopeless.

Back to my mark. "This will be his last over of this spell!" *Right Honourable calls this out loudly. That bloody six-over rule. I've got to come off. They'll have a few overs left to thrash for 250. I must get him out. Three defensives. Jaffa! Best ball of my career! Beats his defence. Everyone's up in the air. But it is only a dot-ball in the scorebook. Big inswinging yorker. Dug out. Last ball, last chance. I've done everything. Except Uncle Frank's fun ball. The one which made me look stupid. Stop dead in my run-up and bowl a wrist-spinner. Yes! He looks stupid. Flat-footed swish. Missed completely. Just past the stumps. But he's still there. Professional failure.*

Scrambled leg bye off Zeke. First-class to face him. Tries to drive him. Not allowed to. Finally he charges. Over his head. Great shot, but a bit desperate.

Criminey, Sam wants me to bowl again! And the good guy's just got a single. He'll be facing,

"Trust yourself. Sam thinks you're the best bowler for this situation. Three wickets to get with your name on them."

Same field as last time. Batsman's impatient. No, I'll bowl when I'm ready. Steve told me that.

He skips down the pitch. Cover drive, four runs. Applause from his team. Handshake from Sam. That's his hundred. I couldn't give a toss.

"Relax! It was a good ball!"

"I know." **I love him to bits but don't interrupt me right now!**

Cal stops in his run and swats at a wasp. I couldn't see it. Bowls. Batsman down the track again. Not there. Spins back on him. This time Johnny gathers. Stumped by miles! That wonderful Chinaman.

"Well bowled, son." *Cheesy smile. Don't you dare pretend that you were giving your wicket away after your hundred! Cal doesn't even look at him. I join the others mobbing him.*

"Beautiful ball. He didn't read it. Was the swat the secret signal to Johnny?"

"Not telling you!"

Number ten comes in. Orthodox, flighted ball. Stabbing defence. Jeers from his team mates. Same ball again. Big flash. "Great catch, Ernie!" *It was. Threw his hands up over his head.*

Number eleven. The zooter. I knew he couldn't resist it. Hit on the pad. In front. Big appeal. Pleading, puppy-dog eyes. Blimey, he's given it. Maybe he has a heart after all. We've dismissed them for 220.

"Lead us off, Cal. Three wickets."

Blush. "Don't want to."

"Then I'll carry him off!"

Squeal. "Marjorie, let go!"

She hoisted him and turned to Right Honourable. "I'm having a quickie with my toy boy. Could you save some tea for us?"

Chapter 25 Late Result

Edwin's mum had supervised the tea. It was the first time I had met her. He looked like her, not his dad. She seemed really tired, but brightened when Cal asked for the recipe for her lemon cake.

"Steve! Cal! You haven't met our scorer. Dorothy, this is Steve, our new fast bowler and Cal, our new spinner." *She was a bit plump and even I could tell that her blonde hair was dyed and she had a bit too much make-up. Married 45 years and he was still thrilled that she was his wife. I got a bit teary again and could barely make out my figures of 12-3-36-1.*

Cal admired the scorebook. "Dorothy, that's beautiful. You must be an artist like me!"

"Funny you should say that. The man who taught me to score – people said he was an artist. And he was called Mr Scorer. I was his secretary when Ernie had a shop in London. Lovely man. In finance. Shame he went to prison."[19]

The Right Honourable was booming through the pavilion. "Hope to see a bit more of you at the crease this year, young Edwin. Shame you're not at Upvern. Remember the coach there, Sam? How he bawled us out if we backed away?" *More mind games. You're a coward and your father's broke. I saw Sam and Edwin flush. I walked up to them. Ignoring the Right Honourable I said* "Hey Edwin, do you want to warm up?"

"You've just bowled twelve overs flat out."

"I've got plenty more like that. Of course if you're scared…"

"Fuck off."

He padded up. "Take my chest protector."

"You'll need it."

"I'll be down the order."

---

[19] See "Final Score" in <u>A Tale Of Ten Wickets</u>.

"I'll give it back to you when you join me." *Confidence! David Court padded up too. My heart went out to him. Marjorie's dad, who didn't really like cricket, taking the heat as opener. Sam was giving Dorothy the batting order. I went over to check.* "Number six? I'll get a nose bleed at that height! Swap me with Marjorie. She's better than me."

"We may need eight an over when number six comes in. That's asking a lot from her. We may need to block it out when number eight comes in. That's asking a lot of you." *Good thinking!*

"Cal, number 10?"

"Fraid so. Unfair, I know, but I can't ask the grown-ups to drop below him. Except for Ernie, who probably can't bat anyway. Everyone's already dropped one for my son. What if he's out cheaply? They'll say it's favoritism and the Davisons were right."

"Bollocks. But I'll tell Cal."

He was eating more lemon cake. "Look, they've put you number 10, it's not because you're no good, but in teams like this…" *He waved me aside.* "Win without me. Tell me if I'm needed. I'm going to play with Billy. That will help Luke. He's a god. Edwin and David are waiting for you."

Marjorie and Luke were at the nets too. We bowled alternate overs at each opener. I was glad to see David stand up straight and Edwin look implacable. I worked up to full pace. No alarms for either, but oww! Bloody shoulder.

The openers went out. David to take first strike. I watched their opening bowler take a long run-up. Out first ball to Cal. He might be angry. Close catchers all around. First ball. On target. No great venom. Nice one, David. Push for two.

"He's not as fast as you." *Luke was watching too.*

"Maybe he's not warmed up."

"Not as good an action as you." *He certainly doesn't look like a glad animal.*

"He's played first class."

"Plenty of donkeys in the first-class paddock." *We watched the other opener. Just a little medium-pace dobber.* "That's the danger man." *I bowled at him in tandem with Marjorie, to simulate their attack. He played us both with so much time.*

He is a god. Why didn't he play first class? "Try and bounce me, please." *I hurled one halfway down. Mega-oww! And he pulled it like Ricky Ponting!* "Thanks." "Young Steve, get out of there at once!" *Ernie pulled me away and made me lie face down. He worked and worked my shoulder. Torture but it freed up again. I tried to get up.* "You stay, there. You'll not be needed awhile."

He was right. David and Edwin were accumulating without alarm. As I expected, Right Honourable was a fussy captain. Lots of field changes to unsettle the batsmen. And use up overs. He stationed himself right in Edwin's face at silly mid off. Two balls defended then bang! And he's on his arse again!

Luke tapped my other shoulder and pointed. Cal and Billy were solemnly drawing each of the twelve teddy bears.

They're starting to fret about the run rate. Relax, Luke to come. Quick singles. Careful, they can all field. Especially the guy who subbed for Ernie and made such an effort for us. (Not.) Punch from Edwin. Wide of mid-off. Easy single. David wants another. Good pick up by the guy who was sub. David could struggle. "Bowler's end." *Bullet throw. Slight fumble from bowler. David's got a chance.* "Howzat?" *Borderline. Oh shit, it's their umpire. 42 for 1.* "Break both legs, Luke."

Laura gives him a huge kiss. Great warm-up routine, Luke, but remember the two-minute rule!

Takes middle-and-leg. Their fast bowler comes in. Crash. Driven straight past him for four off the back foot. Casual. All the time in the world. Where did Luke learn to play? One defence, one leave-alone. Another four. Front foot, on the up. Deliberate, no hurry. Over.

Short conference with Edwin, who relaxes visibly. Knows Luke will take over responsibility for scoring rate. The tiddly medium-pacer. Edwin watches very carefully. Single. Luke takes guard. Respect. Single off last ball to keep strike.

Fast bowler back. More fussy field changes. Much more defensive. Crash. Four. Force off back foot. Hardly short at all. Loads of time. Bowler and Right Honourable look a bit sick. Next ball: straight drive. Four. Nearly kills their umpire. Shame (about the miss).

Next ball very wide of off stump. No wide given. Same again. Next ball short on off stump. Swivels, tries to pull. Underneath it, taken by wicketkeeper. Appeal from Right Honourable at slip! Joined by keeper and bowler. Luke looks unconcerned. Zeke unmoved at square leg umpire.

Out! Given by their umpire. No conferring with Zeke. Our best batsman triggered. Victor Marks murmurs "Oh dear!" on TMS. Luke looks thunderstruck. Says something to Right Honourable. Stomps back. Mutters to Sam, next batsman. No one goes near him except Laura, who hugs him. He calms down. Finally I nerve myself to talk to him.

"Of course I didn't touch it. Keeper did not even appeal until Right Honourable Cheatingsod."

"What did you say?"

"Just reminded him of what he said to Cal when he batted. The stuff about spirit of the game and not appealing unless you're certain. Listen, there's nothing out there to worry about."

Edwin's lecturing his dad. First time that's happened? Quite right, Edwin's the senior man. Sam takes guard. Right Honourable booms something at slip. Ignored. Sam settles in. Right Honourable moves a fielder, so Sam has to look up and settle in again. More gamesmanship.

Edwin takes six off next over. Right Honourable tells tiddly medium-pacer to take a blow. Luke pleased with Edwin. "He was their best bowler."

Fast bowler back. No worries for Sam. No god like Luke but a well-organized, determined batsman. He had not needed any technical advice when I coached. Slow left-arm replaces tiddly medium- pacer. Accurate but no mystery balls! Cal's more of a threat. Five off first over, no risks.

Fast man makes final big effort at Edwin. Actually looks fast for first time. Bouncer. Hooked. In front of square. Four! Where did that come from? We never practised that!

Partnership building nicely. Slow left-arm bowling wide of off-stump. One turns. Watched by Edwin.

Another fast bowler. Very long run-up. They don't rate him, he didn't get new ball. Thank you. Eight off over.

No worries. I look away at Cal, still drawing teddy bears with Billy. Maybe there are more important things than cricket?

Appeal. Sam's walking back. Shaking head. Hurls down gloves. "My own bloody fault! I know this team. I know this umpire. So why do I pad up?" *Another trigger victim. Hell, I've got to pad up. Luke relieves Zeke at square leg umpire. Doesn't speak to any of their team.*

Adam's in. Hope he will play straight occasionally. Conference. Edwin's in charge. . Listen, Adam!

Edwin's milking the slow left-arm. Well, he is a farm boy! Adam's infuriating the fast man. Everything glibly glanced or glided. [Alliterative Wordpower!] Well, he is an artist! More bad body language from fielding side. We're on top again. Drinks. David brings them out. Must be last 20 overs.

Out! Adam lbw. Occupational hazard of compulsive leg-glancer. Might actually have been out this time.

I'm in. Check kit. Edwin's still got my chest protector. He can keep it. Don't want to break his concentration and these bowlers are pie-throwers. Check score. 90 for 4. Six point five an over needed. Edwin's well set. I'm the last big hitter. If we get a good partnership we'll win.

Please let us win. We deserve it. We're the good guys. The little village with old men and kids against the swells. Who cheat. If we win I'll trade the rest of my career… and care for children, beggars, endangered species … and free hostages in terrorist camps.

"There's nothing special, Steve. Trust your feet."

End of the over. Edwin to face slow left-arm. Easy single. "Leg stump, please umpire."

Watch. Slow, doodling ball. Feet say go down the pitch, drive it over his head. Message over-ride – not first ball. You're the club professional. They need you. Check stroke. Dreadful smear, just wide of backward point. Lucky not to be caught.

"Yes!" *Edwin calls the single. Summons me. Quite right.* "Listen to your feet, Steve. That's what you told us."

Next ball he gives perfect demonstration. Pupil teaching coach. Down the track, first-bounce four.

Next ball, short and wide. Attempted cut. Mistimed. Fielded on the bounce by Right Honourable at wide slip.

My God, he's appealed. And he's staring at the umpire who's in his pay. Umpire's sweating. Come on. You were first-class once. Be true to yourself.

Finger goes up. "He hit that into the ground." *Couldn't help myself. Look at the bowler. Isn't he going to say anything? He looks away from me.*

"That's out." *Umpire can't look at me or Edwin. He is sweating really badly now. And should be.*

Walk off with Edwin. Put my arm round him. Some stares from them. Who are you looking at? "Great batting, Edwin. They cheated you of fifty."

"Don't care. Just beat them." *Glimpse at scoreboard. 96 for 5.*

Edwin gets standing ovation. Not just from our team and supporters, but from strangers. And quite right. He disappears under group hug.

Johnny's in. Wicketkeeper. Good eye, light on feet. A bit short of power. "Johnny, they're crap. They're also cheating scum." *Were you listening, Mr Multicoloured Cap?* "We're not blocking for a draw. Can you give me the strike?"

He grinned at me. "Suits me, Psycho." *My nickname must have leaked out.*

Good as his word. Sharp single off first ball. Umpire has to move quickly. "Ooh! Feel a bit giddy. Sorry, skipper." *He looks terrible. Right Honourable looks sick too.*

David rushes on. "Let me through, I'm a pharmacist." *Pushes past Right Honourable. Puts umpire into recovery position. Feels pulse and forehead.* "This man has a serious heatstroke. I'm taking him to my pharmacy. I have a remedy."

"There's not many overs left. Surely he just needs water?"

"Don't be ridiculous. If this man stays in this heat I won't answer for what happens to him. He needs special hydration and then at least an hour in a darkened room. You and you, give him a chair lift to my car!" *Instant obedience. After all, he's a professional.*

"I'll take his place." *Sam took over the umpire's coat.* "Luke and I will do alternate ends." *A break for us at last. Now they'll actually have to get us out.*

Last ball. To me. Thrown wide. No problem at all. My feet can get me there. Thwack. Six over extra cover. Crowd noise, including squeal. Glad Cal saw that. Hundred up.

Self-styled fast bowler back against Johnny. Another sharp single. I love you so much, Johnny. I'm leaving you everything in my will! Think you're a fast bowler? Pass the pies. Thank you for twelve. Missed one down leg side. "Yes!" *Johnny, my dreamboat! Taking a bye to the keeper.* "There when we want it, Steve. He doesn't take cleanly and he can't throw."

A lot of fussy field changes. Why bother – you have to bowl another 18 overs? But wasting time now might mean bad light at the end. He thinks of everything, Right Honourable Scumbag.

Slow left-arm again. Feet say go down the pitch, hit a first-bounce four. Quicker ball, feet say block it outside off stump. Hit on pad. Silly appeal. Bowler's forgotten that there's now a proper umpire. Tossed up. Obey feet again. Ball sails over mid wicket boundary. Tossed wider. No problem, feet move again. Missed. Dart back into crease but bails are off.

"Owzat?" *Stumped. Stupid, arrogant, unprofessional ghit. I've lost us the match.*

"Not out."

Protest. I must say, Luke, I would like a reason myself. "Ball was not in his gloves." *You mean they cheated again. Calm down. Keep focus. Defend the rest of the over.*

Tiddly medium pacer back at the other end. Johnny to face. Luke whispers to me to watch him. Johnny's defending carefully. Keeper back. Johnny leaves one. Bad take. "Yes." *I'll have the bye for that because you're no good at your job.*

"He really should not mask the keeper." *Right Honourable complaining that we're unfair?*

Luke, why do you rate this bowler? My feet say walk into the buffet and help yourself. Another straight drive. And just to show them something new, a whip through midwicket. Eight more.

What is so hard about this batting game? Your feet take you somewhere and you hit the ball. Right Honourable shuffles his attack, but these aren't bowlers, they're waiters. Johnny tries for another single, times it so well he gets four. "Sorry, Steve." *Don't be silly, Johnny, you're allowed to enjoy the menu as well.*

Applause with mingled squeal for 50 partnership. I must have scored most of it.

Right Honourable puts himself on. Johnny facing. Please let me face the Right Honourable. I refuse to believe that he is any good. I'm going to humiliate him.

Reverse sweep a six with one hand. For starters. Everyone available stopping one. Okay then, three or five, please Johnny.

Unbelievably slow. Johnny waits. But not for long enough. Great flailing mow. Huge skyer. "Mine!" *That bastard again who made no effort for us. Now he runs back full tilt, catches it over his shoulder. Right Honourable congratulates fielder but I know he thinks himself a tactical genius.*

Johnny stomps back in a flood of self-loathing. I know what he feels. Out to that filth. 150 for 6.

Heart skips a beat. Marjorie's next in. Rush to meet her. Hug her without thinking. Whistles from opposition. Embarassment. Start babbling advice. "Relax. Don't worry about me. Keep going. Psycho."

Johnny and I crossed. Me to face. Fielders scatter to boundaries. Right Honourable ambles in. Even more unbelievably slow. Feet twitch. Message override – no, it would be unbearable to get out to him. Another horrible smear. Lucky it falls into a gap. Bowler throws up hands, theatrically.

"No!" *I think Marjorie meant the shot, not the run. Summons me to mid-pitch conference.* "It's filth. He's filth. Listen to your feet and clear away the filth."

Of course. Straight boundary is shortest. Two sixes there. One over cover point, because I've got a fan there. Lots of noise. Renewed when crowd realizes that my fifty came up with the second six. Helmet off, point bat. Hug from Marjorie. Malcolm on TMS reads out the stats.

"Very well batted." *The tiddly medium-pacer is the only opponent to congratulate me. Ignore the last ball of the over, well wide. Need to think. Another conference.*

"Well ahead of the run rate. Don't need big shots now, let's just work singles."

"Don't be stupid. Carry on. They're cheating scum and we want to rub their noses up their arses."

"Ouch!"

She defends an entire over of the tiddly medium-pacer. And she needs to. You were right, Luke. "Maiden to the maiden!" *Right Honourable cackles and his team join in. Must be the way he tells them*

Opening fast bowler back again. Packed offside field. Wide of off stump. No, I'm not buying. More like that and a couple of bouncers. Watch these over left shoulder. Eleven dot balls. Fans silent. Feet say they've had enough. Short again. Feet say open the body up and hook. Good effort by deep square leg but it's still six. Fans erupt in relief. Normal service resumed, but suddenly I'm tired. 174 for 6. Nearly fifty to go.

Marjorie, my darling. It's you I really love. Sorry, Johnny. I rewrite my will. She takes over the strike for a while. She must know. She takes ten while I rest at the non-striker's end. But it does take some time. 37 now to win, five overs left. We need one more big over. Another conference. "Thanks. I needed the break. I'm great now."

She's facing. Right Honourable brings back slow left arm. Good move. No bye to keeper. Everyone on the single. Two good shots but straight to fielders. She's fretful. Next ball. Attempted sweep. Not her best shot. Bounces a little. Top edge. Caught by Right Honourable. Fury. Anyone but him. 184 for 7.

Zeke is in. Clean hitter. Non-existent defence. No sense telling him to block. More pernickety field changes. First ball tossed up. Foot down the pitch. Pulled. Miles over midwicket. 190. 31 to make, 26 balls. Conference? He once played for Barbados. I don't feel right about telling him what to do. Instead, "How many to come?" *I ask Sam loudly.* "Two left this over." *Equally loudly. Subtext: block them. Next ball, much the same. He thinks of pulling it again, changes his mind. Straight up in the air. Caught by bowler.*

Another triumph for the professional. Too wimpy to take charge. Instead I mess partner's mind with subtext.

Oh no. Cal's next man in. All his protective gear on. He looks tiny. Rush out to meet him. Hug. Don't care what anyone thinks. Conference. Now I am taking charge.

"One ball this over. Ignore it if it's off the wicket. Otherwise block it. I do all the calling. We are going to win because we are good and they are going to lose because they are cheating scum and their bowlers are pie throwers."

"Yeah." *Was he listening?*

Even more fiddly field changes. Right Honourable hauls people in. "He won't hit it off the square."

"I'm left handed." *Exasperation from Right Honourable. He has to move fielders. First trick to Cal. Stupid of Right Honourable. He should not have set field until he knew, and he could have looked at Cal's gloves.* "Leg stump, please, Sam." *Copying me. Now he knows he can kick away anything which pitches outside his legs.*

Last ball, tossed up. Down the track. Over bowler's head. No one there because he wouldn't hit it off the square. Four. Over. 27 to make. 24 balls. Two wickets. Me to face. Find eight or ten off the next over and pinch the strike. Conference.

"Great block, Cal."

"I listened to my feet, like you told us. I better do the scoring now. You're stuffed. You're not fit like me." *He always winds me up that way.*

First-class fast bowler back on again. Field setting now takes ridiculous amount of time. Light's really closing in. But maybe they don't know how to set the field to me? Finally they decide to offer me a single.

First ball. Short, outside off stump. Boundary potential. Force off the back foot. Not timed, but extra cover has a little ground to make. Single completed "Look for two."

"No!" *Firm. I dart back to bowler's end.* "My call!" *Reproving. Takes guard from Luke. This time centre.*

"Left hander." *More field shuttling. Hordes of close catchers. Staying over the wicket, trying to push it across him. Fast, but offline. On his hip. Reflex shot. Flick. Safe. Four runs.*

"Did he get bat on that?"

"Did I signal leg byes?"

"Round the wicket." *Short legs brought into place.*

Bouncer! In bad light. Cal jerks head away at last second.

Bastard! I don't care about the match now, I'm going to punch his lights out!

"Stay there, Steve! I'm in charge. Captain, he bowls one more like that I no-ball him and send him off."

"If he can't take it, he shouldn't be playing."

"Ten years old." *I see Cal about to protest and say twelve, but I stop him. He looks ten and it strengthens Luke's point.* "If he can't dismiss a ten-year-old without bouncing him in bad light <u>he</u> shouldn't be playing. One more like that and I'll get him banned. His choice."

Ostentatious new run-up of just four paces. Attempted yorker. Full toss. Surprise to Cal (maybe he's still in shock?) Jabbed away at last second. Squirts just past gully. "Yes!" *One more. I've now got the last two balls.*

"Right hander."

"What am I allowed to bowl at him?"

"Whatever you bloody like."

"Hold on, Steve. The light is now poor. The captain should take him off and complete the over with a slow bowler."

"No. Leave him on."

Next ball. I can't see it. Back my hunch that it's short. Hook. Too late. Top edge. This is the end. No. I've got more on it than I thought. Light's bad for them too. Fine leg hasn't picked it up. Six! Thank you, whoever. You can have everything I promised before, and I'll find a cure for cancer.

Fifteen to win. Less than a run a ball. Just get the strike.

Last ball of the over. There to be driven but I just want to push for a single. Aggh! Bad choice. Thin edge. Concerted appeal from behind. It's all over. Can't move. It's too cruel.

Sudden silence. Luke is frowning. He did not detect the nick. Or maybe he did. But either way he's going to give me not out. Serve them right, the way they've played.

Cal's at the other end. That settles it. Can't play like them. It would betray him. Destroy everything that's gone right since I met him. "That's out." *I walk away.*

"Very well batted." *Tiddly medium-pacer again. Joined by slow left arm this time.*

I trudge off. Henry Blofeld on TMS says "He's getting a standing ovation. We'll ask Malcolm for his stats …" *Don't bother. I don't care. We've lost.*

"Just a minute, Steve." *Henry is cut off. It's Ernie.* "It's asking a lot but can you be my runner?"

"Of course. Honoured." *Brave old man with your bad knee. But I've left you and Cal too much. Fifteen. Three overs to get them, but in bad light.*

"Eighty four. Great knock." *I could have whacked four more fours, won the match and got my first hundred. Now I'm just a proxy.*

Lightning three-man conference. "Ernie? I do all the calling, not you. How's your knee? Can you move?"

"I can bloody dance."

"Great. The bat is Dorothy. Take Dorothy to the ball." *Suddenly realize that's a pun. Wordpower!* "Both of you, trust your feet. Enjoy! They're not!" *True. They're arguing.*

Right Honourable objects to my being a runner! Unfair advantage! After 12 overs flat out, running round the outfield and whacking 84? Over-ruled by Sam, who maintains Luke's ruling on the light. "I'm not allowing a fast bowler. Keeper up to the stumps."

Right Honourable wants the tiddly medium pacer. Cal facing. Round the wicket, close fielders including two short legs. Keeper does not want to stand up to him in bad light. Even with helmet. Fair enough, although I can't imagine Johnny objecting. Eventually Tiddly agrees to slow down. Bad idea. Sure enough it spoils his rhythm.

"Wide ball!" *14 to get, still 18 balls. Angry with himself. Goes back to his old pace, fires it behind Cal. No chance for keeper. Four byes! 10 to get, 17 balls. Right Honourable summons third man to fine leg. Bowler mutters. In again.* "No ball!" *Called by Luke. Instant change of shot to wild slash. Over slips. To now vacant third man boundary.* "Three men behind square on the leg side." *Recriminations. Captain's fault! 5 added, still 17 balls. Just survive.*

Jaffa! How did it miss everything? Cal pretending he didn't play at it! 5 needed off 16 balls.

Another good ball. Blocked. Pointless dive by silly mid-off. 5 off 15 balls. Next one pitched up. Drive. Not quite there. Loops over silly mid off. "Yes!" *Bloody hell, Cal. Ball retrieved, hurled in. I dive full length for batting crease. Big appeal.* "Not out. Light's too poor to judge because of all the time-wasting." *I love Luke. Now <u>he's</u> getting all my money.*

"Sorry. I thought it was easy. Forgot you were stuffed." *Win or lose, you are dead meat, Cal! 4 to make. 14 balls. Can Ernie survive two of them?* "Right-hander." *This time elaborate checks on legside field. Leave it or block it, Ernie.*

Straight, well pitched up. And he dances. Takes Dorothy to the ball. Drives, past the bowler.

"Yes. At least two!" *But they've given up on it! Enough on it to make the rope. We've won!*

I'm on my knees. Babbling thanks. Everything I've already promised and I'll clean the Taj Mahal with a toothbrush.

Chapter 26   After Match

Steve has just puked his guts out. I hope it will be good for the clematis. He looked green in the car and bolted as soon as we reached the house. Teenage rite of passage. I administer the remedies I use when Cal pukes (chocolate, brushing teeth, wrap in rug). He rallies enough to hug Cal good night and then subsides on the couch. I force Cal to brush his teeth before allowing him to crash with Bungle. Back to the casualty. A little colour. I think he'll live.

"Oh God, I'm so sorry!"

"Why? You held it together until we reached the garden. Very considerate."

He still looked miserable, so I simply took his head in my lap.

"The head must lie upon the block…"

"That was wont to lie in Queen Catherine's lap." He was pleased that I remembered. His uncle Frank's story has some deep meaning for him. I stroked his hair. "Growing out. We'll be able to take you to Yasmin soon. How much did you have to drink?"

"Can't really remember. I had to buy a jug for my fifty. I had some from that and Ernie bought me a pint. I didn't want to refuse him. But Joe said never drink when you're thirsty so I had two pints of cranberry soda first."

"Beer on top of cranberry could give you a jumpy stomach. On top of excitement. How does it feel, being the hero of the day?"

"Amazing. I never thought anything like this could ever happen to me."

"You paid a lot for this day, sweetheart. Enjoy every minute. And remember there will be more."

"I had to sign autographs! Cal too."

"Hmm, I bet his took longer than yours."

"Way longer."

"He did his special signature. You were ages getting to the pub. Would the fans not let you go?"

"No. Right Honourable made a speech…"

***

"Mr Speaker... Sorry, force of habit..."

"He's been out for ages. One of the first losers of 97. Other people had a Portillo moment. Laura and I had a Russell moment, actually a bit more, right on the floor of the laundrette." *Luke is such a god. Must find out more about him from Joe.*

"Anyway, Sam, before we move off to Lord Illwynde's place for tomorrow's fixture, I just want to thank you on behalf of us all for such a brilliant match – rather more competitive than in previous years, thanks to your astute dealings in the transfer market" *Glance of loathing at me.* "Thank you also for looking after our umpire so well at a critical stage, and we would like that formula from your pharmacist for heatstroke..."

"What <u>did</u> you give him?"

"Sugar, water, colouring and a little oil of clove to make it nasty."

"Now we have a little presentation for you. First, a new edition of my biography of F S Jackson, the England cricketer who had a sad decline and became chairman of the Conservative party." *Laughter from his team.* "We've signed it but the unsigned ones are much more valuable. There are copies of this book lying unread in dressing rooms all over the world." *Laughter and assent from his team.* "And another presentation. As in previous years, Sam, here is a cheque for a thousand pounds. Sorry it can't be more, but blame Gordon Brown. May I suggest you spend it removing the new ridge in your pitch at the far end?"

***

"And he went on for a bit, hinting that we had cheated."

"It's common for guilty people to accuse others of their own crime." Long silence. I recognized Steve struggling to say something important. "Then something else happened, didn't it?"

"I went to have a piss and Right Honourable came beside me."

"Oh my God!"

"No, it wasn't that. Although I did wonder. He made sure we were alone and then whispered 'Young man. About that trial at the MCC. I would look somewhere else. I'm on the MCC Committee. You had fun today on a bad pitch but it was a bad career move.' Could he really stop me getting a trial?"

"I doubt it. I'll write to him in London as your lawyer." But I could not help being nervous that Steve now had a rich, powerful enemy. And Cal.

"Don't care anyway. I'll play here for the rest of my life. If they still want me as their professional. I love our team. I loved helping them … to play better and… achieve something… and feel happy."

"Steve, you have to be a teacher."

"Did you see Johnny, adding the word Victory to the chalk notice about the barbecue tomorrow? Are we going?"

"You bet we're going. I want to hear the Sixties tribute band. The Small Fakes. I told you my uncle Cal used to jam with the real Small Faces."

"Shame Luke had to go early, but we had a really good chat."

***

"Luke, thanks for being umpire. Over that stumping."

"No need to thank me. You weren't out. He was a cheat. Like most of their team."

"You didn't take any crap from any of them."

"You don't get anywhere in the laundry business by letting people wash over you."

"Wordpower!"

"I don't see why we should play them ever again. I'll get in touch with Joe, see if we can get the Frenetics together and bring them down here. It would be a much better game."

"Luke. I heard people talking. Wondering why you aren't playing for Illsleigh. Bigger club, better fixture list and right on your doorstep."

"They failed the Billy test. Looking at him as if he had no right to be out in public. The South African professional, angry because Billy held up his net session to pick a daisy. I prefer the professional here. And his assistant."

***

I smiled. My boys have also gained a rich, powerful friend. Oops! That plural is way premature.

"Did you see that amazing blonde?"

"Who didn't? She's living with Adam Sawyer. Apparently there's a new one each summer. And none of them ever speaks."

"I don't think I could live like that."

"I'm sure you couldn't, Steve."

"Alice?"

"Steve?"

"Are there lots of people like Ernie and Dorothy? Still mad about each other after 45 years?"

"You're asking the wrong girl, Steve. I haven't met many. And certainly not among my clients."

"Oh. Sorry."

"Stop being sorry. You didn't do or say anything wrong. And stop being so polite. You're a teenager, you're sullen, surly and a brat." I tickled him as if he were Cal and he squealed as if he were Cal. "Surrender and say 'I am sullen and surly.'"

"Fuck off."

"Yes!! At last." I went back to stroking his hair. "Steve, I think there is a very high chance you will meet your Dorothy. But she isn't going to be delivered to you in a parcel, with a big label. You have to search out and discover her. Or him. But when you do I am certain that you will have the same feelings in 50 years as you do now."

He smiled happily and dozed off in my lap.

Steve slept in <u>again.</u> He really isn't fit. I biked around for a bit and had to sign <u>more</u> autographs for the fans. And promise to get them Steve's. When I got back I tried to get him out on his bike but he just flopped about and when I tried to beat him up he said it wasn't fair because I was a superhero.

"If you're just going to flop, I'll draw you."

"All right." But just when I wanted him to flop he kept moving about so I had to pose him. "That doesn't feel right."

"Trust me, I'm an artist." Then he went into a kind of trance and his lips moved in and out and then he started singing. Aaagh!

"Super Cal... is so artistic... expertly he poses..." He looked really proud of himself and he sang it again. And I got it and he sang it again and Mum rushed out.

"Steve, you promised! No singing." But then Mum got it and we all sang it.

"Super Cal is so artistic, expertly he poses."

"Quadruple pun. Maximum Wordpower!"

Steve's created a family joke.

I made us a light lunch and we set off for the beach. Laura and Luke are bringing Billy. I made us go by bike because I don't want to become a fat slag. Steve's worse than me about checking Cal's helmet and taking his lifejacket. Memo to myself: he needn't be so protective.

"Do you mind walking a bit? To Billy's beach. He found it."
Billy took Cal's hand and led us right to the end of the main beach. We then scrambled along a rough path and over rocks. We had to climb a little bit of cliff. Steve really isn't good at heights but he forced himself through.

"Look! That's the haunted house."

"Not today, and keep up with Billy."

Finally we got to a brilliant little beach. A strip of sand and some rock pools. And all to ourselves. "Billy the explorer! Great discovery."

"I'll add it to my map." I knew that Cal could do that from memory.

Billy walked a little way into the sea and bobbed up in his lifejacket. Laura quickly joined him. "Billy can actually swim. He's fine in a pool. But he has no spatial awareness. He could easily go miles out without noticing. So he always wears the jacket in the sea. And Laura has to do all the patrolling, since I'm crap at swimming." The boys looked astonished at this confession from their god.

Steve started to say something but I got in front of him. "Please put your jacket on too, sweetheart. Make me happy. New beach, just us here." Reluctant assent.

"You can save me, Cal." He brightened when Luke accepted his hand.

"Quite a sharp drop off. I can't stand." Steve had gone a little way out. He took a step further and disappeared. "It's going to get wavy soon. We can have a wave-riding contest. Cal versus Billy." Right on cue, a decent-sized wave. The two of us launched Cal. Squeal. Billy gave a matching squeal and presented himself to his parents for a launch.

After about half an hour Billy was declared the contest winner. We presented him with a handsome shell. We removed the lifejackets and he hugged Cal for a long time.

"Do you want to show me the rock pools, Billy?"

Luke and Laura looked awed. "He's done more for Billy than months of therapy. He's talking."

"Billy's doing a lot for Cal. Gives him a chance to pay forward what Steve does for him."

"Billy found Mrs Crab. Let's take her home again, the little Crab children will miss her. Then shall we draw something in the sand, Billy?"

We watched them digging and sculpting. Billy doing an equal share.

"Go away, we're not finished." Eventually we were allowed to look at their sand sculpture. "Do you want to tell them what it is, Billy?"

"Bear."

"Wait, we haven't signed it." Cal did some fancy work in the sand with the spade, then passed it to Billy. With a little help Billy completed a signature as well. "What's that one say?"

"Cat."

"Very close. Try again."

"Cal."

"And the other one."

"Billy."

Laura and Luke were wide-eyed. A wave snapped near the sand teddy bear's feet. Laura grabbed their camera and peeled off dozens of pictures. We passed the camera round to get different combinations of us with the bear. Finally Luke set up a time exposure, to get all of us in.

I'm keeping those pictures for life.

"Ladies and gentlemen, that is the end of the food, unless someone wants us to roast another pig." Noise. "Someone other than Cal. Now we come to the second part of our victory celebration…" Johnny had organized the barbecue and the band. I had always found him very laid-back. This evening he was dynamic and decisive. Another secret talent. "Now we travel in time. Please welcome those style-setting mod icons of the Sixties, and a truly great band – brought back to us by the Small Fakes!"

I gasped. Their lead singer stepped straight out of the pictures in Uncle Cal's trunk. He was Steve Marriott reincarnated. And not just the look. I recognized the guitar licks and the vocals from my uncle's 45s. The keyboard player was very accomplished too. The new Ian Maclagan. Poor Uncle Cal claimed to have sat in for him on several Small Faces recordings. "I want you to know that I love you, baby, I want you to know that I care. I'm so happy when you're around me but I'm sad when you're not there…"

Cal started the dancing. "Whatcha gonna do about it, Marjorie?" He pulled her away and began to gyrate. Edwin looked a bit sick. Steve looked amazed. Some older couples drifted into the dance space but Cal was still the star. Edwin's parents joined in and he cringed. Will I embarrass Cal in public when he's a teenager? Actually they both moved rather well. Much better than Adam the artist and his silent blonde.

"I'm just a little tin soldier, that wants to jump into your fire…"

"My toy-boy's dumped me." Cal had started dancing with a girl around his own age. To be precise, dancing in front of her. "Help me out, Steve."

"Marjorie, when I dance they call for paramedics."

"Trust your feet, Steve. That's what you tell us…" After a little while the music did its work on him.

Ernie and Dorothy stopped by. "I knew them. The Small Faces. I used to cut the hair of their roadie."

"Ernie, did you ever know my uncle, Cal Devane, same as Cal? He was a rock musician. He jammed with the Small Faces."

"Er… Fraid not." I was not surprised. Poor Uncle Cal. Nearly famous. Now remembered only by rock anoraks.

Steve didn't so much dance as move in rhythm. I recognized a faraway expression and was frightened that he might start his run-up again. Marjorie hauled him back into his surroundings. Edwin looked even sicker.

"Edwin, go right out there and ask her for a dance."

"She won't want to now."

"Trust me. No girl ever minds being asked to dance. Especially by a boy like you." I recognized the band's next number. "Listen now, it's an omen."

"I knew everything's gonna be all right, Sha-Na-Na-Na-Na-Nee." Smile. I watched him walk over to the other two. A quick conversation and Steve walked away with a smile. Edwin seized Marjorie's hand and pulled her into space. She looked startled. Still clinging awkwardly to her hand he completed the rest of the number and then, obligingly, the band switched to a slow one. He wrapped both arms around her and they moved very slowly in their own tiny space.

"I've got mine…" Cal was cutting a swathe through the room. Steve was dancing with his discards! It gave me a little chill. Not a future I want for either of them.

The band switched to a long number, allowing Edwin to continue with his armlock around Marjorie. "Oh baby, you need cooling, I'm gonna send you back to schooling…"

"Mum, come and have a dance!"

"Run out of hearts to break?"

He looked hurt. "Mum, it's just dancing."

"Maybe to you but what about all those girls? Do they know you're unavailable?"

"Mum. I just asked them for a dance. I didn't say 'I love you' or anything. Was that wrong?"

This wasn't the time to say that his father was a selfish, charming shit who danced with people's lives and then disappeared. I wondered when I would ever be able to say that to him? He looked up at me, almost pleading, and joined the words of the song "I know how to pony…"

I gave in. "Okay, show me how to pony…" He did some intricate moves of his own. I gave up trying to follow and shuffled rhythmically between feet. Other couples yielded us the spotlight. Edwin and Marjorie stayed in their own world.

Applause but he didn't milk it. Maybe I had been too hard on him.

"Nice moves, mister, but you haven't asked the best dancer in the room."

"Who?" I whispered. He looked amazed, but I insisted. "Dorothy, may I have a dance with you? Do you mind, Ernie?" They both blushed, but very politely he offered his arm and guided her to the floor.

"Which way do you wanna go? To the left or the right…" To match the words, he moved sinuously in each direction. Maybe he is a cat after all. She watched him briefly and then followed him move for move. Everybody stopped to look at them.

"I can't move to the way you're dancing, you've got to see me move when it comes to romancing…"

"We're not dead yet, are we, Alice?" Ernie held out his hand to me.

"Like hell we are." We took to the floor.

"Look out, 'cos I'm on your trail…" It was a long number anyway and the band extended it. We swapped partners. Ernie and Dorothy did a kind of slow-motion jive. Cal suddenly collapsed into my arms. I had upset him. Some tears. We went on dancing and I don't think anyone else knew that he was my little baby.

The number finished. To give Cal more cover I whistled loudly and bigged it up for the band. People were startled, especially Steve.

"Mum! Embarrassing." Cal had recovered.

"Thank you, thank you so much. You've been the best audience we ever had. Well, you've been the first audience we ever had. First one to pay." I warmed to him. More than a Steve Marriott clone. A sense of humour and a mind. "We're going to end with my personal favourite…"

Good grief. Brief guitar lick and then sudden rich organ chords. It was my uncle's favourite too. The one he played over and over, making me listen out for the organ part. Cal squeezed my hand. He never knew his great-uncle but he always knows when I'm thinking of him. "Don't burst my bubble, leave my bubble alone."

I bigged it up for them again and asked Johnny to set up a beer for them all.

"Not for the singer. He's only 15. And his brother's only 17."

"His brother's the keyboardist?"

"They're American. I think his father's a spy at that top secret US base, which is only known to every pub in Devon."

The boys were thrilled, but the father, Sean Kinch, looked more like a college professor when Johnny introduced us to the band. He described himself as being an IT consultant. He was acting as roadie. It was indeed the band's first paid gig. They had come a long way to get it. Johnny had signed them from his sister's school dance.

Jesse the singer looked heartbreakingly young as a Steve Marriott clone. His brother Rick was dark and intense. He had made much less effort to style himself as a Small Face. "Jesse. You're an American teenager. What draws you to an English singer from another era?"

"I saw one clip on You Tube. Watcha Gonna Do About It? And I just felt electric. Everything about him, singing, performing – you know he was a great child actor as well? – the words, the music, the clothes, girls going crazy in those weird hairdos, and feeling I was right there with everybody, with the sweat and the cheap perfume… I went through every clip from You Tube of his great songs and I wanted to be Steve Marriott. I mean not the stuff about drink and drugs and burning himself to death but the… electricity."

"You should see his room. It's a shrine."

"Beats Oscar Peterson."

I looked at his brother as they bickered. "When we went to London, we didn't see any sights. One went to Ronnie Scott's and the other went to every place that Steve Marriott lived in."

"My outfit's all real, Alice. I mean from the Sixties. I bought it on eBay."

"I have some memorabilia of Steve Marriott in London. They came to me from my uncle, Cal Devane."

"Cal Devane? Of Calamity? He used to jam with the Small Faces. He filled in once or twice for Mac Maclagan. Ohmigod, you're his niece?" He threw himself on the floor. "I want to kiss your feet."

I raised him gently and looked in his eyes. "Jesse, you're an awesome Steve Marriott and you electrified this crowd. But I think you are an awesome Jesse Kinch as well. Even I can tell you're a superb guitarist and you've got great pipes and huge stage presence. You can produce electricity as you, not borrowing from a dead rock star."

"He's written loads of songs. Let's give them Timeless Rider and Cutter[20]?"

"No. Not in public!"

"Jesse. I'll offer a deal. You visit us in London. I show you my uncle's trunk. Anything you like about Steve Marriott, you can keep it or I make you a copy. I also introduce you and Rick to a friend of mine who knocked around with my uncle and Steve Marriott. Ray Corvino. He's now a top music agent. But on two conditions. First, you bring me a tape of your own material. Second, can you loan me Rick from your band? Starting now, Sean, for maybe half an hour?" Agreement. "Rick, do I understand that you like jazz?"

"Do cows fart? Oops, sorry dad."

"Would you like to work with a local jazz singer? Marjorie?"
She unclamped herself from Edwin and came over. I introduced her to Rick. "Marjorie, I've forgotten too much and it's time you worked with a professional accompanist. Do you want to try some numbers with Rick?"

"I've never used a mike."

Jesse took charge and positioned her. "You're not planning to move, are you? Sing anything. Johnny will get your levels."

She did a few bars of Day In, Day Out. Rick sat up. "I love that song. But we don't have it. Just only Small Faces stuff."

---

[20] Real songs by the real and multitalented Jesse Kinch, for whom see www.jessekinch.com He has never been in a Small Faces tribute band.

"I have it. And others." I held up a case of sheet music I had brought from the house. "Just in case. Just in <u>case.</u> Never mind." Must be the way I tell them.

"Omigod! Ricky Rubato. I saw that 20 times."

"We know Howard Foy." Well, we're going to.

This time Rick threw himself to the floor. "I want to kiss your feet." I stopped him. "What's he like? Howard Foy?"

Oops! "Surprisingly shy. Keeps himself to himself." Not defamatory but reckless as to the truth. It seemed to satisfy Rick.

"Are you happy with this key, Marjorie?"

"I don't know. Is it what Alice played?"

They started on Day In, Day Out. She was hesitant at first, but Rick was a much better accompanist than me and Johnny quickly worked the sound system to good effect. (Another hidden talent). She gained confidence and asked to do it again. The second time she let herself go and Rick went with her. People stopped talking and ordering drinks. Ernie murmured. "Proper music."

They did a selection from Ricky Rubato. Blue Train knocked them dead. Then they switched to a Frank Sinatra number which Ray used to massacre. Come Dance With Me. She made it light and airy and strictly a tempo and the lyrics sounded fresh, coming from a girl not a man. Ernie led Dorothy to the floor and they whispered a few requests. Marjorie did I'm In The Mood For Love and Pick Yourself Up. Rick caught a signal from his father and they finished with Who's Taking You Home Tonight? Ernie and Dorothy waltzed adoringly and we all got a bit teary.

The final chord was hardly played when Edwin rushed forward to answer the question for Marjorie.

Johnny took over the mike. "Ladies and gentlemen, remember in years to come that right here in Glendon Courtenay you saw the world debut of jazz diva, Marjorie Court!"

Suddenly I'm hustling two major talents. Maybe I should take over from Simon Cowell?

Chapter 27   Night Match

Mum's still angry with me and I don't really know why. She gave me her you've-done-something-wrong-but-I-love-you-anyway hug last night and again this morning. Was it about all those girls at the barbie? It was only dancing and having a laugh and maybe becoming Facebook friends. Mum says I'm a heartbreaker. Does Steve think that too?

I hate to see him in tears. Or hurt or frightened. I have to do something about it right away. He sobbed on my shoulder and then sobbed again because he thought he'd spoiled one of my good Ursinho shirts. Finally he choked out his problem.

"Of course I don't think you're a heartbreaker. You have the biggest heart in the northern hemisphere." *We had a silly argument about the southern hemisphere and I knew he was on the mend. It reminded me to write to Brendon and Daniel about the match and stuff. He went off to work on his map of Billy's beach.*

I found Alice in the garden, gardening. I asked if she had any unskilled manual work (I'm not up to more than lawnmowing) and she set me to remove a dead tree stump. It was a tough job, in spite of my magnificent physical conditioning. She was grateful and I took the chance put in a word for Cal. She cut me short.

"Steve, you don't have to be the peacemaker. Cal and I sometimes make each other unhappy. That happens sometimes with people who love each other. You get through it. Sometimes one of the people is unfair on the other – you get through that too. I think I was unfair to call him a heartbreaker. He was just showing off and having fun. But I want him to take responsibility for other people's feelings. I would hate it if he made people love him and then just walked away. Like his father." *She snapped off a big dead geranium.* "It's true what they say about tough love, Steve. Sometimes you say 'no, you're not wonderful, no, you're not doing that.' I would love to hear you say no to him. Especially when he turns on the charm. Now do you see this stuff? It's called Jacob's ladder. Do you think you can go round the garden and remove it? Only if it looks like that. If you're in any doubt, leave it in the earth. It's about time Cal and I made up."

Mum and I are OK again. We had a talk about other people's feelings and never leading people on. Then we had the I-love-you-to-bits hug, then best of all...

"Stop working, Steve. We've decided that the rest of the day is treating Steve day and you get to do everything you want."

"You haven't seen the haunted house yet."

"Not today. What I'd really like is to go to Bee World."

"Bee World?"

"My mates in New Zealand have a hive on their farm. I'd like to see one."

Actually the bees were cool. Steve said something really weird to the people in the hive. "Do you ever get any bishops in here?" And he totally lost it. Laughed so hard and started rolling about. The bees got really wound up, It's the first time we've seen him really let go. The bee people must have thought he was weird.

"Our new hive was blessed by the Rural Dean." That set him off again.

We had a bit of a walk and Steve told Mum a story about Brendon and Daniel's dad on their farm and a bishop.

Cal's always been a terrible walker. He bounces and darts about and scurries back for physical contact – handholding, mini-hugs or even piggy backs. Steve's now getting this treatment. He's always available. Sweet to watch, but I wish he would push Cal away sometimes.

We went back to the shop and tried all the honeys (well, only I did them all) and we bought his favourites and then we drove back in time for a swim at the main beach, Edwin and Marjorie were there and they waved but they didn't come and join us.

A flash of jealousy. Steve is not certain he wants to let her go. I'm going to make him ask her out on a date. Just the two of them.

He was moping a bit on the beach so I jumped on his back.

"Just for that, I'm throwing you into the sea."

"I want to be thrown into the sea."

I raced him and Mum to the red buoy. I ran out of puff again in the last stretch and they had to tread water to let me win. We practised lifesaving each other and Mum told me not to scream so much and save it for the real thing. I was still out of puff but Steve told me to flop like Bungle and go to sleep and the tide would carry me in. It did.

We walked a bit in the wet sand. "Look, Mum, my prints are almost as big as Steve's. That means I'm going to be bigger than him, doesn't it? Imagine carrying Steve" and I tried to lift him and I actually did for two seconds. Everyone was surprised.

Mum took us to the Chinese that used to be the post office and we all got a free spring roll because of Steve's performance in the cricket match. And mine! Mr Wu played cricket in Hong Kong. He's a left armer like me.

Mum bought Steve's favourite ice cream, mint chocolate chip (now mine as well) and we went home and played Monopoly and Bungle let him win.

"Now, it's still Treat-Steve Day, so what do you want to do next?"

"Listen to you play the piano."

"Puh-lease! I've warned you before about being polite."

"I'm not being polite. I love hearing you play the piano. It makes me feel… at home."

Mum played some songs by someone called Johnny Mercer. Steve stretched out on the couch and I held his hand and it was like he was just floating. Then Mum came over and put his head in her lap. That doesn't do anything for me but it was Treat-Steve Day.

"The head must lie upon the block…"

"That was wont to lie on Queen Catherine's lap." And Steve told the story of Owen Tudor and Queen Catherine. Really sad, but he must like it so I'll do a drawing. Then I got up on the couch as well and we held him for a bit.

And that was the end of Treat-Steve Day. I don't know when the next one will be, after this holiday. I hope this one made him feel special and that he'll remember it. I worry about his life after we go home. We will see him again. Whenever we can. And he will get a trial with the MCC, even if I have to go to court.

Future Zoe (is there one?)

We'll we're back in London. Felt sick on plane. Mum blames airport café. I blame Steve. Nothing from him since cricket match. Hope he's having fabtastic time but not with Devon hussy! Plead with Mum to send me to Devon in time to watch next cricket match. And Robert desperate to see Cal. Fears he met Devon hunk. Rbt much hunkier himself – we did swimming and fitness regime - and me much hussier (I think). Mum sez wrong to chase Steve (and Cal). But suppose he decides to stay in Devon for ever? They've given him dream job as cricket professional. That plus beach, plus hussy ... Only one hope for me – Howard back in London and Steve wants to meet him. Will introduce them only if he is free of Devon hussy!

Zoe Present

It took ages to wind Steve up to phone Marjorie and ask her for a date. They swam and played cricket together several times but he couldn't ask her in front of Edwin. Instead his fingers hovered over his mobile and he actually made notes of what he wanted to say. His only previous experience of dating was in his sad relationship with Angie. It wouldn't give him much confidence.

He was surprised at how easy it was to persuade Marjorie to go out with him to a jazz club in a fashionable resort town. I would drive them there, after dropping Cal at Laura and Luke's new house. He was staying overnight to play and draw with Billy. Steve would pay for a taxi home.

"I feel you've had enough of her, Steve."

"You bet. She's not a patch on you."

"Steve! She's famous, she's recorded, she's on TV regularly…"

"Sssh!"

"This is Marjorie Court. Book now for her show here in a year's time. No one will talk through her."

She punched me but I think she was pleased. I paid our bill.

"Would you like something to eat? That was terrible. Totally inedible. Couldn't force it down. And such a small portion!" *Giggle. Thanks, Uncle Frank, I nicked that from you.*

"There's a kind of tradition that you don't eat well at a jazz club. I don't know why. I wouldn't do things that way at my club."

"Your club?" *For some reason she blushed.*

"Oh, as if. It's hot as hell and you're wearing that leather jacket again."

Now I blushed. "I thought you liked it. Do you want to share it?" *I gave her an arm. We stood outside the club for a while. I felt that we were one being, a single perfect machine. I suppose that's intimacy, again. We could still hear the Famous Singer in the club.*

"She sounds better at a distance. You sound better close to."

"Steve, don't be such a flatterer. It will take me years to get close to her technique and control."

"Don't care about technique and control. When you do something extra to a song it's because you mean it and when she does something it's because she can do it and she wants us to know."

She thought about this. "I do think about songs. What they're trying to say. What they might mean to people. Like Ernie and Dorothy when they're dancing. When it comes right, it feels as though I'm not singing at all. The song takes over and I'm just a kind of outlet. I might take acting lessons as well as singing lessons."

"How are you going to fit all that in when you're playing for the England Test team? With me. And Cal. And Edwin."

"No chance!"

"Why not? Who says we won't have an integrated team?"

"You could get there, Steve, but we'll just be your entourage. We'll all play with you in the nets. Keep your confidence up when it's down. Cal will be your official artist, Edwin will be your accountant. I'll be… your personal laundress. I'll go to work with Luke and Laura.."

"Laundress?"

"Only for you, Steve." *Fantasy, but I think she would do my laundry, and all.* "Who does it now? Will they manage this ketchup stain?" *She fingered a point on my shirt. It felt tingly. I let her go on for a while.* "How's your shoulder?" *She started working that too. I blissed out.*

"Marjorie, can I cancel the taxi so we can stay here for ever?" *Warm night, warm bodies, distant jazz.*

"Too late, Steve." *A taxi drew up asking for my name.* "And we couldn't miss the Illsleigh match. What a news story! 'Star All Rounder Elopes With Club Professional. Club Date Leads To Night Of Shame'. Exclusive to the Argus." *Beautiful, cricketer, fabulous voice. Add sense of humour. And now we're getting into a taxi. Like Emma Bovary and Leon in the closed carriage at Rouen. Shall I seal the blinds and order the driver all over town?*

There were no blinds and Marjorie ordered him to return to Glendon Courtenay.

"I can't remember when I was last in a taxi."

"London ones are different." *Man of the world! As if I take them constantly. She nestles against me. Does she feel sophisticated? Adventurous? Happy? Safe? I want her to.*

The taxi driver was a grumbler. On the outskirts of Glendon Courtenay I caught her eye. "This will do. We can walk from here." *I hurled money at the driver and waved away change and the offer of blank receipts. Why would anyone want a blank taxi receipt? He drove away. I started to fold her into a kiss. A car flashed by and honked. Spell broken.*

"It's surprisingly busy this road. This way, Steve, we can walk home along the beach."

I gave her some leather jacket again. We walked along a footpath. "I like your perfume."

"I nicked it from Mum."

"You're a Bad Daughter and I'm a Bad Son! I nicked my dad's special fragrance and put it in my trainers!" *We both lost it and writhed hysterically on the footpath. We ended on our backs, looking up at the stars.* "That has to be Venus. Nothing else that bright. Venus can cast shadows."

"I know. Dad once showed me when I was little."

"That is terribly lucky! Seeing the Venus shadow. My mate Nick told me." *And I found myself telling her about him being nuts on astronomy and discovering an asteroid and naming it after me.*

"Asteroid Steve! Where? I want to see it!" *But I felt such a bighead.*

"It's only a little tiddler and no one else bothered to discover it. I could ask him to discover Asteroid Marjorie but it wouldn't be fair."

"Why not?"

"Because you're going to be such a huge star on Earth it would be greedy to give you another up there."

"Sweet." *I hope so but it suddenly felt phoney as well. I jumped up. She looked surprised.*

"I want to see the sea. At night."

"Take this little path." *She led me to this little beach.*

"Wicked. Like Billy's beach."

"There's a chain of them, if you're willing to walk. Some are dangerous. Which one's Billy's?" *I tried to describe the route we had taken.*

"I'm not sure I know that one and I've lived here for ages."

"I need Cal here to draw the map in the sand."

"I love Cal even more after seeing him with Billy. He's not just my little cutie-pie. Dead calm."

"Cal? No way."

"The sea, silly. I'll bet there'll be phosphorescence. Come on, last one in's the world's biggest wuss." *She threw her clothes off and ran towards the sea.*

"Marjorie, we can't!"

"Who says? No one else here. Keep those expensive clothes on if you're embarrassed. This is a safe beach. I'm going in and I'm still a fraidycat but you're a brilliant swimmer." *She squealed when she hit the water. I threw my clothes off. I just wanted to. I thought of leaving my pants on but they weren't hiding anything anyway.*

Sudden cold water cured my problem down there, instantly. I squealed too. Okay, I'm a wuss. We splashed around. She didn't act like a fraidycat. I worried when she got a bit far out and some waves began, and gently led her back into the shallows.

"Steve, you're so protective."

"Sorry."

"Don't be sorry. It's nice to feel safe and looked-after. But make sure you're getting looked after yourself. Look, there is phosphorescence." *She drew her hand through the clear water and created a streak of luminous green light.*

"I've seen that in the Med. What is it?"

"Tiny creatures. Emitting light to scare us." *We made some more luminous streaks. She started to shiver.*

"Better go in. How are we going to get dry?"

"Like this." *She ran up and down the beach. Grace, energy. Glad animal.*

"Great, but practise your action!" *We both practised our bowling actions. Two glad naked animals. One naked part of me started to feel particularly glad.* "Your left knee's collapsing on this dodgy wicket." *I stood behind her, took both arms and corrected her action. Excessive gladness down there!*

She broke away gently. "No Steve. No night of shame with the club professional. Not right for either of us. Not fair on Edwin. I'm his girlfriend now." *Surprise. Guilt. Rapid diminution of gladness.*

"Let's get dressed and I'll tell you." *We were now dry enough and dressed quickly. I gave her all of my leather jacket. We walked towards the main beach. Two people suddenly waved at us. I jumped nine feet (estimate).*

"That was Adam. And his amazing blonde. Do you suppose they saw us?"

"So what – unless he paints us. He's pretty bad. His annual show never sells much. I've seen him here a lot. With each year's model. That's all they are, models. He takes them here to paint them. I don't want anyone to paint me except Cal."

We walked on for a little bit and looked back. Sure enough, Adam was posing the blonde. She looked extra-amazing against the sea. Shame he couldn't paint!

"Steve, it would be so easy to fall in love with you. You're a girl's fantasy – gorgeous, talented, strong, funny, caring. I almost decided to run away to London, even if you didn't want me to, just to be within reach of you.

"But that's just it – you'll always be out of reach. Out of reach as a cricketer – you are going to heights I can never get to. Out of reach as a brain – I can barely read cricket magazines."

"You can read music."

"True. But I think that's part of me that will always be out of reach to you. I know you like my singing, but do you really know what's going on for me in a song? And could you help me with it? We're never going to sing duets." *She squeezed my hand.* "And then there's that giant heart of yours, Steve. There are parts of that I can never reach. Your relationship with Cal, even though I love him too. You and Cal and Alice, the way you're a unit. Your London girlfriend." *Guilt.* "She means a lot to you. I can tell. You let go of my hand, like it was scalding. Honestly, Steve, I'm glad. I want you to have a girl who loves you in the place where you live. And Steve … this next bit's hard… You love everybody. Anybody you meet, you want to make them happy."

"Hell, that sounds like a compulsion. Maybe it is. I had three years without any real happiness at all and then suddenly everything turned magic…"

"Steve, you don't have to explain. You love people. You love all of our cricket team, that's why you've coached us all so brilliantly."

"I don't love the Undecim lot. I hate their captain."

"Because they were bad to the people you love. I saw your whole body change when their captain wound up Cal. If they had been ordinary people you would have bowled flat out for our team but you would still have tried to make sure they were having a nice day." *I think that's true. Should I play only against nasty teams?*

"Steve. I would always have to share you. With anybody you meet you think you could give something to. I'm not as nice as you, Steve, and I'm not a sharer. With Edwin I get all of him. All the time. Greedy bitch. You are allowed to think that! But I do love him to bits. It's your fault, Steve, you taught him to bat."

"I showed him that he could bat."

"If you like. But when he stood up to you bowling flat out, it opened my eyes. I saw guts and determination. And then I saw everything else. Loyalty, commitment. Look at the way he helps Sam maintain the pitch. And he's got a mega-brain. He really understands money. He does his dad's accounts. He's made money for my dad already, just by re-organizing his bill payments. And he's got a plan for our future.

"I go on playing cricket because I can't stop and I get as far as I can. But I also take voice lessons – and acting. I work with Rick Kinch as much as I can, before his dad has to spy somewhere else. Rick's not just a great keyboard player, he's a top-notch arranger. We'll work out my best songs and he'll leave me arrangements for another pianist, when he has to go. When I think I'm ready I meet Alice's friend, Ray Corvino, the music agent.

"But whatever he thinks of me I want to stay based here in Glendon Courtenay. I'll perform in local clubs, like tonight's, and get a following. Edwin will be my personal manager. As soon as he leaves school he'll qualify as an accountant. And he'll get a job with Ray or someone else where he can learn the music business. Then he'll come back here and look after me – money, contracts, supporting musicians – everything I need done so I can concentrate on singing. And he'll work for Luke."

"Luke?"

"Luke wants to invest money in local people. Luke thinks Edwin is talented. He's promised him a job any time he wants.

"When I've got a bit of a following and some money in the bank, Edwin and I are going to open a jazz club. We've got a name for it already – Café Society. Johnny will manage it. He's a great organizer – the barbecue was all his show – and we trust him. A jazz club makes sense around here – young people go down the coast for the surf beaches. We'd get the older crowd. We'd offer them good performers – I'd do a residency myself – and decent food. And as an extra stream of income we'll have a recording studio as well. Luke's already said he'll back us if we have a proper business plan. Edwin will draw that up. We'll ask you to come down for opening night – and to bring the rest of the England cricket team with you. And the wives and girl friends. And we'll ask Cal to supervise the décor."

"You've really thought about this."

"Edwin did most of the thinking, but we are in it together. You see, we want to make our future here, Steve. Until this summer we couldn't wait to get away. Again, it's your fault, Steve. What you did to the team. Making them winners, who don't roll over to money and power. Winning last week seems to have brought the whole place to life. Loads of people now want to join the team, people I'd forgotten about. The nets will be really crowded this week. Edwin and I will take them over when you go. Doing what you did. Wait till you see us next year. You will come back, you are the club professional?"

"Of course. But what I can't get over… you weren't happy when we first met. Now you've got this whole new life worked out – just because of a cricket match?"

"Not only that. Alice did a lot too. But you started a chain reaction through the cricket. You showed me everything was possible. Here, take back your jacket." *She gave it to me and added a kiss. I was too stunned to make it last. She skipped away from me.* "I'm sorted, Steve. Thank you. For ever."

Suddenly she started singing. "Don't worry about me I get along, don't worry about me, be happy my love…" *I had never heard that one before. It was slow and achingly beautiful. The waves seemed to keep time with her.* "…If you can forget, don't worry about me."

"I don't want to forget you, Marjorie. You're wonderful. But I won't worry about you." *This time I gave her a long kiss. Finally we both decided it was time to walk her home. She told me about the song. It was from her gran's record collection.*

"Thanks for a wonderful evening. Thanks for saving me from those terrifying waves. Thanks for the rest of my life. See you at the nets." *A quick peck this time and she slipped into her home. No one else seemed to be up. Phew! I didn't really want to explain why we were back so late.*

I walked back to our place, brooding about the chain reaction. I teach someone to play cricket and people get a whole new life? Why not, it happened to me?

I missed our place again in the dark! Bloody clever architect. Retrace steps. No one awake. Good. Quick shower. Admire myself again in the mirror. Start out for kitchen.

Remember I'm not alone in house, and slip on swimming trunks. Gulp milk (Alice lays in giant supply for me) and head for computer.

"Dear Zoe." *Correction.* "Darling Zoe..."

I found Steve crashed out in front of the computer, and woke him gently. "I haven't read this. Did you want all those repeated Xs at the end or did you fall asleep on the key?"

"Leave them in." He hit Send without signing it. I think she'll know whom it's from.

Chapter 28   Caught In The Deep

Steve was still fast asleep when Luke delivered Cal, but he leapt out of bed at the sound of his god.

"You have to see what Cal gave us. It's totally beautiful."

I could see it was much more painstaking than his usual style. The faces were real portraits rather than cartoony and he had given each a meticulous reflection. Himself and Billy at the rock pool at Billy's beach. Beside it a little poem in a clear handwriting I had not seen from him before.

"That's Cal-ligraphy." We all booed.

Steve read out the poem. "Where the pools are bright and deep Where the grey trout lies asleep Up the river and o'er the lea That's the way for Billy and me."

"Laura and I love that poem. It's by James Hogg. It's been Billy's lullaby."

"I did a crab not a trout because Billy found a crab."

"This is the best copy we could do. Please keep it. Then we'll have it done professionally. Thank you. Thank you." He was choked. He mumbled some excuse and drove away.

"Darling, that is your masterpiece." For once he did not hop around and look away. He just looked at the copy and nodded.

"I think it should be Treat-Cal Day."

"Motion carried. Everything he wants to do."

"Haunted house."

"Everything without ghosts."

"Cricket."

"Club practice this evening."

"Cricket just with Steve. Like when we first met." *Only a few weeks ago...*

"We'll go early. What else?"

"Swimming to the red buoy and not letting me win. Picnic. Then going to the top of the cliff."

"I don't like the sound of that word 'top.'"

"There's a great view which he likes to draw. Steve, there's a path."

"Going to tea with Dorothy because I'm invited. Then the cricket. Then Chinese at Mr Wu's. Then … I don't know."

"I'm sure you'll think of something."

This time I was last to the red buoy but I wasn't out of puff and I went back. There were some waves and I got wiped out.

"I'm OK. Don't wet yourself, Steve, we're in the sea already!" but I was glad Mum said we should go in and eat the picnic. Then we started up the cliff. Mum and I did it easily but Steve started puffing and sweating. He's not fit like me!

"Give me the backpack, Steve. There's only water and his sketching stuff."

"Are we nearly there yet?"

Steve got slower and slower and stopped. "Just admiring the view."

"It's way better at the top."

Then we got to the bad bit where you have to know where the path is. Steve stopped again. He was sweating a lot and hanging on to this broken post. "I can't do this."

Mum was ahead of us. "Mum, you go on. This is a job for… The Cat!" I went down to him again. "Steve, put your other hand on my shoulder." He gripped me really tight and it hurt but I didn't say anything. "I've got you. Now hold my other shoulder." Very slowly he let go of the post and grabbed my other shoulder. "Now count to ten backwards." I don't know what that's supposed to do but he once told me to do it. "Now Steve, just follow me. I'm a weed and you're a god so if I can do it, you can."

"Yes, but you're a cat and I'm a … prat." We both laughed but he still didn't let go of me.

I had a great idea. "Okay, Steve, we're going to dance. Pretend it's the barbie. Pretend I'm Marjorie." He got tense. Have they had a row? "Pretend I'm Zoe." He did a silly smile. That's on again. No time to think about that now. "Anyway, listen to the song and dance. Trust your feet!" Another smile. "Which way do you wanna go? To the left or the right?..." Hey. I'm good! By the time I finished the song we had danced to the top of the cliff.

"Bad shame!"

"Don't worry, you're still my hero." And I gave him my biggest hug but he still looked miserable. Mum hugged him too.

"Steve, you made it. That makes you a bigger hero." But he still looked mis.

"Now that we're here, look at that view."

"Can I look at your drawing instead, when it's finished." He walked quite a way from the edge of the cliff and flopped on a flat bit of grass. I didn't bother with the drawing - I've done it before - I sat beside him, holding his hand. Mum sat down and held the other. After a bit he lay back and fell asleep.

We all had quite a long nap. "Okay, people, we'd better go back."

I jumped up to join Mum, but Steve just sat up. "Down's worse than up, isn't it?"

"Steve, there is a very gentle path in the other direction. It's well marked and you can't miss it. That will take you to the road. Cal and I will take the short way down. I pick up the car, I drop him at Ernie and Dorothy, I pick you up on the road."

"That is way too much trouble."

"It is not. We want to do this, Steve. Do you love us?"

"Yes."

"When you really love somebody, you admit that sometimes you need them to take care of you." He agreed. Mum always wins arguments like that.

When I picked up Steve in the road he was fine again. "Dorothy's teaching him the tango. We'd better hurry and save her toes."

But when we got there they were moving together silkily to an old-fashioned gramophone. "He's a natural. Almost as good as Ernie. You're sure you don't want another scone, Cal? You hardly ate a thing." I saw the remains of a clotted cream tea.

"Oh, I couldn't, Dorothy. I'll have to tango all night to work off my tea. Thank you for everything, it was totally brilliant." He gave her his best hug and kiss. I love seeing that, when he means it. I thanked Dorothy and Ernie and promised he would come again before we left.

"All your cricket stuff's in the car so you can go straight to the nets."

Mum dropped us and yes! We had the nets to ourselves. I got excited because I'm still a baby and I jumped on his back.

"Get off, fat boy!"

"Ooh, I am a fat boy today. I couldn't finish Dorothy's cream tea."

"That must be a first. Congratulations, Dorothy! You'd better bowl first, work off some of that stodge and podge." *But he didn't get down.*

"Steve?"

"Cal?"

"When you're famous will you still come and play with me in the nets?"

"Try and stop me. Now get down." *This time he did. I padded up.* "Okay, fatty, see if you can waddle up to the stumps."

"Waddle!" *He ran in, full tilt. Like me. And the ball actually jumped. Like mine. I had to jab it down.*

"Good grief. Now's he's a seamer as well."

"Just wanted to see if I could do it."

"Keep it as another surprise. Make sure you warn Johnny."

He gave me a really good workout. Going through all his variations with much less chatter and squealing. One professional to another.

We swapped places. "Come on, bounce me!"

"Saving my shoulder." *True, but I still can't bear to bounce him.*

There were new people at the nets. Kids and grown-ups. Not much good except Mr Wu. I whispered to Steve "Now they'll have another Chinaman bowler when I've gone." He laughed but told me not to be racist.

"If I play, you'll have a Chinaman bowler!" Mr Wu laughed fit to bust. We compared grips. Jesse and Rick arrived, from the band. They had come from miles away. They'd only played baseball. They couldn't believe you had to catch a cricket ball without a glove. They laughed when Steve asked them to love Johnny and hug the teddy bear. They were ace in the deep. Steve had them give a demonstration. Batting, Jesse carted everything over midwicket. He was a home run specialist at baseball. Steve called him a cross-batted slogger and Jesse carted him! I had to get him out with the zooter.

The new players gave us a selection problem. It was quickly solved.

"I'll come and umpire. More use to you there than in the field with my knee."

"Ernie, you always play in the Illsleigh match."

"And I will again, but we've got two lads we'll never see again."

"I'll stand down too, Sam. I'm a very slow opener and I could use the time to master Edwin's new payment system. Marjorie will uphold the family honour."

"I'll be your official artist for the day. I've always wanted to do a painting of the team."

"Oh. Adam. That really would be… marvellous." *Respect for Sam! He really sounded as though he meant it.* "If you three are sure, that means we can give those brothers a game. They're brilliant in the field. And Mr Wu is a real find as a bowler. Must sort out his first name."

I asked him about the match. " Fixture's been going over 150 years. We haven't won for ages. The Illsleigh lot look down on us. Probably worse now that they've got the Davisons. I suppose I'll open again, instead of David."

"May I suggest Marjorie? I think she and Edwin would have a good understanding."

I was hungry again when Steve finished the meeting. Mr Wu handed out more giant spring rolls to celebrate his selection! I was stuffed again so I walked home with Steve.

"You're such a restless person to walk with. Worse than Tigger."

"In that case you can carry me." **Jump!**

"Off! You're too fat." **But he didn't throw me off.**

"You've gone past the house!"

"Bloody architect!" **He did throw me off.**

"Welcome back, sweetheart. There's still some Treat-Cal day left. What would you like to do?"

He thought for a while and then did a sudden bounce. "Mum, have you got any tango music?"

"I know one by heart." I went to the piano and picked off Kurt Weill's Tango-Ballade from The Threepenny Opera.

"Look. Dorothy taught me this. Steve, you've got to be her because she taught me to be the man. I'm going to lead." Steve took his hands, awkwardly. "Stay close, Steve. Trust your feet!" He got hysterics and had to start over. I vamped the opening bars over and over again. "Closer, Steve!" I started the tune. He glided about, languorously but dramatically. He held Steve and tried to make him follow, but he was clearly embarrassed. I put him out of his misery.

"I don't think Steve's up for that after cricket. He's not fit like you." I knew Cal's tease by now. "Give us a solo." I replayed the Tango-Ballade and he disappeared into the music. My little boy became someone else. A gigolo. I didn't like it, but I finished the number and bigged it up for him. "Sorry, but that's the only tango I know." (Not true). "Let's play Monopoly. Go and get Bungle."

"Rather play gin rummy. Mum, can you go on playing? Stuff like that?" I felt a stab. Is he done with Monopoly? Is he done with Bungle? But I went on playing. It was his treat to choose. He played the card game very intently. None of the noise that he makes playing Monopoly. He called "Gin" regularly. I hoped Steve wasn't letting him win.

"You've cleaned me out."

"I will show mercy. Thanks for playing." He turned to me. "And thanks for playing." Not a great joke but it sent him into hysterics. He recovered and went back to being my little boy. Big hugs for us both. "Thank you for treating me." We dispersed to bed.

I lay in bed and had another go at Slim: Defeat Into Victory. Uncle Frank had made a little pencil note: "Beats himself up!" I realized what he meant. Slim never gave himself excuses.

Cal slipped into my room, in just a pair of pants. I noticed they were Ursinhos, like mine. "I can't sleep."

"I can." *Hint ignored. He looked at himself in my mirror for a long time.*

"Steve, do you really think I'm getting fat?"

"Of course not. But you are getting shoulders. And muscle." *Preen.*

He came over to look at my book. "That's not Slim, it's heavy!" *More hysterics. It was funny, but I didn't want to join him.* "Steve?"

"Cal?"

"Can I sleep with you tonight?"

"Bungle will miss you."

Mistake. Flash of anger. "Bungle's a toy. It's stupid of me to keep him. Makes everyone think I'm a baby."

"Bungle's your past and your memories. It's never stupid to keep those. I've told you I wish I still had Sergeant Bear."

"Yes. But you do think I'm a baby."

"Wrong. I know you're not a baby. That's why I don't think you should sleep here all night."

"I don't want to have sex or anything. I just want to hug you and spoon up to you. We have loads of hugs during the day, what's the difference with hugging all night?"

"It wouldn't feel right to me, Cal. I think it would … change everything."

"Nothing would change for me. I loved you the minute I saw you. I still love you. You don't love me. You're just kind. Like you're kind to everyone you coach in the nets. Don't want to sleep here. I hate you!"

He rushed out. As usual, it tore me up seeing him unhappy, and even worse because it was due to me. I could have followed him, talked to him, maybe convinced him that I had not let him in because I loved him. But I was in turmoil myself. Maybe he was right. Maybe I am just kind to people. Being kind keeps people away, keeps you in control. Like being a cricket coach.

He hugged me the next morning as if nothing had happened. But he still seemed to be wired up. And Alice seemed really ragged. None of us said much at breakfast and we didn't make any plans. Alice mooched back to bed, he went off to draw, I went to the garden with Lord Slim.

She came out to me after about an hour. "Steve, a favour. I need a floppy day and he's having a fidgety day and we're getting on each other's nerves. Can you take him somewhere and feed him and I'll call you when I'm flopped out?"

"Of course."

I found him glaring at a drawing of the house. It looked fine to me. "You have some leftover time from Treat Cal Day. Would you like to go somewhere? Your mum's tired, so I'm afraid it has to be with me."

Oh hell. Does that sound like I'm just being kind to him and her? He bounced around and looked away. His usual routine for giving someone a drawing, but I didn't think that was it. "Do you want to go out with me? I'm so stupid."

"I really, really, want to go somewhere with you and right now."

"I do love you and I hate myself for being stupid. And selfish."

"You're not."

"I am!"

"Your mum's trying to sleep so if you want to argue you have to do it somewhere else. Pick somewhere you'd like to go. Somewhere that would be Treat-Cal day."

Thought. "Billy's beach."

"Long trek, but no problem."

"I know another way. Shorter. Just follow Cat-Nav!" *Joke and self-esteem. He was on the mend.*

"I'll get water and snacks and sunblock and the big back pack. You meet me here with sketching stuff, lifejacket and towel."

"Do I have to?"

"No, you don't have to bring a towel."

"Ha-ha. You know what I meant."

"And you know what I meant. 'We had a great time at Billy's beach. By the way, Cal drowned.' No, I'm not having that conversation with your mum."

"Okay, don't wet yourself." *He was back to normal.*

We assembled everything, I packed it expertly (Uncle Frank's training again) and we set off. Suddenly he swerved off the road onto a tiny path.

"Does this go up anything?"

"No, very gently down. It winds around a bit but we'll get to Billy's beach. Trust Cat-Nav."

He stopped suddenly. "There's the haunted house."

"So there is." *I moved on. He didn't.*

"We're at the back of it. There's a drive at the front but there's a big locked gate."

"Really."

"I don't think anyone knows about this path. You can get in easily this way."

"Really." *He bounced about again and looked at the ground. Something important coming.*

"I'd like to draw it." *Big pleading eyes.*

"Your mum doesn't like this place."

"She's never said I can't go. And I don't want to go in, just draw it from the outside." *A treat for him. And a small adventure. What could go wrong? They won't have laid mines in the grounds, or set wild dogs loose.* "Mum doesn't mind where we go if you're with me. She told me." *Wonder if that's true. He sounded sincere.*

"Do we have to climb something to get in the grounds?"

"No, just go through this hole in the fence."

Easy. Suddenly we were in forbidden space. Once it was a garden. We were on a lawn. Madly overgrown. Horror to mow even to an expert like me.

Years ago with Uncle Frank. Breaking into another big garden behind another big house. Uncle Frank telling me the owners were spies, and to follow him and not make a sound. Me believing him. Scared but thinking it must be OK if I'm with him. I took Cal's hand and gave it a squeeze. He squeezed back. "Sketch. I'm staying here. I won't make a sound."

He sketched. I looked and listened for spies, spooks or spectres [Wordpower!] 360 degrees like Uncle Frank taught me. Not just looking at the obvious places. He showed me his sketch. I nodded approval. He had made the house look very sinister.

"Now we're here, let's explore a bit." *Hand slipped into mine. We moved slowly across the former lawn, me still doing the 360-degree watch. Sudden stop. He pointed excitedly. There was almost nothing left but it could only be the remains of a cricket net.*

"The ghosts play cricket." *Giggle but with extra hand squeeze.*

We circled round the house. "It's way bigger than it looks. I wonder if we can get inside?" *And right on cue he spotted a slightly open window.* "No trouble at all for – the Cat!"

I stopped him. I knew that we shouldn't go into the house. I also knew that I wouldn't be forgiven if we didn't. If we let someone else discover the stolen treasure. Or even the dead body.

I compromised. "I can do that too. I go first. I make sure everything's OK. Like there's no rotten floor or something. If I call you, you can follow. If you don't hear from me in five minutes, or if you hear anything you don't like, you run away and call the police on your mobile. Promise. No heroics."

"Promise." *Excited. New possibilities in the adventure. The window was easy. Too easy? Who had left it open? Was our hero walking into a trap?*

In fact, I walked into one empty room after another. Dust and cobwebs but the floors were sound. One room had a hammer on the floor, another a sweet wrapper. They both looked quite new. The biggest room had candle stubs. Arranged in holders in front of one wall. The walls had all been painted, but badly and I could see an image behind the paint. Jesus being crucified. Some elaborate lettering: Sinners Redeemed. Was this place a church?

A piece of paper on the floor. I picked it up. Not paper. An old faded photograph. I looked at it. I jammed it into my T-shirt. I knew we both had to be out of there.

A boy playing cricket. Batting. Years ago. No helmet and an old-fashioned hairstyle. Ernie would know what to call it.

A blond boy. And left-handed.

I ran to the open window and leapt out. Cal was not there! Panic.

"Steve!!" *Hell, he can be loud. I jumped, but in relief. I knew the happy squeal by now.* "Come here! There's a beach." *I followed the squeal.* "It's fabulous!" *He was right. A small strip of pure sand. Shimmering, calm sea. Narrow inlet bounded by rocks. Where the hell were we? You couldn't possibly get there except from the empty house. Or I suppose by boat. But why would you go there by boat, except to get to the house?* "Let's go in."

He had taken off his T-shirt and trainers already. "HELLO!!!" *I jumped out of my skin. His shout echoed back off the rocks. No reply.* "There's no one else here."

"Why not?"

"Because… we're explorers and no one else is!" *Spooky. A phrase my uncle Frank used regularly. He stuck a toe in the water. Huge challenge to the owners. Or the spooks.* "It's well warm". *Both feet in the water. Nothing happened.* "Only up to my waist." *Now the challenge was to me.* "<u>And</u> I'll wear my lifejacket."

"You will." *I knew I had given in. But I did say No last night. And now it would take so little to make him happy. He darted off to fetch the jacket. I made a fuss of doing up the straps. I slipped off my T-shirt, taking care to hide the photograph.*

"Put the back pack under that rock."

"Why? It won't get stolen."

"Keep it cool, stop my sketch paper curling up." *I obeyed.*

"Wait. I'm going first." *Futile attempt to regain my authority. But I walked quite a long way out.* "All right. There's no drop-off and it's calm as."

We didn't swim much. He wanted to do the same stunt over and over, jumping off my shoulders. Twinge of pain in right shoulder, but he was having fun. Then we both lay on our backs and blissed out. He held my hand, weightless and adrift in the lifejacket. I shut my eyes too. Hot sun, warm sea. Total peace, not even a sea bird.

"Cal, wake up! We need to swim in a bit." *The shore was further away than it should be.* "Front crawl, hard, with me." *We churned through the water but then he had to stop. Was the shore any closer? I couldn't put my feet down. I held him.* "A bit more."

"Can't keep up with you. You hold your breath too long. Edwin says so."

"Okay. I'm going to be the shark again. I throw you and if you get to the shore ahead of me you've escaped. You can put your feet down and walk when you can, but just get to the shore first." *Just playing a game. I hoped I didn't sound anxious. I trod water and threw him towards the shore as hard as I could. My right shoulder really hurt. He churned again, breathing his way. We made ground and I caught him up.*

"You're allowed to stand up."

"Can't." *Me neither. And for all the ground we had made, the shore seemed no nearer.*

"Cal, this is serious. We're caught in the tide. We can't fight it."

"You could make it. Let me go. I've got a lifejacket, I can just float. You could get in and get the mobile and call the lifeboat or something."

"No! We stay together. We find some calm water where we can swim in or we get spotted and picked up. We just have to keep warm. Which means that you hug me. Pretend that you like me." *Smile. Hug.*

"Well, if I die at least I'll die in your arms!"

"Don't be a silly little drama queen!" *But he wasn't. He had wound me up deliberately. He must have sensed I was scared. Smart. Brave. It made me calmer.*

"This is called the HELP position. Heat Escape Lessening Position. My uncle Frank taught me."

"Help. HELLPP!!!" *I would have jumped again. The scream bounced around all the rocks and then died into silence.*

"Jesus. What was that for?"

"Just in case there's someone around." *The silence seemed thicker.* "But there isn't. And no one comes here. And no one knows we're here." *Bad train of thought. End in tears. Change the subject.*

"Do you suppose Illsleigh are any good?"

"Don't know. And we're not going to play. I'm sorry." *Real tears. Bad change of subject.*

"Look, there's a seal!"

"Where?" *I pointed to a half-submerged rock.* "That's not a seal, stupid, that's a rock."

"It's a seal. It's basking. Like us. Not moving a muscle. Just floating in this beautiful calm sea."

"Rock."

"Seal." *Good change of subject!*

"Bet you three million pounds it's a rock. Let's swim there and check it out." *He let go of me and we both churned towards the rock/seal.* "We're not getting anywhere." *More serious tears. I hugged him again.*

"Stop crying now! It makes you colder. My uncle Frank told me." *Lies on my part, but they worked.* "Hug me tighter. Pretend you <u>love</u> me." *I almost got choked but I didn't mind.* "Good. We're warm and we're safe. I'm not swimming now. Your lifejacket's holding me up as well as you." *I did stop swimming and hoped I was right. We did not sink. Relief.* "Now listen to this because you're going to take it over." *I stopped and tried to remember which voice I was going to do.* "This is Jonathan Agnew and welcome to Test Match Special. Start of the deciding Ashes Test. Andrew Strauss won the toss and he surprised everyone by asking Australia to bat. The England team are on the field followed by the Australian openers, Shane Watson and Simon Katich. And here is another surprise, Strauss is throwing the ball to England's new mystery spinner, Cal Devane, in his very first Test. Tremendous gesture of confidence in this young man, just four foot seven inches tall..."

"Four feet ten and a bit!" *Successful distraction. The old routines never fail.*

"Malcolm our scorer corrects me on the height of Cal Devane. Four foot ten plus. Those extra inches could be vital. He'll bowl the first ball to the right-handed Watson, and I'm going to ask Phil Tufnell who's in the box with me to give his field settings and comment on them..."

"Three slips, two gullies, point, silly mid off, short mid off for the checked drive and on the onside leg slip, short leg." *Giggle.*

"Very aggressive field. Strauss must have huge confidence in his new spin bowler. Phil, you're a left-arm spinner. Is Devane the greatest of all time?"

"Totally." *Succession of giggles.*

"What makes him so great? Is it the variety of deliveries? What have you seen him bowl?"

"Ordinary slow left arm, a straight one, an arm ball, the Chinaman, and the zooter. And now he can bowl fast too."

"And can you tell when he's bowling the zooter?"

"Nobody can. It is a total mystery." *Giggle.*

"Anyway here he is, bowling to Watson. First ball, full length. Watson forward – and he's bowled! Sensational start! Australia 0 for 1. Let's see it on replay. Was that the zooter? Phil?"

"No. Not the zooter. He did tell me he was working on a new mystery ball."

"What's that one called?"

"The… the… zamboni." *Giggles turned into hysterics.*

"Ricky Ponting in, much earlier than he would have liked. One of the greatest batsmen of all time. What will he make of this new bowler?"

Ponting only just survived the rest of the over, but scrambled a single off the last ball.

"I'm speechless, Jonathan. That was the best over I've ever seen."

"At the other end, Steve Helson, England's leading fast bowler. Fifty Test Matches but they gave Devane, the newcomer, the choice of ends. Helson will bowl to Ponting. Not such an aggressive field as Devane's…" *I gave it.* "He bowls now to Ponting… Fast, good length…"

"And that's six. Straight back over the bowler's head." *More hysterics.*

And that was the pattern of the match as we drifted further out to sea. The genius Devane carrying all before him and trundler Helson getting battered. But by the time he had taken the sixth wicket in a row the giggles were less and less frequent and his input falling off. It was all I could do to get him to finish off the innings. "That's all ten wickets to Devane. Ten for 47. The best bowling figures in Test Match history." *No response. He was pale and his lips were blue.* "Strauss has no hesitation in enforcing the follow-on." *I then realized that England had not batted at all but he did not correct my mistake.*

"Don't want to do any more. Tired. Going to sleep."

"No!" *I shook him.* "You can't go to sleep. Uncle Frank said so."

"Fuck Uncle Frank." *He shut his eyes. I shook him again and he opened them briefly and then wider.* "Boat!" *He pointed. A small boat in the distance.*

"I'm going to lift you. Scream and wave one arm from side to side."

"HELLPP!!!" *He startled a sea gull. But we didn't see any response from the boat.*

Chapter 29   Declaration

The boat got smaller. I started to cry. I didn't care if he saw. I had failed him and Alice and we were going to die.

"One more time, Steve." *Just for something to do I lifted him again.*

"HELLPP!!! PLEASE!!!" *Manners! It made me giggle.*

And it worked. The boat stopped. It changed course, in our direction. My eyes were full of salt. I could just make out a man and a woman in the boat. The boat stopped near us and idled in neutral. The man threw a lifebelt near us. I grabbed it. Nice throw! It was Adam, from the cricket team. And the amazing blonde!

He pulled us in with the lifebelt. He said a few words to the AB and we got hauled into the boat, first Cal, then me. He threw the engine into gear and we headed off. I couldn't make out the coast or the inlet to the haunted house.

He seemed to be a completely different person in the boat. Efficient, in charge. We were given water and towels. Cal was shivering. The AB removed his lifejacket (he wanted to keep it) and hugged him tight, wrapping her survival jacket around him. Envy! Cal stopped shivering but stayed in the hug.

"What are you two doing out here? No one comes here except us. There's a small island we go to… You can thank Anya. I thought you were seals. She told me that wasn't a seal and I came over to look. Saw Cal's lifejacket."

"Steve made me wear it." *Not really true. He was lying already, to protect me.*

"Adam, Anya, thank you, but have you got a mobile? We need to phone Alice." *He fished a mobile from his survival jacket and gave them both to me. He was prepared. Unlike me.*

Cal had to remind me of Alice's mobile number. She answered instantly.
"Steve? Where are you? Where's Cal?"

"He's with me. He's fine."

I passed him the phone. "I'm fine," *he murmured and passed it back.*

"I've been phoning for hours. You didn't answer. I phoned the police and the coastguard."

"We're fine. Really. We're in Adam's boat. Adam from the cricket team. We went swimming. We got swept out to sea. It … was my fault. Adam picked us up in his boat."

"Swimming where? What on earth were you up to?" *Adam signalled to me to give him the mobile.*

"Alice, there's time for Steve to talk to you later. He needs more water now. Trust me, he and Cal are fine. I know the sea. I've seen this situation before. I'm now going to tell you where I'm going to drop them. You can pick them up by car. You could take them to hospital but I wouldn't bother. You'll just wait around for hours when they could be having a hot bath. That's really all they need. And water and sleep. And Alice? They did all the right things." *He gave directions to his mooring and made Alice repeat them. He reminded her to call off the police and coastguard and snapped the mobile shut. Totally in charge.*

He issued more water and handed out Kendal Mint Cake. I recognized it from Uncle Frank. I revived, Cal too. Anya kept hugging him in the big jacket. That would be a good reviver.

"If you feel up to it, can you tell us where you went swimming?"

"Cal and I know it only as the haunted house."

"Good Lord. If you mean Caslon House… No one goes there. I was warned off the inlet when I bought the boat. It's really treacherous. Hell, I wish you had asked someone first, somebody local."

"Does no one live there?"

"Not for years."

"Is it haunted?"

"Don't know. But you survived. Cal survived." *He stared at him.* "That might be important… No more talking now. Get you home."

Alice was a few minutes late at his mooring. "Sorry. Bloody car wouldn't start."

I remembered an experience with Jimmy's Alfa and blurted "Did you try in fourth?"

"Steve, I can deal with the car." *Clipped. Cold. Deserved that. Stupid, she had far more important things to think about. She swept Cal into her arms. Looked at him, felt his forehead.*

"I'm fine, Mum. Really. Steve saved my life." *She did not look at me.*

"Adam." *She realized she did not know Anya's name and Cal prompted her.* "Anya. Thank you for saving my son's life." *I took a pace back. He dropped from her arms and hugged Adam and Anya. She put him in the front seat of the car and handed him more water. I said thank you to Adam and Anya. Alice motioned me into the back seat and pointed to a water bottle.*

The car started reluctantly. She drove back in silence. "I'm taking Adam's advice about hospital. If you feel hot or shivery or odd later on, I'll have you checked. You're probably hungry but I'm not up to cooking. Can you get by on cereal? Drink lots of milk anyway. I'm running Cal a bath." *Still hardly looking at me.*

I got the cereals. Steve looked utterly mis. I wolfed mine, he hardly ate his. "It will be OK, just give Mum some time." I squeezed his hand but he didn't squeeze back.

Mum came back. "Steve, can you go on fending for yourself? Cal and I will be some time." He nodded. Mum took me to the bathroom. She checked the bath water and made me check it. Perfect. She stayed while I got in. She washed my hair. And Bungle was there to watch me being brave when the shampoo got in my eyes. Everything just as when I was little.

"It was my fault, Mum. We were walking by the haunted house…" Suddenly she yanked a bit of my hair and I squawked and she said sorry. "And I begged Steve to let me see it, just from the outside to do a sketch. And he didn't let me go inside, just himself so that he could be sure it was safe. Then I went exploring and I found this fantastic beach and I wanted to go in but again Steve went in first to make sure it was safe. And Steve made me wear my lifejacket." That bit wasn't really true. I hope Mum believed me. "We mucked around in the water …" I told her all the rest and I think she almost smiled at Steve's Test Match. "He did everything right, Mum. In the water. Adam said so. Steve saved our lives!"

"Darling… That's a fine speech for the defence. Believe it or not, I'm not so worried about what happened in the water. I am still terrified that you nearly drowned, but there's something else on my mind. Come on, let's get you dry." She wrapped me in a big towel, ran her hairdryer over me and styled my hair. Just as when I was little. My hair's getting long. I'll go to Yasmin when we get back. Steve was supposed to come with me. Will he? That's when I lost it. I burst into tears and couldn't stop. Mum switched off the dryer and held me for a long time.

"It's OK. Everything's going to be OK." She scooped up Bungle and carried us back to my bed. "You're going to have a little sleep. Bungle's going to watch over you. When you wake up, everything's going to be fine." But that was when I was little... I wanted to say that and some other stuff, but I just gave in and fell asleep.

Cal fell asleep. My little boy, back again, with his bear. I looked at them for a minute and tiptoed out of the room.

Steve was still in the kitchen, staring at a cereal bowl. I knew that he felt guilty and tormented, but just then he irritated me. I couldn't even look at him.

She couldn't even look at me. I didn't blame her.

"Steve, we need to have a conversation but I'm too overwrought to have it now. It's not just about doing something stupid and reckless and nearly drowning my son. It's about why you did that. It's about him twisting you round his little finger. Did he look up at you with the big puppy-dog eyes and get you to do exactly what he wanted? How many conversations have we had about that? When are you ever going to say no to him?" I saw him twitch.

Oh God, young man, if you value your life don't start to argue with me now.

I poured on and didn't give him the chance. "What will it be next time, when you can't say no? Will it be drugs? Or sex? Or letting him fuck over somebody and then walk away? Like his father. We could have that conversation, but what's the point? We had that conversation and it didn't do any good."

He looked really terrible. I had been very unfair, a total bitch. But who was this stranger to judge me? Make me feel like a bitch. My anger was eating itself. I forced myself to look at him. Calmly. "Steve, we must talk again later. Calmly. Right now I think you should have a shower and think and reflect. Oh, leave the bloody cereal bowls!"

Stupid of me. At that point she didn't need domestic help.

I had a long shower. The shampoo stung my eyes. I howled. Baby! I dealt with it, rinsed and dried.

It was still light. Way too early for bed. I looked for some clothes to put on. Nothing but my great Ursinho stuff. Suddenly I hated it all. Everything with the little bear logo. My makeover clothes, for my new life. What new life? I had it and then I threw it away, because I'm stupid. I never deserved it. Now they'll take me back to London and throw me back to my old life.

I chucked all the Ursinho clothes around the room. Finally I found some old stuff. Boring, stupid. Like me. I stuck it on. And my old trainers. Maybe I could just run and run and run and not even have to say goodbye.

Instead I picked up Lord Slim and started reading. He had made a bad decision and the Gallabat campaign was a failure and he was beating himself up. How appropriate!

A few hours' responsibility. That was all she asked of me. And I've been weak and stupid and nearly killed her son. After all they've done for me. I don't belong with people like that. Or the Barneses. Joe and Belinda trusted me to look after their children. I can't ask them to trust me again.

I can't come back here. As if they would ask me. I can't be the professional for Glendon Courtenay. Professional. Someone who makes good decisions. Adam will have told everybody now. Steve's a weakling and a fool.

Maybe I could go to New Zealand. Oh yes, that would be a great email to send to Brendon and Daniel. 'Remember I told you about Cal and Alice and how much they were doing for me? Well, I let them down completely so I thought I would come over and do the same to you…'

Cal slipped in. This time dressed, shorts, T-shirt, trainers. "Mum's asleep. I can't. Do you want to run somewhere? Bloody hell, what have you done with your clothes? You'll wreck them." *He started to pick them up.*

"Leave them!" *He jumped and dropped them.* "You can have them all."

"What happened?"

"I let Mum down."

"That's the first time you've called her Mum."

"Well, she's not going to be my mum now, is she?"

He tore past me out of the room. "Steve, Steve! Where are you going?" I ran after him, out of the house. "Steve, wait up!" He didn't stop. He was way faster than me. I tried to hang in and watch him. I was gasping and had to stop.

I saw him swerve suddenly off the road. He took the little path. Towards the haunted house.

I stumbled back to our house. "Mum! MUM!! Wake up! Please!"

She woke up and held out her arms. "Don't worry, sweetheart, it was only a nightmare. You're safe now."

"Mum, it's Steve! We've got to go after Steve! He's running to the haunted house."

"Steve? Steve often goes running." She didn't seem to be awake. I forced myself to be really slow.

"Mum, Steve is really angry with himself and we can't leave him alone." Then I suddenly realized. "Mum, he's going to the beach. He's going to drown himself!"

Cal burst into tears, great gasping sobs. I was wide awake. No time for comfort. I just grabbed his hand. "Car. With me. Now." I seized the car keys and some shoes. "Do you know how to get there by road?"

"Yes, but it's miles!"

And damn it, the car didn't want to start. "Mum, do something!"

"We have to wait, otherwise we flood the engine."

"Try starting in fourth, the way Steve said." The least I could do, and it worked. I managed to keep the engine running along our drive.

"Left!" I had to wait before I could pull into the road. "Go now!"

"Let me decide. Won't help Steve if we crash." It was getting dark and it was a narrow, unlit road. Cal was frantic at my chosen speed. "Next right!"

"Next right? Sure?"

"Of course I'm bloody sure!" I turned right and followed more directions. He was right. "Park here and follow me! That gate is locked but we can still get to the beach." Before leaving the car I gave a long blast on the horn. He jumped. "What was that for?"

"He'll know we're here."

"Oh yeah. STEEEVVE!!!" He was almost as loud as the horn. He tugged me round the side of the house. I stumbled and cursed myself for not bringing a torch. The Cat of course had no trouble staying on his feet. We reached the back of the house and he yanked me through the hole in the fence. We hurtled towards the beach. Empty.

Another scream for Steve. Echo off the rocks and then silence. He burst into tears again. But my brain was working and I needed answers, quickly. Again no time for comfort. I smacked my darling in the face.

"Sorry. I always wondered if that worked. What was Steve wearing when he ran off?"

"T-shirt, shorts, trainers."

"Where are they? He drowns himself in trainers?"

"He would drown faster!" More tears. Stupid of me. A better idea came to me. Another slap.

"You had the big back pack. Where is it?"

"I made him leave it behind this rock in the shade. To save my paper. Not there!"

"Steve drowns himself <u>with</u> your phone and <u>with</u> your sketchbook? I think not. Had you done a sketch?"

"Yeah."

"You know our Steve…" I paused. Had he noticed the 'our Steve'? Yes. His whole body relaxed. "You've gone somewhere and you've left a sketch behind. Our Steve finds it. What do you think our Steve would do with it?"

"Give it back to our Cal." Huge smile.

"He's gone home, sweetheart. Trust me."

We retraced our path to the car, Cal guiding me, not hurrying me. The same in the car, for the route home. It started instantly. No excitement until I told him my proposal. Carried nem con. Stop for hug and kiss. A few tears. I forgot the torch but I'm never out of tissues.

Steve was sitting in front of the door, with the backpack. A beaten soldier, knees drawn up.

"Steve, I think we left it open. Come inside, anyway. Did you go for the backpack? Very considerate, as always." Gently, matter-of-fact. I signalled to Cal to do nothing dramatic but I didn't need to. "You two are grounded tomorrow. And on work detail – good time to do some jobs and leave this house ready for Portia. Now we're putting today to bed. We've all thought about it enough. We know how we can all stop it from happening again. No more talking. I want to sit on the couch with my boys."

I sat them on each side of me and put an arm round each. I waited until I heard Steve's breathing slow down. Then I took a deep breath myself. "You heard me say 'my boys', Steve. Boys, plural. I want you to be part of our family. So does Cal. When we go back to London I'm giving you a key to our place. You use it when you want. You respect our home, because it's your home too. Until you make your own way. We love you, Steve. We look out for you as you look out for us. You're stuck with us, for as long as you want."

And I went on holding my boys.

Chapter 30 Bits And Pieces Player

Foy, Howard (Shackleton) *Author, broadcaster. Trustee:*
Literary Benevolent Fund, Human Capital Trust, Chairman
of the Governors, Marian's College (independent).
Consultant (former copywriter) to Barnes, Dorman, Sharp
(advertising). Married Marian Stone (decd), no children.
Publications: The Speculator (novel and screenplay),
McMaster: Hero Of Zero (biographical novel), For Napoleon
(novel), Living Death In The Buying Department (novel, as
R Bristow), Who Killed Aunt Agatha? (also television
play, and 8 other Bertie Wooster mysteries), The Mind Of
Cricket (edited), Batting With Tigers (cricket manual,
with Tim Morrow), Dead White Men: A Defence (criticism),
It Almost Makes You Think (collected journalism).
Screenplays: Rob Patty Runs Out Of Luck (full-length
feature, and 26 episodes of TV series), Turkey (with P
Hobby), Your Very Own Ricky Rubato (Kleenex Award) and
numerous contributions to other films and television
dramas. Radio: creator/presenter of You're Booked! Many
other broadcasts.

That's enough, I'm sure. Yes, I'm that Howard Foy.
Wordsmith. Spacefiller. Always available for the snappy
quote or interview or an op-ed or review piece on any
cultural phenomenon. Urbane. Fluent.

But when I first met Alice Devane I became instantly a
gibbering idiot. A blusher, a babbler, a burbler. And
thoroughly impatient. I have got far ahead of events.
Blame her…

I met her boys first. I returned from the Cape Verde
Islands, lecturing for the British Council and meeting
the benefactor of the Human Capital Trust. (Let us call
him a retired businessman.) I was instantly bombarded by
requests from the Barnes children to meet their new
friends (and to bring my cricket stuff when I did). I was
happy to oblige. Being a self-employed man of letters
(indeed, being an unemployed man of letters) means being
able to play cricket at will and to play indulgent Uncle
Howard.

I met Zoe and Robert at the usual nets. Joe and Belinda
were back at their boutique agency, rejecting undesired
clients. One of the new friends was Steve, 16, an
athletic, serious young man, with unusually good manners
and a rich vocabulary. I could not resist some wordplay.

"Helson? The perfect name for a fast bowler. As soon as you come on, the Barmy Army will call out 'Give'em Hell, son!' Try to take 6 for 66 so the papers can headline 'The Spell From Hel'" He laughed (polite?), the others booed.

"Can I tell him your nickname, Steve?"

"See if he can guess from my bowling, Zoe. My psychotic bowling, ooh what a giveaway!" Psycho Helson. Not this boy, draped around Zoe, taking endless play punches from the younger boys.

The other friend was Cal, 12 (I guessed younger), a bouncy, blond chatterbox. Were they brothers? They did not look alike but seemed exceptionally close. (My brother and I never liked each other.) Steve was a fast bowler of quality and an aggressive batsman, Cal a left-arm spinning all-rounder with a proud array of mystery balls. Both required my full reserves of low cunning with both bat and ball.

"Howard, I hate you! You're the most boring batsman in the world! You've no backlift, you wait until the last minute and then punch everything away."

"Yeah, Howard, and you never try to hit the zooter and the zamboni!"

"Temper, temper, boys! I learnt that from my boyhood idol, Basil D'Oliveira. He learnt it when he was a boy because he was a non-white South African and he was never allowed to play on the good pitches with the white boys. My friend Peter Oborne wrote a good book about him.[21] I'll lend it to you."

"I read it!" Tribute. Robert claimed he never read books. "Howard played minor counties. Three seasons for Hertfordshire!"

"Robert's my stats guru. Only in holidays. Just a bits and pieces player. Like my writing." Start of loyal protests from the Barneses. I cut them short. It's true. "Now, let's see if you can handle bits and pieces bowling."

The new friends had produced astonishing changes in Zoe and Robert. They had abandoned, apparently overnight, their racking feud and enjoyed each other's society. Robert had lost weight and gained courage. Zoe, my there-is-no-goddaughter, was far prettier and far less anxious, her conversation more intelligent and less affected. It

---

[21] True.

was hard to prise her away from Steve (I felt that Robert wanted to put the same lock on Cal but still lacked the nerve to do so in a public park).

They did not affect only the Barnes children. I enjoyed myself. Not having to act out funny old Uncle Howard. Just bowling my little bits and pieces. "Howard, you're such a dreary bowler. Just sitting back of a length and waiting for mistakes. I hate bowlers like you!" Feeling good that the two new boys could go straight to 'Howard', and abuse me as just another cricketer. I made a mental note to inquire about their schooling and whether they might want to follow Zoe and Robert into Marian's. Only one parent was mentioned, Cal's mother, Alice. Who had piloted these children? I was already curious to meet her but nothing prepared me…

But I am again rushing ahead of events. We have finished playing cricket. I am treating all the children in the park café. They are chattering excitedly about a dramatic sea rescue, two cricket matches, a house with a curse, a holiday treat, a vital family meeting. Be patient, Howard, let the children finish these stories. You might by then find coherent words to describe Alice Devane.

"We were in the paper!"

"You sent it to us. BOY CRICKET HEROES IN SEA ESCAPE."

"Guess who wrote that headline?"

"I had to help that reporter. He didn't even want to call you an MCC triallist."

"I'm not an MCC triallist. Howard, can I ask you something later?"

"Of course. Now, can you both continue, because I didn't catch the North Devon Argus…"

"I had to tell that reporter everything, like my great-uncle Cal being a big rock star and me being a famous artist…" Boos. "Mum had to shut me up but eventually he got enough tape and he said 'I'm going to get a splash out of this' and I said 'we're the ones that had the splash, we were in the sea for hours!'" More boos.

* * *

"I've got the story from them and statements from Adam Sawyer and Anya Tukhachevsky."

"She speaks!"

"Loads."

"Respect to you!"

"Mostly about Cal." *Preen. Max Foggo, the reporter, looked at his notes.* "One thing I need to get straight. Cal says Steve saved them and Steve says Cal saved them. Which do you want us to print?"

"Both." *We hugged. Didn't care what Max thinks. Actually he gave us a big smile.*

"We'll go with 'Both'. Alice, I've got your statement on safety and keeping people off that beach. Are you really suing the owners of Caslon House?"

"Possibly, but keep that off the record. Tell me about that house. Somebody must own it. Why is no one living there? Go to your newspaper morgue, feed me everything you have about the place and its owners. In exchange I'll give you a second story."

"It's owned by some religious group. There's a legal dispute over it. I pulled out some cuts but they are full of legal red ink. But I'll give you what we have. Now, can I take pictures of Steve and Cal? We're a poor paper, I have to be the snapper too."

"I give permission for Cal, if I approve the published picture and the caption. I can't give permission for Steve. I'm not actually his mother. Cal and Steve are friends – as you've heard."

I wanted to have my picture, with Cal and Alice, in his paper. What did it have to do with my parents? They didn't care what happened to the real me, why would they bother about my image? But I didn't want Max to know that part of my story.

"Alice, in the absence of my parents, can't my lawyer give consent? I'm sixteen. I know my mind. My picture might stop kids my age swimming there and drowning."

"A good argument from public policy. You may take my client's picture."

"Can you do it in cricket whites? Me bowling, Cal batting? You could wait for the Illsleigh match and do it for real."

"Now's better for me." We changed. He shot off shed loads of pics of my glorious action in the garden. "Now you, Cal. Can you get rid of the helmet so the readers get your handsome face?" *Preen. Many poses. Much laughter, but I got spooked again. I knew we all had to confront something.*

I pulled out the photo I had found in the house. "Max, everybody? Ignore the hair. Do you think Cal looks quite a lot like this?"

***

"Admirable story-telling, Steve, beautifully constructed."

"That's what happened, Howard."

"Sorry. I deserved that. Please continue."

***

We were all more or less spooked.

"Is that me?"

"No, sweetheart. You are not the only blond, lefthanded boy who plays cricket." *Max wanted to say something but Alice cut him off.* "This boy is at least thirty now. Perhaps he would like his picture back. Max will take copies but give me back the original. And now Max, I told you long ago that the boys are grounded and have jobs around the house. You have enough, begone!" *She shooshed him out and returned.*

"Work detail. Cal the Cat, clear guttering and clean upper windows. Don't wet yourself, Steve, he did it last year. You are my Ground Force. Mowing both lawns, removing another dead stump and remaining Jacob's ladder. Myself, two washes and polish all polishable surfaces. No communication except as absolutely necessary. Take water and snack supply with you. Go!"

We worked flat tack. I got the heebie-jeebies when Cal climbed on the roof. Couldn't help it.

Alice called us in with her giant whistle. Where did she learn it? She gave us sandwiches and milk. "Boys, are your jobs finished? Honest answer."

"Honest yes."

"Lawns mowed. Stump removed. Some Jacob's ladder standing."

"Remove it. Then your grounding is lifted. By request of your public.
Everyone wants to see you. First call, Adam and Anya, with a thank you gift.
Second call, Ernie and Dorothy, where Cal is to tango. Mr Wu wants to give
you a free meal. The team wants to buy you drinks at the pub. I think there
will also be requests for autographs. And we are going to the main beach to
swim to the red buoy and back. You up for that, sweetheart? With us but no
lifejacket. I'm keeping that for the Cal Devane Museum."

"Okay." *Not totally sold.*

*Adam showed us all his work in progress. Seascapes, nude studies of Anya, still lifes.
Even I could tell that it wasn't terribly good. Cal did his bounce and look away
routine.* "Adam, Anya. Thank you for saving our lives. I hope you like
these." *Sketches of them in their boat, from memory. And some cartoon basking seals
crying for help. They were moved.*

"Cal, you're an artist. Way ahead of where I was when I was your age. There
is a tradition that artists exchange. Would you like something of mine?" *He
thought hard and very carefully picked out the least bad seascape. Not by a flicker did
he suggest that Adam was getting the better of the exchange. Respect!*

"Adam, Anya, I want to say thank you too. I can't give you anything
personal, but Adam, could I commission the picture you're doing tomorrow
of the cricket team? One for them, and a copy for me?" *He looked choked and a
bit confused. I forced him to accept £500. I don't think he gets many commissions.
We said goodbye. Hugs and tears. Me too, of course, meet Mr Mushy!* "Very
nicely done. I'm proud of you both. Now, quick visit to the main beach."

*We went into the sea together, up to his waist. He stopped and held hands. We
stopped too and paid no attention. He let go suddenly.* "First to the buoy gets ice
cream!" *We went with him in close convoy but he didn't stop or grab.* "First one
back gets another ice cream!" *Mission accomplished.*

"Well done. I needn't cancel Treat-Cal-and-Steve-Day." *Had to be something
sea-based, but we could not wheedle more out of her.*

*This time Cal had help with Dorothy's clotted cream tea but it still defeated us. We
all watched Ernie and Dorothy waltz and foxtrot. Cal took over for the tango.*

"Never got on terms with the tango. Too liquid for me." *Cal and Dorothy did some dramatic steps and he nearly fell over but they finished to wild applause.*

"Ernie, do you know anything about Caslon House?"

"Before my time. But Noel Felix told me. He used to be President of the cricket club." *He shut his eyes. Trying to remember, or just being a drama queen? I can also be Mr Cynic!* "Caslons were American. Mum, Dad, two older kids, one younger boy. Very rich, very religious. Travelling around these parts, looking for ancestors. Then the spirit told them to stop here and buy Caslon House. Used to be called something else. Way too big for one family, but they had these sort of priests with them, called themselves the Redeemers.

"Caslons hardly came into town. Children didn't go to school, parents didn't shop or go to the pub. Stayed at their place with the Redeemers. Just one thing. The younger boy was dead keen on cricket and they let him play. We had a kids' team then. Josiah. That was his name. It's in the Bible. Always Josiah in full, never Jo or Josh. Some Redeemer always drove him to practice or matches in his whites. He was never allowed to change with the rest of the team, or stay on after. Driven straight home. Good bat though, said Eric. Left-handed. Like Cal." *Another long pause. I dared him to light a pipe.*

"Then Josiah drowned. Off their private beach. There were questions asked. He was a small, slight kid. What were they doing, letting him swim there?" *I blushed.* "There were stories of baptisms in the sea by the Redeemers."

Alice suddenly went rigid with tension. "That's potentially manslaughter."

"Body never found. Inquest gave a verdict of misadventure. Sympathy for the family. Parents went mad with grief. More gossip. They had taken Josiah's death as punishment for their sins and pride. Anyway, they gave their house to the Redeemers."

"That must be voidable. Undue influence, lack of consideration. Mala fides – bad faith."

"The Caslons disappeared not long afterwards. The rest of the family. Left the house empty. People would come for weekends and then leave. And sometimes people to clean, or repair things. I think they must have been Redeemers. Never came to the village."

I thought for a bit. "Big empty house and a good bit of land. Wouldn't they want to sell it? The Redeemers?"

"They had a big bust-up amongst themselves. Two different lots calling themselves the true Redeemers. Neither letting the other lot sell the place."

"Possible. The parents might have set up a trust and the trustees could not agree. Or they might be afraid to sell. Might expose the way they got the place, and show that they never had good title to it."

"Who would own it if it isn't the Redeemers?"

"The older children, unless the parents made a will and said something different. Ernie, do you know how old they were when this happened?"

"No. But they both believed in the Redeemers."

"Cal and I got in really easily. Have there been squatters… travellers?"

Dorothy cut in. "I know some travellers. They won't go near it. They think it's cursed."

"There was a squat a few years back. Someone cleared them out in the middle of the night. Just disappeared without trace. People go there from time to time. Security, cleaning, maintenance. Plain white vans. Never come to town."

"Not enough maintenance. I'm going to sue them for negligence. Cal and Steve were trespassers but they are still liable in negligence. Keep that to yourselves, please, that I'm suing. It's the only way I have locus – grounds to act against the owners. These Redeemers. Scum who preyed on parents in grief and stole from children."

"They're dead meat now. Mum never loses."

"I do sometimes, sweetheart. But wait till they meet Portia. Ernie, Dorothy? What do you think? Would you help me? I can find out the owner from the Land Registry. But I need more. I've got the reporter who interviewed Cal and Steve. Max Foggo from the Argus. But you have local knowledge. Somebody's watching over the property. Paying council tax. Providing the security and maintenance. Somebody local? Did the Caslons use a local lawyer to buy the place, or a local estate agent? They had a child not going to school. Did they get visited by social workers? Any information like that. Would you help me?"

Dorothy and Ernie looked at each other, then at Cal.

"We will. For that boy who played cricket."

***

Zoe and Robert and I were spellbound. Steve was a natural
storyteller. We looked at Cal. Another Josiah? But he
survived. Some kind of symbolic death and rebirth? Tosh,
Howard, but I could not help thinking about it. And I
had another reason for thinking about him. Robert broke
my reveries.

"What happened in the Illsleigh match?"

"It was a bit boring really."

"Just because you didn't get 84 again!"

"What did he get?" Zoe on the edge of her seat.

"Only 12. Singles. Giving Luke Marriott the strike to get his hundred. What a
god! You must know him, Howard, he knows Joe and he played for the
Frenetics. He plays really late like you, only proper shots with a big backlift!"

"Luke Marriott. Yes, I do know him. I taught him. My favourite pupil. I was
briefly a prep school master. Traditional occupation for struggling writers.
Luke was a wonderful bat and a terrific kid. Helped me pull out from the Lost
Years of Howard Foy. Along with Joe. I stole Luke's name for the boy in my
first novel. The Speculator. A cricketer. I thought Luke would be
embarrassed. So I turned his namesake into a blond and made him left-
handed. And now I've just met a blond left-handed boy who's a wonderful
cricketer and a terrific kid. Some sort of circle. Pah. No mumbo-jumbo. I'm
delighted you both met Luke. I lost track of him. Shame on my part. I will ask
you a lot more about him and Laura. They've got a son, haven't they? But for
now, go back to his innings."

"We batted first. Sam usually bats second and hopes for a draw but we all felt
up for it after beating Undecim. Anyway, we had a good opening stand from
Edwin and Marjorie."

"Marjorie?" Zoe, suddenly tense.

"Don't worry, I'm her toy boy and she's my fag hag. Actually, she and
Edwin are an item." Zoe relieved. Steve took her hand.

302

"They had this South African professional as their opener. Faster than me."

"He wasn't faster than you and he was a nob. Ordering everyone around when he's not the captain and when he's not even bowling. And they had another nob opening with him called Davison, who used to play for us, only Steve threw him out, and Luke said they were both nobs, well not quite…"

***

"This is stupid bowling. Really slow wicket and they're trying to bang it in. Pass the buffet. You're not going to bowl like that, are you Steve?"

***

"Marjorie and Edwin pretty much helped themselves and Marjorie got out and Edwin got out soon after but only because I think he wanted to be with Marjorie. Anyway, Luke was number 3 and he took 12 off his first three balls from the South African and he said his ankle hurt and took himself off.

"Sam was in and he's a good bat but he just handed Luke the strike. They had some good bowlers apart from their openers but Luke just decided when he wanted to score off them. That was what it was like to watch, Howard. Lots of footwork, right forward or right back, and then waiting for the ball and saying 'shall I have six or four or just take a rest and put Sam in with a single?' Sam got caught in the deep and I came in and Luke said 'Do you mind, Steve?' As if! I just gave him the strike, like Sam, and he got his hundred and then there was this nice kid, about my age, bowling off spin and Luke got himself stumped to him. I had a big whack and got out - really unprofessional - but we had made around 200 with plenty of time before tea. Everyone else just tucked in and we declared on 320 for 9. It was a record."

"How many did Cal get?" Now Robert on the edge of his seat.

"11. And a six off the South African."

"Top edge!"

"Calculated uppercut. Cal-culated." I already loved the way those two boys argued. For pleasure, totally secure with each other. Like me and Marian in the good years.

"Jesse hit two sixes in two balls off him and Rick put him into the river."

"Cross-batted slogging. No cal-culation."

"We had tea. Cal ate mine while I was talking to Luke."

***

"Luke, I can't believe you never played first class."

"I've never thought anything to it. Cricket. It's just a bit of fun. You just hit the ball or stop it or catch it. I never bowled. That would have been hard work. I never did any hard work until I met Laura. Then I threw myself into laundry." Like me until I met Marian, only with writing. Must meet him again.

***

"What about their innings?"

"All out 150. Never in it. Marjorie and Mr Wu put them under the cosh."

***

"Not your sort of wicket, Steve. Low and slow. Holding you back in case we need an enforcer."

***

"But Steve did bowl?"

"He got three for 15 including the South African bighead."

"He was stumped. Brilliant work by Johnny. I bowled medium pace. It didn't feel right. Underhand. Not a glad animal."

"Frank Tyson."

"You know him?" Steve seemed transfixed. I had made some connexion.

"Of course. His book is a classic. I quoted a lot in my book, The Mind Of Cricket."

"My uncle Frank gave it to me." Tremor in the voice. A powerful connexion.

"Did Cal bowl?" Robert again.

"Sam kept me back for ages and then Marjorie bowled number 10 and their number 11 came in and then she said 'ooh, ow, I've hurt my ankle, can't go on', not, but making sure the South African could hear, and Sam asked me to complete her over."

***

"Nothing fancy, Cal, just a straight ball."

***

"So I did and number 11 had a whack and I bowled him."

***

"Congratulations, Cal, Hat trick! You took two with your last two balls against Undecim so that's a hat trick and you buy us all a jug. Clem is the worst batsman in Devon. Probably in the northern hemisphere."

***

"Mum bought my jug but no beer for Steve because he pukes." Zoe looked at him adoringly, as if puking was godly.

More bickering and then more story-telling. Celebrating the historic victory, looking at Adam's sketches of the match ("Way better, almost as good as mine!") and then Cal spending the night with Billy ("We talk now on the phone. And scan drawings.") Loyal to stay in touch with Billy. Must get this boy into Marian's.

"They dropped me back and we packed up and got the place ready for Portia." Portia Harper. Another Frenetic connexion. And Alice a partner in her firm. "We drove off."

***

"Mum, wrong way."

"Right way. Didn't put today's destination into Cat-Nav."

***

"Mum drove to Clovelly only we didn't stay there long because it's too pretty-pretty and Mum took us to this boat and said we were going to Lundy Island to swim with the seals."

***

"You don't have to if you feel nervous. You can see them from the boat."

"Mum, I want to try this wetsuit. Do I look like Steve?"

"It will help you float a bit, as well as keeping you warm."

***

"We all got in the water and it was deep and a bit wavy and I almost panicked but then I looked round and I knew I would be looked after."

"By Steve?" Zoe, gazing at him with big eyes.

"By the seals!" Hysterics. "They came out to play and they were just so cute..." He gave us the name of each seal and its special trick. "So that was Treat-Cal-And-Treat-Steve-Day." Memorable. The stuff of family legend. I wanted even more to meet this woman, who had given it to her boys.

I offered more ice cream, cakes, tea, drinks. All refused. No reason not to leave, except that Steve seemed to have more to say.

"Steve, I heard you say something about a special meeting, but you don't have to talk about it."

"I want to. Maybe some water after all, Howard. Please."

***

We got home. Yes, home. Went to my room.

"Alice, are you sure? You're going to lose your study. You don't have to move these law books. I've only got Uncle Frank's trunk to move in."

"This is your space now, Steve. Only your stuff goes in here and no one goes in unless you let them. We'll find you a proper cricketer's bed and some clever storage."

I phoned my mother and father. No special rejoicing that I was back. No curiosity about my holiday. Good. I wanted things low-key. Made an appointment for me and

Alice to see them next evening. An appointment to see my parents in my home. I nearly got angry, but I wanted things to be businesslike.

I couldn't sleep. All sorts of worries. What happens now? Do I get my MCC trial? How? Will the Right Honourable really stop me? What if I fail? Do I get more education, I'm not stupid? Or a job? How will they get a decent bed in here?

I threw some running stuff on. Not supposed to be such a good neighbourhood as my old one, but I didn't see any winos or creepy people. Rehearsed my glad animal action. Hell, I would hate to become a tiddly medium-pacer. I asked Malcolm on TMS to strike those Illsleigh wickets from my career stats.

Got back. Crashed on the bed in my stinky running stuff. Slob - wrong in Alice's study. Still couldn't quite believe it was my room, but I fell asleep anyway.

Awake in time to see Alice off to work. Hugs, casual banter between the three of us. No more waking up alone after a run (or wandering in the nude admiring myself!)

Dozens of missed calls from Zoe already, this early in the morning. Phoned her back. Instant answer. I hardly did any talking, just reassured her that Cal and I were fine after our ordeal (had told her about it). Accepted invitation for Cal and me to play cricket with Howard in the park. (Cal had already accepted invite for us from Robert!)

"Do you mind if we talk tomorrow? I've got to do something today and it's on my mind." *Felt awful about shutting her out. But I did say* "Nearly drowning wasn't great but the worst thing was you sending me all those beach snaps and then you not being there." *Hoped she believed that. Was it a bit glib? And we did say Love you-Love you to each other about 30 times until Cal dragged me off to Mrs K.*

We gardened and she said I was handsome as sin with my long hair. Cal said Mum had made appointment for us with Yasmin. Then he got tearful. Mrs K administered pastries. He got better.

"You're edgy. Do you want to be on your own? You don't have to look after me." *Felt bad but rode my bike to the crematorium. Looked at the tablet for Uncle Frank. Why? It meant nothing to me, never has. Biked back home. Back home. Read more of Lord Slim. He was starting to win against the Japs. Omen for me?*

Alice came back and fed Cal. I couldn't eat. She drove me to my old house. I noticed how nice the lawn looked. Were they using the Ahmads? They didn't need me.

"Hello stranger." *My mother should not have said that. She wanted to make a light remark but it was too true. I had been a stranger for sixteen years. I snapped off that thought: don't be a silly little drama queen. This was a business meeting.*

"You remember Alice? Is Dad in the living room? Can we start?" *We all sat down. Alice and I facing them. Then I nearly lost it but I kept things detached, businesslike (I hope).* "Mum, do you mind putting your manuscript in another room? And Dad, the same for your spreadsheet?" *For the only time in my life I wanted undivided attention. They complied and returned.*

"This isn't easy to say. I better come straight to the point. Alice has offered me a home with her and Cal and I want to live there. I'm sixteen and I can do this. I'm sorry if this is a shock and if I've upset you but this is my decision and I hope we can get everything sorted."

They didn't look upset. My father did look shocked and my mother looked furious. Not at me but at Alice. I remembered that someone had taken the man she really wanted to marry. Now she was losing another man. Alice was the Other Woman.

My father finally broke the silence. "Steve? Son? This is a shock. I know we've had our ups and downs, especially about cricket. I know things haven't been right for you since Frank died but … leaving? Living somewhere else?" *I think he wanted to add 'with someone you've just met,' but it must have seemed like bad manners.* "This is your home and we've tried to make a life for you and we love you…" *And now my mother was crying and he went over to hold her and comfort her. I felt guilty and terrible but I had to go on.*

"Dad… Mum. I'm sorry. I'm not saying I hate you, you're bad people. Just what I feel. I am not certain that you love me. I don't think you're really interested in me, except when I annoy you. I'm not happy here. I get by. I know that Alice loves me. And Cal. That they care about me all the time and that I'm happy with them. So I want to live with them."

"We can change things here, son."

"It won't make a difference."

"I could give up work." *My mother at last saying something. Too late, and I never minded her work. I wanted her to give up the Novel and the script of her life, and my part in it.*

"Please… this is my decision. It's about me, not about you."

"Steve's just said a very wise thing. Donald, Desiree, you might hate me at this moment but I hope you'll listen to me. I'm a children's and family lawyer. I've seen many break-ups. It's vital in these situations that people don't pass judgment on each other, or on themselves. Please take Steve's decision that way. My son and I have offered him a different kind of home life. He wants it. Forgive me, but you cannot stop him taking it. I hope we can work through the practical consequences. You may like to know that Steve will be going to a home with rules and structure. He's not going to be allowed off the rails or to be a bad influence on my son. He will work hard at what he chooses to do – but that you ought to know already. Steve is a conscientious young man. Our problem is getting him to relax."

"This is your final answer? Absolutely final, final answer? Don't want to phone a friend?"

Respect to Dad. Trying for a little humour. I replied in kind "Final, final answer. Have I won one million pounds?" *It reminded me of something, with a jolt.* "Uncle Frank's money. What he left to me. I want it. I can't have Alice paying for me for everything."

"It's invested for you, Steve. Everything's set to come to you on your eighteenth birthday. It would be very disadvantageous to encash it now."

"Fuck that. I just want what he left me. Well, plus what it might have got in the Post Office. Is that fair? You can keep everything else. And I want Uncle Frank's trunk. Is that too much to ask? You won't have to keep me any more and you might even rent my room…"

"Steve. I think your father and I can have a discussion about your money. And make arrangements to send your uncle's trunk. Can I assume now that you accept Steve's decision?"

"Yes." *Both of them. Calm, no edge.*

"Well, here's my key."

"Keep it, son. Use it whenever you want. You don't have to tell us in advance. Please stay in touch. Oh, I suppose your GCSEs will arrive soon. We'll send them on but tell us what happens. Please."

"Okay, dad. Thanks."

***

"And then I said goodbye and that was it. There's some legal stuff to do, but well… Alice and Cal are now my family." A bit choked. Me too, urbane Howard Foy. The other children looked at him and then barrelled into him for a gigantic group hug. Right there in the crowded café. Then Zoe and Robert pulled me into it and kept us all prisoner.

In which felicitous position I first met Alice Devane.

Chapter 31   Taking Guard

"Children! Release Mr Foy at once. He's a famous writer."

A small woman. Fine-boned. Office clothes. Hair beginning
to escape from attempt at severe style. Smile definitely
escaping from attempt at severe style. Why am I so
nervous? As if I'm taking guard against a fast bowler?

"Too kind. A mere entertainer. Another performing flea, like my master P G
Wodehouse." Shame, Howard. Babbling, and affected!

He freed himself and came over to greet me. Faultless whites, MCC sweater, but
untidy. Tall, shambling. A bear. Cal will like him. Obviously loves children.

And now they all rush to hug her. Gives me the chance to
reply in kind. "Children! Release Ms Devane at once. She's a famous
lawyer. She will serve you all with writs of fieri facias and nemo me impune
lacessit." A tiny extra smile at my legal gibberish. Firm
handshake. "It is Alice, isn't it? Delighted to meet you. Howard Foy.
Writer. Of sorts. But Steve has been the master story teller today. He told us
he had joined your family. Congratulations. That's a wonderful thing to do."

Nice. Meant it.

"We were celebrating. Will you join us in a potation? I know the maitre d
here. Alfonso, we will move to my usual table when that pigeon has finished
with it."

Clowning again. Why?

Idiotic. Behaving like someone in my novels. Wanting to
know somebody and then not letting her know me. Using
words as an clown's make-up.

"Some tea would be nice."

I order tea. I think I sound quite normal. Tea is served.

"Thank you for playing cricket with my boys, Howard." Faintest
emphasis on the plural, tiny private smile between her
and Steve. "Was Cal bumptious?"

"No. I would use the term 'bouncy'. Letting people know when he feels
happy or brilliant."

"And Steve? Was he too polite?"

"No. He sledged me as a fast bowler should. I would be glad to play with them again. Anybody would."

Nice. Meant it again.

"I'm a member of the MCC. I would be glad to take Steve and Cal to the Indoor School. Robert and I have been known to go there in the winter. It's not intolerable, is it Robert?" Assent. "And we have sometimes fortuitously met Tim Morrow and Tom O'Ryan." Cal, wide-eyed, looks at Robert, who gives a confirmatory nod. Steve looks worried.

"Howard, do you know someone called Right Honourable Paul Russell?"

"Unfortunately. He's an arsehole. In fact he's an arsehole of international class. They had an international scientific convention a while back to set the standard arsehole, as you have a standard metre and a standard second. Well, Paul Russell led the British delegation and when he started speaking everyone said 'Problem solved. That is the standard arsehole.' Every other arsehole in the world, in the universe, is calibrated against Paul Russell."

Everyone in the café is looking at him. He doesn't mind. Only cares about making the children laugh. And me. I am laughing. Robert and Zoe are laughing. Cal's in hysterics. Only Steve's still worried.

"I bowled some throat balls at him in the Undecim match."

"Good."

"I hit him once or twice."

"You'd have hit him more only he fell on his arse!"

"Fell on his arse… Perfect! Did anyone take pictures?"

"No. But it was a bit like… this."

Cal grabs pencil and pad from his backpack and sketches rapidly.

"Brilliant!"

"I know."

"That so is Paul Russell, falling on his arse. Mind you, there's nothing else he could fall on!"

Now he's hysterical at his own joke. Like Cal, when he thinks he's done a good one. He stops instantly when he realizes Steve has more to say.

"Well, he told me afterwards that he was on the MCC Committee and he would stop me getting a trial at Lords and I should go somewhere else."

White fury. "Paul Russell is not on the MCC Committee. He is an unelected member of the Library Committee because he gave a pile of historic manuscripts to the Library. He does not decide who gets trials at the MCC. If he tries to interfere in any way with Steve's life I will … personally … do something to him which will hurt more than facing Steve without a box."

He means that too. He hardly knows us but he's in our corner.

"Steve, do you want to be a professional cricketer? I mean, for a county as well as for Glendon Courtenay?"

"I would like to try for it."

"What do you think, Robert? Could Steve make it as a professional?"

"Of course."

"I'm not so sure. I think we should ask a real professional not a bits and pieces player. Let's get him bowling at Tim."

"Cal too!"

"Definitely. See if he can pick the zamboni. Will you fix it, Robert, or shall I?"

This man is not only offering my boys the biggest treat they could imagine but including Robert as one of the providers.

"One condition, Steve. I want you to do a coaching course at the first opportunity. You are a natural. Don't you think, Robert? You will learn something on the course and you will get a bit of paper, saying that you are a cricket coach. Today's world is full of people with bits of paper who can't teach and full of people without bits of paper who can. Don't start me on that. Level One takes a few days. Try and get it done before school."

"I've left school. I was supposed to go to business college."

Guilt. Steve's future. Cal's school. Issues not faced. I've let this holiday run too long.

"You clearly don't want to go there and you don't have to. Have you thought about anything else?"

"Only cricket. But … I don't think I'm stupid."

"Come to Marian's." `Zoe. Imploring.`

"Yeah, and Cal! You don't have to take exams, just do an interview with the head and all he did was talk about my photos, and swimming, and whether I'd be happy there and make other kids happy there. And there's no bullies, ever, and everyone gets to play on the cricket team if they practice, well, I got in and Cal would just piss through. Sorry."

"Rupert would want Steve, wouldn't he? To do A Levels."

"Mr Giles, or Yes sir, to you, young lady. Our head teacher. Rod of iron. Personally selected by me from the Wackford Squeers academy."

"By you?"

"Yeah, it's Howard's school." `Zoe punches him, but it is too late. I see Alice recoil. Fool, Howard, you gave Robert the opening. This woman does not want favours.`

"Robert, full attention please." `Of course, I really wanted Alice's.` "I founded Marian's College, with others, in memory of my wife, who was a teacher. It is named for her. It is a school where she would have been able to teach as she knew how but found impossible in the state system. It is independent. We have an endowment from… a benefactor. I am chair of the governors. I am regularly outvoted. The governors are not allowed any say on admissions – or expulsions. Your parents entered you and Zoe for Marian's because they love you. Rupert selected you and her because he wanted you. If you imagine that I had anything to do with that you are taking away from your parents, from Rupert, Zoe and from yourself. If I ever see you on school premises you call me Sir or Mr Foy until I tell you <u>and</u> other children to use Howard."

"Sorry." `Not far from tears. Too hard on him, Howard. Straining to impress Alice.`

"I need to run round the field. I did nothing but watch. I'm Miss Slacker Queen!" Zoe leapt to her feet.

"I'll come with you!" Steve on his feet.

"I'll come with you!" Cal on his feet.

"I'll come with you!" Robert on his feet. Thank you, Zoe. Leaving me alone with Alice.

"First back gets ice cream!" Alice and I watching running styles. Zoe and Robert pushing themselves, Cal scuttling back and forth encouraging, Steve well within himself. Watching over the rest.

"What I said was true. I can do you no favours at Marian's. Rupert will meet the three of you and interview them if you like what you see and hear. It would be a favour to the school and me if you looked at it. We're only two years old. We want to build up numbers, especially in the sixth form. We want leaders and doers and – energizers – like Cal and Steve."

"It's private. I couldn't afford that for Cal alone, let alone Steve as well. He's got some tiny inheritance from an uncle. That wouldn't go far even if I was willing to touch it."

"There's no set fees. We have an endowment and bursaries."

"Do you control them?"

"Awards are made on the basis of need. When a pupil's accepted we work out what his or her carers can afford. Carers can pay part of their fees in labour or teaching or lecturing. So can pupils. Steve will almost certainly earn money off as a cricket coach. There is a cricket team, as Robert said. The one thing I insisted on."

"Where's the money come from, Howard?" Pause. Don't make it too long, Howard, she'll know that you're making up a lie. Trust her. Bring her into that small circle who know. Make her an honorary Frenetic. "Give me a pound, Howard. Engage me as your lawyer. Our conversation then becomes privileged."

"Thank you. An excellent stratagem, and I suspect well used. Not necessary. Our conversation is privileged because it's a privilege to talk to you." Oh that's so … literary. She didn't like it. "I trust you."

Much better.

"The ultimate benefactor of Marian's, through a special vehicle called the Human Capital Trust, is Antony Scorer." `Struggling for recognition.` "Large-scale fraudster. Stephen Duveen wrote a good book about him, but he didn't tell all of it.[22] He scored for the Frenetics. Joe and I and Luke Marriott knew him well. So did Portia. I was closer than most, still closer when he went to prison. Antony had much more money than the authorities recovered. He cleansed it, made it untraceable. He didn't need it in prison. He never needed it for himself. He liked to help people, especially the Frenetics. He funnelled money to us all, especially if we were in trouble. You could say it was a power trip, but it changed other people's lives, not his own. He wanted to go on using money that way, so I became his sort of almoner. I devised the Trust for him to channel money to talented people in need, and when I needed the money to start up Marian's, he made it available.

"They let him out of prison early. They use his skills to trace dirty money. If they know about his unrecovered money they ignore it. That's all I'm going to say. He lives in a small house in a small island. He's a big local benefactor, and they take care of him. I report to him regularly on Marian's, on the Trust, on the people he's helping.

"If Steve and Cal go to Marian's they will be profiting from a secret criminal. Like Pip and Magwitch in Great Expectations. If that bothers you, pull out now and no offence."

`She thought for a while.` "Did he serve the sentence for his crimes imposed by the court?"

"Not in full. Executive release."

"Something provided in law. Did his frauds harm poor people?"

"Not directly. He targeted rich individuals and financial institutions. Some may have recovered their losses through burdens on poor people. He's not a Robert Maxwell."

"I don't think I really care, but I wouldn't want my boys to know about him. If they were to go to Marian's I would like you to act as a firebreak between them. Thank you for trusting me."

---

[22] See 'Final Score' from <u>A Tale Of Ten Wickets.</u>

"Does this mean you'll give Marian's a trial?"

"The boys and I will look at it. I need somewhere badly for Cal. Hell, I'd look at anything that isn't an academy." Deep draught of tea, stare into empty cup. "Why, Howard?"

"Why what?"

"Why do you want to help my boys? You've hardly met them and you pull out a giant treat and a possible future. Why?"

Thought. Good, no slick answer. But don't think too long, Mr Novelist, I might think you are making things up.

"Because I've had a happy day. Because I haven't … done much since Marian died. Just filled space. Newspapers, magazines, radio, TV. Instantly forgettable. Your boys gave me a glimpse of something better. And because of what they've done for Zoe and Robert, the children I love, for… lack of my own. The children I love were deeply unhappy. Your boys changed their lives, almost instantly. Those four are now a unit."

And, obligingly on cue, the four children come into sight. Robert in the lead, puffing gallantly. Zoe and Cal holding Steve back.

"Robert wins the ice cream!"

"Share it." Gasp. "Still on diet. Three kilos left." Prods diminished stomach. I pass over a note, don't notice the amount, wave them all over to the ice cream counter.

"A unit. I can't now think of Zoe and Robert without thinking of Cal and Steve. If I add something to Cal and Steve I'm adding to the unit."

Yes. Believe that. But there's more. Keep silent and he'll say it.

Now the children are arguing. One ice cream to share. Each argues for <u>another</u> child's favourite flavour.

"Peace, children. Buy one apiece in the flavour you like. You've all earned it. Robert, if you're afraid that the big bad Diet Fairy will see you, share yours."

Four ice creams bought. Zoe leads them to a bench outdoors.

Distraction over. No escape through the children. And no help from me. Examines hands, examines floor, reads café menu and hygiene notice. He's worse than Cal giving someone a drawing!

"And there's something else. I would like to help Cal and Steve because I would like to know you better. And that's all wrong, isn't it? Trying to buy my way into your life. You've every right to say that's creepy and manipulative, and that you'll go your own way…"

"Howard! Don't beat yourself up! And don't put words in my mouth. I'm not a character in one of your novels."

"Sorry."

"And don't say sorry! Steve drives me crazy saying sorry. I far prefer 'shut up, you stupid bitch!' Try that for me."

"If you must… **Shut up, you stupid bitch!**" Looks of alarm from Zoe and Robert, conspiratorial smiles from Steve and Cal, followed by whisper. Resumption of ice creams.

"Now, Howard. If I thought you were a bad man with bad motives I would keep you away from Cal and Steve. I would also tell Belinda and Joe. I think no such thing, and I want my boys to have all the love and support they can get. Make sure you sometimes say No to Cal, especially when he's being extra cute, and don't let Steve be too polite and helpful. And Howard, I want to know you better. You're not in the least like a Great Writer."

Oh hell. That came out all wrong. He never heard the ironic capital letters.

"Well, that's true enough. I was not in the least like a Great Writer even when I was a writer. I mean, a real writer, of books, not just a spacefiller. I thought I was an entertainer. When Marian… became ill my work didn't seem entertaining, it seemed unbearably trivial."

"Howard! I'm so sorry. I said something awful by mistake. I actually meant it as a compliment. I've suffered in my life from Great Artists, capital G, capital A. People who think that because they have a specialized talent they're gods and they act like gods and the rest of us worship them… Well, you're not like that. I got worried when you started clowning. Did you want me to think 'wow, he's so funny!' and go weak at the knees?"

"Well… maybe."

"No Howard. I think you wanted to make me laugh. And the children."

Not ruined! But must remember not to clown so much.

"So there is a remote possibility that you would come with me to the annual reception of the Literary Benevolent Fund next month, to be attended by writers who are household names in their own households. They will include a holder of the Order of Merit but the merit in the room will increase by a factor of ten if you were to enter."

Aaggh! Clowning again! What is it about her that makes me do it?

"Oh, Howard. A little mouse like me would get lost with all those literary lions." Serves me right. But wait, she's clowning too. Meeting me.   "Who's the Order of Merit?"

"Mary Varley."

"Oh my God! I adored 'Victory'. Just about the last novel I read."
Aaagh! Another faux pas. What is it about him that makes me do it?

"If you must abandon fiction, an excellent farewell choice. Way above mine."

Serves me right. But wait, this time he's just playing. Sharing a game with me.

Ice creams finished. Four children staring at us.

"We need to go home. Lots to do."

"Do you want a lift?"

"Your car's at our place, Howard."

"Doh! I knew that. Can I summon you a taxi?"

"We like walking."

"Ah yes." Standing about like a lemon. Silly, lemons don't stand. Instant glance between Steve and Cal.

"Thank you for playing cricket with us, Howard, and all the treats. Don't forget your drawing."

"Paul Russell on his arse? How could I?" But I nearly did. Shame.

"I'll do a better one. I don't want you to think that is representative of my work." Means that. Serious artist. Reply in kind, no clowning!

"I think it is very accomplished for an instant sketch, but I would certainly like to view your finished work. Perhaps your mother could fix an appointment. Here are my contact details." I passed Alice my personal card with the private numbers. Oh so casually.

"Thanks for the treats, Howard, but no thanks at all for the cricket because you're a boring batsman and I hate you." Alice pleased.

"Boys, aren't you going to say goodbye to Zoe and Robert or don't you like them any more?"

Enormous four-way hug. Alice pulled into it. Then me.

"Unit, Howard. Be part of the unit." Whispered. Not noticed by children. Finally the six breaks into two times three.

Watching their unit walking across the park. Steve hauling heavy bag, Cal trying to sneak rides and piggy backs. Alice and Steve swatting him away. Remembering our unit. Hauling our bag. Arm around Zoe. No spare arm for Robert. "Come on, Slim. Take a ride on my back."

Dear Mrs Helson (looking much more likely. Five minute hug from Steve on meeting. Delayed start of cricket!!!)

Howard's smitten with Alice!!! Acting like gawky teenager (on which am expert). Had to herd others to give him space. Brilliant! If they marry would make Steve my step-there-is-no-god-brother. But would I then be allowed to marry Steve? Check with lawyer (not Alice of course).

Howard extra nice to us. Effect of love. Hope I'm being extra nice to everyone. Think so, but will also take soup to beggar children.

Zoe Past

Chapter 32 Square Cut

I have a busy law practice and I have just doubled my parenting responsibilities and I still feel as though I'm on holiday.

I blame that Howard Foy.

He fancies me. Now that hasn't been totally unknown, but Howard Foy. He's a Famous Writer. Awful about his wife, but if he's really on the market again there must be hundreds of women who would throw themselves at his feet. Glamorous, sophisticated women, who know about Writing. I haven't read anything more than a law book for years. Or dear old Rosie M Banks. But Howard wants to take me to his literary reception. What am I going to wear? I've got nothing but my work gear (my "law suits" says Cal, ha-ha) or my floppy wear.

Must read something of Howard's. I look him up on Amazon and order the lot! I'll be reading for ever, like poor Steve. Steve! Must get back to work. Must draw up application to court and get necessary signatures. But here I am, adding all of Howard's DVDs to my Amazon order. People who bought Howard Foy also bought P G Wodehouse, Scott Fitzgerald and George Gershwin. That's promising.

Maybe his work will help me understand him. He's light-headed and he makes me feel light-headed. "Makes"? What's that present tense doing, we're not in a relationship? But there's a core of deep feelings. Not just about his wife. Glad he's in my corner, and the boys'. Sense that we can trust him. Sense that he would go to the limits for us if we need it.

Must tidy him up a little bit. Unfair to judge after he's played cricket all afternoon? But he's got strong features, he's in terrific shape and he's rich. Should look a little more kempt. Wonder if he would like to go to Yasmin's? Yasmin's. Where the boys need to go fast! Before I take them to Marian's. Marian's. Time to do some parenting. Remember that? Parenting. Book boys into Yasmin's. Send texts. They're at the pool with Zoe and Robert.

Find number for Marian's. No trouble fixing visit. It's open all year. Secretary, who's also a parent, says some teachers are there every day and parents and "visiting lecturers." Head is there almost every day. Pupils can come in when they like. Like the sound of that, and of "visiting lecturers." Looking forward to visit. Think school will tell me more about Howard.

All right, I fancy Howard. Now that's out of the way, can I get some work done?

Catch-up meeting with Portia. Review my ongoing clients. Accept her suggestion of replacement lawyer for Steve.

"Oh, by the way, the boys introduced me to Howard Foy. He asked to be remembered to you." Actually he didn't. An excuse to mention him and pump her.

"Howard? Haven't seen him for ages. Not since I watched the Frenetics." Looking at me, daring me to ask more.

"What was he like then?"

"Very good player. All-rounder. Very hard to dismiss, and could bowl all day." She knows that's not what interests me! "Go-to man on the team. Good in a crisis." Still teasing me. "Off the field as well as on. Anyone with a problem, Howard would go to work for them. Him and Antony Scorer. They worked together. Antony would fix money, Howard would fix everything else."

"I heard about Antony. Did Howard know he was a fraud?"

"I'm sure he didn't. None of us did. I didn't know and I did his legal work. Everything I saw was on the up and up."

"Was he married then?"

"Antony's never been married, as far as I know." Oh please! "Oh you mean, Howard? Yes. To Marian. Terrific woman. Everybody adored her. Extrovert, noisy. Amazing cheerleader at cricket matches." Oh. Not like me. "She could do this astonishing whistle when anybody did something good, or something terrible." Must do mine for Howard! "They were great together, in company. Drew everybody to them. Howard was witty and affable and she was really … empathetic. Interested in everyone she met. Could listen to people for hours, even bores." Yes, I think I can do empathy.

Portia looks at me, totally undeceived by my casual throwaway remark. "Howard was distraught when Marian died. If he's come to life again… Tell him I'd love to see him. Howard? Hmm. I owe you and Cal for John Westaway."

Portia on the case. Poor Howard, you haven't a chance. Neither have I.

Dear Mrs Helson,

Really confident now, after fabulous time at pool. First time I've seen Steve with nothing on except Ursinho swim trunks I got him. Nearly fainted! Amazing tone, amazing tan. Better than ours from Corfu. Hair longer – not a soldier now but a poet (Romantic era, but not Shelley who could not swim!) Cal brown too, and starting to fill out. Hair bleached and wild.

Made Robert drool and breathe in to hide last spare tyre. (Still worried about mine so selected sleek one-piece swimsuit).

Steve and Cal so tight together. After surviving together. And now elective brothers (Steve's phrase). Memo to Mrs H: there's a Cal part of Steve you won't reach.

Steve still worried about Cal in water. Whispers to me and Robert that one of us must always be close to him. As if he needed to ask Robert! Meet Steve's lifeguard friend Phil. Nice. As would expect of any friend of Steve. We do some lengths in fitness pool. Steve swims like a missile. But Robert's almost as good. I am back marker (pretending to watch over Cal but actually puffed).

Cal and Steve start doing stunts so Phil throws us out to fun pool! Says Steve was "wild child" at last school. Oh sure!

"They let him do GSCEs in the punishment block with his probation officer. Had your results?"

"Any day. They're looking for a new category above A Star."

The usual waves and flume in fun pool. Crowded but people seem to make space around us. Can see lots of people eyeing Steve. Girls and boys. And women and men! Steve doesn't notice. Looking out for Cal and Robert, but mostly paying attention to me. Me. Making sure I'm having fun. Making sure I'm close and safe. All that, but also just glancing and gazing at me. For no reason. And lots of little touches. A soft kiss when the others are away. The most beautiful being in the universe belongs to me!!! Zoe the Monkey. You others all want him but this one's mine!!!

Waves begin. Cal and Robert back to join us.

"Ohmigod, giant waves! We're being swept away. Grab Steve everybody, HELP position." Crafty Cal makes excuse to look onto Steve. Me and Robert quickly follow. Steve folding us all in, treading water. Keeping us all above the waves. Pool subsides. Dash to flume. Too late, big queue.

"Hello, Psy… Steve." Oh no! Steve's ex. In front of him. Never seen her before but I can tell. Mum said you can always tell your beloved's exes. The air changes around them when they meet. Big, blonde, blowsy girl. Almost fat. Surely not his type? Great tits. Oh hell, he's a tit man. I've no chance.

"Hello, Angie." Totally cool. "This is my brother Cal. This is Zoe." Squeezes my hand. Then arm round me, in case Angie's totally thick. Giant neon arrows pointing at me: Steve's Girlfriend. YESSS!!! "This is her brother Robert."

She can't look at me. Locks onto Cal instead. "I didn't know you had a brother, Steve. Especially such a cute one." Preen from Cal The Vain, R and me call him that too!

"I've got a new family now, Angie. I'm not living with… where you came." No move to give her new contact details. Suddenly I feel sorry for her. Who's she with? Looks like no one. "How about you, Angie? What's going on for you?" Genuinely interested.

"I'm back with Johnny." *Johnny? From Glendon Courtenay?* "From the football team." *Oh yeah. From my school. Seems a million years ago. Or like another person's life.* "He's getting a trial at Fulham."

"I really hope that works for him. And you, Angie. You'd be wonderful as a footballer's WAG. You'll have your own fashion house, like Victoria Beckham, only stacks better, and you'll go partying and get in all the celeb mags and you'll get banned by Fabio Cappello. You deserve all that, Angie." She looked happy. He wanted her to be happy.

"Your turn, Angie." *She slid out of our lives. Our turn. Two spaces side-by-side on the flume. Holding my hand. Speeding, bouncing, still holding my hand. Giant splash landing, still holding my hand!!!!*

I believe that in some countries that's classed as marriage.

Zoe Past.

Texts for me and Cal.

"Mum's fixed hair appointments for us at Yasmin's." *Still gives me a buzz to call Alice Mum. But then feel instantly guilty about my other one, in tears.*

"Brilliant! Robert, can you do before and after photos of both of us?" *Robert delighted.*

"Are you sure you've got enough film for Cal The Vain?" *For once I don't let him beat me up. He walks away with Robert. I hear them discussing bowling grips. I might have a little time with Zoe before we reach the bus stop.*

"Have a bit of my jacket, Zoe?" *Still hot, and the last thing either of us needs is a leather jacket. But she takes the offer eagerly. Arm around her. Awful to compare but can't help remembering Marjorie outside that jazz club. Zoe's smaller, not nearly as athletic. But more liquid, almost melting into my body. I so want this girl to be safe and happy for the rest of her life. With me, or with whomever. Arm a little tighter.*

"I knew Angie at our school. She was my girlfriend for a while."

"I know." *I knew she knew. Phil told me girls always knew that about each other.*

"It was a mistake. We never had much in common. I'm never doing that again, having a … relationship just for its own sake. You're more alone when you're tied to a stranger than you are on your own." *I so nearly start talking about Jean-Paul Sartre! Fatal. Save myself just in time, to talk about what really matters.* "Zoe. The best thing about being on holiday was knowing that I missed you. The best thing about not drowning – well, apart from not drowning – was knowing I was going to see you again. I really, really want to get into Marian's so we're at school together. If we are, can I carry your books? Even if I don't make it and can't carry your books, will you, I mean, would you like to, do you want to be my girlfriend?"

Do I want to go on breathing?

"Hurry up, bus!" **Thanks, Robert. Perfect timing. Would never happen in a Howard Foy movie! Gasp out "Yes" as I puff towards bus. Think he heard.**

Robert's before-Yasmin photo shoot took ages! He's a total perfectionist and Cal is totally vain. Insisted on lots of different angles. Told my multiple pun "Super Cal is so artistic…" She got it right away.

"Cal, say thank you to the nice people but we can't stay. Mum wants us home. Why don't you come to ours tomorrow for the after photo-shoot?" *Still getting a buzz saying Mum for Alice and ours for our home, including me.*

Mum had her this-is-serious-listen voice. I can recognize it. "Steve, Cal? When you finish at Yasmin's tomorrow, can you step into my office? I want to see what she has done, and I need a few minutes with Steve. Now I want to explain the next steps legally for Steve. As a 16-year-old he can live with us for as long as he wants. But he's still legally a child and there are many decisions he can't make for himself, such as medical treatment. He needs a responsible adult who can make those decisions until his 18th birthday. That is why I am applying to court to be what is called his Special Guardian. It makes me effectively his day-to-day parent but unlike adoption it doesn't end his relationship with his natural parents. They will sign the application as well. So will Steve, although it will have no force, to show that is what he wants."

"Can I sign it?"

"I don't see why not. It will not have any legal force, any more than Steve's but it would be a declaration of your wishes. We'll draw up a form of words."

"Just say I want Steve to live in our home and be my special brother."

"What happens after we all sign?"

"Our local authority sends a social worker to see if I am a suitable person to be your Special Guardian."

"What a waste of money!"

"Thank you, Steve, but it is important. I don't know whom they will send. I know everyone in the children's department. Now, this brings me to an issue we need to face together. Cal is gay, Steve. He loves you sexually as well as emotionally. That's true, isn't it?"

"Yes."

"No one may have a sexual relationship with Cal until he is 16. Steve, you may not have a sexual relationship with anyone else under 16. That is the law. Even if the person under 16 wants and encourages a sexual act. That simply doesn't count to the law. Now I totally trust you both. Have done from the beginning. But I have to warn you now, it is even more important that you don't do anything sexual. Or anything that might lead an outsider to think that you might be having a sexual relationship. If a social worker ever thought that, we could lose everything. Steve would not be allowed to live here or see us. I might be tagged as an unfit mother – I could lose Cal as well as Steve. I have won cases against the police, schools, local authorities. I have got a lot of personal enemies there. They would love to get back at me in that way. You need to know this."

Silence. They both looked scared, as I intended.

"What does a sexual relationship mean?"

"Any relationship with sexual acts. To make that very simple, any acts involving pricks, arses or cunts which make someone feel sexually excited."

More silence. "What about hugs and kisses?"

"They're OK. But they could be misinterpreted. To a sensible person, they mean physical affection. They also mean trust, self-confidence, someone who likes to show other people he loves them. I've always been pleased that you're a major-league hugger and kisser. When you mean it. But some people aren't sensible and some people like to have an excuse for hating other people. Hell, you know that from those bloody kids at school."

"Would it be bad for us if the social worker saw me hug Steve?"

"Maybe. Do you think you could hold off when the social worker visits?"

"How long will that be?"

"Can't tell. Maybe an hour?"

"No chance! I don't think I could get through five seconds!" He plunged into Steve's arms. My son the drama queen. Steve ruffled his over-long hair and whispered something and he broke away.

"The other big issue for the social worker will be education. He will not let us be Steve's family if I let you both run wild. You have to be educated somehow, Steve has to be educated or trained or employed. We're going to Marian's the day after tomorrow. That might be the answer. If not, I have to work very fast. I'm still out on a limb for pulling you out of that bloody school." They looked anxious. "Come here, both of you." Arm around each. "You're my family. Nobody breaks up my family. Now get the family bear and the family Monopoly board."

A million years ago I waited ages in a salon for Angie to get her hair done. Never dreamt I would go to that kind of place myself. Ernie Walt with his clippers was more my style. Cal of course was like visiting royalty. Yasmin wasn't ready, and Cal pointed out her colleague Michael. "Watch him a minute, he's an artist like me." *There was a sad-looking man in his chair, but as Michael started shaping his hair he looked magically younger and almost successful. Finally Yasmin was ready.*

"You go first, I need to think about mine." *Yasmin hardly looked older than me. Cal told me she was in demand by actors and footballers.* "Now she can say she does two famous cricketers." *Yasmin looked at me from all angles and moved my head around. Then she said* "Mmmh!" *[True!] and sent me to have my hair washed. I accepted the offer of a scalp massage (nice) and returned to her chair. I started to say something.* "Shut up, Steve! Yasmin knows what to do, but please remember he's a fast bowler. He's got to look evil but also keep the hair out of his eyes." *He went away to a chair and started sketching.*

It didn't seem as though Yasmin was cutting at all. She just seemed to glide through my hair. What with the drier, it made me feel quite dozy and I hardly spoke to her. Rude! Luckily she chattered away non-stop. She adored Alice and Cal. Alice had been her lawyer when she ran away from her family.

"Okay, Steve. Take a look. If you hate it, I'll take it all off and you can have a buzz cut."

I was stunned. Was the person in the mirror my secret identity? Why had I never met him for sixteen years? "Yasmin, it's wonderful. You've made me ... a glad animal." *There was just enough space at the back for me to practise my delivery stride. Yes! I've hit Right Honourable again!*

"Umm, Mr Yummy! Put his photo in the window and take down Frank Lampard." *Cal hugged me right in front of everyone. Drama queen! There was a soap actress in one of the chairs. She looked jealous!*

On his turn Cal did his usual bounce-and-look-away act. "Steve, do you mind not looking until I've finished? Why not go to Selfridges because they've got Ursinho clothes on the first floor." *Trust him to know.* "Come back at 12."

I went to Selfridges but I forgot all about Ursinho because I mooched about in the sports section and bought some out-of-season cricket gear for us.

Yasmin kept asking if I was sure, but I said yes, I really wanted to look older.

"On your own head be it!" Steve made that joke. Will he like it? And should I have warned Mum? No, it's my decision.

I got back just as Yasmin was finishing. I was stunned again. His hair was really short. Not the funny little kid I met in the park. He looked older and harder.

He doesn't like it. He hates it.

I thought he was going to cry. Now he was that funny little kid all over again, whom I can't bear to be unhappy. I hugged him. The soap actress looked jealous again!

"Cal! It was a shock. You look amazing."

"I wanted to look older. It's time I was older. Let go, I'm fine. I'll pay. You don't know what to do about the tips."

We walked to Mum's office. Just plain walked, none of his usual bouncing and scuttling and pretending to be annoyed when I look after him. No chattering either. Two people on business, walking in step together to a conference. It felt lonely. Suddenly he took my hand, but I think he was just looking after my feelings.

The receptionist at the office gawped at the new Cal and simply gestured us towards Alice's office. We went in.

She was horrified. She recovered quickly but I could tell. "Oh my god, sweetheart, what have you done? Where's my baby boy? I thought he'd been kidnapped."

"Sorry, Mum. I should have given you a warning. You hate it."

"No, but I am shocked. You're someone else." *She looked at some papers on her desk.*

"No, I'm still me but I wanted to look older. Just to see. It will grow out again." *She put down the papers and gazed at him. I felt she was adding back his old hair.* "Isn't Steve yummy? One out of two isn't bad."

"Steve is yummy. Actually this meeting's about Steve, and we're going to Portia's office. Do you mind waiting here? You have a choice as always, drawing or reading Cheshire on Contract."

Before we went out the door he leapt up and gave her one of his giant hugs. But I think he was looking after her feelings.

"Sorry, Steve, that was my second shock today. The first was about your inheritance. We'll go through that in Portia's office."

There was another woman in Portia's office. She looked like someone's gran. Portia introduced us. "Liz, this is our former client, Steve Helson. Steve, please meet Liz Smallgood. She was the head of my firm when I met Alan. Smallgood and Long. Alan thought that was a good name for a law firm. That's why he chose us, why I eventually met him.[23]" *For a second her eyes went from steely to misty.* "Liz is now retired but she has some personal clients and would be glad to act for you."

"I can't be your lawyer any more, Steve. I might be a rotten guardian and you might have to sue me. And Portia cannot act for you against one of her own partners. We both strongly urge you to engage Liz. Give her the usual pound." *I had to scrape it together in small coins. Embarrassment.*

"Thank you, Steve. Here are my numbers. You can talk to me at any time, and on your own." *I looked at Liz's card and put it in my wallet.* "Now Steve, please be ready for a shock about your inheritance."

It's bloody gone! I never wanted money from Uncle Frank but he wanted me to have what was left and my dad lost it. That's why he never told me anything about it.

"We had an up-to-date reckoning from your father today." *Lying crap. Just tell me, without bullshit.* "Your inheritance is worth just over £120,000."

---

[23] See "Death Wish" from <u>A Tale Of Ten Wickets.</u>

I felt dizzy. And ashamed. "Your uncle spent very little of his pay over the years. He invested his savings during his army career on a very simple plan. If he came across a good bit of kit he bought shares in the company that made it, and if he came across a bad bit of kit he sold them short. It worked very well – outperformed a lot of funds. Then he picked up a lot of useful tips from Russian billionaires when he went into private security.

"As you know he left money to a forces charity, but the balance, to you, was already substantial. Your father has managed it exceptionally well. His plan will mature for you on your eighteenth birthday. Portia and I agree that you should leave your money with him."

My father. He was, is, really good at his job. All that time he was looking after me. I wish I had known. "There's more. Your mother and father have some funds invested of their own. They propose cashing them in two stages. They would like to give you £10,000 now and another £10,000 in a year's time. To spend as you want." *Twenty thousand. On top of Uncle Frank's money. Maybe I was a Good Son after all.*

"That could pay for me at Marian's. Cal too. If we get in."

"You possibly. I'm not taking your money for Cal."

"Why not? You told me to let you and Cal help me, because you loved me. When I panicked. On the cliff. Why won't you let me help you?"

"I think I need a few moments alone with my client." *Liz looks like a dear old thing but I wouldn't want to be on the opposite side to her. Mum and Portia left us.* "Steve. Take my advice. Don't make any decisions about your money. A few treats maybe, but no big decisions. You may not know it but you are in shock. You are certainly absorbing a lot of new information all at once, and you need to make sense of it. Not just financial sense but emotional sense. All of us predicted your first reaction – that you would want to help Alice and Cal. We also knew that Alice would refuse. Not out of pride, although she is a proud woman, but because money's a very dangerous thing for relationships. Imagine that you did pay for Cal's education from your own money. And imagine Cal wasted it. People change. He could turn into a slacker or worse. You would resent that, think him ungrateful. Eventually you would hate him. Alice too. She is not up for that risk."

No chance. I will love them for the rest of my life. "Steve, I know you don't believe that could happen, but please respect Alice's thinking. Now, can I assume that you accept your parents' offer? It sounds like a lot but you're sixteen. It works out at £1250 for each year of your life. As your lawyer, I must ask you if you want me to press for more."

"I never wanted money from them. I didn't even ask them to love me. I just wanted to know that they didn't think I was a bad son. Now I know. That's enough."

"Professionally, I accept your instruction. Unprofessionally, I think you are an exceptional young man. A credit to every family you belong to." *I might have teared up again because I'm such a mush lately, but I still felt dizzy. I agreed that Liz would manage my £20K and pay something regular to Mum for my keep. After all, she keeps pumping protein into me.*

Mum hated my hair. She pretended not to, but she kept looking at it. Can't understand why, it's only hair. She looked a bit weird in her office and almost forgot to kiss us goodbye when we left. And Steve was miles away and didn't hold my hand like he usually does when we cross a busy street. My fault for looking older!

"What's wrong with you and Mum?"

"Nothing really, we're just thinking."

"Well, don't. I never do."

"Can't help it. Cal, I'm rich. My uncle Frank left me much more money than I dreamt of and my… other mum and my dad gave me £20,000 on top."

"Cool."

"I can't make out my dad, that's all. He knows I've got lots of money, he can afford to give me a lot more, but he won't even let me think about cricket, or going to uni, or going round the world or just having fun. Instead I had to work flat tack and earn money."

"Well, you don't have to do what he wants any more. Only what Mum wants. And you'd better, because when Mum loses it she throws plates around and twists all the cutlery and makes the whole house shake."

"She does all that to you?"

"You bet. I have to hide under the bed with Bungle." I got a bit of a smile out of him. As if. But I wish that Mum were like that sometimes, instead of like today when she won't let me know what I've done wrong.

Zoe hates my hair too. She almost screamed when she and Robert came round to our place for the after-photos.

"Perfect! I get the greatest haircut of my life and you can only look at Cal's."

"Sorry, Steve, yours is totally dreamy but that's not a surprise. It's just that Cal… is someone else." He's changed our balance. It used to be me and Steve and him and Robert. Now he's the same age as me and Steve and Robert's the odd one out. Robert feels that. He's hurt. Hiding behind his camera.

First time they've been to our place. I show them everything including all my drawings but nobody seems to be having fun. And Steve's room isn't really Steve's room yet. Still Mum's study. "We're getting Steve a proper cricketer's bed. Until then, Steve should sleep in my bed." The others all looked panicked. "Not with me, but he can have Bungle." Some giggling. "I can sleep on this sofa bed because I'm still only a weed. And besides, I want a futon like Robert's."

"Cal looks like Michael Clarke." First thing Robert's said.

"He does a bit, only Clarke's right-handed. Ohmigod!" Steve looked transfixed. "Cal, can you put your whites on and your batting stuff but only pads and gloves?" Cal rushed off. "Now Cal, playing forward. Nothing fancy. Robert, can you take his picture, left profile?"

We looked at Robert's images. Even in miniature we could see what Steve saw. "Cal looks like the boy who drowned. At the haunted house."

"Is that why you've all been acting spooked? I thought you just hated my new hair."

"I just feel that the boy's story isn't over, and Cal is somehow part of it. And that Cal needs to be free of him."

"Steve, that's so melodramatic. And a bit of a cliché."

"Clichés become clichés because they're true." I have to say we did all feel a bit spooked (although it was nice to imagine Steve protecting me – zero points for me as a feminist). Cal got changed and made us all play Monopoly with Bungle. He made a big deal of the bear. Alice came back and joined in but I could tell her heart was not really in it. I took Robert home. Steve of course wanted to see us back safely.

"Thank you, Steve, but it is still light and Robert and I have ridden a London bus before. I think Alice needs you here. There's something going on in your family." His face lit up for a second when I said "your family". As I meant it to.

I did manage a long kiss with Zoe and when I got back Cal was pampering Mum, making her lie on the couch, fixing her a gin-and-tonic, long cuddle, even administering Bungle. He insisted on making dinner (giant stirfry, extra bean curd (protein!) for me.) We ate it and then he put her back on the couch. I made her decent coffee (my only skill) and he gave her another long cuddle. I took up his usual position on the floor and held her hand.

"Thanks, boys. Men. Hard day. A lot going on for me."

"Mum, I've decided Steve and I should swap beds until we get him a real one. He's a fast bowler and he needs support for his back and I'm only a spinner. And he's going to have Bungle from now on!" *Giggle, turning into hysterics.*

"You've decided? I suppose it makes sense. I'll have to change the sheets."

"I've done it. I'm sleepy." *Stage yawn. Drama queen!* "Honestly, Mum, I'll be fine on the sofa bed." *He disappeared and came back in what must have been some really old pyjamas which he had outgrown.*

"You're too fat for those."

"Am not and just for that you'll carry me and you can't have Bungle."

"If you're worried about my back it's not fair to make me carry you and that fat bear." *Something told me he wanted Mum to carry him. I stretched out on the floor and made a big show of being unavailable. Drama queen! Mum hoisted him. She was away for a long time.*

"Mum, is everything OK?" Poor Steve. I offer to take care of him and suddenly I'm in turmoil. Don't want him to be the peacemaker in our new family, trapped in a war of competing wills. He had that for sixteen years. "It's his hair. You've not been the same since you saw his hair. Should he have discussed it with you first? He sent me out of the salon. Maybe I should have stayed there…"

"Steve, stop! Right now. Don't take responsibility, don't think you have to fix everything. I'm the parent here. Tell me one thing – Cal's behaviour tonight, being, well, extra cute and loveable. Was that real or just a performance?"

I thought hard. "I think it was both. We both tease him but I think he is a natural drama queen. And when he feels something he really wants to act it out so that everyone knows. Especially when he loves somebody."

"That's very thoughtful, Steve. I wish I could be absolutely certain. I better tell you why his hair gave me such a shock. It made him look just like his father. And you know already, that's what scares me. That I'm raising another charmer and another taker."

"Charmer, yes, but definitely not a taker. He's a giver. He makes people happy. People he doesn't even know, people he doesn't expect to see again. And when he gives he gives totally, to you, to me, to … Billy! Think about him and Billy. And he still talks to Billy, sometimes for hours. Shuts me up, if I try to interrupt, because it's Billy time."

"Thank you, Steve. What you say is true but I'm still scared. Of Cal's inheritance. His father looked like a wonderful, caring man. He was brilliant at making people feel good and making people feel good about him. He knew what pleased people and how to perform it. He knows I love him as my little boy and you love your cute little brother. Is all that real or just to please us?"

"I think that Cal really, really likes to make us happy, and other people. But maybe he needs to know that he doesn't always have to be cute. I mean, I really love it when he teaches me about drawing. Or when we're playing cricket really seriously, just batting and bowling and working for each other, like two professionals."

"That's very wise, Steve. Yes, do reward the serious, mature Cal. But it's not the answer, and anyway, it's not fair on you to give the answer. Steve, I am 99 per cent certain that Cal is my wonderful son. It's the other 1 per cent that terrifies me. The chance that he's a prototype for his father. The chance that there is stuff in there I can't change, can't even reach."

"Does Cal know about all this? That you're afraid he's going to be his father?"

"No. I've never thought that's fair. Telling him not to become someone he does not even know but still can't escape. I tried to fill in all the squares as a parent, but as he got older I knew there were some I couldn't fill. I so believed John Westaway was going to fill them, and I gave up, but then you came into his life and Steve, that is so unfair on you!" *She burst into tears and I held her.*

"Mum! Do you know what a buzz it is to call you Mum? We're a family and that means we all help each other and we do everything we can."

"Thank you, my wonderful son. Now go to bed and don't read any of your heavy books."

"S for Solzhenitsyn, August 1914."

"No chance, I'm giving you a Rosie M Banks. You need a good night's sleep, we're all going to Marian's tomorrow."

He is a wonderful son and it's not fair to expect more. Least of all, being a substitute father and providing a vision of maleness. Long hug and then shoo him away. Find the number I've been keeping.

"Howard? It's Alice. Devane. Is this a good time to talk?"

Chapter 33   New Pitch Inspection

Late at night. Composing another facile 800 words.
Interrupted by the voice I haven't nerved myself to
telephone, asking if it's a good time to talk. Something
urgent, even desperate. No more clowning from me!

"Howard, you're a writer. Can I ask you what you think of Cal?"

"Charming." Actual shriek from her. Precisely the wrong
word. Breathless, disjointed narrative. A new haircut, a
sudden reminder of the absent selfish father. The terror
of raising a cruel, manipulative charmer.

"Stop! If you value my opinion as a writer, you're talking complete bollocks.
Cal is charming but he is also loyal, generous, affectionate. By nature and by
upbringing. Trust him. Trust yourself."

"I know you're right. At least I hope… God, I'm sorry to dump all that on
you. I got a shock, and such a bad feeling. Stupid."

"Feelings are never stupid. They may be misguided but never stupid."

"I said that once to Steve."

"Then you know I'm right."

"I hate charm." Must remember. Cut the charm. Laconic,
Howard. Even hit the surly button. "It's so bloody… British."
Now I'm stuck. I'm as British as they come. My books
never translated well. Never took off in the USA. "I mean,
being allowed to be a shit if you're entertaining."

"But you can be entertaining without being a shit. You can be entertaining
because you like to see people entertained. Or because it's a substitute for
being angry or fearful or guilty."

"Do you think Cal is angry or fearful or guilty?"

"I've no idea, Alice. I've never had any children. I've only other people's to go
on, and then only as a teacher, a long time ago, or as a spoiler. Uncle Howard,
the treat machine. I only know that children are different from us. Things
matter to them which we don't know about, can't imagine."

"That's true enough. I know that from my work. I once had to write a residency clause for a little girl's rabbit."

"I can give you a theory about Cal. He was bullied, wasn't he? Zoe told me."

"Yes."

"And that came out of the blue, didn't it? Betrayed by his best mate and suddenly turning from being Mr Popular to Mr Outcast. That's devastating for anybody. Could have left him pretty insecure. Then suddenly his life turns round. He meets Steve – and you let him keep him. He meets Robert and Zoe, and Joe and Belinda and me. And there's a promise of a new school, and playing cricket with Tim Morrow, and all manner of other treats."

"Where's this going, Howard?"

"He's got a wonderful new world, Alice. But it's barely a month old. Lose it and he could be Mr Outcast again. Now think of the new haircut in that context. He tries out a new Cal – and you all hate it. So he thinks. Robert, Zoe, Steve and you. The guardians of the new world. Maybe you'll all throw him out. Wouldn't he scuttle back to the old Cal, the one you all loved?"

"That's very wise of you, Howard. Why didn't I work that out?"

"It's only a theory, Alice. I may be totally wrong."

"It's a good theory, Howard. Better than my hysterics." I could have argued, told her not to beat herself up. Something told me to listen instead. "Howard, I've suddenly doubled my parenting responsibilities. Steve's a terrific kid but he's a lot of work. I thought I had Cal pretty taped. Now I'm not thinking straight about him. I need help, Howard."

"I'm not sure how much help I can give, Alice."

"I'm sorry. I had no right to ask. You must put your work first."

"If by work you mean filling space with words, that is far less important than what you have just asked me. What worries me is this. I can do the easy stuff - outings, treats, attention. I do that for Zoe and Robert and your two are almost joined at the hip with them, so it's no problem to add them to any treat. In fact, I will ask them now to come to the Literary Benevolent Fund reception. Zoe and Robert are going – as my assistant and official photographer. Cal could do cartoons, Steve I'll add to my staff. But beyond treats, handling the deep emotions, I'm not sure I'm much use. I couldn't cope with Zoe and Robert during their poisonous feud. Couldn't even persuade them to come out with me on the same treat. What happens if I get all the fun stuff as Uncle Howard and you get stuck with all the hard parenting?"

"We can all face that, Howard, if it seems to be happening. What's good enough for me, for us, right now is attention, interest, observation. Can I ask you for that?"

"Of course. Beginning tomorrow because I want a debrief on your visit to Marian's. And I have been promised a private view of Cal's drawings. I think it would be good for him to ask me, but since you're checking, tomorrow evening would be good for me."

"Thank you, Howard. I think that would be very good for us too. I… we… would all like to know you better."

Mild argument about eating arrangements. I suggest takeout or restaurant, will she want to cook after long visit to Marian's? She says Cal does cooking for special occasions. Agreement to leave decision to him. She inquires about article I'm writing. Typical late-period Howard Foy. Instantly readable, instantly forgettable. She actually seems interested. Desultory conversation. Reluctance on both sides to hang up. As it used to be with Marian. Final goodbye. Return to the article in the wordprocessor. Slick, empty. Start again, Howard, your public deserves better.

Nice of Cal to hand over his bed but I still can't sleep. Thinking about Marian's. Sounds brilliant. Bet they'll take Cal but why should they take me? I'm good at cricket (I think) and I've read a lot of books which were left to me. Anything else to offer? Er… I can swim. I'm OK as a left back. I don't mind heavy lifting. Next, please! Might just as well go for a run. Maybe they'll take me for my body.

Last to breakfast. Mum has saved mine from Cal.

Messenger at door with special-delivery envelope. My GCSE results. Sent on from my former home. Hell, that sounds cold. Sent on from my birth parents. Big card from them, with a cricketer. Tom O'Ryan bowling flat out. They must have thought about it, made some effort to get it. Message inside. "Dear Steve. Hope this is cricketer you like! We haven't opened the envelope but congratulations for all your hard work. Hope you get what you deserve. Let us know some time. Mum and Dad." *Suddenly they are Mum and Dad, when it's too late.*

Well, open it! "Bloody hell!" *Stunned. Can't read it out. Pass it on to Cal.*

"Four A Stars, four As, two Cs. And he still loses to Bungle!" *Giant hug from the two of them.*

"Nice of them to send it on that way. I ought to tell them."

Phone up Dad's counting house. That's how I always thought of it, like Dickens. Actually it's totally modern. Put through straight away. Usually I had to wait or let him call back. He seemed really pleased. "Sorry about the Cs. Maths and Business Studies." *His subjects!*

"It doesn't matter, Steve. I don't suppose you'll be going to business college now. Tell us how you get on at Marian's today. And Steve? I'm proud of you. I don't suppose you remember our agreement, but you kept it." *I had forgotten. It doesn't matter. He has no power over me.*

Phone up Mum's office. Again put through straight away. "I always said you were a genius!" *No you didn't. Pleased at my A-Stars in English Language and Literature (her subjects) contrasted with my Cs in his subjects. That will come up at dinner – but I won't be there!*

Mum wouldn't let us take the cricket bag to Marian's.

"They've got proper nets, Robert says so."

"You haven't got a place yet, sweetheart. You can't help yourself to their facilities. And besides, we're not going by car. No one's allowed to go to that school by car – that's part of the deal. It's going to be a long return trip for you. At least it's against the stream of traffic, both ways. And you'll be with Robert and Zoe."

"And Steve. I'm not going without Steve."

"Time out, sweetheart." **Mum had the 'serious' face.** "That's very loyal, but that is not a decision for you. It would be great if you both went to the same school, and convenient for me, but it might not happen. We need to make the best available choice for each of you. Steve does not have to go to school at all - he could go to sixth-form college, he could work. We still have to get him his trial at Lords. Even if Steve does go to school with you he'll be doing A Levels and you may not see much of him. And he'll leave that school in two years and do something else. Travel, work, go to uni. You understand what I'm saying, don't you?"

"He's older than me and he's got his own life." **Without me!**

"Got it in one. Now you know our Steve. Do you think he would ever lead that life without thinking about us? Just use our home like a hotel and check out one day without saying goodbye?"

"No and no."

"And do you think that our Steve would be happy if you got into a great school where you're happy?"

"Yes." **As if I'd be happy at any school without Steve!** "Now you've packed the sketch bag and a selection of the best late-period Devanes?"

"The copy of the Billy drawing. And some of Shithead falling on his arse. And Steve bowling. And reading."

"Good picks. I think you could also pack two cricket balls, but don't use without permission."

It would not be an easy journey, especially at night, and yes, I would be happier if Steve were with him. Nice grounds. Converted from a mental hospital. School seems full of children, even though it is still holidays. Tennis players, skaters, basketball, footballers, trampoline, martial arts. Table tennis, but in some new, anarchic version: someone penalized for jumping onto the table. Some strange dancers. An indoor swimming pool. The familiar clonk of cricket ball on cricket bat: I had to stop my boys from following the sound.

Big reception area. Photograph of Marian, Howard's dead wife. Formerly his editor, became a teacher in a state school. Forced to act as a social worker and paperkeeper above being a teacher. This school created as one where she would have wanted to teach.

A tall, dramatic-looking woman with dark hair. Polar opposite to me! What was she like otherwise? What did Howard love? Brief inscription with her dates. Followed by the school motto: Act For Others, Think For Yourself. Good choice. Suspect it was Howard's. A special board labelled Company Notices. Documents from limited companies in correct legal form: Marian's Childcare … Marian's Design and Media… Marian's Auto Workshop…

Met by school secretary. Flustered, apologetic. The head, Rupert Giles, has gone walkabout. I was ready for this: his official nickname is Perpetual Motion. "It's an interesting typeface, isn't it?" Had not noticed, but in fact it is. "It's called

Marian's. It was designed here, in our studio. We've started to earn money from it."

The head was finally located in the school's newspaper office in the studio. She led us there, narrowly avoiding some tap dancers and a pantomime horse. Every bit of wall space was filled with works of art. Some were terrible and I could sense Cal about to criticise but she got in front of him. "Anyone who wants to exhibit gets wall space. That's our policy. So long as the work isn't obscene or vicious. And we try to sell it if the artist wants. The market tends to weed out the lesser artists over time. Not always. That basket of puppies will easily make its reserve."

We stuck our heads into the theatre. "Good grief, isn't that Sheila Fereday?" Household-name actress, taking direction from a diminutive girl.

"She's one of our supporters." I bet Howard recruited her. "She's taken a small part in Marie's production. You should have heard Marie chew her out for upstaging."

The school newspaper office was marked by a giant poster: COSY MOMENTS WILL NOT BE MUZZLED! Steve began to ask a question, but the head was talking.

"Ivan, you know that I have never censored Cosy Moments for content, but I refuse to let you attack the English faculty with a split infinitive. Remove it, and if you persist in using 'challenge' as a substitute for 'problem' you will become a management consultant and serve you right. Good grief, it's Ms Devane, isn't it? And Steve and Cal? How do you do? Rupert Giles. Ivan Murray, current editor of Cosy Moments." About Steve's age. Untidy, but less so than his headmaster - small, rumpled suit, every pocket filled with notebooks or phones. And a cricket ball! He looked younger than me. "I do apologize for missing our appointment, but you will have learnt more about our school from walking here than from sitting in my office. I hope it looked like a happy place. If it didn't, we have failed and you can go home. Happiness is our formula, Ms Devane."

"Alice, please."

"Alice." Sudden piercing stare. Remembering my name, and signalling strength behind the patter. Like Howard! "If our children are happy they want to learn and achieve and we barely have to teach them at all. Look at Ivan here. He's happy. He's even happy when his headmaster embarrasses him in front of strangers. People come to this school as pupils, as teachers, helpers, lecturers, supporters, because they make the school happier. If they don't, they leave it. We have Happy lessons – the only ones which are compulsory - in happymaking behaviour. To give their technical name, Social and

Emotional Aspects of Learning and Roots of Empathy. It includes taking care of a baby. First a dummy one, then a real one. We need a constant supply…"

"The school did seem happy. It also seems incredibly full for a holiday."

"As I think you know, we don't really have holidays, Alice. Only voluntary days. We try to stay open every day of the year. Not necessarily teaching or lecturing but providing some kind of facility which children can use with supervision. Not just our own. Local children can come here with a free swipe card. And no junk food." Steve beamed approval. "There are few rules here but that one is rigidly enforced. We want happy, active children here and we can't get them if they are full of fat, salt, sugar and chemicals. We treat possession of junk food with intent to supply as seriously as we would treat cannabis or ecstasy. But we administer free cereal bars, trail mix, fruit at break times, and water, pure juice or smoothies. Extra rations as rewards." Cal beamed approval.

All the while the head had been pacing more and more furiously, scrawling things into one of his notebooks. "Winston! You're a slacker and a disgrace to the school! Get on with your work!" We looked for another pupil, until Ivan lifted an overweight black cat.

"Winston?"

"I thought everyone knew that Winston is the janitor's cat in Bash Street School in the Beano. That Winston's a worker, this one's a waste of space."

"But does he make the school happier?"

"Good point, Cal. His official duty is to catch mice but the children keep feeding him. Come to that, they keep feeding the mice. We've never killed a rodent on the premises but we've buried three health inspectors."

My boys laughed but Ivan sighed deeply. "Wait till you're on kitchen duty. Hygiene overkill."

"Each class works for a whole day in the kitchen. Helping to make and serve lunch and clean up afterwards. Apart from food preparation and fanatical hygiene they learn nutrition and health, interpersonal skills, biology, chemistry, physics, mathematics, languages, geography, business methods and economics, international trade, transport, art and design, history…"

"History?"

"Certainly, Cal. All food has a history. Who ate the first pineapple to come to Britain? Shut up, Ivan. If you come here, you'll find out. Correction, you'll be invited to find out for yourself. Just as Steve will find out why the school newspaper is called Cosy Moments." I was impressed that he remembered a question that Steve had not even spoken.

He gave a final instruction to Ivan to exterminate clichés like cockroaches. "We try not to teach anything in an abstract, academic, atomic way. We try to connect learning and make it relevant to everyday life. You may have noticed already that there are many businesses run from this school. Almost everything we do here generates some kind of business. Real businesses, selling real goods and services for money, although we do a lot of things pro bono as well. The pupils run the businesses themselves on co-operative lines although we have to have adults to act as directors and sign contracts. But it is the pupils who make the policy decisions. We have a catering business and we are going to publish a recipe book, we have an entertainments business, a design business, an IT business, a local advertising agency, a child care business, a car repair business. I've lost track. When our pupils get involved in a business they have to learn every aspect of it and every skill that goes into it. No privileges for the board room. Excuse me…"

He took a call from one of his mobile phones. "I didn't invite the rabbi so he can wait with the plumber. If he wants to help with the blocked toilet, he's welcome." That sent Steve into hysterics. "I'll invite you to share the joke when you've recovered. If there were more plumbers and fewer priests the world would be a better place. Some people don't like the way we teach religion. As a theory, not as a fact. A bad theory, because it fails Popper's test. Shut up again, Ivan. They can discover Popper's test by themselves, if they choose."

He led us out into the school grounds but his attempt at a guided tour was constantly interrupted by children greeting him.

"Kulabesh Mishabob, sir!"

"Kulabesh Mishabob, Tony, Adrian." Two boys about Cal's size swept past us, chattering apparent gibberish. "One of our classes is inventing a language. It's a good way of teaching the principles of language. I don't think theirs will catch on, if you need that mouthful just to say hello."

"Sir, sir, watch this!" We stopped frequently so that children could show something off to their head. If Cal comes here he would never get away!

"We hand out a lot of admiration, Alice. We aim for 90 per cent admiration against 10 per cent admonition."

"Wordpower! Oops, sorry."

"Don't be sorry, Steve, I'll take that as admiration. The pupils are expected to follow that ratio amongst themselves. Admiration for effort, not necessarily for result. If we criticize the result we often use hyperbole. Someone hands in a bad history essay, the teacher won't say 'this is a bad history essay,' but something like 'this is the worst history essay in history.'"

"Just like Steve when he's coaching."

"Coaching what, Cal?"

"Coaching cricket. He makes you feel brilliant even when you do something crap. Oops, sorry. He coached me, and Robert who's coming here and Marjorie and Edwin and all the team at Glendon Courtenay. In Devon. He's their professional."

"That's excellent. Are you a qualified coach, Steve?"

"Well, not really but I'm going to do a course. When I met Cal I found myself teaching the way my uncle Frank taught me. My uncle Frank played for the Army but when he joined the SAS he really only played with me on his leaves. He did hyperbole and two guns for bowling and pace is your friend for batting and…"

"Show me at the nets." Predictably, it took ages to get there. We detoured past an enormous library ("We still use it to contain books"), a science block ("we can do anything in here. We had UN weapons inspectors round last month"), their version of Companies House and the lecture hall. "Every pupil here gives a public lecture here once a year on a subject of his or her choice. And I mean lecture, not presentation. We teach public speaking – rhetoric. We invite family members and friends to lecture too, on anything which they know about. We also invite them to be coaches, trainers, supervisors – make any contribution they can. On any given day we have dozens of part-timers and volunteers on the premises. I wish the government would let us choose who comes into our school and trust us to keep out the weirdoes instead of making us wait eternally for the CRB…" He was starting to get heated but silenced himself for the Meditation Room. He made a note to remove a distracting stain on one of the bare walls. "Is it not like a whale?" My boys looked blank. With a flash of anger I realized that none of their previous schools had led them to Hamlet.

"And here is the Bocardo room, where we teach formal logic and argument. Named Bocardo, why? Another thing to find out."

We passed a climbing wall and before anyone could stop him, Cal shinned up it. "Another day's work for … the Cat!"

"Cal, you have to wear safety gear and be roped and supervised by a qualified climber. Please come down at once before we get prosecuted."

He shinned down again. "Catch, Steve!" and Steve did so, comfortably.

The head sighed. "However did we manage before Health and Safety?"

At the Music School a punk-rock band was rehearsing. Even by punk standards they were awful. "Sometimes it's very hard to maintain 90 per cent admiration." He led us into the studio and the din subsided. Three boys and a girl. At their head's entrance they became another set of children wanting to show off for their head. They started a long explanation of their style: 'post-thrash sub-techno garage.'

"Why do you call yourselves Three AM Kebab?"

"Because we're terrible. Like the kebab you eat at three am because you can't get anything else." Ray Corvino would love them.

After we left, the head told us that two were aiming for the Royal College of Music. "And listen to the drummer for a minute." I hate drum solos but I was mesmerized, as were the boys. Aggressive, yes, fluent yes, tricky cross-rhythms yes, but much more. Another world. "Some echoes of John Bonham, but principally Brandon Vessio. American.[24] I think his father is some kind of spy."

"Like J…" Steve stopped him before he could blurt the name of Sean Kinch, although he seemed to be known as a spy all over Devon.

"We know another. The music gene seems to go with the espionage gene."

"We're often described as a progressive school. We're not in the least progressive about technical standards. Especially in so-called creative subjects. We make them learn the rules so that they know how and when to break them."

We nearly lost Cal in the Art and Design complex. "I think we have all media covered. We have a tension we have not quite resolved, between participation

---

[24] He's for real too, but not in London.

and achievement. We want students to express themselves in art. We exhibit all their work. Some are terrible. Is that fair to the good students? I don't know. I am sorry Mr Gray is not here today, our head of art. We would have a vigorous debate. He used to teach at the Royal Academy Schools. He wants us to be more selective. We reached a compromise – a tougher programme for specialists but more exhibition time and space. Same problem with our sports teams. We select by rotation. Everyone who turns up to practice and training plays for the school. Is that fair on the best players?"

Appropriately, we had by now reached the cricket nets. "Sir, sir! We want to shred the head."

"I used to play a bit. If anyone can bowl me, he or she earns ten thousand marks for the celebration. I should have explained about the celebration. It plays a big role in this school. Each year gets an annual celebration, which they organize themselves. It could be an outing, or a party, or a meeting with a celebrity or all of these things. But they have to earn it. They have to achieve at least a million marks, collectively, during the year. If they earn more than a million they get more time and more money for their celebration. So if they have a wonderful year they might be able to book … Radiohead. If they have a mediocre year they could only book Three AM Kebab." All his listeners shuddered. He pulled us aside. "Marks are given for work and behaviour – and can be taken away. A year can easily fall to minus a million, or even more. Behaviour and attitude count for a lot. They earn a big plus for any behaviour which makes other people happy or achieve something and a big minus for any behaviour which is destructive or negative or makes people unhappy. But when and if such behaviour is corrected the minus is cancelled."

"Collective reward and collective punishment?"

"Not legally sound, is it, Alice? But it promotes group discipline. Our students share responsibility for behaviour and attitude. And we have a court system to express that formally – I'll tell you more later. Now then, you pampered jades, you pampered jades of Asia, what hope do you have of shredding the head's stumps? I will face you all. What do we have – three Marians and two visitors? Add two new visitors – Steve here says he is a fast bowler and a professional and Cal here claims to be a mystery spinner. Usual rules. If a Marian bowls me it's ten thousand marks for the celebration and if a visitor bowls me he or she gets a fiver. But neither of these events will happen." By now he was padded up.

Steve looked uneasy. "I don't like bowling at people without a helmet."

"Then wear a helmet." He laughed uproariously at his own joke. "Don't worry, Steve. I was on the Middlesex staff. I've not forgotten everything."

"Did you play first-class?"

"A bit. Then I discovered something else to do with my life."

Even I could see that he was a brilliant batsman. I was pleased that my boys seemed better than the other bowlers, but he played them with ease, even Steve at his fastest. One of the others bowled him a wild, head-high ball. He smacked it away.

"Sorry, sir."

"Minus five thousand, Charlie. A beamer is either vicious or abysmally incompetent. One more and you will be savagely punished, worse than Emperor Bajazeth!" Someone else for Steve to look up. Charlie looked crestfallen.

I switched off for a while. I loved this school and this head, but I still had questions. Suddenly I heard a clunk and a familiar squeal.

"Zamboni!"

"Glare in my eyes off the science block." Not long after, Steve was celebrating.

"Yorker! Reversed!"

"Movement from behind your arm in the science block." And a little later he was bowled by Charlie. I think that he meant to be. "I'm going to tear down that science block. Ten thousand marks to Year Ten for Charlie, five thousand net of the beamer. Five pounds each for Cal and Steve."

My boys exchanged a quick glance. "Can we donate ten thousand instead?"

"As you wish. Ten thousand each to Years Eight and Eleven." He scrawled a note. "Carry on. Helmet for batters. Watch the ball not the science block."

The head and I walked away. "Oh hell, that poor plumber and that dratted rabbi. Excuse me." He spoke briefly into one of his phones. "Good old Ella. She's sent the plumber to the toilet and the rabbi to the basketball court. That was a generous gesture by your boys. If it implies that they like this school and would like to come here I would be glad to interview them. Today if you wish. But I'm sure you have questions. That must have seemed a very disjointed visit. We are actually more structured, sometimes."

"Your notebooks tell me that. I don't think much escapes you. I do have questions. First, Cal. I had to pull him out of his last school because of homophobic bullying. He's gay. Will he have any problems here? Might he get bullied for any other reason? He might seem cocky or lippy sometimes. Will someone think they have to knock that out of him?"

"As to being gay – he'll be under pressure to come out because his year gets ten thousand marks towards its celebration when someone comes out. Yes, it's on a par with bowling the head. To be fair to the straight kids, so that they can earn marks too, they are encouraged to come out about anything in their lives which attracts mockery or prejudice. It might be … stammering or being fat. It might seem completely trivial, like enjoying the wrong computer game or the wrong kind of music. That's actually helpful, because it makes all prejudice seem equally silly.

"As to being bullied – we've already taken a lot of refugees from bullying. I can't guarantee that it won't happen but we really try to get in front of it. First of all, the way we define it. Bullying means any deliberate conduct which makes another person unhappy, or, in some cases, reckless conduct which makes another person unhappy. You're a lawyer, Alice, so I imagine those concepts are familiar to you."

"Indeed. Do you mean conduct which would make a reasonable person unhappy?"

"No. What makes an actual person unhappy. We react to that whenever it happens. If we know about it. We start at the top. If a teacher does it, more than once, he's out. If a teacher ignores it, he's out. Some teachers in other schools are too weak, some teachers are too tired, some teachers collude or even ally with bullies to help them control their classes. We don't have that sort of teacher here. We have dozens of applicants for every post, because we shield our teachers from government targets and paperwork and actually let them teach creatively. And, being honest, because we give them small classes of carefully selected children. Selected because we think they will make other people happy…

"So we weed out a lot of potential bullies before they come here. We give everyone here a stimulating, energetic place, with plenty to do. The children eat properly and are hydrated. They have to do at least two bursts of intense physical activity every day. We use virtually every inch of our space. There are very few isolated places, where someone can physically intimidate someone else without being detected.

"All those measures, we think, are good for behaviour generally and discourage bullying. Add to that, the baby care and the rest of the empathy programme. Our students discover the power to recognize unhappiness in someone vulnerable and make him or her happy instead. They enjoy this. Add to that, we provide very good counselling. Bullies are nearly always unhappy about something themselves. We guarantee that they can talk to somebody about it before they take it out on someone else. Talk in confidence, without being judged or condemned, and get the power to overcome their unhappiness, stand up to anyone dishing it out to them.

"Add to that the collective reward and penalty system I described. It seems to work. Each year's students follow their collective scores carefully. They themselves reward the people who earn marks for the year, they shun the people who lose them. But we can't stand Uriah Heep children, so if anyone makes a big show of good behaviour he gets minus marks not plus ones.

"In spite of all that, we do get cases of bullying. Both perpetrators and victims are often a big surprise. When it happens, the perpetrator can either accept a summary penalty from the head of year or go to trial. If he goes to trial, head of year is the judge, but jury, counsel for both sides are students. He might get off but he might get a higher penalty. Penalties are minus marks and something personal – maybe a fine, maybe suspension from a sports team or a company or some other desired activity. And they always include restitution to the victim. When all that is done, especially the restitution, the penalty is purged and the minus marks disappear. I might add that there are big penalties for making a false accusation against anybody.

"If bullying is serious enough to cross the threshold of crime we always bring in the police. We had a lot of argument about this, but we decided that it's right to remind our children that they are members of wider society and that they have to respect the law. And if bullying that serious is proved we will almost certainly expel. Double jeopardy? Too bad. Everyone knows that's our policy. It's only happened once in two years – but we made sure everyone knew about it. I'm sorry to go on so long."

"Don't worry, it was important."

"You had another point which I have now forgotten."

"Cal can seem cocky and lippy."

"All of our children seem cocky and lippy a lot of the time. Cal will not stand out for that reason. Tell me what else is on your mind."

"Mr Gray, your head of art, makes me feel nervous. Cal is very opinionated about drawing and art. He has to discover things for himself. He does not take kindly to formal instruction."

"I honestly do not think you need to worry. Mr Gray is demanding but not didactic. He is strong on technique but he gives his artists their head on vision and execution. I hope that he would make Cal progress faster to where he wants to go. And he is not the only art teacher. We have three others on the staff, and regular visitors and all the specialist students are encouraged to teach each other."

I've delayed long enough. Tell him my real worry. "I can't afford this."

"Wrong, by definition. If we offer places to Cal and Steve, you'll pay what you can afford. Cal might also gain an art scholarship – that decision is with Mr Gray. Steve could get a credit for cricket coaching and perhaps other assistance. He seems a very responsible young man. And you're a children's lawyer. I am sure that there are ways you could help us. And we have long-term loan schemes on very good terms. I really ask you to put finance out of your mind. I am ready to interview Cal and Steve and assess what we could offer each other. If you would like more time to think about us, or discover more, or look at other schools please take it."

"The interview alone decides whether you offer them a place?"

"Yes."

"In that case, would you do it today?"

We walked back towards the nets. Another interruption. "Sir, there's a mad rabbi on the basketball court!"

"How do you know he's mad? Is he talking about religion?"

"No, he's scored two hundred points."

"Then learn from him."

At the nets Steve was coaching a small horde of children. Cal was sketching. We watched for a few minutes. By now I recognized Steve's schtick. Wild praise or criticism, mock commentaries, making sure the weaker ones achieve something memorable. I felt this would do Steve more good than any interview. Whisper: "I think I'll take Steve first. He's a worrier." Good assessment. Aloud: "I'm afraid I need to borrow Steve for half an hour."

Hell. I'm all sweaty and I'm going for an interview. Won't matter. This is a genius school and I'm no genius. Cal will get in as an artist. He'll be happy here and he won't need me.

Steve's interview. Will they know he's a god? He doesn't know he's a god himself!

I bowled him! Was that a good idea? When I bowled Right Honourable he hated me. This one was really nice about it. What are we going to talk about? Hell, where's my GCSE results!

Steve bowled him! And he's better than Luke. I bowled him too, and Charlie, but I'm not sure he was trying. He was trying against Steve and he still got bowled. He must know Steve's a god.

Steve's forgotten his GSCE results! Rush up and hand them over. Head distracted by yet another child. Take chance to whisper. "Be yourself. Remember we love you."

Chapter 34   Day/Night Fixture

Dear Mrs H (Zoe Future)

Steve's coming to Marian's!!!!! I knew it would happen but I still got a thrill when he phoned...

"Can I carry your books this winter?"

Of course he's doing A Levels and he's going to be a cricket coach and maybe other sports so we won't have the same timetable but we will go in together on the train and eat lunch and he will carry my books and people will see us, and I could take up cricket because it's for girls too and he could coach me, only Robert says I'm crap. And we'll both write for Cosy Moments, and do homework together and go to lectures together and be in the play together because I can act and they'll cast him for looks if he can't!!! Cal got in too (nice)...

***

"We'd be glad to have both of them, Alice. The interviews were rather sweet. Cal kept talking up Steve, and Steve kept talking up Cal. 'My elective brother', a nice phrase. If I may say so, it was wonderful of you to give him a home with you. He's come through a lot of adversity. There's still a legacy, isn't there? We'll work through that together. He was very worried about an incident at X School, I hope I reassured him that makes no difference here. He'll be a huge asset as an extra cricket coach. I was very impressed with Cal's drawings and I've kept the one of me. Mr Gray will make the judgment on the art scholarship, but I would like to have Cal here on character. He's a generous and exhilarating person ... Let Ella know if you need a discussion with the finance committee. I hope we'll see them on Induction day on the 8th but they can come round earlier, we'll issue swipe cards... Excuse me a moment. Rabbi! Delighted to meet you. We have no need of your religious function here but I hope you might accept a post as our basketball coach..."

***

I asked Howard to dinner! He phoned up to wish luck before Marian's and to fix time to see my drawings (he remembered) and tonight was best for him. He likes anything with lime in it...

"Mum, there's loads of time if everyone does what I say! Steve, squeeze all those limes. Not in your hand, we know you're strong, but use the squeezer. Don't throw away the skins. Mum, give me zest from one lime, then beat egg whites. Cal, melt butter and honey, dissolve jelly, add extra lime juice, crush bikkies for pastry..."

It's so hard to get good help these days.

"Pie phase completed. Mum, complete margarita phase. Steve, commence chicken phase. Rub whole body with lime skins, garlic clove. Put two more lime skins inside with one more clove of garlic and pass to me. Cal – improve boring supermarket guacamole phase.

Dinner is a bit easier with Steve here, even though he doesn't know anything.

"You are peeling the carrots and parsnips because I'm left-handed and I can't use a right-handed peeler. And then you can peel the rice..." *Hysterics, but even I know you don't peel rice.*

Howard was on time, curse it!

"Steve, crush ice! Mum, let him in and entertain him. Play the piano or something. Vamp him!" *Hysterics.*

"Sweetheart, go and greet your guest. Show him the drawings he came to see. Steve and I will finish up here."

They have half a nice house in a cul-de-sac. Could be tight with Steve living there.

"Hello, Howard. Mum will like those..." (Will she? Those flowers suddenly look terribly hackneyed) "I will like those... (Expensive chocolates, ditto). "Steve and I got into Marian's!"

"Cal! You were going to wait for us!" She sweeps me into a living room.

He's wearing an expensive suit. Trying to impress me? Flattered, but didn't he notice the frayed pocket and the stain on the Garrick Club tie? Needs an inspector for public appearances!

Light. Uncluttered, unlike mine. A good piano! Fight down urge to play it. I can empty parties. Even the dead-drunk arise and go home. I take the couch. Steve comes in with a tray bearing guacamole and an evident margarita.

"Howard, I hope you really, really like lime because Cal's put lime into everything. Do you want this margarita, we have alternatives?"

"I like margaritas. And I walked here. I don't drive much, except for cricket."

"You don't drive much at cricket!" She looks pleased at Steve's sally. Must encourage him.

"Blame the dreary defensive bowlers I face. Mmm, brilliant margarita!"

"Should be – Mum did enough sampling in the kitchen."

"Cal, that's defamatory." She's having one too. Good. Don't want to drink alone. Don't want special treatment here – as a visitor.

"I am very, very happy that you are both going to Marian's." I am. Very very happy. A strange, forgotten feeling. Would it be premature to hug the daylights out of them all? Prevented by the offer of guacamole.

"It's only supermarket, but I've perked it up. Extra lime juice. And those are lime-flavoured tortilla chips." Chomping and sipping. The boys are drinking Rose's lime juice. By choice, or in my honour?

"Who plays the piano?"

"Mum. She was a professional."

"Cal, don't boost me! Accompanist to Ray Corvino. One step below Beppo The Wonder Dog." She knows Ricky Rubato!

"I would like to hear her later. But may I look at your drawings now?" Well done, Howard. That was why he invited you. I would have hated you to forget.

"Take a refill, Howard, you could be gone for some time. Which reminds me, were you named after the Polar explorer?"

She's looked me up in the reference books! No one else
bothers with my middle name.

"I wasn't. My father named me after Hampshire's naggingly accurate opening bowler. My elder brother was Derek. That left me Shackleton."

Astonishingly neat child's bedroom. Tidied up for me?

"Steve's sleeping here for a bit, because of his back. I packed up my stuff to make room for his." Of course. Don't be silly, Howard.

Album after album of drawings. They all seem very
accomplished to me but he is fiercely self-critical. "I am
ashamed of most of my early work. I've kept it mostly because of the subjects, holidays or places or people. We don't take many photos, Mum and me, so we keep my drawings instead. And it's worth learning from my mistakes. When I was little I tried to put everything in which I could see, instead of the important things. Look, this is the Penguin Pool at the Zoo when I was eight and this is when I went back last year."

"Last year is … better organized. You've focused on the penguins and you've given them all some personality. This one's the chief penguin, isn't he? But don't despise the eight-year-old's drawing. It may seem disorganized but maybe the Zoo's like that. I mean, it isn't just about the creatures in the cages but the creatures looking at them, or not looking at them. You tried to put all the people into that drawing, and they all have their own story. This family isn't even looking at the penguins, they're arguing, aren't they?… And this couple's in love with each other… And this boy wanted to be somewhere else… And this dad's lifting two huge children…"

"They weren't that big, I just didn't draw them properly!"

"Maybe. But why lift two children at once? Most parents would do them in turns? Is the dad showing off his strength? Or is he trying to be fair to each child? Oh, this is so not the way you're supposed to look at pictures. Trying to turn them into stories."

"I like drawing stories. But you've got to decide what the story is. And chuck everything else out."

"That's the hardest part about writing. The chucking out. But it's still worth creating the things you chuck out. People, scenes, dialogue, thoughts. They're never wasted. You might want to come back to them and use them somewhere else. And they may guide you to what you really want to create. And you probably can't stop yourself creating them anyway." You hypocrite, Howard. You've stopped creating. And you've chucked out all the people you created. Get back to him. "No paintings, Cal?"

"Colour gets in the way for me. I do a colour wash for some subjects. But I really don't want to paint. I can't even draw yet." Wistful.

"You might enjoy experimenting. Not just in paint but in other media. You'll be able to do that at Marian's." More hypocrisy, Howard. When did you experiment? One 'serious' psychological novel. It flopped and you scuttled back to what you knew. Lightweight comic characters. Get back to him again. "What are you working on now?"

"An alphabet for Billy. Mostly animals. He likes animals." Reminder: must write to Luke.

"That's a wonderful thing to do. You'll have a tough job with X. Hmm… do you ever work from photographs?"

"Can do."

"Robert might like to take some."

"Maybe. But Robert's … awesome. Almost a pro." Genuine doubt about his right to work with Robert, who would kill to work with him!

Shouted summons to kitchen. Of course I don't mind eating at the kitchen table. More intimate.

"Chicken with lime. Carrots and parsnips with lime glaze. Lime in the water jug. Nothing in the rice. Or the wine." Fleurie. Luck. One of my favourites. Drinking for pleasure again, not at a business lunch or on parade at a literary gathering. I don't drink alone.

"Cal, this is really good."

"I needed Mum and Steve."

"I'm sorry. Cal, Alice and Steve, this is really good."

"Weren't the carrots peeled well? And the parsnips."

"You kept sending them back."

"Your recipes, Cal?"

"Yes. I can't do stuff from a book. Like drawing. I have to invent everything myself. But it's worse with cooking. I mean, you can hide a bad drawing or throw it away. But Mum's had to eat all my cooking mistakes."

```
Two helpings of his chicken. Two slices of his lime pie.
Glad I chose this suit which hides a paunch. Cal manages
three.
```
"Steve says I'm an ectomorph."
```
                                                    Proud.
```

"Thank you, everybody. That was a wonderful dinner."
```
                                                    Now can I get
her to the piano?
```

"Hope you know how to play Monopoly, Howard."
```
                                                    Not yet. There's a
family ritual, and I'm invited. Quick visit to loo. Lime
cologne over basin! Discourteous not to use some. On
return, table cleared and Monopoly set up - for five.
```

"So this is the famous Bungle. Zoe and Robert warned me about him."
```
Rapid explanation of special rules for bear.
```

```
I am the first to be wiped out by the uber-ursine.
```
"Howard, you've left yourself cash-short by buying so much property. I learnt that from my dad."
```
                                        Significant glance between Alice and
Steve. Squeeze of his hand. Clearly some big moment for
him.
```

```
Monopoly finished (another triumph for Bungle). Now for
the piano?
```

"Howard, could you do something for me?"

"Of course, Steve."

"You're a writer. Could you look at the books my uncle Frank left me?"

```
He takes me to a small room. Once her study. Computer and
law books still there. Temporary cupboard and chest.
Sofabed. Locked trunk. Opened with great care. Some
photographs: mostly the two of them playing cricket.
Steve takes after him, and has inherited his bowling
```

action. One of them with a teddy bear. "That was Sergeant Bear. My Bungle. He was given away."

His uncle Frank's Military Cross. "I don't know what it was for."

"Bravery. The details don't really matter." Finally, the books. Carefully packed, in strict alphabetical order. One gap, at letter S. No F for Foy! I nearly make a joke about this but check myself in time. These books are sacred relics. My opinion matters.

"These were the books your uncle wanted to keep, and wanted you to read?"

"Yes."

"This is a remarkable collection. Some titles would be on almost everyone's list of great books. Many are about war and soldiering. Some are about young men, looking for identity. The X for Xenophon is a military classic but I think he couldn't resist completing the alphabet. I'm glad he gave you a W for Wodehouse, as light relief. There's humour in the H for Heller and the V for Vonnegut but it is dark. Was he a serious-minded man?"

"He made loads of jokes with me and his army mates. But I know he was a loner and he ended up really bitter and stressed and he did not even see me when he left the army and drank himself to death." Voice starting to shake. I put my arm around him.

"You're not bitter and stressed. You don't drink. You're not a loner. You have a home because two people love you very much and want you to live with them. All the Barneses love you and care about you. I ... think you're a very fine person. I would be glad to help you in any part of your life. You're about to go to a good school, full of interesting people who are going to like you and support you. Steve, you're in charge of your future. And you're in charge of your past. You can pick and choose among your memories, use the ones which enrich your life." More hypocrisy, Howard. You haven't done that with Marian. Turn the agenda back to him, as I did with Cal. "What are you reading now?"

"S for Solzhenitsyn. August 1914."

"Another book about war. And one competent soldier fighting against incompetent leadership. But can I ask you to skip out of sequence and read V for Varley?"

"Mary Varley? Victory?"

"I would like you to meet her. At the Literary Benevolent Fund reception in a few week's time. Your mother's kindly agreed to join me. I hope you and Cal will join us. Zoe and Robert will be there."

"Meeting one of uncle Frank's authors. I thought they were all dead."

"Mary Varley admits to 92 but she's as sharp as a tack."

"Cliché, Howard!"

"I'm taking that as a yes. You'll enjoy Victory, and I think you'll see below the surface. Shall we join the others?"

Mary Varley's book. What a stroke of luck. Unconventional and perceptive choice by his uncle. The trunk relocked with care. One last plea for reassurance.

"They are good books, aren't they Howard?"

"Definitely. You are already exceptionally well read and there are more to come. And it's not over at Z for Zola. You'll read many more great books. You might well write some."

At last I was back in the room with the piano. And Alice.

"Coffee, Howard?"

"It's the only thing I can do. I can put lime in it?"

"Thank you, Steve, but do it normally. For me, black with nothing." He scurried away. She and Cal were on the couch, she stroking the hair which had given her such a fright. "What a beautiful piano..."

"Help yourself, Howard."

"Mum, are you sure? Zoe said..."

"Manners, Cal!" But I was glad he didn't treat me as a guest. What had Zoe said? Infamy! I play my show-off pieces, Milestones and Riders On The Storm. Respectful silence! Steve back with coffee.

"Way better than my piano."

"Er, Howard, I'm not surprised. You're on the loud pedal the whole time. It's like driving a car with your foot on the clutch."

"Did you get that from Ricky Rubato?" Flattered.

"Yes. I haven't seen it, Howard. I read it. I wanted to read you without the actors and the director. And the dog." Even more flattered. "Now I've heard Ricky in private performance. Like the Queen!"

"Marian gave him to me. At a dinner party. We were talking about piano players and she suddenly said 'if Howard ever turned professional he would have to call himself Howie Rubato.' I made it Ricky for alliteration, and his story wrote itself. Beppo The Wonder Dog pushed his way in. And the Queen and Metallurgy In Turkestan.[25]"

"I liked it, Howard. And you got it right – about the music, I mean." Only about the music? It was supposed to be a love story. "I've played a lot of Ricky music. Professionally. Accompanying a real Ricky in settings like the Polo Lunge. It does take people into another world."

"Do you still play Ricky music?"

"Yes."

"To get to another world?" With me, perhaps?

"I'm happy enough with the world I've got." Serve me right! Steve now with her on the couch. Arm around each of her boys. "I play Ricky music for pleasure."

"May I hear some?" I yield her the piano stool. She picks up a thick volume of Frank Sinatra favourites. "May I turn your pages?" Sudden spasm.

"I'm sorry, did I say something wrong?"

"No, Howard, that line simply has a memory for me. Now, you'll know this one." Day In, Day Out. One of my favourites, stuck into Ricky Rubato. Did she know? I can't stop myself crooning

---

[25] See Your Very Own Ricky Rubato in www.richardheller.co.uk

the words. "Nicely, Howard. Better than poor old Ray. You could turn professional."

"Only with the right accompanist." We get through Night And Day and Moonlight In Vermont, before we both notice Cal asleep on the couch. Steve fighting hard not to join him. We go over to them.

"You've had a massive day, sweethearts plural. Try and get a massive sleep."

"It might be another massive day tomorrow. Do you have plans?"

"Talking to Billy. Annoying Steve."

"Talking to Zoe."

"Will that conversation end by the afternoon?"

"No chance! 'Love you... love you... love you... love you...'" Affectionate, but an undercurrent of jealousy.

"Something important may happen in the afternoon, so can you be ready to say goodbye?" Assent: both too tired to ask me why. "Good night. Thank you very much for my wonderful dinner. Thank you, Cal, for showing me your drawings. Thank you, Steve, for showing me your books."

Cal jumps up and hugs me, without reserve. "Good night, Howard. Come again soon." Steve is hesitant. I offer a hug and let him decide how much he wants and how long. Then she gets a long hug from both of them. Then Cal jumps on Steve's back and is carried away.

"My son the eight-year-old and my son the forty-year-old."

"Elective brother. Steve's phrase, Zoe told me. I like it. Makes me wish I loved my real brother. Or even liked him."

"I don't like my real brother, and I don't miss him. He lives in Capetown."

"I don't miss mine and he lives in Basingstoke. Where we were born. He took over my father's garden centre. And he grew it, ha-ha, although I helped him out when he over-borrowed. He's always resented that – the grafter bailed out by the dilettante. He's not a bad man at all, just boring. He's raised boring children. No curiosity at all. Marian and I tried to take them out and spoil them and they never got excited by anything except meeting people who'd been on TV. Hell, suddenly that seems cheap and unfair." `And poor tactics, Howard. Hoping to join a new family and badmouthing the one you've got. Course correction.` "Maybe I'm the one who's bored them."

"Howard, don't beat yourself up. I don't know what went on in your family but I know that families tend to write a script for themselves and act on it. If you don't like the script, change it."

"I hope you're right. You should know – you change the script for people. All day as a lawyer and then home to write a new script for Steve. And Cal."

"Thank you, Howard, but please don't make me into some kind of heroine. Certainly not about Steve. He's a great kid. I'm lucky to get him as an extra son. But he's come through many troubles and he still thinks, deep down, that he deserved them in some way."

"I told him he has power over his past and that he can pick and choose among his memories."

"Oh Howard, just the right message! I'm so glad he can talk to you. Thank you for taking him seriously – and Cal."

"Thank you for letting me take them seriously, and trusting me to talk about things that matter to them." `She's struggling to say something more.`

"Oh god, Howard, I never said thank you for Marian's. Nor did they. How awful, how ungrateful." `That wasn't the something else.`

"I only pointed you at Marian's. You and they did the rest."

"If you hadn't pointed we wouldn't have tried. I think Marian's will make them and me very happy. Where did you find that headmaster?"

"The other governors accused me of choosing the best cricketer. But we were unanimous. There were hundreds of applicants but Rupert was a standout. He was the one who focused first on making children happy." `She's still struggling with something else. Don't prattle, Howard.`

"Maybe I need Steve more than he needs me. To be a success story for me. My life isn't a great success, Howard. I've raised a kid who doesn't even know his own father and I'm scared to even talk to him about him. My attempt at a replacement was a failure. I'm frightened about my kid all the time – frightened that he's immature, frightened when he tries to grow up. Frightened when he's charming, frightened when he's not. Frightened of him clinging to me, frightened of him going away. And Howard, don't get any illusions about my work as a lawyer. I do divorce, and family disputes and children in trouble. Dealing every day with dysfunction and failure. Usually the script is handed to me and there's no chance of a happy ending."

"Don't beat yourself up, Alice." We're both a little shocked. My first departure from Mr Nice Guy. "I don't know about your life. Tell me as much as you like, whenever you like. But I know already that your life is real. Unlike my… stuff. Where you know everything's going to come out fine and even when Rob Patty gets knocked down you know he'll be back next week, full of hope. Another entertainment by Howard Foy." A beat. I could tell her how little my stuff means to me now. Not fair to her. She went out of her way to read Ricky Rubato and she liked him. "Sorry about that. Nothing more boring than authors who turn against their work."

"What are you working on now, Howard?"

"My immediate project is to write a review of Scarlett Ferber's first novel. I detect your grimace. It was a Celebrity Novel, published only because she has a following from her newspaper column and her TV show. The novel is a shocker in every sense. Formula characters, mechanical plot, gratuitous sex, drugs and money. It's nasty and it rips off anyone who buys it. If I were a hero, I would say so out loud. I am not a hero, and I am doing it for her own newspaper for a substantial sum. So I will write something with heavy subtext – something the publisher can quote and put on the back of the paperback edition but will still tell the discerning reader that it's crap. Although of course any discerning reader would not buy it anyway. You are entitled to grimace again. At me."

"I don't grimace. I'm not judging you for writing that review. I just wonder why. I don't believe you need the money. It sounds like a punishment."

Perceptive. But this is not the time to tell her about Marian. "Sometimes you take on jobs to prevent someone else doing them. I once asked that Scarlett if she was related to Edna Ferber. She didn't know whom I meant."

"I don't know whom you mean, Howard." Faintest teasing of my pedantry.

"She was a really good writer, but there's no reason for you to have heard of her. Scarlett says she's a writer. She should have known. Instead, she was indignant that someone else had used her name. She gets big money for being strident and stupid. I wouldn't care if it weren't for the good writers I know who have nothing. The ones we support in the Benevolent Fund."

"Easy, tiger! I think that coffee cup's in danger."

"Sorry."

"Don't be. I'm glad you care about your profession. Listen, I have a problem about the Benevolent Fund reception."

"You can't come!" Blurted. Couldn't help it. Hope she was flattered.

"I can come, Howard, but in what? All my clothes are either sloppy or starchy."

"The most elegant woman there will be Mary Varley, 92 at least, in her wheelchair. You will be Number 2 in anything you choose to wear. Think cocktail dress."

"Howard, I don't have a cocktail dress. That's not part of my world."

"Then … would you like to look for a cocktail dress? And then give it a test run over cocktails?" Brief shudder. "Did I say the wrong thing again?"

"No, Howard. Just another memory – having clothes chosen for me… But I think I would like to shop with you, on one condition."

"Of course."

"You let me help you choose a suit."

"You don't like this one."

"Too stuffy, Howard. Too old."

"It's a deal." Shopping with Marian. The one infallible happy day. The resolution of all quarrels. Unable to choose between two outfits – you must have them both, darling. And then the same rule for me. Every expedition buying something frivolous and mad for both of us. Cupboards still full of them at home. Home. A sudden jar, and a new issue to think about.

"More coffee, Howard?"

"No, thank you. I'm hyper already. Your house is very stimulating even without coffee. I ought to go. Thank you for having me." Shared laughter at the formula taught to polite children. "You must all come round to my place. Except that it needs a little work. I've let it become... an office in which I live."

"Where do you live, Howard? Do you need a taxi?"

"Clerkenwell, and no, thank you I'll walk."

"That's miles."

"A light stretch. It will work off two helpings of Cal's chicken and two of his pie." And remind me of walking home when I met Marian.

"If you're sure..."

"Sure. Thank you again. Perhaps I'll see you tomorrow if I do something with the boys."

"That would be nice."

"Well, goodbye." Time for a kiss. But I'm out of practice. Nothing lately but public social kisses. Come on, Howard? Pretend it's one of your movies! Mmm, that felt right – not kissy-kissy but not too passionate. A base camp kiss, with plenty of climbing left. Did it feel right for her?

The front door shut behind her. Lingering in the street for a last look at her home. Tosh, Howard, you're not Freddie in My Fair Lady!

Composing that cursed book review as I walk. Suddenly it's a piece of piss. "Scarlett Ferber's first novel is a real surprise. The outrageous columnist and TV personality has produced a serious, studious critique of

our current society." <u>That</u> should knock fifty thousand
off her sales! "She writes like Zola on speed." More like
Gorgonzola. Over-ripe and cheesy. "With ~~brilliant~~
mordant insight, she exposes the hollowness of our
celebrity idols. Every single one of her characters is
spoilt, self-centred, treacherous – and stupid. Even the
children and the pets. And their dialogue is universally
strident, dishonest and empty. To expose this each week
in a newspaper column is achievement in itself – to
sustain this vacuity over 400 pages is a triumph." Great
subtext, Howard. She'll love it, the publisher will love
it, the newspaper will love it – and my public will love
it.

Back at the flat. Straight onto the wordprocessor it
goes. A teeny bit short on word count. Can't resist a
flattering comparison with her namesake Edna.

Still wide awake. Two more important things to write.

"Dear Luke

I feel really guilty about losing touch, but have just discovered that you and
Laura and Billy are living in Devon, and that's because I've just met Alice
Devane and her two sons, Steve and Cal, who met you in Glendon Courtenay
and think you're a god…"

"Dear Derek

No special motive for writing except to say that things aren't right between us
and maybe we should change the script…"

Chapter 35   Test Trial

Dear Mrs H (Zoe in Year ????)

Steve is the most perfect being that ever walked the Earth but he has no sense of news value. I want him to call me about anything important, ie his entire life!!! ("Hello, I'm on a run... Hello, I'm on the loo...") He waits for something mega ("Hello, our house has burnt down"). But there's no excuse for keeping me waiting to hear about Howard's visit. Mega by anyone's standards.

10am. Will he be asleep? We'll need the same rhythm ~~when if~~ when we sleep together. I'll have to train him, like Mum trained Dad.

"Hello, it's me."

"No, I'm me, you must be an impostor."

"Are you awake?"

"No, I'm only dreaming that you would call."

"Drop everything and come over."

"Can't drop the coffee jug, it would break. I'm washing up after last night because I'm a Good Son." **Sudden choke.**

"Steve, is everything all right?"

"Sometimes I get reminded of how … things were. I used to wash up a lot at … my other home. To be a Good Son. And because the kitchen was a safe place."

"That's finished, Steve. You can wash up if you want to. You don't have to prove anything to your mum. Or hide away in your home."

"It still gives me a buzz when people call Alice my mum and this place my home."

Sad. Means he still doesn't believe in himself. Don't know how to change that. Let that go for now. "Look, do you want to come over and talk about Howard? Bring Cal."

"He's talking to Billy. That always has to wait until Billy's finished."

"Sweet. Well, just you come over?" Trying to sound casual.

"That would mean choosing clothes and I haven't got time because somebody bought me so many."

"What are you wearing now?"

"Some sweaty running shorts. My maniah."

"In that case, can I come to you?"

"You only love me for my body."

"That's right. You're just eye-candy and you haven't got a brain in your head and it will waste my time to talk to you for the next three hours. But since I've finished doing my nails and our goldfish is busy I thought I would phone and see if you remember anything about Howard's visit."

"Howard? Who's Howard?"

"He's a cricketer."

"Oh yeah. Dead boring. I remember. He came round here. Cal made dinner. I peeled the veg. We had to put lime in everything."

"And?"

"He looked at Cal's drawings."

"And?"

"We had dinner. He had two helpings."

"And?"

"We had a really good conversation about Uncle Frank and his books. My books." **Game's over.** "It means a lot to talk about those books. Mum and Cal know they mean a lot to me but they can't talk about them as books. Like Howard. And you." **Now I'm choked up.** "Zoe, is everything OK?"

"Better than OK. What happened then?"

"We played Monopoly. He got wiped out. I told him … what my dad used to say about me." **Long pause.** "Then he played the piano. Like Ricky Rubato, only worse. Then Alice played the piano and he sang a bit. Like Grant Hewson as Ricky only a bit better."

"Duets! On a first date. Brilliant! In Victorian times that meant you were practically married. Then what?"

"Cal fell asleep and we both went to bed."

"Leaving them alone?"

"I suppose so."

"Did he stay the night? No, not on a first date. But did her eyes gobble him up like a child afraid of losing a sweet? And did he look back at her, a man looking at a woman, not a despatch rider handing papers to a clerk. Both of them suddenly, and eternally, AWOL?"

"Who's that?"

"Victoria and the despatch rider. Mary Varley's Victory. It's really good."

"Howard told me to read it. We're going to meet her. A real author."

"Howard's a real author."

"Oh hell, what an awful thing to say."

"Don't worry, I know what you meant. But don't ever let Howard hear anything like that, or think he's heard anything like that. Howard … sweats blood. Light comedy's the hardest thing to do. And he's turned against all his work since Marian died."

"What was she like?"

"Dramatic. You should have heard her watching cricket. Glamorous. Extrovert. Funny. Wonderful with people. Always made them feel she was interested in them."

"Mum's like that. How long were they married?"

"About twenty years. She was Howard's editor. He says he edited him, not just his books. Knocked out the bad bits."

"I can't think of anything bad about Howard."

"Not now, but he had a past. He sometimes talks about Howard Foy, the Lost Years."

"Howard told me you can pick and choose from the past."

"Well, he has."

"Do you mind talking about Marian? She must have meant a lot to you."

"Yes, but I like talking about her. She spoilt us terribly, me and Robert, but we had to have good manners and we were not allowed to be boring. And we had to call her Marian, even when we were little. She loved children – they both did, but they couldn't have any. When she finished editing Howard she trained as a teacher."

"Were they happy?"

"I think so. Certainly they always were with us. I know they argued sometimes. Howard never quite learnt my dad's way of ending arguments."

"You're absolutely right, dear. As always."

"Just you remember that!"

"Of course, dear."

"Howard's way of ending arguments usually involved going shopping. Or to a party where they worked the room together. Or travelling to glamorous places."

"What did she die of?"

"An especially awful cancer. It lasted two years, with bouts of agonizing therapy. Robert and I weren't allowed to see her, except when she was in remission. She'd rally and be what she always was."

"I can't imagine seeing someone you love dying for two years. Howard must have been torn up."

"He was. He spent a lot of time with us. Making an extra-special effort to be Uncle Howard. And holding it together in public."

"Marian died… two years ago?"

"A bit more."

"And he's not seen anyone since?"

"No one we know. And we would be the first to know. Steve, we think Howard's fallen for your mum. And we're thrilled. We're all working on him at our end. Especially my mum, against whom resistance is futile! But you've got to work at your end. You and Cal. If that's what you want. Let your mum know you'd be happy if they got together."

"Cal will do that. I couldn't."

"Why not?"

"I've had so much from her already. I can't ask for Howard as well. That would be greedy."

"Not possible, Steve. Love makes you hungry. The more you get the more you want."

"Who said that?"

"I did. You make me hungry, Steve. I want more every time I think about you."

"I thought it was just my body."

"Steve, take a test. No sport for six weeks and live on pizza, chocolate and beer. Meet me with bad breath and spots and a giant gut and I'll still drool over you."

"I'd hate to look like that."

"Then get Cal to draw it. Is he finished?"

"No. And Billy time is sacred."

"Okay. Maybe I'll see you later. Howard's got some treat going. Robert's very skittish. Steve?"

"Zoe?"

"Love you."

"Love you."

"Love you."

"Love you a billion times so I'm now way ahead."

"Love you a trillion times."

"Love you a quadrillion times."

"Love you googleplex times. Ha, you don't know how much that is so you have to look it up so I win."

"Love you all the atoms in the Universe. Ha back!"

"Love you all the atoms in all the googleplex parallel Universes. Ha, I've won!"

"You're absolutely right, dear. As usual."

The great thing about having that kind of conversation (as if I'm any expert!) is being able to replay it in your head. Which I did, while half-listening to Cal's end of a different kind of conversation with Billy. Most of it listening, just chiming in sometimes to let Billy know there was still someone there. Finally it was over.

"You look zonked."

"It's hard work sometimes. Billy tells me what every single bear has been doing and I have to remember each one's name and if he's a good bear or a naughty bear and what he eats or won't eat. Steve, will Billy ever get better?" *He started to sob and I hugged him.* "It's so unfair!"

"I don't know what will happen to Billy. But I know you've made his life better. Like mine."

"Billy might become a great artist. Maybe I could be his manager and look after him. There are lots of sharks in the art world." *My heart went out to him: Cal, four-foot-ten-and-a-bit-more, fighting off the sharks.*

"It's great that you want to look out for Billy but will you have time when you're a great artist too and playing cricket for England?"

"Not happening. You will but not me. Maybe I'll teach drawing somewhere and cricket and tell the kids I know Billy Marriott and Steve Helson." *More sobs. I hugged him tighter.*

"Cal, what's going on for you? Normally you act like an art genius and a cricket star and it's fun and I love you for it. What's changed?"

"Steve, I didn't just get bullied at my last school because I was gay. They turned on me because I was a bighead and a show off."

"Who says?"

"I say. And other kids. When I do a good drawing or something brilliant at cricket or say something funny I want everyone to know about it. And I get loud and carry on like a great big drama queen. Lots of other kids must have hated that and when I was outed they had an excuse to pay me back."

"Do you think Marian's will be like that? When we played cricket in the nets with Charlie and the other kids you were a big noisy drama queen as usual, and they all enjoyed it. I don't think people get bullied in that school. And I'll be watching out for you."

"No! I won't let you! You must have your own life in that school, in your year. And outside school. I know that. If you have to look after me all the time and have me tagging along to everything you'll hate me." *More sobs. I let him finish, and then pushed him back so that I could look him in his face.*

"Cal. I won't look after you at Marian's. I don't think you'll need it for a minute and it probably wouldn't be good for you, anyway. But you can't stop me thinking about you, sometimes worrying about you. Or wanting to be with you, often. Or needing you to look after me."

"Look after you?"

"You do. Maybe you don't know it. You taught me to be happy. You still do. I need you … for net practice in being happy." *Giggle.* "You were my happy coach. And you still are, but only when you're Cal the Vain, Cal the Genius, Cal with the Big Mouth but the even bigger heart." *[Wordpower! It just came to me in the moment]. I hugged him tight again.*

"Steve?"

"Cal?"

"You need a shower really badly but don't sing!"

He went off. And he didn't sing. He must love me a bit. Robert rang. He was really out of breath and I had to make him slow down.

"Steve! Get out now and into your whites and we've got to be ready with all the cricket stuff and spikes outside the door in twenty minutes."

Easy-peasy. Howard drove up with Robert and Zoe in a big black Saab. Steve got the front seat and Zoe was disappointed (me too).

"Sorry for the short notice. We're going to Lords. Some friends are coming, they're hard to get."

"Zoe, are you playing?"

"Watching and taking pictures as Robert's deputy."

"Cool".

Howard checked seat belts. Worse than Mum! And he was a really cautious driver.

Playing at Lords for the first time! Even if it was only in the nets. It was not a match day and Howard waved a pass and we went to the car park. I pulled out our cricket bag and headed for the Indoor School.

"No, we're using one of the outdoor nets."

"Gosh, I thought only professionals used them."

"You are a professional, at Glendon Courtenay. And probably at Marian's too. Here we are, spikes on. Now do you mind if my friend bats first, he hasn't much time?"

"Hey, Howard. Bang on time, thanks. Zoe, so glamorous! Paps will think you're my new squeeze. 'Cricket star with mystery brunette.' *And who the fuck are you, coming onto my girlfriend?* " Robert, you look fit." *Hugs.* We've not met. I'm Tim Morrow."

Cal was open-mouthed. I must have looked just as stupid. We stuttered our names. A few weeks ago a nobody bowling at nobody in the park nets. Now I'm bowling at Lords at an England star.

"Let's start. Howard, Robert I know but you've also promised me an express bowler and a mystery spinner."

Bowling at a Test star. I've got an audience, kids, tourists, MCC staff. Zoe taking pictures. Line and length, don't bowl any junk. Howard bowling first. Boring, back of a length, where he wanted. Watched onto the bat. Robert, decent, full length. Respected. "Good start, Robert. Big improvement. Who's fixed your action?"

"Steve." *Feel a bit better. Cal bowls, trying to push it through. Crashed off back foot. Me. Thinking about everything, trying to get it right. Full. Too straight. Whipped through midwicket. So much time for the shot.*

Howard and Robert are tidy and he's respectful. Me and Cal are tidy and he treats us like waiters serving the buffet. And as if it couldn't get any worse.

"About time, Tom!" *England opening bowler, Tom O'Ryan. Temperamental. Bad boy.* "Tom's a pushover for any kid wanting an autograph. On the India tour he signed for every kid in Calcutta." *Interesting. Is he a secret softie (like me)?*

Tom's warm-up ball. Bloody hell, about three times quicker than me flat out! Blocked. Robert takes over his camera from Zoe. Howard still bowls his dibbly-dobblers. Me and Cal still try not to look stupid. And he milks us.

Tom's warmed up. His full run-up. Mad animal action. TMS commentators in raptures. I'm never going to be that fast. TMS surprised at O'Ryan's opening partner, a tiddly little medium-pacer. Me.

"Excuse me a second. Robert, you promised me a new express bowler and a mystery spinner. I've had pizza delivered faster than the express bowler."

Piss off! Don't sledge Steve!

"And as for the mystery spinner, the only mystery is why he's called a spinner. He spins like the Moon, once every 28 days."

Arrogant prick! Just like the Right Honourable, sledging a twelve-year-old. Hah! That hurried you up. At last. As I walk back to my mark, I hear a familiar squeal. "Not out. Span and bounced too much. Good variation." *Cal's Chinaman.*

We're both in the zone, now. Dying to run in and bowl. Not even looking at Tom O'Ryan, England bowler, just wanting our turn. Howard drops out to give us more bowling. Howard, I love you for ever. And Robert. Sometimes we get hit by the Test batsman, but we're not waiters any more. Cal's doing all his tricks. He's noisy and being a drama queen. I'm quiet but I'm being a drama queen too, glaring at him when he has a play-and-miss or gets hit on the pads.

Massive squeal, Robert joining in. What happened? I've bowled him! Didn't even see the greatest delivery of my career! "Well bowled. Inside edge but you earned it." *The others tell me it nipped back. He walks out of the net.* "Great bowling, both of you. Much better when you got angry. One lesson: never respect the batsman. Never bowl to his reputation. When you're bowling all batters are the same. And Tom, what are they?"

"Filth."

"And what do we do with filth?"

"Clean it away."

Whisper from Robert. "Tim's worked at my dad's agency. His stepdad's a partner."

"Who's going to be the next piece of filth?"

"Steve!" *Unanimous vote. Howard makes sure I put on every bit of protective gear. As if I would face Tom O'Ryan without it.*

"Now Steve, you're a batsman and all the bowlers are …?"

"Waiters."

"Hmm. Like it. I'm nicking that for my newspaper column. Which I write myself. Unlike people Tom and I know. When I'm batting I like to think I'm the star and the bowler's a supporting actor giving me my cue. Do what works for you, but dominate."

Bowled first ball by Tom! That's dominating.

"Right shot, just not in time. Make your decision a fraction quicker. And stick to it." *I've said that kind of thing myself.*

Tim bowls. Never seen him bowl but he must know how. Slow somethings. Wow! Huge leg break. Grope forward, fizzing past outside edge. "I'm not allowed to do that in Test matches. Only in dead games."

"Six Test wickets at 32.33. First-class 176 at 29.07." *Robert should be the TMS statistician.*

Robert, Cal, Howard bowl. Decent but familiar. I take the chance to get feet moving. Tom back again. Yes, behind it. Solid. And suddenly I'm in Glendon Courtenay again. Moving my feet somewhere and hitting the ball. Plenty of near misses and appeals but boundaries too – and against Tom. He's trying. Bouncer! Move towards off stump, watch it over left shoulder. Cal's zooter. Spot it and plunge forward. Robert's yorker. Dig it out. Howard's boring back of a length – down the track and lever it over midwicket. Almost killed by rebound off the net. Tim's big leg break. A bit short, backfoot drive. Tom again. Hook! Can't help it! Top edge over keeper. Probable six. Tom in my face.

"Filth."

"Waiter."

"Next batsman. Steve, I like your feet. They will have to move even quicker against quality bowlers and you're not ready to hook Tom. But it's a good attitude. Now Tom, do you think Felix should take a look at him?"

"Dunno. Felix hates wasting his time on second-raters."

"I think I'll send Felix an email. Steve, can I have contact details?" *He hands me a notebook. I can barely write them down, I'm getting all weepy again. Pathetic little drama queen! But Tim Morrow doesn't think I'm second-rate.*

I choke out "Who's Felix?"

"Felix Lindsay. The Doctor. The best coach in the world. Says he's retired, but he works with individual players, including me and Tom, and manages youth teams." *Working with me?* "Who's batting now?"

"Haven't you two got a sponsor event?"

"It's voluntary, Howard."

"You'll get another black mark."

"Tom and I are cricketers not corporate assets. Four batsmen left. Well, three and Tom." *Glare.* "I want to see Robert and Cal bat."

Cal's bouncing and looking away again. "Tim, I don't want you to get into trouble because of me and besides, I don't want to pee in my pants when Tom bowls at me." *Hysterics from him and Robert.*

"Okay, if Tom drives to the corporate event we've just got time for a session with Robert."

Robert facing Tom O'Ryan? Whisper to him: "Pace is your friend."

"I know."

Out a few times but not worried by Howard, me or Tom. Sometimes lost against Cal and Tim.

"Hey, we've gotta run. Can't afford to lose my licence again."

"Okay. Goodbye, Howard. Goodbye, mystery brunette. Goodbye, Robert. You're unrecognisable. What did Steve tell you?"

"Pace is your friend."

"Good thought. Are you a coach, Steve?"

"Going to get a certificate."

"Good, but you'll learn way more about coaching from Felix. Goodbye, Cal. Are you going to show me how you bowl the zamboni?"

"No way. You're filth. Maybe Tom."

"Goodbye, Steve. Be ready to hear from Felix." *Hugs for everybody, from everybody.* "Wait! Steve and Cal haven't met you-know-who." *He opens his cricket coffin and unwraps his precious toy tiger mascot. Two pictures from Robert: me and Cal, each holding Tiger, with him and Tom.*

"Wait! Can I have one with everybody?" *Robert passes camera to some watching kid. Several pictures. Then takes picture of kid and friends, with Tim and Tom, but Tiger put away first.*

Whisper from Howard. "Congratulations! You and Cal have been admitted to the Order of the Tiger."

"Come on, Tom, no more autographs. They only want swaps, anyway. Ten of yours for one of mine." *Fighting each other on the way to the car. Like Cal and me!*

"Steve, you're shaking!"

"Oh my god, Zoe. I can't believe that happened."

"I saw it, Steve. It was amazing. I've never seen you play as if you meant it."

"What did I look like? Was I a glad animal?"

"You looked more like a warrior. A young squire knighted on the battlefield."

"Really?" *Impatient sound.* "Hell, sorry. I haven't bowled at Cal and Howard."

I make a special effort to maintain the intensity when I slow down for the others. As I would have to do in a Test Match. All batsmen are filth. Including my wonderful elective brother. And Howard, my what?

We drive home via Marine Ices of Camden. Double scoops all round. Ten flavours. and we all trade. Robert defies Diet Fairy. He's hardly fat at all now.

Mum's at home when we arrive. Howard can't stay, he's promised to take Zoe to the movies. (Revival of Bringing Up Baby – must check). Zoe wants to let him off, Mum won't hear of it. Worry – doesn't she like Howard after last night? They seem OK. Think she just wants him to keep promise. Quick view of images in Robert's camera. My action's like Tom's! But too round-arm on outswinger. Sudden start when looking at closing "Tiger" image. Me standing next to Tom.

"How tall is Tom?"

"Six foot one and a half." *Robert the infallible statistician.*

"I think I've got taller!" *And I thought I was stuck on five foot ten for ever!*

Chapter 36   Change Of Kit

" *Nick,*

"How many more asteroids do you think you've discovered? Because I need one more, an asteroid Howard. You told me once that some asteroids have weird orbits, like they can spend years in deep space and then suddenly hurtle towards the Sun. I think that's what's happening to me this summer…"

"Brendon Daniel

"Well, your dad seems A-1 now and I really think that religious people would learn to avoid him. What did the Mormon missionary think he was going to do at the duck pond? Conduct a baptism? We had a problem with a rabbi at my new school but the head got him a job as a basketball coach instead! Hell, I don't think I told you about my new school but first, guess whom I bowled at Lord's yesterday (yes, Lord's)?…

"… well, if you've read right through to the end of this email you'd better know that I bowled Tim Morrow of Northamptonshire and England (current average 45.43 according to Robert) and it was an even better delivery than the one that castled B in the park nets. Howard arranged that and he has fixed for me to go to this big writers' party and he seems really stuck on my (new) Mum. Listen, how much did you spend on that maniah you gave me? Has it got extra power, because everything's turned round since I've had it…"

Dear Mrs Helson (ci-devant Barnes)

My parents have just given one of their famous brunches. Primarily to showcase Howard's legendary Bloody Mary to Alice. Not a great success. She took some polite sips but most of it ended down the dreary banking neighbours. And Howard – who got too sozzled to play cricket with the boys! There's a big Frenetic cricket match next weekend at Arthur Fraser's country house. Howard's going but not Alice!! Split already? Mum tells me not to worry.

Followed the boys to the cricket nets where something unbelievably brilliant happened…

"Steve, you've got a zit!"

"No… Impossible. I never get zits."

"You have now. On your shoulder. It could affect your bowling. Let me pop it, I've got a clean tissue."

And he let me!!! And of course my beloved has the most beautiful pus in the world. Mum told me later it was a huge sign of trust. Cal jealous! Steve's promised him the next one.

I've got to accept that I can't play cricket. Steve's incredibly patient – but not Robert and Cal.

"You can't bowl legally, you can't throw or catch and you can't hit lollipops."

"I'd have given you one if you'd fainted." Steve's phrase. But he gives me a ten for spectating. I wonder if I'll ever get tired of watching him and the boys. They're now completely at ease with each other, actors improvising around a familiar script. Cal's histrionic, Robert's phlegmatic. He never whines any more. A lot of that was my fault. Steve is the dream-master (and dreamboat!), using fantasy to take them all to higher places. They're all very intense because they're making their debuts for the Frenetics next weekend.

Steve is always willing to let others share the net.

"It's payback. Where would I be now if I had never shared these nets?"

A dramatic text from Alice.

"Shopping for dresses with Howard. For me not H. Then drinking again. Eat stale bread in house for dinner. Bad Mum XXXOOO."

Two hours, at least twenty dresses tried on, nothing bought and he did not even twitch! "Howard, you're a saint! Can you bear to go back to Nicole Farhi?"

"Only if you try on the deep purple again."

"If you liked it, Howard, why didn't you say so? I could have bought it there and then."

"Because I wanted to make sure that it was calling to you. That's the rule..." Sudden stop.

"Whose rule? Yours and Marian's?"

"Yes. I'm sorry. This is you and me shopping. We don't have to follow Marian's rules."

"I think it's a nice rule. It shows you were thinking about her. I'd like to keep it. And Howard... What did we say about picking and choosing from our past? I don't want you to eliminate yours. I want to hear about Marian, anything you want to tell me."

"Yes. Thank you. And of course I want to hear everything you want to tell me about your past. But sometimes I wonder whether it's right, what we've told Steve. Can you really pick and choose? Open up one bit of the past and aren't you asking all of it to fly out at you? And this would be just the wrong moment. There's a dress calling you in Nicole Farhi." Sudden dazzling smile to patient assistant. "Eve, that indigo number is marvellous but we need to hear it calling. Could you very kindly hold it until close of play?"

He swept me away. "Howard, we're not catching a train."

"I don't trust that Janine in Nicole Farhi. She could sell that deep purple to someone totally unsuitable just to get her commission." But it is still there, when we arrive, panting and giggling like children. I tried it on again. "Now, is it calling to you?"

"Yes."

"Good. Take it at once, or spend a lifetime of regret." I passed over some plastic in a daze. "But now listen again... Do you hear a sad, mysterious music? From the direction of Karen Millen. 'You ain't been blue ... till you're in that mood indigo.'"

"Howard, please! You're off key."

"Am not and I will sing at full volume until you go back with me to the radiant Eve."

"Don't be silly, Howard. I've bought a dress for the reception. I can't buy two."

"Of course you can. I'll ask for legal advice and you can charge me."

"Advice on what?"

"Advice on … whether indigo is really a colour or whether innocent shoppers are being induced to buy that dress on a false trade description." And sure enough we hurtled back to Nicole Farhi. "Eve. We're back. May we have another look at the purported indigo?" And I tried it on again and admitted that it was calling to me. Another wave of the plastic. "Brilliant. There'll be nae shoes for the bairns this winter. Shoes! Accessories! We need them. Even I know you mustn't let down a great dress with bad accessories. Besides, the purple is very dramatic, and needs to be calmed down, and the indigo is very classical and needs to be warmed up."

"Howard, I'm already way over budget. I can't take any more from my boys."

"Alice, I don't think you could give any more to your boys. Except the pleasure of seeing you getting a treat for once."

"That sounds a bit glib, Howard."

"Glib doesn't necessarily mean wrong."

"Two complete outfits in my wardrobe for one reception. That does seem wrong."

"When that reception comes round, don't you think you deserve a choice? Going dramatic or going classical? And who says there will only be one reception? If you enjoy it, I know it will lead to dozens more receptions. And salons and soirees and concerts and conversaziones and lunches and launches. People will send out invitations 'To Meet Alice Devane', the poster girl of literary London. And you won't dare be seen twice in the same outfit."

"Doesn't sound like my world."

"Doesn't have to be. But I would like you to know you have visiting rights. Listen, would you feel embarrassed if I treated you to the accessories? As a thank you."

"Thank you for what?"

"For a fun afternoon. And I don't want it to end."

"You're worse than Cal!"

"Maybe. I haven't had much fun lately. Cue violins! My money hasn't had much fun lately. Ask my accountant. Alice, I wasn't a particularly good writer but I was a lucky one. Like Michael Arlen, I may have been a flash in the pan, but there was gold dust in the pan. People liked my stories, my characters. Marian helped to polish them when they were young, but then they became reliable performers. Not just in books but in movies and TV. They've never stopped making money. Accessories of quality for those dresses … they'd represent one day in the earning life of Rob Patty. Not boasting, fact."

"Okay, Howard. I'll hit your plastic. On one condition. Never use the past tense again when you say you're a writer."

So we bought accessories. Howard was right – one set to jazz up the indigo, another to calm down the purple. He has a good eye. Just before closing time I darted into Aerospatiale and bought three lurid ties.

"The boys will fight over them. Why three?"

"First pick to you, Howard."

"I can't wear any of those, I'm a man of letters."

"They're not as lurid as your Garrick club tie – or should it be Garish Club? Or even the Gravy Club because there's a souvenir on it. I'm going to burn it, Howard. And the stained MCC one, which you should rename the Madras Curry Club."

"You're absolutely right, dear, as always."

"Good response, Howard."

"It always worked for Joe and me." Hmm. Was Marian like Belinda? Is that what he wants? Someone assertive who always wins the argument? If you care about someone, don't you want to win the arguments sometimes? And is he really that rich? Portia would know, or would know how to find out. I'd hate to be a gold digger. But we had fun, shopping. Me and him. Why stop him having fun?

"Now, can I make one last effort to persuade you to come to the Frenetic match? Arthur Fraser is quite a host."

"I'm really sorry, Howard. I have to give up that day to my only rich client." Claude's visiting. Double guilt – over Howard, who doesn't know about him, over Claude who doesn't know yet about Howard. Then inspiration: "Portia's thinking of going. She would like to reconnect with the team." And she might open him up. Why has he turned against his writing? Few people can resist a Portia interrogation.

"I'll ask her. Now - cocktail time. It's the thirsty hour on a Sunday, we'll go to one of my clubs."

"The Garrick?"

"Heavens no. Makes me feel ancient. 'Waiter, either remove Judge Twinfeet or have him stuffed. He's been dead for three days.' Taxi!"

We went to some dim street near Tottenham Court Road. "Fitzrovia. Mary Varley cut a swathe through here in the Forties. If there was a blue plaque for every bonk you couldn't see the houses in between."

"The Low Dive?"

"It's a club. The founder believed in Ronseal advertising. Does what it says on the tin. Mary made me join, years ago."

It did live up to its name. I wondered if it had ever seen daylight. I could just make out an ancient piano and a matching barman, reading a book. And a lone drinker in a corner table.

"Isn't that Damien Hirst?"

"Yes, but don't remind him, poor thing, his last show was a bit of a frost."

The barman looked up from his book. I glimpsed at the title: <u>Wittgenstein and the art of Origami</u>. "Evening, Howard. The usual?"

"Haven't been here for three years but he never forgets a cocktail. No thank you, Arthur. I think, a Negroni. Alice, Arthur, Arthur, Alice."

"Pleasedtomeetcha, miss. Will it be a sweet sherry or a port and lemon?"

"Fuck off, Arthur. I'll have a Negroni too, but just for that I'll have it in a folded paper glass." He smiled and I knew I had passed some kind of test.

"Arthur, nobody's fooled by that title." Howard took the book from his hands and showed me the true content: <u>No Orchids For Miss Whiplash.</u> We sipped our Negronis. "My usual usual was a margarita. But I'm never drinking another unless you make it. Are you enjoying that? You didn't like my Bloody Mary."

"A bit too early for me. I know it's supposed to be a breakfast food, but it felt like a drink."

"I could do you a Virgin one next time."

"Tomato juice dressed in Nicole Farhi?"

"I'm stealing that."

"Only if you put it into something good."

"What's something good?"

"You decide, Howard. Something you actually love to write. Not something you write as some kind of punishment. Your characters made you money because you loved them."

"Yes. I think I did… How <u>is</u> that Negroni?"

"It's very good, Howard." Past tense again, about his writing. Why? Must find out – but not now. Time to stay in a nice, comfortable, companionable present. "It's fun being here. Drinking for pleasure. Not something I do much lately."

"Me neither. Pleasure. It's very important. Pleasure." He frowned deeply. Something struggling for expression: I couldn't help him. "Would it give you pleasure to have another Negroni?"

"Yes, but that's it and can I pay?"

"Not allowed. Club rules."

"Which I think you've just made up. But if you want to pay from your literary fortune, go ahead and I can buy more stale bread for my starving bairns."

A low exchange between him and Arthur and he returned with refills. "You know, Howard, I realize that I don't mind you paying for things. Within reason. I'm glad you let me pay for the two dresses."

"I wanted you to feel you had chosen them both. If I'd paid for one it might have become 'the one Howard likes' and you might have worn it even though you liked the other."

"That was very thoughtful. I told you, shopping has some painful memories for me. Men using money to take power over me. I feel safe with you. I'd like to go shopping again. Within reason."

"It'd be my pleasure." He took both my hands in his. They're huge. I wonder what he can span on the piano. "I'd really like it if we could … have more pleasure together."

"That would be very pleasant, Howard." Still some unspoken agenda.

"That piano's in tune, you know."

Mum came back rat-arsed! She tried to buy us off with a couple of ties.

"I'm sorry I'm such a bad mummy and it will happen again. Howard took me to a club and guess who I played the piano for?"

"Beppo The Wonder Dog?"

"Damien Hirst. He was singing with Howard and Arthur the barman."

"I hope he can sing better than Howard because he can't draw better than Howard."

"You haven't seen Howard draw."

"But I have seen Damien Hirst!"

Even I could tell that Mum had bought some fabulous clothes. She says Howard has a good eye. They had fun. Mum says we've all got to help Howard buy a suit for the reception because his are too old. Not sure. He still plays cricket but I can't imagine Howard as a young person. I think they wore flares then!

Both boys are really rooting for Howard. Steve won't say so but Cal's direct.

"Mum, I don't mind you getting rat-arsed with Howard but if it's anyone else will you run him past Steve and me?"

"Fair enough. I'm not a great picker, after all. But you approve of Howard?"

"Of course."

"I'd be interested to know why."

"Because he's a non-stop treat machine."

"I know that's not the reason."

"Well… he makes me laugh but he takes things seriously when they mean something to me, like drawing and cricket. And in some ways, I think he's like Steve, like, when we're doing something he tries to make me feel really excited but also really looked after. He's such a boring driver. I think we got passed by a pram on the way to Lords." Interesting but that could drive me crazy! "And, I think, Howard … likes me as I am. I mean he does not think I'm a baby or stupid or a drama queen, even when I am, and I know he doesn't mind about me being gay. And being in love with Steve. Because I am and don't worry, I won't do anything stupid, but I am. I always will be. And I think Howard takes all that and he doesn't want to change anything." And Howard doesn't have a family on his back trying to change him!

"Thank you for that, sweetheart. Now Howard's like Steve in another way – he's come through pain and a terrible loss and he hasn't talked about it all yet. Or written about it. And I think we should do what we did for Steve – have fun together and show that we care about him."

"No change there then."

Chapter 37 More Kit Changes

Howard's shopping trip must have gone brilliantly because Steve wants to go shopping with me!

"Are you sure, Steve? I was trained to shop by my mum!"

"Go ahead – and just think Emma Bovary."

Just him and me for once. Cal and Robert are at the Zoo together, to make an animal alphabet for Billy. (They haven't told me what they've got for X). Steve insists on going to MegaMall again.

"You've turned into a fashion queen like Cal! You only want to go back to Ursinho and buy for yourself!"

"We're only going to the girly section."

"My god, you've turned into a trannie."

We had to take loads of buses. Steve will be driving next year! Wonder if I can get Mum to give him the BMW (she's getting bored with it!) Sure enough, we did go into Ursinho and Emerson remembered him from the makeover. (Remembered? He practically swooned). "Welcome back! Do you have two hours? We have all the new lines in for autumn."

"Thanks, but we're here for my girlfriend today."

"Of course and Jessica here will be delighted to serve you. But before I hand over, please don't be offended but that shirt and those trousers you're wearing - I remember selling them to you like it was yesterday – well, they're now both too short."

"Really? It's true then. I'm taller." He did his bowling action! Some people applauded. "Thanks, Emerson, you don't know what you've said. Wait! If this is really too short, do you think it might look better on Zoe?" And he peeled the shirt right off! Emerson had to hold onto the counter but I'm now used to my beloved's astonishing upper body (plus Devon tan).

Of course I loved wearing his shirt (wish I could bottle his aroma) and I thought it looked good on me (kind to my lingering spare tyre!) Emerson sold him two longer replacements and some trousers.

"I was right. You're a total fashion queen and I'm only going to get your castoffs!"

"Jessica, how big is the girly section? To save time we'll take everything you've got in Size Perfect…"

But actually Steve was really nitpicking. I might have thought that he was protecting his plastic except that some of the stuff he did go for was really expensive.

"What have you got against that top, Steve? I think it's fabbo and it really goes with those trousers."

"There's nothing wrong with it, but it just doesn't have … Zoeness."

We went round Ursinho and picked up a good haul, including shirts for Robert and Cal. Steve ordered everything delivered (vy grown-up) Then he insisted we go to Nicole Farhi. "Howard took Mum there. It must be a bit special." I felt a bit hesitant but Steve soon attracted two competing assistants. "We're looking for something to wear to a literary reception with famous writers and even people who've been on TV. For my girlfriend, not for me." The assistant who had won the contest smiled and gave me a long look. Breathe in, boobs out, tummy in! She showed us a few party frocks but nothing did anything for us. Then Steve said "I like what's on the mannequin."

"Steve, I can't. Siena Miller wore that in <u>Serenissima!</u>" But he insisted. I felt strange. As if I was rich. In my own right, not just

because of Mum and Dad. "You've got a cocktail glass in your hand. Gin-and-It. Like the girls in Victory." **What does that make Steve? The despatch rider? The black marketeer? The commando? Surely the commando? I took an imaginary sip and flicked ash from my cigarette (ugh) in its long holder.** "Sure it's not too tight?" **Still worried about accursed tummy! Crash diet? Running? Tight pants?**

"I think it's got Zoeness."

"Steve, you can't spend all that. I want to go halfsies."

"Would that make you happier?"

"Yes. And halfsies on the accessories. Mum will send it straight back if it's not accessorized properly".

"Your Mum and Dad? Are they going to feel … all right about… this?"

"Me going shopping with my rich boy friend? Steve, Mum and Dad really like you. If they ever stopped liking you, they'd let you know. Especially Mum. Come on, Lucy's waiting to show us accessories." **We kept things very simple, but our plastic still took a battering. Apparently simple means expensive. Again we ordered everything delivered (in our usual way).**

We collapsed into the mall café. "I'm exhausted. I'd rather bowl twenty overs flat out than go shopping again. Oh, but Mum and Cal and I have to shop with Howard. Then we're going to his place. What's it like?"

"Big flat in an old building. What Americans call a duplex. Haven't been there for a while. He doesn't see people there much, since Marian died." **Sudden panic, could Alice move in there? Steve would be much further away. And it would be much harder for him to carry my books to school. A bored waitress came round, saw Steve and became instantly animated.**

"One regular black coffee and one…"

"The lady will have a regular black coffee too."

"Sorry. But you always have cappuccino."

"Not if my tummy has to get into that dress."

"I like that tummy. I couldn't see enough of it when you sent all those sultry beach snaps."

"I think you see too much of it. And adjoining bum and thighs."

"Impossible. They've got Zoeness."

"You keep saying that and what's Zoeness?"

"Don't put me on the spot. It's like that bit in Victory when Elizabeth is waiting at the railway station and all the men come off the train, same uniform, same kit, but she can pick out her man instantly. From tiny details. And that song they hear on their last night together – They Can't Take That Away From Me."

"Yes, but Steve, why do you want Zoeness? You could have anybody, you must know that by now. You could have our waitress." *Right on cue, she deposited our coffees as sultrily (? Adverb) as she could manage.* "Seriously, Steve. Why me?"

"Because I can't imagine Zoelessness. I think it was the holiday. Best one I've ever had (apart from nearly drowning and nearly losing Mum and Cal) but otherwise non-stop fabulous and I did meet another girl I really liked – well, fancied – and I still want to play cricket with her and listen to her sing and be her friend but at the end of it all I felt Zoeless."

"Steve… if you ever wanted to be Zoeless, you would tell me? You wouldn't … hang on because you felt guilty."

"Only if you make the same promise when you want to be Steveless. Zoe, all I know is I want you to be part of everything good in my life. I really, really wanted to go to your school, so we could share that. I want you to be part of my home, with Mum and Cal. I want us to be there for our brothers. I want you to watch every cricket match I play. I want us to read books, and meet writers, and go shopping and travel and … go swimming with seals. 'I want you to know that I love you baby, I want you to know that I care…'"

"Please, Steve, no singing."

"Can't stop. 'I'm so happy when you're around me but I'm SAD when you're not there.' I want people to stare at us!"

And as if they weren't doing that already, he jumped up, lifted me and gave me our longest-ever kiss (3.04 minutes, official time).

We didn't say much on the way back, just held hands. It should have really peaceful but he was restless.

"Are you worried about your plastic? I can take stuff back."

"No, nothing like that. I haven't heard from Felix Lindsay. Tim's cricket coach. I wonder if Tim changed his mind about me?"

"We've known Tim a long time and if he promises you something he'll always come through with it."

"I'm sure of that but I still get nervous. I think sometimes that this summer was not really meant for me at all. There's a big Sorting Office somewhere about to say 'I'm afraid there's been a big mistake and the parcel was meant for someone else.'"

"Steve, that's crap and you know it." I surprised us both. "I'm not a parcel, given to you for being a good boy. Everyone you've met this summer wants to be part of your life. They chose you. Now deal with it."

"You're absolutely right, dear. As usual."

I spend all my time these days buying clothes. Mum and Cal and I forced Howard into the new Ursinho section in Selfridge's.

"I can't have that. That's the kind of suit Ricky Rubato would wear."

"We all like Ricky Rubato, Howard. Close your eyes and think of your royalties."

Howard took us to his place. It was a bit gloomy. "I'm sorry, I've let things slip a bit. Marian always said I had no sense of surroundings. I think she was right. I always have trouble writing descriptions of places. It's much easier in movies. Just 'INT. HOWARD'S FLAT. DAY.'"

"Gosh, Howard, you've got tons of awards." *Cal started reading them out. Some for cricket but mostly for writing. He looked a bit embarrassed.*

"How about this one? Kleenex Award for most sentimental movie of the year. Ricky Rubato. It was the dog wot won it."

"You don't list the BAFTAs in your biographies, Howard." But he did mention the Kleenex Award. Why has he taken against his work?

"Help yourself to the piano, Alice. It's just had its annual service and MoT." The piano's always his emergency escape! It was a very decent upright Broadwood.

"I can tell you play this piano a lot." Loud pedal almost permanently down!

"The neighbours pound on the walls and ceilings to hear more."

My mobile rang. I can tell if it's Zoe without looking at caller display. Her ring's always a bit breathless. But this time it was somebody else.

"Hello, am I speaking to Steve Helson?" *Man's voice. For a micro-second I thought it was Brendon or Daniel.* "Felix Lindsay here. Tim Morrow gave me your number. Sorry, I haven't been in touch earlier, I was in Afghanistan. You're a fast bowling all-rounder and you're under 19, right? Do you think you could help me out of a jam?"

Steve went white! He stammered out his email and hung up.

"That was Felix Lindsay. Tim's cricket coach. He wants me to play for him – for an England under19 squad. He's the manager. Against Emerging Players of Mumbai. All day. Uxbridge. They play first-class there. Tuesday. That's the day after the literary reception."

"Excellent. You'll be busy on Monday evening and you won't have time to get nervous. And the Frenetic match before to tune up. Oh, and congratulations!"

"Howard, I can't play at that level. Not yet. There'll be people with counties, who've played first class."

"How do you know what you can do? Suppose I'd said I wasn't ready to write my first novel. I'd never have done The Speculator." First time Howard's taken pride in his work. For Steve's benefit. "Now then, strict curfew for you until Tuesday. No night clubs, no drinking."

"As if. He pukes."

"You're his minder, Cal. Especially at the reception. It will be full of drink-crazed writers. I assume you want to go the match. Now, Steve, you might want to tell Zoe. She and Robert will want to come. Joe and Belinda will try to come but they have a busy agency to run. I will come because I am a mere man of letters. Alice, you're a busy lawyer."

"Just try and keep me away. I've given up the Frenetic weekend to be with a client. The firm can give me back Tuesday. Now Steve, wait till we're at home to phone Zoe, because your conversations are unbearably long and gooey." And Cal gets jealous.

We cut the visit short. Whatever happens with Howard, we're not living there. But how would he fit in here? I'm already over-run with cricketers (and fashion queens).

Steve was still uptight. I made him lie on the couch with his head in my lap. Cal held his hand. Our usual double act. We said his grace. "The head must lie upon the block…"

"That was wont to lie on Queen Catherine's lap."

"Steve, we love you and we're proud of you. Whatever cricket team you play for and if you never played again in your life."

"Thank you. I know that and you know I really love you. And nothing can change that but I still don't want to bowl like a dead gerbil on Tuesday."

I stroked his hair (much more satisfying now) and Cal went on squeezing his hand. Eventually he unwound. "Now before that endless conversation with Zoe, I think it would be nice if you rang your parents and gave them an update of all your major news." Some tension returned. "They're not the enemy, Steve. That would not be good for any of us."

Mum was right of course. I called my former home. They both seemed genuinely glad to hear from me. They invited me over straight away to hear my news but I didn't feel ready to go back. Maybe I never will. I fixed for us to meet at Paparazzo's. Once our local Italian. Source of my birthday lunch each year. Always better with Uncle Frank but okay even without him. In Paparazzo's we were always a normal family. I excused myself and picked out my bike. Cal shouted out "Helmet!"

Luigi at Paparazzo was a bit surprised when we arrived separately. He pointed a safe place to park my bike and I whispered that I had left home to become a cricket professional. I promised him a signed photo to go with all the other Celebrities on his wall (whom I'd never recognized!)

Former Mum and Dad (feel bad calling them that but can't think what else) just had coffee and water. They insisted I eat. I remembered a profile of Tom O'Ryan and ordered the house pasta and a giant salad.

"Thanks for coming here. I still don't feel quite … right going back to the house."

"It's okay, Steve. In your own time. It's always your home." *I got a bit teary again. What's happened to me? How can I be a fast bowler?*

"We'd like to see your new home, but we don't feel quite ready for that. But we can tell that you're happy. You look great." *She meant it. My birth mother did care about me. I was going to cry majorly. Suddenly all my news poured out in a rush, me and Zoe, getting into Marian's, Howard and the literary reception, being picked for the cricket match. They just listened. He perked up when I told him that kids run businesses at Marian's.*

"That's very interesting. Would they… may I come and visit some time?"

"Of course. Whenever. They have loads of visitors and supporters. It would be brilliant if you and … Mum" *(hope she didn't notice microscopic pause!)* "could become supporters."

"It might be possible to release some of your inheritance."

"We can get by. Cal got an art scholarship" *(inevitably)* "and I'm going to get money off for coaching and sports assistance."

"Leave it with me."

"Of course. Thanks, Dad." *I know that I can trust him totally over money.*

When I rattled on about Howard and the reception I could tell that she was really envious. Wouldn't she have loved to have Howard as a friend and go hobnobbing with other famous writers? All of a sudden I felt pity for her. Aspiring so desperately to be a Writer and losing all the other life she might have had.

"I'm rewriting my novel completely. One of the characters was totally wrong." *The one who was me! Thanks. I couldn't tell her I'd secretly read it. Perhaps she knew.*

They both seemed really interested in the match. They asked intelligent questions and they knew who Tim and Tom were. "Do you want to come?"

They both smiled ruefully. "Your mother and I had lots of chances to see you play cricket. I don't think it would be fair to crowd in on your big match. But we are proud of you." *He sighed heavily.* "I was wrong about your cricket. I had reasons for discouraging you, some good, some bad." *He sighed again and signalled for the bill.*

"We've saved you our biscotti." *Just like when I was a little boy. We were a family sometimes. We had rituals. I took the biscotti in acknowledgement, even though I had never liked them.*

Steve's playing cricket for England!!! Sort of. Howard's organized everyone in a rota to keep him busy until Tuesday. Poor Steve still can't believe he's a god. When something brilliant happens, he still worries that he doesn't deserve it.

We all biked to Marian's. All tired – even superfit Steve. Not an option for term time in the winter. Carrying stuff. Steve and Cal were recognized and dragged to cricket net to "shred the head." They both failed but Robert succeeded and earned "celebration points" for his year. Had feeling head wanted this. And S and C.

R and C went to Media Centre to do stuff for Billy's alphabet. (Still haven't found out letter X). S and I just drifted around for a bit. Lots of people looked at him, girls and boys. Felt brilliant, like three girls in "Victory" in public with their men. Yes, he's mine and if you ever get him it's only a loan.

Finished up in theatre. "Sheila!" Sheila Fereday rehearsing! I screamed out her name without thinking. At my last school that started off all the bullying. Here it just seemed natural.

"Zoe!" Kissy-kissy. Steve was awed. I introduced him and she flicked me a little smile of approval (of course).

"Sorry to be so dumb but I really loved you in Rob Patty."

"Well, thank you. I'd love to do another series. Zoe, tell Howard. Actually, I'll tell him myself, Alex is playing for the Frenetics this weekend."

"Sheila, did I say take five?"

"Sorry, Marie." Tiny Marian's girl bossing a theatre idol! Sheila hissed to us "She's tougher than Clint Eastwood. She'll cut my line again."

R and C caught up with us and we all had a go at badminton. S got beaten!!!! Low cunning prevailed over power. He pretended to sulk. "Silly game, but hard work. Does anyone else feel stiff? Good, Robert. Do you think you might say, if someone asked you, that you were a little stiff from badminton? Try it."

"I'm a little stiff from badminton."

"There's no need to be ashamed of your birthplace." He laughed loudly. None of us did. "That was one of my uncle Frank's. He told lots of crap jokes." First time I had heard even faint criticism of his uncle Frank.

When we biked home Cal was so zonked that Mum phoned Alice and put him straight to bed in Robert's room. Steve carried him (sweet). Robert donated his Ted Luger (sweet). He looked at Cal in his bed for a long time and then rolled out a futon for himself (sweet but sad too).

Boring banker neighbours dropped by. Sat and sat. Dad's too polite! Mum caught me yawning and said "Zoe! Have you been to the café yet to deliver that poster? You promised it before they shut this evening?" As I said before she's a terrible actress but neighbours did not notice! "Steve, would you mind going with? I'm way over-protective but it's not very far." We escaped and I shared Steve's bike! No helmets! BAD kids.

"Not-A-Meating-Place? Aaagh!"

"Don't be rude, the owner's a friend. It's vegan." We ordered two herb teas and a bit of non-animal fruit cake. While waiting we looked over a bookshelf full of old books. "Ohmigod!" I showed Steve a first edition of "Victory."

"Spooky! How are you getting on with it?"

"Just finished."

"Don't tell me what happens!"

"Steve, it's not a mystery!"

"Even so."

"OK. How are you getting on with it?"

"It's fantastic but a bit weird. Most of Uncle Frank's books are about people hating war but the three girls … seem to like it."

"Are you sure they like it? Don't you think they're all a bit desperate, all their partying, all their sex, just grabbing their chances because they and their men could be dead tomorrow?"

"Yeah but I still think there's a level where they actually like the war, certainly better than the life they had before." Suddenly he started laughing hysterically.

"What is it? Choke it out!"

"I just thought. Are we Britain's most boring teenagers? Like all over the country now, there's teenagers … clubbing… partying… drinking vodka and Red Bull … doing E or something… and making out… And we're in a vegan café drinking herb tea talking about a book. A book!" **More hysterics.**

"Shall we go wild? Two more herb teas, please? But this time, in dirty cups!"

Chapter 38   Team Reunion

All the clothes arrived - spent <u>the whole day</u> trying them on for him. R and C out on their animal alphabet project for Billy.

Mum amazed at my Nicole Farhi. "Steve! A-Star for shopping! That dress is so Forties." So he was right about making me look like one of the Victory girls. She restyled my hair instantly and passed me a cocktail glass (with Steve's cranberry mix).
"Now, come and raid my jewel box."

"Mum, if it's all the same I know what I want to wear with this."

Dad was embarrassing. "I've lost my little girl. For ever."

"Dad, you're such a bad actor. You'd fail an audition for the Ferrero Rochet commercial."

"Not one of ours."

R and C came back. They have finished the alphabet – even the X. R took dozens of pix of us and C rushed off some sketches. Alice arrived – with Howard (!) More admiration from them. Then Howard tried on new suit they made him buy – he looked younger. And Alice asked for votes between her Nicole F and her Karen Millen. Split decision so she'll leave it to the mood of the moment for the big reception.

Then Dad got all solemn and I thought he was going to do some more awful melodrama but I realized he was serious.

"Steve, Cal, Belinda and I thought it would be right … well, we hope our children agree because they haven't been consulted, sorry… anyway, we'd like you to feel that you're at home here and can come here when you like so we would like you each to have a key."

"Steve had the key of my heart the minute I saw him."

"Zoe! Now who's the melodrama queen? Anyway, Robert will give you the combination to switch off the alarm."

"4-0-0-6. Just think of Basil D'Oliveira's Test batting average."

At the beginning of this holiday I used to hide in the kitchen. Now I seem to have three homes. Mum caught the eye of Joe and Belinda and cleared her throat.

"Zoe and Robert, we all feel the same about you. Here's a key to our place. No alarm system yet."

"Madness. When my drawings are worth millions."

"Namaste!" *Our host, Arthur Fraser, was a big, overweight man in this long Indian jacket. He had an Indian wife. Howard and Portia told me and Cal about him on the way to Upton Chesney.*

"Head of Megalopolitan TV in its great days. Invented Ted Luger – Bearvate Eye – and climbed to power with a string of great ideas. Then went to India and made a second fortune in Indian media."

"And got married, Howard."

"And got married, Portia. Came back to Upton Chesney, which was always the Frenetics' favourite ground, and bought the local manor. Became the President of Upton Chesney, which is why we are playing today as the President's Eleven. It's always all day and we stay overnight at his house. There will be a wonderful Indian lunch at the match – Cal, get ready, and Steve, don't be too polite. Arthur expects people to enjoy his hospitality. He may hand out oracular advice, so just listen and chime when you need to. Oh, and don't bet on him catching anything at slip."

Another one of them. But I just don't care. I know I ought to. My debut for the Frenetics. Joe's team, Howard's team. Tim's team – he's their President. Of course he's at the Test but his dad's playing. I want to do well for them but all I can think about is the match on Tuesday. My sort-of-England debut. Zoe thinks I should wish myself the worst. Stage superstition. Okay, I'm going to bowl non-stop pies, miss easy catches, and out first ball. And split my trousers.

Howard and Portia keep talking about a Frenetic called Pat Hobby. Screenwriter (not). Howard used him for Rob Patty.

"Do you remember when Pat got locked in his own coffin?"

"Was that when Anthony Scorer drove him home in his boot?"

"No, I'm sure that was another match, when Pat was hiding from Edwin Shaw."

"Who would hide from Edwin, he's shorter than Cal!"

"Edwin lent him money. Some Frenetics never learn."

"What about the time that Pat wanted to pitch his screenplay at George Galvan and ran out his little boy before he'd faced a ball?"[26]

"He was a terrific opening bowler. Best we ever had before Steve. But that was all he could do."

Hmm. Maybe that's all I can do. And suppose I'm not even a good opening bowler?

Howard is such a boring driver. We got overtaken by a garden gnome!

"Cal, stop twitching and fidgeting. I'm stopping the car up ahead, where's there's a big open space. Steve, chase him away somewhere and don't bring him back until he's zonked."

```
Portia and I watched Steve chase him until he escaped up
a tree.
```

"Good to have them in your world, isn't it, Howard? Alice too."

"It's wonderful, Portia, but I worry about whether I belong in their world."

"Howard, look at me. I know lots of men who have deserted people who love them, who all used that shitty line, 'I am not worthy of you.' I won't believe that you are that kind of shit. If you were, I'd kill you."

"If I were, I hope you would. Hear me out, Portia. I need to say this. My world is all… surface. People don't have deep feelings there. They have fun and nothing bad ever happens. When it does, people say a few funny lines or do something entertaining or maybe even sing a song, and all the pain goes

---

[26] See "Pat Hobby Runs Out Of Luck" in <u>A Tale Of Ten Wickets</u>

away. Everyone gets a happy ending. If I could stay in that world, everything would be fine.

"When Marian got cancer..." `She looked at me for a long time. I so wanted to tell her everything. Rehearse, polish the lines I would have to say to Alice. Despicable! Treating Marian as just another script to be doctored. I stumbled on.` "The pain never went away. Well, I just couldn't cope at all. It was so out of my range. Anyway, Alice and Steve and Cal, they're different. They have... big feelings and they've coped with big crises in their life. If we could all live in my world, for ever, I think we would all be fine. But if I had to move into their world – real dramas, deep emotions – I would let them down."

"Howard, I think you treat your life like a screenplay. In which you're the hero and you always have to look good and say wonderful lines. Fuck that. Do you love Alice?"

"Yes."

"Well, Howard, that is all the script you get given. 'Howard loves Alice.' The rest you improvise."

"I know that you're right, but it still frightens me. The thought of letting her down. And the boys. Not being what they want and deserve. Not coming through on a promise."

"I hope you get over that, Howard. I really do. If it makes any difference to you I think I made the wrong choice after Alan died. Deciding to be a one-man woman. Defining myself as his widow. Never letting anyone else get close. I feel that was wrong. Every time I see Cal." `Returning to the car, staggering under his attempt to carry Steve in a fireman's lift.`

"Namaste," *our host repeated.* "You're Steve, the new Pat Hobby. But only on the field! And this is Cal, the mystery spinner. I'm afraid our captain, Joel, does most of the mystery spin on our team. It's certainly a mystery to him. My wife, Anjali. Darling, you know Howard. And this is Portia. Portia Harper. I'm so glad to see you." *He gave her a giant hug.* "Now some tea. I know Howard's driving, you must have been on the road for six hours."

"And yet we're the first."

We had tea and he took us all round his house. It was huge and he actually got lost and Anjali had to get him back on track. "Not bad, eh? And all because I made two good decisions. The first was to get out of a lift at the right time.[27] Steve, Cal, whatever you do in your life always be ready to get out of the lift if the floor looks more interesting than the one you're going to. And my second good decision was to play cricket in India with my friend Mihir Bose. No one should have any cricket career without playing cricket in India with Mihir Bose. There may be a last-hurrah tour next year, did you know, Howard? Anyway, by going to India with Mihir Bose I met Anjali."

"You also met Ashok and his television network and a few million rupees."

"They only reminded me of you."

He eventually found a big bedroom which Steve and I were to share (yes!)

He showed us a big bedroom, murmuring vaguely that it was for "all the kids" and I wondered if that would include Zoe. Right on cue, all the Barneses arrived. Felt a buzz seeing Zoe again – after seeing her yesterday! If we live together, will I still get excited when she comes in from the next room? And then came Luke, Laura and Billy.

I could see Billy getting very tense because of the strange people, so I took his hand and we went to look at an elephant. There were elephants all over that house, especially if you included the god Ganesh. The others were talking for ever, so we started drawing and then Robert came over and let Billy use his camera.

Everyone got emotional at seeing Portia and Howard was really choked over seeing Luke and Laura. I'd thought the Frenetics were a bit of a joke – bad shame! They care about each other. I will bowl flat out tomorrow and stuff my England debut.

After a bit they all started talking about Pat Hobby again. "Do you remember the summer that Pat got writer's block?"

"Which one would that be? Summer 76, 77, 78? Do I hear 79? 80? 81?"

"Writing Happy Birthday on a card was a day's work for Pat, and only if he could steal it."

Sheila arrived. Kissy-kissy. And her husband, Alex. Nice man and rich but never understood why she went for him. (Sorry, Alex). But they are really happy. They always treat

---

[27] See "Lift Off" in <u>A Tale Of Ten Wickets</u>

the Upton Chesney match as their anniversary. It saved their marriage years ago.[28]

Alex Bramley. Married to Sheila Fereday. Apparently he's an ace fielder. Doesn't look it. Fat, with glasses. More Pat Hobby stories.

"Pat made a pass at me on the set of Rob Patty. A bit creepy. The real Rob Patty trying to play his pretend self."

"What was Pat like as an actor?"

"Terrible. Worse than your dad, Zoe. Now, Howard, when are you going to write me another series?"

Howard suddenly looked really tense, then he gave a smile. I've learnt to recognize it as his "company" smile. "Sheila, I'm like Rob Patty myself. I've run out of ideas. And who would I cast as Rob?"

"Jeffrey Archer?"

John Morrow arrived. Tim's dad. He acts as his agent. Surprised that he's not at the Test Match, but Tim doesn't allow him to miss the Upton Chesney match. It seems to be important to these people. I will bowl flat out.

"Steve, good to meet you. Tim told me about you." *Really?* "A new Pat Hobby at last. I'll just hold the other end for you." *He started to tell Howard about Tim's latest row with the England management but Howard cut him off and they went back to swapping Pat Hobby stories.*

"Do you remember when Pat stole the script for the nursery school play?"

```
Luke and Laura aren't getting as much from the reunion as
the rest of us. They're in a constant state of vigilance
over Billy. I couldn't handle that.
```

"Me and Robert are going to take Billy on an elephant hunt. Is that OK?"

"That's sweet of you both. Just ask Arthur and Anjali." `Permission granted and for the first time Luke and Laura relaxed.` "Cal's been wonderful for Billy and now it looks as though he's got Robert as well. If it ever gets too much for them we need to know."

---

[28] See "An Excellent Moment" from <u>A Tale Of Ten Wickets</u>

Edwin Shaw arrived. Opening bat. Are all Edwins opening bats? Small thin man with small thin wife. Then our captain Joel Hegarty. Flurried. Rapid speech and gestures. No wife. "Anjali! Arthur! Sorry to be late." *He wasn't. Nothing was happening.* "My life's a little…"

"FRENETIC!" *The others all shouted. That's how the club got its name.*

More emotional reunions with Portia. Years on, everyone feels real sorrow over Alan's death.

More Pat Hobby stories and then someone asked about Jim Wyatt, another absent star.

"Doing brilliantly in Brazil. Married, kids. In partnership with his best friend and they've got some Scorer money behind them. I get a long postcard from him, every year. From Porto Alegre."[29]

Anthony Scorer. International Man of Mystery! He seems to have helped everyone in this team. And he funds Marian's College. So he's helping me and Cal. People started asking Howard about him.

"He's very happy. Living in a small but beautiful house in a small but beautiful island. He plants orchids and he plants money. And, John, he still scores all of Tim's innings for England, by radio. Still in that beautiful multi-coloured handwriting."[30]

Cal and Robert and Billy came back.

"There are 173 elephants."

"And Billy took a picture of each one."

"Thank you very much, Billy. Anjali and I lost count at 89."

"Robert, you must be the last person in England to have a Ted Luger T-Shirt." *Arthur and Joel looked really wistful.*

"I've got him with me."

---

[29] See "Porto Alegre" from <u>A Tale Of Ten Wickets.</u>

[30] See <u>A Tale Of Ten Wickets</u> *passim*, especially "Final Score".

"Try and part him from Ted Luger. It's worse than Tim and Tiger." *I used to give Robert a terrible time over Ted Luger and his other cuddlies. Until I met my own giant cuddly.*

"It was stupid they took his gun away. How could he be a bearvate eye without a Luger? And it only fired blancmange."

"Now then…" *Arthur suddenly pulled out a big voice. I could see how he became boss of a big company. The whole room was silent except for Sheila finishing off another story about Pat Hobby.* "… he was furious with the bishop for stealing his line about faith, hope and charity."

"Thank you, Sheila, and did you ever see Pat's rewrite of the Ten Commandments?"

"Thou shalt covet thy neighbour's plot and dialogue, even to the last syllable. Thou shalt steal."

"Verily. A few short service announcements. Anjali will reveal the remaining room allocations. Cricket stuff is safe in cars and the boot room. Dinner is a cold collation here. Black tie is optional. We recommend the pools for anyone under 36. That is, 36 waist." *He prodded his paunch ruefully.*

I helped people with their luggage. Zoe not in "kids' room" after all, given small one of her own near parents. Safe from my raging teen hormones. (Actually, I was a bit relieved). Luke and Laura worried about Billy.

"Anjali, he doesn't cope very well with strange houses. I think he had better sleep in our room."

"Robert and I can look after him." *They each took his hands.*

"Do you want to be with Cal and Robert?"

"Yes." *They looked like they'd been given a surprise present.*

Arthur meant it when he said "pools". There was one indoor and one outside and a hot tub.

"Billy's ace at swimming."

"Better than you, Cal."

"You're going to be drowned to death for that." *He made a futile attempt to wrestle me under. No bad memory of our ordeal in the sea – but Mum's still suing the Redeemers for negligence and claiming he's totally traumatized. Serve them right, the shits. Ernie and Max Foggo, the reporter, are still on their case. Luke didn't go in. Still can't believe the god's a non-swimmer. He was in the hot tub clinging to the rail! Cal and I joined him and got an update on Glendon Courtenay.*

"We can't stop winning now. Four on the bounce after the Undecim."

"How many centuries have you made?"

"Three, as it happens, but all against pie-throwers. Edwin got one."

"Bet you helped him."

"Marjorie's taken over the coaching. Way stricter than you, Steve. You'll be fighting for your job next year. And she's doing jazz sessions with Rick and Jesse."

"Who's doing the pace bowling?"

"Zeke, Marjorie, she's become a real spitfire – and Mark Davison. Walked out on his dad and Ilminster and asked if he could play for us. Marjorie's teaching him to bowl like you, Steve. You've left a legacy. Oh and so have you, Cal. Anna and Adam are getting married. When they pulled you out of the sea they decided they wanted children."

"What about Steve?"

"Well… He clinched the deal."

Client meeting, that's what I told Howard. *Suppressio veri.* I was meeting Claude as my fancy man. For the last time. I had two lovers who could not manage a face-to-face goodbye. He deserves better.

He has chosen another fine concert, Il Festino, In St John's Smith Square. Baroque, not usually my tasse de thé. Brilliant young harpsichordist – make a note of her name. Claire Williams.[31] I praise them extravagantly at dinner, but nothing gets past Claude.

"Who is the new man, Alice?"

---

[31] A real person and a superb musician, for whom see www.clairewilliams.co.uk

"Oh Claude, I'm so sorry. Is it so obvious?"

"This has happened to me before. Quite often. I have learnt to recognize the signs. New shoes. That's often a sign. And today I also see new handbag, new scarf, new brooch. All of high quality. I know that you do not spend that kind of money on yourself. And other signs. Not looking at me in the usual way at the concert. Studying the programme intensely. Talking about the music afterwards – in great detail. To delay the news."

Oh hell. Why can't he be angry or vain or cynical? That would make it so much easier. Or even cry. I'm used to crying people. I'm very bad at it myself.

"Alice, look at me." He took my hands across the table. His are beautiful – much better than the concert pianists I've known. Howard's are battered – he says from writing, I say from cricket. "Alice, I never thought you would be satisfied for ever with an arrangement like ours. I was certain that you would meet a man to share your whole life. To bring home to your boy."

"Boys. Plural. Steve – the boy I told you about last time. You said take him on holiday. Well, he's now my son too."

"Wonderful. But twice as many reasons why you would want a real man to bring into your home, not one who cheats on his wife."

"That's not what you are!"

"Well then, a man with arrangements. A man who's too vain to change them – or too weak. Believe me, Alice, I am happy that you found somebody. I want you to be happy with all my heart."

"Claude, you'll find somebody too. I know it – you're clever and funny, handsome, sexy and you're kind. You're a very, very kind man. They're rare."

"If I'm kind, you're one of a kind." His jokes have never been very good in English (perhaps they're not very good in French either) but I recognized an attempt, We both smiled. Then he squeezed my hands very hard. "You know, Alice, that I have arrangements in other cities. But you were the one who meant the most." Past tense. He's accepted it. "You made me think there was more to life. I loved every moment we were together. Look, please refuse instantly if you feel wrong about this, but would you remain as my lawyer?"

"Claude, I've hardly given you any legal advice in ages and you're still paying a retainer as well as the concerts, the dinners, the hotels."

"Our business is expanding in this country."

"Then you'll need a good commercial lawyer, not a family one. But of course you might also need a litigant. My partner Portia is the best in England…"

The cold collation was humungous. English not Indian. Beef, chicken, fresh salmon, pies. Howard seized a piece of chicken and started singing. "You must remember this, a cuisse is but a cuisse, a thigh is but a thigh." *Nobody laughed. I didn't get it and I think the others had heard it before.*

There weren't enough chairs so I pulled Zoe onto my lap. Mistake! And she must have known it. I was relieved when Robert brought her one of her own.

I thought Cal would go mental at the collation but instead he helped Billy choose. That took ages. He didn't take much himself and then started drawing everybody.

Everyone came up to admire my drawings except Edwin. He looked at my sketch pad!

"Top quality. May I ask how much you paid for it?"

"Eight quid and I really get through them and Mum says we'll have to sell the house."

He passed me a card. "Put your mum in contact and we'll deliver them at wholesale prices. And whatever else you need. Art supplies are my business."

"Wow, thanks Edwin!" **I'll show him my zamboni tomorrow. Not Steve!**

They went on and on telling Pat Hobby stories. I recognized some from Howard's Rob Patty on TV. I asked Arthur, who seemed to be in touch with ex-Frenetics, what had happened to him. He laughed. "Steve, he did the only thing possible. Pat couldn't write any more but he was brilliant at stealing other people's talent. So he became a studio executive. He's number 3 at Paraversal. People defer to him, grovel to him for five seconds of his time – just as he used to do to important people when he was Rob Patty."

Claude and I had a nice dinner. No agonizing farewell. He wanted to draw me out about Howard. It didn't yet feel right yet to claim Howard as my man. Evasively. I called him a journalist. Well, that's all he does nowadays. I'm not letting him reject his real writing. I talked about Portia and he was interested. Could be an inspiration!

We finished the cold collation. Luke and Laura began to prepare Billy for bed. I could see this takes a long time. Cal and Robert caught each other's eye – and yawned. They were worse actors than Joe! They announced that they were tired. Hugs for and from everybody and they took Billy away themselves.

"Steve gets the big bed because of his back. We'll set up these folding ones, so you're between me and Robert."

"Do you want Ted Luger, Billy? He'll keep you really safe."

"Wait till you see Billy's, Robert."

"Criminey. Twelve bears, Billy. Worse than me."

Robert listened to all the bears' names and what they eat and whether they're good or naughty. And he let Billy take pictures of each with his good camera. He's another giant softie, like Steve.

We went into a big living room for coffee and liqueurs (no thanks!) Arthur set up a card table. He and Anjali started to play bridge with Edwin and his wife (never got her name). Joel came up and pointed an accusing finger. "The Devil's Playthings!" I thought he was just doing a melodrama turn like Joe when he wants to embarrass Zoe but there was a sudden tension.

"Social bridge, Joel. A game of genuine skill and no money at stake."

"Sorry, everybody. Steve's looking worried. He doesn't know that I used to be a compulsive gambler. In my view, compulsive is redundant next to gambler. Anyway I gambled, badly but incessantly, and I nearly lost my wife and kids. Then I got cleaned out at a poker game. I gave up and it saved my marriage.[32] Then my business hit the skids. Thanks to Arthur," *Short bow.* "I got the franchise for Ted Luger merchandise. Then they took his gun away and the character lost favour. I staked a lot on a new character – Premier Bear – a teddy bear who moonlights as a soccer star. He… never got off the bench. I started gambling again to refinance my business. Spread betting. The most poisonous form of gambling there is. Makes you believe you can win, by skill and knowledge. Crap. Steve, the more you gamble the more you lose. That's all you need to know. I lost my money, my business and my family. I quit.

---

[32] See "High Low" from A Tale Of Ten Wickets.

Anthony Scorer kept me afloat," *(him again- absent benefactor)* "while I qualified as a therapist. I treat gamblers. I can't even bear to toss the coin for the Frenetics. Arthur will do it tomorrow."

The other grown-ups were having a long catch-up with Portia. Zoe and I slipped away into the library.

"Look, Steve. Tons of Howard's scripts – and a whole shelf of Pat Hobby's. Arthur had a special stamp made to say REJECT."

There was a noise behind a sofa and we both jumped. I put my arm around her. Hope she never finds out I'm actually a coward. John Morrow lifted his head.

"Sorry. I have read my son's book a thousand times and I still choke up and the chapter about me and him and Tiger.[33]"

"He'll be batting tomorrow in the Test. Won't you want to be there?"

"I can't bear to watch him bat. I'm just a great puddle of nerves. Just like when he was eight. I go to his matches as little as I can. I don't want to pass on my tension. I don't even watch him on TV in case I give him bad vibes."

Hell, what a sacrifice. "You'll miss his century tomorrow."

"Shut up, Steve!" **I could have smacked him.** "Walk three times anti-clockwise round the room." *I obeyed.* "John, you'll miss his golden duck and his broken leg!"

"And his trousers will split! John, whatever happens to him or me, having that net with Tim will always be the high point of my cricket life."

"Thanks. I'll tell him. That's what counts to him. That's why he plays cricket at all. To connect with people and give them an exciting and beautiful part of their lives. True. He'd play for nothing if he could, just like the amateurs used to do. Most of my job as his agent is turning offers away."

"I don't want to hear anything I shouldn't but is it true that the England management don't like him? And some of the players?"

"I'm afraid it is. His nickname in the dressing room is Goody. It's not an affectionate one, although the player who gave it to him is quite happy to take

---

[33] See "The Tiger Will Bite Your Legs" from <u>A Tale Of Ten Wickets.</u>

his share of his prize money and the sponsorship and perks he doesn't want. His only real friend is Tom O'Ryan. They've got tagged as the rebels. And when they got set up in that so-called night club in Australia – actually it was a music club – management left them high and dry. I had to take on the Sun to clear his name."

"Get Mum as his lawyer. Or Portia. They're terrifying."

"I just might, because there will be a next time. Tim's always been a loner. The only coach he's ever liked and trusted is Felix Lindsay."

"And you!"

"And me, I suppose, and his step-dad Steve. But he overtook both of us when he was little. Me first, then Steve."

It still hurts after years. Steve taking over his son.

"Tim's biggest black mark with management is that he bars some of the products which promote themselves through cricket. You know his drink-drive video?"

"Getting bowled by David Brent after two pints of beer?"[34]

"Tim made sure that the beer they used was the official beer of the England cricket team. Steve shot it brilliantly. It's not named but you can tell which one it is. Lovely script by your dad, Zoe."

He sighed heavily. "In the dark hours, in hotel rooms, Tim sometimes thinks he's wasted his whole life on cricket. Don't be shocked, Steve! He thinks he's living in a bubble and that real life is outside. He talks to me for hours, or Howard. It's the fans that keep him going. He signs more autographs than any other player except Tom, who's a total pushover. It meant a lot to him to meet you and Cal. I'm not just saying that. He will always look out for you."

"Why are you three frowsting in here? John, can you sit in for me and stop my wife over-bidding? You young people, walk at once in the moonlit garden where the sweet woodbine flowers are closing."

Always obey your host. Zoe and I strolled into the garden. The air was lush and langourous [Wordpower].

---

[34] The script for this exists and is available from www.richardheller.co.uk

"They've imported plants from India. They've really thrived this summer."

"Nice. Zoe?"

"Steve?"

"You know I talked about Zoeness when we went shopping?"

"How can I forget? But I still don't know what it is."

"I don't either, but it's driving me crazy. It's a feeling you give me. It's something like ... bowling the best ball of my life at cricket. But that's not even on the scale. And bowling, well I work and I practise and a coach can help me get better. But with you, I can't practise at all, things just happen."

"I wouldn't want you to practise. I love things that just happen."

"One thing mustn't happen yet, Zoe. You must know that you turn me on. Even a touch."

"I had noticed. Don't be embarrassed."

"I am with other people. I had to hide in the hot tub today. And if Robert hadn't found you a chair… Zoe, I'm scared that I won't be able to wait. And that could ruin everything. Mum said I mustn't have sex with anyone under age because I mightn't be able to live with her. And your parents, who've been good to me and trust me and have just let me into your home, what would they think? But that's not really it… Zoe, I have had sex and it wasn't happy. It just kind of took over me, and I didn't care who I was or who she was. That was the scariest thing – not caring who we were. And we did it again, quite a few times, for all kinds of reasons. Because I wanted to defy my parents, because our school mates expected and because, well be honest, we liked the sensation. But always the same thing going on for me – not caring who we were."

"Steve, shut up." *I did.* "Good. Instant obedience. That's what keeps relationships going. Walk around their beautiful garden with me. Use all your senses one by one. Look at the flowers, the moonlight – and me. Listen to the nightingale – and me. Touch … that blossom – and me. Smell – all the flowers – and me. Taste – the air on your lips and then taste mine." *I did. For about three minutes.*

"I think that's our record. Now Steve, that was exciting wasn't it?"

"Yeah."

"I could tell and don't be embarrassed. But we were still Steve and Zoe, weren't we?"

"Yes. I suppose that's intimacy."

"It's love, Steve. Choosing where you want to be together, the feelings you want to share. Being at one with somebody and still being totally yourself."

"Wordpower, Zoe! So, what do you choose?"

"Steve, you've got enough on your mind. New family, new school, trying to be a great cricketer. Good reasons to wait. I've got my reasons too. New school means a lot to me too. A big adjustment even if it's wonderful. My family. I've only just got them back, thanks to you and Cal. I'd like to … enjoy them. And Steve, I only know sex through novels. And all I know is that it changes people. I'm not ready for that. What it might do for me, and you and our families and everyone else in our world. If I'm happy where we are and you're happy too, let's stay here for a bit."

"You're absolutely right, dear. As usual. Can we … do the five senses again?" *But this time we didn't get very far.* "That's not a nightingale, that's Howard at the piano." *And pretty soon after we met Luke and Laura, and Edwin and his wife, and Joe and Belinda. And our host and hostess.*

"A scented garden by moonlight. Irresistible to any romantic couple. And Howard does sound better at a distance."

We sat on a bench for a while and watched all the other couples gliding in their own space. I felt really ashamed of not knowing the name of Edwin's wife, because he adored her. "We've got a lot to live up to, Zoe. To be like them. And wait till you meet Ernie and Dorothy in Glendon Courtenay."

We all mooched back and said good nights. I didn't get long with Zoe but I said something I'd forgotten earlier. "Good night, Zoe, and remember there'll never be another." *So wait as long as you like.*

"Don't be certain, Steve. Every girl in Marian's will be after you and quite a few boys."

"They've got no chance. Unless they remind me of you."

"Good night, bad Psycho."

"Good night, wise Monkey."

Laura and Luke came with me to check on Billy. Fast asleep between Cal and Robert. Ted Luger and eleven other bears on patrol around them. One bear left for me. Kisses for Billy and they tiptoed away.

The bear they left me kept me awake all night. That and my nerves. My "England debut" was bad enough. Now I cared about the Frenetics as well. I'd hate to let them down. Five am. I glared at the bear. What did he have to smile about? Then I gave up and went for a run.

"Zoe! What are you doing up?"

"Waiting for you, Steve. I could tell you were restless and I know what you do when you are. Come back to bed. You've got an all-day game and a lot of bowling and you need more sleep. Your bed. Mine's terrible."

"Yes, dear. Anything you say, dear."

She smoothed out my bed and sat at the head. "Now, my love, lie here. Don't worry, we're choosing to be at peace together. Put your head on my lap."

She stroked my hair. I'm such a pushover for that. "The head must lie upon the block…"

"That was wont to lie on Queen Catherine's lap." He slept. I slept. The bear slept. At some point, Robert, Cal and Billy crept in with all the remaining bears. We all slept until woken by Arthur banging an Indian gong.

Chapter 39   Debut Match (1)

Breakfast was English, Indian or Continental. Cal tried all three, I fashioned my usual Sportsman's Special, imitated by Robert. Zoe's on a diet (she says) but she ate Cal's rejects because other people's food has no calories.

Cal did his bounce-and-look-at-the-ground routine, when he wants to give away something, and now he's got Robert doing it. They whispered to me and I managed to detach Luke and Laura and Billy from the others. They handed over a CD.

"This is an alphabet for Billy. With animals. And some people. I did the drawings and Robert took the pictures of the animals. We'll send you a better one later. But we got all the letters, even X." We borrowed a computer from Arthur and looked. I thought it was really good and Howard said they should send a version to a children's publisher. "There's B for Billy and B for bear... C for Cal and C for Cat ... R for Robert and R for Rhinoceros" Unfair, he's lost sheds of weight. "And here's the real X for X-Ray fish."

"We had to go to a tropical fish shop. You can see the name reflected on the fish tank. Product placement."

"Thank you Cal, thank you Robert. I love Cal. I love Robert."

Howard beckoned me and Cal to talk to Edwin. "Tell him about your run-in with Paul Russell" *so I did and Cal knocked off an instant sketch of him on his arse and Edwin fell about laughing and then got serious.* "I was with him at school. Same year, same house. He was my total hero. I even entered a boxing tournament for him – although I thought I would get beaten to a pulp.[35] He was a rebel but he changed sides to become a prefect and I'm sure he betrayed his best friend, Charles Markham and got him expelled. They were rivals for a younger boy called Johnny Linder, and he chose Charles and that's when Paul Russell suddenly became a puritan."

"Did you know Sam Carter, my captain at Glendon Courtenay?"

"Yes, he was a younger kid in our house. One of Russell's disciples."

---

[35] See "The Undisputed Champion Of The World" from <u>A Tale Of Ten Wickets.</u>

"I think he still is."

"These things can last a long time, Steve. When you've been a disciple it's hard to let go of the image of your god. I still remember Paul Russell as he was – funny and brilliant and subversive. Pity he was immoral, too."

The Upton Chesney ground had a fabulous pavilion. Arthur was too modest to say so but I could tell that he had given it to them. It was full of Indian stuff.

"There are 26 elephants."

"Thank you, Billy."

Issue of Frenetic shirts to me and Cal, in Belinda's eccentric typeface. It seemed to tell me not to take this team seriously. Our fielding practice had the same message. Joe hit up this huge skyer and three of them shouted "Yours!" I was too shy to take over but Cal wasn't and he took them through my "hug-the-teddy-bear" routine. Fat Alex Bramley had a bullet throw, smack into Joe's gloves. I complimented him.

"Thanks. Years ago I did a throw here and it saved my marriage. That was a fluke, so now I work on it."

Joel gave us a tactical talk. "We're going to attack all out unless we're forced to defend, in which case we do a holding operation. All-out pace is our main weapon but we have the option of spin and medium. It's going to be very hot, especially if we bowl first, so it will be short spells unless somebody runs through them or we need to seal an end. We'll have fielders close to the bat, but we don't want free singles or boundaries."

More usefully, he pointed out their leading players. "Frank Wall's been their captain for ever. Still a very sound bat but not at ease against spin. The McFarlane brothers. They used to be teen terrors. Good all-rounders and they'll almost certainly open their bowling. That must be the latest Turner in their side. There's a family gene which produces flighty slow bowlers and it is fatal to hit them. Now there's the danger man. Roy Gribben. Wonderful bat. I can remember when he was a podgy kid who was scared of the ball."

"Like me."

"Like you before Steve." *Cal was right. I have made a difference to Robert. That feeling keeps Tim Morrow going.*

John Morrow cleared his throat. "Our President regrets that he is unable to join us, owing to business commitments at the Oval. He wishes us all ill fortune, injured limbs and injured pride. Our mascot regrets his absence with our President but he has sent his deputy."

He reached into his cricket bag and pulled out a toy tiger, a smaller version of Tim's. The older Frenetics suddenly chanted together. "Stiffen the sinews, summon up the blood and imitate the action of the Tiger." *It made me feel serious again. I loved this team. They had stuck together all these years and now they had let me into their world. Six weeks ago none of them knew me. I was going to bowl out of my skin.*

Arthur (as Joel's proxy) lost the toss. Upton Chesney, predictably, batted first. Hot day, perfect wicket. Tailor-made for me.

Laura gave Luke his usual pre-match pep talk. Zoe looked amazed.

"Does that help?"

"Works for Luke."

"Into battle, my hero." *Long kiss. Stopped finally by Cal saying they were waiting for me to set my field.*

New ball in my hand. I wanted to let go but I liked the Upton Chesney people. Fool. They were not people, they were batsmen. Filth, to clear away.

"Steve, awesome. The oppo were terrified. Can't believe it's only two wickets."

We were at the first drinks break. "Your dad's catch was the best ever taken off me. I told him. The ball broke back and took the inside edge and your dad had to change direction. But I needed to get that Roy Gribben. He's quality."

"Arthur dropped him off you."

"Yeah but he's probably not used to catching anything at my pace. It wasn't clever bowling. If you don't expect slip catches, don't bowl for them."

"You're such a perfectionist. Why did they take you off?"

"They had to. Because I'm only sixteen and I have to lie down with my teddy bear after six overs."

"Into battle again, my hero."

Amazing lunch. Twelve kinds of curry on hot plates. It's what they do in India. Anjali gives cookery classes in the village. Cal wanted to sign up and she gave him a recipe book and a case of spices. But he didn't eat much.

"Excuse me, Zoe, but I need to cheer up Cal."

"Why was he taken off?"

"He was taking some stick and Joel thought it would be bad for his morale and that if anyone was going to take stick it should be him as the captain. So he put himself on."

"Is that good captaincy?"

"Er… no."

I found him glaring at an elephant, and hugged him. Cal, not the elephant.

"Listen, everyone knows that you should be bowling and not Joel. But this isn't just a cricket team it's a set of people who've stuck together and who care about each other. Joel's a very good person and he really did care about you when he took you off and put himself on instead."

"I know and I'm being a baby."

"You're being a frustrated artist. I think you'll be back. Howard and Luke and I will lobby for you. But whatever you're asked to do, be noisy and bouncy and a drama queen. Big mouth and big heart."

"What about Robert's catch? I'd have peed my pants."

Normal service restored.

"Lead us off, Steve. Five wickets. Jug tonight." *Three wickets in my final burst. Helped by the heavy atmosphere. They say locally we're in for a storm.*

"Where's Cal? Is he OK?" *Took a screaming catch off me at backward point. Portia was putting ice on his hand. Luckily his right, the non-bowling, non-drawing one.*

"Howard, do you have any-driver insurance? I'm taking him to hospital for an X-ray. No arguing, sweetie, just a precaution. And I'll go because I'm a professional at terrorizing hospitals." *As if on cue, a flash of lightning and very shortly after, a clap of thunder.*

"That's close." *Frank Wall, their captain, gave orders to get the covers on. To his fury, they were locked in a shed and the key was missing. While it was located, a lot of rain fell on the pitch.*

"Are we going to win?"

"Maybe. Depends how much time we lose to the rain. I didn't see what they finished on. Let's see the scorebook." *Not quite the truth. I wanted to see my figures. Their scorer was Sam Gribben, Roy's younger brother.*

"Sam, what an amazing book!" *Like Dorothy at Glendon Courtenay.*

"Your Mr Scorer taught me when I was a kid." *Him again! Same teacher as Dorothy's.*

"What do Steve's numbers mean?"

"Twelve overs, two maidens, five wickets for 54. Three no-balls." *Aagh! Unprofessional. Can't bowl them on my "England debut." And 4.5 an over. Small ground, fast outfield, but still expensive.* "Run out Bramley. My brother's an idiot. I put that in year after year." *Sam had added some editorial in minute writing to each dismissal. His brother was indeed an idiot. Alex's other run out was rightly attributed to "panic". Joe, Cal and Arthur got credit for "brilliant catches" off me and their position, but my other wickets were both "too fast". Howard's wicket was "bored, tried to slog." John Morrow's lbw "too plumb, even for Bert", Joel's wicket "huge skyer, midwkt, kid kept nerve."*

"We need 250. We could have gone for it but we're going to lose too much time to the rain and it will change the pitch and slow the outfield. It's a time game. We'll have to fight for a draw."

The rain finally stopped and we got the covers off. Some standing water got mopped away. Still dangerous to bowl on. Hot sun back and we waited for it to dry the pitch and the run-ups. Steam coming off the wicket! I think this is called a "sticky dog." I've never played on one. We're going to have to fight really hard for a draw.

"I'm not interested in a draw. We're going for the win."

I caught Howard's eye. He whispered. "Joel is the only captain in the world who thinks we could get nine an over on a sticky dog. We play it his way."

"I think we need to change the regular batting order. Luke, will you open? And I'm going to open with you, try and rattle them a bit."

"What's his batting like?"

"Random."

"Arthur three, Joe four. Steve, five." *What?* "Edwin six, Alex seven, Howard eight in case we have to defend, John nine, Robert ten and who knows if Cal will be able to bat?"

Howard's way too low, but he's not complaining. Edwin's a specialist opener down at six. Not complaining either. They like Joel although he's a daft captain.

"Steve! Three sixes. They think one's a local record!"

"Shouldn't have tried for another. We're actually up with the run rate, but Joel's run out Luke and your father and he thinks he's got to take over the scoring." *Random was the right description for Joel's batting. But it was impossible to set a field to him and he riled their deadly spin bowler, Turner, so much that he lost his length. Edwin was a decent bat and so, to my surprise, was Alex, but when Howard came in at the fall of the sixth wicket we needed 11 an over.*

A ridiculous single forced Howard to fling himself full length but gave Joel his fifty. Big applause and I joined in, but I couldn't help whispering to Zoe "That was the worst fifty in the history of the universe. Not one shot went to the right place. Wonder if Sam did a scoring chart."

At last he was out. Sam wrote "attempted cut, holed out mid on (!)"

"It's still in range, Howard." `No, it isn't Joel. John and I know what to do.`

Cal returned with Portia. "I think they knew who I was. They took dozens of X-rays. No break anywhere, bruising, possibly tendon damage. Two fingers taped as precaution against lawsuit. No cricket for two weeks." *Protest over-ruled. He was even more gutted to have missed my sixes but Robert had pictures. He brightened up and asked Joel to talk him through his fifty, the little star.*

Howard took over most of the strike. The ball was now jumping and squatting unpredictably. I saw for the first time the merits of his no-backlift. After three overs yielding 4, Joel changed his game plan. "Probably have to block it out now, you two."

John Morrow plunged forward at every opportunity. Eventually one bounced on him and he was caught behind. "Robert, you're in!" *Loads of encouragement from everyone, especially his family. Ignored, with a set face. Robert was in the zone. Four overs to survive. Zoe had his camera on him. Cal did a drawing.*

"NO!"

"You tell him, Robert."

"What happened there? Look at Robert!" *Zoe passed me the camera. He looked imperious, waving Howard back to his crease.*

"Howard wanted a single to face the next over. Robert sent him back. He was right, it was his call, and he's ready to take the next over himself."

The deadly spinner back on the awful track. Every fielder in Robert's pocket.

"Footwork, Robert!" *At the pitch, each one safely stunned. Maiden over.*

Howard blocked five balls, then a big hit over the infield. Easy single to keep the strike, but the crafty sods let it run for four.

"Steve, why didn't he stop it?"

"To make Robert face the next over."

Robert, my beauty! Safe single off the second ball of the deadly spinner. Two blocks from Howard. Then he tried for a single. Ball stopped on him. Caught at mid on. We've lost.

"I'm going in!"

"Cal, you are not!"

"Pad me now. Hurry, so I'm not timed out. One ball to face, Portia. I'll bat it one-handed only if I have to. And he's really slow. If I survive, Robert can face all the last over."

We got all his gear on bar one glove and he marched onto the pitch, to surprise and then general applause. He asked for "Leg stump" in a loud voice and Luke gave it to him. He marked his guard ostentatiously and took his stance with one hand on the bat. Minor adjustments of the field for the left-hander.

Another deadly flighted ball. But pitching outside leg stump. Padded away, dropping the bat, disdainful look at fielder making futile appeal. Maximum drama queen!

Robert produced six more blocks in the last over. Cal screamed "NO!" to each one. Otiose [Wordpower] and I don't think Robert even noticed. "Over!" Match drawn. Pitch invasion. Both batsmen carried off.

Robert got the Man of the Match award. I bought my jug in the Bat and Ball pub, but managed to avoid drinking any beer myself and so did not puke. On TV we were able to see highlights of Tim Morrow's century at the Oval.

If all their matches are like this I'll play for the Frenetics all my life and stuff my England career.

Chapter 40 Debut Match (2)

If I weren't a partner I would sack myself from my law firm. I have done almost nothing all day except wonder to wear to wear the new indigo Nicole Farhi or the new deep purple Karen Millen to this evening's reception. Howard was no help when he brought back my two (zonked) boys back after the Upton Chesney match. "One will speak to you." Well, actually they're both screaming in my ear.

Portia was no help to me either. She had plenty to say about the match and a long medical bulletin on Cal's hand. As to Howard, "He's got some ideas fixed in his head. Hear them out and then smack his head to get rid of them."

Steve rang me at work. Unusual. I feared a domestic emergency. No worse than losing the cufflinks for his good shirt. Really a pretext. He's a bag of nerves.

"There's going to be famous writers and important people tonight and they're going to wonder what on earth I'm doing there."

"Same for me, kid."

"No it isn't. You're Britain's top children's lawyer."

"I wish."

"You are and you're grown up and you're brilliant and I'm just a … kid."

"As are Cal and Zoe and Robert."

"Cal will be drawing and Robert will be taking photographs. Like professionals. And I'll just be standing around like a lemon."

"Like Zoe."

"Zoe's clever, especially about books. She gets things in books way quicker than I do."

"That's what really scares you. Zoe might think you're stupid."

"Yes. Well, and all of you and I especially don't want to let down Howard, but Zoe especially might think I'm stupid."

"Won't happen. Trust me. And if it did, you'll both get over it. Real people are sometimes stupid. Only people in movies are never stupid." Suddenly that seemed disloyal to Howard. But I think he sometimes works too hard on his dialogue.

"Steve, take a tip from me. I have met a few famous people and they all loved talking about themselves. You'll go a long way this evening as a listener. If there is any pause after a famous person speaks, just say 'how marvellous' (or just possibly, 'how terrible') and add 'what happened then?' Everyone will think you're brilliant." Laugh, but we weren't finished. He was scared about his big cricket match.

"I know it's not proper England, we're just Under-19 Emerging Players but suppose I don't? Emerge?"

"You have emerged already, Steve. Two England players rated you. A legendary coach rates you."

"He hasn't seen me and he needed me to make up the numbers. Suppose he thinks I'm an idiot and then I've let you all down and Tim and Tom."

"Terrible. Give me his number. I'll call him and say you've got a cold and you can spend tomorrow in bed with Bungle."

"Too late. He called already to confirm I was playing. We had a long chat."

"About how useless you are but he needed to make up the numbers."

"No! Actually mostly about Afghanistan. He's been out there to coach and they've got some great young players, and I told him Uncle Frank had been there and hated it, but I felt better now because they had good cricketers. And then we talked about Uncle Frank for a long time and what he'd taught me."

***

"I'd like to have met your uncle. I do a lot of my work on the same lines. Now, Steve, you know the time and place tomorrow. We do some team warm-ups and drills but get there earlier and I'll help you with any personal routine. Any questions?"

"Who are the other players?"

"There are six batsmen including the wicketkeeper, three specialist bowlers, two seam, one slow left-arm, one other all-rounder."

"Other all-rounder?"

"Number seven. A batsman that bowls, you're eight, a bowler that bats."

"But… are they with counties? Have they played first-class?"

"Some, but that doesn't matter to me." *Cripes. Will they care about Glendon Courtenay or Upton Chesney?* "Any other questions?"

"Felix, are you a New Zealander?"

"Can you still hear it? Yeah, but I'm having a long Overseas Experience."

"Do you know the McConnel twins? Daniel and Brendon? I've played with them. I bowled Brendon."

"Bloody hell, mate. They've had a Test trial back in the old country." *Cripes again. They never told me.*

***

"Then we talked about Tim's century and whether Tom could bowl the Aussies out today on a slow pitch, and…"

"Steve. What do you think of Felix Lindsay?"

"Great bloke. That makes it worse. I wouldn't mind bowling like a drain if he was a shit or a dweeb." Aaggh! Determined to look on the dark side.

"Steve, put Cal on." We had a short discussion and came up with a plan.

Cal brought Steve over to watch the last day of the Test on our giant screen (bigger than most pubs!) We threw him onto the couch, ourselves afterwards.

"Steve, you're here until you go home to change for the reception. You're not allowed up except for the toilet. You can't speak unless it's about the Test Match or to ask for a drink or a snack."

He fell asleep! What is it about our couch? We only woke him up when Tim came on to bowl. Then we watched the dream finish. Tim getting the breakthrough wicket, Tom blasting out the tail. Winning the Ashes just in time for us to change.

"You look stunning. So the indigo was the one that finally spoke."

"They both spoke to me non-stop but this one said 'you want to be dramatic but in that crowd everyone else will be dramatic so the only way you can go dramatic is to be classic and understated.'"

"Convoluted logic but wonderful result. Reminds me of an old Jewish story. Jewish mother, trying as always to make her son feel guilty, buys him two beautiful shirts for his birthday. He wears one, she says 'the other one you didn't like?'"

"Howard, are you Jewish?"

"No. French by descent. Foy as in 'ma foi' – my word. A mild expletive."

"I thought it meant faith." Troubled look. Why? Must smack his head soon.

"I parked the children ahead of time at Omnium House. Richard will find work for them."

"Richard?"

"Richard Heller. Secretary of the Fund. Actually its first beneficiary. Sad chap. Very decent writer, fifteen books, but none of them caught on. Even his book on failure was a failure." And then, right there in my dusty legal office, he seized me, lifted me up (a good distance) and kissed me. Not complete abandon, but way on the scale above social. And he made it last! "Sorry."

"I'm not."

"I'm just… indescribably happy that you're coming with me."

"Not indescribably, Howard. You're a writer."

"You're … real life." He looked at my new dress and his new suit. Nothing out of place, after a serious clinch. "Good tailoring."

Zoe was wearing my monkey brooch! Didn't think it went with the dress but was too chuffed to care. Howard left us all with the Fund Secretary, Richard Heller. Small man, a bit flustered. Suddenly I realized I'd seen him before – the sad man having a great haircut when Cal and I went to Yasmin. He's met Zoe before but he didn't recognize her! "Zoe, I'm so sorry. I thought you were one of the writers. Oh hell, what a thing to say. Why shouldn't you be a writer? Look, can anyone see my to-do list?" **I found it. Item 1 said "Make To-Do list" and had a tic.**

"Thank you. Now, Cal and Robert, sketch artist and photographer, do you need to … scout locations?"

"No."

"Oh. I thought you people always had to scout locations. Look here, can you help Steve move that table and chairs to the other end of the room? Zoe, not you in that sensational frock. Count the olive bowls, I think we've been short changed by the caterers."

I had to move a gigantic vase. "Stephanie!" *I nearly dropped it and it was worth thousands.*

"Xan! What are you doing here?"

"My last play closed out of town. Audience – you could have stored meat in them. I'm a barman tonight. You learn other jobs when you're an actor. Especially a middle-aged actor. You remember Eileen?"

"Al… Yes, Eileen?"

"Making much more than me. She's paying our rent. Oh, not that way. As a specialized car mechanic. Although I'm surprised she can get underneath many cars, we can't keep her out of the cookie jar. We've got Jimmy's Alfa while he's away." *He looked anxiously at me.*

"Don't you mean Jemima?"

We both laughed. I had put Jimmy into the safe category of Xan's cricket queens. "Look, here's my email. You don't have to give me yours."

"Here's my email. I'd like to see you, and him."

"And why are you here? With Miss Cutie Pie, and Miss Snapper and Miss Real Girl?"

"We're here with Howard Foy."

"Ooh, best behaviour. You never want to get on the wrong side of Howard."

"Really? He's been brilliant to me. Us."

"A very powerful man, Howard, and un homme serieux. He's the only cricketer I know that I have never given a girl's name."

Howard and Mum arrived. The four of us scurried over. I'd seen Mum try on her dress but I was still gobsmacked. Robert took dozens of pics of her, alone and with Howard. They looked… famous. Richard bustled over with his to-do list, to report, but Howard waved him aside.

"Richard, it will be another triumph. Now Robert and Cal, you have your jobs. Steve and Zoe, I would like you to be Mary Varley's minders while she's here. Steve can take over her wheelchair from her driver and hand her back. Zoe, you're her lady-in-waiting. Oh yes, she's the real royalty here, not the ersatz Highness. Now, I think we should all have a little private gargle before the ghastly guests arrive." *We all went over to the bar. Champagne for the adults, juice for us four. I might have had champagne but I thought of the match tomorrow. Xan served us. The biggest drama queen I knew (bigger than Cal) but he made himself anonymous. He is a good actor.*

"Howard, a quick whisper?" He took me aside. "I feel a bit nervous about talking to writers when I don't know any of their work."

"Why should you? They don't know anything about yours. Writers always think that people should be interested in them. Why? They play with imaginary lives, you deal with real ones."

"But this is a writers' occasion."

"Please trust me, Alice. All the writers who are worth anything here will know right away that you're amazing."

"Okay, Howard. But I have some bad times with geniuses."

"Then stay right with me and you'll be fine."

The room slowly started to fill. Everyone knew Howard. I was his friend, Alice Devane, and one of England's leading lawyers, but strictly off-duty tonight. Some of the women looked me up and down. I didn't mind at all. Suddenly I felt like a few million dollars. As I had expected, my part of the conversation was generally easy. "How marvellous! And what happened then?" Steve got the giggles but Howard flashed him a look and he quelled them. A new side of their relationship.

Just once did I see Howard off-balance. "Howie! Howie, come here!" She looked like the Red Queen, shouting 'Off with his head!"

"Hell, it's Scarlett Ferber. I tore her book to shreds. Metaphorically. Now she's going to tear me to shreds. Literally."

She hurled herself at him, knocking over a well-known librettist. "Howie! Your review of my book. Genius. You were the only reviewer who realized that it was a serious social study. And that wonderful phrase. 'She writes like Zola on speed.' Mind you, I wonder how many people remember Zola Budd?"

She swept away again. This time the casualty was a TV historian. Howard recovered. "Was that last remark stupid or post-modern irony? We'll never know."

Richard Heller bustled over again. I noticed that he had a very good suit but was wearing it very badly. "HIRH is here. And the Minister."

"Damn. Still I suppose it was inevitable."

"HIRH?"

"Her Imperial and Royal Highness. Don't be frightened of the Imperial, it's only Brazilian. Our Royal Patron. She writes history books which nobody reads but she does attract money to help indigent writers. Much more than the Minister attracts from the government. Now I have to crawl for few minutes. It's not pretty and I don't want you to see. These two are much better company. Claire, Michael, may I introduce my friend Alice Devane?"

Howard didn't give me their second names. Older than him. Evidently writers but they seemed kindly. They didn't talk about themselves at all but asked about me and Howard. They seemed to care about him, and they were interested in me and my children and the law. I was in full flow but got cut off by Howard. He had leapt onto a chair. "Your Imperial and Royal Highness. Your Grace. Your Excellencies. Minister. My Lords. Members of Her Majesty's Privy Council. Ladies and gentlemen of all ages. I will not detain you long, but I propose on this occasion to feel compelled to say a few auspicious words. I must first auspiciously thank his Grace for these wonderful auspices, here in Omnium House, so rich in its literary heritage. We are indeed privileged, as we are by the gracious presence of our Royal Patron and that of the minister. I am saying nothing about the Fund and our year's activities, for I would merely duplicate the elegant but lucid account given in the annual report by our excellent secretary." General applause, from which Richard Heller shrank. "Generous support from patrons and other donors, combined with rigorous administration, have enabled us to assist more needy writers than ever before. But then, there are more needy writers than ever before. Now that the government has finished bailing out Britain's banks (we hope), may I ask the minister to consider a bail-out for Britain's authors?" General laughter, forced smile from minister. "It would be more popular. Britain's authors have their faults, but none of them has sentenced a small business to death or repossessed a family home. However, in fairness, I must say that Britain's banks in recent years have produced far more original fiction than Britain's novelists." More laughter. Minister attempted to join in, as a good sport.

"Before delivering my auspicious and compelling thanks to everyone for coming I have a short business announcement. In this room are a talented young photographer and a talented young caricaturist. The young photographer is no paparazzo. His usual subject is wildlife, which makes him ideal for literary lions. He will take your photograph only if you wish. If you like any image, his fee of £10 will go to the Fund. The same terms for the caricaturist. Thank you for coming. Please enjoy yourselves."

General applause, much glad-handing as he made his way back to us.

"Excellent, Howard. Claire and I have to go now, but we never miss your Gussie Fink-Nottle passage." They slipped away without fuss.

"They were lovely, Howard, but you never gave me their last names."

"Oh, sorry. Claire Tomalin and Michael Frayn. Two of the most talented people in the room and two of the nicest. Those things can go together. I'm worried about Mary. She's late. God, I hope nothing's happened to her. She's at least 92."

"Traffic's bad, Howard. You'd have heard if there was anything worse."

"You're absolutely right, dear. As always."

All this time, Steve and Zoe had been following in our slipstream. Zoe was poised and pert, Steve polite but withdrawn. Suddenly he came to life. "That's Roy Hodgson! The Fulham manager. Howard, is he a writer?"

"Much more important, he's a reader. Roy! Sebastian!"

They came over. Howard's a god here! We got introduced. The other bloke was Sebastian Faulks. Howard whispered that he's a really good writer, and plays cricket. "Mr Hodgson, er Roy, you've just signed a kid from my school, I mean my last school. Johnny Palladino." Idiot! As if the manager would know or care about some sixteen-year-old schoolboy. But he did know him! I suddenly felt really happy for Johnny. His career was in good hands.

"A midfield schemer. What can you tell me about him?"

"Great ball control, both feet, brilliant passer. Sometimes too ambitious, can get caught in possession."

"Thank you. I'll remember." *He actually made a note!* "How about yourself? Anything we should see?"

"Left back in the school team. Nothing special. Just pace and fitness. Get my man and hoof the ball away. I want to be a professional cricketer and I've got this sort of England game tomorrow and I was just a park player a few weeks ago…" *Oh hell, as if they want to hear that? But they did. They both kept asking me questions, and Sebastian Faulks asked if I'd bowl at him some day because he's an opening bat and he needs to tighten up against the outswinger. They let me burble on for ages and then Roy cut in quietly.*

"Howard says you're a great reader. Keep it up. Sport can be terribly boring, rehearsing the same skill over and over. Books are another world. Give me your email. We'll compare favourites and you can meet Brede Hangeland – he's reading right through Dickens. Here's one for your list. Saul Bellow, The Adventures Of Augie March. Good luck with the cricket. If it doesn't work out, ask me for a trial. Left backs are hard to find." *I handed over my email details in a daze. They were really interested in me, not just polite.*

"Howie! Howie baby!" *It was the awful Scarlett woman again. I suddenly remembered I'd sat under her (non)celebrity photo with my (former) parents in Paparazzo's restaurant. She knocked over an ambassador (I think). Cal and Robert were in her wake, looking embarrassed.* "These little cuties are geniuses!"

Robert whispered "She's spent £500 on snaps and sketches."

"I want them for the gutter." *Howard looked blank.* "The Gutter. My new review."

"Scarlett! What an honour for them!" *Expansive gesture!* "But alas, they are already under contract to Cosy Moments." *Cal was about to blurt that this was the Marian's School magazine, but Howard headed him off at the pass.* "Magazine. Launching next month – you'll be asked of course. Cosy Moments is so cutting edge you could shave with it." *He blushed and I saw that she had a bit of a moustache! She didn't react and he hurried on* "Cosy Moments will be positivement le dernier cri of the avant-garde of the nouvelle vague."

"Mot Pouvoir, Howard."

She looked at me for a long time. I could sense a wheel turning slowly, as if propelled by an arthritic hamster. Then she completed the translation. "Mot Pouvoir!" Cacchination. "I'm stealing that." She swept off. The Duke of Omnium jumped out of her way in the nick of time.

Everybody needed a drink after that. I took orders and headed off for Xan.

"Good god! Who let you in here?" *My blood ran cold. Sorry for the cliché but it did. The Right Honourable Paul Russell. Barring my path to the bar. I just stood there (what a wuss, but my blood was still cold).* "And your little friend, I see?" *That heated my blood instantly and I nearly hit him but Howard was suddenly there..*

"Paul! Marvellous… Now I think you've met Steve before. He's got a sort of England debut tomorrow. Steve, if you bowl as slowly as you fetch drinks you're going to get pasted."

I escaped to Xan. "Look at little Pauline, she's wetting her knickers."

`He's sweating. Give him a moment more of silence. That's` `what Bertie Wooster, the Drones Detective, would have` `done in my stories.` "Paul. First time you've been to one of these. Glad to have the chance of a word. You have indeed met Steve and Cal and their mother, Alice. They are friends of mine. I take it very badly if my friends face any kind of threat or hostility in anything they do. You have made your mark in conventional politics but you now want to advance in literary politics. These are much nastier than conventional politics and as anyone here will tell you, I am the Peter Mandelson of literary politics. Another thing, Paul. I have had several reports of that match you played against Steve's village in Devon, with that team you've bought for yourself. You were wearing MCC colours, which the Club doesn't like when you're playing for other clubs. And there were incidents which were not totally in line with the Spirit of Cricket. Club likes that even less. Now I've been a dreadful slacker with that MCC committee on which we both serve, but I will be attending much more regularly, and liaising with the full Committee… Ah, Jeffrey! Of course you know each other and of course you've read his novel on Mallory. The climber. Jeffrey, you reached new heights…"

`I think he got my message. I released him to the custody` `of Jeffrey Archer and signalled to Richard Heller.`

"Richard, who let in the Right Honourable Arsehole?"

"He is a writer, Howard, and he became a patron. Came through with a big donation while you were away in the Cape Verdes. Mary Varley's arrived."

"Thank God." I despatched Steve and Zoe to meet her at the main entrance. What had kept her? She was usually the first to arrive and the last to leave, but my worrying was stopped by Cal.

"Howard, who's the wicketkeeper?"

"Wicketkeeper?"

"Yeah. Tall guy. I was just practising some grips with an orange and he talked to me for ages and said he was a wicketkeeper and I taught him to read my zooter. Look, this is him." He showed me a caricature. Funny but accurate as always.

"That is Sir Tom Stoppard. One of our greatest playwrights."

No interest. "He knew loads about wicketkeeping. I thought he'd been a professional."

Mary Varley. One of Uncle Frank's authors. Tiny woman, in a wheelchair. All I could do was gawp. Zoe had to take charge.

"How do you do, Mrs Varley?"

"Mary, please. The Varleys never liked me."

"I'm Zoe, and this is Steve. Howard sent us. I'm your lady-in-waiting and he's … your personal slave."

"Good. Does that mean he has to satisfy my every want?" *She checked me out and she's over 90! I shifted behind her wheelchair and started pushing towards the reception. There was a back way, with ramps.* "Is he your sweetheart?"

"Yes."

"Then I won't move on him unless you loan him to me. That was our code. Will you loan him to me?"

"Sorry."

"That's your privilege, he's your sweetheart. But you haven't had sex yet."

"No."

"One can tell. Quite right, there isn't a war on. You do not have to cheat death. Wait and enjoy it. Pretty dress. I had one like it in the war."

"I love yours, Mary."

"My friend Jean Muir made it for me. We used to knock around a lot. Sadly she died." *That's what I'd hate about being old. Surviving people. I hate surviving Uncle Frank.* "Pretty brooch too. Do you want to swap it for my medal? It's quite rare. Only 24."

"Sorry."

"Steve gave it to you, didn't he? Otherwise you might not have worn it with that dress. Well, Howard got me this medal. Thought I would have to settle for a Companion of Honour, but its colours aren't nearly as becoming. Howard was implacable. Demanded the Order of Merit for me. Nice session with HM. Ran overtime. She was in the ATS in the war. She could still service a lorry if she had to."

"That was in Victory, wasn't it? I mean, not the Queen, but women servicing lorries, and building planes, and telling the Spitfires where to go."

"The slave speaks! And the slave watches television."

"No, Mary, in the book. It was in my Uncle Frank's collection. I hadn't got to authors V but I read it ahead of time when I knew I was going to meet you. Me and Zoe. It's wonderful. Up with the Dickens, the Flaubert, the Stendhal. Not that it's the same, but just in making you want to read and read."

"Thank you." *She stopped the chair, just short of the reception.* "Who was your uncle Frank that put me in such distinguished company?"

"He was a soldier. He's dead."

"I'm sorry. We used to collect books for soldiers in the war and they had forces editions. On incredibly thin paper. The forces then seemed to have a great appetite for books. I'm not sure they do now. Nor anybody else. Well, what did you both make of Victory?"

"I… we… Well, I think it's really sad. Not just in the characters who get killed and wounded, but the ending. The girls aren't happy at all, even when they're celebrating with their… sweethearts. They know that they're going back to their old lives."

"Victory's an ironic title, isn't it?"

"Good." *She sighed deeply.* "They missed that completely in the television series. It had far too much patriotism and far too little sex. They lost their nerve. Shocking to think that the heroines actually enjoyed the war and were sorry it was over. Still, it paid my debts and it did wonders for sales. I wanted Howard to adapt it."

"Howard?"

"Definitely. Don't think he's just a comedian. Now, before you push me into the reception I have to teach Lady-in-Waiting my handbag signals. I learnt these from the real Queen. Keep an eye on my handbag. If hold it thus it means I need the loo. Thus means this person's a bore, get me out of here. Thus means whisper me his name. Thus is the one you'll see most often. One of mine, meaning 'what does a girl have to do to get a drink around here?'"

I pushed her into the reception. There was a sudden hush. She really was Royalty. Howard scuttled to her, Mum close behind.

"Mary, wonderful to see you. We were worried."

"One tiny bomb scare and all the London traffic paralysed. I'd have got here easier in the Blitz, when real bombs were falling everywhere. Who is this nice woman in the beautiful indigo dress? She's much too smart to be a writer."

Zoe and I caught the drink signal with the handbag. She whispered "My usual" *and I went off to Xan.*

Inspecting me. She's Howard's replacement mother. Pulling out all that devotion, anxiety, protectiveness, need for approval. Will Steve feel the same about me? Does he already? "Thank you, Mary, but I might say the same of you. I'm Alice Devane and I'm a lawyer. Mostly children and families."

"Are you anything to do with these nice children?"

"Steve is my son." No hesitation. I'm glad because he returned right then with a gin-and-Italian for her. The drink of the Victory girls. "I have a younger son, over there, who's drawing. The other boy, taking photographs, is Zoe's brother, Robert. Howard kindly brought us all."

"You can all tell Howard he's a very, very bad man. Why aren't you writing, Howard? Proper writing. You do nothing but journalism and literary politics. Where are those entertaining people you used to give us? Ricky Rubato, Rob Patty, even Bertie Wooster, although he wasn't yours to begin with?"

"I'm sorry, Mary, but I just don't feel like writing about them any more."

"Well, think of some other entertaining people. These are bad times, Howard. People need entertainment, escape. During the Depression the Mayor of New York ordered the cinemas to show only happy films. He was right. I met him. Gentleman Jimmy Walker. One of the last men to wear spats."

"I just can't get a head of steam."

"Pah! I'm 92, I think, and I'm doing one more novel. As soon as that old fart dies and the injunction dies with him. I must be the oldest person ever to get a Carter-Ruck letter. I've asked for an entry in the Guinness Book Of Records."

There was now a long queue of people waiting to be presented to her. Like the Queen. Howard took refuge from her strictures by acting as major-domo. "Now Mary, you remember Her Imperial and Royal Highness…" Nod. "Our host the Duke…"

"Dukey, your back stairs are in a shocking state."

"The Minister."

"Have you come far?" Fixed smile from the minister. Taking the send-up like a good sport. Or perhaps not knowing it was a send-up.

Shedloads of people wanted to see her. Many wanted pictures, but she would not let Robert take any. She gave the drinks signal again and then the one for get-me-away-from-this-bore. "You might as well take me to the loo", she hissed as we pulled away from Scarlett Ferber. By the time we got back, the party was breaking up. Robert had downloaded his photos of people. He was clever and made them all look better. He was doing a roaring trade as people left. So was Cal with his sketches. They had to endure kisses from Scarlett.

Finally it was just Howard and us and Mary. And Richard Heller. I feel bad about forgetting him!

"Now, young man, I would like to be photographed with the people in this room." *Robert did different combinations and then handed the camera to Xan to do some with himself. Xan was still totally anonymous to everyone but me. Respect! Cal was introduced, and sketched furiously.*

"Alice, do you mind taking me to the loo again?" She stopped me when we were out of the room. "You must be very proud of your boys. They have different fathers, don't they?"

"Er, yes."

"You were ridiculously young when you had Steve."

"I'm not Steve's biological mother."

"You're a very good one. I wasn't. Didn't like my son. Shocking, isn't it? Left him with others and went with strange men into low dives."

"Howard took me to one of your low dives. That's what it was called."

"That place." Brief smile. "There was a lot of bad behaviour there. I hope you both behaved badly."

"Howard sang."

"Bad enough." She looked me up and down. "Howard's a good person. He needs to be happy again and to write properly."

"We're working on both. Me and the boys."

"Yes, I can see you are. That's enough time to imagine I've been to the loo."

I wheeled her back. "Goodbye. It was a lovely party. I really liked meeting all of you. Thank you two for the photographs and sketches. Now, I'd like Howard to take me to the car."

I was ready for another long lecture about writing again but she simply said **"Marry that woman, Howard."**

"If you say so, Mary."

"I do say so. Do some courting if you must but remember I haven't much longer. Make it a short story not a novel."

Chapter 41   Debut Match (3)

Mary Varley left and that was the end of the party. Cal and Robert sat down with Richard Heller and worked out how much they had raised for the fund with their sketches and photos.

"Over two thousand pounds. Such is the vanity of writers. Oh, and a huge tribute to your work. Look, it's not much of a thank-you but you might enjoy this. You're too old to have teddy bears" Double blush! "But there's some humour, even satire. And the illustrations are brilliant. Anyway, it's the story of the first teddy bear to become an MP. And he plays cricket."

"Membear of Parliament. Oh, ha-ha. Will Tubby. Good name for a teddy bear artist."[36]

"Would you like some more? I've got plenty of them." I felt a surge of pity for him, having to give his books away. I thought of a failed solicitor I knew, who handed out free legal advice in pubs. Howard and I each had children to take home and we all had a big day tomorrow. The goodbyes were a bit desultory, even between Steve and Zoe who normally have to be prised apart. But we had a quick exchange.

"That was a wonderful evening, Howard. A total thrill to meet Mary Varley, and Claire and Michael and everyone. But you ran the show, Howard. Everyone wanted to schmooze with you."

"They wanted to meet you. I told you people would climb on chairs. Look, are you free some evening later this week? I'd like some alone time. To talk."

"Me too, Howard. I can park the boys. They'll be starting at Marian's, I'm sure they could hang out at the Barneses."

"You tell me when and where. I'll be free." Slightly disappointing kiss. Something was on his mind. We would need a long evening. I had stuff to empty too.

"Young Steve, stop prowling. You're worse than the troops of Midian. On the couch, now." We all assumed the usual unclench-Steve positions and I completed his customary grace. I stroked his hair, now almost too long. "You haven't told me about yesterday's match, so talk me through all of your five wickets. Not just what happened but what it felt like."

"You'll be bored."

---

[36] This work exists. See www.harrybearforparliament.org.uk

"Try me. Close your eyes." To be brutal, it was a bit boring. But as I had hoped, he was the first to fall asleep. We gave him some time and slipped away.

I woke up at 3-30. What is it about me and couches? I didn't remember the duvet or Bungle. I did remember talking about my five-for. Had I reached my second wicket or my third? I thought about going to bed properly. No, definitely my third wicket. Second spell, very slightly downhill…

"Better wake up, Steve. Howard will be here soon with Zoe and Robert and we're going in convoy."

"Mum, do we have to follow Howard? You'll go mad."

"He knows the way. Steve, you know where the bathroom is. Have a proper shave, unless you think that stubble makes you look more threatening." Suddenly he has got stubble. Not like the first time he used the bathroom.

"Steve's got a zit again! Can't bowl with a zit on your back. This one's mine!" Good grief. Steve will have to start selling tickets.

"Is that enough sportsman's breakfast? Check your kit one last time." Add Bungle if you want to."

Hesitation, resolved by Cal. "I think Bungle should stay here. We don't know the rest of the team. Someone might make a remark and Steve might have to punch him, like Tim with Tiger."

Horn outside. Quickly into my car, since Howard's double parked. Hell, Cal was right about Howard's driving. Nice to know that my boys are more likely to die of old age in his car than in an accident. Even with Howard's driving we were almost the first to arrive. The only other car was astonishingly grubby, and jampacked with cricket kit.

The biggest ground I'd ever played on. Electronic scoreboard. I suddenly felt sick. Had to think of something else quickly.

Inspiration. "Howard, do you know an actor called Xan McVeigh?"

"I've played cricket with him a few times. The fastest queen in the West."

"I think he'd be really good as the next Rob Patty."

"Hmm. Rob Patty is many things but not a screamer."

"Xan does not always scream. Did you know he was there last night? As a barman."

"No. I didn't. You've almost made me think."

I got a text message. Still doesn't happen often, and a strange number. "STIFFEN SINEWS SUMMON BLOOD IMITATE ACTION OF…" *And before I could read further Zoe leapt on me from Howard's car.* "Tim and John want you to have Deputy Tiger for the day and loads of luck." *Robert struggled out of the car loaded with photographic stuff, and the Frenetic mascot round his neck.*

"I'm guessing that you're Steve. Felix Lindsay." *Tim's guru was small and if not shabby certainly less than kempt. [Wordpower].* "Howard I know but who are all the other groupies?" *I introduced everybody and he repeated all the names. He wanted to remember them. Up to me to make sure he would meet them again!* "Glad you've brought such a big crowd, do you blokes mind helping me shift this lot into the pav?"

We moved everything from his car and he slit open a big paper parcel. "This one's yours, Steve." *He tossed me a new shirt.* "Only one size, hope there are no fat bastards on the team they gave me. Had a big row with the ECB, but I managed to get the word England into the description." *I looked down.* "All-England Emerging U-19s." *I didn't hear Felix explaining to Howard how the team was made up.* "Finally I told them, call this team England and you pull in some sponsorship money. That swayed them."

"All-England. That's early Victorian. You'll have to bowl round-arm, Steve."

Felix handed me a scorecard. I was Number 8. S F Helson. I hoped no one would ask my middle name. My (former) mum insisted on Feodor. She took a fancy to it. I'm going to say it's Francis, for Uncle Frank.

Biggest dressing room I'd ever been in, even at X school. I changed quickly, and put on the familiar space-material shirt under the new All-England one. The one I wore when I first played with Cal. I wouldn't need the new All-England sweater, but definitely the cap. It was heading to be another scorcher.

"You're nervous."

"Yes."

"If you hadn't been I'd have sent you home. You'll probably feel better bowling a few in the net. Nothing flat tack."

Terrific net. Almost as good as Sam Carter's masterpiece at Glendon Courtenay. I bowled six balls into it and retrieved them. How many times have I done that?

"Like the look of that, Steve. Nice action, you could be in for a long spell. Very attacking length, you going to stay there if they get after you?"

"I think so. That's what Uncle Frank always wanted."

"Good enough, but in that case have you got some mix-up balls? Cutters, slower balls, skidders."

"He's got everything except a zooter and a zamboni!" *Cal and Robert had joined us.*

"Go away, Cal. No cricket for you for two weeks."

"I don't need my right hand. Look!" *He bowled the two mystery balls.*

"On the money. We'll talk about them later, young man, but the others have started to arrive. Now, Robert, what sort of camera is that?"

Some kids came with parents, a few had driven themselves. Most seemed to know each other, as did the parents. I didn't take to any of them much. Pushy dads and standoffish mums. And all terribly blasé about the match. I think their sons had been talent-spotted early and hot-housed. One nice couple – so obviously professors they could have been sent by Central Casting. And their boy was very polite.

Some of them were with counties. Hell. They'd come in sponsored cars. They were all a bit up themselves. It was like my last term at X school. Would the captain be a shit and would I hit him? Not a shit, I decided, but well up himself. Asked who I was because he had to and couldn't imagine why I was there. Well, fuck off, Did he want to play with ten? One good joker. Number 4 bat. Francis. Omen? His parents looked like total boffs but they were nice too.

"Steve, I hate waiting. Do you mind bowling a few? Don't strain yourself."

"Sure." *Francis was quality. All right, I wasn't at full pace but he had so much time. Like Tim. He was playing regularly for Oxfordshire but not first-class. Two other pace bowlers joined in. Also below full pace, but I could tell they would be quicker than me. Well, had I really expected the new ball?*

Francis stepped out of the net and took me aside. "You'll get a lot of bowling today." *Good, but how did he know? He looked up at his parents and smiled. His dad was doing some kind of giant calculation on paper and his mother was correcting proofs.* "They don't understand cricket and they always take work with them but they come to every big match. Is that your mum talking to them? She looks too young. And that's Howard Foy, isn't it? I've seen him interviewed. Is he your dad?"

"Not yet. That sounds weird but my whole set-up's a bit unusual. I've been sort of adopted. That's my new mum and the kid with the sketchbook is her son and my elective brother and the kid with the cameras is his friend and that's his sister."

"Your girlfriend."

"Obvious?"

"Obvious." *Good.* "You're lucky. To have one who likes cricket. Mine didn't."

"I'm sorry."

"It's an ordeal sometimes. Cricket, I mean. Playing day after day. I'm not sure I could stick it as a living. Like James Marriner-Goldschmidt. Ten wickets on his Test debut, the new Shane Warne, and he preferred to become a chef. But cricket's all I'm good at. I've picked up some rogue cricket gene in our family. My double great-grandfather was captain of Oxford but after that everyone was some kind of genius like Mum and Dad." *He smiled at them again as they both worked away. I thought sharply of my (former) parents, with the constant spreadsheet and the constant Novel. But this family was at peace with each other.* "I haven't got a hope of Oxford. I haven't got a brain, like the Scarecrow." *He danced like the Scarecrow. Brilliantly and I cracked up. Great footwork for batting.*

"But the Scarecrow actually has a brain all along." *Mum taught me that, on the night I told her everything.*

He thought for a second. "You're right. But I don't think he'd get into Oxford."

"If you're not going to play cricket what would you like to do?"

"Be an astronomer. An old-fashioned one with an optical telescope because I haven't got the brain to be a radio astronomer."

"Hell, you should meet my friend Nick. He's in the desert in the States somewhere. He's mad on astronomy. He's found an asteroid and he…" *Nearly said he'd named it after me but that felt like such an ego trip.* "He's looking for others." *I wanted one for everybody. He hadn't found any more, the slacker!*

"That is so brilliant. Can you give me his e-mail? What about you? If you're not going to play cricket what would you like to do?"

"Teach cricket." *I had that one ready.*

The Indian team coach arrived and we lined up to greet them. All in team blazers. A few looked well over 19 and one looked about 12. Some maharajah was managing them. Felix called him "Your Highness" and he meant it. While they got changed Felix gave us a quick team talk. "This is not an official England match but I expect you to play as if you are representing your country. I want respect for our visitors and the umpires and if any of you sledge or dissent or cheat I will make sure that the right people know. You've all had a tough season and it may be hard for some of you to pump yourselves up for an extra one-off match but that's what I want to see. I want workhorses not show ponies and I want teamwork. Now if it makes you feel like a team, go and huddle but personally, I think that's all bollocks. I want you to huddle your minds." *Captain looked anxious and Francis smiled.*

"This is a time game. That's what they wanted and it's what I like. Lunch at 1-30. Tea between innings. Twenty overs from 6. Now you're all here because you've been recommended and you know how to play. You will make your own decisions. I've only one instruction. Win the toss."

He did a few warm-up fielding drills. Nothing out of the ordinary except that he suddenly started reciting random bits of poetry. I started to listen – and dropped a catch. "I wondered if we had any poetry lovers among us. Wonderful thing poetry, but it takes your mind away. 'At the round earth's imagined corners blow your trumpets, angels'" *But this time I caught it. Got the message: keep my mind on the game.*

We weren't a unit. The captain preferred the players he knew, the other bowlers all fancied themselves. The keeper was flashy. I'd have to force myself to love him. Shame he wasn't Joe or Johnny.

We lost the toss. They batted. Shock. Another perfect wicket for Helson S F to bowl uphill on a scorching day. Not that he was going to bowl for a while.

We went off and waited for the umpires to lead us on. Some of the fathers hissed instructions, and Felix looked narked. "You know how to play by now otherwise you wouldn't be here." *All of my "groupies" came and hugged me. A few surprised looks. Well, fuck off: I had some people who still love me.*

"Filth" *said Cal and Robert.* "Clean up the filth."

"Give them hell, son," *said Howard and Mum. He must have taught it to her.*

"Into battle my hero," *said Zoe. Massive kiss. Sniggers and a long whistle. Fuck off, again. Just because your girlfriend was more interested in her nails.*

The umpires moved off. I followed (last in line) and stepped on the field. Even if I fainted, I had now officially played for All-England.

I was sent to third man. Predictable. And a good place to watch the first over and get used to things. I made a decent stop and pinged it into the keeper. "Played, Steve!" *Francis, not the captain. Assorted shouts and squeals from my fan club.*

Second over I was the only fielder in front of square on the leg side. Two boundaries clipped past me. Bowler glared at me. I glared back. Fuck off and bowl in the right place.

Their openers were phenomenal. 70 for none off the first nine overs. It would be 100+ before I got on. Then suddenly I was wanted. Bighead Bowler 2 had a niggle. Hmm.

Uphill. But the ball still quite new and hard. Could do something with it. Except that I wasn't even getting a slip. "Sorry, Steve, but we've just got to plug the gaps. Until things happen."

"Sure." *I hoped the keeper would go for every nick. He fancied himself.*

I marked out my run-up. I looked round and saw my fan club. All unknown to me a few weeks ago when I was the lost boy of the nets. Now I was bowling in front of them for All-England. How could I be angry? "Truly fast bowling carries with it a sensation of pleasure; it is to be borne along in a sense of elation." Frank Tyson. I emptied myself of all feeling except my glad animal action.

"Nought for 120! Twenty off the last over."

"They were going to declare. Nobody else wanted to bowl it."

"I bowled pies all day. They just helped themselves. 'Hi, I'm Steve and I'll have the pleasure of serving you. Our speciality today is pies. And more pies. And still more pies.'"

"You could have had three wickets, at least. Two catches dropped and the keeper didn't even try for one."

"You can't blame fielders. I dropped a catch myself. Right in front of Felix."

"You did well to get there. Mid-wicket should have gone for it."

"Well I went for it and I got there and all I had to do was hug it like I've told you two, millions of times."

"Anyway, come to the reception. Everyone's waiting and Howard's talking non-stop to the Maharajah about Mihir Bose to delay the speeches."

"You can see all the pictures I took. Zoe's showing them to Francis. I only did him and you from our team. Didn't like the others."

"Same here for my drawings."

"Thanks, guys. I'm just not quite up to it yet. Tell them I'm looking for a contact lens."

"You don't wear contact lenses."

"That explains why it's so hard to find."

I knew I was being stupid but I couldn't face all those people thinking, what the fuck was he doing here? They disappeared. I glared at my All-England kit. I nearly threw it all away, but then decided Cal and Robert might like it.

"Steve, are you decent?"

"Yeah."

"Shame."

"Zoe, you can't come in here."

"Then come and join me. Us. Your mum's anxious and Howard's angry."

"I will, in a sec."

"What happened batting? I was on the loo."

"Out first ball. Caught and bowled."

"The boys said it was a brilliant catch."

"It was a stupid shot. We're trying to save the game, we're a man short, and I try to hit a boundary first ball. Stupid, selfish. If I'd stayed a bit Francis might have got his hundred. He's been great to me all day and I couldn't even stay with him to his hundred. What's he going to think of me? At least Felix didn't see my innings. He took our player to hospital." *He looked in agony. But why was he playing football?*

"Felix told Howard you bowled well with no luck."

"Felix was being nice or maybe it's because Howard's important."

"I don't think so, Steve, but anyway, come to the reception."

"I will. In a tic."

"You're still my hero." *Great exit line, Zoe.*

"This will not do." *Howard this time. Icy but scary.* "Hiding in here and being a big drama queen in a sulk. You are being abominably rude to everybody. Including your mother and me. And Cal and Robert who want to show you their work today. And Zoe who wants to be with you. Back out there with me right now. Or say goodbye. And say goodbye to Tim and Felix. I'll tell them you're not a real cricketer, you're just a snivelling, selfish wimp."

"Felix won't want to see me again anyway."

"You know that? No. But you can make it a certainty by sitting here and beating yourself up instead of following me and being gracious in defeat."

"I'm coming."

"About time. Oh, and give me £20. For your Primary Club[37] membership."

I handed it over. "I'm sorry, Howard."

"Say sorry to the others too. And plenty of listening and pleasant conversation for everyone else in that room."

I think I did all right. The Indians were nice – especially the one who hit 175. Mostly off me. The maharajah said I'd bowled well. "Thank you, sir. I'm glad I didn't bowl badly, you'd have made 500." *I hoped that didn't sound sarky. Evidently not, because Howard laughed, for real, not his "company laugh".*

The maharajah thought for a second and said "We'd have made less. Fewer." *He had to be an English nut. Then he made a speech, thanking us for a good contest (victory by 150 runs in a one-day match!) and telling anecdotes about Mihir Bose. (Had to meet this guy!) Felix was still absent and no one on our side offered a reply. Howard stepped forward.* "Accustomed as I am to public speaking, I propose on this occasion to feel compelled to say a few auspicious words." *He never wastes any material! He kept it short and the party broke up.*

The Indians all made a point of saying goodbye to me. Must remember their names. When they break into their Test team I'll be able to say I once played against them.

Francis came up with his parents. "Great meeting you, Steve. See you again."

"Doubt it! Maybe in the desert, if we go and see my friend Nick."

"Yeah. I'm writing to him. Thanks. And thanks for bowling at me."

"A trip to the pie factory."

Back to the cars with our lot. "Thanks for coming. I'm sorry I played like a dead gerbil and I'm even more sorry I was such a baby afterwards. Thanks for kicking my head in Howard." *Mum flashed him a look.* "Making it as a cricketer kept me going for a long time, so it hit me hard learning that I'm not going to make it. Not at this level. But I've got Glendon Courtenay and the Frenetics, and maybe Marian's. If they'll have me. And you. If you'll still have me."

---

[37] A charitable club which provides sport and recreational facilities for blind and partially sighted people. Cricketers are expected to join if they are out first ball when batting. See www.primaryclub.org

I think they will. Major goodbyes from Robert and Howard and a maximum from Zoe. Then Mum and Cal drove me home. Home.

Almost dead. Fifteen overs on the field, quite a few more in the nets. Running round the deep. But I had to fire off some emails

"Brendon/Daniel, You would think by now all religions would learn to stay away from your dad. Asking the imam to prune the quince tree – it was bound to end in tears. Listen, you never told me you'd had a test trial. Felix Lindsay told me. Yes, the legendary coach. I met him but I won't be seeing him again…"

"Dear Nick, You'll be hearing from this great guy called Francis who's a cricketer I met and who's nuts about astronomy. Sadly, Asteroid Steve crashed out of the cricket universe today. Will spare details, but hurry up with all the others you promised me."

Chapter 42   Declaration

"Wake up, Steve! Felix wants to talk to you."

"Hmmph?"

"You got an extra half hour's sleep because he talked to me about my zooter and my zamboni."

"Maybe he'll sign you."

"Oh and Tim phoned and asked about the match and I said you were crap and he doesn't want to see you again."

"Thanks for speaking up for me. Gimme my phone, you've cost Felix a packet." *Nice of him to call.*

"Steve? Listen mate, I'll come straight to the point. Would you like to work with me at Lords? I'll be there Sunday mornings through the close season and I'd like to give you an hour one-to-one. And maybe some sessions with Francis as well."

"What? Me?"

"You got some other Steve staying with you?"

"But I was... crap."

"You had crap figures. That doesn't mean you were crap. Indian boys didn't think so Most of them have played first class. Ranji trophy. The bloke who scored 175, he's Virender Sehwag's cousin? You bowled fifteen overs flat tack on a flat track. There's a poem there somewhere. You were always trying to get wickets. Anyway, I saw plenty that I liked. Sorry I missed your batting."

"I'm not. Out first ball. Great catch but what was I doing?"

"Your brother told me. Took him longer to tell than your entire innings. Listen, was the ball there to be hit?"

"Yes, but first ball?"

"The second ball could have been unplayable and you'd have missed four."

"What happened to Jack? In hospital?"

"Bad. Ruptured Achilles tendon. I knew that but it took them four hours to tell us. Now, you haven't told me you want to work with me?"

"Hell, yes."

"Look, I've got to sort this out with your mum. You never told me you were 16. We need to keep stumm about that. I could get into trouble. You weren't allowed to bowl all those overs. Nanny says so. I'm going to suggest that you register with Tim's country, Northants, as an Academy player. I'm one of the coaches there, but it's a fair tramp to Northampton so we'll work at Lords. They pay my fees. You'll be committed to them for at least two years – unless I chuck you out. You progress and you come to Northampton pre-season, work with the other players, maybe play a few second-team games. But your education comes first. Your mum and Howard said you're going to a new school. You and that mad brother of yours and your girlfriend and her brother. I had a laugh about all your groupies but that was really important to me. You've got people who care about you. They'll keep you on the rails, help you through the bad times. Which there will be."

"I let them down a bit. After the match. I hid in the dressing room. Howard had to kick my head in."

"Good. Proves my point. Listen mate, you know what really sold me on you? You bowled those fifteen overs – and then you bowled flat tack at our top four in the nets. Did anyone bowl at you before your innings?"

"Howard and Cal and Robert but some official came and said the nets were for players only."

"Glad I wasn't there, you'd have heard words spoken and language used. Steve, if you want to be a professional, find a way of handling stupid officials. If you do, you'll be one step ahead of Tim and Tom. And me. See you round, mate. When we're sorted with your mum."

"Felix. Thank you. Oh, wait. Which hospital is Jack in?"

"Your brother knows. He already asked me." *I might have known.*

"Oh, Felix? When did the McConnel twins get their Test trial?"

"Mate, I hate to tell you this but I've never heard of them. I thought it might boost your confidence. But from now on in, I'll tell you the truth and you'll have to make the most of it."

"You can't fall asleep again. We're going shopping for Marian's. Mum's left a list and some cash. This bed's crap. Can't believe I ever slept here. Mum's getting me a new one. Elevated. No good for you because you're scared of heights, but just right for … the Cat! By the way, Tim doesn't think you're crap and he's having dinner with us at the Barneses tonight."

Big noisy dinner at the Barneses. Belinda's so cool. Gets everyone organized, never seems to be working herself. She's a designer. I think she designs people too.

Tim was there with both of his dads, and Mary, his mum. She's a systems analyst (?) First time I'd met Steve (namesake!) his stepdad. Joe's and Belinda's partner. Makes their commercials and videos. Brilliant cricketer (like me). Self-confident, extrovert (not like me). Met Mary and Tim at a Frenetic match and they went to live with him. Can't imagine that – taking the family of someone in your team. But they get on brilliantly and Tim loves them all. Maybe things will work out with my… Must stop calling them (former). Will call them first mum and dad and no insulting brackets.

Tim really chuffed about me and Felix. Says I'll learn lots of poetry too. He knew Deputy Tiger would work!

Howard full of jokes but subdued with Mum. Why? Now I'm even more nervous.

Howard was bang on time for our head-clearing evening.

"Howard, this bottle is way too good for Chinese takeaway. Feast for two – I didn't let you choose, it's pretty good and it leaves the maximum time for talking. Boys are parked at the Barneses overnight."

"How did induction day go at Marian's?"

"Howard, is this a diversion? I genuinely don't know. Steve hasn't been back at all and Cal swept in with Robert and three other kids, two boys, one girl. Noisy but good-mannered. The new ones passed the Bungle test. They ate everything that wasn't nailed down and swept away again. I asked Cal how was school and he said brilliant over his shoulder. That's enough for me. We've got other things to talk about. Things we want each other to know."

"Yes." Deep sigh. "I asked for this and now I wish I hadn't. I wish we were having cocktails, or shopping, or in a room full of interesting people. Or spoiling your boys. Just having fun. And that's exactly what I have to talk to you about." Deeper sigh. He was really struggling. He got a reprieve as the Chinese takeaway arrived. He was complimentary. Genuine, the food was good, but it was also an excuse not to talk. He told me a long story about a visit to Macau, when it was still Portuguese. Interesting but not intimate. He speared the last piece of pineapple. I cleared everything away and returned.

"That's it, Howard. Unless the Jehovah's Witnesses come calling we won't be interrupted again. We both wanted to talk. I'm going to flip a coin for who goes first. Don't be like Cal and say 'best of three' if you lose."

But I lost the toss. "Okay, me first. That wasn't the first bad call I've made in my life…" and I told Howard my past, as I had told Steve but in less detail. I didn't think I needed to explain so much to a mature writer. He listened attentively, sometimes asking a question but more for my sake than his, to give me time to think or calm down. When he heard about each of the men who deserted me he clenched his fists and could barely sit still. Finally I caught up with the present.

He took my hands. "I knew some of that but it's even more wonderful now. Your life. What you've faced, what you've done, virtually on your own. Raising Cal, taking on Steve, what you do as a lawyer for other children. And being funny and sharp and lighting up a room when you come into it. And being real and deep. Oh hell, me now. Saying what I have to. And you've made it so much harder."

"Just say it, Howard. It doesn't have to be good dialogue, say it as it comes. Trust me, Howard, nothing you can say will shock me or repel me, except…"

Suddenly she was shaking and crying. I held her. The crying stopped and her breathing slowed down. Then she broke away violently.

"Oh God, Howard, if you're leaving… Is that what you want to say? Well, goodbye is fine. Christ almighty, I've had two men leave me. One did it by lawyer's letter, another did it by phone. I guess it's progress that you're doing it face to face. But the first man fucked up one life, the second fucked up two, and now the third wants to fuck up three…"

"No!" I held her again for a long time, until we were both breathing slowly. "That's not why I came at all. I want to stay with you for ever. But you have to know something about me."

Another deep sigh.

"I betrayed Marian."

"You had an affair with someone?"

"No. Much worse. I betrayed Marian on the first day of our marriage. No, on the first day of our relationship. I made her a promise I didn't keep, didn't understand when I made it. Never understood."

Suddenly he relaxed. I've seen it so often with clients, friends, my children. The moment they've decided to let go.

"You know that Marian was my editor. My first novel, The Speculator, was accepted by Random Harvest. It was way over-written. They gave it to Marian. The greatest bit of luck in my career. A brilliant editor and a wonderful woman. Beautiful, passionate, exciting, magnetic. Like you. But taller, and more extrovert. Phenomenal with people – like you but I think more willing to let rip when she was for someone or against them. The Bible says somewhere 'let your yay be yay and your nay be nay'. Never a doubt over Marian's yeas and nays." He closed his eyes, clearly remembering a few.

"Almost instantly I fell in love with her – as a person. And yet it's important to remember that we were also writer and editor. That relationship – it's always different. It's like being in the office compared to being at home. You act differently. In a way, we never left the office. No!"

He was furious with himself. "I'm preparing a defence and it's a rotten one. 'I'm a writer and writers are different'. Crap. Writers should behave decently and take responsibility when they don't."

He glared at his fingernails. "But Marian was a wonderful editor. She taught me William Faulkner's rule of good writing. 'All your little darlings must be killed.' We had some real up-and-downers over her … homicides. But she was right. By targeting the passages I was most in love with she hit the ones that were likely to mean least to readers. Marian taught me a great deal more. Vital skills, which I use now. How to give interviews, how to broadcast, how to schmooze critics, how to review other people honestly but without making enemies, how to write slick 800-word articles on demand. And she taught me literary politics, which are much more poisonous than conventional politics. Think – after-dinner mints at the Borgias."

A bit prepared, but he was a writer. "Marian taught me to dress, how to get by in company. Howard Foy, Mr Urbane, he was her work. I wasn't a total mess when I met her but I wasn't sorted. I had an unhappy love affair in my twenties and I decided – in a typically immature male way – to punish my ex by trashing my life. Howard Foy: the Lost Years. Walking out of two good jobs. Walking out of my cricket team. I was Minor County, you know." I really tried to look impressed.

"I made stupid bets, even worse than Joel Hegarty of the Frenetics. Lots of one-night stands. Drink and drugs – and driving under their influence. I did jail time. Does that explain the way I drive now? The good thing about jail: I got the idea for my first novel, The Speculator. It came terribly easily – like all my stuff – but for one fatal weakness in the plot. I came out of jail and my good friend Joe Barnes got some of my life back on track. Found me jobs as a copywriter, introduced me to the Frenetics, where for the first time I met…?"

"Anthony Scorer."

"Is the right answer. And Anthony Scorer fixed me a job teaching English in a prep school who were not fussed about my jail sentence. I don't think that could happen now. It turned out that I was a good teacher – I ran the cricket as well as the English and they had their best-ever season. Mind you, that was Luke as much as me. Luke Marriott. A wonderful batsman and the nicest kid you could imagine. I know teachers find them occasionally – the kid who makes it all worthwhile. And without knowing it, Luke solved the plot problem in The Speculator and gave me a major new character. I gave him Luke's first name in his honour but changed everything else. I was vain enough to believe that The Speculator would be a worldwide bestseller and I didn't want Luke to be trapped in it like a boy in amber. Christopher Robin Milne wrote a sad book about that…" Just like Steve – using literary flannel to delay the painful part.

"I brought Luke into the Frenetics and he was a star batsman. I think he could have gone as far as Tim Morrow. But you know what happened to him instead. That is so amazing, your meeting him and the boys…" More flannel!

"Anyway, all this is to say when I met Marian I was half-finished – as a writer and as a human being. I always told her 'you edited my book and then you edited me.'" Laughter, but uneasy.

"Marian and I clicked together and we had a lot of fun. Lots of parties and literary events and then replaying them afterwards and jeering the famous people there. We used to play this game of going to restaurants with celebrity photographs on the walls. You know the kind of thing: 'to Elena, with thanks for your wonderful zabaglione!'[38] under a cheesy smile. And we'd find some

---

[38] In homage to the legendary Elena Salvoni, of Bianchi's, L'Escargot and L'Etoile.

celebrity we didn't like and have this loud conversation, saying 'who the hell's that?' or 'wasn't he in the National's Hamlet? I think he played Yorick.'"

I remembered just in time that Yorick was a skull, and laughed dutifully, but he was far away. "We did a lot of shopping, mostly for me, turning me into a fashionable new writer. Marian pulled me in some jobs as a travel writer and we blagged some great free trips. Best of all, Marian loved cricket. She was the noisiest spectator in history. When I played for the Frenetics in Dudbury – the village where time goes to sleep – she made me feel that I was in front of the Saturday crowd at the Lords Test. Anyway, we had a lot of fun. It was even fun to have screaming rows over her editing."

Another heavy sigh. He was running out of flannel and could no longer delay the confession, whatever it was. "But eventually, we had a serious conversation. We discussed children. We both loved them but I couldn't give her any. A legacy of Howard Foy, the Lost Years, and permanent, as you know. We talked vaguely about adoption or fostering but I knew that she would be making a sacrifice if we stayed together. Then she told me what a relationship meant to her. Emotional security. Being able to share your emotions without ever feeling that you have to hide anything, or trim or compromise, because it's a bad feeling and it might hurt your partner and make him feel bad about you."

He was shaking. "And she asked whether I was up for that and I said, yes, definitely. And that was the betrayal. I was totally sincere, which makes it worse. I signed up for something I didn't understand at all. I knew as much about real feelings as … Bertie Wooster. And I found real feelings as scary as … Honoria Glossop." He smacked his fist. "God, how clever that sounds! How 'literary'. But that's just it. I can't cope with real feelings at all. They have to be dressed in clever language and witty dialogue, like guests at a fancy party. Feelings have to be good-mannered and charming. Emotions are just scenes from musical comedy – the love scene, the quarrel scene, the sad scene, and always the happy ending scene. Listen, I'm at it again! But that is true, and I knew it then but I didn't tell Marian. I made her that promise which I couldn't even understand, let alone keep.

"But she believed me and we got engaged. At her suggestion we announced it at the launch of The Speculator, because it would create a story, and she made a big gag of my being a cheapskate and wanting to marry her to save her fee for editing, and I made a gag about her being wanted for the murder of ten characters in The Speculator, and yes, she was right, we became a story, we became Britain's newest, smartest, funniest literary couple, and it really helped the sales. And we stayed that way, right through our marriage. Because that was the only way I could make it work."

He closed his eyes. "I treated marriage like a club. Marian wanted a marriage that was a home. Wouldn't you?"

He opened them again to look at me but I wasn't going to give him any help. He had to work through this himself. "We had a wonderful social life. We made a great team and you could always count on the Foys at parties and openings and launches and readings. We had open house. Fridays became Foydays where smart, funny people could just drop in. Of course there were freeloaders among them but we accepted this. When we wanted people to go home I started playing the piano. Cricket matches every weekend in summer and a winter tour.

"If we couldn't have company we gave ourselves lots of surprises and treats – trips and shopping. If the Foys were sighted in a store the news was flashed to the City and the store's share price would go up. When we went to India to play cricket with Mihir Bose the rupee rose dramatically against the pound. It sounds so shallow that life but we were happy there. I really think… Marian too. And I know we made other people happy. On one of our cricket tours … No. Forget it." Another long sigh.

"But when all the people had gone, and all the shops were shut and there was nowhere to visit, when Marian and I were alone and she wanted to talk about something important – that's when it all went wrong. Anything with real emotional content for her. I really couldn't understand her. It was like an exam in a foreign language I didn't know. I'm actually poor at other languages and none of my books has ever translated well…"

Another flight into literary flannel. He checked himself. "Anyway those conversations always failed. She would always get angry and I would always panic and she would always get angrier and we would quarrel, and as we quarrelled we would get more and more convinced that the other was being unfair. The quarrels never got resolved and we always ended up in separate rooms. And eventually we would patch up. Usually by going shopping. And every time I would replay the quarrel and work out logically, rationally, what I could have said and done instead, and file it away for next time. But next time we'd have the same sort of quarrel all over again, because I said and did the same things all over again. Eventually I did find something to say to head off the quarrels."

"You're absolutely right, dear, as usual."

"Joe's phrase with Belinda. Now for them it's a shared joke, a sign of intimacy. It never got that way for me and Marian. For me, it was just a plea to be let off the serious stuff and allowed to go away and play again. And Marian would agree. So she never got any emotional life at all, not even through the quarrels."

I wanted to say something but he pushed on. "Of course I worked terribly hard as well. Genuine creative frenzy, I really, really loved my writing then, but there was another reason. It kept us both in the writer/editor space, not the husband and wife space. That caused another problem, because my writing got better. I learnt to edit myself and I needed her less and less at a professional level. It got so that I would occasionally make deliberate bad judgements in my writing, so that she could go on picking them up. And I would quarrel with her because those quarrels were safe and fun, not like the real ones. How sad is that, as the children might say? Making myself write badly. Mind you, it was good training for writing Rob Patty."

Sorry, Howard, I'm not going to pick up that ball for you. "By the same token, I asked Marian for lots of advice about interviews, broadcasts, journalism, literary politics – all the stuff she had taught me. But I had learnt it all myself by then, and I think she saw through me.

"Then we got one great piece of luck. I landed an interview with Mary Varley and Marian came too, she was one of her heroines. Mary really took to us both. We were a substitute family for the one she didn't like. That gave us both a shared emotional life. We also got a shared professional purpose because Mary was at a low ebb then, financially and critically. Marian and I re-launched her. We got the great Victory trilogy re-published and rediscovered. I didn't like the TV series but it solved her financial worries and made her an icon. She did two more novels, edited her diaries and letters, did some worthwhile non-fiction. There's another novel in waiting which no one's seen… Scandalous. It's been injuncted.

"But eventually Mary could look after herself again, in the literary world, and so could I, which left Marian a little in the cold. She took on some other writers, but no one she actually cared about. So that emotional outlet was gone. She was back in the Eternal Sunshine world of Howard Foy.

He stared at a picture of Cal, aged 8, with Bungle. "It might have been different if we'd had children, but I was … not suitable to be an adopter or a foster carer. Because of the Lost Years."

I felt a flash of anger. Bloody agencies and children's departments with their tick-boxes. Howard and Marian could have given a child a wonderful home. "I was saying that Marian eventually trained as a teacher."

"I'm so sorry, Howard. A stray thought."

"Very dangerous, thoughts. They should be banned. Teaching was a very logical move for Marian. Being with children, doing something creative and with emotional content. And a world of her own, not being an endless … performer in mine. We gave up our Fridays, dropped some of the flakier people in our entourage. We still had a pretty major social life, and kept up our treats, but we focused on people and things we really enjoyed. But then things got worse again, because Marian got so frustrated and tired. There were a lot of dysfunctional children and families at her school, but what really got her down was the endless paperwork, controls, directives. That's what drove her to rage – above all, being ordered to teach English badly. And having to get permission to do anything imaginative.

"And I would listen and sympathize and sometimes help her fight back, but I never really understood how much this was taking out of her and what was going on for her, in her soul. Because all that sort of stuff was beyond me.

"And then Marian got cancer." Struggling very hard. Looking away. "Of course I couldn't cope with that at all. Hope and despair, pain and terror. Not my repertoire. And I couldn't give Marian a safe place to pour that out. I just got lost and choked and tried to pull us back into our… old world. Where *I* was comfortable. That's what I did to Marian, whom I thought I loved. Poor Marian got more support from her girl friends. Even from some of the children she taught."

He looked back at me. "That's what I wanted you to know. You with your real life, you could be letting yourself in for someone without one. Just like my characters. When Marian died, I hated them all, with their silly, slick, facile dialogue, living in their synthetic worlds with their cartoon emotions…"

"For God's sake, Howard, don't be such a drama queen!"

He looked shocked, as I hoped, and shut up, as I planned.

I continued more gently. "Howard, you have been pouring out grief and guilt and I know it's genuine but I also think it's become a script for you, which has taken you over. I assume you're looking for something different because you've taken up with me and my boys. Well, now it's time to choose. I'm going to run a bath. There's room for two, even with a big cricket-player like you. If you still want the new life, it's in the bath. If you want to continue with your script, stay here as long as you like and let yourself out."

I swept away. Was I being a drama queen? I lit some candles and ran the bath.

"Lime-scented candles. Are they your favourite too?"

"Not specially."

"So you thought I would come?"

"I had my hopes."

"Beating myself up for the rest of my life or sharing a bath with you. That was a tough decision."

He tore off his very good clothes with flattering speed. "Are you sure there's room?"

"Yes, if you cuddle me." He stepped in and held me and we got comfortable. For a small eternity (that's in Ricky Rubato although I think he nicked it from Mary Varley!) we closed our eyes and blissed out.

He opened his first, and then turned my head around. "It's silly to come all this way and not look at you. You're so beautiful, Alice."

"You're not so dusty yourself, Howard. You're in great shape."

A momentary frisson. "You nearly added 'for a man of your years.' More than twenty years older than you. Does that worry you?"

"Howard, the only thing that's worried me since you came into my life is that you might leave. Like the others."

He almost hugged the breath out of me. To give me time to catch it again I ran some more hot water. "Howard, this is hard to say but… please don't think you know what would worry me about you, or not like. I'll always tell you. And I want you to do the same for me. And the boys. Agreed?"

"Agreed."

"You told me a lot about Marian. You're afraid you're going to let me down as you think you let her down. Are you certain you let her down? After all, she stayed with you. Marian was a beautiful, brilliant woman who earned her own living. With any reasonable divorce settlement from you she would have been pretty rich. I'm sure there were loads of other men she could have gone off with. She stayed with you. Go figure. Howard, I can't unpick your relationship with her, because I never knew her. But it always takes two to make a relationship work and it always takes two to make it go wrong. Trust me on this, I'm a divorce lawyer.

"Now, accepting only for purposes of argument that you did let Marian down because you could not deal with deep feelings, I would also like you to remember that I'm not Marian. Perhaps I don't need to talk about deep feelings, or perhaps I can talk about them to someone else. I listen to deep feelings at work, maybe I'd like to get away from them into the fun world of Howard Foy. I've had a ball so far. Maybe all I want is … the kindest, funniest man in the world, who loves treating me and my boys but is also there for us in the bad times, and who makes us all feel special and loved. Howard, if you cry in here the bath will overflow."

"Sorry."

"I've told you not to say sorry!"

"Sorry."

We both laughed. "Wasn't that nice, Howard? Shared joke. Personal ritual. Now, before we go further, can I tell you the things that are important to me? Then you can do the same for yourself."

"Of course."

"This house to be respected. Hell, you can see that I'm not fanatical about housework – that's Steve – but I hate seeing anything that spells mess or neglect. Along with that, no freeloaders."

"They will be excluded. I have a little list and they'll none of them be missed."

"I'm still not at ease with some of your literary friends, Howard, and I'm not sure I could spend every Friday evening in a room full of them."

"No more Foydays. Perhaps we could play a little Parcheesi."

"That must have sounded really controlling. I'm sorry."

"Who's sorry now? Who's sorry now…"

"I think we may need rules on singing and piano-playing. Nothing after ten thirty, nothing above top E flat."

"I once lived in an apartment block with an opera singer in the top E flat."

"Was that a little darling that got killed?"

"In the massacre on the first day of Ricky Rubato."

"I'd like you to write again, Howard." Momentary tension. "That sounds snide about your journalism, but I really would like to see you writing about characters you care about. Either the old ones or some new ones. You're wrong about the old ones. No one had to read about them or watch them. People chose to, because you made them loved. And times are hard, Howard. People want to be entertained and spend a little time with characters who take them into a … nicer world."

"Mary said the same. I do have some ideas for another Rob Patty series."

"Do you love Rob Patty?"

"Yes, although he's such a louse."

"Then write about him again. I would know that you loved yourself."

"Well, Rob Patty then…" Trance. I think he had begun instantly. "What else?"

"Don't be too indulgent, Howard. Especially towards Cal, with his dangerous charm. I was glad when you cracked down on Steve when he sulked in the dressing room. And don't spare my feelings, when you're angry with me."

"All right, you stupid old bat."

"Needs more work. Now your turn."

"There's nothing I want beyond seeing you."

"Sweet, but don't be silly."

"All right. If I'm going to write – properly – you will have to be indulgent when it takes over and I can't think of anything else. My idol, P G Wodehouse, called writing a series of spasms and you never know when they are going to come on."

"Accepted."

"And writing is a sedentary occupation so none of Cal's rich desserts for me. Some ignorant people have mistaken this wall of muscle for a paunch."

"You won't get fat in this house. Cal will burn it off you, so will Steve. And so, I hope, will me. What else?"

"Being indulgent. I know why you're worried about this but I really, really would like to treat you all, regularly. I made a lot of money and Marian taught me to spend it creatively and Anthony Scorer taught me how to make more of it. It would make me happy to spend money on all of you, if you could feel happy to receive it."

"You mean hoovering Nicole Farhi and Karen Millen each weekend? I could just force myself…"

The which being agreed, we stepped out of the bath and dried each other, slowly and tenderly. We glided to my bedroom and I had a sudden, unfamiliar dilemma.

"Howard, I've actually never had a man in here. I've had affairs but always away from here. Do you … need to sleep on one side or the other? Do you like a glass of water? Do you need a reading light?"

He crashed onto my bed and lay face up. "I need you to get comfortable."

Which I did, in his arms. "But not too comfortable. Because I'd like us to paint each other. With our bodies. We've just had a water colour but now let's try a big painting in oil. Like the Pointillistes. You know them, Seurat and Signac. Tiny dots of paint. Like this." A series of very light kisses. "And like this." A series of very light touches. "And we'll find that some of these dots explode into light and colour and some are subdued."

So we explored, but long before our canvases were completed they took a very different direction. "My God, Howard, that's not Seurat that's Jackson Pollock!"

And we both hooted with laughter. As we did again the following morning. As we did again, still in the nude, when Howard tried to play and sing "Too Marvellous For Words" at my piano, when the boys came back from the Barneses.

Chapter 43   More Highlights

"Howard, it was so embarrassing!"

"Why, was I off-key?"

"I wouldn't know. But it was a shock."

"Why was it a shock that I should want to tell your mum that she was too marvellous for words?"

"But you had no clothes on."

"Sometimes these things have to be said right away."

"Howard?"

"Steve?"

"Do you really think I'm a writer?"

"Yes.That's why I brought you here to meet Elena. No one's allowed to be a writer in London until they've met Elena. Marian told me that."

"Do you mind talking about Marian?"

"Not any more. Your mum got me through that. And you and Cal. You can be haunted by your past or enriched by it. The choice is yours. I used to say that all the time, now I believe it. And you're learning that about your childhood, aren't you? I'm glad you're on terms with your birth mother and father."

"They'd like me to visit them at … home. I haven't managed that yet. We still meet in restaurants. Like acquaintances."

"I had a good talk with them. They're working for the school, you know. Your father's got our money working much more efficiently. Your mother's helped some of the Marian's companies with marketing and promotion."

"Really? They never told me."

"I can't tell you more. I think it would be good for you to see them at home. Now then, you wanted to talk to me about a literary problem?"

"Yeah… it's just that I don't know where to stop. My story, I mean. You got me started and it's all poured out and I can't believe that there's so much already, and you and Mum and Cal and Zoe don't help when you take over, we all seem to have so much to say. There's tons more and if we do it all my story's going to be like Bleak House."

"All right. Let's go through everything else you might want to tell them. Your devoted public."

"As if… Do you really think people are going to be interested in some schoolkid who's a bit sad but then gets lucky?"

"Perhaps not. But perhaps they'll like the people he meets, the sparky younger kid, his amazing mother, the sassy but vulnerable girlfriend, or the witty, urbane writer haunted by self-inflicted guilt. And the sharply-drawn minor characters."

"Sorry. It isn't just about me."

"Don't worry. I think they will care about the sixteen-year-old schoolkid who keeps his giant mind and his giant heart in adversity and who gets everything he deserves. Don't be afraid of giving them a happy ending. It always worked for me. Anyway, what's left to tell?"

"Well, Mum got approved as my special guardian."

"Not much to tell there. It was over in five minutes, wasn't it?"

"Yeah. Should I tell them what happened at Marian's? Not just to me, but Zoe and Cal and Robert?"

"The four of you cut a swathe through the place in your first term. They can read about you pretty much non-stop in Cosy Moments. It's like the Old Testament: 'and the rest of the acts of Stephen and all that he did, and the acts of Zoe and Calum and Robert, and all that they did, are they not written in the book of the chronicles of the kings of Israel?'"

"So nothing about the football season?"

"You could mention en passant that they elected you captain of the team, and that your friend Roy Hodgson came down to do some training sessions and converted you into a defensive midfielder, and you went right back to B for Bellow to thank him. And that Robert's turned into a really solid centre-back.

And that you couldn't entice Cal to play football but mad Rabbi Glick turned him into a basketball star."

"He jumps like a maniac but he doesn't take it seriously. He just says 'another day's work for … The Cat.'"

"Anyway, all of that is in Cosy Moments. So is your lecture on 'Some Great Authors A to S' and Zoe's on Mary Varley. More triumphs."

"Mary wrote most of that herself, when you set up that evening with her. It seemed a bit unfair."

"Those lectures are not a contest, Steve. You're not doing someone else down, if you make them as interesting as you can."

"That's true. And it meant a lot to Zoe, after what happened at her last school when she said she knew Sheila Fereday. She didn't get picked on for knowing somebody famous, everyone was really glad that she'd shared it. But what about her in the pantomime?"

"Cinderella is fully reviewed in Cosy Moments."

"And I suppose they can see Cal's drawings all over Cosy Moments, and Robert's photographs, and the photomontages they did together. They're doing one for all of us for Christmas, so try to look surprised."

"All of us? How big is this thing?"

"I think they've hired a lorry to take it out of Marian's. Last Christmas they could have put all of my life on a postage stamp." *Oops! Self-pity again. Bad Steve! I should be over that.*

"Steve, remember our pact we made? Repeat with me, 'I deserve everyone.'"

"I deserve everyone. Now you."

"I deserve everyone." *Elena came up and offered us some more coffee and it gave me a little thinking time. I know Howard's right and I know I deserve everyone in my life now, but sometimes I still think I need to earn them. And Howard sometimes feels the same way about Mum and Cal and me. Elena asked about Mary Varley, and Howard made sure I told her as much as he did. Putting me in the space for Famous Writers Whom Elena Knows! Eventually we were alone again.*

"All right, so I leave out first term at Marian's, except that it was brilliant for all of us. We're the Gang of Four, although Cal of course has his own 'posse' as well. Do they want to know about winter cricket with Felix?"

"I will simply tell them that he's given you an extra yard of pace and I can't keep you out even with my no backlift."

"Well, that's not quite true but I do hurry you. Felix said I shouldn't leap so much, because I was losing pace. I've always been hung up about my height."

"Wordpower!"

"But not any more and I seem to be getting a spurt anyway. Felix thinks it's because I'm happier."

"A plausible theory."

"You know, he hardly talks about cricket at all in our sessions. Philosophy, psychology, astronomy – he looks for asteroids too, like my mate Nick - and of course, buckets of poetry. Then just as a throwaway he says, 'try holding the seam like this, see if it works for you.' Same for my batting. 'The world's whole sap is sunk, the general balm the hydroptic earth hath drunk, why not shift your left hand an hour anti-clockwise on the bat?'"

"I think you can see why Tim works with him. How about your own coaching, at Marian's?"

"I did the coaching course, but I feel I got more from Uncle Frank and Felix."

"Rupert says he's never had so many volunteers for cricket."

"I had to do a kind of coaching course of my own, for staff members and older kids. Robert and Cal did a manual for me, with pix and drawings. Rabbi Glick's a psycho fast bowler, way worse than me!"

"So your cricket is booming. That's enough. And you're still going to play for Glendon Courtenay as their professional."

"Hell yes! If they'll have me."

"They might like to know about Marjorie."

"Turning professional as a singer? Edwin's her personal manager and accountant, but Mum's friend Ray Corvino is her agent. He makes me laugh."

"Maybe, but he's a huge power in the music business."

"You know what he said? Marjorie was the first singer he'd ever known to turn 'He's A Tramp' into a sad song. That happened with Mum at the piano in Glendon Courtney. And Ray got a recording contract for Jesse and Rick Kinch. Not as a tribute band but in their own right. They are bringing out a CD called Peace Bullet.[39]

"Ernie and Dorothy won another dance contest, but she wants Cal back again for the Latin American section. Luke and Laura are investing money, their own and Anthony Scorer's. They've got more time and energy, because Billy is so much calmer. The hour each week with Cal and Robert makes a big difference. And trading drawings and photos. Billy time is totally inviolable."

"Luke and Laura are backing Marjorie. They're going to set up a club for her and Johnny's going to run it."

"But Howard, if we tell them where that club is, we've got to tell them about you and Mum in Glendon Courtenay."

"It was your mum. I just sat in silent admiration."

"Come on, Howard, you found Miss Caslon."

"Yes, but Max Foggo's doing the story about the Redeemers. It should be his big breakthrough. It wouldn't be fair to spoil his exclusive."

"He's getting all the rest, surely we can have Mum and you and Miss Caslon?"

"Very well. You did set up a sort of ghost story and it should be left unfinished."

***

"Howard, could you give me some child care for a few days? I need to go to Glendon Courtenay in a hurry. Ernie says there's activity at Caslon House. Lots of repair work and maintenance. But also a woman, alone, with flowers."

---

[39] True and an excellent one. See www.jessekinch.com

"A mystery woman, who could be the sister with all the secrets? I'd like to come with you. Remember, I'm a detective writer even if my detective is silly-ass Bertie Wooster and the country house is full of corpses before he has a clue who did it."

"I don't think I need a master detective, Howard. Ernie's looking for her and I just want a conversation."

"Forget detecting, Alice. I don't want you to go alone into a nest of religious fanatics. We can park Cal and Steve with the Barneses – or leave them here."

It was a mistake to tell the boys where we were going and why. "We're coming! You'll need me, the Cat, to break in and Steve for muscle."

"We don't need your special skills, Howard will do any rough stuff and you two have school."

"Take your bat with you, Howard and smack a few Redeemers."

"I did not hear that offence of incitement. We're away for five days, maximum. You okay here for that time?"

"Yay! Party!"

"Steve will be in charge."

"Gloom. Housework."

We were going to share the driving but Alice gets too impatient with mine.

"This is silly, Howard. Ernie can't find this woman with all his local knowledge. How am I going to find her, even with the help of ace gumshoe Bertie Wooster?"

We stayed with Luke and Laura and Billy. We had a conference in Glendon Courtenay with Ernie and Dorothy. They confirmed one sighting of a mysterious lady at Caslon House. In the evening. Clear night with full moon. On foot, with flowers. At the front gate, then walking round the perimeter fencing. Back at the front gate, half an hour later, no flowers. Then she'd disappeared. Ernie and Dorothy didn't want us to talk to their informant (I think he might have been a poacher).

Where was she staying? Had she hired a car? Did she take a meal anywhere? Ernie and Dorothy had checked everyone they knew and drawn a blank. "I'm sorry to have got you down. She might come back. I could watch the place for you."

"Thanks, Ernie, but that's too much to ask." We switched to the sudden flurry of repairs and maintenance. Same as before, all done by strangers in plain white vans. Nothing to learn from them.

We went back to Luke's and Laura's and I ran through all I knew, from Ernie and Max Foggo. "Present owner, The Reverend Doctor Elisha Hoover, of Reading. Still styled Leader of the Church of Redemption, but there is a schismatic faction led by The Reverend Malachi Fitzsimmons. It's a very small church, but very rich. Principally property, but some publishing. They had a religious publishing venture in Britain for a short time and guess who was a non-executive director? Our favourite cricketer, the Right Honourable Paul Russell." Some whistles.

"Doctor Hoover often feels the call to minister to vulnerable people with valuable assets. He has a long record of litigation involving disputed wills and settlements of property. There's a current appeal involving his Reading property – son trying to set aside a deathbed gift by his mother. He was really blackened by Dr Hoover and his counsel in the lower court."

"What response did you get to your threat to sue him, Alice?"

"Sharp letter back from his lawyer, denying any liability for Caslon House because it was not occupied by him or anyone acting for him. My suit was never really going to trouble him. And I couldn't truthfully claim that Cal and Steve had been traumatized by their ordeal in the sea. Imagine them in the courtroom. Cal would over-act wildly and Steve wouldn't try. We have to find Miss Caslon and get her to take on the Redeemers. They stole her home and her life. The courts could give her home back, and maybe her life with it."

For lack of anything better to do we went to Caslon House ourselves the next morning. "They've done a lot of work, Howard. That's where Cal and Steve walked in and I don't think even a real cat could get in there now. How did Miss Caslon break in? She must be middle-aged."

"Middle-aged, eh? Doddering, probably drooling."

"Sorry, Howard. But where would you even try to break in, with your magnificent physique?"

"You've stumped me there. And where did she go afterwards? On foot. One road. Takes you back to Glendon Courtenay, where she was not seen, or goes miles into nowhere in the other direction. Surely somebody met her, in a car?"

"Who knows? We've come here, I might as well leave her the letter. The ad will go in Max's paper tomorrow, asking her to contact me. Then all we can do is wait."

We went to the pub in Glendon Courtenay for an early lunch. My treat. Minor problem – the pub had a giant chalked notice: SORRY WE CANNOT TAKE CARDS TODAY.

"Cash point at the bank next door."

But the one outside wasn't working, so I had to queue for the one inside. I vaguely noticed a middle-aged woman doing some business with the lone clerk at the counter.

"Thank you very much, Miss Garamond." Suddenly, I was very alert.

"Excuse me, ma'am," I put on my most disarming smile. "But were you once known as Miss Caslon? Please don't be alarmed…" However, she didn't look alarmed. More stunned. I'm not good on expressions, only dialogue and plot, but I thought that she also looked relieved. "Miss Caslon or Miss Garamond. Forgive me, but someone must have said 'you're just my type.'"

Instant pallid smile. "My late father was fond of that joke."

"My name is Howard Foy." No recognition, and served me right. "I'm really just a courier." Another instant smile. She got it. "A courier for my principal, who would very much like to meet you. She's a.. a…" I couldn't think up another punning typeface but I came up with "… a very bold type of person." By now I had eased us both to the threshold of the pub. She stopped dead.

"Liquor was made by Satan and this house is his temple."

"Pack my box with five dozen liquor jugs. Have you seen that one in either of your typefaces, Miss Garamond or Miss Caslon? It's one of the sentences printers use for demonstrations. It uses each letter of the alphabet, although some more than once, so it's not a pure pangram."

This drivel served its purpose of distracting her mind and I could see her counting out the letters in the sentence. By the time she had got them all, I had eased her through Satan's doorway to Alice's table. "Alice darling, may I introduce Miss Garamond, who has also been known as Miss Caslon?"

"Talitha. My father liked to pretend that he could not remember our names. Amos was Mr Bodoni. I was Miss Garamond. Jo... Josiah was Master Zapf." Tremor in her voice. "That was when we were little, before the Lord's messenger came to us. When my grandmother … tried to take me from the Lord she bade me choose another name. That was all I could think of." Really? Or had she chosen the name that might get her discovered?

"Please sit with us, Talitha. Howard will bring us all lime juice with soda."

Gray hair, but she's not old, ugly, short crop. No make-up. Dark shapeless clothes.

"I need to go to the house again. And then I must return to the community of the Redeeming Lord and atone for my sins of pride and deceit."

"Howard and I will take you back to the house. But I think it is your house, Talitha, and you can go there when you wish."

I slipped back with the drinks but she ignored me and looked straight into Alice's eyes. "Who are you?"

"I'm a lawyer, Talitha. I will explain why I wanted to see you, but may I show you something first?" She pulled out a snapshot from her handbag and passed it to Talitha. She looked at it and began to shake. "How came you by this? Was this sent by him or the Evil One?"

"That is not who you think, Talitha. That is my son, Cal. After a new haircut. He is very like Josiah, isn't he?"

"Jo."

"Jo. Same age, left-handed, loves cricket. They are very alike, aren't they?" She handed over another snapshot.

"But that one is Jo. I took it."

"My elder son found it in your house. May I tell you the story of my boys and your house?" I told it in my most "lawyerly" way. Just the facts, no emotion until

475

they were saved from the sea, when I could not help myself. Howard took my hand. She followed every word intently.

"The Lord took Jo but spared your boy."

"I don't know about that. His brother was with him and had made him wear a lifejacket. He is not a believer, neither am I, and your community would think us both very sinful."

She pondered this briefly and then asked "This happened when?"

"In August. The 23rd to be exact."

"That's when the Lord sent me the vision of Jo, calling for me. In the sea, only I could not get to him."

She started to shake again. Alice took her hands. "You were not to blame. You were his loving sister. You are here for him now."

"It took time. To be alone. To become Miss Garamond. To find my friend in England who would help me go to him. They have found her and I will go back to them. The lost sheep shall stray no more."

"May I ask you first to read something? It will be painful. This is the local newspaper's account of the inquest into your brother. I don't think you were there. You didn't give any evidence. Most of it was offered by Elder Hoover."

"The Shepherd." I handed over a photocopy of the story Max had retrieved from his paper's archive. She read it briefly. "That's a lie!" People looked round but she didn't care. She read "'Josiah was an adventurous boy who loved the sea.' Lies! Jo was terrified of the sea and he howled and cried when they tried to force him into it. Which they did. Hoover and Fitzsimmons. All of them. Taunting him for lack of faith. Telling him he must be born again and baptized or he would burn in hell. I stopped them dragging him in. But that day, I wasn't there for him!" She cried. Gasping, racking sobs. Like Steve when he finally let go. I took her hands again and Howard stared down all the other people who had started to stare at us.

The sobs reduced and her breathing became normal. "You are still his loving sister. It was you who gave him his cricket, I know."

"I told them it was a gift from God, which he would use to display the glory of God, and it would be a sin to deny it."

"Indeed. And you got your father to put up the cricket net in the garden and I think it was you who bowled to Jo, for ever and ever. He was a very good batsman, wasn't he? And you said he must play for the boys' team, in Glendon Courtenay."

"They went with him. I wasn't allowed. Because… Well, I wasn't. But Jo told me everything that happened, in every match. Not just to him but what everyone else did."

"Sweet. I get the same from my little one. He and you were different, weren't you? You knew there was a life outside."

"I knew all the secret ways in and out, which they knew not." Flash of pride, but then she went rigid. "But those paths were shown me by the Tempter, to lead me away into Hell!" Some people started to look again, but Howard quelled them instantly. "The Tempter led me away from him when they forced him into the sea and when he was crying for me!"

"But they took advantage of the Tempter, didn't they?" For the first time, she looked at Howard. "You always resisted them. All alone. Your parents and your elder brother were in their power totally. But you held them off. All alone, because you loved your little brother. And your love was too strong for them. They made sure you were away, that's when they forced Jo into the water. Did they pull him in themselves or simply taunt him to go in himself? And that bay is terribly dangerous, even for a strong swimmer and one with a lifejacket. I'd like to think one of them tried to save him. Or did they all just fall on their knees, praying and wailing, and then deciding how to lie?"

"Howard!" I thought that too, but it wasn't on my agenda. I took her hands once again and made her look into my eyes. "Who was it, Talitha? The person you went to meet."

"Dave. Jo's cricket coach. He was still only a boy, but an incredibly fast bowler. At least I thought so. And really sweet and kind and a brilliant coach for the younger kids. Made them laugh even when they did something bad."

"Just like our Steve. Perhaps he too was meant to close the circle."

"I met him just before the season began. They let me go with Jo to a practice. Dave taught me to bowl so that I could bowl at Jo. And we… talked afterwards. They noticed and took Jo and me away, but he managed to slip me a note. Contact details – useless for me, I had no use of a phone or computer. But also a place we could meet in the woods. I was banned from going to matches, but I found the place and the ways to get to it. We left notes there for each other and when we could, we met. We just talked. And held hands. He promised to wait for me until I was 18 and could leave the house."

"I wish you'd had a lawyer. You could have left at sixteen, or even earlier and asked to live with another carer."

"We kissed for the first time, on … that day. Nothing more, but we talked and talked. When I got back, I heard that Jo had drowned. Everyone was deadly calm and saying it was the Lord's will but I got hysterical. And Elder Hoover said that a great judgement had been brought down on our family because there was a sinner amongst us and I knew he meant me and I got more hysterical and he said the devil was in me…"

She stared far into the distance, and her lips moved in and out with no sound. "Talitha. I can sense that you are in deep conflict. Part of you thinks that Elder Hoover was wrong and wicked, but another part of you cannot give him up, or the faith and the community on which you built your life. May I make another suggestion? Howard and I can take you to our friends, who are very good people. You will see that right away, especially when you meet their little boy who is … afflicted. You can stay with them as long as you like. No one will see you or speak to you unless you wish. You could seek guidance from the Lord and reach your decision. I promise that we'll respect it."

"Honey, the Lord's telling me loud and clear that I've been suckered for years and I want you to get my house back for me and put that swindling, murdering son of a bitch behind bars."

Missouri. Her accent. A legacy of her grandmother. We heard her full history at Luke's and Laura's. We picked up her bags from the farmhouse B&B where she'd been staying. She had left her English friend (another breakaway from the Redeemers) after a threatening phone call, which they thought came from the sect. The cult. The crooks. I made a note of the friend's name, to persuade her to talk to Max Foggo. I didn't want to give him Talitha.

Her father seemed to be clever and charming but also a weak, feckless man. He had inherited money, and made and married more of it. Their family had led a rootless life, shifting between countries, communities – and charlatans. None of the charlatans had been so costly, financially or emotionally, as the Reverend Doctor Elisha Hoover.

"Guilt. That's what he was good at. Making people feel guilty because they didn't believe in him enough. Mom and Dad were easy victims. So was Amos. They all died in the care of the Redeemers. They have houses where doubters are sent away for fasting and prayer. Fasting was clever – saved feeding them and gave them hallucinations which they could say were visions from God. I was sent to one of those houses, after Jo's death. I met my friend there. We held out for a while but then we gave ourselves to the Holy Spirit, aka the Reverend Doctor Elisha Hoover."

"Forgive me, but did he have or attempt…"

"Sex. Feel free to say it, Alice. No. I don't think that interested him at all. Only fucking with minds, and money. He collected weak minds with a lot of money. That caused the Great Schism. He didn't give enough of the take to his sidekick, who tried to take over, and now the little Church of Redemption has Pope Elisha and Anti-Pope Malachi. And they've now come to believe that their dispute is about religion, not money, so they cannot strike a deal."

"You've been with Pope… in Doctor Hoover's community all this time."

"Grandmother Caslon got me away from him for a time. She set up a passport, bank accounts, identity for me as Miss Garamond. But I went back to him because I felt lost and sinful and in terror of hell because we are in the last days and only a very few will be redeemed. And when I returned to the church I felt happy and very close to our Lord. And there were the orphans."

"Orphans?"

"The church had orphanages, in the Balkans, Latin America, Africa. He taught redemption by work as well as by faith. I was … called to work in two of them. In Albania and Angola. Both desperately poor. Now I raise money for them. And they did… good work in the Lord's name. Food, shelter, education, care and love. And we were never allowed to preach at the children to join the Redeemers." I bet you weren't: they didn't have any money. Clever move by Doctor Elisha. Orphanages. Something to put in the shop window for investigators and critics, another excuse to raise money, a cheap place to park doubters and something that would make it much harder for them to leave and denounce the Redeemers.

"But you kept your doubts, didn't you? You maintained 'Miss Garamond', you were in contact with your English friend who broke away and, above all, you remembered your brother."

"That was the one thing I could never believe. That his death was the Lord's will. Or punishment for my sins. If I was the sinner, why didn't the Lord drown me? The Redeemers couldn't explain that one. They just said I lacked faith. I put my doubts aside, mostly for the orphans' sake but partly because I was afraid of being lost again. But then, last August, I had that vision of my brother and I had to see the house again. As his sister, not as a Redeemer."

We all sat around for a long time. With a visible effort, Alice then said "Talitha, would you please give me a pound?" She did so, and Alice skipped over to Luke's computer and printed out a receipt. "I am now your solicitor. You have instructed me to act against Dr Elisha Hoover. I am therefore abandoning my son's action against this individual. I will draw up an affidavit for you to sign. I will also need a copy of the deed which your father used to transfer Caslon House to the Redeemers. Can you get that?"

"I have a copy. Grandmother Caslon gave it to me. Alice, what if we win? What am I going to do there, in that house? I have no life over here, I have no life anywhere."

"Hello. I'm Billy. Have you come to see the bears?"

He took her away without even bothering with her name. I saw Alice crying and shaking. I led her into another room and held her. "I'm sorry, Howard. I hear so many sad stories. I don't know why hers should get to me. I'm too close, I'll give her to Portia…"

"She trusts you and you will do a wonderful job. But now I think you should go back home and see your boys. You pack, I'll sort everything with Luke and Laura. Talitha will be fine here. Billy's taking care of her. And I'm driving."

Talitha eventually returned. She seemed much happier. "That Bruno's a bad, bad bear. Here's the deed my father executed."

"Undue influence… There's precedent." Alice sounded like an automaton. We said goodbyes and drove away. For miles Alice was silent and she shivered although the heating was on full. Eventually she dozed and woke up on the motorway. "Howard, you're allowed to do 70 here. It's called a motorway."

"I hope that means you're better. You want me to put my foot on that pedal?"

"You bet."

"Then would you marry me?"

"What?"

"You heard. If you want me on my knees, I'll pull over to the hard shoulder. But I mean it. We don't have to be married but I would like to be … the one who's around when you've given out too much and you need to be taken care of. Who takes care of you the way you want. Who even learns to drive the car the way you want."

"I want to marry you, Howard. Everything else you say would be nice too."

I put my foot down. Vroom! I could get used to this. I took a break for a pee and a quick phone call home. Home. When I went back to the car, Alice was wildly excited. She waved the deed which Talitha had given her.

"That darling man, Mr Caslon. He stuck in a reverter clause."

"Meaning?"

"The house is given in trust 'as a place of daily prayer and worship by the Church of the Redemption.' If not used in that way, it reverts back to the original owner and his heirs. It is not used in that way. Dr Hoover told me, through his lawyer, that Caslon House was not occupied. That is beautiful. She hates the Redeemers but she can get her house back from them because they don't use it for their worship!"

When we arrived home (!) the place was spotless (Steve) and aromatic with kitchen smells (Cal). "Mum's favourite. It's called chanfana. It's Portuguese. But there's lime pie after." We all ate heaps and then played Monopoly, and Bungle let her win. I caught her eye and we told the boys we were engaged.

"About time," said Cal but neither of them could keep the indifference going for very long and we collected protracted hugs. They let go only when Alice fell asleep.

* * *

"Well, after that Howard, surely we've got to give them your engagement party? With Mary Varley and everybody at the Low Dive."

"It was leaked into the papers. Robert got an offer for his exclusive pictures, but it was very disappointing. They paid more for those sneak shots of Simon Cowell's goldfish. Anyway, it's official. Your mum and I are engaged."

"I'm glad your brother came, pity about Mum's parents. Howard?"

"Steve?"

"Wasn't it a brilliant idea of Cal's, for you to rent a floor from Mrs K next door as your office?"

"Yes, it was, and the new series of Rob Patty advances in giant spasms and your idea of Xan McVeigh was inspired because it means I can make Rob a cricketer. But I've learnt a bit from your mum, and that isn't what you wanted to talk about."

"Howard, did you mean what you said to me and Cal after the engagement party?"

"Oh no, we're not repeating that, it was so 'literary' and over-prepared."

"Stendhal once said that a son is a debtor given to us by nature, but a stepson is a debtor given to us by love."

"Aaagh!"

"Which book by Stendhal?"

"Lucien Leuwen. It was unfinished."

"But you did mean it?"

"Totally. And we're going to be blubbing again in a second. There's a lot of blubbing in your story. Don't worry, there's nothing wrong with a few tears. People used to weep all the time, women and men. The Victorians introduced that stiff-upper-lip nonsense. Anyway, it is true. I'm thrilled to have you and Cal in my life and I want you both to be the happiest kids in the world. And if you aren't, you will be savagely punished to within an inch of your lives."

"Marian's! That's what Rupert says to everyone at the beginning of term. Did he get it from you?"

"That doesn't matter. But your public will want to know whether you are the happiest kids in the world."

"Let's see, great school, working with the best cricket coach in the world, fantastic home, another fantastic home I can go to any time,"

"Two other homes where you can go to any time."

"Oh. Yeah. Fantastic mum, fantastic brother, fantastic stepfather to be, girl friend who makes me feel … electric every time she comes into the room. What a crap life."

"Do you really feel that way about Zoe?"

"Totally."

"Good. Because your mum does that to me."

"Howard?"

"Steve?"

"We've stuck to our pact. Me and Zoe. About full-on sex, I mean. But the nice thing is, I think we know more about our bodies than if we'd just gone straight into it, like me and Angie."

"That's one of the great rewards from the choice you've made."

"Do you know, Howard, that when we lie close together our heartbeats actually synchronize?"

"I thought that only happened in silly romantic novels by Howard Foy."

"Well, it's a medical fact. When I get uptight, I put my head in her lap, and when she gets uptight I put my arms around her and she kind of burrows into my chest and we always end up with the same heartbeat. Howard?"

"Steve?"

"Was I … more interesting when I was unhappy and misunderstood?"

"No. That's just a literary convention, especially for characters of your age in fiction."

"I worry about that. I mean, I'd hate to get… complacent."

"Steve, you don't do complacent. You drive yourself in everything, cricket, writing, teaching other kids. You can't … fill the dishwasher without thinking how you could do it better next time. And there's no one who worries more about other people. When you got flu you went to pieces because you couldn't take Zoe and Cal and Robert to and from Marian's. And guess what, they made it under their own power. And they enjoyed looking after you."

"Cal went mental with chicken soup every hour. Maximum drama queen as usual. Do you think Mum will like her Christmas present?"

"I think she'll love her Christmas present, and it was a brilliant idea and a great way to use the extra day you had to spend at home."

"His writing was well hard to read at times and even when you could read it, lots of stuff made no sense."

"You did a really good edit. Anyone can write but only a real pro can edit. Marian always said that."

"Howard?"

"Steve?"

"I do worry about Cal. A lot."

"You always have."

"As soon as I met him I wanted to look after him. And even more, after he led me to everybody. And after I nearly lost him because I was stupid and weak. And nearly lost everyone. I still feel the same way. And I still get eaten up if he's unhappy and I can't do anything about it."

"Steve, that's never been your responsibility. It's not mine, either, or even Mum's. People need to be unhappy and scared – sometimes – and they learn to cope with it themselves. Our only job is to love Cal and make sure he knows that when he is having a bad time. Is he having a bad time? Never looks like it, but is there something Mum and I should know?"

"He beats himself up a lot about his art work. Mr Gray pushes him and he's made him paint, but he says he hates his paintings. He really respects Mr Gray, which makes it worse."

"I hope and believe that's a temporary problem. He is a maximum drama queen, so his work is going to be either rubbish or genius. Nothing in between. We must wait, and meanwhile be absolutely honest about his work. That's not what's really worrying you."

"He's still in love with me. As in… eventually becoming lovers. As in … living together for ever."

"He's told you this?"

"He's drawn it. I found them at home, when he asked me to find some drawings of you and Mum. Drawings of us when we're older. Brilliant but spooky – like those computer-generated images of missing children when they're years older. Us together in our 20s, 30s, even older. Not having sex, but just … well, intimate. Maybe I was meant to find them. But anyway, I hate the idea of telling him that's not going to happen."

"Have you discussed this with your mum?"

"Yes. She said…"

"Don't tell me what she said! Then if I agree with her you won't think I'm just agreeing with her. I think … you should give everyone all the love that you can, and not worry about the love that you can't give them."

"Wordpower, Howard! Did you just think of that one?"

"Yes. Although I might have read it in Woman's Own."

"I still feel really guilty. Whenever Cal hugs me, jumps on me, has a play fight, I know that he wants more, and that he wants it for ever."

"Guilt is a really bad emotion. Trust me, I'm an expert. You feel guilty about Cal, so you are going to push him away? Because he loves you more than you think you can give back, you give him nothing at all? Cal hugs everybody in his world, and jumps on them like a cat. You're going to be the only exception?"

"That's pretty much what Mum said."

"People want to love you, Steve. Don't deny them their pleasure."

"Mum said that ages ago. And Zoe."

"And your response?"

"You're absolutely right. As always."

"Is the right answer. And Steve?"

"Howard?"

"Do you think Cal would ever have trouble finding a partner? Or a solo life without you?"

"Hell, no. I wish he'd ... get together with Robert."

"Wouldn't that be neat? Tie up all the loose ends, wouldn't it? Might happen, but nothing we can do about it. He's nervous about being Robert's boyfriend because he thinks it might affect their relationship as artists. I can understand that. Now, Steve. Elena's too polite to throw us out. No more talking."

"So we jump straight to the big Christmas scene?"

"Always worked for Dickens."

Chapter 44 Christmas Extended Highlights

Dear Mrs H

Even now, looking back over 50 years of a wonderful marriage (!), Steve and I agree that our first term at Marian's was the happiest time of our lives...

I was nervous about Marian's because I thought Robert and I might get picked on again. But no. That just didn't happen. There was always something going on that people want you to join but if you didn't want to join you were left alone. And if you knew someone interesting people liked you to share them.

And I was nervous about losing Steve. To competition. But no. He never noticed people drooling over him. I noticed them all the time, and lots of the girls had better tits than me, or tum or thighs, and faces and hair but he just said they didn't have Zoeness, even Caitlin who had all those and read more books than me. He spent every spare minute with me – carrying my books everywhere in a marked manner. Not that he had many spare minutes. Student Council, football coach to juniors, cricket coach to everybody (juniors, seniors and staff), constantly in demand to 'shred the head' (bowl out Rupert in nets) and earn celebration points.

I retired from cricket. And all other ball games, where I'm equally hopeless. Dad's genes missed me completely. Worried it would mean less Steve time, but he did so much running, biking, swimming as well (with me).

S and I had lots of dates. I took him back to Ursinho's – not to buy anything but to show him off to Emerson (cruel?) We joked often about being Britain's most boring teenagers.

Went to regular poetry readings (coach Felix switched him onto poetry) in vegan café. Lots of other Marian couples wanted to double-date with us because we made them happy. Steve more ~~gorgeous~~ beautiful than ever. He was really made up about being taller (the old one was quite enough for me but it helps his bowling) and his upper body got stronger. (He forgot this sometimes when he hugged me!)

I wanted him to go out for Prince Charming in panto. Refused point-blank (had to be girl anyway. Vapid Vicky. Bigger thighs than Steve's! Bitchy, but true) But he signed up for sceneshifting. Sheila came to last perf. Maximum kissy-kissy. "Darling. Wonderful performance. Such emotion. Gave us all the subtext."

"Thank you, Sheila, but didn't the scenery move beautifully? That's what made the performance."

Did something unprofessional when I saw her and Howard in audience. Adlibbed a line when Fairy Godmother promised me the transformations. Big laugh from her and H but not many others. And S said something really wistful when I replayed it. "I have always relied on the kindness of strangers."

"That should be my line." S still surprised at being loved. His upbringing... Big step for him to go to first home on Christmas Day.

And I was nervous about Robert. No need. He kept the weight off, made swimming team and year football team as centre-half (S's coaching!) and took millions of photos. Could have made squillions as celeb portraitist (even flattered Vapid Vicky) but still preferred wildlife. And of course he joined Cal's posse (ultimate in-group). They worked a lot together, multimedia, esp huge secret project in R's room (evident Christmas present). Easier to board aeroplane to New York than enter R's room. Wanted so much for R and Cal to get together, but Mum said don't push it. Would tie things up so beautifully. Instead – R secretly pining for C secretly pining for S secretly guilty about C and secretly guilty about Z (for feeling secretly guilty about C) while Z secretly angry with C (for hold over S and R) but also secretly remorseful because not C's fault for pining for S (and C brought S to Z in first place).

None of which stopped us being the Gang of Four. Maybe we clung on to the Gang of Four, all just kids who really like each other and have fun and never have to make hard choices...The Gang of Four still becomes the Couch of Four if we see S lying down on one! And we do really like each other and the Gang do have fun and I love seeing S with R and C because I get a picture of him with our kids...

S and I keeping to pact. Tough sometimes, but lots of discoveries. Feel as though we are having our Christmas stockings but big presents still waiting!

Will close now – summoned by Mum for kitchen duty. Huge meal for everyone here on the day (goose not turkey, as in Dickens). All presents bought (had inspiration for S's!) Will try to write again on the Day, but may be blotto on the Couch of Four!)

Love to Futureself from the former Zoe Barnes

Everything would be totally brilliant if I weren't such a crap painter. And Steve.

"Don't look at this! It was brilliantly drawn and now it's a mess. I told you ages ago colour just gets in the way."

489

"I'm not an expert, but it still looks brilliantly drawn to me, especially my hands and you said hands are really hard and that's why painters always put one of Napoleon's inside his waistcoat."

"Can you just... take it away?"

"Where to? Howard's office?"

"No, not fair on him. It already looks like a Salon des Refusés. Charity shop. Anywhere. That's my last ever painting. I'm telling Mr Gray-A-R-A, I'm sticking to what I know."

"Cal, suppose you'd done that at cricket? You'd have stuck to orthodox slow left arm and you would never have learnt to bowl the Chinaman, the zooter, the zamboni or the zombie." *Flicker of vanity at his new mystery ball and then all serious again.*

"Steve, I wish you wouldn't be so nice all the time. You said you had a bad side. The first day we met. Well, I've seen you at full moon and you still recycle newspapers. You still look after me, and Zoe and Robert. You always talk to me even when you'd rather read or do your homework. You always let me feel brilliant when I think I'm brilliant and if I'm not brilliant you say I'm not as brilliant as last time and you never say I'm stupid even when I am and I wish you weren't nice all the time because then I wouldn't love you so much." *Major display of the bounce and look-away routine.*

"Why don't you want to love me?"

"I do, but not as much because it's just... not fair. On you and everyone else."

"Cal?"

"Steve?"

"I'm no expert on love but I learnt a bit about it this year. From everyone but starting with you. Anyway, it's not like a recipe book where you measure everything out – so many ounces of love to Mum, so many to Howard, so many to Steve. You just pour out what you can, to everybody. And the more you give to anybody, the more you find yourself giving to everyone else." *Sudden inspiration.* "Look, I'll prove it to you mathematically." *His best subject, other than art. Leonardo was brilliant at maths too (he told me).* "When I met you, how many people did you know whom you loved?"

"Mum." *A beat.* "Portia and Mrs K."

"Let's stick with Mum for convenience. Now let's look at your world now. Mum, me, Howard, Robert, Zoe, Belinda, Joe, Tim, Billy, Laura and Luke, everyone else at Glendon Courtenay, all the Frenetics, your posse at Marian's, your basketball team and Mad Rabbi Glick, your climbing club, Mr Gray, even when you're furious at having to paint not draw... Probably some other teachers I don't know."

"So?"

"So do you love Mum any less than when I met you? Not the way it looks to me. Or her."

"Some days I hardly see Mum at all."

"Doesn't matter and you know it. Think about my question. Do you love Mum less, about the same, more compared to summer?" *Thought.*

"More. It wasn't always... right between us in the summer."

"QED. Now, fast forward to Christmas Day. Don't know about you, but it's going to be completely different for me." *I froze up. I remembered Christmases past. Everything as it should be, presents, turkey, crackers, hats, the Queen, family game, but feeling all the time that they were doing it out of duty. And Uncle Frank never coming till Boxing Day, even if he had Christmas leave, because he didn't feel right about being there on the day itself. Would I get through my visit this year.*

My brother was looking at me. Not anxious, not even sympathetic, just being there for me if I wanted to spill. "Totally different and I want to soak it all up. And the only thing that could spoil it would be my brother, not jumping on me and hugging me like he does everyone else." *Predictable response.*

"I think you've made a thousand hugs this season. Who says you're not an all-rounder?"

Howard's settled really easily into our household. A little too easily. I want him to stamp a little more of himself on it. That said, he does drive me nuts when he plays my piano. His pedalling. Or rather not-pedalling. My training kicks in and I have to kick him off. But he is useful when we want the boys to go to bed.

He does sound better at a distance. He moved his own piano into Mrs K's. That was an inspired idea of Cal's. She gets company and he's insisted on a realistic rent. She's taken herself off to Prague for the first time in years. He's rented his old flat and he'll sell it when the market revives. Good. It was no place for him to live alone, beating himself up. He's moved his precious stuff over. We made him bring all his awards and they're on display in our living room. Domestic God Steve dusts them each day. Domestic Disaster Cal polishes the silver ones.

I've had to ban him from making ageist jokes about himself. He's still nervous about the age gap between us. He has no reason to be, either vertically or horizontally.

We've had plenty of time together. For some reason, work has been a total doddle. I was ready for a long battle with the Redeemers. Talitha came to London and we drew up an affidavit based on what she had told us. I was preparing two different routes to getting her house back – enforcing the reverter clause and a claim of undue influence by the Redeemers when Mr Caslon executed the deed. But Dr Hoover surrendered without firing a shot. It would have caused him major damage if the story of Caslon House had come out in open court. I checked something in my criminal law books. Dr Hoover and Reverend Fitzsimmons committed a criminal act of perjury when they lied to the inquest on Josiah's death. There is no time-limit for charges.

Talitha regained her property. She removed all traces of the Redeemers and leased it forthwith to Laura and Luke. She gave money in memory of Josiah to Glendon Courtenay cricket club, and his picture is in the pavilion. She accepted the post of Vice-President. She's still living with Luke and Laura, and training to work with autistic children. She attends regular Anglican services (traditional and not happy-clappy) and has stepped out twice with the widowed vicar. As you may have gathered, Caslon House is being converted, under the supervision of Johnny and Edwin, into a jazz club, where Marjorie will have a residency.

One of my other cases did depress me, and Howard dropped everything (he's writing a storm again, and proper writing), poured out a large gin-and-tonic and listened to me. Every now and again he chimed "How terrible, and what happened then?" to let me draw breath. That was all I wanted. No good dialogue. No analysis, no solutions. Just attention and feeling safe and loved.

Howard still loves treating us, and will use any sort of excuse. "I've just written a cracking scene in Rob Patty… Tim's made a century in India…" Once he claimed it was St Willibrord's Day (there is one!) Suddenly we have to go shopping, or out to a meal or a movie or concert, and he'll sweep up Zoe and Robert too, and the rest of Cal's posse, if they are around (which they are, often). I take Howard to task and he repents briefly but then will come another excuse. "I've mastered 'Falling In Love Again' on the piano. We have to celebrate…" and he takes me off to look at more Karen Millen or Nicole Farhi.

I am not sure I want us to overcome this problem.

Steve wanted me to have a farewell piece. I have written much more than the other characters, so I won't make this long. Not even a reliable Howard Foy 800-worder.

Alice and I will marry next spring. We all wanted it to be formal. Mary Varley is pleased with the tempo. I would like Alice to come together again with her mother and father. She will feel better, just as I did when we all went to see my brother and his family in Basingstoke.

My old friend Joe Barnes hates public speaking and made a frightful hash of it when I married Marian. I hope that the boys might do that best man's job instead.

I had astonishing luck in connecting with Alice, Steve and Cal. If I wrote any more it could go straight into Hello magazine: FAMED WRITER HOWARD FOY FINDS LOVE AGAIN AND SHARES THE SECRETS OF HIS NEW HAPPY LIFE.

"Are you awake?"

"No, I'm asleep. Open your Christmas stocking, that's what it's for."

"I did an hour ago. I ate everything edible and played Owzat against Bungle."

"I can't sleep either. Remember the pact. Mum and Howard get ninety minutes more. Let's run, make room for your mince pies. Wrap up, it's cold."

"You're worse than Mum. Worse even than Howard."

Cold and clear. We didn't say anything but somehow I knew we were going to run to the park. We stopped at the nets. Just the surface and the structure, the netting was down for the winter.

"Come on, face me!" *He put a strong but mis-shapen stick in my hand and showed me a roundish stone, about the right size. I obeyed.*

Squeal. "Out! Right in front. You still can't read the Chinaman!" *I didn't argue. We turned back. Before I could stop him he started up the tall tree.* "Don't need a start from you any more. Closing in on five foot." *He had put on a spurt, like me.*

"Cal, get down, it's icy!"

"What's a little ice to … the Cat?" *He did a few more branches to show that he could. Then some manoeuvring.* "Ready? Catch!"

This time I was better positioned and I'd got stronger, so he didn't knock me over. He hung on. "You're still a giant softie and you couldn't squash a tomato!"

"You're still an ectomorph."

"Thank you." *We hung on, till the memories stopped. Then ran back to our home.*

Showers, dressing (basics not smart for later), and it was at last time to wake Mum and Howard. Scrambled egg breakfast with Bungle (ritual: me and Howard there for the first time). Finally present opening.

New cricket stuff for me, pads, gloves, sleeveless sweater. Thought that might happen because I knew Cal had been through my bag. Howard added signed photos of Frank Tyson in his glad animal action. I think his arm's lower than mine! And an application form: Associate Membership of the MCC. Signed by him and two other Famous People. The family present to me was a giant bookcase, but I had to assemble it myself.

"Idiotproof instructions."

"But not Steveproof. Give them to Bungle." *Hysterics.*

Howard collected a cocktail shaker, silk dressing gown (no excuse now to be nude at the piano again), cravat (as in illustrations for Bertie Wooster, ace detective), emphatic shirt and tie (chosen by me and Zoe at Ursinho, helped by Emerson). The family present to him was a lime tree.

"It might do miniatures if you point it south and keep it out of the wind. We got it through your brother."

"So that was the giant conspiracy in Basingstoke. Thank you. A beautiful thought."

Cal got a giant set of cal-ligraphic pens (left-handed), basketball and hoop (me), and shed loads of white T-shirts and paints and dyes for them. Howard gave him an edition of Vasari's Lives Of The Artists (quite rare). The family present presented a presentational problem [Wordpower]. He looked puzzled when he unwrapped the stuffed toy cat.

"Cute." *Couldn't keep disappointment from showing.*

"I told you he wouldn't read the card."

"Can be traded at Battersea Cats Home. Mum, are you serious?"

494

"You are a cat so you should know how to look after one." *His face lit up and he chattered away about possible names. And I could tell he wasn't going to give up the toy one.*

Howard says that the new washing machine should not count as Mum's Christmas present, because it was a necessity now that she had three dirty men in her house instead of one. Instead she collected a gym and spa membership (to get a break from us), a Turkestan silk shawl (Ricky Rubato!), a magnifying glass for legal small print (gold, antique) and a complete set of Misleading Cases (signed by A P Herbert).

I was nervous about my present and did a fair imitation of Cal, bouncing and looking away. "It's kind of edited highlights from your uncle Cal's trunk. On CD as well. I started it when I got over the flu. Bits of diary and letters he wrote, and loads of pix with him with other musicians, especially Steve Marriott – I sent some copies to Jesse, do you mind? – and Robert photographed them, so that I could scan them. Oh, and there's an unpublished song. The words are a bit sad, it's called Mr Nearly."[40]

"That was the story of his life. This is wonderful, Steve. It means so much. I love you." *Guess what, I got all teary again.* "I'm going to play Mr Nearly."

"Wait a moment, and unwrap your family present." *New piano stool.*

"And open it, please." *Big album of Kurt Weill songs. Signed by him and Lotte somebody. Where does Howard find these things? She was ecstatic. And there was something else.*

"This looks jolly, Howard, but why?"

"Look at the composer." *Don Bradman!*

Mr Nearly had interesting chords (said Mum) but it didn't seem like hit material. Every Day's A Rainbow Day For Me was much catchier. "Of course, it's catchy it's written by a cricketer!" *We all beat Cal up.*

Then we had another ritual. Cal always gave a set of drawings to Mum each Christmas, his highlights of the year. This time Howard and me (I?) got one too. Mine had loads of our first day together at the nets, and of course I got teary all over again. Mind you, Howard wasn't much better. I packed my drawings carefully and took all my loot back to my room.

---

[40] See Appendix.

I took ages to shower and change. Vanity? Difficulty choosing from my now huge wardrobe? Yes, but also putting off the bike ride to my first parents. Snapped myself out of it – bad manners to make them wait. My final sartorial selection was approved. I stuck their presents into my backpack and gathered my bike.

"Helmet!" *Cal loves paying me back. But I would have done anyway. Icy roads. Had brief nightmare of falling off, hitting head, coma, losing everybody... In the event, easy journey to Kenborne Vale. Same winos in streets where I used to run and pretend I was a fast bowler.*

Nearly missed former home. Bright new front door and loads of plants (presumably winter bloomers). Hall looked brighter too, but didn't really notice because they hugged me right away. And for real, not the pseudo and social ones I used to get.

"Hello, darling."

"Hello, Steve."

"Hello... Mum, Dad." *Oh shit! I didn't want to pause. I rehearsed this but I still paused. Did they notice?* "Happy Christmas!" *I handed over their presents to cover myself. Emperor-sized containers of his cologne and her massage oil. They'd taken a giant bite from my plastic. Made me feel a super-Bad Son for nicking them so often!*

"You remembered. Thank you, darling. Shall we see if Santa came?" *Stab of pain returned. Her ritual phrase each Christmas Day. Not like the rituals I had just shared, between Mum and Cal who loved each other, but ritual as in routine, dutiful performance. Stopped brooding when we reached living room and I saw her in the light. She looked way younger.* "Mum!" *Brilliant, it came straight out.* "So glamorous! Who's the visitor?"

"A handsome man." *Coy. Took a second to realize she meant me. I'm really dense, sometimes.* "Well, looky there? Darling, did you put those things under the tree?"

"Not me. There was some kind of commotion on the roof last night..." *They were trying a bit too hard but I decided to play my part in the play.*

"Gimme, gimme, gimme!" *That was it – the horrid spoilt brat. Bad Son! One small package, one tiny. The small one first, wanted time to guess the tiny.* "Love from Mum." *Back to my present self. It was a quality laptop and some extra CDs.*

"Hope it might help your writing, Steve." *Shy.* "And the CDs... Maybe they'll give you extra... Wordpower." *She knew about that? Thought it had just been between me and Uncle Frank. I looked at the CDs. Dictionary, quotations, style tips...*

"Great! This has got a full set of figures of speech. Howard's a maniac for figures of speech..." *Shit! Had resolved not to bring up new family. Looked at last CD. Plotting tips for fiction writers.*

"That one never worked for me. I only had one script and I couldn't change it."

"Or me." *Both looking at each other. Wry but intimate. Couldn't remember that from before. I gawped at them like a giant newt and then remembered the tiny present.* "Love from Dad."

A miniature Tim Morrow cricket bat. Unlike Cal, I read cards with presents. To be exchanged at Tim's bat maker for custom-made one. "Dad!"

"I've got the right cricketer, haven't I?" *He knew he had.*

I hugged them both. For real, but I think they knew I was a bit... confused. She helped me out. "Let's have some coffee. You like coffee now, don't you, Steve?" *She knew. She was interested in me. I got up.* "No. You did it often enough." *She headed off for the kitchen.*

We couldn't think of anything to say, Dad and me. Or maybe we thought of too much. Eventually I broke the silence. "House looks great, Dad. Didn't recognize the front, with the door and the plants."

He was grateful for a diversion. "Come and see the back garden."

"Bloody hell! Way better than when I looked after it!"

"The Ahmad brothers. Your recommendation. That little Ijaz. He's a genius for business." *Wished I'd been like that. What he wanted.* "He's doing some work with me, part-time." *Maybe he would get the son he wanted, at least as a timeshare. Wordpower? Or self-pity again? Always seemed to hit me there. We were summoned back for coffee. My favourite blend, the one Mrs K used to convert me. Mum _was_ interested in me. She poured mine and then sat beside him. Holding hands.*

"Strange to you, isn't it, Steve? We really quite like each other now."

"Shame to lose our wonderful son to discover that." *Mutual wry smile, intimate again. I wasn't prepared for that. I'd met them intermittently, but always in restaurants. Making conversation as acquaintances, not really interested in them. Payback. Hope it was subconscious. My mother continued.* "After you left I found something you'd written. To Frank. Long after his death. Was there really nobody else to talk to?"

I couldn't answer, but that was my answer. My father continued "My family's a battlefield and I'm just a small hill which each side occupies to fire on the other." *His quotation was spot on.* "It was the right image."

"We were at war and that's all we could think about. Knowing you – now," *She gave another wry smile.* "I'm sure you've read the books Frank left you." *Flash of guilt at skipping over giant T for Tolstoy!* "You know that war takes people over, they have no life, no meaning outside the war. People in war say and do terrible things because the war is all that counts. That's not an excuse for… giving you no childhood. We just want you to know, don't we, darling? So you don't think at any level that it was your fault."

"That's absolutely right."

"I did think I was… a bad son. I put it in caps to make it seem funny. But I did think it without caps."

Long silence. My mother poured more coffee. I'm sure none of us wanted any but it filled space as well as cups. [Wordpower!]

"There was something I could never figure out. Cricket. The only thing I was any good at and it never made you… think better of me." *I bottled out of saying "love me", but I think they knew.* "At most, you put up with it. You paid for my kit and you turned up at my first matches, but I was glad when you stopped because you so obviously didn't want to be there. And you were glad when other people took over my cricket life. Frank. And Jimmy." *They looked really guilty over Jimmy. Well, that bit I'm not letting them off. Sorry.* "I'm over Jimmy. Alice sorted that for me."

They wanted to say something, but I wouldn't let them. "Anyway, I couldn't figure it out. Mum, I thought you found cricket boring, but Dad, you seemed to hate it. Last few years, especially. When I had to leave X school, you parked me in Cibber which had no cricket at all. You wouldn't drive me to any club matches, and I didn't feel safe on my own because there might have been another Jimmy, and I could play at all only if it helped your business. And you were always on at me to work in the holidays. You hated cricket, which was the best thing I did, so you must have hated me. That's what it felt like. I do need to get my head around you hating cricket."

He looked into his coffee cup. No answer there, so he looked at me. "I'll give you the best answers I can. There is more than one answer. Part of it was for your sake, Steve. I was genuinely afraid that you'd waste your life on a dream. You might remember I said this when we first met Alice. It happened to my best friends at school. One failed actor, one failed writer and one dead footballer. By his own hand. I was the plodder. I think they only put up with me because I did their homework while they were having fun. I was so unfair on you, because you always did your homework. You really do give 110 per cent in everything. Do football managers still say that?" *No. I wasn't going to let him escape into a chat about language. I have learnt a bit from Alice.* "I was genuinely frightened that you were going to waste your life like them. But there was much more."

Now he seemed in real pain, and I did want to give him some help. "I thought you might be jealous of Uncle Frank. Preferring cricket with him to fishing with you and, well, wanting to be with him all the time."

"You were only a little kid! How could you help your feelings? But yes, I was jealous of Frank." *He struggled to say more. I remained silent. Alice taught me the power of silence. He had to fill it.* "It was the war again. The endless war between me and your mother. Cricket came to you from her, at least her side of the family, so it belonged to the enemy. It was worse when you went to X school. God, I hated that place! People looking down on me from the first minute I set foot there. When your mother and I went there together I felt people thinking 'God, she married beneath her.'" *My mother blushed deeply.* "They may not have thought that at all but that's what I felt. And she seemed perfectly comfortable there."

"Not really. But I wasn't going to let you know." *The tension eased.*

"When you got that scholarship I didn't want you to take it. X school was enemy territory. Her territory. If you went there, I thought you would join the enemy for good and... look down on me. God, that was even more unfair on you! Nobody could ask for a better son. Nobody!" *He choked up. She held him and eventually he continued in a calm, almost mechanical way.* "When you got into trouble there, I saw it as my chance to remove you. I persuaded myself that it was for your own good. I thought that X school was a thoroughly corrupt institution. But removing you was also a big conquest – taking you off her territory and putting you firmly onto mine."

"I think I can understand that, but why then send me to Cibber? I actually thought you'd picked it because it didn't have any kind of cricket."

He sighed deeply. "I'm afraid that was an attraction. But the most important factor was that I went there."

"What? You never told me!"

"It was called Tate School then, and it was better than Cibber is now. It had a bad patch later and they … repackaged it with a new brand name." *Looking at my mother, recognizing her expertise. She nodded approval.* "Cibber was intended to turn you into me. I did start working for money at 13 and I actually wanted to work full-time at 16 to get out of Tate. I hoped that you would feel the same if you went to Cibber."

I thought for a bit and then asked "Did Mum know that you went there?"

"I'm afraid so." *That's what really mattered. His conquest. I didn't matter at all.* "I'm sorry you had to hear all this, today of all days. But please take one thing away. Your mother said it already. Nothing was your fault. Nothing. I… we… failed our wonderful son. We didn't even know our wonderful son. Until we lost our wonderful son."

"Wordpower!" *My mother and I blurted it together.*

"Dad, you used a figure of speech! Three sentences with the same ending. I'll look it up on my new CD."

"Son, I'm sorry about Cibber."

"And I'm sorry about X. But we're so happy that you're now at Marian's."

"I never knew you both were helping them. Howard told me."

"It keeps us in touch. Loads of people ask if we're related to the brilliant, popular Steve Helson, but we say no."

"I don't want you to do that!"

"Thank you, son. But I .. we…" *She nodded to him again.* "Your mother and I had a long discussion after you left. We actually took a week away together." *Could not remember that, ever. Duty holidays with me, but never time together.* "We made one decision before any other. You must enjoy your new life with the people giving it to you. We're never… going to make a claim on you. But this is always your home. Come here whenever you like."

"Well, maybe phone first in case we're having an orgy." *She gave a whooping laugh, like Sybil Fawlty.* "We'll tell you when we're going away and then you can use it for an orgy."

"As if... Teenagers do still say 'as if,' don't they Steve?" *The heavy stuff was over. Time to move to the safe haven of language.*

"We still say that. And (Not) in brackets, and..."

"Steve, we love you but you're going to be late for lunch. We mustn't keep you." *Double meaning. I think, intentional.* "Thank you for our wonderful presents. You shouldn't have spent so much. Now can you manage yours?"

"I can easily give you a lift to the Barneses." *He thought for a second and added* "Or order you a taxi." *Afraid he would embarrass me? Suddenly I felt sorry for them. I almost asked them both for a lift. Knowing Belinda, she would ask them to stay to lunch. No – that would be too much responsibility for everyone. Having to be polite to strangers. And I didn't have enough of something to go round...*

"Thanks, Dad. But the roads are empty and I need the bike ride to work off a bit of lunch, and I can get my wonderful presents easily into the backpack."

More hugs in the hall. Genuine. Then I went to get my bike. "Helmet!" *Well, she was my mother.*

Whizzed to Barneses (hoping new deodorant was working!), parked and locked bike. Stopped and looked at all the keys on my chain. Mostly new this year. Last Christmas I had no real parents and no real home. [Drama queen!] This Christmas I have four parents and keys to three homes.

They opened champagne when I arrived. We all had some, even the little boys. [They'll hate that. Heh-heh.] More present giving. Robert's was dead easy, just pick from his wish-list of photographic stuff, but hoped Howard was right about Zoe. She opened up big silver bracelet. Colossal snog. Thanks, Howard: you can't go wrong with jewellery.

She gave me a small package. "Examine this carefully, Steve."

"A wrist watch. And quality. Oh..." *I caught sight of the brand and spelled out the letters to myself. S-E-I-K-O.* "It's a Psycho!"

"Payback at last for him." *She was wearing my monkey brooch. Another snog, but cut short to watch the Queen's message. Howard corrected a grammatical slip. We then pigged out on the Barneses' goose and veggies, followed by Cal's mince pies and brandy butter. (Secret ballot showed no support for Christmas pudding.)*

Cal and Robert scuttled off to Robert's sealed room, and came back staggering under an enormous whiteboard, covered with a sheet. They propped it on two chairs and both did the bounce-and-look- away routine. Finally they pulled back the sheet.

"It's a montage. It's a Lord's Test match with everybody. My drawings, and nearly all pix are Robert's and he edited them all."

"Steve's bowling of course. And he's put the Right Honourable on his arse again! The other batsman's wetting himself! Dad's wicketkeeping. Cal's at slip, I'm on the leg side. Howard at gully. Tim's at cover point. Tom at fine leg, he's going to bowl the next over. Luke just backward of square leg, so you can see his face. Rupert's in the field and so are Felix and Francis."

"Both Mums and Zoe in the crowd going mental! And Laura. And Portia. Oh, we put in your … first mum and dad. Is that right?"

"Totally right."

"These are Frenetic spectators – we even found Pat Hobby."

"There's a complete Glendon Courtenay contingent in the Members' section, because they've taken over the club and expelled the Right Honourable. I had to draw most of them, but we used Marjorie's new promo picture, and Jesse's and Rick's."

"There's everyone else from Marian's. And there's a toy section. Billy's in charge of it. See there's Bungle, and Ted Luger and the rest of mine, and Tiger and Deputy Tiger, and all of Billy's bears."

"And here's a writers' section. Mary Varley in front. And famous people from the party. And poor Richard Heller."

"All those people are modelling Ursinho. And there's Emerson."

"There's Steve's New Zealand pals, Daniel and Brendon, who scared me, and Phil from the pool and his mate Nick, only I don't know his face so he's looking up at the sky for an asteroid."

"The rest of the crowd are just extras, and there's thousands more trying to get in and watch Steve. But we got Antony Scorer into the scorebox."

"I hope we got everybody. You don't have to say it's brilliant, but in case you do Robert's photographed it professionally so we can copy it."

"That is totally awesome." *It was. Everyone was gobsmacked. I took advantage of the silence.* "Er, if I could have everyone's attention? I will not detain you long, but I propose on this occasion to feel compelled to say a few auspicious words." *Whistles from those who had heard this before from Howard. (Everyone.)* "I must first thank Joe and Belinda for having us in these wonderful auspices and Belinda and Cal, well, everybody, but especially Belinda and Cal, for the auspicious lunch. There is one other present I'd like for everyone to have. I've got this around my neck. Daniel and Brendon gave it to me. It's a maniah and it's supposed to be a protective spirit. Anyway, it's totally worked for me, because as soon as I wore it I met Cal, and then everybody who's come into that picture. Now each of these spirits looks out for each other, but you can't give one to yourself and I'd really like all of you to have one, because, well, I suppose technically you're not my family but…" *Inevitably I started to tear up again, but Cal saved me by nearly choking on one of his mince pies.*

"We may not be family but we're a network because we do so much net work!" *Hysterics. We all beat him up.*

I'm going to stop there. My life's sorted and despite what Howard says I don't think anybody would want to go on reading about a totally happy teenager.

I still sometimes have trouble believing that I got my Network, but I did, and just because I played cricket one day with another lonely kid.

I like to think everyone's got a Network in waiting.

THE END

Appendix : Blue Train   by Howard Foy (from <u>Your Very Own Ricky Rubato)</u>

I watched you fade away
Through the steam
Goodbye for ever, love,
Goodbye dream.

I've caught
The Blue Train
From Nothing to Nowhere,
Full speed
Through the night.
Freight cars
Full of spaces
Only lit by
Passing stars.

I'm on
The Blue Train
With no destination,
No stops,
No returns.
I've got
Nothing with me
Just your picture
On the pane.

I thought your sun would never go in,
You were my only fire.
One day I caught you looking at me
And saw the evening in your face.

I'm on
The Blue Train
From Nothing to Nowhere
Midnight
Lost on the plains.
Next day
You'll forget me,.
I'm moving,
I'm travelling,
Unravelling,
On the Blue Train.

Appendix: Anywhere But Here   (words and music by Cal Devane senior, of Calamity)

I live in a time that is full of lies
By hollow men with cheating eyes
Telling us all what to think and feel.
Without you there would be nothing real.

They've trashed the world which they say is mine
We're running on empty but they say we're fine
Air and sky full of poisoned rain
But when I'm with you I can breathe again.

I wanna live
Anywhere but here
Any time but now, with
No one else but you

Why… do we both have to take it?
Why… can't we simply forsake it?
Me and you… we really could make it.

Plastic rose on the teacher's desk.
Worn-out lessons from a worn-out text.
Preparing for life in a plastic mould
But lovers belong in the world of gold. *Some people hate this verse*

I wanna live
Anywhere but here
Any time but now
With no one else but you.

Why… do we have to receive it?
Why … do we have to believe it?
Love … we can surely achieve it?

The world may be crowded with cheats and fools
But lovers can make up their own rules
We can hold time hostage till the break of day
And make night listen to the words we say.

Night … is our time so let's seize it
Now… hold my hand tight and squeeze it
Now … take this moment and freeze it.

If I must live
In a place called here
In a time called now -
Let it be with you.

Appendix: Short Story (words and music by Cal Devane senior, of Calamity)

The first time I saw her waiting in the school canteen,
I thought she'd escaped from the cover of a magazine,
And every time she moved my eyes did a photo call,
Cos she's drop-dead-gorgeous – but man, that girl is tall.

She's the one and only in the world I ever wanted to love me,
But she's not in my world at all, she's so far above me.

Well, I'm not the kind of guy who would ever stand out in a crowd,
And there she is standing with her head kind of touching the clouds,
I tried to say "Hi!" but my tongue seemed to turn into glue
And she looked as if she'd heard a little mouse squeak by her shoe.

She's the one and only in the world I ever wanted to love me,
But she's not in my world at all, she's so far above me.

A month's gone by but I still haven't found my voice
I look up to her so much but then I really haven't got much choice.
If she stooped down low, she might just hear my beating heart
But as things stand I guess we'll have to spend our lives apart.

She's the one and only in the world I ever wanted to love me,
But she's not in my world at all, she's so far above me.

I'd love to be her toy boy or maybe her teddy bear
I'd nestle on her pillow and smell her fragrant hair.
I'd keep all her secrets and listen to her hopes and fears
And I'd be there for her when there's no one else to mop her tears.

She's the one and only in the world I ever wanted to love me,
But she's not in my world at all, she's so far above me.

I'm back in the canteen although I never want a thing to eat,
When she walks up beside me and sits down on the next door seat,
She says "I can't wait any longer, I've simply got to let you know,
"I've watched you for a month, and I so wished you'd say Hello."

She's the one and only in the world I ever wanted to love me
And now we're holding hands, although she's still so far
Above me.

Appendix: Mr Nearly: Words and music by Cal Devane senior, of Calamity

I once flew solo across the Atlantic Ocean -
Nearly.
I discovered the long-lost secret of perpetual motion -
Nearly.
I nearly became the first man on the moon,
I nearly played the hero in High Noon,
But in all of my life there could never, never be
Anything worse than that you nearly loved me.

They call me Mr Nearly,
The one who loved you dearly
And told you most sincerely,
And you nearly loved me.

I climbed all alone to the top of Mount Everest -
Nearly.
I scored 300 when I took my intelligence test -
Nearly.
I nearly won the Derby on a veteran horse,
I nearly set the record for completing the course.
But in all of my life there could never, never be
Anything worse than that you nearly loved me.

They call me Mr Nearly,
And all because I merely
Told you I loved you dearly:
And you nearly loved me.

I don't want you as my friend
And if you can't really love me
I'd rather my life end.

I don't want you to like me
And if you can't really love me
I'd rather you strike me
Dead…

I painted the smile on the Mona Lisa -
Nearly.
I straightened out the leaning Tower of Pisa -

Nearly
I nearly won a boxing match with King Kong
I nearly nearly nearly wrote a number-one song.
But in all of my life there could never, never be
Anything worse than that you nearly loved me.

Even when thousands cheer me,
I see it very clearly
That I'm always Mr Nearly,
And you nearly loved me.